WEST

BY PENELOPE WILLIAMSON

HEART
OF THE
WEST

PENELOPE
WILLIAMSON

POCKET BOOKS

New York London Toronto Sydney New Delhi

Pocket Books
A Division of Simon & Schuster, Inc.
1230 Avenue of the Americas
New York, NY 10020

This book is a work of fiction. Any references to historical events, real people, or real places are used fictitiously. Other names, characters, places, and events are products of the author's imagination, and any resemblance to actual events or places or persons, living or dead, is entirely coincidental.

First Pocket Books paperback edition July 2013

POCKET and colophon are registered trademarks of Simon & Schuster, Inc.

For information about special discounts for bulk purchases, please contact Simon & Schuster Special Sales at 1-866-506-1949 or business@simonandschuster.com.

The Simon & Schuster Speakers Bureau can bring authors to your live event. For more information or to book an event contact the Simon & Schuster Speakers Bureau at 1-866-248-3049 or visit our website at www.simonspeakers.com.

Designed by Lewelin Polanco

Manufactured in the United States of America

10 9 8 7 6 5 4 3 2 1

ISBN 978-1-4767-3100-1
ISBN 978-1-4767-4006-5 (ebook)

For my mother, Bernadine Wegmann Proctor,
and for her mother, Elizabeth Bonhage Wegmann . . .
You showed me how.

PART ONE
1879

1

HE WASN'T COMING. OH, God, he wasn't coming after all!

Clementine Kennicutt paced back and forth across the shell-patterned carpet, kicking at her skirts with the patent leather toes of her walking boots so that the stiffened muslin whispered in the too silent night.

She paced her dark and quiet bedroom. Down to the black walnut wardrobe. Over to the four-poster bed, all swaddled in white chintz and eyelet lace. Across to the fireplace. A lyre clock sat on the green marble mantel, its pendulum silently swinging. She had to lean close to its porcelain face to see the time. Ten minutes past midnight, ten minutes late. He wasn't coming, wasn't coming . . .

Back to the window, where faint light spilled in from outside. She pushed aside the voile undercurtains to peer down at the street. The glass was smeared with rain, and moist air made halos around the streetlamps. Moonlight lanced through melting storm clouds. The iron fence around Louisburg Square cast spiky shadows onto cobblestones that were slick with water and deserted.

There—surely that was a coach light flickering through the elm trees across the square. She pressed her face against the pane, trying to see better, but her breath fogged the glass. She flipped up the latch and pulled open the window.

The hinges squealed and she froze, her heart thudding in her throat. She eased the window open more slowly then. She could hear the wind now and the harshness of her own breathing.

A gust ruffled the green velvet drapes, slapping them against the casement. Behind her the crystal lusters on the mantel lamps tinkled. She leaned out the window, feeling the wind cool on her face. It smelled of the rain and of coal smoke. The street, shining with the wet, was empty still. He wasn't coming.

"What are you doing?"

She whirled, almost stumbling. Light from the silver chamber stick in her mother's hand threw huge shadows on the cream silk-covered walls. Clementine's heart beat hard against the clenched fist she had pressed to her breast. "Mama, you frightened me."

The flame flared and jumped as Julia Kennicutt lifted the chamber stick. Her gaze traveled the length of her daughter, assessing the steamer cloak that covered a plain maroon walking dress, the kid gloves and black beaver bonnet, the bulging carpetbag at the girl's feet. "You are running away," she said. Her gaze went to the unlit candle waiting on the window seat and the china safe filled with matches. "With someone. You're running off with someone."

"Mama, don't . . ." Clementine shot a glance to the open doorway, expecting to see her father looming there. He always seemed to swell when he was angry, and the air around him would quiver. "I'll put everything away and go to bed, and no one but you and I need ever know. Only don't tell—"

Her mother left, shutting the door and taking the candle with her, plunging the room once again into darkness.

Clementine sank onto the chintz-skirted stool before her dressing table. The fear she so despised within herself clogged her throat, thick and sour like old grease. She heard a scraping noise outside, and her head whipped around. But it was only the wind slapping a tree branch against the corner lamppost. She stared with hopeless yearning at the window. If he came now, it would be too late. He wasn't coming anyway.

The door opened. She stood, squaring her shoulders as she began to draw deep within herself, away from the hurt. So battened down was she against the gale of her father's fury that it took Clementine a moment to realize her mother had come back without him.

Julia Kennicutt set the chamber stick among the glass bottles and enameled boxes on the dressing table. The beveled mirror reflected fractured light onto the two women. In her white nightdress and with her pale, unbound hair, Julia almost seemed the younger. "Clementine . . ." She lifted a hand as if to touch her daughter's cheek, then didn't. "You must take this with you."

She gripped Clementine's wrist, pressing something into her palm. The weight of the object surprised the girl, and she almost dropped it. It was a heart-shaped sachet embroidered with silk flowers and decorated with lace. The smell of roses clung to it, but it was too heavy and lumpy to be filled with sweet-scented powder or herbs. Clementine hefted it in her hand and heard the clink of coins.

"It's not a lot," her mother was saying in a strained whisper. "Not more than a hundred dollars. But it would be a good start for you, should you ever need to run away someday from this man you are running off with now."

Clementine looked down at the small bag in her hand. She had a wisp of memory, of having seen it once years ago among her mother's underthings—a place where her father was unlikely to go snooping, where a heart-shaped sachet smelling of roses would never seem out of place.

She looked back up to her mother's white face. "You were going to use it yourself," she said. "All these years you've just been waiting for a chance—"

"No, no." Julia gave a sharp shake of her head, and her hair swung free, slapping against her cheek. "I won't leave this house. I haven't the courage."

Clementine tried to thrust the sachet back into her mother's hands. "But you can come with us. We're going to the Montana Territory—"

Julia made a soft, strangled sound. "Montana . . . oh, my. What a whimsical, fey child you've always been. What would your young man think of a girl who dragged her mother along on their elopement? And to such a wilderness, no less. Can you imagine me among those horrid buffalo and Indians? Oh, child . . ." She lifted her hand, and this time she did touch her daughter's cheek. "You are so very young. You think you'll have such grand adventures, and you will—though not, I expect, the sort you're dreaming of."

"But, Mama—"

"Hush now, and listen for once. There is something to be said for safety and security, for staying close to the life you've always known. So at least take the money, since you'll probably need every bit of it on the day your grand adventures cease to be so grand." Her fingers slid off her daughter's cheek, and she sighed. "I have only this one thing to give you, and even it was stolen from him."

Clementine felt the hardness of the coins through the thin silk, felt their weight. And the weight of all the words that had always remained unspoken between them. She imagined pulling the hoarded words out of her heart, holding them out to this woman, her mother. *This one thing I have to give you.* Like coins in a silk cachet smelling of roses.

"Clementine, this man you are running off with . . ."

"He is nothing like Father." She put the sachet into the pocket of her cloak, and put away those other words she didn't know how to speak. "He's a kind man, a laughing, gentle man. I am sure of it." But she wasn't sure of it, for she barely knew him; indeed, she knew him not at all. And she had this sinking feeling, like a weight of soggy dough in her belly, that he wasn't coming for her anyway. She squinted, trying to read the lyre clock. "You won't believe this, Mama—but he's a cowboy, a real cowboy."

"Oh, heavens . . . I think you had better spare me the details." Her mother tried a smile, but the hand she laid on Clementine's arm trembled. "No matter what sort of man you believe him to be, promise me you'll keep the money

as your own secret from him. Otherwise he will think it his
by right and—"

The rattle of carriage wheels on cobblestones sent Clementine flying to the window. "Quick, Mama, douse your light."

A small black gig rolled down the street, wavering
in and out of the shadows and pools of lamplight. It was
tattered and mud-splattered and missing its hood, yet to
Clementine's eyes it looked as magical as would a gilded
coach pulled by white unicorns. She dropped one match
and broke another before she managed to light her candle.
She waved it twice across the window, then blew it out.

She snatched up the carpetbag, its weight dragging
against her arm. She had crammed as much as she possibly could into it, for she couldn't begin to envision all the
things she would come to need in a wilderness like Montana. She almost laughed aloud. He had come. Her cowboy
had come for her after all.

She turned away from the window. Shadows obscured
her mother's face. Yet she heard Julia's sharp intake of
breath as if she were choking back her own unspeakable
words. "Go with joy, child," Julia said. She gripped the
sides of her daughter's head, squeezing hard. "Go with joy."

They stayed in this awkward embrace a moment before Clementine pulled away. But at the door she turned.
"Good-bye, Mama," she said softly to this woman, her
mother, who stood in silence. A shadow among shadows.

Clementine's feet made no sound on the hall's thick
runner, and she gripped the heavy bag against her chest to
keep it from banging against the wainscoted walls. But the
servants' stairs were narrow and twisting, and she caught
her toe in the hem of her skirt and tripped, dropping the
valise. The bag thumped and clattered its way into the
kitchen, spilling open. Trinket boxes, balls of cambric
stockings, and a fluting iron rolled beneath the big block
table and behind the icebox, getting lost among the coal
scuttle and lard buckets.

Clementine's breath left her in a gasp. She had made

enough noise to rouse all of Beacon Hill, to awaken her
father surely. Her father . . . She stuffed what she could find
back inside the bag, managing to refasten only one clasp.

A row of copper pan bottoms reflected her white face
as she ran to the door that led to the mews out back, where
her cowboy was to go after he had seen her signal. Her
bootheels clicked on the brick floor. The sachet of coins in
her pocket bounced heavily against her thigh.

The bolt stuck, and she bruised her knuckles trying to
force it. The door scraped like a rusty chain as she yanked
it open. She spilled out onto the stoop and came to a stumbling and breathless stop in front of a tall man, made taller
by the deep crown of his wide-brimmed hat.

"Mr. McQueen . . ." She had to stop to suck in a deep
breath. "I am here."

His laugh was young and carefree, and his teeth flashed
white beneath the long drooping curve of his mustache. "I
heard you coming, Miss Kennicutt. Me and all the rest of
Boston." He took her valise, trailing a petticoat and corset
laces, and tossed it into the gig. He stretched out his hand
to take hers.

"Wait, there is another," she said, pointing. "Over
there behind the dustbin, beneath that pile of old gunnysacks." The rotting sacks hid a calfskin trunk fitted with
brass hardware and banded with copper. A piece at a time
she had smuggled its contents through the house and out
to the mews.

"What've you got in here"—he grunted as he wrestled
with the trunk, trying to wedge it into the narrow space
between the small gig's leather seat and the splashboard—
"bricks and cobblestones?"

"It's just a camera," she said quickly, afraid that he
would ask her to leave it behind, that she would have to
choose between her new life and the only part of her old
life that mattered. "And glass plates and chemicals and
such things. There'll be room for it, won't there? It's not
too heavy, is it? I can manage—"

He turned and gripped her face the way her mother had. Only he kissed her. A man's kiss that was hard and fierce and left her feeling excited and breathless. "I knew you'd come with me, girl. I just knew it."

His strong hands spanned her waist and lifted her into the cart. He leaped onto the seat beside her, spanked the reins against the horse's rump, and they clattered out of the alley, turning toward the river.

Clementine Kennicutt looked back to the house, to the window of the room that had been hers for all of her life. A flickering light flashed once and was gone—her mother lifting a candle in a brief and lonely farewell.

She watched the dark window until the house was swallowed by the shadows of the elms. She turned and there ahead of her, floating above the mansard roofs of Beacon Hill, was the moon, round and plump as a Christmas orange.

Her head fell back and she laughed softly into the night sky.

"What?" said the young man beside her. He tugged at the reins, and the horse high-stepped around the corner. Louisburg Square and her father's house disappeared forever, but the moon stayed with her.

She laughed again, stretching out her hand to the moon, her fingers spread wide. But it remained just out of reach.

If one's life, Clementine Kennicutt had often thought, could be written out like a tale in a yellowback novel, then in her story she was fated to end up married to a cowboy.

Actually whenever she'd done her imagining, it was she who had chased wild mustangs across the range, taken a bead on a stampeding buffalo, and whooped it up at the end of the trail in Dodge City. Still, one had to be practical. Even in daydreams little girls did not grow up to be cowboys. But they *did* grow up to be wives, and if . . . well, just suppose . . . But even that, she knew in her most practical moments, was stretching things for a girl whose father was minister to Tremont Temple in Boston, Massachusetts. A girl whose way of life was as different from a cowboy's as was cheese from the moon.

The union of her parents had been a marriage of convenience and money. Julia Patterson had brought with her to the altar an inheritance of fifty thousand dollars and a house on Beacon Hill. The Reverend Theodore Kennicutt brought his fine old Boston name, along with his godly self. Clementine was their only child, and the Reverend Mr. Kennicutt did know his duty as a parent and a servant of God. Daughters were weak vessels, prey to vanity and instability. A pretty face didn't mirror a pure soul. No one was allowed to coddle or pet or make a fuss over little Clementine.

Sometimes, when she was supposed to be contemplating her sins, she would follow her thoughts back as far as they would go, back even before she knew about the cowboys. She thought she must have been four that summer her grandfather took her to the bleachery and she discovered what life could be.

Grandfather Patterson had a smiling face, ruddy as an overripe apple, and a great booming laugh that jiggled his big belly. He owned numerous textile finishing plants, and on that day he took Clementine and her mother on an outing into the country where he had his bleachery. It was an enormous brick building with a belching smokestack. Inside, great bubbling vats emitted billowing clouds of steam. Hundreds of pipes crisscrossed like netting over the ceiling and dripped onto her head. Fumes pinched her nose and made her eyes water. Mama said the bleachery put her in mind of the cauldrons of hell, and Clementine loved it. The clattering noise, the fearsome stink, the hustle and bustle of it, the *life* of it. Even now when she thought of the fullness of what life could be, she was put in mind of that noisy, smelly bleachery. She had loved that place and she'd waited with barely controlled excitement to go back, but they never did.

Yet that summer held its magic anyway, for Mama smiled a lot and began to get a big belly like Grandfather Patterson's. Cook said her mother was growing a baby, but Clementine didn't believe it until the day Mama took her hand and let her feel the baby's foot kicking against the tautly stretched yellow dimity of her mother's morning dress.

She laughed at the wonder of it. "But how could a baby get inside you?"

"Hush," her mother scolded. "Never ask such naughty questions." Yet they laughed together when the baby kicked again.

She always smiled when she remembered how she and Mama had laughed together. But thoughts have a way of flowing one into the other, and the laughter could become screams and footsteps pounding down the hall in the middle of the night, and a pair of servants whispering outside her nursery door, that the Mrs. Reverend was surely dying and little Clementine would be a poor motherless child come morning.

Clementine had lain stiff in her bed that night, listening to her mother's screams. She watched the shadows melt and sunshine filter through the sawtoothed leaves of the elms in the park. She heard the chirp of sparrows and the rattle and clatter of the milk wagon.

And then she heard the screaming stop.

By morning, the whispers had said. By morning her mother would be dead and she would be a motherless child.

The sun had been up for hours before the Reverend Mr. Kennicutt came to her. Although he frightened her at times, Clementine loved the way her father looked. He was so tall it seemed his head must surely touch the top of the sky. His beard was long and thick, parting and curling up on the ends like a pair of milk jug handles. It was the same color as his hair—the shiny black of spilled ink. His eyes shone, too, especially on the evenings he came to pray with her. He made words with his deep voice that were like the songs the wind made in the trees. She didn't understand all the words, but she loved the sound of them. He told her how God judged the righteous and was angry with the wicked every day, and she thought he must be God, for he was so large and so splendid, and she longed to please him.

"Please, Father," she'd said that day, careful to keep her eyes humbly downcast, although her chest felt pinched for air. She wasn't sure what dying meant. "Am I a poor mother-less child?"

"Your mother lies near death," he said, "and all you can think of is yourself. There is a sinfulness in you, daughter. Such a wildness and a willfulness that at times I do fear for your immortal soul. 'If thy eye be evil, thy whole body shall be full of darkness.'"

Clementine flung her head up and clenched her fists. "But I've been good. I *have* been good!" Her chest hitched as she stared up into his face. "And my eyes have been good, too, Father. Truly they have."

He heaved a deep, sad sigh. "You must remember our Lord sees everything, Clementine. Not only all we do, but what is in our thoughts and in our hearts. Come now, we must pray." He led her into the middle of the room and pressed her onto her knees. He lifted his big, heavy hand and laid it on her head, on the plain rough cotton cap that always covered her hair to keep her from vanity. "Dear Lord, when in thine infinite mercy, thou . . ." His voice trailed off. His daughter's head was not bent in prayer. His fingers tightened their grip, but he said gently, "Your baby sister has passed on, Clementine. She has gone to the glory of heaven."

She cocked her head beneath his hand as she considered the meaning of his words. She had never been able to picture heaven very well, but she thought of what Mama had said about the bleachery and the cauldrons of hell, and she smiled. "Oh, I do hope not, Father. I hope she went to hell instead."

The reverend's hand jerked off his daughter's head. "What manner of child *are* you?"

"I am Clementine," she had said.

Clementine was forbidden to leave the nursery that day. In the hour before bed, her father came again and read to her from the Bible about a lake of fire and brimstone, and a righteous anger that would show no mercy when she died. Even the angels who had sinned had not been spared, the reverend told her, but had been cast down into hell to suffer for all eternity.

Her father came again and again over the next two days, morning, noon, and evening, to read more to her of hell. But it was the upstairs maid who told her that her mother would live.

On the morning of the funeral all the mirrors and windows of the house were draped in black crepe, and flowers filled the hall, choking the air with their smell. A hearse pulled by horses sporting curling black plumes carried the tiny casket to the Old Granary Burying Ground. The wind stung cold on Clementine's face and slapped dead leaves against the gravestones. She knew all about hell now, and it was nothing like her grandfather's bleachery.

Sometimes the thoughts would flow on to that Easter when Aunt Etta and the twins came for a visit. These boy cousins, who were seven years older than Clementine, had just returned from a trip to Paris, where they had acquired a miniature guillotine. Clementine was excited to see this marvel, for she was allowed few toys of her own to distract her from her lessons and prayers.

The boys had offered to show her how the guillotine worked. And she, so pleased with the attention they were paying her, had smiled at the wonder of it. And was smiling still . . . until they set it up on the table where she took her morning porridge and milk, and they cut off the head of her only doll.

"Please, stop," she said, careful to be polite and careful not to cry as she watched the porcelain head bouncing bloodless across the white painted surface. "You're hurting her." But her cousins only laughed, the tin blade fell with a shriek, and a pink dimpled arm went rolling onto the floor.

Clementine didn't hurry, for she was forbidden to run. She didn't cry. Stiff in her starched pinafore and cap, she walked soundlessly through the big house in search of someone to stop the slaughter, while her little chest shuddered, and her eyes stared wide and unblinking.

Lilting laughter floated out the open doors of the morning room. She stopped at the threshold, so enthralled she forgot about the murder of her doll. Mama and Aunt Etta sat knee to knee in white rattan chairs, heads bent over teacups. Aunt Etta had brought Easter lilies, and their thick sweet smell mixed with the melody of laughter and chatter. Sunlight poured through the tall windows, gilding her mother's hair.

Julia leaned forward and gripped her sister's arm. "Then Dr. Osgood said in that gruff-kind voice of his, 'If you want to go on living, madam, you are not to try to have any more babies. I've told Mr. Kennicutt that if he cannot reconcile his conscience to birth control, then he must reconcile himself to abstinence. To behave otherwise is tantamount to murder, and I have told him that as well.' Oh, Etta, the good doctor broke this news as if it were a tragedy. How could he know the utter, utter *relief* I felt?" Julia laughed, then her shoulders hunched. Aunt Etta gathered her into her arms. "The utter relief," she sobbed into Aunt Etta's plump bosom. "The utter, utter relief."

"Hush, Jule, hush. At least from now on, you'll be spared his bed."

Clementine hadn't understood the words they spoke, but she so had wished she could be Aunt Etta. She wanted fiercely to be able to wrap her arms around her mother and make her smile. But she wanted to be Mama, too, to be stroked and held and comforted, to feel safe and loved.

She wanted, wanted, wanted . . . Yet she had no words to describe the things she wanted.

That was the first time she could remember feeling them, those yearnings that were to come to her more often as she grew older. She felt and wanted things, but she didn't know what they were. At times she would be almost choked with a tumult of feelings, of wantings, she couldn't name.

She was nine when she first learned about the cowboys.

It came about when Cook hired a new scullery maid. Shona MacDonald was her name, and she had hair the bright red of a fire wagon and a smile that beamed from her face like the summer sun.

The first time they met, Shona knelt and pulled Clementine to her breast in a crushing hug. The smell of lavender water filled Clementine's nose almost making her sneeze, and rough, work-chapped hands rubbed circles on her shoulders. Then Shona gripped her arms and leaned back, smiling. "My, what a bonnie lassie ye be," she said. "Never have I seen such eyes. Like a loch at dusk, they are. All stormy green and brooding, and filled with secrets and mysteries."

Clementine stared at her, mesmerized by the lilting words and the brightness of her smile. No one had ever hugged her before; she wished the girl would do it again. She tried a smile of her own. "What is a loch?"

"Why, a loch is a . . . a gret big puddle of water, ye ken?"

Shona laughed. The sound was like rose petals, sweet and soft. Clementine studied the shiny black toes of her shoes, afraid to look, almost afraid to ask. "Do you think you could be my friend?" she said.

Shona's strong, bony arms enveloped her again. "Och, ye puir wee thing. Of course I'll be yer friend." And Clementine was almost giddy from the happiness that came from these words.

Sunday afternoon was Cook's time off. It was a quiet time in the house, between church services, and Clementine was supposed to spend the hours at prayer. Instead she spent them in the kitchen with her friend. *My friend.* How she loved the sound of those words. She would say them to herself as she crept down the servants' stairs: *My friend, my friend . . . I am going to visit my friend.*

Shona had a passion for yellowback novels, and she spent most of her meager salary on weekly editions of the Five Cent Wide Awake Library's Wild West series. The books were a treasure trove of dreams, and she didn't mind sharing them on those secret Sunday afternoons.

Clementine would sit on top the flour bin, swinging her legs, reading aloud these tales filled with gun-toting cowboys and wild mustangs, wicked cattle rustlers and scalping Indians. Shona would scrub the copper pans with a paste of lemon juice and salt, stopping to peer at the pictures and interject comments in her Scottish burr. "And who cares whether that cowboy was caught red-handed thievin' them horses? The man is too bonnie to hang. A guid woman is what he needs. A wife to love him and turn him away from the pathways of sin."

"I think I should like to marry a cowboy when I grow up," Clementine said, almost shivering with the wonder of the idea.

"Och, wouldna we all, Miss Clementine? But cowboys, they're like wild horses, them mustangs. They love their roamin' ways too much. There's no harm in dreamin' about lassoin' such a man, though, no harm t'all."

The odor of the lemon paste would mix with the other kitchen smells, of yeast and coffee beans and salted cod. But Clementine's nose wouldn't be in Boston. It would be on the prairie and filled with the smell of sagebrush and buffalo hides and woodsmoke carried on the western wind.

One Sunday Shona was given the day off to be with her family, who lived a ferry ride across the Charles River. Clementine spent the precious hours that they normally shared by herself in the kitchen. She sat at the block table, her elbows on the knife-scarred wood, her cheeks on her fists, poring over Shona's collection of souvenir cards of famous bandits and cowboys. And dreaming.

She didn't know her father had come into the room until his shadow fell across the table. She tried to hide the cards beneath a pile of freshly laundered towels. He said nothing, simply snapped his fingers and held out his hand until she put the cards into it.

She stared at the tabletop while her father slowly assessed her crime, shuffling through the souvenir cards one by one.

"I trusted you to be at your prayers, and instead I find you here, looking at this . . . this . . ." His fists crushed the cards, and the stiff pasteboard cracked and popped. "Where did you get these? Who dared to give you this lurid filth?"

She lifted her head. "Nobody. I found them."

The air began to shiver as if a wind had stolen into the sun-bright kitchen. "Recite Proverbs Twelve: Thirteen, daughter."

"'The wicked is snared by the transgression of his lips.'"

"Proverbs Twelve: Twenty-two."

"'Lying lips are an abomination to the Lord.' But I found them, Father. Truly I did. On the back stoop. Maybe the ragman left them there. He's always looking at lurid filth."

He said nothing more, only pointed up the back stairs. She walked past his outstretched arm. "I found them," she said, not caring if the lie would damn her soul forever to the lake of fire and brimstone.

In her room Clementine knelt on the seat before her window and watched the gulls dip and soar among the elms and over the gray slate rooftops. Slowly the sunshine was washed from the day. A lamplighter walked down the street with his long pole, and small points of light began to appear behind him one after the other, like a string of

dancing fireflies. She heard the sound of a door opening and
closing below and heels clicking on the granite steps of the
servants' entrance. The frayed crown of a straw hat topped
the wrought-iron railing below, followed by a fat red braid
bouncing against the back of a faded Indian shawl. A cheap
straw suitcase dangled from a work-chapped hand.

"Shona!" Clementine threw open the window, shouting at the green and blue plaid shawl as it disappeared into
the dusk. "Shona!" She leaned so far out that the edge of
the wooden sill bit into her stomach. "I didn't tell him.
Shona, wait—I didn't tell!"

Shona picked up her pace, almost running, and the
straw suitcase bounced against her legs. Although Clementine continued to scream her name, she didn't once look
back.

"Clementine."

She spun around, almost falling off the window seat.
Her father stood over her and he had his cane with him.
"Stand up and hold out your hands, daughter."

It was the punishment he meted out for the direst
transgressions. Three lashes across the palms of her hands
with his malacca cane. It hurt terribly, but she had borne
it before and she thought that this time she would not cry.
She wouldn't cry because this time she wasn't sorry.

She held out her hands, palms up, and they only trembled a little.

The cane rose and fell, cutting through the air with a
hiss, lashing her flesh. Clementine swayed and she nearly
bit through her lip. But she didn't cry out. The whiplike
rattan left a red and fiery welt.

My friend, she said to herself with each blow, *my friend,
my friend.* The words came like an incantation. Or a prayer.

When he was done, he blew the air out of his chest in
a great gust and tossed the hair back from his eyes. "Onto
your knees now and beg forgiveness of the Lord."

Her hands burned. She stared up at him, mute, her
eyes wide open and unblinking.

"Clementine, daughter . . . The face of the Almighty turns against you when you give in to the wildness in your heart."

"But I am not sorry! I would do it again and again and again. I am not sorry."

His fingers gripped the cane so tightly it trembled. "Put out your hands, then, for I am not done."

She held out her hands.

The fifth stroke, two more than she'd ever been given before, broke the skin. Her whole body shuddered. But she didn't utter a sound. Again and again the cane slashed across her lacerated hands. She knew that all she had to do was scream or plead that she was sorry, but she wasn't going to give in to him, never would she give in to him, and so the cane rose and fell, again and again and again.

"Theo, stop! Oh, God, stop, stop!"

"I cannot stop. For her soul's sake I *must* not stop!"

"But she's only a child. Look what you've done . . . She's only a child."

Clementine heard the shouting voices through a thick rushing in her ears. Shudder after shudder racked her thin body. The flesh of her palms gaped open in long cuts. Blood welled up, splashing onto the shell-patterned carpet. She thought she could taste the blood in the back of her throat, strong and hot.

Her mother's arms, the smell of roses . . . She wanted to press her face to that rose-scented breast, but she couldn't seem to make any part of her body move. Her father still held the cane gripped tightly in both hands, but tears ran from his eyes into his beard. His voice trembled. "'Thou shalt beat thy child with the rod, and thou shalt deliver a soul from hell.' What kind of father would I be if I allowed her to take these paths of wickedness? She is wild and full of sin—"

"But, Theo, you go too *far.*"

A sob tore out of his throat. The cane clattered to the floor, and he fell to his knees. His hands groped the air. "Come, daughter, we must pray. Hell is a lake of fire that can never be quenched, but I will show you the way to the Lord—"

"But I'm not sorry! I'm not sorry!" She screamed the words. But she didn't cry.

"I don't want to pray." To pray was to admit that she was sorry.

The mattress sighed, and her father's frock coat rustled as he shifted his weight. He sat beside her on the bed. She lay on her back with her hands outside the covers. Her mother had smoothed ointment on the cuts and bandaged them, but even her mother's tears hadn't stopped them from hurting. *She* hadn't cried, though. She had set her will to the thought that she would never cry again.

He shifted again and sighed himself. "Child, child . . ." He rarely touched her, but now he cupped her cheek with his big hand. "What I have done, what I do, is for love of you. So that you may grow up pure in the eyes of the Lord."

Clementine stared up at her father's face. She didn't believe him, for how could he truly love her when she remained wicked and full of wildness? And she wasn't even sorry for it.

"I don't want to pray," she said again.

He bowed his head. He was silent for so long she thought he must be praying to himself. But then he said, "Kiss me good night, then, daughter."

He leaned over her, bringing his face so close she could smell the spice of his shaving soap and the starch in his shirt. She lifted her head and brushed her lips across the soft black whiskers on his cheek. She lay back on the pillows and held herself still until he left the room, and then she rubbed her mouth with the back of her hand, over and over until her lips burned.

She slid a cracked and bent souvenir card from beneath her pillow. Again and again she tried to smooth it with her fingertips, which were swaddled in bandages. A cowboy's smiling face looked back at her. A cowboy in a fringed shirt and a ten-gallon hat, swinging a lariat with a loop as big as a haystack over his head.

She stared at him so long and hard that it seemed with just a little more effort she ought to be able to conjure him into full-blooded, laughing life.

"You are a woman grown."

So her mother said on the day Clementine turned sixteen. That morning she was allowed to pin up her hair in a thick roll at the back of her neck. A woman grown. She peered at her face in the beveled mirror of her dressing table, but she saw only herself.

But no more caps! she thought with a sudden smile. Wrinkling her nose, she picked up the one she had worn only yesterday and flung it into the fire. No more caps and a woman grown. She spun around on her toes and laughed.

It was her birthday and the day before Christmas, and they were going to a photographic gallery to have their portraits taken. They made a family outing of it, her father doing the driving himself in his new black brougham. The roofs and treetops all wore white bonnets. The winter air pinched her nose and chaffed her cheeks and smelled of the holidays— of wood fires and roasting chestnuts and evergreen boughs.

They passed the Common, where children raced their sleds down ice-crusted paths. One, a girl, must have struck a root, for her sled stopped but she kept going, tumbling head over heels, turning into a squall of blue skirts, red stockings, and flying snow. Her shrieking laughter bounced against the flat winter sky, and, oh, how Clementine yearned to be that girl. She longed for it with a fierce ache that pressed onto her heart like a pile of stones. She had never ridden a sled, never ice-skated on Jamaica Pond or thrown snowballs, and now she was too old, a woman grown. It made her think of all the things she had already missed in her life. All the things she was missing now.

Her father stopped the surrey to let a beer wagon cross in front of them. In the corner house, a boy and a woman stood in a big bow window pooled in yellow gaslight. The woman's hands rested on the boy's shoulders as they watched the snow fall. A man came up behind them, and the woman lifted her head and turned her face around, and Clementine held her breath, for she thought the man was going to kiss the woman, there in the window for all the world to see.

"Clementine, you are gawking," her mother said. "Ladies do not gawk."

Clementine leaned back against the leather squabs and sighed. Her soul felt chaffed raw with a restless longing. Something was missing from her life, missing, missing, missing . . . She thought she would almost rather feel dead inside, wooden and dry like winter branches that would never grow leaves, than have this constant, changeless longing for things unknown, unnamed. The missing things.

Stanley Addison's Photographic Gallery was in the top flat of a brownstone on Milk Street. Mr. Addison was not a genteel man. He wore a striped waistcoat of a garish lime color and a paper collar. He sported a mustache so thin it looked inked onto the flesh beneath his nose. But Clementine barely noticed the man. She was mesmerized by the samples of his art, photographs and tintypes, that hung on the dull maroon gallery walls.

She circled the room, studying each portrait. Men of serious demeanor and pompous poses, actresses and opera singers in fanciful costumes, families of mother and father and stepping blocks of children . . . She stopped, a little hum of delight escaping through her lips.

Here was a cowboy. But a real one, not a made-up man on a souvenir card. He was decked out in silver-studded *chaparejos* and a fringed vest, with a scarf knotted flamboyantly around his neck. He sat on a hay bale, his booted legs rigid and braced apart as if he was more used to straddling a horse. A coiled lariat hung over one knee and a shotgun rode across his lap. He must have had a taste for violence, for a pair of pearl-handled six-shooters was strapped around his waist as well. His mustache grew thick and long, falling over the corners of his mouth and hiding the shape of it, just as the low-brimmed hat shadowed his eyes. He looked wild and young and fierce and noble, as untamed as the land he roamed.

Clementine swung around to the hovering Mr. Addison. She sent a barrage of questions at the man. She wanted to know how a photograph was made. She wanted to make one herself. She ignored her father's scowls, nor did she notice how Mr. Addison flushed and stammered as he led them to what he called his camera room, where he proposed to take their portrait.

To Clementine this place was even more fascinating than the gallery. An enormous window had been cut into the roof so that the room was washed in light. Painted screens lined the walls depicting trellised gardens and colonnaded porches; there was even one of the Egyptian pyramids. Among the screens stood several mirrors of various sizes and an enormous sheet of foiled tin on rollers.

The camera, a large wooden box with an accordion-like bellows, sat on a wheeled dolly. Clementine circled the thing, trying to puzzle out how it worked. She gave Mr. Addison a shy, tentative smile and asked him if she might view the world through the big unblinking eye of his camera.

He blushed and nearly tripped over his own feet as he showed her where to look. Clementine pressed her eye to a hole in the top of the box and saw the Reverend Mr. Kennicutt and his wife.

A canvas backdrop, painted to resemble a cozy sitting room, was stretched on a screen behind them. Her father sat on a fringed red velvet chair; Julia stood behind him. Her hand rested on his shoulder and he held it in place with his own hand, as if he feared she would bolt from the room if he didn't restrain her. A potted palm balanced the grouping, its fronds sheltering their heads like a big green umbrella.

Seeing them through the camera lens was to Clementine like looking at them from a great distance, as if they were not of this world. Or, no—as if they were still of the world but she had gone to a place beyond. Her father shifted his feet, uncomfortable in his ruffled dignity. The palm fronds cast small bars of shadow across her mother's face.

Clementine knew she looked like her mother. They had the same ash-fair hair and shadow-green eyes, the same air of porcelain fragility. A woman growing, a woman grown. She tried to see in the face of her mother the woman she was becoming. There were so many questions she wanted to ask of that woman. Why did you laugh when the doctor said you could have no more children? Have you ever wanted to stand at the window and lift your face to a man's to be kissed? Are there empty places inside you, yearnings you cannot name? She wanted to make photographs of her mother's face and study them for the answers.

"Miss Kennicutt, I believe your father grows impatient."

She left the camera to join her parents next to the potted palm. Aware now of the camera's eye, she kept herself apart from them. Even when Mr. Addison asked her to move in closer, she took care that no part of her person, not even her sleeve or the hem of her skirt, touched the man and woman who had given her life.

Mr. Addison fixed iron clamps behind their heads to assist them in holding still. He disappeared into a small closet, and a sharp, stinging smell like rubbing alcohol permeated the room. He emerged moments later, his movements rushed and jerky like a rabbit's. He carried a rectangular wooden box, which he slid into a slot in the camera. "Raise your chin, please, Mrs. Kennicutt. Er, Reverend, if you could give your vest a tug. Now, each of you draw in a deep breath and hold it, hold it, hold it . . . Miss Kennicutt, if I could coax from you a smile."

Clementine didn't smile. She wanted to memorize all that he was doing, to understand. Her deep, wide-spaced gaze went from the wondrous wooden box to the papier-mâché props and painted screens. A growing excitement filled her until she felt that she was humming and crackling inside, like the new telephones that graced the lobby of the Tremont House hotel.

She was beginning to grasp, to know, what of life she wanted. And so it was that on that day over a year later when a cowboy from Montana knocked her down with his big-wheeled bicycle, Clementine Kennicutt was ready for him.

It would never have happened at all if a wheel hadn't come loose on her father's black brougham. It began to wobble when they turned onto Tremont Street, and soon the whole carriage was shuddering. Her father pulled over to let Clementine out. As they were only two blocks from the Tremont House, where she was to meet her mother and Aunt Etta for tea, Clementine was allowed to go on without him.

She walked slowly, savoring the glorious day. Shop awnings shielded the street from an unusually strong February sun, but the warmth of it was in the breeze and felt like milk against her skin. The strains of a waltz tinkled through the open doors of a pianoforte salesroom. She had to stiffen her back against a wild urge to go dancing down the sidewalk.

She paused before a milliner's window to stare with longing at a spring bonnet of white rice straw. A thick crimson plume flowed over the crown and was fastened onto one side with a plate buckle. A lady, Clementine knew, would have labeled the hat vulgar, but she loved it. It was like a peacock, flashy and gaudy, and it shouted to the world: "Look at me. I am beautiful!"

A delicious smell of chocolate and marshmallow wafted from the shop next door. She drifted down the street, following the smell, until she came face to face with a pyramid of candy. Sighing, she pressed her nose to the window glass. She was never given any money to spend on herself; otherwise she would have entered the shop and bought a dozen of the treats. She would have eaten each one slowly, licking the chocolate coating off first before biting into the gooey white center.

The frantic clatter of a trolley bell jangled through the air, followed by a scream and angry bellows. A silver flash caught her eye—the spokes of an enormous wheel weaving through the jam of traffic in the street.

She had seen a drawing once of such a machine in the newspaper. It was an ordinary, or a bicycle, as they were coming to be called. The advertisement had claimed it could distance the best horse in a clay's run, although seeing one now, Clementine wondered how a person even managed to stay astraddle of it.

The monstrous front wheel of this ordinary was nose-high to a man. Connected to it by a curved pipelike rod was a small trailer wheel the size of a plate. The wheelman perched on a tiny leather saddle atop the big wheel, his feet pedaling madly. His mustached mouth was open in a scream of terror or laughter, Clementine couldn't tell which over the noise he was leaving in his wake. Vehicles and pedestrians all scattered before him like frightened quail.

He bounced across the tracks directly in the path of a trolley. The horses reared in their traces, and the driver's arm pumped hard as he rang the warning bell. The bicycle narrowly avoided slamming into an elegant lady in an osier wood phaeton and struck a street-cleaning wagon instead, sending the wagon up onto the sidewalk with its sprinkler spinning in a wild arc and raining water onto the shoppers in front of Harrison's Dry Goods.

Miraculously the bicycle was still upright, although wobbling now like a drunken sailor. It hit an awry cobblestone and leaped the curb onto the sidewalk, narrowly missed a whip peddler's stand, clipped the back end of a chestnut cart, and headed for Clementine Kennicutt.

She told her legs to move, but they wouldn't obey. It never occurred to her to scream, for she had been taught to retain her dignity regardless of the provocation. Instead she simply stood there and watched the giant wheel come straight at her as if someone had aimed and shot it.

At last the man noticed her in his path and tried to swerve by yanking the wheel crosswise. The ordinary balked at this rough treatment. The tire shrieked as it skidded on the granite sidewalk, and Clementine got a whiff of hot rubber before the wheelman sailed over the handlebars and slammed into her hard, knocking her flat on her back and driving the air from her lungs.

Her chest strained as she wheezed, and her eyes opened wide onto the candy shop's awning. The green-and-white-striped canvas billowed and blurred.

"Well, hell." A man's face hovered above her, blocking out the light and the awning. It was a nice face with strong bones and a wide mouth framed by a mustache that was thick and long and the golden brown of maple syrup.

"Well, hell," he said again. He pushed a big soft gray hat off his forehead, uncovering a hank of sun-tipped light brown hair. He wore a strange, bemused look, like a little boy who's suddenly awakened from a nap and doesn't know where he is. Clementine had the strangest impulse to pat him on the cheek as if she would comfort him. Yet he was the one at fault, sailing cat-in-the-pan over the big front wheel of his ordinary and into her.

She pushed herself up onto her elbows, and he grabbed her arm. "Take it slow and easy, now," he said. In the next instant he lifted her to her feet with one hand and a hard strength that she felt all the way to the bone.

"Thank you for assisting me, sir." Her plain black straw hat was tilted askew over one eye, and he helped her to straighten it. She started to thank him for that as well and then lost her thought as she stared into eyes the color of a summer sky and filled with laughter.

"I'm sorry I stampeded over you like that," he said.

"What? Oh, no, please . . . No harm was done."

His mouth broke into a smile that blazed across his face like the explosion of light from a photographer's flash. "Not to you, maybe. And not to me. But just look at my poor bicycle."

The big wheel's spokes were bent, and the red India rubber tire lay in the gutter. But she barely gave the ordinary a glance. I must be dreaming this, she thought. Surely she must be dreaming; otherwise how would a cowboy have found his way into Boston, Massachusetts?

His pants of rough and riveted canvas were tucked into tooled leather boots with elevated heels. His blue flannel shirt gaped open at the collar and a loosely knotted red handkerchief sagged from a throat that was strong and sun-browned. He needed silver spurs on his boots and a pair of pearl-handled six-shooters, and he could have stepped straight off one of Shona's souvenir cards.

He kicked at the loose tire with the pointed toe of one of those boots and shook his head, although the bright laughter never left his face. "These things have got more pitch to them than a Montana cayuse."

"Montana . . ." The wonder of him stole her breath. His talk was all drawl and it resounded through her blood like the pipe organ in her father's church. "What is a Montana cayuse?"

"A cow pony that can run all day and turn on a nickel, and is all wild."

He had a way of smiling, she thought, that was just with his eyes. She stared into his smiling eyes as his long brown fingers tugged loose the knot in the kerchief around his neck. He pulled it off, then leaned toward her. He took one corner of the soft cotton and rubbed it along the side of her mouth. He did it gently, like the brush of a feather across silk. "Grease," he said.

"Oh." She swallowed so hard her throat made a funny clicking noise. "Are you real?"

"Last time I pinched myself I yelped, so I guess I must be real."

"I meant are you a real cowboy?" she said, and she smiled.

Clementine had no idea what her mouth did when she smiled. The man stared at her, not moving, not breathing, looking as if he'd been hit between the eyes with his own ordinary. "I, uh . . . I'm . . . well, hell."

"And if you are a cowboy, then where are your silver spurs and your *chaparejos* and your fringed vest and your pearl-handled six-shooters? And why are you riding an ordinary instead of a cayuse?" she said, and then she smiled again so that he would know she was teasing.

His head fell back and he laughed, a wild, joyous sound. "I made a bet with my cousin that an old bronco-busting cowpuncher like me could break in a Boston bicycle and look the part while he's doing it. But if I'd've put on all those duds you mentioned, I'd be looking like a greenhorn on his first roundup."

"You make me smile, the way you talk," she said, only she wasn't smiling this time. She was looking at him, lost in looking at him.

The laughter left his face and he stared back at her for the space of three slow, thunderous heartbeats. She was surprised he couldn't hear it, the beating of her heart.

He reached up and rubbed the place alongside her mouth where the grease had been. "This cousin of mine, he's got a whole factory full of these bicycles. He's putting on a demonstration race tomorrow, and somehow I've let myself get talked into riding in it. Why don't you come along with me and watch me make a fool of myself some more?"

She had never seen a race of any kind, but she thought they must be wonderful things. Of course her father would never allow her to attend such a vulgar event, let alone in the company of a man who was a stranger to the Kennicutt family. "We haven't been properly introduced."

"Gus McQueen, ma'am." He swept off his big western hat with a flourish and performed a sweeping bow that was self-mocking and yet oddly graceful for such a large man. "I own a ranch in the middle of the RainDance country, where I run a few hundred head of scraggly cows. I also got me twenty percent interest in a silver mine, which so far as I know has produced nothing but muck and gumbo. So I guess you could say my prospects are of the promising sort, and my antecedents are . . . well, if not strictly respectable, at least there's none in jail that I know of."

His gaze dropped to the hat he held in his hands. He pulled the soft brim around and around through his fingers. "As for myself, the man—I don't lay claim to being a saint, but I don't lie or cheat at cards or drink whiskey or chase after loose women. I've never put my brand on another man's calf, and when I give my word, I keep it. And I . . ." His fingers tightened on his hat, as if he struggled for the words to impress upon her that there was more to him than the cowboy she saw. He couldn't know that what she saw she thought was wonderful.

But when he looked back up at her, his eyes were laughing. "And I'm not usually one of those mannerless rascals that cusses in front of a lady, even if you did manage to pull three *hells* out of my mouth in the space of as many minutes."

She tried to act indignant, but inside she wanted to clap her hands and spin around on her toes and laugh over the delight of him. "You are unfair, sir, to lay the blame for your sins at my feet."

"Oh, but it is all your fault, ma'am, every bit of it. For I've never in all of my life come across a girl prettier than you. And when you smile . . . when you smile, my, but you are truly something wonderful to see."

He was the wonder. The way he talked and the brightness of his laughter that was like a glow on his face. And the way he simply was: built tall and broad-shouldered and strong, as a cowboy was meant to be.

"Now that I've given you my name," he said, "why don't we make it a fair swap?"

"What? Oh, it's Clementine . . . Clementine Kennicutt."

"And will you come with me and watch me race tomorrow, Miss Clementine Kennicutt?"

"Oh, no, no . . . I could never."

"Of course you can."

A strange, tingly excitement bubbled inside her. She didn't smile at him again; she only wanted to.

"What time do you race, Mr. McQueen?" she heard herself ask.

"Straight up noon."

"Do you know where the Park Street Church is, just down the block from here?" The daring of what she was doing left her light-headed, making all of her feel lighter than air, making her fly. "I'll meet you beneath the elms in front of the Park Street Church tomorrow at eleven."

He put his hat back on and he looked at her from beneath the shadowed brim of it, so that she couldn't see the expression in his eyes. "Well, I don't know if I feel right about that," he said. "Not meeting your father and getting his permission to court you proper."

"He would never give his permission, Mr. McQueen." She punctuated the words with sharp shakes of her head, while her throat grew so tight with wrenching disappointment that she could barely breathe. "Never. Never."

He looked down at her, stroking his mustache with the pad of one thumb. She waited, staring back up at him with her still, wide-open gaze. She wanted to see that race, and she wanted other things, too, things having to do with him that made her stomach clench with excitement. She wanted to see him again, to talk with him and make him laugh.

"I suppose," he finally said, "that we'll have to do it your way."

He held out his hand, and she placed hers within it.

His hand was large and rough, and it swallowed hers. He rubbed his thumb over her palm, as if he knew of the scars hidden by her glove and was trying to erase them. "Just one more thing . . . Will you marry me, Miss Clementine Kennicutt?"

She stiffened and pulled her hand from his. Something caught at her chest, something that tore through her and hurt and left her feeling empty. "You are ridiculing me."

"Oh, no, never that. Not that I don't enjoy a good joke—there's too much pain and sadness in living not to crack wise about it every now and then. But when things get real bad . . ." He flashed a sudden smile. "Say I'm trailing cows through a blue norther and the snow is stinging my face and the wind is howling like a lost soul in hell, it's the dreams I make up in my head that see me through it. Dreams like having someone waiting at home for me, with a fire going and a pot of some good-smelling thing cooking on the stove. A gal, say, with wheat-colored hair and big green eyes . . ." His words trailed off as he stared at her face, and though she blushed, she could not look away.

He shook his head, his eyes still smiling at her. "Nope, when it comes to my dreams, Miss Clementine Kennicutt, you'll always find me a dead serious man."

"Dreams . . ." she echoed.

He raised his hat. "Tomorrow, Miss Kennicutt."

He lifted the battered ordinary out of the gutter as if it weighed no more than a stocking stuffed with feathers. She watched him walk away from her, watched the people in his path part before his wide shoulders, watched his gray western hat bobbing among black silk top hats and beaver bowlers, watched until there was nothing left of him to see.

She climbed the broad granite steps and passed through the columned entrance of the Tremont House in a daze. A gentleman does not ask a girl he scarcely knows, knows not at all, to be his wife. A gentleman is one who has known you forever, whose parents have known your parents forever. A gentleman wears a frock coat and a top hat, and he does not ride an ordinary pell-mell through the streets. A gentleman—

Her mother's voice, though never loud, still managed to reach her over the refined whispers and rustling silk in the hotel lobby. "Clementine, what on earth has happened to you? Your bonnet is askew and you've *dirt* on your face, and look, there's a rip in the sleeve of your new jersey."

Clementine blinked and saw her mother and Aunt Etta standing beside her. "I was struck by an ordinary," she said.

"Gracious." Julia Kennicutt expelled a sharp breath, and Aunt Etta echoed her gasp. "Those devil-driven wheels will be the death of us all," Julia said and her sister clucked her agreement. "They shouldn't be allowed on the streets. Only a hooligan would even think of driving such a . . . a boneshaker."

To hear slang on her mother's lips nearly shocked a smile out of Clementine. "He's not a hooligan," she said, and then a laugh did roll up and out of her throat, a laugh that was loud and rather unseemly. And quite shocking, coming as it did from a girl who rarely laughed. "He's a cowboy."

The clock on the square white tower of the Park Street Church showed that it lacked five minutes to eleven. Clementine pulled her cloak close around her neck. It was more seasonably cold than yesterday. The big elms cast deep shadows onto the sidewalk, and a stiff breeze blew in off the bay.

She paced the length of the wrought-iron fence that separated the street from the tombstones of the Old Granary Burial Ground. She looked again at the clock on the tower. A long, agonizing minute had passed.

She decided to play a little game with herself. She would walk along the fence to the Egyptian-style gateway that led into the cemetery, and when she turned around, he would be there—

"Miss Kennicutt!"

A black rattletrap gig pulled up beside her with a protesting creak of its wheels, and she looked up into a man's
sun-browned, smiling face that was shaded by the broad
brim of a big gray hat.

"You're here," he said. "I wasn't sure you would be."

"I wasn't sure you would be either."

Laughing, he leaped down and helped her into the gig.
"Sorry about the shabbiness of this conveyance, ma'am," he
said as he climbed back onto the seat beside her. "My uncle
has five sons, and there's always a shortage of vehicles in
the family stables— Get up, there!" he yelled to the horse,
and they pulled out into the street at such a spanking pace
she instinctively gripped her hat. The motion jostled her
so that she fell against him. He was solid and surprisingly
warm. She stiffened, scooting away from him as far as she
could, until her arm and hip were pressed into the iron
railing that wrapped around the seat.

His eyes smiled at her. "I probably don't want to know
this, but just how old are you, Miss Kennicutt?"

Her gaze fell to the gloved hands she had clasped so
tightly in her lap. She thought about lying, but he had said
he was a man of his word and she wanted to be worthy of
his regard. "I am seventeen."

"Seventeen . . . Oh, Lord, help me."

She looked behind her, into the empty space where the
gig's hood would have been folded, if it'd had one. "Where
is your ordinary?"

"I left my cousin to rope and saddle it. I figure if he
wants me to race, he can supply the mount."

"You do make me smile, sir—the way you talk."

"Uh-uh. So far I've only managed to do it twice. But
I aim to keep on trying until . . ." He was staring at her
mouth so intently she had to bite her lower lip to stop its
trembling. "Until I can get you to smile at me again."

She jerked her gaze away from his. But a moment later
she was trying to look at him out the corner of her eye.

Today he was dressed more properly for cycling, in blue knee breeches, yellow gaiters, and a seal-brown corduroy reefer jacket. The thin velvet breeches fit tight across the muscles of his thighs, which looked strong from busting broncos and trailing cattle. She thought that riding an ordinary probably seemed tame stuff to such a man.

There were so many things she wanted to say to him; so many questions crowded her mouth. But the one that fell out made her flush with the stupidity of it. "Is it true what they say about Montana, that a person can ride from one end to the other of it without crossing a fence?"

He laughed, as she had known he would. But she didn't mind, for she liked his laugh. "I suppose you might come upon a drift fence or two here and there," he said. "And there are some mighty big mountains that'll give you pause."

She had read about such mountains, but she had never been able to draw a picture of them in her mind. She had known only the low bluffs and drumlins that rose above the salt marshes around Boston.

They had reached one of the busiest thoroughfares, and he gave his attention to the traffic now, so she was able to study him. He was so large he seemed to fill all of the gig's seat. There was a joyous shine to him, like a brand-new copper penny. "What brings you all this way to Boston, Mr. McQueen?"

He turned his head and his gaze met hers. She had forgotten that his eyes were such a deep, clear blue. The Montana sky would be that blue, she thought.

"My mother was a long time dying," he said. "She asked to see me before she went, and so I came. I'll be leaving again, though, come the end of the week."

"I'm sorry," she said, and then added hastily, lest he misunderstand her, "Sorry, I mean, about your mother's death."

A shadow crossed his face, like clouds scudding across the sun. "I left her and Boston when I was seventeen, the same age as you, and I wasn't always very good about writing."

"Did you run away?"

He cast a glance at her, then made a clicking noise in his mouth, urging the horse around an ice wagon that had rolled into their path. "In a manner of speaking, yeah, I guess I did. I wanted to see the elephant." At her quizzical look, he laughed. "I wanted to see the marvels of the great Wild West. Indians and buffalo and grizzly bears and rivers of gold."

How she yearned to see such marvels herself. Yet it all seemed so far beyond her reach and doomed forever to remain so. "And was he as wonderful as you thought he would be—your elephant?"

She watched him as he took a moment to think about it; there was an excitement about him, a shining, that stirred something deep within her.

"There's a bigness about Montana that tends to frighten a lot of people. But it's not so big you can't find what you're looking for, if you know what that something is." His eyes met hers, and the stirring within her quickened. "Sometimes, Miss Kennicutt, all a body needs is a place to run to."

She didn't know what she was looking for. The missing things, she supposed, but she couldn't have defined them, even to herself. She only knew that in this one moment she felt alive. The wind was stiff with the bite of salt in it, and late winter sunlight dappled the shop awnings and made the windows shimmer, and she was going to see a bicycle race in the company of a man, a cowboy.

He pulled the horse to a halt in the middle of the street, ignoring the shouts that came from the carriages and wagons stalled behind them. He turned to her, and although his eyes were still wreathed with laugh lines, his mouth was set serious. "Yesterday I told you one of my dreams. Now how about sharing one of yours. What do you dream of, Miss Kennicutt?"

She felt suddenly breathless, as if she'd just sprinted to the top of one of his big Montana mountains. "I don't know," she said, but of course she did know. She dreamed of him. She'd been dreaming of him all her life.

"I'm twenty-five years old," he said, his gaze probing hers, pulling at her, "and I've done a fair amount of wandering in my time. When a man's seen as much of the world as I have, he gets to knowing right off what he wants when he comes across it." His thumb stroked the bone of her jaw, and the smile his mouth made did something more to her breath. "Or *runs* over it, as the case may be. You and me, girl, we're a fit. I could take my time at courting you, showing you how we're meant to be together, but either you see it now—this rightness of us—or you don't. And no flower bouquets and serenades are going to change what is already the truth."

She marveled at him, that he could speak of dreams in one breath and of certainties in the next. She had never been on a horse in her life, but in that moment she felt as if she were riding one of his cayuses that could run all day and turn on a nickel and was all wild.

She turned her head away, her heart pounding so hard she wondered that he couldn't hear it. "I can't think about this yet," she said.

His words came to her, riding on the salty wind. "You're already thinking about it, Miss Kennicutt. Shoot, you're halfway to Montana already."

2

GUS MCQUEEN'S YOUNG BRIDE stood on the grassy levee and looked over the straggling line of weather-rotten buildings and jerry-built shacks that passed for the town of Fort Benton, Montana. She wasn't going to let herself be disappointed. She had never seen a real elephant before, either, but she supposed that up close they all must be smelly, dirty beasts.

No sooner had the steamboat deposited them and their baggage onto the levee than Gus informed her he would have to check immediately for a freight wagon leaving in the direction of the RainDance country, for it was not a route often traveled. "Wait for me right here, Clementine," he said to her, pointing to the ground as if he thought she was too dense to understand what "here" meant. "Don't move from this spot."

She opened her mouth to ask if she could at least do her waiting out of the sun, but he was already striding away from her. Her gaze followed him as he crossed the road and disappeared into the yawning doors of a livery barn. Gus McQueen. Her husband. Sometimes, for no reason, looking at him made her chest ache. It was the tall, strong, splendid sight of him, she supposed.

A departing steamboat held her interest for a while as she watched clouds of inky smoke billow from its double stacks. The giant paddles of its stern wheel churned the coffee-colored water, splashing the bank and stirring up a stink of dead fish and rotting weeds. The boat pulled out into the river with a bleat of its whistle and a hiss of steam, and she turned her attention back across the dusty road. They had been traveling six weeks to reach this nothing place.

A few of the ramshackle buildings sported rough signs. She was able to identify a mercantile, a hotel with a sagging porch, and a saddle and harness shop. The mercantile's tall false front provided the only dab of shade on this side of the river.

She was surprised to notice a number of women strolling up and down the boardwalk. Some walked alone, but most were in pairs, arm in arm, laughing and chatting. Many were dressed quite finely in hats trimmed with ostrich plumes and silk flowers and dresses with long pleated and ruched trains of bright rainbow colors. Clementine watched the pleasant scene with wistful longing. Her black sarcenet parasol seemed to draw the unusually warm spring sun down upon her head. Trickles of sweat rolled down her sides and between her breasts. In her cambric chemise, long flannel drawers, steel busk corset, quilted eiderdown petticoat with two flounces, nainsook camisole, and oatmeal serge traveling suit with velvet-trimmed waistcoat, she was stifling.

She looked toward the livery for a sign of Gus. She didn't see him, nor did she see Indians or bank robbers or any other obvious perils. With so many other women about, she could hardly be in any danger. She couldn't see what harm it would do to cross over to the mercantile for a few moments of blessed relief in the shade. Especially if she was careful to keep an eye on their baggage.

She had to lift her skirts high in order to pick her way around the horse apples and bull pies that littered the wide and wagon-rutted street. As she stepped onto the boardwalk she looked up and saw that a man lounging on the hotel porch in a willow rocker was staring rudely at her legs. She lowered her skirt, even though the warped boards were stained with dried mud and tobacco spit. At least her traveling suit had only a modest train.

She had started toward the shade of the mercantile

when she noticed that next door was a saloon. Curious, she peered over the top of the slatted swinging doors. Through a haze of tobacco smoke she saw a garish oil painting of a woman who was as plump as a corn-fed chicken and quite naked. Men were lined up along a counter facing the naked woman, standing slightly bent over and hipshot, like horses at a hitching rack. The saloon was filled with a kaleidoscope of men who looked as if they could have stepped right out of a drawing in one of Shona's Wild West novels. Soldiers in blue, miners in their rough clothes, professional gamblers in black suits and ruffled white shirts. The air that wafted out the slatted doors reeked of spilled whiskey and un-washed bodies. A clink of glass against glass was followed by a roar of laughter and an explosion of pungent profanity. Clementine realized with a start that even in Montana it probably wasn't quite the proper thing for a lady to allow her eyes and ears to linger on such a sight.

As she turned away, she felt a tug on her skirt. She looked down to discover the rowel of a spur hooked in her train. Her gaze followed the length of the man from his glossy boot up to his face. It was the man from the hotel porch.

He must surely be an army scout, she thought, with his long blond hair and fringed buckskin shirt, and his knife sheath decorated with brass studs. But tobacco juice stained his yellow goatee, and his hands, she noticed as he raised his hat to her, were dirty. "Howdy do, ma'am," he said.

"How do you do," she said, nodding politely. Of course they hadn't been properly introduced, but Gus had already explained to her how westerners were freer in their ways. She gave a slight pull on the train of her traveling suit. "I fear, sir, that your spur has become entangled with my skirt."

He looked down, opening his eyes wide in exaggerated surprise. "Why, so it is. I do beg your pardon."

He bent over and unhooked her train off the sharp rowel, lifting her skirt indecently high to do so. When he straightened up, he was grinning. "You appear to be a mite hot, ma'am, if you don't mind my sayin' so." He slipped his hand beneath her elbow. "How 'bout if I buy you something cool and wet to put out the fire in them pretty li'l cheeks—"

"Take your hand off her!"

Clementine swung her head around to see her husband striding down the walk so fast the rotting boards groaned beneath his weight. "I said, let her go, damn you." Gus planted himself before the man. His hands hung loose at his sides, but the rest of him had drawn up tall and taut, and his eyes glittered with a coldness she had never seen before. He was also wearing a gun she had never seen before, its holster hanging heavily from a gun belt strapped around his waist.

She tried to pull her arm from the man's grasp, but he tightened his grip. He hawked and shot a wad of tobacco onto the toe of Gus's boot. "You're rustling on my territory here, cowboy," he said, and his voice, which had been so friendly before, now turned mean. "I found the lady first."

"The *lady* is my wife."

The men stared at each other and the moment lengthened, grew tight, and there was the danger of impending violence in the air that could be smelled, sharp as gunpowder.

The man's gaze flickered away from Gus's. "My mistake," he said. He released her and stepped back, his hands spread wide in an attitude of surrender.

Gus seized her arm and hauled her down into the street so abruptly her teeth cracked together. "I told you to stay put, girl. Did you think I was talking just to exercise my tongue?"

She dug in her heels and jerked her arm out of his grasp, forcing him to turn and face her. A spring wagon clipped past, its wheels sending a cloud of dust drifting over them. "You flung an order at my head, Mr. McQueen, and walked off. If you had exercised your tongue a little more and given me a reason—"

He leaned over to shout at her. "You want a reason? Because it's the middle of the afternoon, when the chippies go on parade. Any woman who walks along Front Street during this time of day is likely to be taken for one of their kind. Is that what you want everyone to think, Clementine—that you're a chippy?"

His hands had clenched into fists, and she took a deep breath. She would not fear him the way she feared her father.

"You still haven't explained yourself adequately, sir. What is a chippy?"

For a moment he simply stared at her, breathing heavily, then the anger collapsed within him. He reached out and pulled her to his chest, rubbing her back with his big hands. "Aw, Clementine, you're such a sweet innocent. A chippy is a soiled dove. A fancy woman who sells her body to a man for his pleasure."

She felt small tremors rippling through him, and she realized suddenly that he had been more frightened than angry. The thought disturbed her—that he could be frightened. "I didn't know of this western custom, this chippy parade."

"Clementine." He gripped her arms and set her away from him. "You mustn't use that word, not even with me."

"What am I to call them, then?"

"Nothing. You're not supposed to know about them."

"But it was because I didn't know about them that I got us into trouble. Surely you must see that ignorance does not help in this sort of situation. I'm not a child; I am a woman grown."

He was becoming angry with her again. She could see it in the flush of color on his cheeks and the pulse pounding hard and fast in his neck. "I'm not going to stand here in the middle of the street and discuss the conduct of lewd women with you. Come along." He spun around and stalked away from her. "I got a room for us at the hotel."

They carried their baggage into the hotel with its

sagging front porch. No sooner were they settled in their room than he told her he had to leave again to track down a mule skinner who was rumored to be heading west in the morning. He tugged his hat tighter on his head, picked up the key, and headed for the door.

"You can't be meaning to lock me in," she said. The words weren't loud, but they were as sharp as a scream.

He swung back around. There was a tautness about him that had nothing to do with what had happened down in the street. Or not only to do with that, for she felt it within herself as well. Like a length of silk thread being stretched so tight it was in danger of snapping. He wasn't a wild-riding cowboy come to life off a souvenir card. He was a man, her man now, and yet she suddenly realized she didn't know him at all. Looking up into his sun-browned face, into those vivid Montana-sky eyes, she thought how she so wanted to come to know him.

His breath left him in a soft sound that was like a sigh. He tossed the key back on the table; it made a loud clatter in the dense silence. "I wasn't going to lock the door to keep you in, only to keep the scalawags out. There aren't a lot of decent women out here, and some men forget how to behave."

His gaze came back to hers and then settled hard and long on her mouth. Her lips felt as if they were burning. It was all she could do not to wet them with her tongue or to cover them with her fingers. *Hold me,* she suddenly wanted to say to him. *Kiss me.*

"Why don't you go ahead and wash up?" he said, and an instant later the door shut behind him.

She curled her hand into a fist and pressed it to her mouth.

The room was the size of a horse stall, part of a larger room that had been broken up with calico partitions. One of the partitions went up to the middle of the room's only window, and there was a three-inch gap between the deep-set sashed panes and the calico wall. She could hear men moving about and talking on the other side of the thin cloth, which had once been red but was now faded to a dusty rose. She saw the flash of a brown flannel sleeve through the gap when one of the men came up to the window.

Through the dust-streaked glass Clementine could look down on the chippies she must pretend did not exist as they strolled like pretty birds along the boardwalk in their bright plumes and ruched trains. Soiled doves, Gus had called them, these women who sold themselves for a man's pleasure outside the sanctity of the marriage bed.

The marriage bed.

She stared at the jack bed built into the corner, with its moth-eaten gray army blanket and lumpy straw ticking. There were intimacies between husband and wife that went beyond kissing and a man holding his woman in his arms. To share his bed, to lie with him, to become one flesh. *"I am my beloved's, and his desire is toward me."* Words—sly, whispered words, the sacred, solemn words of Scripture—words were all she knew of the physical act of loving. She was Gus McQueen's wife, but there had been no marriage bed for them as yet.

They had passed the train ride from Boston to Saint Louis on hard wooden benches, pressed knee to knee with a family of German immigrants. The swaying, smoking kerosene lamps and the reek of sausage and sauerkraut had Clementine passing the hours in a haze of nausea. The one night they'd spent in a hotel in Saint Louis had been in separate rooms, for they hadn't yet become husband and wife. The next morning they'd been married by a judge, and they'd gone from the courthouse straight to the levee and boarded the steamboat that would take them up the Missouri River to Fort Benton.

The steamer was making its first run of the year, over a month earlier than usual because of a light winter. They were only a day out of Saint Louis when the captain spotted the smoke of a rival boat, and it became a race to see who could navigate the tricky waters of the river faster. They dodged ice floes and uprooted trees in the rough current. They stopped rarely, only to wood up, even traveling at night and sounding the channel by lantern light.

She had seen buffalo once, an enormous herd that was a black smudge on the horizon. Once they'd been fired upon by hostile Indians that Gus said were the same Sioux who'd massacred General Custer at the Little Big Horn only three years before. But they'd been too far away for her to see so much as a feather on their war bonnets, and their shots had fallen harmlessly in the water, sounding like a string of firecrackers.

To Clementine, safe on the riverboat, it had all been so exciting, like living an adventure out of one of Shona's novels. Gus had been less a husband to her than a companion in that adventure, the wood-wise scout to her intrepid explorer. Their nights they'd spent sleeping in the common room of some woodyard with the steamer's roustabouts. Or in cots on the second deck with only a canvas tarp to shelter them and no privacy at all—

"I thought you were going to wash up."

She swung around, startled, for she hadn't heard the door open. Gus shut it with the heel of his boot. He came right up to her until only a handspan separated them, and she had never been more aware of him as a man, of his man's great size and his man's hard strength. She thought of the jack bed waiting in the corner, her marriage bed. She tried to swallow and couldn't; her mouth was as dry as the dusty road outside the window.

"Would you do something for me, girl?"

She nodded dumbly, unable even to breathe. A man hawked and spat in the room next door, and the other man cursed foully, and then there was a thump, like a boot hitting a far wall, and another curse.

"Would you let down your hair for me?"

Her hands trembled once as she lifted them to take off her felt bonnet, plain and black and without any plumes. He took the hat from her and tossed it onto the bed, his gaze not leaving her face. One by one, she pulled the pins out of her hair, and it began to fall in thick hanks over her shoulders. She shook her head, and it settled heavily on her back, falling to her waist.

He ran his hands through it, lifting it and letting it fall, watching it slide through his fingers. "You got hair like molded butter, Clem, and just as soft. All of you is so soft. So soft and fine."

He lowered his head and she thought: He is going to kiss me. He had kissed her before, but she knew this kiss would be different; it would lead to a thing that would change her forever, mark her, like a brand.

"Let him kiss me with the kisses of his mouth: for thy love is better than wine." Oh, how she wanted this. She wanted him.

"Clementine."

She tried to make her mouth smile, to stop the shaking in her legs. "Please . . ." But there were no words within her experience to tell him what she wanted.

He tightened his grip on her hair, as he mistook her trembling and her pleas for resistance. "You're my legal wife, girl. I'm entitled."

"I know, I know." Her eyes fluttered closed. *"Let him kiss me with the kisses of his mouth . . . Let him kiss me . . ."*

One of the men next door began to relieve himself into a tin chamber pot, clattering, splattering, and then he let out a rude noise suitable only for the privy house. Clementine jerked back, and hot color flooded her face as the appalling noises went on and on, echoing like a Boston Bay foghorn.

"Well, hell," Gus said when the room next door at last fell silent. He smiled, a shining, laughing Gus McQueen smile. He lowered his head again, but he only rubbed the tip of her nose with his.

"A man can't marry himself a lady and then make love to her for the first time in a place like this, where you can practically spit through the walls. I want it to be good for you, good and decently done, as it should be between man and wife."

He slid his hands through her hair and lifted it to his

mouth as if he would drink of it. Her breath caught, and she trembled.

"I know you're scared, girl, but then, a man doesn't expect a wife who's been gently reared the way you have to be easy about the goings-on that take place in the bedroom. I reckon if I've waited my whole life for you, I can wait awhile longer. I don't suppose it would kill me to court you a little more first."

He was breathing heavily, as she was. Trembling deep inside himself, as she was. It was Clementine's thought that he could court her just as easily in bed as out of it, but she held it back. She was a lady, gently reared and innocent of the goings-on that took place in a bedroom.

"Christ, Jeb," a gruff voice bellowed next door. "You got it smellin' like the back end of a cow in here."

Gus's head fell forward, nearly bumping with hers. He was laughing. She did so love his laugh. "I reckon this here is more parts of the elephant you ever thought or hoped to make the acquaintance of," he said, and his laughter caused his breath to flutter soft and warm against her neck.

"I don't mind," she said. His breath on her neck was making her shiver and tighten up inside, tighter and tighter, so that she had to bite her lip to keep from moaning.

"Of course you mind. But things'll get better, you'll see. More what you're used to." His hand, gentle, so very gentle, stroked down the length of her neck to her shoulders. "The first night at our place, that's when I'm going to make you mine."

"Put a nickel twixt his ears, boy," the mule skinner said. "And quit grinnin' like a jackass eatin' cactus."

Gus McQueen kept a tight line on his mouth, but his eyes creased with laughter as he fingered a coin out of his vest pocket. He ambled his horse to the head of the team and, leaning over, placed the nickel between the floppy ears of the lead mule. The mules, all sixteen of them, stood gray and still as corpses in the middle of the Montana prairie.

His bride watched, perched beside the mule skinner on the wagon's plank seat. The skinner was a woman, although one wouldn't have known it to look at her. Her face was as brown and weathered as saddle leather. She wore man-sized boots and britches so caked with grease they crackled when she sat. Her cropped hair was covered with a battered slouch hat, its brim pinned up in the front with thorns. It was the filthiest hat Clementine had ever seen.

The skinner made a show of taking off her oilskin duster and rolling up the sleeves of her homespun shirt. Her arms were like a man's, knotty and thick as pine logs. She peeled the buckskin gauntlets off her hand and spat into bear-paw palms. Slowly she lifted the heavy braided rawhide out of the whip socket.

Nickel Annie claimed she was a rarity, being the only female in Montana to skin a mule train. Her wagon, built for heavy loads and rough terrain, was piled high with mining machinery, furniture, barrels, a bundle of buffalo hides that gave off a sour smell, and a piano bound for the only honky-tonk in Rainbow Springs, which was the only town in the RainDance country. Annie called her eight yoke of mules her babies. But she drove them the way a man would, by filling their ears with curses and cracking a whip over their heads.

The skinner gripped the whip's lead-filled hickory stock with both hands. She shifted the cud of tobacco in her mouth from one cheek to the other and grinned at Clementine. "You folk ready for this?"

"Ready?" Gus McQueen said. "I've been ready so long I've grown moss on my head."

Clementine pursed her lips to keep from laughing. A hawk hung in the air, the drone of the wind filled her ears. Suddenly the skinner's arm went back and forward in a blur. Twenty-five feet of braided rawhide unfurled and popped like a Fourth of July firecracker. The nickel went spinning up, up, up until it winked like a raindrop in the sun. Gus tried to snatch it out of the air and missed. The mules stood, not a tail flickering, not a hair stirring.

"And that," the mule skinner said with another brown-toothed grin that split her face in two, "is why they call me Nickel Annie."

"Well, shucks. And here all this time I thought it was 'cause you're so cheap," Gus drawled, and Clementine covered a smile with her hand.

"A nickel nurser—ha!" The skinner flung back her head and let out a bray of laughter. "A nickel nurser!" She shot a glob of tobacco juice out the corner of her mouth and gathered up the jerk line. The wagon lurched, and Clementine gripped the seat to keep from tumbling headfirst into rocks and ironweed and prairie grass. Gus nudged his horse into a walk beside them.

"Fetch me back my nickel, boy," Annie said after a couple of minutes had passed in silence.

"That's my nickel."

"Not any more it ain't. I earned it off you fair 'n' square. 'Sides, it don't seem right to leave a nickel a-lyin' there in the middle of the range where just any innocent might come acrost it. Why, a jackrabbit could swaller it, mistakin' it for a thistle, and give hisself a bellyache. Or an Injun could find it, spend it getting hisself all liquored up, and go on a scalpin' rampage and we'd all wind up dead as General Custer. Why, the more I think on it, boy, you owe it to man and animalkind to fetch me back my nickel."

Clementine looked behind them at the ruts that passed for a road. The wind tattered the worm of dust left by their passing. There was nothing to mark the place where the nickel had landed.

Gus heaved a put-upon sigh and pulled his horse around. He pushed his hat down on his head, thrust his boots deep into the stirrups, and shortened the reins. Without warning, it seemed, for she had seen no signal pass between the man and his mount, the horse broke into a wild gallop back down the trail.

Gus leaned far over sideways out of the saddle. His hand dug into the tall grass, his fingers scraping the ground. He was barely upright again before he had reined into a turn so tight the horse did it on its haunches. He laughed as he galloped back toward them, passing the wagon and tossing the nickel at the mule skinner on the fly. Annie pawed the coin out of the air, bit it, and stuffed it into the pocket of her leather britches. Gus kept going, disappearing over a hill of dusty sage.

Clementine watched him with her heart in her eyes. He rode by the seat of his pants and the tips of his spurs, and her chest wanted to swell with pride for him. Her man. Her cowboy.

She wasn't sure she liked it, though, when he rode ahead of them, leaving her alone in Nickel Annie's raw-boned company. She had the feeling the mule skinner kept testing her and thus far had found her sadly wanting. "It takes a gritty heart to come out to this country and meet it on its own terms," Nickel Annie had once said, implying that Clementine's heart wasn't near gritty enough.

Normally the skinner drove her team by riding on the back of the left wheel mule. But today she'd chosen to ride with Clementine up on the seat, which wasn't anything more than a rough plank nailed between the wagon's tall slat-board sides.

Clementine clung to the splintery board eight feet in the air with a white-knuckled grip. The ground was pocked and rutted, and the wagon swayed and lurched over it like a rowboat in a heavy swell. She could see why these wagons were called spine-pounders. She felt the jar of every mile deep in her bones.

Miles. There had been an endless number of them in the week since they had left the steamboat and Fort Benton. Flat miles of olive sage and wind-ruffled grass. But today the buttes, which had been but blurred humps in the distance, were now suddenly upon them. It was like the quickening swell of an ocean wave, the way the plains rolled into ridges studded with yellow pines and dipped into coulees choked with brush and old snowdrifts.

A gust of wind buffeted her and drove stinging dirt into her face. The day was raw, the sun hidden behind clouds as thick and woolly as a horse blanket. Yesterday that same sun had been brittle and hot. Clementine had never sweated before in her life, but she could feel the residue of yesterday's sweat on her skin, gritty and sticky. She thought she probably stank, but she couldn't smell herself over the rank odor emanating from the green buffalo hides and Nickel Annie, who probably hadn't bathed since Lee surrendered at Appomattox.

At the road ranch where they'd spent last night, there had certainly been little opportunity to get clean. The place had been nothing more than a sod shack. When Clementine went to wash up before a dinner of boiled potatoes and canned corn, she found only an inch of wet scum in the wash trough and a sliver of soap the size of a thumbnail in an empty sardine can. The tow towel on the roller had been as black as the bottom of a coal scuttle. Their beds that night had been just as horrid: rough bunks lined with coarse ticking stuffed with prairie grass—what Gus had laughingly called Montana feathers. The wall next to the bunks had been smeared with smashed bedbugs.

Clementine shuddered now at the memory. A lick of wind tore at the ground and sent more dust swirling into her face. She wiped her cheeks and forehead with a grimy handkerchief and licked the prairie of her teeth. Already she knew she would come to hate this about her husband's country, this inability to keep clean.

Her husband. She could see him riding through a line of cottonwoods in the distance, sitting tall and loose in the saddle on the dun-colored mare he had bought in Fort Benton. She felt a sweet warmth when she looked at him. He was such a flamboyant man, with his ready smile and big laugh. As if he'd been dipped in gold with his sun-tanned face and tawny hair, and his melodious voice.

"An infinity of grass, Clementine," he had said, with that shining look he got on his face whenever he talked of his dream: to build his Rocking R into a cattle ranch the likes of which the world had yet to see. "Montana is an infinity of grass, and it's all there practically free for the taking." When he talked about the RainDance country, about its wild beauty and the miles of open range, she would feel something like music humming in her blood.

An infinity of grass. She would never have believed it without seeing it for herself. This endless vista of riffling yellow and green, always being stirred by the wind and smelling of the sage. She lifted her gaze to the looming mountains, black and gray and peaked with snow. There was such a great vastness to this country. What Gus called elbow room for the heart. But all this land and sky—there was a raw emptiness to it that sometimes touched her soul with fear.

The rawhide whip snapped twice through the air, crackling like gunfire over the head of a mule lagging in harness, breaking her reverie. "Gee, Annabel!" the skinner bellowed. "Gee, you twice-damned daughter of a whoring bitch!"

Clementine had to struggle to hide another smile, although she thought she could almost feel her ears burning. The mule skinner was not at all genteel. Indeed, Nickel Annie was proud of her leather lungs and her salty mouth, which she liked to boast could cuss the hide off her mules slicker than any whip.

The skinner pulled a twist of tobacco out of her boot and tore off a hunk with her mulelike teeth. She worked her jaw awhile, then tongued home the chaw. Clementine tensed as a brown stream whizzed past her face to land on the wagon tongue with a splat. But for the first time that week she didn't flinch.

"You was sayin' yesterday," Annie began in a voice gentle enough to lull a baby to sleep, "that your daddy is preacher to some temple back in Boston?"

An old tumbleweed tore loose from a rock and bounced away, startling a sage chicken. The bird made a strange whirring noise as it took to the air, but Clementine's gaze did not follow its flight. She knew the skinner was setting her up like a wooden duck at a county fair, only to shoot something outrageous out of her mouth that would bring a blush to Clementine's cheeks.

"Tremont Temple, yes. Perhaps you've been there?" she said with a Beacon Hill parlor smile. She was determined to hold her own against the vexing woman.

The skinner's lips pulled back from her teeth in a tobacco-stained grin. "Well, Gus's daddy is a Bible banger, too, but you probably already knew that. A circuit-ridin' preacher is Gus's daddy. Not like yourn, who does his sermonizing in a proper church. A temple, even . . . Now, there's a funny thing I've noticed about preachers' sons over the years," she added as if the thought had just occurred to her. "They're either hell-bent boys or they're all lassoed up tight in their own righteousness like your Gus. No betwixes and no betweens."

Clementine watched the wagon ruts unwind before her like ribbons across the prairie. Gus hadn't told her that his father was a servant of God. Odd that they had this in common, yet he hadn't seen fit to mention it. "Mr. McQueen is a good man," she said aloud, then wished she hadn't, for it sounded too much as if she was trying to convince herself that Gus was nothing like her righteous father.

Annie let out a liquid chuckle. "Oh, a regular saint is your husband Gus. Just like 'a hell-bent boy' do sure enough describe your brother-in-law."

She cast a smirking look at Clementine's wind-chaffed face. "Surely your Gus must've told you about his brother. They're partners in the Rocking R, each owning half and each tryin' to run it like he owned the whole shebang. Bets are on in Rainbow Springs as to how long it's going to last. Nope, there ain't two more different snowflakes than Gus McQueen and Zach Rafferty."

Not a word of it. He hadn't told her a word of this. Only yesterday he had accused her of having a jaw as tight as a beaver trap because she found it so hard to share her thoughts and feelings. But he had been keeping secrets of his own. So many times he had described his ranch in dream words—the meadows of sweet grass and wildflowers ringed by surging buttes and tall, timbered ridges. Not once had he mentioned that he shared the ownership of all that with a brother.

So many wonderings arose within her: whether this brother was younger or older than Gus, and why they didn't share the same name. But it was her husband's place to tell her these things. To discuss him and his brother behind his back was a disloyal thing, what her mother would call perfidious gossip. She decided not to say another word and let Nickel Annie stew in the silence.

The wagon's big hickory axle creaked; the iron tires crunched over the rocky ground; the wind whined. Clementine cleared her throat. "In what way are the brothers different?"

Nickel Annie's grin pleated her leathery face. She sent another brown stream splatting onto the wagon tongue and settled her shoulders for a long gab. "To begin with, Gus spent his boyhood with his ma, getting an East Coast shine on him, while Rafferty was rawhiding around rough country, growing up wild as a corncrib rat. I suppose you could say Gus's been tamed and Rafferty ain't.

"And then there's Rafferty's sinnin' ways, which Gus can't abide. The drinkin' and the gamblin' and the whoring—especially the whoring. 'Course that might've just been jealousy workin' through Gus's guts. Mebbe it explains why he up and married you, him bein' a man for all his righteous ways, and men always do tend to end up thinking with their tallywhackers. And genu-ine ladies like you are as scarce out here as sunflowers in January."

Clementine supposed she was being complimented. Or maybe not. People out here, she was learning, took a perverse pride in their rough edges, flaunting them like medals. "Thank you," she said, a bit stiffly.

"You're welcome. Out here, you see, women're either whores or they're like me, thinking that all men are snakes and seein' no sense in bedding down with a snake. Which is why all the cowpunchers and sheep-coddlers, all the wolvers and dirt-grubbers—hell, you name it, they're all gonna come riding from miles around just to eyeball you, you bein' such a rarity. There ain't a man out here who wouldn't give his left ballock to be gettin' the cook, housekeeper, laundress, and all-round slave that you're gonna be to your man. Yup, slave and broodmare and bedmate all done up in the starchy trappings of an honest-to-God lady—Christ, the wonder of it stretches the mind." She hooted a laugh. "Dearie, you ain't only a rarity, you're a damned luxury!"

Annie paused, and the whining wind immediately rose up to fill the silence. One of the mules flapped its ears and let out a snort, but Clementine held herself still. *I will not let her provoke me,* she vowed. There was grit in her heart and she would prove it.

"Nope," the skinner went on with an exaggerated sigh. "Rafferty sure ain't gonna like findin' out his brother brought hisself back a wife with notions to go and civilize things. But Gus is the one comin' in for the real surprise."

"What do you mean?" Clementine asked in spite of herself.

Nickel Annie leaned so close that the stink of her tobacco breath washed over Clementine's face. "You, Mrs. McQueen. Ye're the surprise. 'Cause underneath that goody-goody shy-and-sweet air you wear on the skin side is a hot-blooded woman just waitin' for an excuse to bust out. Only Gus, he don't see it. Yet."

"I cannot imagine what you are talking about," Clementine said, her mouth tightening around the lie. Somehow the mule skinner had seen the wildness in her, the wickedness. Just as her father had. As Gus had not, and never would if she could help it.

"I am not like that. Like what you said." She smoothed her nubby wool skirt over her lap. She ensured that the pins were still in place in the thick Roman knot of hair at the back of her head. She felt disheveled . . . hot-blooded. "And as for Mr. Rafferty, he'll just have to accept the fact that his brother is married, and that is that."

"That is that, hunh?" Nickel Annie brayed a laugh. "Hell, with Rafferty that ain't *never* that."

They made camp that night on the side of the road beneath a lightning-scarred box elder tree. Nickel Annie fixed a supper of sowbelly beans and canned corn and showed Clementine how to bake biscuits in a fry-pan.

Clementine ate her meal sitting on the wagon tongue, apart from Annie and Gus and a smelly fire of sagebrush and buffalo dung. She swung her dangling feet back and forth, back and forth, watching the toes of her high-buttoned black kid shoes make parallel ruts, like miniature wagon tracks, through the tall prairie grass. But these marks, she knew, would be only temporary. The land was so empty, so vast it could swallow a hundred Clementines and leave not a trace.

The loneliness of the thought disturbed her, frightened her even. She set her empty plate aside, stood and stretched, reaching up with her hands as if to grab a piece of the sky. She sighed, breathing deeply the stink of burning buffalo chips and sweaty mules.

She turned to catch Gus watching her. He sat on a log, his hands wrapped around a cup of coffee. With the steam wreathing his face and the brim of his hat shading his eyes, she couldn't read his thoughts. Her husband's moods could take a brooding turn, Clementine had discovered, when he wasn't smiling and laughing and spinning dreams with words. He hadn't opened his mouth in hours, and Nickel Annie, after that morning's loquaciousness, had also fallen silent.

It was that quiet time of the day anyway, when the earth seemed to be holding its breath, waiting to go from daylight to darkness. The thick white clouds had acquired black streaks along the edges, like bands of mourning crepe, and the wind had died. There would be no stars tonight.

Clementine settled onto the log beside Gus, not an easy maneuver in her narrow, looped skirt and the long-waisted, stoutly boned cuirass bodice that fit so tightly over her hips. She wished she could capture with her camera the way the box elder's black twisted branches clawed at the blanched sky. But she would have needed to set up a dark tent in order to develop the wet plate immediately after exposure—though she could have done that, for she had such a tent in her trunk. No, the truth was, she feared what Gus would say. She needed to accustom him gradually to the thought that his wife pursued an avocation most would call unconventional, even unseemly, for a woman.

"I owe it to myself!" Nickel Annie said out of nowhere and so loudly that Clementine jumped. "By damn, I owe it to myself, and I ain't never been a woman to welsh on a debt."

The skinner lurched to her feet and lumbered over to the wagon. Standing one-footed on the wheel hub, she hefted a barrel out of the bed. She rolled the barrel back over to the fire with the toe of her boot. She set the barrel upright, then hunkered down before it.

Out of the cavernous pockets of her oilskin duster, she took a chisel and a nail. She pried one of the hoops out of place with the chisel, then bored a little hole in a stave with the nail. A tiny stream of brown liquid spurted out the hole and Clementine caught the tangy whiff of whiskey. Annie picked up her coffee cup, tossed out the dregs, then set the cup below the hole to catch the stream. The whiskey rang as it hit the tin.

She slanted a broad wink over her shoulder at Clementine and Gus. "This here is what us folk in the freighting business call eee-vaporation."

"That's what decent folk would call stealing," Gus said.

"Guess that means you won't be wantin' any, then,

you bein' so temp'rate and of the decent sort. And Mrs. McQueen, bein' such a la-di-da lady and the daughter of a preacher an' all—she sure ain't gonna want to stain her saintly lips with the devil's brew."

Annie cast Clementine one of her sly looks. "Yup, a real starched-up wife you got yerself there, Gus McQueen." The whiskey had reached the cup brim and was now over-flowing. "Just as well," she said, as she plugged the hole with a broken matchstick and pounded the hoop back into place, "the laws of nature only allowin' for so much eee-vaporation."

She took a long; deep swallow. She shuddered dramat-ically and smacked her lips together with the pleasure of it. Gus watched her antics with a sour mouth, as if he wanted to say something more and only the distaste of the words was stopping him. In that moment Clementine thought he did seem all lassoed up tight in his own righteousness. Not at all the man with the laughing eyes who had come flying into her life on a big-wheeled ordinary.

There was a tetchiness now to the silence that came over the camp. "I think I would like some of that coffee after all," Clementine said for the sake of making noise. She hadn't yet acquired a taste for the brew that westerners insisted had to be thick enough to float a horseshoe.

Gus's hand fell on her shoulder, holding her down. "I'll get it."

She watched him pour from the giant blackened pot. As he put the cup into her hands, their fingers brushed and she felt a soothing warmth from the coffee and from touching him. She gave him one of her rare smiles. "Thank you, Mr. McQueen."

"You could try putting your tongue around my given name, Clementine."

The smile faded. "I will. I promise. Just give me a little more time."

He said nothing. But he picked up a stick and punched

it deep into the fire. She didn't understand this stubbornness in herself. She yearned for the intimacy of his touch, yet she couldn't bring herself to the intimacy of calling him by his given name. It was as if it was a way of keeping one small part of her newfound woman's self to herself and apart from him for a while longer.

She turned the cup around in her hands, staring into the coffee, dark and oily as ink. Her father's pulpit voice echoed in her head: "Wives submit yourselves unto your own husbands, as unto the Lord." All of her life she had spent in battle with her father; she didn't want to fight her husband as well, and yet she was doing it. Already.

"The first night at our place, that's when I'm going to make you mine," Gus had said. They were the words of a man planning to take possession. Soon they would be at his ranch, and he would take from her body the sort of pleasure the chippies sold. To think about it made her ache deep inside as she had one rainy day when she'd sneaked outside and taken off her shoes and stockings to play barefoot in the garden. When she had stood in mud that was as soft and slippery as buttered silk and squeezed her toes and felt the wet mud ooze up between them, and the pleasure of it had pierced her so that she had to set her teeth. Not to stop herself from laughing but to stop a scream.

She stole a glance at this man, her husband. He sat with his forearms braced on his thighs, staring into the fire. She wondered if he, too, thought of that first night. The first night of the rest of her life in the RainDance country, and the first night that he would make her his.

She sighed silently, deep within herself, and drew her steamer cloak tighter around her throat. The air had gone still and heavy, and there was an odd smell to it, like cold metal.

A wet drop struck her wrist; another glanced off her cheek. Sparkling pinwheels fell into the flames with a gentle hiss. She flung her head back, staring into a sky of swirling cottony flakes. "Oh, look!" she exclaimed. "It's snowing!"

Gus held out his open palm and laughed. "Darned if it isn't. Fat, wet snow, too. What we cowmen call a grass bringer."

Nickel Annie belched and gestured with her half-empty cup of whiskey evaporation. "Hell, we're liable to get two or three more blizzards before spring honestly arrives, and even then you ain't safe. That's Montana for you, dearie. Hot as hell one day and snowing to beat the band the next. Why, it snowed just last year on the Fourth of July. Goddamn perverse bitch, is Montana."

The snow came down heavy and lumpy, like wet oatmeal. Clementine turned her face, flushed and warm from the fire, up to the sky. She stuck out her tongue and laughed as the snow fell cold and wet into her mouth.

"Clementine . . ." She turned to find Gus staring at her. There was that tenseness about him, a tautness around his mouth. It wasn't anger; she knew what it was. "Let's go to bed," he said.

Away from the fire their breath trailed in little white ribbons from their mouths. The snow fell around them in a cloaking silence. Gus hung a lantern from the wagon tongue and unrolled the thick, closely woven quilts called soogans that he had bought before leaving Fort Benton.

He knelt on the ground, arranging the soogans beneath the wagon's high bed. She looked at his bent back, so strong and wide. "That was wonderful what you did today," she said, "scooping that nickel up off the ground from out of the saddle and without even having to slow down your horse."

He was quiet a moment, resting his elbow on his bent knee, staring at the ground. He rubbed a hand over his face and looked up at her. "That wasn't the same nickel; that was another one I fetched out of my pocket." In the lantern's feeble light she could see he was smiling. He stood up and wrapped his arms around her waist. "How did you think I was going to spot a thing as small as a nickel in the middle of all that grass and rocks?"

She leaned back within the circle of his arms and stared up at him. "I guess I think you can do anything."

He pressed her head against his chest. "Don't . . . don't ever think that."

Clementine shivered. She hadn't liked those words or the timbre of worry she heard in his voice. He wasn't supposed to have doubts, only certainties. He was supposed to have enough certainties for both of them.

Gus blew out the lantern, and they took off their boots and shoes and crawled fully dressed into the soogans. When they had burrowed into the quilted warmth, he enfolded her in his arms, surrounding her with his hard man's body. His breath stirred her hair, blowing hot on her throat; then his lips brushed her cheek, seeking her mouth. His lips slanted back and forth across hers, gently at first, then with more urgency. An odd tenseness began to burn inside her, low in her belly. She squirmed, pressing harder against him.

His fist gripped her hair, pulling their mouths apart. "Clementine, don't."

He said it harshly, yet his arms tightened around her, crushing her to his chest. Her cheek rubbed against the rough wool of his coat. It smelled of prairie dust and woodsmoke, and she could feel a trembling deep within him, within the hardness of him.

He released her, breathing heavily. He turned her around within the circle of his arms so that they lay back to front. He took her hands, rubbing his thumbs over the ridges of scars. "When are you going to tell me how you got these?"

It was a question he'd asked her at least a dozen times since he'd first seen them. But to tell him about the caning seemed as intimate a thing as standing naked in front of him, and she hadn't done that yet, either.

She felt his sigh warm against the back of her neck. "How can I get to know you, girl, if you won't talk to me?"

She didn't want him to get to know her, for she seemed to have brought all her failings along with her into this marriage. Unlike her, Gus McQueen had never pretended to be other than what he was: a good man, a decent man, one who would provide for her and keep her safe. He believed he had married a proper young miss, someone who would always be a virtuous, obedient wife. A starched wife. A genu-ine lady. He knew nothing of what she really was.

"Clementine—"

"I wish to go to sleep now, Mr. McQueen," she said. She thought he would draw away from her then, but he didn't.

Away from the light of the fading fire, the dark was thick and deep. A coyote cried, a high quavering that sounded lonely. Clementine rubbed her tongue over her lips, tasting him.

They lay together, snug in the soogans. He slept, his arm resting on her hipbone, his hand warm on her stomach. She could feel him along the length of her, from feet to knees to his chest pressed against her back.

Moments ago she had been laughing at the snow. Now she felt an aching sadness that she couldn't understand, a hollow emptiness. A fear began to grow in her that was as wide and raw as the Montana sky. A fear that somehow she had brought the loneliness of her father's house with her.

3

GUS MCQUEEN HELD HIS horse still a moment as he looked across the valley that was his home.

He felt a piercing joy as the word formed in his mind. The sky was a clear blue, stretching to the end of the world. The copper sun put a shimmer on the Rainbow River as it wound through sweet-grass meadows carpeted with pale purple windflowers and pink bitterroot. Mile after mile of fat, rich grass rolled into tree-furred mountains and the slope-shouldered buttes with their scattering of pines. Seen like this, today, the RainDance country looked almost pretty and tame. Not wild as he knew it was. And possessed of a loneliness that could seep into you if you weren't careful, to lie there like an ache on the bone.

He turned his gaze from the horizon to his wife. She sat the high, hard seat of the mule skinner's wagon as if it were a throne. Her pale face was chapped by the wind, her fashionable clothes grimed with dust and dried mud. But just as a good cow pony could be told in the way it moved and held its head, there was no doubting the quality of Clementine. She was prime. She was a lady.

Clementine . . . Even the echo of her name in his mind made him ache. He remembered how she had lifted her laughing face up to the sky the night it snowed, how she had made his body hard and trembling with wanting her. The snow was gone now. Spring snows never stayed long on the ground. Not like in the winter when the stuff piled up in drifts higher than the ranch house roof, and it got so cold a man's breath froze in his chest. Montana winters could defeat a woman, grind her down like fodder beneath a stone. The winter and the wind.

Longing and fear swelled within Gus's chest as he stared at his wife. She was more precious than the land, and he had never believed he would think that of a woman. She stole a man's breath. Her hair was as golden as the light of the dawn sun, her eyes deep green and rippling like range grass in spring. All of her was as fragile and delicate as heired china.

She ought to be preserved in a glass bell, he thought, so that she wouldn't get broken and her purity would never be tainted. The winter and the wind. He knew what Montana could do to a woman.

She turned her head just then and caught him looking

at her, and her mouth curved into a shy smile. A smile that made his body grow hard. He felt ashamed sometimes of the raw lust he felt for his wife.

"I like your RainDance country, Mr. McQueen," she said. "It is truly as beautiful as you said it would be."

He felt an easing deep within his chest at her words. Until that moment he hadn't realized what it was he'd been dreading. That once she had a look at the place he'd brought her to, she'd want to go back—back to Boston and civilization and the life she'd been raised to. A broad smile stretched across his face. They could be happy here in the RainDance, he and Clementine.

"If you think this is pretty, Clem," he said, laughing with joy over life, over her, "just wait until you see the ranch."

Nickel Annie made a snorting sound like a pig at feeding time. "Yup. The prettiest place in the world to work yourself to death."

Clementine McQueen had to stiffen her back to keep from squirming in her excitement. Weeks of days with the constant wind sanding her face raw, whipping at her clothes and hair, coating her teeth with the grit of prairie dust. Weeks of nights spent on the hard ground or in the lumpy, bug-infested bed of some dismal road ranch. Weeks of mile after lurching, bumping mile, perched like a sparrow on the freight wagon's seat, dodging Nickel Annie's taunts and tobacco spittle. Weeks of days and nights and miles that had to be endured somehow and that now at last, at last, were almost over.

In these last days they had ridden through stands of fir and larch pines whose great needled boughs filtered the sun and caught the wind and whose beauty made her ache. Then yesterday they had emerged from a pass through glacier-sheared mountains to look out over a valley that stretched raw and empty, like the Montana sky. Gus had pointed to a slope-sided hill that thrust up out of the rolling rangeland, a butte shaped like the crown of a hat. "At the foot of that butte is Rainbow Springs, and on the other side of it is my ranch. Our ranch," he'd amended, and the words warmed her, making her smile.

"It's how the RainDance country got its name, from that butte," he went on, spinning dreams out of words. "The story goes that once long ago a Blackfeet girl lost her lover during a time of great famine, because he had hunted only to feed the others of his tribe and saved nothing to fill his own belly. The morning of his death, she carried his body up to the top of the butte. There she danced in her grief and wept so hard her tears fell like rain upon the valley, and that summer the buffalo grass grew taller than a brave on horseback and thicker than a grizzly's coat, and her people grew fat off the land." He cocked his head at her, smiling with his eyes. "And some of that story might even be true."

Clementine didn't care whether the story was true. It was sad and beautiful, and she thought of it often while she watched the butte grow larger as they meandered across the valley, following the serpentine curves of the river. Now at last, at last, she could see the sun slanting off the tin roofs of Rainbow Springs, Gus's town. Her town now, her home.

Quaking aspens lined the river as it flowed around the butte where the Indian girl had mourned her man with a rain dance. Snug on the river's far bank a lone smoke-stained tipi rose tan-white in the sun. Clementine searched for signs of life, for an Indian maiden and her brave lover, but the tipi appeared abandoned. The wide road—wide enough to give a span of mules maneuvering room, so Nickel Annie said—was deserted as well. It ended at the slope of the butte, which was pocked with the holes of abandoned mine shafts.

A pile of tin cans and bottles marked the beginning of what Clementine had come to learn was Montana's idea of a town—a scattering of log shacks weathered to the gray-yellow of old bones, their tin roofs striped with rust. Two sported signboards: The Best in the West Casino and Sam Woo's General Mercantile. The lettering had been painted by the same person, who liked putting elaborate curlicues on his capitals.

But Clementine's most vivid first impression of Rainbow Springs was of the mud. The mules' hooves made sucking, popping sounds in the soupy mud. The wagon wheels sank half up to their hubs in mud and sent mud splattering in red globules onto Clementine's skirts. Nickel Annie cursed and whipped the air above the mules' heads as they strained to pull the heavy wagon through the mud. Gumbo was what they called such mud, Gus had told her. It was red and glutinous and had a swampy, feral smell to it.

The wagon squelched to a stop in front of a livery barn. Attached to the barn was a blacksmith's shop. Within the shadow of the forge, a man with a long, tangled gray beard and a belly that rode low over a leather apron was fitting the lid onto a fresh pine coffin.

Gus dismounted just as the slam of a door smacked against the crisp air. A woman in a ruched and draped gown the vivid hue of hothouse violets came running. She lifted her skirts high and hopscotched on the planks and boards that had been laid down in the mud, flaunting red-tasseled shoes, pink-and-lilac-striped petticoats, and royal purple silk stockings.

"Oh, Annie, you darling!" the woman cried, laughing as she ran. "You've brought it at last. You've brought my piano!"

At the sight of Gus the woman stumbled to a stop and lowered her skirts. Rich color flooded her cheeks as she smoothed flyaway strands of hair that was of a deep beech red. She had a face and body meant to go with red hair and a violet dress—dimpled and naughtily seductive.

"Well, how there, Gus," she said in a voice that was rough and breaking like a boy's. "You were gone so long I reckon even I was starting to miss you."

Gus walked past her as if she were a ghost he couldn't see.

With Gus's help, Clementine climbed off the tall wagon, using the wheel rim and hub as a ladder. The woman had run around to the other side to throw her arms around Nickel Annie, and she was now climbing up the wheel for a better look at her piano, not caring that she exposed the red tassels on her shoes and her purple silk stockings. Clementine was fascinated by this woman in her vibrant violet silk dress. Her mother would have called the gown vulgar, Clementine knew. She herself had never been allowed to wear anything that wasn't some refined shade of gray or brown. She wondered how she would look, how she would feel, wearing such a gaudy dress.

"God almighty, if it ain't Gus McQueen!" The blacksmith loped up to them, his leather apron slapping his shins. He grinned to reveal a checkerboard row of black gaps and stubby teeth. He smelled of horse liniment. "Howdy, stranger." He bellowed a laugh and thumped Gus on the back with a meaty fist. "We ain't caught sight of your ugly face around these parts in a coon's age."

"Howdy, Snake-Eye. Who's the toe-pincher for?" Gus said, nodding at the casket. Resting on a sawhorse, it had been fashioned of rough pine boards, broad at the top and narrow at the foot, and built long for a tall man.

"That Scotchman, MacDonald, got hisself kilt," the blacksmith said, and Clementine, who had her hand on Gus's arm, felt him relax as if he'd been fearing the answer. "He was found out on his north range, shot in the back. We're all figuring it was Iron Nose and his boys what did it. The poor bastard probably caught 'em laying rope on his spring calves, and they plugged him when he tried to stop 'em. Some of us've been saying it's about time we formed ourselves up a lynching party to track them renegades down and string 'em up."

The blacksmith's gaze had been bouncing between Gus and Clementine like a ball on a string. Now he paused

and looked at Gus, a frank question in his eyes, which were
as small and pale as pumpkin seeds.

Gus slipped his arm around Clementine's waist.
"Snake-Eye, I'd like for you to meet my wife. Snake-Eye
runs the livery, does the blacksmithing, and passes for the
town's undertaker when it's needed."

Clementine nodded politely. "How do you do, Mr. . . ."
She faltered. "Mr. Snake-Eye" sounded ridiculous.

Snake-Eye stared at her, his mouth hanging open. He
shut it with an audible click of his few teeth. "Well, shi—
shucks, Gus. You went and brought yerself back a wife.
Well, shucks."

"Welcome to Rainbow Springs, Mrs. McQueen." The
woman in the purple dress had come up behind them, and
at the sound of her husky voice, Clementine turned.

The high color on her face came partly from paint,
Clementine realized. A friendly smile put deep dimples in
her cheeks. But her coffee-brown eyes held a touch of wariness and vulnerability as her gaze flickered from Clementine to Gus.

Gus tightened his embrace of Clementine's waist,
swinging her away from the woman. "Be back in a shake,
Snake-Eye," he said. He took her elbow, pulling her after
him. "Come along, Clementine."

The woman's voice, dry and taunting now, followed
after them: "My, but if some folk don't have no more manners than cows in a stampede."

Clementine's shoes sucked and popped in the thick
red mud. She grappled one-handed with her skirts, trying
to find a safe island on one of the planks and boards that lay
haphazardly across the road. "Wait, please, Mr. McQueen.
I am floundering in this mud."

"You may as well get used to it, girl," he flung back at
her over his shoulder. "It's here to stay till June."

"Will you at least tell me where we are going in such a
hurry? And why are you behaving so rudely to that woman?"

"I'm not introducing my wife to the town harlot."

The town harlot. Clementine wanted to turn around for another look at the woman. The memory of that violet silk dress, rich and so gay, was bright in her mind. She could see why they were called fancy women.

The town's few buildings were made of rough-hewn logs. Only one, the hurdy-gurdy hall, was the least bit dandified, with whitewashed chinking and a rack of deer antlers over the double front doors. But as they passed by the saloon, Clementine saw in back of it a house nestled in a grove of quaking aspen and pines. A two-story white frame house made of sawed lumber, with wood-carved rosettes and teardrops festooned along the top of the front gallery and a balcony with a spooled railing. "Who lives in that house?" she wondered aloud.

"You saw her. Hannah Yorke, owner of the Best in the West and the town harlot. *Mrs.* Yorke, she styles herself, although if she's ever been married to any of the men she's had in her bed, I'll eat my horse—hooves, tail and all. Put her out of your mind now, Clementine. You'll be wanting no truck with her."

There must be a profit in it, Clementine thought. This selling of one's body for a man's pleasure. After seeing all those places where they'd spent the nights on the trail, those road ranches and claim cabins, she'd begun to fear her husband's place would also turn out to be little better than a sod shack. But surely, she thought now, their house must be at least as nice as the town harlot's.

Gus came to such an abrupt halt that she almost walked up the back of his boots. "This here's the mercantile," he said, waving at a square, squat building that boasted a single window with a sack stuffed in one broken pane and the others so filthy that all Clementine could see of the inside was the dim flicker of a lantern. "Why don't you go on in and have a look around? I'm going back to the livery to see about borrowing a buckboard to take us out to the ranch. If you find anything you'd like, just have Sam Woo mark it down on the ranch account."

Clementine watched her husband's long legs plow
back through the mud toward the livery stable and Nickel
Annie's freight wagon. He had brought her over here to
the mercantile just so she wouldn't become soiled by contact with the town harlot. Yet the woman hadn't seemed at
all wicked. Only cheerful, and perhaps a little shy.

Clementine watched Hannah Yorke as she circled the
freight wagon almost skipping in her joy, like a bright bird
in her violet plumage. Nickel Annie and Snake-Eye were
wrestling with the piano, trying to get a rope around it so
that it could be winched out of the wagon bed. The woman's laughter, light and tinkling as silver bells, joined with
the mule skinner's hearty, liquid guffaws. They are friends,
Clementine thought, Hannah Yorke, Nickel Annie, and
Snake-Eye. Watching them, hearing their easy laughter,
she felt a strange and wistful envy.

She turned her back on the livery stable and climbed
the two sagging steps to the mercantile's front door. It was
already slightly ajar, and she pushed it open, knocking into
a pair of cowbells that announced her arrival with a loud
jangle. She looked for a mat on which to wipe her feet and
saw that it would be pointless. The warped puncheon floor
was only slightly less muddy than the road outside.

She lifted her skirt to step over the high threshold and
raised her eyes to find three men staring at her as if she'd
just come crawling out of a bog.

Two of the men were toasting their backs before a
small black potbellied stove. One was a tall string bean
of a person with eyes as wide and serious as a barn owl's
and a sunken, toothless mouth. The other was short and
round. His head was as bald as a china doorknob, but his
beard grew long and thick to the middle of his chest and
was the flat yellow color of old wax. Because of the red clay
that stained their clothes and their hobnailed boots, she
thought the men must be prospectors. They both appeared
to patronize the same tailor as Nickel Annie.

Behind a counter of rough planks laid between two

pickle barrels was obviously the Sam Woo memorialized in fancy script on the signboard outside. He stared at her from behind a pair of spectacles, mostly hidden beneath a green eyeshade pulled low on his forehead. He had a flat-boned face and a set of ink-black chin whiskers so stiff and sparse they looked like the bristles on a horse brush.

Clementine took a single step across the threshold, and the breath seemed to leave the three men in a collective sigh.

"Well, I'll be . . ." the tall, thin man began.

"Damned," the small, fat man finished for him.

"Holy God," said Sam Woo.

Clementine gave them all a polite little nod, feeling shy and as though she were on display.

The Chinese man put his palms together and bowed, his long queue swinging past his waist. He spoke in an odd singsong that seemed to be mocking her. "Sam Woo welcomes you to his humble mercantile, madam. This wretched self is honored. Tell me how I may serve you."

Clementine wet her lips and swallowed. "I should only like to look today, thank you. I'm not yet sure of all that I will come to need." She waved a hand at the two prospectors. "Please, continue helping these gentlemen."

Sam Woo bowed again, the lenses of his thick spectacles winking in the dim light as he straightened. Uncomfortable with the men's goggle-eyed scrutiny, Clementine turned away, pretending interest in a wrought-iron bird-cage that was still littered with the feathers of some long gone canary. After a long, uncomfortable silence, the men gave up staring at her and huddled together, bending over a dog-eared catalog that lay spread open on the counter.

Never had Clementine seen so many disparate things all gathered together in one place. Her nose twitched at the strong smells of coal oil and saddle soap, cured fish and wheels of moldy cheese. A set of checkers lay atop a stack of frypans, which in turn balanced precariously on a pile of lard buckets. Brass lanterns were displayed next to men's unmentionables, little cans of crimson paste next to boxes of Goodwin candles. Something brushed against her head, becoming entangled in her bonnet, and she looked up to see an old-fashioned crinoline hanging from the ceiling.

On the counter, next to a box advertising rose toilet soap, she spotted a pair of scales, which she knew from Shona's novels were used for weighing gold dust. She stepped up for a closer look, and the smell of attar of roses grabbed her senses and sent them spinning back into the house on Louisburg Square. Her mother's face appeared before her, and her fingers clenched around the sachet of coins that she still carried deep in her cloak pocket.

She looked around the mercantile with its crowded, splintering, and sagging shelves, its grimy window and mud-splattered floor; at the walls made of logs so rough they still had bark peeling off in places in soft gray curls. The flickering coal-oil lamp released an oily, smelly smoke, and she could hear rats or snakes or some other vile creatures scuttling around in the open rafters. She was in the middle of a wilderness, a world of nowhere and nothing, and so far from Boston she would never find her way back. She felt hollow inside, utterly alone, and for the first time truly afraid of what she had done.

She became aware that the fat prospector was shouting. It was the odd sound of his voice that first penetrated her thoughts, for it was high and squeaky like a rusty pump. But the subject was so startling that she forgot her own wretchedness and drew closer to eavesdrop.

"It ain't legal, Sam," he was saying, thumping the catalog with a gnarled finger to make his point. "Buying a slave. Don't you know how we fought a war a while back just to make the point that we're all free and equal citizens of these United States and her territories. Even the coloreds are free now. Well, the Injuns—they ain't exactly equal. And women, they ain't equal, either, bein' female. But they're all free—leastaways in a manner of speakin' they are. Dammit, Nash, did you swaller yer tongue? Explain to the man here what it is I'm tryin' to say."

The skinny prospector pulled the catalog out from beneath his partner's tapping finger and held it up to the dubious light of the window. "He's saying you can't go buying yourself a woman, Sam, not even a Chinee woman. How much she gonna cost you anyways?"

"You don't understand, fellas. I marry her, so it is a bride-price I pay her protector, sort of dowry in reverse, you savvy." Sam Woo leaned over the counter to point at a picture of a girl in a high-collared robe. The entire catalog, Clementine saw, was filled with wood engravings of women's faces. "This one here," Sam Woo said. "You like her, huh? She's a pretty bit of calico, yes sirree? A thousand dollars she would cost me."

"A thousand bucks? Crucified Jesus!"

The tall, skinny man whipped off his hat and smacked it hard across the little man's stomach, raising a puff of dust. "Watch your stampeding mouth, Pogey."

The fat man opened his mouth to protest, and his gaze fell on Clementine. He stared at her, tugging at first one ear, then the other—ears that were as big and round as one of Nickel Annie's flapjacks. "Ma'am, I don't wanna seem like a pryin' man," he said to her. "But are you one of Mrs. Yorke's new gals? I only ask 'cause you shore as hell don't look like any sportin' gal I ever seen—shit!" he exclaimed as he was slapped again with his partner's floppy hat. "What the hell you keep hittin' me for, Nash?"

"Watch your language, you ol' bunkhouse rooster."

"Watch my . . . hell." He rubbed his belly and cast a look full of woeful injury heavenward. "Why is it that I can't even break wind without you wantin' to issue a declaration and read me a lecture about it?"

"I'm sayin' there's a lady present. I'm saying a gentleman ain't supposed to cuss in front of a lady."

"Well, good God almighty, hellfire, and damnation. What's talk without a cussword or two for spice?"

"I'm saying if you got an itch where it ain't polite to scratch, you don't scratch."

"You don't talk sense, you know that, Nash? Not once in all the days that I knowed you have you ever made a lick of sense. At least a lady can understand what's coming outta my mouth, which is more'n a soul can say about yours. Yap, yap, yap, like a damned coyote, and not once has there ever come out of them flappin' gums of yours a single sentence that makes any goddamned sense!"

"Anyone with a brain bigger'n a pea would know what I'm saying. I'm saying you should watch your manners, Pogey. That's all I'm saying."

Whatever Pogey was going to say to that remained unspoken, for just then the cowbells jangled with the opening of the door.

An Indian girl stood poised on the threshold, tensed to bolt at any moment. She had a child of about two cradled on one hip and an infant in a papoose basket slung on her back. Her small, thin body was clothed in a simple red calico smock over leather leggings, and she wore moccasins that were decorated with dyed quills and colorful glass trade beads. A small gold papist cross hung around her neck. She was young, barely more than a child herself. But her round copper face was pinched tight, her dark gaze hollow and flickering from one man to the other.

"Please, Mr. Sam," she said, and took two tentative, shuffling steps. "Could you give me milk tins for my baby? She's sick, and my breasts don't feed her enough anymore."

Pogey scowled at the girl, giving his flapjack ear a sharp tug. "What for are you lettin' them war whoops in here, Sam?"

"I'm not letting them in, no sirree jingle." Sam Woo rushed out from behind the counter, flapping his apron and shooing at the Indian and her child as if they were chickens. "No milk without money, squaw-girl, do you hear? No money, no milk. Out, out, out!"

The girl spun around so fast her black braids flew out straight behind her and the cradleboard slapped hard against her hip. She yanked open the door, bounced off

Gus McQueen's chest, and ran out into the mud-choked road.

Gus looked after her a moment, then came inside, shutting the door behind him. His gaze swept the gathering at the counter. "How, fellas. I see y'all have met my wife."

This announcement was greeted with the same stunned looks and long silence Clementine had received upon entering the store. A slow smile stretched across Sam Woo's lips. He bowed low. "It big, wonderful pleasure to meet you, Mrs. McQueen."

"Well, I'll be . . ." Nash's face split into a wide grin, showing off a pair of toothless gums.

"Damned," Pogey finished for him.

Gus leaned over to peer into Nash's face. "What in the blazes've you done with your teeth?"

"Huh?" Nash slapped a hand over his mouth, then tried to talk around it.

Pogey thumped him in the ribs with an elbow. "You can't talk sense, Nash, even without your fist in your mouth. Let me tell him . . . Nash and me, we had ourselves a go at the pasteboards with that tinhorn gambler who's put down squatting rights on a table over at the Best in the West. We staked them store-boughten teeth of Nash's to a heart flush and damned—durned if we didn't draw a deuce of clubs. But we'll get 'em back soon enough, now that we've—uhh!" he wheezed as his partner slapped him hard in the belly with his hat. "Uh, we'll talk to you 'bout that part later, Gus."

Gus gave the two men a sharp look. But when they said nothing more, only grinned at him, he shrugged. "Well, we ought to be making tracks. I got the buckboard all loaded up, Clem, and it's a good two hours yet out to the ranch." He put a hand in the small of her back and pushed her toward the door.

"It was a pleasure meeting . . . so many of my new neighbors all at once," Clementine said, and produced one of her rare smiles.

The door shut behind them with the clatter of cowbells, and a silence descended over the mercantile—a silence so complete you could hear the crackers breaking in the bottom of the barrel.

"The country's goin' tame on us, Pogey," Nash said after a moment with a sorrowful shake of his head.

"Tame as a cream-fed kitten." Pogey pulled at his ear and sighed. "Drag out the bottle, Sam, and start pourin'. We're gonna need to get ourselves pie-eyed just to weather the shock."

"Makes a man want to bawl in his booze, it does," Nash said. "First come the women, and the next thing you know you got fences and schools." He shuddered. "And tea parties and church socials."

"Holy God," Sam Woo said, pulling a whiskey bottle from beneath the counter. The men contemplated the sad state of encroaching civilization in silence for a while.

"I thought Gus went back to the States to visit his dying mother," Nash said.

Pogey heaved another sigh. "Lost hisself a mother and gained hisself a wife."

"A daisy-do wife."

"A ginger cakes and lemonade sort of wife."

"Holy God," Sam Woo said. He drank straight from the neck of the bottle and passed it into Pogey's waiting hand.

"Wonder if Rafferty knows about this yet," Nash said.

"Holy God," Sam Woo said again.

Lilting her skirts high, Clementine waded into the middle of the road. The Indian girl, having to shuffle through the thick gumbo under her heavy burden, hadn't gone far.

"Wait!" Clementine called out. "Please wait!"

Gus strode after her, grabbing her arm and swinging her around to face him. "What in the blazes are you doing?"

"That Indian girl . . . we must give her money. She needs to buy milk."

He gave a sharp, hard shake of his head. "She's Joe Proud Bear's squaw. If he wants her to eat, he can provide. In fact, I'm surprised he isn't providing her with some of my cows, the filthy, thieving renegade."

"But the baby—"

"Besides which, if I gave her money she wouldn't use it to buy milk. She'd clean Sam Woo out of lemon extract and drink herself insensible."

His grip was hurting her, but she barely felt it. The Indian girl had heard her and was coming back, though slowly as if she sensed danger from Gus and his anger. "I don't understand," Clementine said, her throat tight.

"The saloons aren't allowed to sell to Indians, so they try to get their hands on anything with alcohol in it. If she doesn't want her kids to starve, she can take them up to the agency and collect her beef allotment. She and Joe Proud Bear are both half-breeds, not full bloods, but they got kin up there they can go to."

The girl hadn't asked for lemon extract when she was in the mercantile; she'd begged for milk. But I have money, Clementine thought suddenly. A whole hundred dollars right in her pocket. Sewn up tight in a sachet, though. She'd have to pick the seams apart with her nails. She tugged free of Gus and began ripping off her gloves. The soft kid caught on her wedding ring—

A scream pierced the air. An Indian on a piebald pony came thundering down the road from the direction of the river, throwing up red divots of mud. He was dressed in checkered California pants and a faded blue shirt and would have looked like a cowboy if it hadn't been for the thick copper bracelets around his upper arms and the tufts of owl feathers and bits of fur laced into his braids. He was young, hardly older than Clementine herself. But he looked to her like a savage on the warpath, and she went rigid with fear.

"Clementine," Gus said, his voice harsh in her ear, "get in the buckboard." She could sense the urgency in him, and she ran to the wagon, slipping in the thick mud. With a shove from Gus she clambered onto the seat just as the girl screamed again.

The Indian had untied a lariat of braided rawhide from his saddle. He let out enough to make a noose, which he twirled above his head. The running loop sailed through the air and dropped over the girl's shoulders, wrapping itself snug around the child in her arms and the baby on her back.

The rawhide sang taut. The Indian anchored it with fast hitches around the saddle horn and swung the piebald around, heading back toward the river, pulling the girl and her children after him like a roped calf. Her legs had to work hard to keep from stumbling in the heavy, sucking gumbo.

"Oh, please, make him stop!" Clementine cried. "Make him stop."

Gus didn't move. Mrs. Yorke, Nickel Annie, Snake-Eye—they were all watching and doing nothing to stop it.

Clementine stood up, and Gus whirled, snarling at her with such violence that droplets of spittle laced his mustache. "Sit down! Get back in the damn buckboard!"

She froze, more frightened of him now than of the Indian. "But he's *roped* her. He's dragging her off like an animal."

Gus unhitched the reins and threw himself onto the seat. He grabbed the back of her cloak and yanked her down beside him. The buckboard lurched, and Clementine swayed. She gripped the brass rail, pulling away from her husband.

The buckboard's low-slung axle creaked and groaned as it plowed through the mud. Gus whipped at the horse with the reins. "She shamed him with her begging, Clem," he said, his voice calmer, though the pulse still beat hard and fast in his neck. "And they're man and wife. Indian man and wife, anyway. It isn't our place to interfere."

Clementine's hands clenched, gripping the thick worsted cloth of her cloak.

The wheels clicked off several moments of tense

silence. They were past the piles of tin cans and bottles. The smoke-stained tipi was behind them. Clementine did not look back.

"Things're done differently out here, girl. You got to learn to accept them, to get along."

"I won't accept your different ways, Mr. McQueen. Not all of them."

A startled look came into his eyes; then his mouth tightened. "You will if I say you will."

"I won't."

The thick, pale green buffalo grass lay flattened by the buckboard's passing, like a ship's wake. A strange wind had come up, hot and dry and smelling of wild mustard and pine. The wind drowned out the jingle of the harness and the suck and crunch of the iron tires over the gravelly mud. It drowned out the frightened chuckles of the prairie chickens, and Gus McQueen's silence.

Clementine looked at her husband's closed face. He was maintaining a taut hold on his lips, as if saving up his inventory of words. It was certainly a different anger than she was used to. Silence instead of ranting and praying.

She held on to her own bonnet as she watched the dry, hot wind bend the brim of Gus's hat and flatten his coat against his chest. He was a big man, with broad shoulders and muscular arms. Her gaze went to his hands, which loosely held the reins. Large-boned hands, strong hands. There was a dryness in her mouth and a tightness in her chest that she recognized as fear. Her hands curled around the scars on her palms. He wouldn't beat her. She wouldn't allow him to beat her.

He turned to catch her looking at him. "You feel the wind, Clementine?"

She blinked in confusion. "What?"

"It's called a chinook—this kind of wind. It can melt a blizzard's worth of snow overnight."

"Oh." She wondered if he was trying to show her that he was no longer angry with her. She cast another glance up at his face. She was still somewhat angry with him, but she was willing to let it die if he was.

The wind was indeed hot and thick and heavy. It made her feel sad and lonesome and restless. "How long before we arrive at the ranch?"

"We've been on it the last quarter hour."

Clementine looked around her. At green and buff rolling meadows and hills carpeted with fat grass for grazing. At pine-timbered mountains rimming the blue, cloud-stacked sky. At a sunlit river running fast and bright like quicksilver and bounded by cottonwoods, quaking ash, and willow thickets. At a rich land, an empty land, a wild land. Exactly as he had described it. No, not quite exactly as he had described it; he had left out a few important things, had Gus McQueen.

Again she studied his profile. The stubborn thrust of his jaw, the tight set to his mouth. The flash of blue in his eyes, patches of Montana sky. "Nickel Annie told me about Mr. Rafferty," she said. "Your brother."

A flush of color stained his cheeks; he didn't meet her eyes. "I would've told you soon enough."

"When?"

"Now. I was going to tell you now. Zach and I, we grew up sort of footloose all over down south until our folks separated when we were kids and we got split up. Ma and me went to Boston, and Zach . . . stayed. But we hooked up again three years ago, settling down to work this spread."

She waited, but the well of words appeared to have dried up again. "And what about him? Your brother?"

"I told you. We run the ranch together."

"Is he older or younger?"

"Younger. I was twelve and he was ten when . . . when Ma and I left."

"Do you not share the same father, then?"

"No, we're full brothers. Zach's just . . . well, he changed his name a while back; I don't know what for. Men out here do that sometimes, when they step on the wrong side of the law." A ruffed grouse, plump as a farm-fed chicken, scooted across their path, and the horse skittered sideways in the traces. "Look there, Clementine," Gus said. "See those pale purple blossoms? They're windflowers. The Indians call them 'ears of the earth.' And those pink ones— they're prairie roses. The grouse and quail like to eat 'em. Unfortunately, so do black bears."

She didn't look at the windflowers or the prairie roses. She looked at him, and she felt an odd sort of ache that was a mixture of fondness and frustration. "You have a beaver-trap mouth, Mr. McQueen."

The corners of his mustache twitched. "That a fact?"

"Yup," she said in her best imitation of his drawl. "A carved-in-stone, certified, and notarized fact."

He pulled back on the reins, stopping the buckboard, and turned to look at her. "All right, then. What is it you want to know?"

"Why didn't you tell me your father is also a minister of God?"

He emitted a sharp, harsh laugh. "Because he isn't. Exactly. Well, he styles himself a reverend, but I don't think he's ever been ordained by anyone's authority unless it was the devil's, and the only things he's ever ministered to were his base appetites and other people's money. Though with all his bogus miracles and pious razzle-dazzle, he sure can sell God like nobody's business." His mouth pulled in a funny way and he shook his head, as if what he was saying was so outlandish even he didn't believe it. "But then, he calls himself Doctor and Professor, too, upon occasion. When he's got patent medicine to sell, or salted gold mines. Lord, when he starts his patter you swear he can sell anything."

This father sounded like a veritable rascal. She couldn't imagine this man raising up such a son as Gus. But then, he hadn't, at least not for long. "He must be a smart man, though, Mr. McQueen," she said, for she sensed a shame in him that went deep and was biting. "A learned man at least. If he can sell anything."

"Yeah, well, he's a master of philosophy, or so he claims, and he's even got a piece of parchment with a seal to prove it." He pursed his lips and stared off into the empty Montana sky. "What he's a master at is using a person's need to believe in something, in anything, against them. So I guess you can see why I didn't want to tell you about him—not after having seen for myself where you come from."

He stopped abruptly as if he'd run out of breath. She touched his hands, which were fisted tightly around the reins. "I don't care where you come from. Only where you are now."

He bowed his head and looked at the footboard between his spread knees. "And I didn't want to tell you about Zach because I wanted you to like him, and I know you aren't going to. He's . . . well, some rough and wild in his ways."

For some strange reason she wanted to smile. "Nickel Annie said he's a hell-bent boy."

"It wasn't easy growing up anything else around the Reverend Jack McQueen."

He flicked the reins, and the dun-colored mare jerked into motion. The buckboard rolled through the thick, sodden grass. The wind blew dry and warm still, and a heavy silence settled over her husband's face. Not an angry silence this time. A brooding one.

She wondered what had caused the McQueen family to break apart, and why Gus had gone with their mother to Boston and his brother had stayed behind to grow up to be a hell-bent boy. She had opened her mouth to ask him these things when Gus tensed, half standing as he squinted into the distance. They had just topped a rise and could see now that a man walked the trail ahead of them. A man leading a horse with something that looked dead slung across its saddle.

"It's Zach . . . Zach!" Gus waved a circle in the air with his hat and let go with a high yipping yell. He sprang the horse into a loping canter, and the light wagon lurched and swayed and squelched over the soggy ground.

The man stopped and turned to wait for them. Long and lean, he stood with his booted feet braced apart. He was naked from the waist up, and his chest was sun-browned and strapped with muscle . . . And streaked with blood.

But then as they drew up Clementine saw that the something slung across his saddle was a calf covered with blood itself and so newborn it was still steaming.

Gus wrapped the reins around the brake handle and leaped out of the buckboard. He flung his arms wide to embrace his brother, then thought better of it. "Lord, Zach. You're near as naked and slimy as a mud weasel," he said.

The man, Gus's brother, said nothing. Not even a how or a howdy.

"I bet you'd just about decided I wasn't coming back," Gus said, his face wreathed with his bright, laughing smile.

The man, Zach Rafferty, Gus's brother, took a step toward the buckboard. Every muscle in Clementine's body tightened and her breath caught in her throat. She had never seen a man so near to being naked before. Even her husband had yet to undress down to the skin in front of her. She wanted to look away, yet she could not, for though she was repelled, she was also fascinated. Sweat and blood glistened on his skin, matting the dark hair into swirls around his nipples and trickling in slow rivulets down his belly to leave a spreading dark patch on the waistband of his jeans.

He hooked his thumb in the cartridge belt that slanted low across his hips. His dusty black hat was pulled down over a face that was all sharp planes and harsh angles. The hat's soft brim hooded his eyes. He reeked of blood and the animal odor of birth. The dun mare caught the smell of it and sucked in a snort of fear.

The calf bleated, breaking the taut silence. Gus's smile had dimmed a little. He nodded his chin at the calf. "What happened to the dogie's mother?"

"Dead," Zach Rafferty answered in so thick a southern drawl, the word came out in two syllables. "Timber wolves got her."

Gus hooked his thumbs in his coat pockets and hunched his shoulders. "Well, I guess you figure since I'm back that Ma did pass away. She went slow, but peaceful. We had a fine funeral for her. Lots of people came." He cleared his throat, smoothing down his mustache. "She did ask about you, Zach."

"Yeah, sure she did."

He stepped closer to the buckboard, so close it seemed to Clementine that he was right on top of her. His hat brim raised slightly as he peered at her from underneath it. The restless wind blew between them, like a dry, hot breath fanning her face.

He pushed his hat up with his thumb, the better to stare at her. He had strange eyes—flat and yellow, with the hard, shiny look of polished brass. "So who's the woman?"

Gus jumped and glanced up at her, flushing, as if he'd forgotten all about her. "My wife. She's my wife. Clementine Kennicutt. Well, McQueen now. I met her while I was in Boston, and that's quite a story in itself. You'll have a good laugh at my expense when I tell you about it . . ."

The man's head dipped, the hat shading all of his face again but for his mouth that was set hard and mean. "Jesus Christ and glory, brother," he said. "What in the hell've you gone and done?"

4

CLEMENTINE SAT IN THE buckboard and stared at her husband's house, which wasn't a house at all, but a shack. A weather-rotten shack, sod-roofed and made of hewn logs chinked with clay. It didn't have a spool-railed porch, not even a sagging front stoop. She could feel his eyes on her and she tried to say something, but her lips wouldn't move. The silence stretched between them, filled only with the sad whispering of the wind in the cottonwoods.

A dog's barking shattered the still air. A rangy cur with a pale yellow hide the color of a buckwheat cake burst out of the barn. It pranced crazily around Gus's brother, whining in its joy when the man hunkered down to scratch it behind the ears. "Christ, Atta Boy," he said, laughing like a young boy as the dog's drooling tongue slobbered over his face. "Maybe I shoulda worn my slicker."

The man glanced up and caught her looking at him. He dug a stick out of the mud. Straightening, he hurled the stick through the air with such force it shattered when it struck the ground. "Go on, fetch that, you ol' gimp-legged hound," he said. She heard the raw anger in his voice now and knew that it was meant for her.

The dog had started after the broken stick in his odd lurching gait. But a magpie swooped over the yard, and he chased after it instead.

"Well, no sense in us just sitting here in the buckboard for the rest of the day," Gus said, and Clementine heard a tightness in his voice as well.

He wrapped the reins around the wheel hub and

jumped off the wagon. He helped Clementine down and stood facing her a moment, his hands resting lightly on her hips. He turned without a word and began unloading their baggage.

A log barn, much bigger than the cabin and with an attached smithy, made up one side of a corral of unpeeled poles. Gus's brother led his big gray horse with its burden of newborn calf up to the corral gate. His naked back gleamed brown and sweat-slick; the muscles of his shoulders and arms bunched and flexed as he lifted the top pole.

He turned suddenly. Their gazes clashed and held a moment, until Clementine wrenched her eyes away.

Perhaps the shack—the *house*—wasn't all that bad, she thought as she looked at it again. At least it was neater than the soddies and road ranches she'd seen along the trail. No noisome piles of bottles and tin cans littered the yard. All the glass panes were still intact in the two front windows.

Lifting her mud-stained skirts, she looked up. Nailed over the door was an upside-down horseshoe and mounted above it, a pair of steer horns as thick as tree limbs. Wrapped around the middle of the horns was a piece of leather with the Rocking R brand burned into it. Her husband's brand. And his brother's. Gus had drawn it for her once in the prairie dirt. She told herself he hadn't lied; he'd only omitted some things. And his descriptions, his dream words, had been of the good parts, not the bad. It wasn't his fault that she'd expected more.

Gus brushed past her, carrying her bulky carpetbag. A moth-eaten old buffalo robe hung over the warped front door. He pushed the robe aside, hooking it on a nail. He plucked the peg from the hasp and nudged open the door. With the late afternoon sun already dipping behind the mountains, the cabin was dark inside. But it wasn't musty. In fact, it smelled pleasant. A manly smell of leather and tobacco.

Gus struck a flame to a coal-oil lamp and adjusted the wick, and Clementine swallowed down more disappointment.

The furniture was made of packing crates and tin sheets, except for a sawbuck table covered with worn brown oilcloth and the four empty nail kegs that served as stools. A shelf above the pot and two frypans. Pieces of horse blanket had been nailed here and there over the walls, but slits of light still shone through in places where the chinking was crumbling.

At least the floor was pegged wood instead of tramped earth like so many of the road ranch floors. And it was swept clean in spite of all the churned mud in the yard.

She followed Gus as he carried her valise into another room with a sloped ceiling, like that of a woodshed. An old iron bedstead filled most of the small space. Gus slung her bag into a corner and backed out the doorway fast, as if he couldn't get away from her and that bed quickly enough.

She took off her cloak, gloves, and bonnet, laying them on the table. In the rear of the cabin was the cookstove and a sink soldered out of coal-oil tins. A washpan and dishrag hung on a nail next to the stove. She lifted the rag in her hand; it was worn threadbare in places, but it was clean.

It occurred to her that Gus's brother had been living in this place while Gus was gone. The cleanliness of it was due to him, which seemed odd, cleanliness being next to godliness and Mr. Rafferty looking about as far from godliness as a man could get.

A small, high window above the sink let in weak sunshine. She had to go up on tiptoe to look out of it. She saw that the river curved around in back of the cabin. It was thickly hedged with willows and cottonwoods. A winding, narrow trail led along it to a privy downstream.

She heard Gus's step behind her just as he reached around to work the pump handle. Water splashed into the tin sink with a loud clatter, wetting the front of her skirt. "Look here, Clem," he said, his voice falsely bright. "Indoor plumbing, of a sort."

She moved away from him, rubbing at the wet marks on her plain brown serge dress.

His hands fell heavily on her shoulders, and he turned her around to face him. He lifted her chin with his curled fingers, forcing her to meet his eyes. "I guess it's not a palace, is it?"

"I didn't expect a palace," she said, her throat thick. And although it was true, her disappointment made it sound like a lie.

"You expected better than this, though."

She tried to soften the lie with a smile: "All it needs is a woman's touch."

He let go of her chin, brushing his hand along her neck in a quick and gentle caress. I'll build us a better place this summer. Zach and I were only getting by in this old cabin because we've been too busy working the ranch to worry about anything else. I can have some milled lumber sent over from Deer Lodge." His eyes crinkled, and his face began to shine with the joyous glow of his dreams. "We can order furniture from one of those Chicago wish books. What do you say we make the new house two stories, so's to have lots of bedrooms . . ." His gaze shifted suddenly away from hers as his voice trailed off. He rubbed at his mustache. "You'll come to like it here, Clem, you'll see. You'll be happy."

"Oh . . ." Her throat closed up, and she almost couldn't get the word out. She drew in a deep, shuddering breath. "Gus," she said. "Yes . . . Gus. I will."

His face brightened, and then he laughed. A loud, joyous laugh that rattled the pots and pans above the cookstove. He wrapped his arms around her, drawing her close, so that they were pressed belly to belly and hip to hip. His hands moved over her back, soothing her, warming her. "You called me by my given name. It's about time, wife."

She rubbed her cheek against his neck, and she could feel the beat of his pulse. Steady, solid. He was a good man, a good husband, and she didn't know why she had waited so long to do this one thing that had made him so happy.

She lifted her head and gazed up at him. He cradled her face in his big hands, and the smile he gave back to her was lazy and sweet. He lowered his head, and she held herself still, though her heart was pitching and dipping.

"You gonna leave that horse sweatin' in the harness?"

Gus stiffened, his fingers digging into Clementine's shoulders as he spun around. Zach Rafferty stood in the doorway. He spoke to his brother, but his hooded gaze was riveted on his brother's wife.

"Slave driver," Gus said with an easy smile. "I was about to get better acquainted with my bride." He leaned over and kissed her hard and fast and roughly on the mouth, then set her away from him. At the door he paused, and Clementine thought she caught a flash of triumph on his face as he looked at his brother before he brushed past him and into the yard.

Zach Rafferty stepped inside, hanging his hat on a peg next to the door. His hair wasn't tawny gold like Gus's, but a dark brown, so dark it was almost black. He had washed up and put on clean clothes—a blue chambray shirt that had been scrubbed so many times it looked as soft as French silk and clung to his damp skin.

He came toward her, his plain iron spurs scraping the floor. There was a prowling, coiled restlessness to the way he moved that made her feel that she was being stalked. And there was something about his face, his eyes . . . a stark, mesmerizing quality that held her gaze even when she wanted to look away. There was no laughter in them, only the cold, brassy hardness of a winter sun. They were mean eyes, she decided. Mean and repellent, and fascinating.

He stopped when he was so close to her that she could have reached up and put her palm on his chest. The cloth of his shirt lifted a little as he drew in a deep breath, then settled. The smell of him came to her, of leather and soap and man.

She took a step back. He made her feel hot and uncomfortable, restless, as if her skin was too tight for her body. So as not to look at him she looked around the room. Her eyes took in the table with its ugly oilcloth cover and the four nail-keg stools, the rickety couch improvised out of Arbuckle coffee cases and some boards, with an old soogan for padding.

Against her will, her gaze went back to his. She saw the knowledge of her thoughts reflected in his flat tawny eyes. "You'll find there ain't a lot of Chippendale settees out here like y'all got back in Boston," he said in his molasses-thick drawl.

"And you will find, Mr. Rafferty, that I am not some pampered creature who needs Chippendale settees in order to be content."

"That a fact?"

His hand came up, and she tensed, the breath backing up thick and hot in her throat. He reached past her, his arm brushing her hair, to take something off the shelf above her head—a packet of straw-colored papers and a muslin bag with a red bull printed on it, enclosed with a yellow drawstring.

He stood right next to her, seeming to loom over her, while he poured tobacco out of the bag into one of the papers, licked the edge of it, then rolled it tight. His fingers were long and brown and roughened with scars and calluses.

"Surely, sir," she said, lifting her chin in an unconscious challenge, "you do not intend to smoke that in here?"

He paused in the act of putting the cigarette to his lips. A crease appeared between his dark, flaring brows. "Christ almighty. Now that there's a lady in the house I suppose I'm gonna have to remember to spit outside, too."

"A gentleman does not smoke and most particularly he doesn't spit in mixed company. Nor does he descend to the childish expediency of cursing his God in order to express his thoughts, however meager or base those thoughts might be."

No sooner were the words out of her mouth than she wanted them back. She had sounded so hoity-toity, like Aunt Etta in a pique. Except that Aunt Etta would have sooner choked to death than uttered the word "spit."

And all the while she'd been delivering her little

lecture, he'd been looking her over slow and easy, from the patent leather toes of her walking boots to the pins in her hair. His mouth curved into a hint of a smile that caused a faint indentation to appear and disappear in his cheek. "I always knew there was a damned good reason why I never developed a hankering to visit Boston."

He put the cigarette between his lips and leaned over the flame of the lamp that Gus had lit against the fading afternoon. "Did my brother tell you the story about this here claim cabin?" he said. He blew a thin stream of smoke into her face. "About what happened to the fella who lived here before us?"

She waved at the smoke, swallowing back a cough. She was sure she wasn't going to like hearing this particular tale.

"He was a buffalo runner, was ol' Henry Ames, and you might say it was his occupation that did him in. One day a band of Bloods, who're just about the meanest Injuns living, paid him a visit. They'd taken exception to him poaching off their herds, I reckon." He paused, drawing on the cigarette again, and his voice took on a silky, dangerous edge. "They kilt him slowly . . . with tomahawks."

She felt as if her lungs had shrunk and all the blood had rushed from her heart. "In this house? They killed him in my house?"

"Come here."

A scream nearly jumped out of her throat as he took her by the elbow and led her over to the far wall where a rifle rested on a pair of deer antlers above the coffee-case couch. He let go of her arm, and she rubbed the heavy brown serge of her sleeve where he had touched her. Rubbed hard, trying to erase the imprint of his fingers.

He pointed to a deep gouge in the wall in the shape of a half-moon just below the gun's gleaming oiled stock. "You see that?"

"Yes," she said, her pent-up breath escaping with the word.

"The men who found him figured he lost his right hand first, going for his old Long Tom, which he kept right here where the Winchester's hanging now. He put up a fight—you gotta say that much for him. If you'll look around, you'll see the scars left by the tomahawks, where the Injuns missed poor ol' Henry and took chunks outta the walls instead. Some of the marks are down low," he went on, watching her intently, "near the floor. I reckon toward the end he was fighting them off on his hands and knees . . . or rather"—and his mouth pulled into a mean smite—"his bloody stumps and knees."

She tried to hold herself still, but she was shaking from the inside out. She pressed her fingers to her lips to stop their trembling. She looked at him and saw the cruelty in his ugly yellow eyes. She didn't dislike Zach Rafferty; she hated him.

"Get out," she said, the words grating raw in her throat.

His mouth twisted a little more, looking meaner. "Them Injuns chopped up poor ol' Henry into so many little pieces they had to gather him up in a bucket so's they could bury him."

"Get out of my house."

He leaned into her so close she felt the hot rush of his breath. His eyes, empty and cold, regarded her for two long, slow heartbeats. "I live here, too, damn you."

He spun around on his heel and strode out the door. But he didn't go far. He settled his hip against the hitching rail. He crossed his long booted legs at the ankles, hooked a thumb in his gun belt, and stared out over the yard, the cigarette dangling from his fingers. It was a relaxed pose, but anger twanged in every hardened line of his body.

She walked through the door of the cabin and out to the hitching rail. She stood there looking at his profile. Looking at the sharp protrusion of his cheekbone under the dark, taut skin, at the hard, cruel line of his mouth. "I know what you are trying to do, and you will never succeed. I will not allow you or anything else to frighten me away."

He turned his head, and his uncomfortable eyes stared back at her. The chinook wind blew between them, dry and hot as anger. "I'll bet you whatever you care to name that you'll be scootin' off back home to your mama long before the first snowfall."

Clementine deliberately looked at Gus so that this man—this rough, uncouth, and lawless man—would know that his brother was the reason she would never leave. Gus was leading the dun mare out from between the buckboard's shafts. The big gray gelding in the corral, Rafferty's horse, butted his head against a pole and let out a sharp whinny. The horse suited his master; he was as ugly as a rat and probably just as mean.

"Your horse, Mr. Rafferty," she said. "Will you wager your horse?"

"What in hell would a little gal from Boston want with a horse?"

She turned her head to meet his disturbing eyes, and an unexpected shiver curled up her spine. He provoked her—that was it. The man was able to provoke her just by standing next to her, breathing the same air. She had to swallow twice before she could speak. "I might not know how to ride as yet, but I intend to learn. Do we have a wager?"

"Well, now, Boston, I guess that depends." He drawled the words, pulling them out like taffy, mocking her. "On what you got to ante into the pot."

Her hand went up to the cameo brooch at her neck. She felt almost dizzy for a moment at the thought of her audacity and, yes, her own wickedness. For hadn't she been taught that all wagering was sinful in the sight of God? She fingered the delicately wrought gold for a moment, then unhooked the clasp and pulled it free of the stiff black velvet collar of her dress. She held the cameo up to his face. "I put up my brooch."

He peeled the cigarette off his lower lip and tossed it to the ground, grinding it to ash with the toe of his boot. He took the brooch, his fingers brushing hers with their callused roughness. He rubbed his thumb over the carved agate. "This is a woman's thing," he said. "What would I want with a woman's thing?"

"You could sell it," she retorted, her throat tight, "or give it to one of your chippies. I understand you have dozens of such women whom you doubtless need to keep content by giving them pretty baubles."

He let out a startled snort of laughter. "Only five or six, last time I counted. Trouble is, they're spread out all over to hell and gone. Keep me busy, they do, ridin' to and then fro, not to mention all the ridin' I gotta do while I'm there. Christ, by the time I get to the last one, I'm usually so saddle sore I barely got enough left in me to make her scream at the end of it."

Clementine went rigid, and she felt hot color flood her face. She hadn't quite grasped the meaning of all he'd said, but his raw laughter left her with no doubt it was wholly profane and utterly indecent.

He leaned into her, bringing his face so close to hers she could see the fine lines around his eyes and the stubble of the beard he hadn't bothered to shave off that morning. "I don't need any pretty baubles to keep my women content. Unless, of course, you're talking about *my* baubles."

He took her by the wrist and dropped the cameo into her palm. Her chest swelled as she sucked in a deep, hitching breath. She tried to control the shudders that passed through her. She wouldn't let him see how his touch revolted her; she wouldn't give him the satisfaction.

"Do we have a wager, Mr. Rafferty? Or are you afraid you might lose?"

Something flared bright and hot in his eyes, like throwing quicklime on a fire. The tension was now so taut between them that she was surprised the hot wind didn't twang a note out of it.

"When you run outta here with your tail tucked between your legs, Boston . . ." His fingers moved, sliding
slowly up her wrist until they met the tight cuff of her
sleeve. Then he let her go. She gripped the brooch so hard
the pin dug into her palm, drawing blood. "When you
run," he said in his soft-voiced drawl, "don't forget to leave
your li'l bauble behind."

Gus took the cast-iron pot off the shelf and set it with a
clatter on the little stove. Squatting, he opened the damper
and fanned his hat at the flames. "I think some mulligan
stew for supper would be a nice change from sowbelly
beans and canned corn."

Clementine sat on the woodbox, her hands tucked
between her knees like a child. He looked up at her, his
face flushed by the stove's heat. "There's a sack of spuds in
the food cache," he said. She looked to where he pointed,
at an old apple crate under the sink. "There's some wild
onions growing alongside the river. And if I know Zach,
there's probably some freshly killed venison hanging in the
springhouse." He stoked the fire with a piece of kindling,
then tossed it in.

"Gus . . ."

He looked back up at her, his face still flushed bright,
happy, and she knew it was because he liked hearing her
say his name.

She dragged in a deep breath and let it out in a sigh.
"Gus, in my father's house on Louisburg Square, we had
domestics."

The brightness left him, quick as dousing a candle, and
his mouth tightened. "I'm sorry, girl," he said. "But it can't
be like that for you out here, not yet. If you don't want to
stay, Nickel Annie will be heading east again next week."

"Oh, no . . ." She slipped off the woodbox and knelt
beside him. She laid her palm against his chest. "I would
stay if you said we had to live in a cave. I'm only trying to

tell you that, faced with those potatoes and the pot, I find that I am ignorant. Woefully ignorant."

All the tension went out of his big body. Reaching beneath the sink, he plucked a tin can out of the food cache. He pulled a jackknife out of his pocket, snapping the blade open with a well-oiled *snick*. He held the knife and can up in the air, flashing a big Gus McQueen smile. "This is a knife. And this is a can." He stabbed the knife into the can, and air escaped from the hole in a loud hiss. "Stewed tomatoes." He brought the can up to his nose, sniffing loudly. "I take that back. It's more of that durned corn."

He laughed and she laughed with him. She let it bubble up out of her unchecked like a shaken bottle of effervescent lemon.

He went still, staring at her, his eyes wide and serious. He traced the shape of her lips with his fingers. "I wish I could give you a mansion and servants. And I will someday, I swear it."

"I don't want a mansion or servants. I only want you."

"Do you mean that, girl?"

Beneath the touch of his fingers, her mouth curved into a smile. "Only you, Gus. Only you."

The coal-oil lamp, with its wide bell-like paper shade, threw a warm glow over the table. A pot of fresh coffee burped cheerily on the cookstove, and Clementine felt pleased with herself, for she'd been able to make biscuits in a frypan just like Nickel Annie's. Well, almost like Annie's . . . They were only a little scorched on the bottom.

Gus sat in his shirtsleeves, eating the biscuits and the canned corn with an unfeigned appetite. Her father, Clementine remembered, had always worn his coat to the dinner table. Come to think of it, she had never seen her father without his coat. But tin plates and nail-keg seating weren't the same as starched linen, silver and china, and plush-covered chairs.

Clementine started at the sound of scuffling footsteps at the front door, and her head jerked around. Outside, a dog whined, and Mr. Rafferty's rough voice shushed it. She listened, her back taut, until the footsteps faded into the night sounds of the crickets and the soughing wind.

Clementine noticed how Gus, too, had tensed and then relaxed when his brother didn't come in. "Zach's offered to bed down in the barn for the time being," he said.

"That doesn't sound very comfortable for him," she answered, not meaning a word of it. She hoped the man would be miserable.

Gus shrugged, his gaze going back to the door that was now shutting Zach Rafferty out of his own house. "He's used to sleeping rough."

Gus had been gone for almost a year, yet as far as Clementine could tell, the brothers hadn't exchanged more than two or three sentences since he'd come home. And if they hadn't been getting along before Gus left, her presence was sure going to aggravate whatever was wrong between them.

Clementine hoped this would be so; perhaps Mr. Rafferty would be the one to leave the RainDance country. She peered through the shadows cast by the rafters, trying to make out the gouge in the wall. It could have been carved by a tomahawk. Or it could have been left by the innocent ax that had chopped and hewed the log. She wanted to ask Gus about the man who had lived here before them, about how he had died. But she wanted more to think the story wasn't true, that Zach Rafferty had made it up to frighten her away.

"Clementine . . ."

She looked across the table at her husband. His eyes held a strange and sleepy, heated look, and his voice when he spoke her name had a husky break in it. "Clementine, we're here. At the ranch, that is. And it's time I . . ." The skin across his cheekbones flushed, and he pressed his lips together hard. "I want to be making you my true wife now. In the . . . the physical way."

She couldn't swallow, or even breathe. It was real

suddenly, what would happen between them. And it would happen soon, at last, at last. She was going to lie with him on that big iron bed, and he would make her his true wife. *"I am my beloved's, and his desire is toward me."* She would become his beloved, and he would be hers. Her beloved.

The nail keg scraped across the floor as he stood up. He came around to stand behind her. She drew in a funny little sucked-in breath as he began to take the pins from her hair. His hands smoothed her hair over her shoulders, awkward and yet gentle. The room had gone so quiet she could hear her own breath and the uneven thump of her heart.

He reached around to help her up. She placed her hand, trembling and damp, in his. He led her to the lean-to room. It was barely large enough to hold the bed, the big iron bed made up in trade blankets and pillows cased in flour sacks.

She could feel Gus hovering behind her, hear his rough breathing, but she couldn't bring herself to look at him. "I'll, uh, give you a few minutes alone to get undr—to get, well, ready. Well, hell," he said, laughing shakily. She waited until the door had shut behind him, then eased out her own shaky breath.

She had never seen herself naked. She had even bathed in her shift. But this time she did not drape her night rail over her head like a tent before removing her underclothes. She pulled off petticoats, camisole, corset, and chemise. She hesitated when she came to her shimmy, then tugged free the drawstring and peeled the muslin drawers off her hips and thighs.

The air was cool on her bare skin, and she shivered. Her nipples drew up tight and hard. She touched them, briefly. Her hands drifted down, fluttering over her belly, but went no lower.

Moving quickly she took a fresh night rail and her hairbrush out of her valise. She pulled the nightdress on over her head. The thin batiste settled over her, gentle as a caress.

A clay jug sat atop a tall, thin chest made of more packing crates, beneath a cracked and tarnished hand mirror that had been nailed into the wall. She poured cold water into a tin basin and washed her face and hands quickly, chaffing her skin with the rough towel. She gathered up her hair, pulling it over her shoulder, then reached for her brush. Her fingers gripped the handle, her knuckles whitening. The hairbrush, fashioned of sterling silver etched with elaborate roses and engraved with her initials, had been a gift from her mother. She had a vivid image of her mother and Aunt Etta sitting in a wash of morning sunlight, her mother laughing and then weeping, and Aunt Etta saying, "At least from now on, you'll be spared his bed."

Gus knocked on the door. She dropped the brush and whipped around, her hand fluttering to her breast.

The door eased open. She felt shy, standing before him in nothing but her nightdress. Shy and strangely aware of her own body, of the nakedness of her legs beneath the thin batiste, the heaviness of her breasts, the tightness in her nipples. She could feel her pulse beating hard and fast against the high lace collar. Unconsciously she put her hand up to her throat.

He came at her, the light at his back throwing huge shadows over her. His hands encircled her arms, and her breath left her in a soft huff, fluttering her lips.

He stared at her mouth, his eyes bright, his face taut. "Clementine," he said, and his voice broke into a groan as he lowered his head and kissed her.

He filled her with his breath and taste. She was trembling deep inside herself, and she felt a tugging sensation low in her belly that was strange and rather pleasant. She arched against him, gripping the hard muscles of his back. She could feel the heat of him beneath the soft flannel of his shirt, and a trembling within him as well.

He shuddered hard and tore his mouth off hers. "Get into bed."

The mattress sighed, and the braided rawhide groaned as she lay upon the bed. She pulled the bedcovers up to her chin. The sheet was cold and scratchy beneath her bare legs.

She watched him undo the laces at the sides of his boots and kick them off. She knew men weren't built the same as women in their private places, but she had never seen a naked man to know how they were different. But he undressed only down to his white woolen union suit before pulling back the bedcovers and stretching out beside her. It was so quiet she could hear the rush of her own breathing in her ears. Her body felt weighted, her skin too hot and tight.

He leaned above her on his forearms and traced the features of her face: eyebrows, cheekbones, nose, and mouth. It occurred to her that she could touch him, too, and she did so—his brows, which were darker than his hair and nearly met at the bridge of his nose; the strong, hard bones beneath his eyes; the flat planes of his cheeks, bristly with a day's growth of beard; his mustache, which felt softer than it looked when he kissed her. She wished he would kiss her now.

His mouth moved beneath her fingers. "I'll not lie to you, girl. This will hurt some."

She smiled to show him it would be all right. "I've heard it said, Gus, that it's painful the first time. But I've never been able to understand why. What precisely will you be doing to me?"

"Only what all husbands do. Nothing indecent."

He was lying partly on her now, his big chest crushing her. She liked the feel of his weight. There was something so . . . so intimate about it, as if taking his weight made her more his wife than she had been up to this moment.

"I fear that, as with the potatoes and the pot, I am woefully ignorant about this as well, husband. You will have to instruct me on what to do."

"A man doesn't expect the girl he marries to know a chippy's tricks, Clem. All you got to do is lie quietly. Just lie here and be easy, easy now . . ."

He was stroking her as if he were trying to calm a rope-shy colt, and she almost laughed. She touched a finger to the corner of his mouth, ran it along his lower lip. A man's mouth looked harder than it was. "Will it hurt you, too?"

The flush on his cheekbones deepened, and his gaze broke from hers.

"But then you aren't ignorant," she said. "This isn't your first time."

His head dipped so that she could no longer see his face. He pushed out a deep sigh. "Clementine . . . this just isn't a thing a man can easily discuss with his gently reared, sweetly innocent wife."

She wished he would stop saying that, thinking that. She certainly hadn't been reared gently and she didn't want to be sweetly innocent anymore. She wanted to know what was going to happen. She couldn't get the memory out of her mind of her mother weeping with relief when the doctor told her she mustn't try to have any more babies. Even Gus had warned her it would hurt. And she'd heard talk about how the wifely duty was a thing that had to be endured. It was beginning to sound as bad as a caning.

She thrust her hands down stiffly at her sides and squeezed her eyes shut. "You may do it to me now. I am ready."

He laughed, nuzzling the soft spot between her shoulder and neck. "I love you, Clementine. You are beautiful, and so pure and good."

"I am not pure and good, Gus. Not really."

"So you admit to being beautiful?"

A blush heated her cheeks. He kissed her on the mouth, and his laughter, low and husky, washed over her. She breathed deeply, filling her head with the smell of him.

He rubbed his hand over her breast, kneading it with the heel of his palm, then hefted its fullness, as if testing it for ripeness. He lightly squeezed her nipple between his thumb and finger, rasping the silky batiste, and heat jolted through her, coiling her muscles up tight, tight, until she couldn't bear it. She gripped his wrist, thinking she would die if he didn't stop, that she would die if he did. His other hand cupped her between her legs, and the shock of it, of him touching her there, of the way it felt to be touched there, the exquisite, unbearable shock of it, made her buck hard against him and push against his chest with her hands.

He panted against her face. "Don't be frightened."

"No . . . it's just so . . . oh!" She gasped as he pushed his finger against her woman's opening, as if he was trying to push it inside her. Inside her! She didn't want to lie quietly. She couldn't. A tense, tight feeling curled low in her belly, spreading, filling her chest until she couldn't breathe and the blood rushed in her ears.

His hair brushed her cheek as he lowered his head. He fumbled with the opening to his union suit with one hand while he grasped the hem of her night rail with the other, shoving it up around her waist.

A wet heat was spreading in a growing pool from that part of her as if she were melting down there. "Oh, please," she said again, wanting something, wanting something, wanting something . . .

He grew still above her, his chest heaving. His breathing was heavy and harsh. Lantern light gleamed off the sweat on his neck. "I'm sorry, but I have to be inside you now, girl. I gotta get inside you."

And he did just that: he pushed his hard, stiff man's thing inside her, and she nearly screamed. Only by stuffing her fist in her mouth could she stop it. Her eyes opened wide as he plunged deeper into her; she felt that he was ripping her in two. She struggled against the pain, heaving up against him. He thrust into her again and then again, and then he shuddered, arched his back, and a groan tore out from between his lips.

He collapsed on top of her, panting heavily, his face buried in her hair. She wanted to tell him that he was crushing her, that she couldn't breathe. She was burning between her legs, deep inside her woman's self where he still was, stretching her wide. Invading her.

He pulled out of her and rolled onto his side, gathering her up so that they lay nose to nose. The burning between her thighs eased somewhat. She could feel a hot wetness there now. She wondered if he had torn something inside her, if she was bleeding.

The sheets had gotten shoved to the bottom of the bed, and her night rail was twisted up around her waist. The air was cold on her bare skin. But she couldn't move, even to cover herself. She sucked in a deep, heart-shuddering breath. Her throat felt skinned raw, her chest tight and sore.

He rubbed his curled fingers back and forth across her mouth, pulling at her lower lip. "God, you were so small. I've . . . I never had me a virgin before. I didn't expect you to be so small. I guess it hurt pretty bad, huh?"

"Yes."

"Aw, girl." He rose above her, cupping her face in his big hands. "I wanted you so much, I couldn't seem to . . . Next time I'll go gentler on you, slower."

Her eyes stung and she clenched them shut. It wasn't really the pain of it that made her want to cry. It was the disappointment. Somehow she had thought this moment would change things between them. Make everything right, make it perfect. *"But from the beginning of the creation God made them male and female. For this cause shall a man leave his father and mother, and cleave to his wife; And they twain shall be one flesh . . ."* One flesh. He had taken her, possessed her body. She should be as one with him now. Yet never had she felt more alone.

His mouth sought hers, and she gave it to him. His man's lips that were not as hard as they looked, but warm and soothing, and the tightness in her chest eased somewhat.

"I love you, girl," he said, and then held himself still, and she knew what he was waiting for. "I'd like to think you could see your way to loving me back," he went on, when the silence stretched out and grew tight.

She opened her eyes. His face was floating above her and he was smiling at her with his eyes, and she thought suddenly of that first time she had seen him, the cowboy of her dreams. "I will try to love you, Gus," she said. "I will try."

He sighed a laugh. "Clementine . . . always so serious." He lifted her hand, rubbing his thumb over the scars her father had given her. "No one's gonna hurt you anymore, girl," he said, but she knew he lied. He could hurt her even without meaning to.

Later she lay beside him in the still darkness of the night, listening to his deep, even breathing. She wondered what a chippy's tricks were, if those soiled doves with their violet dresses and red-tasseled shoes and their husky laughter knew of a way to keep it from hurting so much. Her night rail was still twisted up around her waist. She touched her bare belly, inched her fingers slowly down until they brushed the hair between her thighs. And felt the echo of something that, strangely, was more pleasure than pain.

She pushed herself up on one elbow to look at him, but it was too dark to see his face. She knew, though, that even in sleep the laughter showed around his eyes. The laughter that was so much a part of him had already become a part of her as well, so that she could not imagine life without it. Her hand hovered above his cheek. She didn't know why, but she wanted to touch him. Shyness and reserve held her back. It was hard for her to show him how she felt, hard to understand these feelings.

She sat up and slowly eased her legs out of bed, then stood up. Her skin was moist and hot, and there was a hollowness in her chest, an emptiness.

She groped in the dark for the water jug and used the towel to wipe away the stickiness between her thighs, then crept on quiet feet out of the bedroom and across the cabin to the door. She lifted her cloak off the peg and wrapped it around her nightdress. The leather hinges squealed when she opened the door, and she shut it quickly behind her.

The silent mountains cast long, dark shadows over the land. A hard, brittle moon drifted in and out of the clouds, and the tops of the cottonwoods rustled at a touch of the grass-scented wind. The road and corral and the pastures beyond were shot with moonlit patches. The night was beautiful and ominous, and it filled her with a loneliness that was both good and sad.

The moon drew her, and she stepped out into the yard and began walking toward the corral. Cool mud oozed over her bare feet, sending shivers up her legs. A flurry of wind buffeted her. She grew still, for she could hear another, stronger gust coming. A sound like low thunder, then a whistling shriek as it shrilled through the cotton-woods, and the slap of it against her body. It was as if the wind was trying to swat her off the face of the earth. Something within her wanted to shriek back at the wind. Or with it.

A scarf of clouds wrapped itself around the moon, enshrouding the land in darkness. The wind died, leaving a silence that was a sound in itself—a rushing noise in her ears that might have been the wind coming back, or her own breath.

A coyote yipped, breaking the spell. An uneasy tremor ran down her spine. She'd read in Shona's novels that Indians made animal noises, signaling to one another as they crept up on unsuspecting settlements with their scalping knives.

A stick broke, a bush rustled. A silent scream crawled up her throat, choking off her breath. A red eye glowed in the dark—then the scent of tobacco came to her on the wind.

The clouds passed, unveiling the moon. The outline of his body was stark and black against the horizon. Like the pines, he was motionless. But she knew he saw her, had been watching her all along.

The red eye arced and flared in the darkness, trailing sparks. The shadow moved, coming toward her. She whirled and ran for the cabin. She slammed the door behind her and leaned against it, shaking, her eyes closed tight.

He had boasted of how he made his women scream.

She brought a trembling fist up to her breast to quiet the hard, fast thrumming of her heart.

Hot air and the smell of rotgut whiskey and stale sweat hit Zach Rafferty in the face. He let the door swing shut behind him with a loud slap, and everyone turned to look. Everyone except the crimson-haired woman dealing solitaire to herself at a table by the stove.

He hung his cartridge belt on an elk-horn rack beneath a sign that read PARK YOUR GUNS HERE. He headed for the bar, stepping around a puddle of water.

"Evenin', Saphronie," he said to the woman who was swamping the floor. A child of about three clung to her skirts. The child looked up at Rafferty, her blue eyes wide, and a smile began to form around the thumb she had in her mouth. Rafferty ruffled her blond curls, then tugged at her ear, and a coin magically appeared in his hand. "Why, lookit here, little Patsy. You're hatching nickels outta your ears."

The child took the coin, laughing with delight. The woman ducked her head to mumble something, her breath barely fluttering the heavy black net veil she wore over her face.

Rafferty tossed two bits onto a counter ringed with the sweat of glasses. "The good stuff, Shiloh," he said to the gin-slinger. "Not that tanglefoot in the barrel."

The bartender shook his head and chuckled at the joke, for they both knew that what was in the bottles under the bar was the same stuff that was in the barrel on the butcher block behind the bar. It was all rotgut.

Shiloh pulled the cork out with his teeth, then set the bottle down before Rafferty so that he could pour his own shot. He scooped Rafferty's two bits into the money drawer.

Rafferty put another twenty-five cents on the bar. "Pour one for yourself."

The round black face broke into a big smile. "I wouldn't want to hurt your feelings by refusing, no, sir."

Shiloh poured his drink and lifted the glass in a toast. "Here's how."

"How," Rafferty said. He tossed back half the shot, shuddering hard. Somebody had doctored the rotgut with cayenne pepper to give it more fire, and it tore the hell out of his throat going down. It eased his nerves, though, once it hit bottom. Nerves that were stretched fiddle-string tight.

He turned around and settled his back against the bar to survey all the excitement in the Best in the West Casino.

The wind was crying wild under the eaves of the tin roof, stirring up drafts. The two large brass lamps with red glass globes hung from the rafters, creaking and swaying, giving the place a hellish look. A new piano sat against the far wall, its keyboard grinning silently.

Saphronie had finished her mopping and was now emptying the spittoons into a bucket, her daughter still hanging on to her skirts. He wondered how hungry he'd have to be before he'd do that. Probably not all that hungry, for he'd done worse, come to think of it. In the room's red light, the black veil made the woman look mysterious and exotic, like a harem girl in a dime circus. But he'd seen the face beneath the veil once, seen what had been done to her, and it had only left him feeling sad.

Two of the hurdy-gurdy girls sprawled on chairs, looking bored. Since there were normally three of them, he figured the other must be with a customer in the room out back. Only one table was occupied, by three men playing poker. Deep play it must have been, because no one was doing any talking. One of them announced himself as a professional by the tinhorn cut of his clothes.

Shiloh had hung up his fiddle for the night, so no one was dancing. The only noise came from a sheepherder in a black plug hat and bib overalls, who stood at the other end of the bar and talked to himself, because no one else would talk with him. But then, mutton-punchers were about as welcome in cattle country as a whore in a preacher's front parlor.

Rafferty decided to amuse himself by watching Mrs. Yorke. Haughty, naughty Mrs. Yorke, who was working hard at ignoring him.

One of the hurdy-gurdy girls—Nancy, he thought her name was—got up and came sauntering toward him. Her lips, which were painted a boxcar red, greeted him with a tired smile. "You lonesome tonight, Rafferty?"

Rafferty shook his head, smiling to soften the rejection. His gaze went back to Hannah Yorke. She must have lost her game, for she was shuffling the cards, her slender white hands moving as gracefully as a dove's wings. She had eyes that stirred a man, and hair the deep red color that on a horse was called blood bay.

The sheepherder pushed himself off the bar and gave his belt a hitch. Nancy saw him coming and hurried away. A moment later Rafferty's nose was assaulted by the stink of woolly monsters and his ears by a voice that grated like a rusty gate. "If you're savin' yer juice for that Hannah, mister, you kin ferget it."

Rafferty turned to look into a face that the wind and sun had sucked dry. "Yeah?" he said. "And why is that?"

"Keeps herself to herself, does Hannah Yorke. She won't have a man in her bed now—not fer love or money. They say that only two years ago she was workin' the line over in Deadwood. Now thar she sits, with a copper-plated crotch and too hoity-toity to give a man the time of day." He sighed. "Damn. What a waste of a good whore."

Rafferty's lips pulled back from his teeth in a smile. But the sheepherder, who could see his eyes, lost all the color in his face.

The man blinked and scrubbed a hand over his mouth. "Din't mean nothin' by it. Was only talk." He took a step back and then another. "Din't mean nothin'." He kept on backing up until he was standing where he'd been before, mumbling to himself again.

Rafferty's gaze went back to Mrs. Hannah Yorke. The red lanterns cast a glow on her white shoulders and put fiery sparks in her hair. She knew that he was watching her, that he wanted her. Yet she sat over there, playing that game of solitaire, as if she were all alone in the world. And as if she liked it that way.

He'd been trying to charm his way into the woman's bed for months now and gotten nowhere. Maybe that sheepherder had a point, maybe a more direct approach was required.

He set his glass down carefully onto the bar. "Give me a bottle, Shiloh."

"Sure thing." The gin-slinger took an empty bottle from under the counter and filled it from the barrel. He twisted a cork in its mouth and asked Rafferty if he wanted it wrapped.

"No. Thanks. Night, Shiloh."

"Good night, cowboy."

Rafferty tucked the bottle into his coat pocket and picked up his gun on the way out. He didn't look at Hannah Yorke, and she didn't look at him.

A mournful bleat greeted Zach Rafferty at the hitching rack. A sad-eyed, red-and-white face looked up at him, lit by the lampshine coming through the saloon's windows. Sighing, Rafferty draped his gun belt over his shoulder and hunkered on his heels to scratch the calf behind its red ears. "I told you I wasn't gonna be gone long. You're worse than a woman, you know that, dogie? Nagging at a man just for having a little drink."

He hefted the calf into his arms, straightening with a groan. He walked around the saloon to the two-story white frame house in back. A small lean-to for a horse sat detached from the house. No horse was in it tonight, but there was enough straw to make a bed for the dogie.

He didn't go to the front door of the big white house, but went up the side steps instead. He tried the latch and was not surprised to find it locked. He took a gimlet and a piece of crooked wire out of his pocket. Within seconds the bolt was sliding back with a soft click, and he was inside.

The door opened onto a small sitting room. He waited a moment, letting his eyes adjust to the darkness. His boots made no sound on the thick Turkey carpet as he passed through a doorway into the bedroom. He lit a big potbellied lamp, casting a soft yellow glow on curtains of white gauze and crimson damask, on red silk wallpaper, on velvet perfume boxes and a peacock dressing screen, on a black lacquer lady's desk decorated with roses, vines, and gilt.

He hung his cartridge belt on the post of a bedstead carved with bows and flowers and tossed his hat onto the head of the china pug that squatted on a stand beside the hearth. He shrugged out of his long-tailed sourdough overcoat and threw it on a black horsehair fainting coach. He set the whiskey bottle on the papier-mâché table by the bed and stretched out on a feather mattress so thick it sighed with female pleasure as it took his weight. He fluffed up the embroidered pillows behind his back and crossed his spurred boots on the petit point quilt. He pulled out the makings of a cigarette, rolled, and lit it.

He linked his fingers behind his head, his elbows spread wide. He winked at the ceramic cupid that looked down on him from atop the shawl-draped mantel.

He didn't have long to wait. He heard the front door opening downstairs, heard her heels clicking across the hall. Carpet muffled her footsteps now, and then lantern light filled the adjacent sitting room.

Her shadow crossed the threshold first.

In the dim light her eyes were two black holes in a face as pale as birch. Her lips looked stained with blood. She pulled a little ivory-handled pistol out of the pocket of her violet dress and pointed it at his belly. "Stand up, mister," she said in a smoky voice that would have made him hard if he hadn't been that way already. "Slow and easy."

He stood up slow and easy. Even so, the rowel of one of his spurs caught in the finely sewn quilt, ripping it. The little gun in her hand was a two-shot weapon, and at this distance it could blow a hole in his guts big enough to kill him.

"Step out into the middle of the room." She waved the pistol to show him where she wanted him.

He went where she pointed, but he couldn't stop the smile from tugging at the corners of his mouth. "You gonna salute me with that boob gun, Mrs. Yorke? Or shoot me with it?"

The ceramic cupid on the mantel behind him exploded into a thousand shards. The concussion of the shot rang in his ears, and he laughed. He had felt the kiss of the bullet as it passed his cheek, but he hadn't moved so much as a breath. "You missed," he said.

She swung the barrel of the gun over and down until she had drawn a bead on his balls. "I never miss, cowboy."

He tugged at the buckle of his belt and started toward her. "The name is Rafferty, darlin'. And neither do I."

5

THE WIND SMACKED AGAINST the cabin. The log walls trembled and creaked. The wind was a constant thing, settling then blowing, settling then blowing. Clementine tried to breathe in time with the wind. She thought the wind would drive her mad.

Her hands worked a ball of dough, kneading, twisting. It oozed through her fingers, soft and warm and sticky, stirring up a strange, hot restlessness within her.

She punched her fist into the dough and looked down the length of the table to her husband. The sour smell of the beer she'd used for yeast pinched her nose, and the wind shrieked outside. She looked at him and felt a hot pain in her chest, as if she'd laced her corset too tight.

His bare forearms rested on the worn brown oilcloth as he shoveled in the last bite of a stack of flannel cakes. His hat was pushed back from his sweaty face, his collar lay unbuttoned against the grimy neckline of his union suit. He looked so big and rough and masculine sitting at her table. She hadn't known that men could look like him, be like him. Gus glanced up, his gaze meeting hers, and he smiled. And though the strange, hot restlessness within her eased some, the memory of it lingered still, like yesterday's ache.

He stood up, the nail-keg stool scraping across the rough floor. "How about if I pour you some more of my famous horseshoe coffee?" he said, his voice booming in the cabin's stillness.

She wiped a strand of hair out of her eyes, leaving a streak of flour on her cheek. She watched his hands as he poured the coffee, hands that were rough and calloused and strong. Hands that worked her body the way she worked the dough, worked at being gentle when they touched her now at night, gentle and patient. A gentle man . . . Her father was a gentleman, but the only touch of his she remembered was the bite of his cane.

Gus added a dollop of canned milk to her coffee and passed her the tin cup, his hands staying on hers a moment. His smile was pure Gus McQueen, lighting his face like a sunrise; his eyes laughed. "I ought to get you a milch cow so's you can have fresh milk for your coffee. And maybe a flock of laying hens, too."

"You'll spoil me if you aren't careful," she said. She had only the vaguest notion of how to go about milking a cow. And hens. Would she have to do anything to the hens to get them to produce eggs? Yet if other women had managed to learn these things, then so would she.

She felt her husband's gaze on her. His eyes had narrowed to sleepy slits, and there was a tautness to him as he looked at her. She knew that look. She knew he saw a woman's body that belonged to him, and he wanted her.

She turned away, fumbling with her recipe book to cover the wild beating of her heart. She propped the thick book up against the lard bucket. Her fingers, lumpy with drying dough, left stains on the pages. Behind her she heard Gus release his breath as a sigh.

The book was *The Woman's Exchange Compendium.* It instructed a wife on how she must order her life. On Monday, wash; on Tuesday, iron; on Wednesday, scrub the floors and bake. Not until the last Friday of the month would she be able to sit down and rest a spell, for that was the day set aside to polish the silver and clean the crystal lusters on the chandeliers. Even Clementine knew that tin spoons didn't need polishing, and she doubted there was a crystal luster to be found anywhere in western Montana.

On each page was a thought for the day. Today's thought was "It is better to do one thing one hundred times than one hundred things one time." It seemed like a silly sentiment, especially if one had a hundred things to do. The book, with its preachy tone, annoyed her. But then, the wind and everything else was unsettling her today.

She had stolen the book from the kitchen of her father's house on Louisburg Square. At the time she had thought she might find a use for it during her adventures in the Montana wilderness, and, oh, how provident she had been. But the recipes it contained were unforgiving of inexperience. The bread she'd made yesterday had baked up as hard as the seat of a mule skinner's wagon.

She put the dough she'd kneaded on the back of the stove to rise. She moved the stew kettle to a hotter spot on the range and added more water. In another three hours she would be setting the table for dinner. Today was Monday; she should be washing. She could wash tomorrow, but then when would she iron? So much to do . . . She wanted to take her camera out of the trunk, where it had remained hidden from Gus's sight, and photograph the cabin and the cottonwoods and the way the black mountains ringed the valley, looking like a choir of nuns in their stiff white caps of snow. But there was the washing and the ironing and dinner to get and the bread to bake.

Gus scuffed across the floor behind her in his stocking feet, and she went still, wanting him to touch her and yet not wanting it. He reached around and ran his finger slowly through the dusting of flour on her arm. "There's something about a woman up to her elbows in baking that makes a man want to . . ." His words trailed off as his breath fluttered warm on her neck. She felt the heat and urgency within him, and she leaned back into him.

"You smell good," he said.

"I smell like beer."

He hummed and nuzzled her neck. "Beer's good."

He turned her so that they were standing chest to chest. Her breasts tightened, her nipples beading up against his searching fingers. She pulled away from him. "Not in the daylight. It isn't proper," she said, even though she wanted him to take her in and lay her down on that big iron bed and join with her.

"I was only going to kiss you. You want me to kiss you, don't you, Clem? Admit it. In fact, you want me to do more than kiss you."

"Maybe." She ducked her head, hiding the heat in her cheeks. She was coming to like what he did to her in bed at night, although she wasn't sure why, or even if she really *did* like it. It aroused within her such a feverish restlessness, a heat in the blood. And yet it left her feeling hollow inside. And sad and lonely.

He heaved a loud sigh that was mostly put on. "I suppose I oughta get back to fixing that drift fence."

He picked up his work boots from in front of the stove, where they'd been drying out. He sat on the woodbox to tug them on by their mule-ears. Mud drifted in pastrylike flakes onto her kitchen floor. Yesterday it had rained hard, what Gus had called a toad-choker, and the sod roof had dripped mud. She had spent all morning cleaning the floor, and now he was dirtying it again already.

She pointed a finger at the mess he was making. "If you'd done the scrubbing of that floor yourself, Gus McQueen, you'd have more of a care where you go planting your filthy boots."

He looked up in surprise. "What's got you so riled this morn—"

A dreadful howling cut him off in mid-word. Long-noted high-pitched whoops that sounded like a hundred lonesome coyotes all crying at once.

Clementine's gaze flew to the gouge in the wall, and fear clogged her throat, stopping her breath. *Indians.*

The howls died away, and for the space of a heartbeat all was quiet. Then a cacophony of hoots and yips and hollers erupted right outside their door. Clementine's one thought was to run, but when she went to move her legs they were as stiff as stilts.

"What in the blazes . . . ?" Gus stood up, stomping his heels down into his boots. He gripped Clementine's shoulders, propelling her forward, out of his way. "It sounds like we're being shivareed, though it was supposed to've been done on our wedding night, not two months after."

He threw open the door, pushing Clementine out ahead of him, and she thought maybe he was laughing, but she couldn't hear him above all the hooting and hollering. The two old prospectors, Pogey and Nash, were doing a jig in the yard, their hobnailed boots splattering mud. They accompanied themselves by rattling strings of tin cans and pulling a rosined bow across a splintery board.

They stopped when they saw they had an audience. Big grins creased their leathery faces. They managed to look both guilty and proud, like two wolves caught in a henhouse and all set to brag on it.

Clementine's heart still pounded from the fright she'd

had. After all that hollering, it seemed strangely quiet, though the wind whistled through the lattice of cotton-woods along the river and whipped her skirt against her legs. The river was running high from yesterday's rain, rushing as loud as a train through a tunnel.

Gus wrapped his arm around her waist and drawled behind a laugh, "Outraged citizens have been known to tar and feather certain scoundrels for disturbing the peace like that."

Pogey combed his beard with grimy fingers while he eyed Gus slowly up and down, making a show of it. "Looks downright sassy and satisfied in his married state, don't he, Nash? Content, I guess you could say."

Nash nodded in solemn agreement, his big owl eyes unblinking in his bony face. "'Content' is just the word I was searching for. Content as a frog with a bellyful of flies."

"Content as a honeybee in a buckwheat field."

"Content," Nash said, "as a dead pig in pink mud."

Pogey whirled on his partner, flinging his arms wide. "How in hell can a pig be content if'n he's dead? And who ever heard of pink mud? You never do make any sense, Nash. Yap, yap goes yer jaw, flap, flap goes yer tongue, and the two of 'em don't work together long enough to make a lick of sense. Do you think the sun comes up in the mornin' just to hear you crow? Good God almighty—"

Nash whipped the slouch hat off his head and whacked Pogey hard in the stomach with it. "Curb your tongue. You promised you wouldn't cuss."

Pogey's gaze fell to the scuffed toes of his boots. He tugged at the pendulous lobe of one ear, then slanted a sly glance up at Clementine. "Reckon I ain't used to bein' round a genu-ine lady."

Clementine stood with her arms crossed behind her back. The stance squared her shoulders and lifted her chin, making her look even more the lady, though she was un-aware of it. "Thank you, Mr. Pogey, for your consideration of my tenderfoot sensibilities," she said, and she shocked the men by flashing one of her rare and ravishing smiles. "I am pleased to see, Mr. Nash, that you were able to redeem your teeth."

Nash stared at her, his jaw agape. "Huh? Oh." He plucked out his teeth and looked at them as if his mouth was the last place he'd expected to find them.

Pogey tugged on both ears, then scratched his chin through his beard. "Well, hel—shucks, we done brought you a wedding present, Mrs. McQueen."

The men had walked out to the ranch leading an old sway-backed burro that was now tied to the hitching rack in front of the cabin. The burro carried a small pannier, and out of one side of it Pogey took something wrapped in a piece of canvas. With a grin so big it lifted his ears, he gave the canvas to Clementine.

The thing squelched in her hands as she unwrapped it slowly. The rancid smell of butchered meat rose up to sear her nose. The meat was thick and flat and black, and dripping blood onto her gray sateen skirt. It looked like the severed tongue of some monstrous beast.

She tried to keep the horror she felt from showing on her face. "Why . . . thank you, gentlemen."

Gus's eyes laughed at her. "It's a beaver tail, Clem. What you do is make soup out of it. The old mountain men consider it a great delicacy."

"I . . . I'm sure it must be delicious." She wondered if her book had a recipe for beaver tail soup, and the thought made her smile again.

From out the other side of the pannier Nash produced a clay jug with a cork stopper. "We know you're a temperate man, Gus. So we brought us along our own refreshment."

"Don't stand there in the mud," Gus said, laughing. "Come in."

The two old men trailed Gus through the door, tracking more mud onto her floor. Clementine didn't mind; she was pleased that someone had come out to see them. She doubted there would be many others. She knew what they all thought of her, what the RainDance country thought of her—the whole of this merciless, unforgiving place. She was an outsider, a genu-ine starched-up lady with no grit in her heart, and they were all laughing at her for it. Sometimes she felt even the mountains and the wind were laughing at her.

Gus drew himself a small tin pail of home brew. He had two buckets of beer every noon with dinner. Each evening, while Clementine washed up, he took a bucket outside with him to watch the sun set. In Montana drinking beer wasn't considered *drinking*.

The men settled around the table. The prospectors' rank smell overwhelmed the cabin. They not only patronized the same tailor as Nickel Annie, they had her bathing habits as well. Clementine put the beaver tail in the sink. She hoped Gus wouldn't really expect her to make soup out of it.

Pogey lifted the whiskey jug in a toast. "Here's how, Gus. Man, you could've knocked me over with a whistle when you introduced the purtiest gal ever to come to Rainbow Springs as your wife."

Nash rubbed his beaky nose, honking a laugh. "Yup. Pogey here was so surprised his eyes were popping like a stomped-on toad's."

Pogey slammed the jug into his partner's bony chest. "Try corkin' your lips with this, you ol' flannelmouth. Some men talk when they got some-thin' to say. You talk 'cause you figure you always gotta be sayin' some-thin'."

There was a Montana way of doing everything, Clementine realized, and that included arguing and whiskey-drinking. She studied Nash as he curled his forefinger around the handle, rested the jug on his bent elbow, put his mouth to the spout, and tilted his arm. He drank for a long time, and when he lowered the jug his mouth puckered up tight as if pulled by a drawstring. He swallowed, shuddered, and smacked his lips. "What're you acting so proddy about, Pogey? Nobody expects a man to sit silent as a stuffed duck when he comes a-visitin'."

"Nobody expects 'im to gabble like a turkey neither. Gimme that jug before you drink it all."

Clementine went to the low coffee-case couch and settled down on the soogan padding, her stiff sateen skirts rustling loudly in the silence. She leaned forward, wrapping her arms around her bent knees. She wished that Gus would say something, but he had turned brooding of a sudden, cradling the pail between his two big hands and staring down into the dark brew.

"I expect you gentlemen have been friends for a long time," she said.

Pogey wiped his mouth with his sleeve. "I been soppin' gravy out the same skillet with this ol' son of a . . . gun for nigh on fifty years."

It was like a marriage, Clementine thought. Their petty bickering only hiding a deep fondness that had built up over time and shared memories. She tried to imagine how she and Gus would be with each other fifty years from now and found that she could not yet see her future beyond Gus's next bucket of brew and the setting of the sun. "And how do you come to be here in Rainbow Springs?"

Nash grinned, obviously pleased things were taking a turn toward conversation. "Well, we was just passing through, and Pogey was feelin' kinda parched, so we decided to wet our gullets at the Best in the West. We got into a card game, and durned if we didn't win a silver mine off some old geezer who shoulda known better'n to try and draw a fourth jack when Pogey had three queens showing on the table plain as daylight." He chuckled, shaking his head. "We named that mine the Four Jacks as a way of reminding ourselves not to be as big a fools when it comes to the pasteboards as the fella that went before us."

He fell quiet then, and in the shadowed light of the cabin, his gaze searched out Clementine. She imagined she could see a wisdom in his strange owl-like eyes, an understanding. She imagined he knew of those aching, empty places in her heart and of the girlhood that had driven her to marry Gus and follow him out here to this alien place. She imagined that he could name the missing things for her and tell her where to find them.

Nash blinked, his gaze breaking away from hers, and she saw only an old miner who smelled of sour sweat and liked to talk. "We been working that hole off 'n' on ever since. Which reminds me, Gus, of what we rode out here to tell ya—"

"Well, hallelujah," Pogey said. "Ye're finally circlin' up to the point."

Nash turned his big sad eyes onto his partner. "You're wearing me out with all your complaining about my talking. You don't think I can be a pithy man, a man economical with his speech? From now on, if you want pithy, I'll be pithy. I'll boil the whole blamed tellin' of it down to one pithy word . . ." He looked at Gus, licked his lips, and drew in a big breath. "Bonanza."

Gus laughed and wagged his head. "What?"

"There, you see, Pogey, what happens when a man gets pithy? He ain't understood, that's what happens."

"You ain't understood 'cause you never make any sense. Let me tell him, or 'tis never gettin' done." Pogey braced his elbows on the table and leaned forward. "You know the Four Jacks mine . . ."

"I ought to," Gus said. "Aside from the fact that Nash here was just jawing about it, I'm supposed to own a twenty percent share in return for grubstaking you old sourdoughs for the last two years. So far it's been nothing but twenty percent of muck and gangue."

"Yeah, well, we too was beginnin' to think that ol' claim had about as much poke to it as a dead man's dick—ugh!" He grunted as the jug slammed into his belly. A blush spread over his jowls and big ears, turning them the dark purple of overripe apples. "Beg pardon, ma'am."

"Let me tell it," Nash said. "So's the missus can be spared your foul tongue. We was sort of fiddling around one day when Pogey bit into a vein of quartz that looked promising. So we went along to Sam Woo's and got ourselves some—"

"Giant powder," Pogey finished for him. "We had Sam add it to your tick, Gus. Hope you don't mind."

Gus waved a hand. "Why should I mind? The Rocking R's already so deep in debt, what's a little more?"

"That's what we figured." Pogey took a swig of whiskey, then rested the jug on the ledge of his barrel gut. "We blasted out a nice piece of that quartz and sent it to the assayer's office over in Butte Camp, and damned—durned if it didn't prove to be veined with silver."

Nash produced a small flat stone out of his vest pocket. It flashed like a new dime as he dropped it into Gus's hand. "There's a whole lode of it down there where that come from. And it looks to go on for just about forever."

Gus rubbed the silver nugget between his fingers. Then he startled Clementine by leaping to his feet and letting go with a loud yipping yell. He swung her up into his arms and they danced around the table, his laughter bouncing off the rafters.

When he let her go, she was breathing hard. Her cheeks felt flushed, and her hair was tumbling loose from the tight knot at the nape of her neck. Gus's face glowed like a child's with his excitement. "Here you go, girl," he said, tossing the silver stone at her.

She caught it, smiling because this was the Gus McQueen she liked best, the Gus of dreams and laughter, the Gus she knew she could grow to love. She held the stone up to the light of the window, marveling at how it shone. "I don't understand . . . What is it?"

"An assayer's button."

"But what does it mean?" The stone felt warm in her hand, magical. "Are we rich?"

Gus smacked his hands together, laughing some more. "It means maybe we're gonna be twenty percent of rich."

"Thing is, it ain't all high grade," Nash said. "And it's hard rock. It's goin' to be expensive to dig it out."

Gus dropped back onto the nail-keg stool, quieter, though the shine of dreaming still brightened his eyes. "Hard-rock mining does need the proper machinery to drive through the rock to get at the veins, and you need mills and chemists to reduce the ore to metal. Y'all won't be able to do it yourselves. You'll have to lease the mine to a consortium."

Pogey blinked. "Huh?"

"A consortium, a group of investors. Men with the money it takes to run a full-scale hard-rock mining operation. How it works is, you'll lease the Four Jacks to a consortium in return for a piece of the mine's yield. A percentage of the profits, so to speak."

Nash blinked. "Uh . . . we was kinda hoping you'd arrange that for us, Gus. We was figuring them fancy educated ways of yours would set better with the money boys over in Butte Camp and Helena." Nash sighed, and his face took on a mournful cast. "It ain't easy being rich. Already things've got all complicated on us, and we ain't even started yet. There was a time when a man could pull up a sagebrush, shake off a dollar's worth of gold into a pan, call it a day's work, and be satisfied."

Pogey thrust out his chest, hooking his thumbs in his black suspenders. "Me, I like the feel of bein' rich. Some folk who don't know better might call it a complication. Those of us with vision and smarts—we call it progress."

"I suppose I could ride on over to Butte Camp and talk to some of those big leasing outfits," Gus said. "It'll have to wait until after the spring roundup, though."

"You better hop to it with that roundup," Nash said. "Else the calves now sucking your cows are going to be wearing some renegade rustler's brand."

"Yup," Pogey said, shaking his head. "That Iron Nose sure is one hell of an artist with a running iron." He leaned toward Gus and pitched his voice into a rough whisper, as if the rustlers had their ears to the windows even as he spoke. "You heard what happened to poor ol' MacDonald? Well, there's been talk about holding a necktie party for them murdering, cattle-thievin' Injuns." He made a fist and jerked it by his neck as if pulling on a rope. "Some folk are sayin' we oughta start right now with Joe Proud Bear. Others say wait and let him lead us to his pa, then we can have ourselves a family lynchin'."

At the mention of Indians, Clementine's gaze had strayed to the gouge in the wall. She wondered how MacDonald had died—had he been hacked into pieces with a tomahawk? No, she remembered Snake-Eye saying the man had been shot. She had never met MacDonald, only seen his coffin.

Ever since coming to Montana, her thoughts had been haunted by fears of Indians. Late at night, lying beside Gus, the sound of the wind caressing the cottonwoods easily became moccasined feet rustling through the grass outside the window. Yet more than by the massacring savages of her imagination she was haunted by the Indian girl and her babies, and how her man had roped her like an animal and dragged her away because she'd shamed him with her begging. And how everyone in Rainbow Springs, including her, had let it happen.

She was standing by Gus now, and she felt a latent tension within him, like a coiled whip. She laid her hand on his arm; it was hard, muscular, a man's arm with a man's strength and a man's capacity for violence. "That Indian boy," she said, "he has a wife and children. If he's stealing, maybe it's to feed them. It isn't right for ordinary citizens to take the law into their own hands. That's what courts and judges and juries are for."

He swung his head around, and she was startled by the raw anger on his face. "You people from the States, y'all just don't understand. There are stockmen at the railheads who'll buy anything on four hooves, cheap and no questions asked, then ship 'em back to Chicago and make a nice fat profit. Those same stockmen own the judges and the courts and the juries, Clem. They've been letting cattle thieves go for years. There comes a time when a man's got to protect what's his or he can't call himself a man."

"Rustlers have always got their necks stretched first and been tried later," Pogey said. "And these here are renegades we're talkin' about. Half-breeds. Most folk don't think a man with red skin got a right to any trial."

"Breechclouted savages, the lot of them." Gus gripped her arm, pulling her against him, as if he could physically force her to line up on his side. "Don't fret yourself with it, girl. This is men's work and is nothing to do with you."

"But it does have to do with me, and what you are planning is wrong—"

"That's enough!" He slammed the flat of his hand down on the table, knocking over her recipe book and sending a cloud of flour puffing into the air. "That's enough talk about cattle rustling," he said, calmer. "I'll do what's got to be done. You let me take care of it."

She pulled away from him, swallowing down the words she wanted to shout back at him. She rubbed the sting on her arm where he'd held her, where his fingers had bitten into her flesh. He had a right to chastise her. She had shamed him by arguing in front of the other men. He was her husband and he ought to know what was right, except that in this instance she couldn't help but believe he was wrong. And it was so hard to accept, so hard . . .

Gus drew lines through the sweat on the pail of beer he'd barely touched. "You seen my brother in Rainbow Springs any time this past week?" he finally said, after the silence had grown uncomfortable.

Pogey cleared his throat. "Ain't seen him precisely. We heard him. Heard of him, that is."

A muscle bunched in Gus's jaw. "I understand there's a new girl at the Best in the West."

"You mean Nancy? Naw, she ain't up to Rafferty's standards. Not only is she so bucktoothed she could eat an apple through a keyhole, she's as hard-used as a cowpoke's boots." He cast a sheepish look at Clementine. "Pardon me, ma'am. Nope, all the while you been gone, Gus, every man in the RainDance country 'cept Rafferty has been calicoing that Hannah Yorke and gettin' snubbed proper for all their pains. Then last Friday night he saunters on into the Best in the West, gives her a look, and damn—durn if she didn't succumb. He's been pokin' her ever since as if to make up for lost opportunities . . . no offense, ma'am."

Beneath the thick curve of his mustache, Gus's mouth took on a bitter slant. A shadow from the rafters slanted across the upper half of his face, obscuring his eyes, but Clementine didn't need to see his face to know his thoughts. His brother was openly sinning with Mrs. Yorke, a woman who wore violet silk and red-tasseled shoes. Hannah Yorke, the town harlot.

"I reckon we oughta be making tracks," Nash said, creaking to his feet and giving his belt a hitch. He nudged Pogey with the thick round toe of his boot. "Hump yore tail, pard."

Pogey pried himself off the nail keg, belching and scratching and swaying slightly once he got vertical. They took their leave, teasing Gus some more about his contented state of matrimony as they shuffled out the door.

Clementine took shelter out of the sun beneath the eaves to wave them on their way. Gus went with them as far as the corral. Pogey rode the sway-backed burro, and Nash walked alongside. They passed the jug back and forth between them. They didn't look like the owners of a silver mine. She wondered if being rich would change them.

The old biscuit-colored dog raised his head and watched them go, but he didn't leave the shadow of the barn. For hours he'd been lying there, flat on his belly, resting his nose on his paws. He pined for Gus's brother, who had stayed gone for three days, courting Mrs. Yorke, the town harlot. The dog had walked around Clementine and sniffed her once and then ignored her, as if he, too, didn't expect her to be here long. He had a strange milky white cast over one eye. Gus said he'd been bitten by a rattler and should have died. Instead he'd been left blind, or nearly so.

Gus didn't come back to the cabin, but went instead to the side of the barn where the buckboard rested. He'd mumbled something about having to take the buckboard back to Snake-Eye or buy it off him. Clementine knew what he was about. He was going into town to fetch his brother home before the man brought more shame and embarrassment upon the family. Her family now.

The misty light of morning had flattened into day. The meadows of wild hay that ran the length of the valley rippled in the constant wind. She could smell the hay, sweet and green. She tilted her head to watch a lone chicken hawk draw circles in the sky. The sky, always the sky. The vast emptiness of the sky numbed her mind and made her dizzy.

Lifting her skirts high above the mud, she crossed the yard toward Gus. She could feel the mountains, bristling with black pines, watching over her shoulder. The wind and the sky and the mountains always made her uneasy. They lured her, laid claim to her, and they frightened her. They stirred the same sort of restless feelings in her that Gus did in bed at night. And along with the restlessness that gripped her heart, there were still the hollow, echoing spaces that needed to be filled. The yearnings of her childhood had followed her to Montana, or she had brought them with her.

"Gus?" she practically shouted, startling them both. She touched the cameo at her neck, felt the tiny betraying flutter at the base of her throat. "Surely you do not mean to leave me here by myself."

He was working a kink out of the harness chains, and he took a moment to look around at her. His broad shoulders blocked the sun; his hair was shot through with threads of gold. His mouth and eyes were tight with anger. "Of course not. It isn't safe."

She drew in her breath and let it out slowly. "I'll just get ready, then."

"Don't dawdle. I want to be back before it gets dark."

She was about to start toward the cabin when he stopped her. "Clementine. Don't ever challenge my authority like that again."

She clenched her teeth against the surge of rebellious feelings that threatened to choke her.

"It makes me look bad, girl, when you set yourself up against me. Like I'm not the man in my own house."

She stood rigid before him, trying to quiet the shaking that was going on inside her. She wouldn't apologize, nor would she acknowledge that he was right. "I must get my hat and gloves," she said instead. She turned and made her way stiffly across the muddy yard. She could feel his angry gaze stabbing into her back. She kept having to swallow again and again to keep from screaming.

In the lean-to that sheltered the big iron bed, she set about making herself decent enough to be seen in town. The wind and dancing around the table with Gus had made a mess of her hair. She put the curling tongs in the chimney of the lamp, and while they heated, she washed her face and hands. Her face stared back at her from the cracked mirror, wind-chapped and sunburned and a little frightened.

Her cloak hung on a hook beside the makeshift clothespress. The cloak with the heart-shaped secret buried deep in its pocket. She took the sachet out and stood there holding it in her palm, feeling its weight, and hearing the clank of the coins.

She wouldn't leave Gus; she knew that already. But she was tired of always worrying about what was proper, or seemly, or even if she was a good wife. She was a woman grown and she ought to be allowed to think for herself. Like the mountain men and trappers who had come before her to this uncharted wilderness, she wanted to forge her own trails.

She used a butchering knife to slit one of the seams in the sachet. She took out a five-dollar gold piece and then looked around the cabin for a place to hide the rest.

Long and lean and beautiful, the cowboy lay naked on her bed.

He lay on her bed and watched her with wild golden

eyes. Hannah Yorke rose from her bath, stepping with deliberate grace out of the galvanized iron tub. Water ran in smooth streams over her skin, caressing her the way his hands had caressed her an hour ago. Perfumed steam banished three days' worth of stale whiskey and sex. It was late morning, and diffused sunlight shone through the gauzy marquisette curtains on her bedroom window, setting the red silk walls afire and painting a soft pink patina on her naked body.

She felt the heat of his gaze on her as she toweled her body dry, and yet she shivered, mostly from the cool spring air, and maybe a little from those strange yellow eyes. Oh, he was a wild one, all right, and just a little loco, in the way that Joe Proud Bear and Iron Nose and a lobo wolf were all ornery and crazy. Creatures that were loners deep inside themselves and answered to nobody's rules.

She put on an Oriental silk wrapper and sat on the horsehair fainting couch to brush out her hair. Gathering a thick hank of it in one hand, she lifted her arm and pulled the steel teeth through, starting at the crown of her head and going to her waist. Her hair slithered and coiled around her wrists and hands. Her breasts rose and fell, rubbing against the sensuous silk. He watched her, and she knew the pure femaleness of what she was doing stirred him. She shivered faintly again, and her muscles tightened in anticipation, and memory.

She stretched out her legs, digging her toes into the thick Turkey carpet. She loved this room—though, with its red silk wallpaper and the elaborately carved four-poster bed, it looked as if it belonged in a bordello. Which was precisely what it had been before she'd bought it. Now it was just a room in a house. Her house, and she lived in it alone. In the fifteen months she'd been in Rainbow Springs, the cowboy was the first man she'd allowed into her life, into her bed.

A decent woman, she knew, would think Hannah Yorke had been corrupted beyond redemption by her old life, and perhaps that was so. For although she had resisted him hard, the truth was . . . the truth was that she had wanted the cowboy since she first laid eyes on him. Had known right from the start that she would have him, or he would have her. And, oh, they had certainly had at each other these last three days, fucking as if they'd invented the word.

The truth was . . .

She tried not to lie to herself anymore. Once long, long ago she had believed that no matter what she did, no matter what was done to her, nothing would ever be able to touch the heart of her.

Lies, all lies. As deep as hell, that's how deeply she'd been touched by all the days and nights of her life.

Now she knew that if she stopped brushing and turned her head, she would catch her reflection in the large mirror with the fluted gold frame that sat atop her dressing table. And she would see the face and the eyes of a whore.

As if to prove she was tough enough to stand it, she lifted her head and looked in the mirror. She saw her face and, behind it, the reflection of the man on her bed.

His gaze met hers in the glass. The hard, almost cruel look of arousal on his face both excited and frightened her, and she looked away. He hadn't a care for things that could be broken, like hearts. And he made love with a desperate hunger, as though he might die tomorrow.

"Come here," he said. Commanded.

Because she wanted to so badly, she didn't go to him. She went instead to her dressing table with its gold mirror. A fringed Arab scarf covered the top of the table, and on it sat a biscuit bowl of cocoa butter cones soaking in boric acid. The strong sweet-and-sour smell rose up to smother her. She pressed her palm over her womb, sure that she could feel the ache of its emptiness. There would be no baby from what she and the cowboy did on her bed.

Beside the bowl was a posy of wax flowers from a wedding cake preserved under a glass bell. Once, the violets had been the deep purple of royalty, the white roses as pristine as winter's first snow. Now the violets were a faded puce, the roses long since yellowed. She ran her fingers over the smooth glass. Nothing, not even a bell jar, could preserve a thing forever from the ravages of time. The years passed, and memories, like flowers, faded. So every day she made herself look and touch and remember never to believe in lies, not even the ones she told herself.

She turned and looked at the man on her bed. He was young and strong and hard for her. She smiled as she went to him.

"Hannah," he said, hunger in his voice.

She sat beside him. He rose up and she bent down until their lips met. His kiss was raw and smoky, full of need. The scent of his skin swam to her head—heat and man and lust. He pushed his tongue into her mouth, and she curled her arms around his neck. She loved the feel of him beneath her hands, the hard, unyielding muscles beneath the warm silken skin. A fierce longing enveloped her, an urge to press her body against his and hold him close.

He eased her down beside him. His mouth and hands moved low over her belly. She had a tattoo of a rose high on the inside of her thigh. His tongue, hot and wet, traced each petal, licking along the curve of the stem and disappearing into her dense bush of woman's hair. Pleasure . . . She had forgotten that pleasure could be given as well as sold. For two years she had been a red-light girl, working the line in Deadwood, renting a shack furnished with little except a bed. Her name had been burned into the wood above the door. Not her real name, of course. The one she'd worked under . . . Rosie.

The tattoo intrigued him, but he'd asked no questions about it. She wasn't used to a man who didn't want her life story, who didn't want to be told that at heart she wasn't really a whore but the girl next door, the girl he'd left behind.

He moved up to kiss her mouth again, letting her taste herself on his tongue. She loved the weight of him. Her chest tightened with a warm, elusive sweetness. It had been so long since she'd been held by a true lover, since she'd been touched with any tenderness.

She suddenly couldn't bear it. She tore her mouth from his, panting a little. "What're you doing here, Rafferty?"

"You mean you haven't figured that out yet? I guess I need to try harder." He licked the middle of her cheek, where a crescent-shaped crease formed when she was happy. "You got a smile a man would go to hell for, darlin'."

"You didn't need to go to hell for it, only as far as Rainbow Springs."

He rolled off of her, sliding one arm beneath her back so that he was cradling her against him. He cupped her breast in his hand, pulling on her nipple until it was hard and tight. He liked to touch, this man. She had discovered that about him in the beginning hours of the first night. And somewhere along the way, some woman had taught him how to do it well.

"You've been here three days," she said. She raked her fingers through the hair on his chest. "That's a long while to be away from your ranch this time of year."

Beneath her hand his chest moved as if in a sigh, though she didn't hear it. "My brother brought a wife back with him from Boston, and things've turned to teetotaling hell. I could see right off the way it was gonna be. Wipe your feet before you come in the door, take your hat off inside the house, eat like you aren't hungry, and don't call it shit even if it stinks."

His words were mean, but her ears had picked out the note of worry threaded through them. His brother's return to Rainbow Springs with a wife in tow made her uneasy as well. Probably because Mrs. Gus McQueen was only the first of what would soon be a whole plague of respectable busybodies descending on the place to point their horrified fingers at Hannah Yorke and call her a disgrace, a fallen woman.

Well, Hannah Yorke had fallen, all right, but she had picked herself up again. She was a property owner now, never mind that the property was a saloon and a former bawdy house. Those respectable women with their turned-up noses and starched bodices could all go to hell, with Mrs. Gus McQueen leading the way. Because Hannah Yorke *liked* having her own money and making her own way in the world. Especially now that she no longer had to do it lying on her back.

She twisted a thin curl of his chest hair around her finger and tugged on it hard enough to pucker the skin. He didn't even wince. "Your brother's new wife is sure enough a lady," she said. "Y'all could use some civilizing."

"Oh, she's as prim and dainty as a lace curtain, all right. And she'll be just as much use to us out here."

She watched his callused, veined hand fondle her breast. She liked the way his hand looked as he touched her, strong and lean, so dark against the paleness of her skin. "She's got a real pretty face, though," she said.

"Gus better hope he likes lookin' at her pretty face"— he pushed himself up on one elbow to lean over her, and his lips curled into a wicked smile that was all man—"'cause I know women like her, and six days out of the seven lookin' is all she's gonna let him do."

He was done with talking. He covered her, and she felt his cock pressing hard and hot between her legs. She slid up, then back to take him inside her, her fingers digging into his shoulders. He moved deep within her, a slow thrust and drag, and the world tightened and narrowed until all she knew was the heavy thumping of her heart in her chest and her own breath sucking in and out.

6

CLEMENTINE PAUSED UNDER THE jangling cowbells of Sam Woo's General Mercantile, letting her eyes adjust to the dimness. Today the place smelled of smoked meat, new shoes, and the vinegar that dripped from the spigot of a wooden barrel.

Sam Woo leaned on the counter, the bride catalog spread open between his bent elbows. The green eyeshade and spectacles obscured the upper half of his face, but Clementine saw his mouth pull into what could have been a smile. It could also have been a grimace of dismay.

"Mrs. McQueen, holy God!" He looked crisp and clerical in a stiff paper collar and black sateen sleeve protectors. "What a big wonderful surprise this is!"

Clementine had a suspicion that it was not a surprise at all, that as soon as they'd left the ranch this morning an invisible telegraph had begun signaling the imminent arrival of Gus McQueen and his bride in Rainbow Springs.

"Good afternoon, Mr. Woo," she said, nodding stiffly to cover a sudden, agonizing bout of shyness. "I . . ." She fumbled with the pocket of her tight-fitting basque. "I have a letter to mail, and my husband said you could . . ."

"Dispatch it for you. But of course, of course."

Sam Woo whipped the green eyeshade off his head and replaced it with a billed blue twill cap. He went behind a small grilled box that had been set up on one end of the pickle barrel counter above a peeling poster for Rosebud whiskey. Clementine pushed her letter beneath the grille.

She'd held her mother's face in her thoughts, in her

heart, yesterday when she penned the words about Gus and the ranch and the frightening wonder that was Montana. But she knew her father's eyes would be the only ones to see them, for the servants were instructed to bring all correspondence directly to him. Perhaps he would read her letter. More than likely he would toss it onto the fire unopened.

Sam Woo pulled his spectacles to the tip of his nose and peered over the top of them at the address on the envelope. "Massachusetts, huh? It's gonna cost you two dollars."

"Two dollars!"

"Handling fee. Someone's gotta take the letter to Helena, so it can be put on the stagecoach heading east. Helena and the stagecoach are a long way away."

"What someone?"

He shrugged. "Someone I hire. Handling fee."

"You, Mr. Woo, are a splendid example of Yankee greed and ingenuity."

He bowed low, as if acknowledging a compliment. He was a strange little man, she thought, exotic in spite of all his best efforts to seem otherwise. They were both outsiders here, she and Mr. Sam Woo. Two people who would never wholly belong, yet could never return to the places they had come from.

"Have you chosen a bride yet, Mr. Woo?" she asked.

He shook his head, his long queue sliding back and forth over his shoulders. "Not yet, not yet. Soon. Soon as I save up one thousand dollars."

"Which shouldn't be long, if you are given many more letters to dispatch." She slipped the half-eagle beneath the grille. "You may take your exorbitant handling fee out of this. And there are some other things I wish to purchase."

Sam Woo bit into the gold piece, then held it up to the light of the window as if he suspected it of being counterfeit. "Where'd you get money like this?"

"I robbed a bank before leaving Boston. I would like five pounds of flour, please, and one of brown sugar. A bucket of lard and several cans each of corn and tomatoes. Fresh eggs—"

"No eggs. Sorry about that."

"And tins of milk. Lots of milk."

Comprehension dawned in his eyes. "Holy God. Does Gus McQueen know you're doing this?"

"Not yet. But I have no doubt someone will soon tell him."

"Not me, no, ma'am." He shook his head, laughing. A soft, trilling giggle that sounded like a child's. "This Chinaman ain't no Indian-lover, but he's not crazy either, no sirree jingle."

He changed headgear, back to the green eyeshade of the busy businessman. He dumped out a nearly empty candle box and began filling it with her order, muttering to himself in a mixture of English and Chinese.

Clementine looked around the store, noting the recent additions to Mr. Woo's bountiful wares: the smelly bundle of buffalo hides that had been freighted out in Nickel Annie's wagon, jars of white grape jelly, a hooked rug . . . As she crossed the puncheon floor for a closer look at the rug, ashes gritted beneath the soles of her shoes. The stove's belly, she saw, was overflowing. Mr. Woo obviously hadn't emptied it in weeks. She would never understand men: how they could work so hard at some things and be so lazy about others.

She thought the rug was beautiful. A jute gunnysack had been used as the base, and bright scraps of red, yellow, and green calico had been hooked through to resemble a giant spray of spring tulips. The carpets in her father's house had all been thick and expensive and woven of soft, muted colors. Her mother, she knew, would probably label this rug garish, but Clementine loved it.

Sam Woo came up to her, carrying the loaded candle box, his face creased in worry. "It's a good thing, Mrs. McQueen, what you're about to do. But, holy God, it's not smart. They're holding a meeting right now over at Snake-Eye's livery. They aim to form up a posse and hang . . . someone."

He gave the box over to her, and she staggered a bit under its weight. She thought he was going to offer to carry it for her, but he pressed his lips together and retreated behind the counter.

At the door she paused. "Mr. Woo, why aren't you at the meeting?"

"This Chinaman ain't crazy," he said. Only this time he didn't laugh.

The day was cool, but the sun shone, and the labor of struggling through the mud with her burden soon had Clementine flushed and gasping for breath.

She paused to rest, setting the candle box among the thick, gnarly roots of a box elder tree. Her arms ached. Sweat ran down between her breasts to pool around the bones in her corset. Her flannel shimmy clung wetly to her legs, making them itch.

She looked around her. The hat-crowned butte from which the RainDance country took its name stood ragged against the blue sky. The butte's arid slopes were lumpy with dishwater-colored gravel heaps that marked the entrances to the mines, most of them abandoned. She could just make out a crudely lettered sign that read FOUR JACKS next to one of the bigger heaps. Rotting timbers surrounded a hole in the red earth and a dilapidated hand-cranked windlass. The mine didn't look as if it would produce a fortune any time soon.

Her gaze shifted to the tipi that shone rusty white in the spring sun. The river flowed between her and it, rushing fast and loud from the mountain runoff. A rickety bridge, made of stones and old timbers, spanned the water where it elbowed around a stand of quaking aspens. She would have to cross the bridge and approach the tipi in full view of everyone in Rainbow Springs.

Her back prickled, and she twisted her head, peering over her shoulder. The bog that called itself a street was deserted. The buckboard in which she'd ridden to town with Gus stood alone before the livery. The barn's big sliding double doors were closed. Gus and Snake-Eye and the other men of Rainbow Springs were all inside, planning a lynching.

She wiped the sweat off her face with her handkerchief, took a deep breath, picked up the heavy box, and started walking again.

She left the road, taking a narrow path that led through the town's small cemetery. The crude wooden crosses were all leaning and weathered, except one. A pair of man-sized boots hung over the freshly hewn marker. She didn't slow down to read the name burned into the wood. She knew who was buried here—the Scotsman MacDonald, who had been killed by cattle thieves.

She approached the bridge, her skin crawling now as if the leaves of the aspens were a thousand winking eyes, watching her. Zach Rafferty's drawling voice seemed to reverberate like war drums in her blood: "Them Injuns chopped up poor ol' Henry into so many little pieces they had to gather him up in a bucket so's they could bury him." She remembered the sight of Joe Proud Bear galloping down the road, his lariat hissing and whipping through the air. Even in his western clothes, he'd looked pure savage.

As Clementine stepped onto the bridge the heel of her shoe caught in a cracked log. Her knee buckled and she almost stumbled. A strange sound popped out her mouth, like the death cheep of a strangled bird. Don't be a fool, she admonished herself. You are not going to be massacred in broad daylight with all of Rainbow Springs watching.

She approached the Indian camp slowly. She didn't see the piebald pony anywhere, and her breath came a little easier.

The wind had died. Pale smoke from a campfire spiraled into the sky. The aspens shivered like silver raindrops in the sun, casting a dappled shade onto an old buffalo robe that covered the ground in front of the tipi, and onto the small child that sat on it.

Clementine stopped at the edge of the robe and tried to peer through the slit in the cone-shaped tent. Strange effigies had been painted on the sun-bleached hide. "Hey there?" she called out.

No one answered. The child crammed four fingers into its mouth and looked up at her with wide dark eyes.

Clementine set the box of food on the ground and knelt beside the child. The buffalo robe smelled rankly of woodsmoke and stale grease. A kettle hung bubbling over the fire from a trammel supported by stakes driven in the ground.

"Howdy, sweetheart," she said. It was difficult to tell, but she thought the child was a girl. She leaned into her, bringing them nose to nose, and saw her own face reflected back at her from a trader's paper-backed mirror that hung from a rawhide string around the child's neck. The little girl's cheeks were fat, but her body was pathetically thin. She wore buckskin leggings and a blue calico smock that had been lovingly decorated with beads and dyed porcupine quills.

"Where is your mama?" Clementine asked. The child stared back at her, unblinking, even though a fly crawled in the corner of her eye. Clementine shooed it away. "Mama," she said again.

The little girl took her fingers out of her mouth and looked toward the river. Clementine got awkwardly to her feet, fighting with her tight-fitting, heavy sateen skirts.

The child's mother walked toward them with long, free strides. She wore a loose scarlet blanket coat that hung to her knees, and her legs were covered by tall fringed moccasins. Each had been decorated differently, with beads and quills, elks' teeth and bits of scarlet cloth. They were beautiful, more colorful than the rag rug in Sam Woo's mercantile. She carried a hide bucket that dripped water, leaving penny-sized patterns in the dirt.

She saw Clementine, and her steps faltered. She looked quickly around. Her long straight hair whipped back and forth, slapping her face. It glistened blue-black in the sun. "What do you want?" she cried.

"I've brought some canned milk for your baby."

The girl walked past her and set the bucket beside the fire. Her face was expressionless. "She died."

"Oh . . . I'm so sorry." The words sounded so shallow, so pointless. But she didn't know what else to say.

The girl lifted her thin shoulders in a shrug, but Clementine caught the flash of pain in her eyes. "My man would not want you here," she said.

Clementine nodded, her mouth suddenly dry with fear again. She took a step sideways and knocked into one of the trammel stakes. The kettle rocked, slurping gravy into the fire. A good thick stew was cooking in that kettle, filled with lots of meat. She hoped for Joe Proud Bear's sake that it was venison.

She looked up and met the girl's wary eyes. "Warn your man: he should cease riding with the renegade Iron Nose or he will be caught and hanged."

The girl's dark eyes widened. "Joe did not kill that white man, and neither did his father. Oh, they maybe steal a few cows now and then, but—"

Her head swung around at the sound of galloping hooves, and the cross she wore around her neck flashed in the sun. The piebald pony burst out of the copse of aspens, cutting straight across the bow in the river, splashing glittering drops into the air.

She seized Clementine's arm and thrust her toward the bridge. "Go!"

Clementine had barely taken two steps when the Indian was upon her. He reined the piebald to a sudden stop, splattering mud over her skirts. He threw himself out of the saddle, blocking her path. His wife cried out to him, and he shouted something back at her in his harsh guttural tongue, freezing her in place. He looked more than ever like a savage today in bone armor that covered his chest and with slashes of vermilion and ocher greasepaint on his forehead and hollow cheeks. The copper bands around his arms blazed like fire in the sun. He was very young, but he had a warrior's face, full of rage and hate.

He glared at Clementine with fierce dark eyes that were incongruously framed with lashes as long and thick as a girl's. Her stomach knotted, and there was a strange coppery taste in her mouth.

"Paying a social call, white woman?" he sneered.

His wife held out her hand to him, as if beseeching him to understand or forgive her. "Joe, don't . . . She brought milk for the baby."

He barked a harsh, bitter laugh. His eyes narrowed on Clementine. He pursed his lips so hard the sprout of feathers on his head quivered. He leaned into her and shot a thick globule of spit onto her bodice. "That for your charity."

Clementine could do nothing but stand there and shudder. The place where he'd spat on her burned as if he'd branded her through all the layers of her clothes to her skin.

His mouth curled into a mean smile. He leaned into her again, so close she could smell him—woodsmoke and grease, like the buffalo robe. He lifted his hand, and her whole body stiffened up, rigid as a tent pole. He pulled loose a lock of her hair that had started to slip from beneath the brim of her hat. She flinched as he rubbed it between his fingers, making little smacking sounds with his lips.

"You have pretty hair, white woman. Like sun-ripened grass. It would look good decorating a war club."

She jerked back with such violence she nearly fell, and he laughed. Drawing on a childhood of strict training, she lifted her chin in the air and turned her back on him. She tried to walk away with some manner of dignity. But deep inside, all she wanted to do was run.

Hannah Yorke had been sitting in a wicker rocker on the gallery of her white frame house, watching the clouds sail across the big blue emptiness of the Montana sky. For once the wind was tame, only stirring itself enough to quake the aspen leaves. And for the first time all year there was the warm breath of summer in the sun.

The dress she wore that afternoon was the fiery red of spring poppies. Humming softly to herself, she spread her hands over her thighs, taking pleasure in the slick feel of the grosgrain silk and its bright color. In the Kentucky coal-mining town where she'd grown up, everything had been covered with a film of soot. She'd had to leave home to learn that the world was not all shades of gray.

She lifted her hands above her head, stretching, reaching for the sky. She was some sore after all the bed exercise of the last few days. At the thought of the cowboy her mouth curved into a wistful smile. She would regret taking him as a lover, but not yet. Not today. His loving had left her feeling a little sad, because he was so good at making her forget. But it was a good kind of sad. She had been world-soured for so long. And so damned lonely.

From the wicker rocker on her porch she could see the whole of Rainbow Springs. She watched the men gather at Snake-Eye's livery and knew what they were about. They came one at a time, looking over their shoulders before disappearing into the barn. How men did so like to play their silly games, making themselves out to be more important than they really were. Men making themselves out to be *men*. She knew them all, and most would greet her if they passed on the street. A few would not. As Rainbow Springs grew up into its own self-importance, those who thought themselves too fine to acknowledge the town harlot would grow in number as well until someday, she knew, she would no longer be welcome here.

She saw Gus McQueen and his new wife roll into town on the buckboard. The dress Mrs. McQueen had on was the sort you'd lay a corpse out in. A Sunday-go-to-meeting dress. Expensive, though—the gray sateen was of the finest quality, draped and trained and trimmed in burgundy faille. It took a fluting iron and hours of work to put that many pleats into a skirt. Hannah watched the rancher's wife go into Sam Woo's mercantile, noting the dainty buttoned kid shoes when she lifted her train and the plain black felt princess hat perched at just the perfect angle on her head. She carried herself as if she had a fire poker strapped to her spine, but there was a dignity about her that Hannah longed to emulate.

Oh, she was a fourteen-karat lady all right. Hannah thought she probably hated her. All starch and breeding and polished manners.

Several minutes later Mrs. McQueen left the mercantile carrying a heavy box that appeared to be full of blue-labeled cans . . . milk tins? Hannah planted her foot to stop the chair from rocking and sat up straighter. She watched Gus McQueen's wife walk out of town and through the cemetery, toward the bridge and the half-breed camp on the other side of the river. It took a mad kind of courage to go marching alone into a nest of renegade cattle thieves armed only with milk tins.

When Joe Proud Bear came galloping out of the trees, Hannah lurched to her feet, an instinctive cry of warning on her lips that she only managed to stop in time. She knew better than to get involved in something like this. And besides, the girl deserved to get the blue bejesus scared out of her for being such a fool.

Still, a breath of relief shivered out of Hannah's chest as she watched Mrs. McQueen leave the camp unharmed, those dainty kid shoes squelching with dignified purpose through the red mud. When the girl passed Boot Hill, she stopped and stood still for a long time. She pulled a hanky out of her pocket and scrubbed at the front of her dress. When she was through, she balled up the white linen and hurled it away as if it had been defiled. She smoothed her fair hair up beneath her bonnet and resumed her slow, stately walk back to town.

Hannah wasn't sure how she came to be standing outside her gate, on the mud-washed plank walk, waiting for Gus McQueen's lady wife to pass her by. She had learned and accepted long ago the price she paid for being the kind of woman she was, for living her kind of life. Only a fool would think the world had changed just because she had woken up happy this morning.

Company, girls! Sporting girls and fancy girls. Every man's girl and no man's girl. "How do ye do and buy me a drink, mister?" *And maybe pretend, if the night is soft and he is kind, if only for a moment, that you are some man's girl.*

Hannah Yorke lifted her chin in a challenge, fully prepared to have the young woman draw away her skirts in horror when faced with the effrontery of Hannah Yorke's sinful presence. "Good afternoon, Mrs. McQueen."

"Mrs. Yorke," Clementine McQueen replied with quiet courtesy. And she said it with true sincerity, too, as if she didn't know that Hannah was as much a real widow as the ring in a merry-go-round was real gold. *Every man's girl and no man's girl.*

Hannah suddenly realized that she didn't quite know what to do next. She could hardly invite a lady like Mrs. McQueen inside to take tea. *Oh, Hannah, all that cowboy's good lovin' must have softened your head.* It was ludicrous to think she could become a friend to this young woman of breeding and respectability.

Yet she wanted to feel what it would be like to brush up against the fineness of a real lady like Clementine McQueen. Maybe she would feel more like a lady herself then, in the way that rubbing a piece of silver between your fingers could make you feel rich. "I saw what you just did," she said, and she tried on a smile. "That was right nice of you."

The perfect angel's-wing curve of the girl's fair brows came together in a frown. "I was too late. The baby's dead."

The wind picked that moment to start acting up again. A gust swooped down on them, tearing at the treetops and snatching at the brim of the girl's hat. She anchored it onto her head with one hand, and the movement pulled up her sleeve, exposing her fragile wrist and pale skin, smooth as frothed cream.

"You better stay away from Joe Proud Bear," Hannah said. "He's got a bad case of hate in him for anything white."

"They say he's riding with his father, that he's rustling cattle."

Hannah shrugged. McQueen and Rafferty sold most of their cattle to the government, which in turn was supposed to allot it as free beef issue to the Indians on the reservation lands. Everyone knew, though, that only a third of the beef sold to the government agents made it into any hungry red-skinned bellies. The ranchers got paid, and the government agents took their cut, and the Indians were left with a third of not much, lands that grew little food, and a treaty that prohibited them from hunting. It wasn't fair, but it was life.

Mrs. McQueen's shadowed gaze was focused on the distant camp. She had strange eyes, gray-green like the sea and hinting at deep hidden currents. "They're having a meeting in the livery barn right now," she said. "They mean to hang that boy, hang them all, if they catch them at it."

And your Gus will be right up front leading the posse, Hannah thought, but didn't say it. It was nothing to her, what happened to the Indians. It ought to be nothing to this girl. But then, she supposed, only real ladies like Mrs. McQueen could afford to be nice.

"Joe Proud Bear knows what he's risking. If a man is bent on drowning, he'll find a way to do it even in a desert."

"But what will his wife do then, she and her child? She's so young, hardly more than a child herself."

"Don't fret yourself about the squaw. She's tougher than she looks. And I'll wager she's hardly much younger than you."

The girl turned those sea-deep eyes onto Hannah. "How old are you?"

The question so stunned her that for a moment Hannah was breathless. She felt her lips tighten, felt the lines that bracketed her mouth deepen. She felt her skin sag and the sun pick out all the tiny wrinkles around her eyes. She felt the legacy of every man, every disappointment, every broken promise, shine on her face like drops of sweat, like tears, for this girl, this child, to sneer at and pity. Oh, God, worst of all, to pity.

She put on the widest smile she owned. "I'm only twenty-nine, so I ain't countin' the steps to the bone orchard yet. And when it comes to pleasuring a man, honey, there are some who say a talented mouth has got it all over a young twat every time."

Hannah expected the girl to reel back in horror at her shocking, vulgar words. But then, she was such a damned innocent that Hannah might as well have been speaking Chinese, for all the girl had probably understood of it. She just kept staring at Hannah with that deep, still gaze. It made Hannah uncomfortable to be looked at like that, as if the girl could see more than Hannah wanted her to know. More than she knew herself.

"I can't imagine what made me behave so rudely," the girl said. "It's just that people out here seem older than they look."

That's because life out here has a way of aging you fast inside yourself, Hannah thought. Inside yourself you can be dead and buried before you're thirty. "You oughta be getting along, Mrs. McQueen. Rainbow Springs might be a bobtailed town, but she's still got her principles. You shouldn't be seen talking to the likes of me."

"I will talk to whomever I please," she said, and although the words were childish and naive, there was a willful tilt to her chin that surprised Hannah. She looked at the girl in a new way, wondering if she hadn't pegged her all wrong.

She wasn't really a classic beauty, Hannah decided. It was her eyes, so wide-set and slightly prominent. And her mouth—a short upper lip that didn't quite meet her full, pouty lower one. Her porcelain frailty and touch-me-not manner were at odds with that mouth. A mouth like that could earn a fortune on the line in Deadwood.

Right now that mouth appeared to have something it wanted to say, but it was having so much trouble spitting the words out that Hannah couldn't help smiling.

"I wonder, Mrs. Yorke . . ." She stopped, drew in a deep breath, and started over again. "That is, would it be possible someday, if it wouldn't be too much of an inconvenience . . . will you allow me to make your photograph?"

The smile slid off Hannah's face. Nickel Annie had told her that Gus McQueen's new lady wife had dragged a trunk full of picture-taking equipment out here with her, but Hannah hadn't really credited it. Oh, she could just imagine this young woman's rich blue-blood family peering at her likeness with morbid curiosity. *Dear Mama and Papa: There are many poor fallen souls such as she out west. They call themselves sporting gals, and they are a living, burning shame to the fair sex they have disgraced.*

Hannah drew herself up, giving the girl a wary look. "Why would you want to make my photograph?"

"You have an interesting face." A stunning smile came and went. "Good day, Mrs. Yorke. It was pleasant speaking with you. Perhaps we can visit again together someday soon."

Caught off-balance, Hannah could only nod as the girl gathered up her train and started down the boardwalk, sateen skirts softly rustling, shoe heels quietly tapping. The sounds of a lady passing by.

She had taken a couple of steps when she suddenly whirled, walking backward and clutching at her hat against a fresh gust of wind. "Are you enjoying your piano?" she called out above clacking branches of the aspen trees.

Hannah swallowed as if she were choking back a rock. "I ain't found anyone yet who knows how to play it. Shiloh, my bartender, only does the fiddle."

"My father believed that music and dancing and singing all weakened one's character and led to worldliness and sin. I should love to hear your new piano played someday. Oh, I should dearly love to hear it."

She spun around and walked in graceful ladylike strides back toward Sam Woo's mercantile. Hannah imagined holding a recital in the Best in the West Casino, where no respectable woman would be seen dead. She would serve ginger cakes and lemonade from lace-covered tables. All of the ladies would keep their hats and gloves on and sip genteelly from tiny china cups and clap politely when the pianist finished a somber musical interlude. No honky-tonk, of course. Oh, my, that would never do.

Hannah wanted to laugh, but instead her eyes blurred with tears.

Something caught at her throat, something that hurt and made a curious melting feeling deep in her chest. A mixture of sadness and happiness, and a strange sweet ache that after a moment she realized was hope.

"I told you before, cowboy—that critter belongs in a barn."

Rafferty slouched on his tailbone, laid one spurred boot across the other on the table, hooked his hands behind his head, and peered lazily up at Hannah Yorke from beneath the shadow of his hat brim. "There's a number of critters of various persuasions in here. Which particular critter are you talkin' about?"

"The four-legged one." Hannah pointed to the red-and-white calf that stood with all four legs splayed, looking as if it was about to christen the saloon floor. Little Patsy had one dimpled leg across its back, trying to straddle it like a horse.

"Have a heart, darlin'," Rafferty said. His drawl carried with it the Deep South of cypress trees and bayou ballads, and he had enough whiskey in him to make his tongue even slower. With his beard-shadowed cheeks and the dark hair growing long and curling over his collar, he looked disreputable and dangerous and handsome as sin. "That poor little dogie was gettin' lonesome out there in your lean-to with not even an ol' draft horse for company."

"Shiloh's going to quit on me for making him mother that calf, feeding him with a sugar-tit and Lord knows what all."

Rafferty crooked his head back, looking upside down at the gin-slinger, who was busy polishing glasses behind the bar. "He don't mind, do you, Shiloh?"

"No, sir. I don't mind. So long as you pay this child, he's easy."

Rafferty's head fell forward, and a rascal's smile lit up his face. Hannah had to clench her fist to keep from reaching out and trying to capture that smile with her fingertips. And what're you going to do with it, Hannah, you sentimental fool? she asked herself. Preserve it in a glass bell along with the flowers off your wedding cake? Yet there he sprawled, long and lean and smiling up at her, and that same curious melting feeling took hold of her heart again, so that the world suddenly seemed bright and new and full of promise.

She drew in a deep breath, trying to clear her head. If she was falling in love, she would never forgive herself.

"If that animal pees in my tonk, Zach Rafferty, I'm bringing you the mop and pail." She spun on her heel and strode away from him, putting the bar between herself and any long, lean cowboys with rascally smiles. She yanked out the money drawer and pretended to count last night's take, although she didn't really care and she knew Shiloh would never cheat her.

She could feel the gin-slinger's eyes on her and she was aware of the grin making its way to the corners of his mouth. He knew where she'd been for the last three days and nights, and what she'd been doing, and why. They'd been together since Deadwood, she and Shiloh, and he knew her inside and out. Sometimes she could succeed in fooling herself, but she could never fool Shiloh.

She shot him a glare she hoped was hot enough to fry bacon. "Don't say it."

He held a glass up to the light, blew on it, polished it. "Nice weather we're having ourselves today, Miss Hannah.

Sun keeps on shining like she's doing and the mud'll be drying up in no time. Business'll be picking up then, I reckon."

Certainly few men were greasing the bar with their elbows today, sun or no sun. Even the gambler had either moved on to greener parts or was sleeping a bender off somewhere. Hannah had decided that nobody was doing much of anything at the moment, when the door to the back room opened and a powerful stink came out of it, followed by the sheepherder. The man was fastening his pants and talking to himself. Saphronie stumbled at his heels, her eyes on the floor. Clutched in her fist was the veil she usually wore over her face.

Without the tattoos she would have been a plain, ordinary woman. Her hair and eyes were both a prairie-dog brown, her complexion sallow. But the tattoos—those four lines of deep blue marks shaped like giant teardrops that ran from her lips to the bottom of her chin—gave her a terrible ugliness that in a strange way bordered on beauty. It was hard not to look at her.

Saphronie kept her gaze on her shoes as she carefully laid three silver cartwheels on the bar. The heavy coins clattered on the scarred wood. Hannah slipped one into the money drawer. When a girl entertained a gentleman, she kept two dollars for herself and Hannah got one for rent of the back room.

It was a better deal than most tonks gave their pretty waiter girls, and in return Hannah made them abide by her rules. She fired on the spot any girl caught stealing, and she never hired a virgin. They could be widowed, divorced, or fallen, but any sweet young thing looking to give up her innocence had to do it somewhere besides the Best in the West. And no drinking. If a gentleman wanted to buy a sporting gal a drink, she got a jigger of cold tea. There was nothing more pathetic than a whore who was also a lush.

But Hannah couldn't stop looking at Saphronie's face. Not at the tattoos but at the lines around her mouth and the shadows beneath her eyes. Hannah took a whiskey bottle and poured a double shot, then pushed the glass into Saphronie's shaking hands. Saphronie didn't entertain in the back room all that often, and each time she did, she took it like a rape. Like an old broken-down whore, she had to sell it to the dregs—the mule skinners and hide hunters and wolfers. Hannah had hired her to do the swamp work around the saloon; it was her choice to do the other. But it took her three days of doing swamp work to earn what she could get from a ten-minute trip to the back room.

Only trouble was, it took her twice that long to get over the shame of it.

Saphronie drank down the booze in two swallows. She eyed the bottle. Hannah sighed and poured a little more. At this rate she'd be giving away in whiskey what she'd just earned renting her back room. "Did he hurt you, honey?" she asked softly.

Saphronie shook her head. She took another drink, her teeth clinking against the glass. "The whole time he was doing it he just kept staring at me, at my face. He didn't even blink. And afterwards he said . . ." Her lips trembled. She stilled them with her clenched fist, covering the tattoos. "He said he'd never poked a freak before."

Hannah patted her arm, then felt awkward and a fool for doing it. "Nobody's forcing you to go with men like that."

"Men like that are the only kind who want me." Saphronie's gaze went to her daughter, who had succeeded in mounting the calf, although she sat it backwards. The calf threw back its head and bawled, and Saphronie's marred face softened into a smile. "I got to provide a better life for little Patsy."

Hannah sighed again. Little Patsy . . . Sweet and pretty as an angel, she was the product of a back-room liaison no different than the one that had just taken place between her mother and the sheepherder. Saphronie could hope and whore and maybe save a little, but there was never going to be anything better for little Patsy. She would end her life where it got started, poor little bastard—in the back room of some rundown honky-tonk in some nameless, dusty town.

A honky-tonk no different from this one.

Oh, Hannah liked to pretend that the Best in the West was a cut above other dance halls. She'd gone to extra trouble with it, adding nice homey touches like the circus posters on the walls and real china cuspidors. For most of the men in these parts it was in a way the only home they had. They treated it like home, too, getting baths and haircuts before they ambled in to meet the sporting gals, to buy themselves a dance, a drink or two, and a poke, if they could afford it.

But the part of her that couldn't lie to herself knew cheap and shabby and sinful when she saw it. Her family had been coal-dust poor, but what little they did have had always been scrubbed and well cared for and on the side of godliness. Clean inside and out had been Hannah Yorke in those days. She'd never forgotten the first night she spent away from home, in that dingy boardinghouse in Franklin. Lord, she'd found chinch bugs in the bed, and she'd like to have died. She'd spent the night in a chair, horrified at how low she'd sunk. Not knowing then that there were lower places and that she would find them.

Like a crib in the badlands of Deadwood with the name Rosie burned above the door.

There had been a bed in one corner; in another, a stove and a bundle of kindling. A small dresser with a wash-basin on top leaned against the log wall. The other wall was nothing more than a canvas partition separating her crib from the one next door. The room had been hot in the summer and cold in the winter, and it had stunk the year round of hair oil and cheap cologne water and sex.

Most days she'd worn nothing but a gaudy kimono. Across the foot of the bed lay a ragged red blanket that she pulled over herself while she slept. When she entertained, she covered the blanket with a piece of oilcloth to prevent its being dirtied by the boots of her gentlemen friends. They never took off their boots, never took off anything but their hats, those men who came to visit her, and they always called her ma'am. "Howdy-do, ma'am? Where you from, ma'am? I'd like it done this way, if you please, ma'am."

In the early afternoon, before her gentlemen friends came calling, she would lie on the bed and stare at the log rafters, which were watermarked and laced with old webs. Hot, salty tears would form in her eyes and leak out the corners to roll into her ears. I won't cry, she'd say to herself over and over, until one day she hadn't cried. She'd just been tired, so tired, with barely enough strength to get herself up off the bed to clean up between men. If it hadn't been for that crazy old prospector dying and willing her his buckskin bags of gold dust, she would have found a way to die herself that last winter in Deadwood.

Yet now, when she looked around the tonk—*her tonk*—she felt a wistful pride. The red lamps and china cuspidors, the piano grinning in black and white-toothed silence with no one savvy enough to play it, the peeling posters and deer antlers decorating the walls. It wasn't much, but she owned it all free and clear. And she owned herself free and clear. She was Hannah Yorke again, not Rosie, and she wasn't going to die a disease-riddled old whore in some piss-filled alley, even if it had been mostly dumb, blind luck that had saved her. What was done was done and best forgotten. But time wasn't like an hourglass that you could just turn over and watch the grains of sand run back through again. Those years in that Deadwood crib had left scars on her soul.

"The whole town's been talking about how you've taken up with Zach Rafferty," Saphronie said. She was eyeing the bottle again. Hannah put it away.

"The whole town oughta learn to mind its own business."

Saphronie leaned into her and lowered her voice to a soft, eager whisper. "So, then? What's he like?"

Hannah told herself not to look at him and did it anyway. A fast-emptying whiskey bottle sat at his elbow. He'd

put his hat upside down in the middle of the table and was
tossing a deck of cards one at a time into the crown of it. He
was drinking and passing idle time until she was ready to go
with him back to her room with its red silk-papered walls
and big feather bed. He was beautiful and bad and dangerous, and he was going to break her heart. They always did.

"He's no different from any other man," she said, her
voice tart. "Ain't you got something you should be doing?"

A dark flush crept up Saphronie's cheeks. She pushed
the empty glass across the bar with such force it squeaked.
"Thank you for the drink. I know how you feel about . . . I
mean, you never let any of the other girls—"

Hannah trapped the other woman's hand, gripping it
hard between her own. "Don't do it anymore, Saphronie."

She pried her fingers free. "I got to, Mrs. Yorke. For
little Patsy."

The door squealed open just then, letting in a shaft of
sunshine and wind-stirred air. Spurs rasped across the floor.
Saphronie turned, and Hannah looked up to the startling
sight of Gus McQueen walking into her saloon.

7

WELL, LORD, LORD, WILL you look at this, Hannah Yorke
thought with a laugh. Here comes Gus McQueen, comin'
to take his brother home.

Poor Gus. A righteous man like him probably found
his wild, undisciplined brother a trial to him most days.
He also had more guts and less sense than she'd given him
credit for. With Rafferty's blood running about fifty proof,

tangling with him was going to be like poking a stick at a rattler.

Gus McQueen had always put her in mind of a big, tame golden bear. It was the size of him and the way he moved, easy, almost slumberous. He paused now to let his eyes adjust to the sudden dimness and to get his bearings. His eyes were the deep blue of a wind-tossed sky, and the look in them as his gaze raked the room was frigid enough to kill a field of cotton in the dead of summer.

Hannah stepped out from behind the bar. She slipped her hand into her skirt pocket, her fist closing around the ivory stock of the little pistol she always carried. With the cost of shipping freight these days, she wasn't going to put up with any busted chairs and tables. And blood never did scrub easily out of unvarnished floors.

Gus went to stand over his brother. "Here you are," he said.

"Yup," Rafferty said, drawling the word out to its fullest potential. "Here is where I am."

"There's work waiting back at the ranch."

Rafferty sent a queen of clubs sailing toward his hat. "See me when I ain't busy."

Gus snatched the card out of the air, crushing it in his big hand. "You're soused," he said, disgust in his voice.

"Workin' on it." For a moment Rafferty's long fingers had closed into a fist. He uncurled them and wrapped them around the neck of the whiskey bottle instead. He poured the stuff straight into his mouth, not bothering with the glass.

Gus stared down at his brother, longing and revulsion and a baffled anger battling it out on his face. In that moment Hannah almost pitied him. It was hard to love someone, to care, and have him not care back.

"We should have started the branding roundup a week ago," Gus said.

"You're the one stayed gone for nearly a year, and now all of a goddamn sudden the ranch is back to being the most important thing in your life. Excuse me if I can't keep up with your priorities."

"She was your mother, too. You could've come with me."

"I never got sent an invitation to the party." There was a flush on Rafferty's high cheekbones that wasn't only from the booze. "Go away, Gus. You're rilin' me, and when I get riled I start to sweat, and sweating is a waste of good whiskey."

For a moment neither man said a thing, and the tension between them stretched as tight as dried rawhide.

Gus snatched off his hat, shoved his fingers through his hair, then slammed the hat back on his head. "Look, I know you're red-assed with me, and I'll allow as how you might have reason to be. But that's no excuse to go neglecting the ranch by helling it all over town like a green hand with full pockets and no sense."

"In case it's escaped your notice, there ain't no 'all over' in Rainbow Springs." Rafferty made a wide, sweeping gesture with the whiskey bottle. "This is it." His eyes narrowed on his brother. "What's really aggravatin' you, Gus? Has marriage put a burr under your tail already? Why don't you go on home to your woman and leave me to mine?"

"Your woman?" Gus's gaze sought out Hannah, and he looked her up and down, a fine sneer curling around his mustache. "I wouldn't be staking out bragging rights yet on Mrs. Yorke were I you, little brother. For three dollars she's *any* man's woman."

Even Hannah was surprised at how fast Rafferty came out of the chair.

Gus took a step back, then held his ground. He turned his head and jutted his jaw forward, presenting it to his brother as a gift. "You want to hit me, Zach? Go on, take a swing."

Rafferty let out a long, slow breath. "I ain't fightin' with you."

He emptied the cards into a pile on the table, tossed the bonnet strings inside his hat, and anchored it down on his head. He picked up the whiskey bottle and took another swig. Gus stood with his fists clenched at his sides, breathing heavily. In a way, Hannah couldn't blame him for wanting to hit something. This was probably the longest conversation he'd had with his brother in a year, and it had been like trying to talk a gopher into climbing a tree.

Rafferty took a step toward the door. Gus grabbed his arm and swung him around. "You'll fight if I got to knock your teeth through the back of your head."

Rafferty grinned and lifted the whiskey bottle to his mouth. Gus's fist got there first.

The force of the blow turned Rafferty half around on his feet and sent him stumbling against the table. The table slid out from beneath his weight, and he hit the floor with a rattling jar that made the windows vibrate. Somehow he still had the bottle upright in his hand, although most of the whiskey had spilled out of it to douse his face and chest. Rafferty held the bottle up in the air and laughed.

But Hannah hadn't waited to find out if he was going to come up swinging. She whipped the pistol out of her pocket and fired. The shot cracked like thunder on a hot afternoon. The bottle exploded in Rafferty's hand. Glass and whiskey rained down on him in glittering drops and splintered shards.

He looked at the jagged neck of brown glass, which was all that was left of the bottle. "Shit," he said, and laughed again. A wild whoop that started Hannah to laughing as well.

They were laughing still as he wiped slivers of glass off his wet chest. Gus wasn't laughing, he was glowering at Hannah, and she thought she would probably like the man a lot better if he didn't make her feel like he was seeing a Deadwood badlands gal every time he looked at her.

She smiled sweetly at him. "If you gotta beat up on somebody, Mr. McQueen, do it outside of my tonk."

Rafferty pulled himself to his feet with the help of the table. He pressed the back of his hand to his cut lip. He glanced at the smear of blood, then at Hannah as if she'd been the one to bust his mouth. "Christ, woman," he said, "one of these times you're gonna quit missing with that thing and kill someone."

"When I decide to put a hole in something that can bleed, you'll be the first to know it." She waved the pistol. "Now y'all settle your disagreement outside."

"All right, all right. I'm goin'. Hell." He sauntered toward the door. After one final, biting glare at Hannah, Gus followed.

The door swung shut behind Rafferty's back. Gus slammed it back open with the heel of his hand and waltzed right into a sucker punch to his gut.

Gus grunted and doubled over. He wheezed in a breath, then wheezed it out again. He tilted up his head and stared at his brother through watering eyes. "I thought . . . you didn't . . . want to fight."

Rafferty stood with his boots splayed and the weight tilted forward on the balls of his feet, his hands hanging easy at his sides. His tawny eyes were full of laughter and violence. "I lied."

Gus straightened and lunged with a bellow that brought Hannah running outside. She would have caught a flying fist square in the jaw if she hadn't ducked in time. She flattened herself against the saloon doors to watch the fight.

Gus landed a blow to the side of Rafferty's head that sent his hat sailing and his feet pedaling backward. Rafferty answered with another punch to Gus's belly that thunked like an ax blade in wet wood. The brothers staggered backward off the boardwalk, bear-hugging each other. They wrestled and grunted, knocked into the horse trough and slammed against the hitching rail. The rotting pine shattered and splintered beneath them.

They sat in the mud among the ruins of the hitching rail, grinning at each other, their breath sawing in their heaving chests. Then they came up fighting.

Fists smacked against flesh, chests grunted, and blood splattered. It wasn't long before the fracas drew a crowd like a circuit preacher in a town of Baptists. The boys from Snake-Eye's livery ambled over to watch the show. Sam Woo banged out of the mercantile and came clattering down the boardwalk. Mrs. McQueen was fast on his heels, as close to running as Hannah had yet to see her.

A lady, thought Hannah, would feel disgust and horror, maybe even faint. But she felt a flutter low in her belly that she knew was the heat of sexual arousal. He was all hard magnificent masculinity, her man Rafferty was. His lithe and deadly body, the savage power of his blows, the ferocity in his eyes, excited her. He fought the same way he made love. Ruthlessly and taking no prisoners.

Gus clouted a fist into Rafferty's eye and drove another into his ribs. Rafferty careened into the side of the saloon, his body heavy and loose. He bounded upright and landed a punch flush in Gus's face. Gus's head snapped back hard on his neck, blood and saliva flying in strings out of his nose and mouth. He weaved on his feet, his eyelids fluttering like dying moths. He shook his head, spat out a tooth, and waded back into Rafferty's swinging fist.

A slender black-lace-gloved hand clutched at Hannah's arm. "Make them stop," said Gus's wife.

"Honey, nobody's gonna make them two boys stop till one or the other of them is laid out cold. They're riled enough to take a swing at Jesus Christ himself were he to suddenly appear preaching brotherly love and goodwill toward men."

Clementine McQueen lifted the train of her skirt and picked her dainty way around the fighting men. They'd spent most of their steam by now and were huffing like locomotives on a steep grade, mostly swaying and grappling with each other and throwing short, weak punches. She headed for the horse trough, and Hannah thought maybe she'd taken it into her head to splash the men with water as if they were a pair of spitting cats. But instead she bent down, gripped one of the shattered hitching posts in her lace-gloved hands, and lifted it high.

She aimed for her brother-in-law's head and hit his shoulder. It wasn't much of a blow, but it got his attention. He swung around on unsteady legs just as she let fly with another swing, like an amateur boxer throwing a roundhouse punch. Except that at the other end of her fists was a pine post and it smacked into Rafferty's groin with a solid whack. He fell to his knees, hugging his crotch and curling up tight, the breath bleating out of him like a penny whistle.

Mrs. McQueen stood over her brother-in-law, the post in the air, and for a moment Hannah thought from the look on her face that she was going to crease his head with it. But then she dropped it and backed up. The color was high in her cheeks, and she was breathing hard through her open mouth.

Gus was swaying like a cattail in the wind, using his bandanna to soak up the blood that was dribbling from his nose. He poked his tongue at his cheek, feeling for the hole left by his tooth. Rafferty had managed to rise as far as his hands and knees and was throwing up three days' worth of whiskey in the street. Mrs. McQueen looked at him as if he'd just crawled out from beneath the door of a privy.

Gus took a step toward his brother. Hannah put a hand on his chest to stop him. His shirt hung in rags from the neck yoke. Sweat gleamed on his splendid muscles, sweat and so much blood he looked as if he'd been sticking pigs. His face was such a puffy mess she had to smile. "Honey," she cooed, "your lady wife just planted your brother's balls somewhere up next to his ribs, and when he gets his breath back and quits seeing stars, he's gonna want to kill somebody. Now, I reckon you ought to hustle her on home. Don't you?"

Gus nodded, wiped his bleeding mouth and nose, and nodded again.

Hannah's gaze met that of Gus's wife. She was looking mighty pleased with herself. "I hope he hurts," Clementine said. She wasn't talking about her husband.

Rafferty still knelt in the mud, making gagging sounds.

"Oh, he's a-hurtin' all right." Hannah grinned at her, and slowly the girl smiled back. A smile of shared power. It wasn't often that a woman was able to bring a man to his knees.

"The party's over, folks," Hannah said, ushering the crowd toward the doors of her saloon, where she hoped they would belly up to the bar to relive the fight and lubricate the telling of it with bottles of her most expensive booze.

She crouched beside her fallen hero, her poppy-red skirts trailing in the gumbo. He was done with retching up the whiskey and was now working on his guts. She patted his shuddering back. "Don't be such a baby, Rafferty. The only thing she hurt was your pride."

He eased onto his backside and unfolded his lanky body until he was leaning against the horse trough. He cupped the hurting place between his legs and let out a slow, careful breath between clenched teeth. "Fuck."

Hannah laughed. "Later, darlin'. When you're feeling more the thing."

He looked at her with a bloodshot eye—the other was swelling shut. "What the hell're you laughin' at? I wouldn't't've fought him in the first place if he hadn't called you a whore."

"Lord, Rafferty, a whore is what I am. It doesn't matter that I don't sell it anymore—a gal can't escape her past. A rawhidin' cowboy like you ought to've learned that by now. Thank you, Shiloh," she said as the bartender brought out a fresh bottle of whiskey. Rafferty seized it, drinking so fast that the rotgut leaked out the corners of his mouth. The pungent smell of whiskey mixed with that of mud and blood and sweat and violence.

She watched the muscles of his strong brown throat work as he swallowed. "I don't pay any mind to Gus," she said. "He always acts all stiff-backed around me, I expect because his back ain't the only thing that gets stiff. He don't like admitting to himself that he's got weaknesses just like any other man. You're a trial to him, Rafferty, and an aggravation, but only because he cares about you. The man has got his good points. You got to admit that."

He scrubbed his face with his sleeve. "Hell, I know he's got his good points. But that don't mean he needs to be jabbin' me with them all the time like they were spurs." He shifted a hip and groaned. "I think I'll just sit here awhile."

"In the mud?"

"Yeah, the mud is nice. It's soft."

Hannah sat beside him. Mud and blood were splattered in rusty patches over her skirt; she would never get the stains out. What the hell—she was rich and could afford a wagonload of dresses. This cowboy, though, was worth more than she'd first thought. She would keep him for a while.

She slipped her arm through his and leaned her head against his shoulder. "That was sweet of you, Rafferty— defending my honor. No one's ever done that for me before."

"Shit, Hannah." A dark flush spread across his sharp cheekbones, and without even looking at her this time, he stole another tiny piece of her heart. She'd always had a weakness for a man who could blush.

She leaned back on her outstretched arms and looked at the sky. It was like staring into the bottom of a deep blue bowl. Nothing could be so blue and vast and empty as a Montana sky. She felt absurdly happy. She wanted to laugh some more, yet her silly eyes kept filling with tears.

She heard the squeal of a wagon axle, the jangle of harness chains, and she sat up to watch Gus McQueen and his wife leave town. That fourteen-karat lady had had herself quite a busy afternoon, she thought. Tangling with renegade cattle thieves, visiting with a calico queen, and bringing the local wild boy low. It was almost as if she'd made up her mind to get all the pea green rubbed off her in one day.

Hannah swung her head around to look at Rafferty. He, too, watched his brother and his brother's wife as they drove away. It was hard to tell what he was thinking from his bruised and battered face. She tried to read the expression in his eyes, but they were as empty as the blue bowl of the sky overhead.

Clementine pressed a poultice of raw potato onto the swelling bruise beneath his right eye. Gus jerked, the breath hissing out of him on a curse.

"Ow! Jesus . . ."

"If you can't stand the cure, then you shouldn't court the trouble."

"Hunh. You're starting to sound like a wife, Clem. Be careful or someone'll think you love me after all—ouch!" He grasped her wrist, pulling the hand with the poultice away from his face. He gave her an earnest, boyish smile. "It wasn't what you thought."

She tossed the poultice onto the table. It landed on the brown oilcloth with a sodden plop. Her husband, the self-proclaimed teetotaler, reeked of the devil's brew. "I find you brawling with your brother outside that woman's thirst parlor and you have the gall to tell me it wasn't what I thought."

"Because it wasn't. The only reason I went into the Best in the West was to put a stop to Zach's carousing with Hannah Yorke and get him back home here where there's work to be done."

He'd been sitting at the old sawbuck table, but he pushed himself to his feet and paced the small cabin. He moved as stiffly as a rheumatic old man, and his face was as bloodied and raw as a side of beef hanging in a butcher's window. It hurt her to look at him. She didn't understand why he had been fighting with his own brother outside that saloon, swinging his fists and grunting and growling like some animal.

And she didn't understand herself. She had picked up a club of wood and stuck a man down with it, and she'd been glad to do it. No, more than glad—she'd been triumphant.

"That brother of mine gets wilder by the day," Gus was saying, the anger in his voice as raw as his face. "Whiskey, cards, and women are all he cares about."

Clementine didn't like talking about Mr. Rafferty. That man disturbed her, and he fascinated her, when she didn't want him to do anything to her at all. She wanted him gone.

"Maybe he doesn't want to be saved," she said. "Maybe the best thing you can do for both of you is to buy him out of his share in the ranch and let him ride away." *To perdition,* she added to herself.

Gus thrust his fingers through his hair, gripping his scalp. He sighed, his shoulders slumping. "You don't understand."

"Then tell me."

He turned, and she saw that his lips were pressed together tight in that way they did whenever he was facing something distasteful, as if the taste of it was in his mouth.

"That last summer Zach and I were together as kids, you know what that brother of mine did?" He laughed raggedly, shaking his head. "He taught himself how to pick pockets. You see, Clem, while the old man—he was running a traveling salvation show up and down the Mississippi in those days—and while the old man would be up front praying and amening and hallelujahing, Zach would be moving through the crowd and cleaning it out slick as butter. Mostly all he ever got was a few cheap gilt watches and rusty pennies, but there were times when, slim pickings that it was, it kept us from going to bed hungry." He huffed another forced laugh. "That brother of mine . . . he was always trying to protect us from the consequences of the old man's ways and follies."

He paused, his gaze hard on her face, seeing what she made of this.

"Oh, Gus, I would never think to judge you," she said, "or your brother, either, for what happened when you were children."

He shook his head again, hard. "Yeah, but you gotta

understand. I was never good for much of anything except dreaming, making up stories inside my head, and hiding out in them. Not my brother, though. He was born tough—tough as jerked meat. And that last summer . . . well, one night the old man came home—we were living in a tent, and he came stumbling into the tent reeking of blood and whiskey, and missing an eye. Zach was with him and he . . . he had more blood on him than Pa did. His shirt was black and shiny with it, with blood, and it was caked in his hair and stained his hands like Indian war paint. And all the while Pa just sat in the middle of the tent, bleeding and whimpering over and over, 'Son of a bitch took my eye,' Zach went about packing up and striking camp, cool as you please. Except for once when he told Pa to shut up."

He trailed off as if that was the end of it, and Clementine thought it a strange story. And a sad and strange life her husband had led as a boy. Her husband and his brother, who had taught himself how to pick pockets and had been as tough as jerked meat.

"Then a week later," Gus went on abruptly, "in another town I saw a newspaper account of a riverboat gambler who'd been found dead, stabbed through the heart with his own bowie knife."

It took a while for her to see what the one thing had to do with the other, and then she couldn't quite believe . . . "Are you telling me your father—"

"Lordy, no. Not Pa." He gave another of those rough, forced laughs. "You'd know that as soon as you met him. He might be a bunco man and a petty thief, and he might like to bed other men's wives and cheat at cards. But he's always run like a prairie chicken at the first hint of violence."

She understood then, and yet she didn't want to. She didn't want to think what kind of mad courage and wild terror it took for a boy of ten to stab a grown man through the heart with his own bowie knife. She didn't want to think of the kind of mark such a thing would leave on a boy, even one as tough as jerked meat.

"Gus, perhaps—"

"But that brother of mine," Gus said, "he's never run from anything."

She laid her hand on his arm. It was rigid beneath her touch. "If he did such a thing, if he killed that gambler, then perhaps it was to save your father's life. Or perhaps the one thing never had anything to do with the other— what you read in that newspaper and what happened to your father."

Gus pressed his lips together, and she saw his throat move as he swallowed. "Yeah, perhaps . . . It was right after that time, though, right after Pa lost his eye, that we split up. Ma said she was gonna make a trip up north to visit her kin. She took me with her and she left my brother behind, and she knew all along she wasn't coming back.

"Zach might be two years younger than me, but he must've been born old, 'cause he always took care of us, even stealing when he had to. He always took care of us, and we left him, me and Ma. We left him with no one to take care of him."

She looked up into his battered face. There was something in his eyes . . . guilt, she supposed. And fear. And as always, the discovery of fear in him frightened her, for he was supposed to be the one with all the certainties. But she knew him a little better now; she knew that what he feared most was failing himself, not living up to the man he thought he should be.

"I owe him, Clem. I can't let him down a second time."

"No, Gus," she said. "You won't let him down. He is your brother, after all."

The day had started to fade. She took down the coal-oil lantern from its ceiling hook. As she lifted off the paper shade to light the wick, she heard Gus give a little snort, then a rumbling chuckle, then an all-out dish-rattling laugh.

She looked up at him, the match poised to strike. "What?"

"I was just remembering the look on Zach's face when you walloped him with that post." He laughed again, real laughs this time. His shoulders shaking, wheezing and huffing and wincing as the laughter pulled at all the cuts and bruises on his face. "Lord . . . Lord . . . When he does get around to coming home, I reckon he'll think twice about getting within swinging distance of you."

Clementine sucked on her lower lip, wanting to smile and thinking she really ought not to. Gus's laughter wound down though and an uneasy, speculative look came over his face as he stared at her. She knew what he was thinking. What she had done didn't set well with his notion of what a gently reared lady would do.

As she drew water from the pump to boil the potatoes, her mind moved on to tomorrow's chores. First there was the washing to do; she was down to her last clean camisole and shimmy. That lampshade was black with soot; it needed a good scrubbing. They were nearly out of bread again. Maybe she would try baking those sweet biscuit things, those bannocks, that Gus had told her about.

He had gone to the door of the cabin to look out at the yard. The dying sun turned his light brown hair the color of pulled taffy. She felt a softening within her when she looked at him, a tenderness. She thought she must love Gus, but it seemed the feeling should be stronger. Powerful and dangerous and fiery, like lightning flashing across a hot black summer sky. Being in love ought to feel as if you held that bolt of lightning in your hands.

And a fine way to get yourself good and burned, she thought with an inward laugh. She'd better hope the Lord wasn't listening to her silly musings right now, else he'd probably send a lightning bolt straight down through the sod roof of this old cabin to carry her down into the lake of everlasting fire. *It is a fearful thing to fall into the hands of the living God.*

That Hannah Yorke, now, the town harlot. Clementine

wondered if she had ever loved any of those men she'd lain with for money and for pleasure. She had certainly looked like a prime example of tarnished virtue today in that poppy-bright dress of hers and those red-tasseled shoes. Clementine didn't know what to think of her, although she knew what she *ought* to think. She ought to think she was a brazen hussy who was no better than she should be. She ought to cross the street rather than cross shadows with such a soiled dove. She ought to pray for the salvation of Hannah Yorke's soul—but from a safe distance, of course, so that none of the tarnish would rub off on her.

That was what she ought to do. What she *wanted* to do was say to Hannah Yorke: "Tell me what you feel when you lie with a man. Do you hope he will be the one to rescue you from your shame with love and a wedding ring? Or do you revel in the wickedness, those wild impulses that have led you to sin? Are you frightened for your immortal soul or do you feel free?"

Oh, Clementine thought, imagine sitting down to have such a conversation with the town harlot. Imagine asking her if you could try on those red-tasseled shoes—

"Clementine?"

She nearly dropped the stew pot, only catching it in time by one of its handles so that it tipped and splashed water all down the front of her skirt. Her whole body flushed as hot as a coal fire. Imagine if Gus had been able to read her thoughts just then.

"Come here, girl," he was saying, beckoning to her from the door. "Come and watch the sunset."

She went with him out into the yard. They stood side by side and watched the sun sink into a rocky bed of buttes. The wind had come up cold, smelling of last winter's snow and this spring's mud. The sky was a hard, brassy yellow, the color of his eyes.

Not Gus's eyes . . .

She wanted to slide her arm around her husband's waist.

She wanted to lean into him and bury her face in his neck and lick his warm, salty skin. Yet she held herself apart, unable to be the first to touch. She felt so alone of a sudden, so separate from Gus and from everything around her.

"Clementine . . ."

She turned her head. She saw a man's hunger in his eyes, and she was beginning to understand how she could satisfy that. But she saw a soul's need as well, and *that* she despaired of ever knowing how to satisfy. There is something missing in me, she thought. Great empty gaps in my heart. Or it was as if something had seized her heart long ago and squeezed and squeezed, had wrung it dry until it was this hard little shrunken ball in her chest.

Out on the prairie a coyote bayed. There was so much loneliness in the sound, she thought.

8

THE MUSCLES IN CLEMENTINE'S back screamed in protest as she bent over to pick up the last wet shirt from the bottom of the tub. She stayed hunched over a moment, sure that she would never be able to straighten up. Her body was one enormous ache. And on the stove inside the cabin another copper of sheets was boiling. Sheets that still had to be rinsed and wrung out and hung up to dry.

She creaked upright and blew a sigh up into the brim of Gus's old hat, which shaded her face from the burning sun. She stumbled toward the rope that had been strung up between two big cottonwoods. Her shoes, thick with mud, were as heavy and clumsy as wooden clogs. The hem of her sodden skirts trailed in the mud. Frayed threads and gaps showed in the puce dimity where she had ripped off the stylish ruching and train.

She had been reared by a mother who insisted that no true lady should ever be caught looking less than her best. But all of her bonnets were utterly useless against the sun, and the train on her skirt scooped up dirt and debris more proficiently than the cowcatcher on a trolley car.

The soiled clothes and linens in her father's house on Louisburg Square had been handed over to an Irish laundress on Monday to be delivered to their kitchen door the following week in paper-wrapped parcels smelling of soap and starch. Until she had taken it into her head to elope with a cowboy and follow him out to this godforsaken wilderness, Clementine had never appreciated the smelly, sweaty, dirty work involved in keeping clean.

Build up the fire in the range to boil countless kettles of water. Lift the heavy kettle from the stove and empty it into the washtub, again and again and yet again. Plunge your arms up to the elbows in steaming suds and scrub and scrub and try not to whimper when you scrape all the skin off your knuckles on the washboard. Drop the soapy clothes into a rinse tub of more boiling water and stir and stir with a broomstick, then stir some more. And then with what's left of the strength in your two hands, wring and twist the scalding water from each piece of sodden, sopping clothing. With your two hands . . .

She looked at her hands, amazed not to see flames shooting from her wrists, they burned so. Whatever skin she had not scrubbed off had been melted away by boiling water and the caustic soda in the soap, leaving her flesh raw and cracked.

The clothesline had been strung up high where the deer couldn't catch their antlers in it, and so she had to climb up on a stack of empty hardtack boxes to reach it. Just as she flung a shirt over the rope, the wind caught it, slapping its tail against her face. She searched blindly for the split-wood pins she had thrust through the front

placket of her bodice. She wrestled the shirt into place and
anchored it down with the pins.

The wind slammed into her again. She swayed, grabbing for the clothesline. The boxes slid out from under her,
and she landed on her fanny with a splatter of mud and a
teeth-rattling jar.

She sat still for a moment, breathing heavily as the
mud oozed around her. The wet clothes flapped and sang
overhead. She squelched to her feet. She wiped at the mud
on her face with her sleeve, smearing it into her mouth.
A dollop of mud fell off the brim of Gus's hat, splatting
onto her bodice. She looked down at herself and laughed.
She was covered from head to foot with mud. Surely there
wasn't this much mud in all of Massachusetts.

They all thought her too much of a genu-ine starched-
up lady with not enough grit in her heart to survive out
here. Well, she would prove them wrong. She had done
Gus's shirts and her underthings. Now she would tackle
the bed linen. She had just lifted the empty tub onto her
hip when once again the cursed Montana wind came roaring out of the mountains.

A great gust ripped into the wet clothes, whipping
them around the line, snapping the wooden pins free. The
wind shrieked and howled, sending Clementine's entire
wash sailing and scattering across the muddy yard.

The washtub fell from her burning hands. She swayed
beneath the buffeting wind, a scream of frustration welling
up in her breast. It built and built and came bursting out
of her in cries that tore at her throat.

"I can't stand it! I can't stand it! I can't stand it!"

The gust died as suddenly as it had come up. The mountains echoed her words, mocking her: . . . *can't stand it . . . stand
it . . .* A jay flew overhead, laughing at her. She stood in the
boggy yard and waited for the wind to come again, waited,
waited . . . and it didn't come. Even the wind mocked her.

She left the wash to lie where the wind had flung it
and began walking.

She climbed the snake fence that bordered the pas-
turelands around the ranch. She walked along the river,
but after a while the bank steepened and the trail veered off
into a stand of larches and yellow pines. The pine-spiced
wind shrilled through the treetops. The jay followed
after her, hopping from branch to branch. *"Coward,"* it
squawked. *"Quitter, quitter . . ."*

She emerged into a small moon-shaped meadow and
took a deep breath.

The air smelled sweet. Wildflowers decorated the
meadow like the embroidered border of a schoolgirl's sam-
pler. Tiny pink fairy slippers, white pinwheels and bottle-
brush, and cheery yellow blossoms shaped like miniature
sunflowers. The sun floated across a hazeless sky, gilding
the wind-riffled grass with a shimmering light. A meandering line of willows followed the river, casting gentle
shade onto water that rolled and shimmered like spilled
coins.

Oh, how she longed to capture it all in a photograph.

She would do it, do it now. She would photograph this
meadow.

She was almost running by the time she reached the
cabin. Her dark tent, camera, and wet plate apparatus were
already packed in portable cases. Their weight made her
walk with a lopsided lurch, and their handles dug into her
raw palms, but she barely noticed. She crossed the yard
strewn with her wash and didn't see it. Her skirt caught on
a splinter when she climbed the snake fence, pulling free
with a loud rip that she didn't hear.

She arrived back at the meadow panting and with
her hair falling over her face in wet, sticky strands. Yet
she was humming as she set up the camera and dark tent.
She coated a glass plate with a thin layer of albumen, then
coated it with the collodion. Her eyes burned as the ether
alcohol evaporated in her face and the film set, but it was
a familiar sensation, and she blinked it away without
thought. Hooded inside the dark tent, she bathed the film

with a silver sensitizing solution, splashing black stains on
her sore hands. Her mother had always admonished her to
wear gloves when she "pursued that messy, smelly hobby,"
but she always forgot or was in too much of a hurry.

With the wet plate now sensitive to light, she did indeed have to hurry to expose it before it dried. She carried
the plate, enshrouded in its wooden box, back to the camera.
She draped the black focusing cloth over her head, choosing
the river and willows as her subject, adjusting the camera's
focal length and aperture. She capped the lens and swung
the focusing screen out of the way to slide in the wet plate
box, and that was when the moose stepped out of the trees.

He walked clumsily, swinging his big splayed feet.
His massive palmed antlers swayed, as if they were too
heavy even for his thick brown neck. He huffed a loud
snort that fluttered his pendulous upper lip as he lowered
his head to the river. An enormous tongue unfurled out his
mouth and slurped.

Oh, don't go away. She slid the plate box in carefully so
as not to make a sound, although her heart thudded loudly
in her excitement. *Please don't go away.*

The moose lifted his head, perhaps to savor the water
or to listen to the wind. Perhaps he was a vain moose who
fancied the thought of immortality. Whatever the reason,
he lifted his great homely head and stood motionless.

Clementine held her breath, uncovered the plate, and
uncapped the lens.

Zach Rafferty moseyed along the trail toward home. He
walked at a leisurely pace, leading his gray. The calf followed at his heels like a homeless pup. Rafferty looked
down at the dogie and pretended to be disgusted. The stupid critter probably thought he was its mother.

He was walking because his horse had thrown a shoe.
Most of the cowboys he'd trailed with would be morally
outraged at the idea of having to walk. Secretly he liked it.

He liked the soft give of the earth beneath his boots. And he liked the smell of it—fecund and ripe, like the smell of sex with a willing woman.

As he walked, he opened his eyes and breathed deeply, letting the earth and the sky sink into him. He loved this land, loved its wildness and the sad, sweet lonesomeness of it. The way the mountains latched onto the wide and empty sky. The way the sun dusted the buffalo grass with gold. The way the wind howled and lashed in pain and loneliness, as wild as any animal and as unforgiving as time.

He paused on a rise that overlooked the dip in the valley that sheltered the cabin and barn and pastureland of the Rocking R. The timothy grass was ripening; he could smell its sweetness on the wind. It made good hay, and they would mow it next month, he and Gus, and put it up as winter feed for the saddle horses. It was part of a cycle of work that followed the seasons and melded the days and brought him a sense of belonging.

For so long his home had been nothing more than a saddle blanket. For so long he had owned nothing but himself. Now the land owned him, and this frightened him. He didn't like caring so deeply about something he could lose.

Nobody was in the yard to greet him except his old biscuit-colored hound. He hunkered down to ruffle the ears of the ecstatic dog until the calf, feeling jealous, butted its head into his lap.

He saw the laundry strewn in piles beneath the sagging line, and he smiled. A lot of work had gone into scrubbing those shirts of Gus's and all those soft white feminine things. A lot of work that was going to have to be done all over again.

He was still smiling as he led the gray into the barn. He loosened the cinches, took his saddle by the horn, and swung it off the gelding's back. He did a quick currying job, brushing the cakes of mud off the gray's hocks and belly.

"You're a worthless old bangtail, Moses," he said, pouring a can of oats into the feedbox. "You been lazin' in Snake-Eye's barn for over a week, and now all's you want to do is eat." The horse snorted into its feed, and Rafferty slapped it on the rump. He draped his saddlebag over his shoulder and left the barn.

He knocked the dung and mud off his boots at the hitching rack. The latch string was out, but still he hesitated before the door to his own house, undecided about knocking.

"Damn you, Gus," he said beneath his breath, pushing the door open.

The cabin smelled sour, like dead steam and soap, and felt empty even before he called out his brother's name. A tub of gray water sat in a puddle in the middle of the floor. A copper full of sheets had boiled down to a mush on the stove. The fire had gone out. He lifted the lid to the wood-box; it was empty.

He took his wedding gift to Gus out of his saddlebag, still undecided about whether to go through with the giving of it. He didn't want Gus to think he'd come around to accepting the woman—which he hadn't and was never going to.

A rag rug he'd never seen before lay spread on the floor. A bunch of wildflowers—mountain bluebells and pink pussytoes—filled a coffee can in the middle of the table, like something you'd see in a restaurant in San Francisco or Chicago. And she'd gone and strung curtains across the windows. They were fashioned of bleached flour sacks, but she'd made a start on embroidering them with a border of little yellow birds. He slapped his hat against his thigh as he examined the work closely. Little finches, he guessed they were supposed to be. Dainty, feminine, finishing-school fine. He turned and stared at the closed door to the bedroom.

It was her sanctuary now, that room, so he invaded it deliberately. She had left her mark here as well. He looked at her things but didn't touch them. Her silver hairbrush, the bar of fine milled bathing soap that released a smell of wild roses into the air, a green leather Bible with a gold clasp. A pair of photographs in silver frames. Of a black-bearded man with the wild, staring eyes of a fanatic. Of a pale-haired woman with a fragile air and a sad mouth.

Her night rail hung from a hook on the wall. He lifted it in his hands, his callused fingers snagging in the fine batiste. He rubbed his face in it. It, too, smelled of roses, and of her woman's scent.

He went to the window and looked at the laundry scattered in the mud. He looked at it for a long time, his balled fists pressing hard into the cracked sill.

The next thing he knew, he was out the door and following her trail, his boots making no sound in the pine straw. He arrived at the meadow and saw the big bull moose first. He paused, surprised, for though they liked to feed on river plants, you didn't usually come across one so low in the valley this time of year. Then he saw her.

The front half of her was covered with a black hood, and she was bent over . . . damned if it wasn't a camera. The moose caught his scent and lumbered off, splashing through the river. She emerged from beneath the hood, and he thought she might have laughed. She pulled a rectangular wooden case framed in metal from out of the camera box. He took a step, his foot coming down on a dry twig.

She whirled, a splayed hand pressed hard to her breast. She stared at him, her eyes wide and confused, and then he saw recognition dawn and, with it, anger. Her breath shuddered in her throat, but her voice was cool, controlled. "How dare you creep up on me like some savage Indian?"

He said nothing, just came right at her. She watched him come, her eyes growing wider, her nostrils flaring. He stopped when only a hand-space separated them. Her face was pink with sunburn, except for two lines around her mouth that tightened and whitened.

She tried to sidle around him. He blocked her way. She

sucked in a little gasp, and he trotted out his most charming smile. "Now, why do you want to go skittering off like that, Boston? And me wearing my party manners today."

Her gaze flashed to his face, then away. She seemed to draw deep within herself to still her trembling by a force of will. "Kindly remove your loathsome presence from my path, sir." She made to step around him, and this time he let her. "I don't have either the time or the inclination to banter or to trade insults with you."

"Yeah, I can sure see that," he said. He followed her so closely their shadows merged into one. "'Loathsome presence' is a pretty tame insult. Folk out here lean toward 'lickbelly bastard' and 'son of a no-good bitch' when they banter. What in hell are you doing?"

"I am developing the negative, of course."

She had stopped before an odd sort of tent that rested on top of a tripod beneath the shade of the larches. Made of India rubber, like a tarpaulin, it was the size and shape of a hay bale. The front end hung open to reveal a miniature cabinet of drawers and shelves lined with bottles, funnels, and beakers. She set the metal-framed case inside the tent beside a large tray filled with water, and began to button up the flap, speaking to him over her shoulder.

"This is a very delicate process, so I would be grateful if you would leave me in peace to accomplish it." Three sleeves dangled from the front flap. She tossed Gus's old hat on the ground, thrust her arms through two of the contraption's sleeves and her head through the middle one. A moment later her head popped out again. "Do not under any circumstances open this tent," she said, and thrust her head inside again.

He leaned against a larch trunk and stared at the back end of her. Her dress was an ugly liverish color, and it looked like she'd worn it to take a roll in a hog wallow. Fumes wafted from the tent, smelling like the inside of a patent medicine man's wagon. Haughty little bitch. The way she'd said "I am developing the negative, of course," in that uppity Boston accent, like he was too ignorant to be breathing the same air with her high-and-mightiness.

She was a long time with her head and arms stuck in the tent. He heard splashing sounds and a muttered "drat." So she had a temper, did she, beneath all her starch and those tightly laced corset stays? Finally she emerged, all flushed and damp. She put the hat back on and walked out from beneath the trees into the sunshine. She held a glass plate up to the sky, and her face grew vivid.

There she stood in her muddy, ripped dress and one of Gus's old hats, and yet she still had the air of the lady about her. She had the kind of looks that went with rustling silk and soft music. Winter looks, with her ash-fair hair and pale skin and bones that seemed as fragile as a film of spring ice. She breathed a little fluttery sigh. Her lips were lush and wet and parted as if in passion.

He wondered if she looked like that in bed at night when Gus took her.

He peered over her shoulder, trying to see what it was about the—what had she called it?—the negative that had gotten her all dewy and pink and excited.

She spun around, gripping the plate in front of her chest. Her hands, he saw, were blistered red and dotted with black stains.

"Guess your developing didn't work too good, huh?" he said.

She thrust her nose in the air and somehow managed to look down the dainty sunburned length of it, even though she was a good foot shorter than he. "It worked quite nicely, thank you."

"So why won't you let me look at it?"

He reached for the plate, and after a little hesitation, she surrendered it. "Be careful. It's still wet. And I haven't varnished it yet, so please take care not to scratch it. And remember it's a negative," she said, "so light and dark are reversed, of course."

"Of *course*," he mimicked.

It was a ghost moose standing in a black meadow in hell. Yet Rafferty thought he could almost see the animal's powerful muscles quivering on the verge of flight, see the wind ruffling the grass and leaves, see each little ripple in the river. There was something about it that caught at his chest. This was his moose, his meadow. His country, damn her. And he felt violated, as if she had invaded a thing of his that was too private and intense to be shared.

"I've never photographed an animal before," she was saying, and the passion he had seen on her face now textured her voice. "It's difficult to get one to keep still long enough to make the exposure. But the light today is so bright and clear, all it took was ten seconds . . ." She trailed off. "It's a moose."

He gave a belittling snort, handing the plate back to her. "If you say so."

She pushed the negative into a wooden slot in the tent, her movements stiff, her jaw clenched so hard her chin trembled. He had hurt her feelings, poor baby.

She began putting bottles away, emptying pans of smelly water. He draped his arm over the tent's brace, watching her. "You don't usually see a moose this far down in the valley until later in the summer," he said. "He'd be in rut then, of course. A bull male all hot and lusty for a sweet female." He brought his head close to hers, and she went utterly still. His mouth was so close to her face that his breath stirred wisps of her hair. He smelled her scent, an unlikely mixture of photographic chemicals and mud, wild rose and woman. "Bulls in rut can be a whole lot dangerous. They've been known to fight to the death when two of 'em fancy the same piece of tail."

She stepped back, wiping her hands on her skirt. Her face was fresh with color. But her eyes, as she studied him, were as still and deep as a mountain lake. She looked at him for so long that he could feel his cheeks growing warm. "You're wearing a flower in your hat," she finally said.

On his walk home he'd come across a field of blooming

camases, undulating in the wind. For the hell of it he'd picked one of the sweet-smelling flowers and tucked it through the silver-studded band on his Stetson. He had forgotten he'd put it there, and now he felt foolish.

"You got something against flowers?" he said.

"No . . ." Her mouth trembled, then broke into an all-out smile that lit up her face. "Only it's such a splendid contrast, don't you see? That pretty little flower stuck through the band of a battered old black hat above a scowling face with a purple eye and a puffy lip." She bit her own lip, catching back another smile. "Would you let me make a photograph of you?"

He stared at her, his gaze on her mouth. She might have the face of a lady, he decided, but she had the mouth of a whore, her lips full and lush and made for sinning. He ripped the camas off his hat and crushed it in his fist, then flung it away. The wind caught the slender petals, swirling them around in a blue cloud.

A charged silence crackled the air as he stared into her upturned face, and she stared back. She had eyes that were set wide apart and slightly protruding. Eyes the color of the moss that grew in the shaded parts of the river. Dense, dark green.

"Why do you dislike me so?" she said.

His gaze fastened again on her mouth, and he felt his own lips form the words: "I want you gone."

"Why?"

"Because you're gonna ruin . . . things," he said, then wished he hadn't. As it was, he and Gus had been having a hard time trying to make a go of the ranch without bringing a woman into it. And the thought flashed into his head before he could stop it: without bringing a woman between us.

"Well, it's too bad for you, Mr. Rafferty. Because you won't be getting what you want."

She stood before him, straight and delicate as the willows. Their eyes held as if locked. A minute passed when nothing was said and everything was understood. He was in a battle with this woman for the land he loved, and for the heart and loyalty of his brother, whom he loved more.

He felt a strange shakiness in his legs as he turned away from her. He prowled the meadow, restless, his thumbs hooked on his gun belt, the pointed toes of his boots kicking at tufts of grass. From time to time he cast a glance at her as she efficiently packed up her camera and the strange little tent.

He was beside her when she was ready to go. He bent to pick up a case just as she reached for it. Her hand closed around the handle, and his hand closed over hers.

He stared at her bent head, at the taut curve of her back.

"I always carry my own equipment," she said, her voice tight.

He let her go and straightened. "Suit yourself, then."

She stumbled away from him, lurching beneath the weight of the cases, her heels kicking up her skirt tails. He could feel the lingering imprint of her hand on his palm, singeing his skin as if he'd held it too close to the cook-stove on a cold winter's morning.

He stretched out his stride to catch up with her, his boots cutting a swath through the grass. He studied her as they walked side by side in silence. He could see, even with her bundled up toe to neck in layers of starched cotton, that she wasn't much woman. Ass and hips as slender as a boy's, narrow waist, small breasts. She'd rolled the tight sleeves of her dress up to her elbows. Tiny scratches crosshatched the delicate skin of her arms. She was badly sunburned.

He really didn't have to work so hard at driving her away; Montana was already doing it for him. This country was too wild, too harsh. It would destroy her. It would crush her in its fist and toss her away as he had done with the flower.

She didn't protest when he took the cases from her and lifted them over the fence. He climbed the rails first and, without thought, held out his hand to help her after him. And she, without thought, gave her own hand into his keeping.

For a moment so brief he wondered afterward if he had imagined it, they looked into each other's eyes and an invisible skein of lightning wrapped itself around them. He felt the fire of it through all his skin and bones, through his very breath.

She was safely on the other side of the fence, but he still had ahold of her hand. Her bones were small, as fragile as a bird's wing. Her skin warm. Her palm was rough, too rough. He turned it over and saw white weals, like packing twine, curled around her flesh.

"Somebody took a strap to you," he said, shocked at the frayed edge he heard in his own voice.

She twisted her hand free of his grasp, her fingers closing. "It was a cane."

"Why?" He could see her heart beating, a tiny flutter at her throat just above the cameo. "What'd you do that someone would take a cane to you for it?"

"It wasn't *someone*; it was my father," she said in a sudden rush. "He found me looking at souvenir cards of the notorious outlaws of the Wild West. I was only supposed to get three strokes, but I wouldn't say I was sorry for it, and so he gave me more and more and more, and in the end I think he was the sorrier. He cried, but I didn't . . ."

She stiffened her back and raised her chin, as if daring him to ridicule her. Which was what he knew he should do, since he wasn't going to get rid of her by being nice.

But he couldn't do it, not with her standing there looking so proud and vulnerable. He wasn't going to let her completely off the hook, though. He gave her a slow, lazy smile. "I've been whipped a time or two myself for lookin' at naughty pictures. They weren't of notorious outlaws of the Wild West, though."

He smiled to himself at the gleam of interest that sparked in her eyes. Lord, she was such a young innocent

"What were they pictures of?" she asked.

"Why, naked ladies of the Wild West."

He watched the tide of color begin at her neck above the cameo and flood her face. His smile turned wicked. "A curious mind is a dangerous thing," he drawled.

"Oh! You are . . ."

"I'm what?"

She didn't answer him. Instead she walked away fast, almost running, and leaving her cases behind. He caught up with her in two easy strides. "I'm what?"

"It is very obvious that you know well what you are, Mr. Rafferty. After all, why would a man brag if he could show off?"

He laughed out loud at that, and to his delighted surprise she joined him. He liked her laugh; it went well with her mouth.

She stopped it abruptly, though, when she got to the edge of the yard. She looked at the ruined laundry, and the blood came back up rich and high in her cheeks.

The wind, mocking her, lifted Gus's hat off her head and sent it sailing toward the corral. Rafferty caught it and brought it back to her. He held it out like a suitor presenting a violet posy, but she didn't take it. She stood still, looking right at him, but he wasn't sure she really saw him.

He set the hat gently on her head. "'They have sown the wind, and they shall reap the whirlwind,'" he said as he gathered up a loose strand of spindrift hair and tucked it behind her ear. His rough fingers snagged in her hair, the way they had her night rail. The back of his hand brushed her throat where the pulse still throbbed, harder than ever. A shiver rippled across the pale skin, and he heard her breath catch.

She jerked away from him. She started to rub the place on her neck where he had touched her and ended up crossing her arms over her breasts. "You . . . you astonish me, Mr. Rafferty. Although less with your accomplishment than with your courage—that you would dare to stand there beneath the eye of heaven and quote the Word of God."

"Hell, yeah, I can recite whole chapters and verses and

not miss a 'thee' or a 'thou.' And I ain't once been struck by lightning, either. Shocking to think, ain't it, Boston?"

She made a little gurgling sound in her throat. He thought she was about to laugh again, and he held his breath, waiting for it.

His old biscuit-colored hound came tearing around the barn just then, chasing a rabbit and barking. The racket enlarged Rafferty's world, so that it was no longer one small woman with light hair and green eyes.

She began to gather the ruined laundry, tossing it in the tin tub. "I will wash it all again tomorrow," she said. She glared up at him, looking as if she wanted to heave the tub, laundry and all, at his head.

"And the wind'll blow again tomorrow, and the day after that. Most every day right on through the summer. Come winter, though, it'll get so cold you can freeze your wash dry. But then, you probably won't be here come winter."

"Your brother has been teaching me how to ride. Come winter I'll be riding your big gray."

A moment ago he was laughing with her, almost liking her. Now his guts twisted with anger and a terrible longing, and he didn't know where these feelings came from or what they meant. He didn't want her learning how to ride. He wanted her gone.

"When two play, only one can win," he said, his throat gritty. "It won't be you."

"It will."

"It won't, because you don't belong here. We all've met your kind before. Your ass tightens up and your mouth puckers when the wind so much as whispers hell, and you're so starchy you squeak when you walk. You're not only useless, you're a liability. If you were a dogie you wouldn't be worth the slaughtering."

She compressed her lips and spun away from him so fast her skirt whipped his legs, and he found himself trailing after her.

She stopped abruptly at the door to the cabin, and she looked back at him, a startled question in her eyes. She held in her hands a small wreath woven of sweet grass and white sage and decorated with bird feathers and dried wildflowers. It hadn't been there before, which meant they'd had a visitor during the last hour, a visitor who hadn't wanted welcoming.

"It's a dream hoop," he said. "You're supposed to hang it over your bed, and good dreams'll come through the hole in the middle to sweeten your nights. Joe Proud Bear's squaw made them for a time and tried to sell them, but no one was buyin'. I reckon it's her way of thanking you for the milk."

"Oh! But how do you know about that?"

"All of the RainDance country knows, and not many are looking too kindly on you for your Boston drawing-room charity, either."

A faint flush dusted her cheeks. "You are wrong about me. You all are wrong, and I shall prove it to you."

"How? By paying calls on Indian squaws because you think it's something *we* think a respectable lady would never do?"

"But that isn't at all why I . . ." The flush on her face had darkened to crimson and she sucked in a sharp breath. "You are cruel."

"So's Montana."

She studied him as she had before, out in the meadow, with those still, deep eyes that seemed to stir a part of him he didn't know he had. She turned slowly and went through the door, carrying the dream hoop. She stopped again when she saw his gift to Gus—a pair of candlesticks carved of elk horn that had been polished to a lustrous ivory. "Oh, my!" she said, with a funny little sucked-in gasp.

She went to the table and picked one up. She rubbed her fingers over it, gently, as if she were blind and needed touch to see.

He stepped just inside the door and propped the sole of one boot on the jamb behind him. He watched her from beneath the concealing brim of his hat. "I guess it's your day for getting presents," he said. A woman like her, she was probably used to great big silver candelabra all doo-daded up with bows and foofaraws.

She turned, surprise and wariness darkening her eyes. "These are from you?"

He shrugged. "It ain't every day a man's brother takes himself a wife."

"They're lovely," she said. And she smiled. A caressing smile, soft and sultry like the wind on a hot night. A smile that caught at his gut and stopped his heart.

He stared at her, stunned, unable to think. Unable even to breathe. It had begun as a tightening in his chest when he'd first seen her sitting on Snake-Eye's buckboard, all prim and scared, and it had ended here in the cabin with her smile and a hard, throbbing ball of want low in his belly.

He watched her arrange the candlesticks on the table, wanting her. She set one on either side of the coffee can with its pink and blue wildflowers. The candlesticks fit; she was the one who looked out of place. This little woman with fair hair and green eyes and a harlot's mouth.

He wanted to take her with swift, rough lust, not on a bed with embroidered pillows and a feather-filled mattress but on the ground with larch needles for a cushion and the blue sky overhead and a hot wind to fan their naked, sweaty skin and drown out the groaning, sucking, panting sounds of loving. He wanted to make her let go of all that fine drawing-room polish, to make her scream and thrash beneath the hard, thrusting strength of him. He wanted to master her and to own her, and he wanted to make her want him. God help him, he thought as he turned and stumbled through the door, back out into the yard.

He wanted his brother's wife.

Thunder rumbled in the mountains as Gus McQueen raised the ax above his head and brought it down. The iron blade split the wood with a blow that reverberated against the cloud-heavy sky. He lifted the ax again and paused to listen. Not for more thunder. He listened for the rhythmic *pang-ping* of metal banging on metal coming from the smithy.

Shadows danced in the red glow beyond the smithy's open door. With this storm brewing, it was too hot to be shaping a horseshoe. But then, maybe his brother ought to get used to such an environment, Gus thought with a sour frown, hell-bent as the boy was on sin and perdition.

Gus anchored the ax in the chopping block and leaned on the helve, his chest pumping from exertion. He wiped the sweat off his face, but not the frown. He thought about crossing the yard to the forge and clearing the air with his brother. With words for once, not fists. He thought about it and decided against it, then found his boots heading in that direction.

Zach's gelding was tethered just inside the smithy door. Gus ran a hand over the broad gray rump as he skirted around it. Heat and the acrid smell of hot iron and rank sweat washed over him. His brother stood at the stone forge turning a piece of iron in the burning coals. Ruddy light limned his dark hair and glazed the flaring bones of his cheeks, casting deep shadows in the hollows beneath. He looked like the devil come up from hell. A devil who'd had a dandy of a fight along the way, what with his purple eye and scabbed lip.

He acknowledged Gus's presence with a glance but no greeting. He flipped the iron bar over in the coals, and they both watched it heat from red to yellow-hot. The split skin on the knuckles of the hand that gripped the tongs had started to heal. Gus poked his tongue into the gaping hole in his teeth made by those knuckles. He worried that the missing tooth spoiled his looks for Clem. Not that she'd ever mentioned his looks or whether she found them pleasing.

Something cold and wet brushed Gus's hand. It was the calf sniffing him like a slobbering pup. "What do you want to go making a pet out of this acorn calf for?" he said, the first words spoken between them since the fight.

His brother worked the bellows. Air whooshed on the fire, and sparks flew. Orange light flared on his face, highlighting the fading bruises. His eyes were puffy and red and sunken into his head. From the looks of those eyes he had been punishing the whiskey hard.

"You want I should kill it?" Zach said.

"I just don't want to have to watch you nursing a broken heart when he's shipped off for slaughter next fall."

"I reckon my heart's tougher than you think, brother."

"Your face looks kinda tender, though. Brother."

Zach squinted up at him through the murky smoke from the forge. Sweat dripped from the hair that fell over his brow. A smile played at the corner of his mouth, deepening the faint groove in his cheek. "You oughta see the other fella's."

Gus looked at his brother, and a logjam of emotions pressed against his chest. Exasperation and anger, resentment, envy, and love. Mostly love.

He hooked a hip onto a workbench next to the forge. He enjoyed watching Zach work at anything—calf-roping, bronc-busting, shaping a horseshoe. His movements were spare, graceful, but underneath there was always this tension within him that gave an edge to even the most mundane moments. Sometimes, sitting in front of the cabin of an evening after a hard day's work, sharing a bucket of beer, Gus would search out his brother's taut profile in the twilight and he would be put in mind of a Colt with a doctored trigger, liable to go off at any moment.

"I've sent over to Deer Lodge for some milled lumber," Gus said. "We're going to need to build us a bigger house before winter."

Zach laid the white-hot bar of iron across the pointed end of the anvil. He brought the hammer down with an echoing, singing clatter and a strength that made the muscles bulge in his arm and back. "I ain't leavin' here, Gus."

"Who said anything about you leaving?"

The truth was, Gus lived in fear that his brother would simply drift away one day, that he had too much tumbleweed in his blood to light in any one place. There were times, looking over the ranch with clear eyes, when reality intruded on Gus's dreams. In those moments he could see that what they had here at the Rocking R was a cow-pen herd owned by a shirttail outfit. They couldn't even afford to hire extra hands, except for a couple of saddle bums at roundup time. The reality of the ranch was endless days of branding, trailing beeves, cutting hay, and breaking horses. They were a long way from being cattle kings. Gus wanted to make his brother see beyond that, to the potential of the ranch, of life. But even when they were boys he hadn't known what saw Zach through a day. Down in Texas they had a word for cattle or men who stayed apart from the rest of their kind—cimarrones. Gus figured his brother was a cimarron.

"We'll team up all right, the three of us," Gus said. "You, me, and Clementine. This place might be work, but it sure beats ram-jamming around just for beans." He searched his brother's closed face for his thoughts. All he saw was that hair-trigger tension and the sweat of hard work. The combined heat of the forge and the storm was like soup steam. Gus mopped his own face with his bandanna. "We can build the house big. I 'spect you'll be wanting to get married yourself sometime," he added, then wished he hadn't. He had the horrible thought of Zach bringing Hannah Yorke out to the ranch as his bride.

Zach rested the hammer's peen on the anvil and leaned over it, bringing him face to face with Gus, eye to eye, and Gus watched those eyes turn as cold and flat as brass platters. Outside, lightning flashed white as a winter moon, smelling of sulfur, followed almost immediately by a crack of thunder. Even before he spoke, Gus knew his brother had picked up on his last thought as surely as if he'd spoken it aloud.

"The thing I'd like for you to understand is that Mrs. Yorke sells whiskey for a living, not herself."

Other things besides whiskey got sold in the Best in the West, but Gus held his tongue. Mostly held it. He couldn't completely shut his eyes to the fact that Zach had formed a sinful alliance with a trollop. A visit every month or so, maybe—he could allow that a healthy young man had needs. But a week and one day, eight nights in a row, was sinful debauchery.

"But she has done it," Gus said. "Even she would have to admit she's done it in the past."

"She don't do it now."

Gus wondered what she would call what she'd been doing this past week if it wasn't whoring, even if no money changed hands. It baffled him that his brother would feel such loyalty for a woman he barely knew and certainly couldn't respect. A loose woman.

He exhaled a long breath through his teeth. "All right, Zach. Maybe she's reformed then, huh?" he said with a forced smile. He would live with his brother's association with the town harlot. That didn't mean he would tip his hat to the woman when he crossed her path. And he sure as sin wouldn't invite her over to Sunday supper with himself and Clem.

Zach straightened up. He hefted the hammer, and the corner of his mouth tipped up into something just short of a smile. "You ain't gonna turn into even more of a boiled shirt on me, brother? Now that you're married to such a starchy woman?"

Clementine. Just the echo of her name in his thoughts did something to Gus's soul. Marrying her was the single spontaneous act of his life. He had lusted after her, a seventeen-year-old girl, and so he had stolen her away from the bosom of her family and brought her to a life of toil and hardship. What he'd done had been wrong, maybe even a sin, but, oh, Christ, Clementine . . .

The words gushed out of him, heartfelt. "I love her, Zach." He pressed a fist to his breast. "I love her so, it's

like a constant pain, right here in my heart." Immediately
he felt foolish. Men didn't talk of their hearts and of love.

The hammer rang against the anvil. Zach's face had
gone all white and taut. With an almost savage gesture, he
grasped the horseshoe with the tongs and thrust it into the
burning coals.

Gus straightened up and went to him. "Zach . . ." He
wanted to tell his brother that he loved him, too, but men
didn't talk of such things. "Man, you've forgotten more
about busting broncs and whacking bulls than I'll ever
know." He gripped his brother's arm. Zach's shirtsleeve
was soaked with sweat, the taut muscle underneath quivering. "Clementine and me, we need you."

Zach shrugged away from him, turning his back. Gus
swallowed down a protest. His marriage was a sore point
between them only because it had been so unexpected. Zach
would come around to accepting it after a time. "I suppose
you heard about the meeting at Snake-Eye's," he said by way
of changing the subject. "I told the boys we could count on
your gun."

Zach spun back around. There was a wild look on
his face, almost one of fear. But he couldn't imagine his
brother being afraid of a couple of renegade cattle thieves.

"Seems to me there's a lot of energy being wasted on
them half-breeds," Zach said. And the fear, or whatever it
was, roughened his voice. "Hell, they're only butchering
a couple of head now and then for food. We can afford the
charity."

"What about MacDonald? He got a bullet in the back
for his charity."

"Joe Proud Bear sure didn't kill him, and I don't think
Iron Nose did either." The grittiness was gone now from
Zach's voice, and the strange wildness from his eyes. He
pumped the bellows, turning the horseshoe in the coals.
"If you ask me, this necktie party of yours ought to look
closer to home. MacDonald and Horace Graham have been
squabbling over the same piece of bottomland for months.

Now he's dead, and Graham's cows are all over that creek-fed meadow, grazin' and gettin' fat."

"Mr. Graham's got a wife and five children. He reads the psalms during prayer meetings. He doesn't drink, gamble, or whore around, unlike some I might mention. You going to stand up in front of everybody and accuse him of shooting his neighbor in the back?"

Zach cast him a look full of mocking derision as he brought the iron back to the anvil. "You don't think a man can pray and kill all in the same breath?"

Gus stirred the toe of his boot through the links of chain and bent horseshoe nails that littered the floor. "Regardless of who shot who, we can't let those half-breeds get away with their thieving. Otherwise this whole valley'll be overrun with rustlers. Dammit, Zach, Iron Nose and his boy are stealing our beeves."

"That don't make 'em unique. Half the ranchers in this territory got started in the cattle business with a wide loop and other men's calves."

The hammer blows thrummed in Gus's chest and belly as he watched his brother shape the shoe. His skilled, cow-savvy brother, who probably knew all the ways there were to alter a brand and rustle a cow.

Not for the first time he wondered if cattle thieving was the little difficulty with the law that had brought about the change in his brother's last name. What Zach had done, what things were done to him between the time they were split up as boys and nine years later, when their paths had crossed on a cattle drive in west Texas—it was never spoken of between them. Those years had taken a hard boy and hardened him further in ways that Gus didn't quite understand.

But then, how well can you ever really know someone? How much can you ever know of that place deep inside a man's guts where he lives? All those shared hours of their boyhood, they had fought and dreamed and sinned together, and he had never really *known* his brother.

Of all his memories of their shared boyhood it was the last one that haunted him the most. On that day the sun was beating down hot on the steamship's varnished deck. Black-skinned dockworkers were singing gospel as they tossed cotton bales into a dray, and the air was thick with the smell of jute and sugarcane. Zach was standing barefoot on the gray weathered wharf, his hands stuffed deep in the pockets of his ragged britches, and there was this look on his face . . . as if he knew they weren't ever coming back . . .

Lightning flashed and thunder rumbled through the open door, bringing with it the smell of woodsmoke and the coming rain. There was a hot hiss and a plume of steam as Zach plunged the horseshoe into the slake trough. It was one more thing they'd never been able to talk about. That day on the Natchez dock when only one of them had been saved and the other was left behind.

He sucked in a deep breath to ease the raw ache of memory. He pressed his fists into his spine and stretched backward, wincing as the movement pulled on his bruised ribs. "Lord, I'm busted. Next time I pick a fight with you, try harder to talk me out of it. We're getting too old for that kinda horse-mucking around."

Zach tossed a hole punch onto the workbench and flashed him a sudden smile. "But it sure do beat the alternative."

Gus had to purse his mouth against the wealth of emotion brought on by that smile. "Well, hell." He draped his arm across his brother's back, gripping his shoulder hard, shaking him. "I played hooky this afternoon and went fishing. Let's go inside and find out if that wife of mine has learned how to fry a trout without having it come out black as boot leather."

Zach eased out from beneath his embrace. He picked up a handful of clench nails. "You go on ahead," he said, his face averted. "I want to put this shoe on first."

"No, I'll wait," Gus said around a thickness in his throat. "I'll wait."

They were almost at the door to the cabin when the rain came. They stood side by side and watched as it slashed in wind-hurried drifts, flattening the grass and hitting the cottonwoods with a snapping noise, like flags bucking in the wind. Lightning flashed, and the trees and mountains were silhouetted black against a sky of beaten silver.

This land, Gus thought. The RainDance country. You worked it, and fought it and coveted it, and in the end you wound up loving it so much it scared you. He felt Zach as a solid presence beside him. Together they could build this place into the biggest and best spread in western Montana.

So maybe, he thought, it didn't matter that he found it impossible to wholly understand his brother, for he knew one indomitable truth about him: he couldn't be beaten. Hurt, yes. Cut bone-deep and bruised soul-deep, but never beaten. Down deep inside the guts of him—in that secret, vulnerable place within a man where he *lived*—Zach McQueen, or Rafferty or whatever he chose to call himself, had never been beaten. And he never would be.

9

"NOW YOU MUST REMAIN quite still, Mr. Montoya, while I shoot you."

The silver bangles on the boy's sombrero shivered as he laughed. "You hear that, boss? Your wife, she say she goin' to shoot me."

He struck a pose, his hand hooked on the red sash at his waist, one hip cocked. His leather pants were decorated with silver conchas, his boots stitched with flowers.

He had been taken on by the Rocking R to help with the spring roundup. To Clementine's bedazzled eyes he looked as if he'd crossed the Rio Grande only yesterday.

Bent beneath her focusing cloth, she couldn't see her husband's impatience but she could hear it. Boots shuffled behind her, stirring up dust. He slapped a coiled reata against his thigh. "Would you hurry it up, girl?" he finally said. "Those cows won't brand themselves. Sun's been up so long the dew's nearly dried."

The sun had indeed burned off most of the morning haze. Clementine adjusted her lens to allow for it. She would not hurry her photographs. She would *not*. She drew in a deep breath, trying to ease the tightness in her chest caused by Gus's hovering. It seemed she was constantly defying him, testing him, as she had defied and tested her father. And had suffered for it.

She drew in another breath of air that was thick with the grassy, hairy stench of cows. Even with their camp pitched a good distance from the roundup corral, she was still engulfed in the smell and noise of it. The cows bawled like hungry babes as they were choused out of the canyons and pine-studded foothills. The men whistled and yipped, herding the beasts into a bellowing mill of clacking horns. Dust haloed the sun, and hooves pounded the ground until Clementine could feel it hum beneath the soles of her shoes. The din made her ears tingle.

They weren't much to look at, those cows. Their rough hides were mottled red, like withered apples, except for a triangle of white on their foreheads that gave them a bald-faced look. They were called short-horns, though Clementine couldn't imagine why, since their horns were long and bowed and pointed. They were ornery, easily spooked, stupid creatures, and they didn't like her.

The men would have the cattle all settled and grazing by dinnertime, but if Clementine went near them they'd get restless and begin to mill and hump up their tails. Gus said it was her skirts, which rustled when she walked and flapped in the constant wind. Mr. Rafferty said it was the smell of starch they couldn't abide.

Mr. Rafferty.

The cows might not like the sound and smell of her skirts, but that man—his very existence unsettled Clementine. She couldn't name or number all the emotions he aroused in her breast. But two feelings she did recognize all too well: fear and fascination.

The evening of the day he'd come home from his carousing in Rainbow Springs, the day he'd given them the candlesticks, there had been a violent storm. Lightning splintered the dark sky, and thunder boomed so loud it sounded as if the heavens had cracked open to spill out the rain. When he entered the cabin it was as if the lightning had come inside with him, was a part of him, raw and violent and dangerous.

His gaze had followed her every movement while she cooked supper. Those strange yellow eyes piercing the murky gloom lit by a single coal-oil lamp. Lightning eyes, watching her until she felt as if she were standing outside beneath the fury of the storm, alone and naked. She wanted to shout at him to stop his rude staring, but of course he was only doing it to provoke her, to frighten her . . . and it had worked. Oh, yes, it worked so well that she had to go into the bedroom and shut the door on his staring eyes. To lean against the door while the trembling shook her, and press a fist against her lips to stifle a scream from the frantic, frenzied feelings that built and built and built within her chest.

He was utterly lawless, that man, everything she had been raised to despise. Lewd and profane and cruel, he was a drunkard and a rake—and worse, if he had truly killed a man when he was only a boy. An animal, violent in his ways. Yet those times when she had dared to meet his gaze, that night and since, each time, the force of some strange emotion would slam into her chest, leaving her winded.

"And he said unto them, I beheld Satan as lightning fall from heaven."

Like lightning he was . . .

Like lightning.

Clementine added another cottonwood branch to the precarious pile in her arms, anchoring it with her chin. A splinter dug into her neck, and she bit down on an oath before it could come flying out of her mouth.

Squeezing her eyes shut, she stood with an armful of kindling in the middle of a Montana cattle range and fought to gather the fraying edges of her self. *"Whosoever curseth his God shall bear his sin."* Three months ago she hadn't even known the words with which to curse her God. Now, thanks to the education she had received from Nickel Annie and that man, profane words trembled on the tip of her tongue far more often than prayers.

She was halfway from the mess wagon to the cookfire when her toe caught in the root of a rotting stump and she smacked into the ground, branches and river driftwood spilling out of her arms like jackstraws.

She lay still a moment, her chest heaving as she struggled for breath. She rolled onto her back, blinking the dust from her eyes.

The dust and the heat had flattened the morning breeze. The sun beat down on her, hot and dry. It had been so hot this past week that the whole valley had turned from a mud pit into a dust pit. What a hard country this was, she thought. Mercilessly hard, like the ground she lay on.

She lay there and let the sun blister her face. She watched the clouds float across a sky so bright a blue it shimmered, and she thought of home.

She had never before worried about how the coal scuttles came to be full in the house on Louisburg Square. Oh, she did have a vague memory of a bent-backed coal man carrying sacks from his cart to the kitchen cellar. Now if she wanted a fire she had to fetch her own wood. It wasn't such a grand adventure anymore; she was tired and scared. She felt . . . scattered. By coming to this wilderness she had taken everything that she was, everything she understood to be true, shaken it and tossed it in the air like the spilled kindling, letting the pieces fall where they might. Yet underneath the Stetson hat she now wore, and behind her sunburned face, she was still the old Clementine, filled with longings and furies.

On a roundup they carried their fuel from camp to camp in a caboose, a cowhide pouch slung like a hammock beneath the wagon. It was called squaw wood, Gus had told her, because it was easily gathered without chopping. Squaw wood . . . She thought of Joe Proud Bear's wife. She wondered if the Indian girl resented her man and his high-handed ways. And Hannah Yorke, that laughing woman of the violet dress and red-tasseled shoes who offered her body for a man's pleasure only to be scorned for it. She wondered if they, too, awoke in the heavy and lonely hours before dawn suffused and restless with yearnings they couldn't name. Longings and furies and those empty places in the heart.

She laid her forearm across her eyes, blocking out the sky. Her city-bred ears listened to the strange lullaby of insects shrilling in the tall grass and of the river chattering to the rocks and trees. But the sun was hot, and a stick was poking her in the back, so after a moment she pushed herself to her feet.

She picked up a few pieces of the scattered wood and carried them over to the fire. She cracked a branch in two and fed it to the flames. She tossed several handfuls of beans into a camp kettle that hung from a trammel, then filled the pot to the brim with water. As grub slinger for this outfit she got to select the menu for dinner. Well, today it would be beans, bacon, sourdough doughnuts, and coffee. Same as yesterday. Same as the day before yesterday.

The outfit was a small one, consisting only of Gus

and his brother, the Mexican boy, whose name was Palo Montoya, and the RainDance country's resident characters, Pogey and Nash. The two prospectors were helping with the roundup because they weren't going to see much silver out of their mine until Gus could spare the time to go over to Butte Camp and talk with potential investors about putting together a consortium to lease and operate the Four Jacks.

Starting when dawn was just limning the hills, the men rode out to gather the cows, chousing them into a makeshift rope corral out on the range. At ten o'clock they came in to eat dinner, then spent the rest of the day cutting the calves out of the herd for branding.

With the beans on the fire, Clementine decided there was time to take more photographs before the men returned to camp. The first view she took—of the remuda with the cookfire in the foreground—was unsuccessful. The horses were so much in motion that they looked like ghosts on the negative. And the blue smoke of the fire floating up into the trees, an effect she rather liked, had not shown up at all. She took a view of the mess wagon that turned out well. It was an old wagon, missing a canvas cover, so that its bare ribs silhouetted against the sky looked like a weathering carcass of mammoth bones. She took another of a late-born calf suckling at its mother. The calf, all bald face and spindly legs, made her smile. She was still fixing this last negative when she heard a man's voice, rough with anger, shouting her name.

Heat and chemical fumes filled the dark tent. For a moment the voice had sounded so much like her father's that she gasped, and the bad air scorched her lungs. It was an old fear, of male anger and punishment, but so potent that she almost choked on it. Her hands shook, causing her to pour too much potassium cyanide into the fixing bath, spoiling the negative.

She emerged from the tent and buttoned it up. She approached Gus and the cookfire. Her hands curled, her fingers rubbing and rubbing the ridges of scars. I will not fear him as I did my father, she vowed to herself. I will not. Yet it was there, the fear, pressing against her chest, running in rivulets of sweat between her breasts. The beans had swelled up to overflow the pot, smothering most of the fire. Gus watched her come, his face hard.

He whacked his fringed leather gauntlets against his leg. "Where're the sourdoughs?"

"I forgot to make them." She wiped her silver-stained hands on her flour-sack apron. "I became busy and I . . . forgot."

His gaze flashed to the deep shade of the box elders where she'd set up her dark tent. His jaw clenched so hard the muscle jumped. "Clementine, I'll take that blasted thing away from you—"

"You will not!" she said so loud his head snapped back. She started to push past him, then swung around. "And I will not be married to my father! You see my hands, Gus?" she shouted, thrusting them up into his face. "You've wanted to know how I got the scars—my father gave them to me. He beat me until I bled because I wouldn't say I was sorry. I will not be married to my father." She clenched her hands into fists and pounded on his chest, punctuating her words with the blows. "I will not . . . be married . . . to my . . . father!"

He grabbed her wrists, the anger hot and hard in his face. "What in the devil is the matter with you—"

His head snapped around as Palo Montoya rode up with a jangle of silver conchas and spurs, followed by Pogey and Nash and Gus's brother on a foam-lathered horse, the half-blind dog loping at its heels.

Rafferty pulled up, taking the scene in slowly. A lazy smile pulled at his mouth, a smile that for once went all the way to his eyes, as if he enjoyed the sight of her and Gus fighting. "I reckon this is what happens when you bed down with a cactus, boys," he drawled. "You wind up gettin' pricked in places you didn't even know you had."

Only the Mexican boy laughed.

Clementine pried her wrists loose from her husband's grasp. She brushed past him, heading for the mess wagon. "I'll fry up the bacon now."

The men helped themselves to the beans. They ate standing up, washing the meal down with cups of hot coffee. A murmur or two drifted Clementine's way, but they fell quiet when she came up to the cookfire. Even Nash ate without talking. Gus looked grim enough to be chewing on his hat instead of the beans.

Clementine squatted to thrust a three-legged skillet layered with rashers of bacon onto the coals. She stared up at her husband's tight mouth and bunched jaw. *You have no right,* she said silently to his set face. *You have no right, no right, no right.*

"I have come to a decision, Mr. McQueen," she said aloud into the taut silence. "I will submit my best photographic views of your roundup to one of the journals back in the States." Defying, pushing, testing. "I don't believe anyone, not even a man, has photographed such an event before." The bulge in her husband's jaw was now as thick as a burl knot. Defying, pushing, testing—a quiver of guilty joy ran through her. "But there are many more sights I shall need to record. I thought I'd try to take one of a gentleman cow this afternoon."

Pogey spewed a mouthful of coffee into the fire. Nash's jaw fell open so wide his teeth dropped. She refused to look at Mr. Rafferty, although she'd felt the hot intensity of his gaze on her all during her minor rebellion.

All of her attention had been on Gus. Now he startled her by tipping back from the waist and releasing a great boom of laughter into the sky. "Gentleman cow!" he exclaimed and laughed again.

His head fell forward and he rubbed his eyes. He stared down at her a moment, then took her arm, pulling her to her feet. His face grew gentle. He ran the backs of his fingers along her jaw. "Aw, girl," he said softly. "You're such a sweet innocent." He laughed again, then spun around to point his finger at the boy. "Montoya, what're you doing here shoveling beans into your mouth and grinning at my wife? Who's out minding the gentlemen cows?"

Palo scrubbed his face with a flashy red silk bandanna, wiping off his smile. He dumped his dish, cup, and spoon with a rattle into the wooden wreck tub, then headed for the remuda with a jingle of silver and a swivel-hipped gait that held a strange fascination for Clementine.

But this time she paid only scant attention to the Mexican boy. She'd been all primed for another argument, and now she was left feeling deflated by her husband's sudden change of mood. She bent over to shake the skillet with its bubbling bacon, fed more branches into the fire, and rattled the coffee pot to see if there was any left. Straightening, she turned and slammed into the stone wall of Rafferty's chest.

"Whoa, there." He gripped her arms to steady her. She jerked back, nearly sweeping her skirts over the fire. She looked around and was startled to find herself alone with him. Pogey and Nash were saddling fresh mounts, and Gus had walked off downstream to relieve himself.

"What do you want?" she demanded, ashamed of the quaver she heard in her voice. As long as he was aware of her fear he would prey on it in his attempt to drive her away.

He rested his unsettling eyes on her face. "The alkali in the dust is already starting to blister your skin. I always carry some sweet oil in my saddlebag. I thought you might want to rub a little on your exposed parts."

The words "exposed parts" and the smirking way he'd said them made her flush, as he'd meant for them to. But he held a small square brown bottle out to her, seemingly in all earnestness. When she didn't take it, he pulled out the cork with his teeth and poured a dollop of the oil into his palm. She jumped when he took her arm, but she didn't pull away. He rubbed the oil over her hands and as far up her wrists as the tight band of her starched linen cuffs would allow.

She watched mesmerized as his rough fingers massaged circles on her skin. She didn't like him touching her. She had to clench all her muscles to control the fine quivering going on inside her. But the oil was cool and soothing and smelled faintly of olives.

His fingers stopped their rubbing. They both looked up at the same time, and their gazes caught and held. "You should put some on your face as well," he said after a moment.

She breathed, swallowed. "Yes . . . Yes, thank you." She pulled the bottle from his loose fingers and dropped it into her apron pocket. "I'll do it myself. Later." His sudden kindness disturbed her. She was more used to him treating her with cruelty and crudeness. She turned away from him, willing him to leave, and breathed a sigh of relief when he did.

When she looked around again she saw that he had joined Gus. Talking together, the brothers drifted past the box elders to a bend in the river where they could see the branding corral and that morning's herd. They stood side by side, elbows bent, hands stuffed into their back pockets.

It was odd, for she'd always thought Gus was the bigger man, but she noticed now that Rafferty was just as tall. He flexed his elbows, bunching the lean and powerful muscles of his back. His thumbs curled over his pockets, drawing her gaze to the taut curve of his buttocks. *He has a magnificent body.* The startling thought came to her unbidden, yet once there she couldn't dislodge it, couldn't stop noticing things. The way his canvas britches were worn white between his thighs from straddling a horse. The way the breeze molded his shirtsleeve to the bulge in his arm. The way he stood with his feet set wide, pelvis tipped slightly forward, as if flaunting his masculinity. Things no lady ought ever to notice.

Hot grease popped in the frypan, jerking her attention away from that man. She forked the bacon onto her empty plate. She knew she ought to take it to Gus—he'd had only beans for dinner. She was a dismal failure as a wife. The sense of freedom she'd felt in defying him had turned to a bitter shame that made her stomach queasy. She would take him the bacon, and she would apologize.

"I've been thinking we ought to buy us some grade bulls," Gus was saying to his brother as she approached them. "Durhams, maybe, to raise the standard of our herd."

Rafferty ground his cigarette into the dirt. One corner of his mouth curled into a faint sneer. "What're we gonna use for dollars, brother—cow chips? We got us a heap plenty of them at the moment."

Clementine watched the hurt come over her husband's face. He turned without a word and walked toward the branding corral, his shoulders slumped.

"Are you pleased with yourself, Mr. Rafferty?" she said as she came up behind him. When it appeared he would ignore her, she flung the plate of bacon into the dirt and dug her fingers into his arm, pulling him around to face her.

And slammed into the blazing violence in his eyes.

She felt it again, that shocking sense of being winded. His shirtsleeve had been folded up to his elbow, and her hand gripped his naked arm. The world seemed to diminish to nothing but the slick, hot feel of his skin.

She let go of him and wiped her hand on her skirt. "Does it make you feel the big man," she said, "to go trampling on your brother's dreams like a . . . like a stampeding herd of your stupid cows?"

"You"—he thumped a stiff finger on her breastbone—"don't know what the hell you're talking about."

She slapped his hand aside. "I might squeak when I walk and I might not be worth the slaughtering, but at least I can appreciate the power of a dream. You're his brother and he needs you and what good are you to him?"

He sucked in a sharp breath and his eyes narrowed. She thought a scoundrel like him could just as easily strike a woman as a man, yet she would not back down.

"Well, Mr. Rafferty? Of what use are you really to the working of this ranch? You spend most of your days and nights carousing in town, and if you have a moment to spare for Gus it's only to mock him for what he's trying to do for this place . . ."

The words dried up in her mouth as he took a step closer. She watched a bead of sweat form below his ear to run down the pulsing vein in his neck and disappear into the open faded blue collar of his shirt. She cinched her mouth tight because it kept wanting to open with her strained breath.

"Ah, hell and Jesus Christ," he snarled. He spun on his heel and stalked off toward the remuda.

She wrapped both hands around her neck, the heel of one palm pressing hard at the place where her pulse thundered. *Oh, God, what is happening to me?*

It got hotter as the day wore on.

The sun had never felt so hot back in Boston, Clementine thought. And the dust. It stuck to her sweat-slick face and stung her eyes. It burned her nostrils and settled into her clothes so that she sifted like a sack of flour when she moved.

It was certainly too hot and dusty to photograph anything, even if she had dared to in the face of Gus's displeasure. From the beginning he'd ordered her to stay away from the roundup. But without any wind to stir her skirts and disturb the cattle, she saw no reason why she couldn't watch the cutting out and branding.

The dust grew thicker the closer she got to the rope corral. It covered every leaf and blade of grass so that the world had a leached look. A cloud of buffalo gnats suddenly engulfed her, biting at any exposed patch of skin until she wanted to turn and run for the sanctuary of the river. Instead she plowed through the stinging bugs, flapping her hands about her head.

The grassy, gassy smell of dung would have told her she was getting close even if she hadn't been able to see the milling cattle through the haze of dust. She made her way to a large fire that had several branding irons sticking out of it.

Gus came up with a cooling iron, frowning when he caught sight of her. "Go on back to camp, Clem. This isn't a sight for a lady's eyes."

"But I want to stay." *I want to understand so that I can share in your dreaming,* she wanted to say to him. *I am so afraid, you see, that I will never come to like this hard, cruel, barbarous land. This hard, cruel, barbarous life.* But she found it so difficult to speak to him of her thoughts and feelings.

His face set into familiar stubborn lines, and she thought he was going to order her away. But a cry of "Hot iron!" from Nash distracted him.

The Mexican boy was dragging a stiff-legged calf across the roundup ground to the branding fire. The calf had a rawhide rope looped around its neck, the other end wrapped around the horn of Palo's saddle. The calf's mother trotted after them, moaning in alarm and shaking her horns.

The boy's teeth flashed white against the dark skin of his face. "You goin' to fry us up some prairie oysters for supper tonight, Senora McQueen?" he called out to her.

She waved and smiled back at him, not understanding.

Palo pulled the protesting calf over to Pogey and Nash, who took handfuls of loose hide, knocked its legs out from under it, and flipped it like a bale of hay onto its side. Palo cast off his rope while Pogey and Nash held the struggling animal down. The calf's bawls of panic turned to bellows of pain as Gus slashed its ear with a sharp knife, then sliced pieces off its vitals and threw them into a bloodied zinc bucket. He gripped the branding iron in his gloved hands and pressed it into the calf's red flank. There was a sizzle, a curl of white smoke, the stench of burning hair and flesh. And the calf screamed.

Clementine whirled, took three stumbling steps, then bent over at the waist and vomited into the dust-coated grass.

She stayed hunched over as her breath fought its way up into her throat and her heart thundered in her ears. The stink of charred hair clogged her nostrils, and she swallowed hard against a fresh bout of sickness that burned in her throat.

She heard a creak of saddle leather. Lifting her head, she opened blurry eyes onto a horse's flank, a dusty boot thrust through a stirrup iron, and a hand holding a wooden canteen and a clean blue bandanna.

She took the offering without a word. She rinsed out her mouth with the tepid water, spitting like a tobacco-chewing mule skinner. She dampened the bandanna and wiped her face clean, and not once did she look at him.

She gave him back his canteen, still without looking at him. Another calf bellowed, and a fresh stink of burning hair and hide wafted to her on the hot air. She squeezed her eyes shut. "Oh, please tell me . . . does it hurt them unbearably?" she said, the words grating raw in her throat.

"What do you think? If you can't take it, Boston, go home."

"I am home," she said. But she lied, and he knew it.

She heard a step behind her and Gus's voice came to her, taut with anger again. "When're you going to start doing what you're told, girl? You see what I meant about this not being a fit sight for a lady? Get on back to camp now."

"No. I'm staying." She lifted her head. The brim of Rafferty's dusty black Stetson shaded most of his face; she couldn't see his eyes. "I'm staying," she said again. To him.

He touched two fingers to his hat almost as if he were saluting her. He laid his reins against his horse's neck, then pulled its head back around. He stared down at her in silence a moment. "It don't hurt them unbearably," he finally said. "The branding. It only sears off the hair and a bit of hide." He squeezed with his knees, and the horse spun around in a cloud of dust and trotted back to the corral.

Clementine stayed, though she couldn't bear to watch Gus at the branding, for it must surely hurt the calves some, she thought; otherwise they wouldn't scream. She fastened her gaze onto Palo and the biscuit-colored hound, Atta Boy. Though almost blind, the dog wended his way through the milling cattle, unerringly picking out a calf with no brand on its flank and herding it toward the boy's swinging rope. She kept catching whirls of movement out the corner of her eye, but she held herself stiff, for she would not look at that man, she would not, would not look at him.

She looked at him.

Long brown fingers building a loop of rawhide, drawing soft floating circles in the air. Lean muscles bunching, flexing, flowing as his arm whipped across the circles he had drawn. And the lasso sailing, sailing, hanging poised in the air, and then by some miracle sliding beneath the belly of a running calf to snag its hind legs. Hands flashing, dallying the free end of the reata around the saddle horn. Thighs tautening as he braced his weight hard into the stirrups against the plunge of the cow pony driving its feet into the dirt. Rawhide singing taut as the calf hit the end of the rope and flopped to the ground, side up and ready for branding.

She thought she knew how his naked body would be beneath his clothing, how it would feel beneath her hands. The thought, so sinful, stole her breath. Yet she could not stop it, could not stop herself from staring at him.

He turned his head and caught her watching. Their eyes met and held. A rush of blood thrummed through her body. Her skin grew warm, felt raw; her clothes suddenly prickled as if they were made of thistles. His eyes still on her, he swung his arm, and the lasso clutched at air. The calf tossed its head and let out a low bawl, dancing free.

"Hot damn, did ya see that?" Pogey exclaimed. "The boy wasted a loop. First time I ever seen him waste a loop."

"They're bulls."

The breath left Clementine's chest in a sharp gust. "What?"

Zach Rafferty stood before the water butt, a full dipper in his hand, poised to drink. She was three feet away, her hands braced behind her on the mess wagon cook's table. Gus had rigged a canvas fly over the rear of the wagon. It shaded her from the sun, but it also trapped the heat, allowing steam to build up as in a simmering kettle. Sweat crawled over her body. She could smell herself. And she could smell him: leather and horse and male sweat.

"Bulls," he said again. "What you genteel ladies refer to as gentlemen cows . . ." He paused to drink. Water spilled out of the corners of his mouth and ran down his neck. She watched the corded muscles of his throat work as he swallowed, then flushed when he lowered the dipper and caught her looking.

He wiped the wetness off his lips with the back of his hand. "I figure if you're gonna photograph 'em, you ought to know what's bull and what's not. Your cows are more specifically your females, which means they got teats, but none of what you genteel types refer to as the male breeding organ. Now your steers, they're males, so they do sure enough got organs. But they've been castrated, which means they had their breeding potential cut short when . . . Am I rilin' you, Boston? Your cheeks sure are gettin' red."

Her cheeks burned hotter than a branding iron, but she answered his taunting gaze with a level look. "You might well be able to make me blush, sir. But it will take more than your foul tongue to chase me away from here."

"The day is young, and I can get fouler."

"I don't doubt that you can, for you do have a bit of

a talent for it. A talent you are understandably proud of, since you have so few and they are all so small."

He snorted a laugh as he scooped another dipperful of water out of the butt. He pointed the dipper's handle at her chest. "You know, for all your highfalutin, la-di-da ways, you got a tongue on you that could rip the hide off a buffalo. Bet Gus didn't know that about you before he married you, huh? He never has liked uppity women."

She would not discuss Gus with him; she would ignore him. She wanted him to leave her alone. She wanted him to get on his horse and ride off the Rocking R spread and out of the RainDance country and keep on riding until he was back in the hell that had spawned him.

She reached beneath the chuck box and picked up a burlap sack of potatoes. As she set the sack on the cook's table, she heard a shrill buzzing and she tensed, for she hated bugs and it seemed that out west they were everywhere. Gnats, flies, and fleas plagued her constantly. And those hideous black beetles that fell out of the sod roof at night and into her face and hair . . . She shuddered at the thought even as the insect whirred again. A katydid must have hopped into the wagon; the grass was full of them.

She scraped a knife around the scrawny, gnarly potato, watching the brown skin curl free, yet aware still of that man. Sliding quick furtive glances at him.

He had taken off his hat and emptied the dipper over his head. The ends of his hair hung over his collar, dripping water. His shirt, already drenched with sweat, clung to his back. She lowered her gaze to the gun he wore. Blue-black and deadly-looking, it rested in an open leather holster that was looped over a thick cartridge-studded belt and tied to his thigh with a thong. It looked too heavy for his lean hips. Yet he wore it easily, as much a part of him as his hat and boots. Gus had told her that cowboys, when they bothered to carry a gun, wore it on a belt cinched up around the waist. Only lawmen and scoundrels who fancied themselves gunslingers wore them hip-low and tied down at the thigh. She had no doubt which category Zach Rafferty fell into. Why, she wouldn't put it past him to have ridden with the James gang, robbing trains and stagecoaches and gunning down innocent bank tellers in the street—

His gaze whipped around suddenly, clashing with hers, and she jumped.

A tortoiseshell comb slipped out of the coiled bun at her neck, bouncing off her bodice into the dusty folds of her skirt. A hank of hair fell over her shoulder, strands of it sticking to her damp cheek. Her hands full of potato, she turned her head, trying to brush the hair off with her arm.

Suddenly he was standing before her, slipping his hands around her neck. She shuddered violently. "Hold still," he said. "I'm not gonna scalp you."

He tugged loose the thick knot of her hair. More combs and pins fell onto the cook table with soft clicks. Every muscle and nerve in her body hummed taut. Her stomach clenched so tightly she felt dizzy. *Revulsion,* she thought. Her mind might have formed a prurient fascination with this man, but at least her body had the sense to remain revolted by his touch.

He tore a fringe off his chaps and used it to tie her hair back out of her face. She imagined his hands handling her hair the way they had the rope. Expert hands, graceful. Almost gentle.

"This isn't proper," she said, the words strained by the tightness in her throat. Oh, no, it wasn't proper. Allowing him to touch her, even in innocence. Because he . . . because she . . .

He stepped back and took a good gander at her, head to toe, the hardness of his eyes and mouth flattening all expression. She felt indecent now standing before him with her hair hanging free and loose down her back, merely tied back with a piece of leather. But then, the man made her feel hot and disheveled even when every pin was in place.

She tore her gaze away from his and jerked around to face the cook's table. The half-peeled potato in her hand was turning brown in the heat. Bright drops of blood lay scattered like ripped rose petals on the scarred wood. The knife handle was sticky with blood. It bewildered her for a moment until she felt a throbbing pain in the heel of her hand. At some time she must have cut herself.

She heard the scuffle of his boots as he left, and she pushed out a pent-up breath that lifted her breasts. Throughout the afternoon the men were always riding back to the camp to pick up a fresh horse and cool off at the water butt. But she knew he'd come here for another reason entirely. To torment her.

He left a deep stillness behind him, broken only by the whirring katydid. She tossed the potato into the camp pot. She ventured a peek over her shoulder. He hadn't left after all. He stood next to the cookfire, his gaze fastened on her and a strange, dark tension sharpening the harsh bones of his face.

Caught fast by his staring eyes, like a rabbit in a sudden wash of light, she groped behind her for the burlap sack and another potato . . . and the world erupted into a kaleidoscope of sound and movement. The katydid whirred again. Rafferty's hand flashed, shooting fire. A whistling wind pressed against her ear. The sack exploded. Pieces of burlap and potato hit her in the chest and rang against the iron camp pot. Clementine screamed and flung her arms up to cover her face and head.

He came at her. Smoke wisped from the muzzle of his revolver. She backed up with a hard jerk, knocking into the table. He stopped in front of her, the gun pointed at her chest.

She gasped, sucking in a deep, rattled breath. "You tried to kill me!"

His laughter startled her so much, she flinched. "If I was tryin' to kill you, Boston, you'd be dead."

He poked the gun barrel into the remains of the potato sack. With his free hand he picked up what her eyes first saw as a thick piece of rawhide rope. Not until he held it up before her face did she see that it was a snake.

A large snake. With scaly olive-green skin marked with rows of round brown spots, and a tail of hard, horny rinds that fit one into the other. The head was missing, shot away by Zach Rafferty's revolver.

Another scream burst from her throat before she could stop it. She leaned as far back as she could, away from him and the snake, until the edge of the table pressed painfully into the small of her back. She wanted desperately to run, but he had her trapped.

He held the snake pinched between two fingers, swinging it before her wide, unblinking gaze. Her fingers fluttered up to her cameo, where her pulse beat fast in her throat. She realized what she was doing and forced her hand down to her side, clenching her fist. She tried to suck in a deep breath, as if she could retrieve her composure from the very air.

"Take it . . . away," she said.

He clicked his tongue against his teeth. "Nasty, ain't it? Eleven rattles."

It was only a snake, she told herself. Well, a rattle-snake, but it was dead. She refused to let the man taunt her like this. She wouldn't give him the satisfaction.

She straightened, lifting her head. "Eleven rattles, Mr. Rafferty? My, my, I am impressed . . . to discover that you can count past your fingers."

A half smile played upon his lips. "Just another one of my *small* talents, and if you keep strikin' at me with those venomous fangs of yours I just might shoot you after all, like I did this sidewinder. Or maybe . . ." he drawled as he holstered his gun, the words thick as the sorghum syrup Gus poured over his flapjacks, "maybe I'll kill you Indian style. Slow and quiet."

So quickly her mind barely registered the motion, he pulled a wicked-looking knife out of a sheath inside his boot. She jerked backward as the long, pointed blade flashed in the sun and barely missed slicing off her nose.

He slit the belly of the snake instead. A black liquid

oozed out of it to drip in the dirt. Her jaw ached from clenching her teeth, and her muscles from trying not to shudder. She stared up at him wide-eyed, trying to prove that she was brave, that she could take anything he and this country flung at her and not cower or whimper or plead for mercy.

He stared back at her for so long, the world became swallowed by the pounding thunder of her heartbeat. Yet she would not break before him, she would not.

His glaze slid away from hers, and a corner of his mouth twitched in what could almost have been a spasm of regret. "Ah hell, Boston, I shouldn't . . ." A faint band of color darkened his prominent cheekbones. "This skin'll make a nice band for your hat. And the meat fries up tasty."

"Then eat it yourself. And if God is kind, perhaps it will poison you."

As soon as the words were out her mouth she wished them back. They had sounded so petty and mean. He tossed the snake carcass onto the table among the bits of potatoes and the ruins of the burlap sack and spun away from her, muttering a foul word beneath his breath.

She stared at the rattler and thought of the biscuit-colored hound left half blind from a snakebite. Crude and violent the man might be, but he had saved her from such a fate, if not from death. Breeding tells, her mother had always said, and her breeding did not allow for poor manners or ingratitude.

"Mr. Rafferty?" It came out scratchy and uncertain. She cleared her throat. "I must thank you for saving my life."

He turned around. He still had the knife in his hand, and he looked as wild and savage as any Indian of her imagination, especially with his mouth set cruel and hard, and his bronze eyes glittering in the shadow cast by his hat brim.

"Forget it." He wiped the knife on his chaps and slid it back into his boot. "It was a prairie rattler anyway, not a diamondback. Like as not you wouldn't have died even if he'd bitten you. Not with someone around to suck out the poison."

"Still, I must insist."

His hat brim tilted up like a quirked eyebrow. "You *must* insist? Bossy little thing, ain't you? All right, then, I accept your apology."

"Apology! Since when does a polite expression of gratitude become an apology? You're the one—" She stopped, suddenly aware that he was teasing her. Not taunting her, but teasing her, the way a friend might do. The thought flustered her.

They looked at each other, and a silence stretched between them that was fraught with shifting emotions as treacherous as quicksand. She hated and feared him, yet she felt an odd, forbidden exhilaration at the very thought of him.

The spell broke as Gus came galloping into the camp. Rafferty sauntered over to meet him, and they talked, too quietly for her to hear. Once his gaze flashed back to her, and she snapped hers away so fast she made herself dizzy. Yet she remained uncomfortably aware of him until he mounted Gus's horse and rode out of the camp.

She looked at the snake . . . prairie rattler. She ran her finger along the scaly skin. She expected it to be slimy like a fish's. But it was dry and smooth and cool and felt much the way she imagined the barrel of a gun would feel.

Gus came up beside her and blew out a soft whistle. "That's quite a beauty. Do you want me to finish dressing it out for you?"

She swallowed around a cottony dryness in her mouth. Her belly hummed with a terrible excitement that had to do with snakes and guns and a man quick and deadly enough to handle both. "Mr. Rafferty is quite a proficient shot."

"He can drill a hole in a silver dollar from two hundred yards away."

She heard pride in Gus's voice and a gruff affection. She looked at him, at his open, sun-bright face. She felt a rush of fondness for him so strong and full it made her heart swell. She had been so unfair to this man, her husband, blaming him for her own failed expectations. Blaming him for the betrayal that was Montana.

She laid her hand on his arm. "Gus . . . I'm sorry about forgetting to make the sourdoughs and for getting sick during the branding." He turned to look at her, but she averted her face. "I fear that I will never make a good rancher's wife."

"Aw, Clementine." His arms came around her, familiar, strong. "Do you think I care so much about those blasted sourdoughs?" He cupped her cheeks and looked into her eyes. "It's enough that I have you, girl. That we have each other."

Her head fell forward and she burrowed her face into his chest. She pressed against the soft red plaid flannel of his shirt, feeling more than hearing the steady beat of his heart, breathing in the smell of him, of woodsmoke and cow and hard-work sweat. For all of his dreaming ways, Gus McQueen was of the earth, root-bearing and elemental in the way of the earth. Not empty and vast and raw like the sky. He did not frighten her or call to her or stir those lonely places deep within her.

"It's enough that we have each other," Gus said again.

She buried her face deeper in his chest, shutting out the sky.

10

SPARKS FROM THE COOKFIRE spiraled into a late afternoon sky that was the deep blue-gray of gunmetal. The wind had come back up, chasing away the dust and carrying with it the homey scent of coffee and burning cottonwood. In the quiet of the roundup's evening camp, Clementine could almost forget what had come before: the grit and the heat. And the violence.

Hampered by her skirts, she sat on a stump. Gus sat on the ground in front of her, his back braced against her knees. He rubbed the bottom fringe of his mustache while he studied his tally book, trying to estimate how many cows had been lost to winter storms, predatory animals, and Iron Nose's rustling.

The others used their saddles and bedrolls as backrests. Pogey and Nash kept up a steady stream of blather, spiking their coffee from a whiskey flask when they thought Gus wasn't watching. Zach Rafferty sat apart, smoking and cleaning his gun.

Nash had seized onto the subject of rattlesnakes and was worrying it to death like a terrier with a rag bone. "I've heard of sidewinders holing up in some funny places to get outta the sun," he said, "but a sack of potatoes sure do beat all. Now, your soogan's a much more likely place to find a snake when you least want him. I recall a time in Missouri during the year of the great grasshopper storms—"

"Hold on, now," Pogey interrupted, thrusting his feet toward the fire, "let me stretch out my legs so's you can pull 'em both."

"'S God's truth," Nash proclaimed, making a cross over his heart. "'Twere back in 'fifty-nine. Them hoppers were so thick that summer they'd chew on anything green. One old woman walked out her soddy wearing a green dress, and they ate it off her down to the skin." He chuckled and scratched his grizzled jaw. "Now, a body can think by the sound it makes that a big-winged grasshopper is a rattlesnake. So after hearing snakes day in and day out and finding nothing but hoppers, you can't fault me for becoming complacent. One night I crawled boneyard-tired into my soogan without first checkin' for snakes, and durned if I didn't hear a hissin' noise. More of them grasshoppers, I think to myself . . . till I feel something a-slitherin' cold up my belly." He paused to glance around the cookfire, collecting his audience like a tent-show preacher.

"Was it a rattlesnake?" Clementine prompted, to oblige him. She rested her elbows on her thighs and hid a smile by cradling her chin with her clasped hands.

"You bet your last bit 'twere a rattler. A diamondback seven feet long if he were an inch, and fangs on him thick as a wild pig's tusks. I'll be blamed if that snake didn't curl up tight as a lariat right atop my chest and go to sleep. There I lay hour after hour, the sweat meltin' off me like hot tallow. Come mornin' he wakes up—me, I ain't slept a wink—and we're staring eyeball to eyeball and I'm figuring I'm so close to bein' a dead man I might as well take up harp playing . . ."

The prospector paused again, awaiting his cue. In the silence Clementine could hear the tinkle of the remuda's bell mare and the low chorus of cow parlor talk: cud chewing, grunting, and blowing over contented stomachs. "So what did you do, Mr. Nash?"

"Bit off his head before he could bite me!" he exclaimed, slapping his knee. His large putty-colored eyes twinkled at her. "Them was in my younger days. I was quicker then."

Pogey, who'd been following this recital with a pained

look on his face, rolled his eyes heavenward. "Shee-it . . . oot. The only thing ever been quick about you is your tongue. And something else I won't mention, but which the ladies at the Best in the West can all attest to."

Nash's cheeks colored brightly, and the others all laughed except Clementine. She didn't know what was so funny, but she wasn't about to ask.

At the thought of the saloon and the sinning that went on there, her gaze sought out Mr. Rafferty. His long fingers moved over the oily metal of his gun almost lovingly. He must have felt her eyes on him, for he glanced up. For a moment he stared at her in that darkly intense way of his. Then a corner of his mouth curved into a slow smile that indented the faint dimple in his cheek. And caught her like a blow beneath the ribs.

She snapped her attention away from him, yet the pain in her chest lingered. Her head fell back and she stared wide-eyed at the sky. A single star twinkled in the vast emptiness. In another hour or so the heavens would be as thick as clotted cream with stars. Out here they burned so bright and close it seemed she was not under them but among them. A star herself, caught fast by the dark night.

"Looks to be a quiet night," Nash said.

"Quiet for who?" Pogey retorted. He ripped a piece off his tobacco twist and plugged it into his cheek. "Your snoring could give away our camp to a dead Injun."

"Well, if'n he wasn't dead already, the smell of you would sure nuff kill him."

"You sayin' I stink?"

"Whiffier than a dead skunk."

Pogey lifted his arm and sniffed at his stained armpit. He shrugged. "I can't smell nothin', and what's to worry about anyways? We ain't had us a good Injun scare in these parts in so long I've forgot what it feels like. Time was when them Blackfeet were the meanest Injuns living. Time was them Bloods woulda lifted your hair soon as look at you. They've had the starch taken outta them by smallpox and firewater and the army, though. Pride's mostly all gone now."

At the talk of Indians, Clementine had stiffened. She couldn't seem to overcome her fear of the painted devils so luridly described in the yellowback novels she'd read as a child. She glanced up to find Mr. Rafferty's eyes on her. She lifted her chin. "I expect you've seen a lot of Indians in your time, Mr. Pogey?" she said.

Pogey's chest swelled and his cheeks puffed with air, but Nash jumped in first. "If you're lookin' to consult an expert on the subject, I'm your man. Now you take your Salish, they're pretty much peaceable savages, whereas your Crows are thievish and sassy. The Sioux can be mean as snakes when their venom gets stirred up. Take Sitting Bull, for instance. Meanest Injun I ever met was Sitting Bull. I guess you could say we was on pipe-smoking terms for a while before he took to the warpath. What he did to Custer and the boys at the Little Big Horn were not a pretty sight, let me tell you. I was there not an hour after it happened, an' what I saw plumb curdled my blood. Bodies lyin' every whicha way and all too dead to skin."

Pogey sucked in such a hefty snort that tobacco juice dribbled into his beard. "Damn you, Nash, but if you ever did half the things you claim to've done, you woulda been wore to a frazzle long before now. You ain't never been within a hundred miles of Sittin' Bull—"

Nash snatched off his hat, the better to glare at his partner. "Are you callin' me a liar?"

Pogey likewise snatched off his hat, to make the glaring contest even. "I'm saying you bend all hell out of the truth. The closest you've ever been to any Injun with any meanness to speak of is ol' Iron Nose. And the closest you ever been to *him* was to catch a glimpse of the back end of his hoss, and even then you was shakin' like a pup with a chill."

"As I recall, you was there at the time, and I didn't see any fur growin' on your brisket." Nash wedged his hat back on his head, tapping its caved-in crown, settling the argument. "Not that Iron Nose ain't one mean Injun."

"He's a mestee," Pogey explained for Clementine's benefit, "which is to say he's got white in him from both sides of the blanket. But it's his red blood that gets to boilin' when he's riled. Why, he's so mean even the Bloods expelled him from the tribe. Got his nose chewed off in a fight once, and some blacksmith fashioned him a new one. I reckon he ain't been the same ever since."

"Yup, it were losing his nose what took that particular Injun beyond the realm of ornery and into pure meanness," Nash agreed happily. "It wasn't long after he got his nose bit off that he and his kin hacked that buffalo hunter to bits right there in the cabin where y'all are living now—"

Pogey kicked him hard in the shin with his dome-toed boot. "Put a stopper in your mouth, you jughead. Can't you see ye're frightening the missus?"

So the story was true . . . Somehow Clementine had convinced herself it was too horrible to be possible. She could feel the pulse beating wildly against the cameo at her neck. With an effort she kept her hand from going to her throat. She would not look at Mr. Rafferty. She wouldn't give him the satisfaction.

Gus stirred, shutting his tally book and stretching as he got to his feet. He patted her knee. "Don't fret about it, Clem. Except for a spot of thieving, there haven't been any serious hostilities with the Indians in these parts in over two years."

She made herself get up and gather the dishes in the wreck tub for washing. She didn't want to go down to the river, but she had to before it grew too dark. She wanted to ask Gus to come with her, but she decided that she would almost rather be scalped by Iron Nose than parade her foolish fears in front of Mr. Rafferty.

It was darker closer to the river. Stunted willows and wild plum thickets cast shadows over the bank. The blossoming plums filled the air with their sweet scent, as did the heavy white flower clusters that Gus had said were chokecherries. Come fall, he'd said, the fruit would hang fat and purple off the trees and she would be able to make pies and jellies with it. Except that she didn't know the first thing about the making of pies and jellies.

Away from camp the evening seemed quiet, but in truth it was full of noise. Frogs croaked their love songs in a deep-throated chorus. A white-winged magpie fussed at her. The river chattered over its rocky bed. Oh, how she longed for a good soaking bath. Dust caked her face and hair; her skin itched beneath her corset ribs. It seemed she hadn't been truly clean since she left Boston. She probably smelled like the bottom of a horse's hoof, certainly strong enough to rouse a dead Indian. The thought made her smile.

She had just finished rinsing the sand from the last dish when she noticed that the frogs had fallen silent. Even the river had stopped its song. Her breath hung suspended in her throat, her ears tensed. She heard a footfall in the grass and a soft rustle of leaves. Her belly fluttered and her scalp prickled. Slowly she turned her head . . .

The brush crackled as it parted and a man loomed against the lavender sky. She would have pitched headfirst into the river if he hadn't grabbed her shoulder. "Careful, Boston. You're about as goosey tonight as a colicky bronc."

She lurched to her feet, nearly falling in the river again. "You startled me, Mr. Rafferty," she said, careful to keep her face composed even though she could feel heat rising in her cheeks. "But then, I have no doubt that startling me was precisely your intention."

"There you go again, putting all sorts of nasty motivations behind my poor, misguided attempts at being the gentleman. What if my intention was simply to help you with the dishes . . . ?"

He fell silent as the willow brakes rustled loudly, this time across the river. He lifted his head, his nostrils quivering, like a hound fresh on the scent. He leaned into her, so close she felt the hot gust of his breath on her cheek. "Sssh. Can you smell him?"

She couldn't smell anything, because she couldn't breathe. And she couldn't hear much of anything, either, because her heart was now beating right up into her ears. She hated this cowardice in herself and she tried to will it away. But it seemed that fear—of Indians and wild animals, of the wind and the loneliness—was part of a woman's lot out here.

"Roachback," came Rafferty's whisper on another wash of warm breath. A shiver curled up her spine, raising the fine hair on her neck.

"What?" she whispered back, the word a tight little squeak.

He moved his lips closer to her ear. She not only felt the heat of his breath, she felt its moistness. His breath fogged her ear, like blowing on a windowpane. "Grizzly bear. Probably hungry."

She swallowed the salty taste of panic. She remembered a picture she had seen in one of Shona's novels of a great shaggy humpbacked beast with teeth and claws as long and sharp as scimitars. She had to ask it, even if he laughed at her: "Do they eat . . . people?"

His chin brushed up and down against her hair as he nodded. "Been known to. Most likely, though, he's after the chokecherries."

It crossed her mind to wonder how the chokecherry trees could be bearing fruit at the same time that they were blooming. But then the willow brakes rattled again and all coherent thought fled her head. She was sure she could actually feel her heart clubbing against her ribs.

Mr. Rafferty was standing so close to her she could hear his breathing, slow and steady, while her breath came in short, scared pants. His quiet strength was comforting. She edged closer to him, her belly brushing against the hard, cold metal of the revolver at his hip.

She turned her head. His profile looked chiseled from

stone. The fading light glittered in his eyes. "Your gun?" she said softly.

He turned his head. They stood so close together that the movement caused her mouth to accidentally brush his cheek. Startled, she jerked her head back.

"Wouldn't do no good," he said, whispering still, "'cept to rile him even more. Takes a double-loaded scattergun to stop a grizzly. That and a prayer—"

The willow brakes crackled and burst open. Clementine whirled to run and slammed into Rafferty's chest. His arms came around her and she burrowed into the warmth and strength of him. Into the smell of him that was Montana dust and horse and man.

He stiffened and set her away from him. "Christ," he said on a ragged expulsion of breath.

She clung to his shirt as she twisted her head around in time to see a beaver waddle across the rocky bank and slide into the water with a slap of his flat black tail. Stunned, she stared at the widening ripples in the river left by the diving beaver, until she felt Rafferty's chest rumble beneath her clenched fists and knew that he was laughing.

She shoved past him, tripping over a rock in her haste to get away. He grabbed her arms. Her muscles, that had been so tight with fear, now quaked from the sudden release. For a moment the only thing that kept her from sliding to the ground was the grip of his hands.

"Release me at once," she demanded, but her voice broke and trembled on the words.

His breathing was fast and uneven, as if he'd just sprinted across the prairie. "My, my, do I hear the sound of starch cracking?"

She pushed him away with the butts of both hands. But she only managed two steps before she swayed on her feet. She was still shaking so hard she was surprised he couldn't hear her bones rattling. She had let it be so easy for him to make an utter fool of her. Her tremulous voice echoed in her head: *Do they eat people?* The man's self-control must be astounding, that he hadn't burst into uproarious hilarity right then.

Suddenly she felt something shatter inside her. She snatched a tin plate out of the wreck bucket and whirled, flinging it at his head.

She missed him and struck a tree instead, and he laughed again, firing her anger like bellows to a forge. "Christ, Boston, you even throw like a greenhorn."

"Go to blazes on a jackass, you arrogant swine!"

"And you cuss like a greenhorn, too. But I reckon even a dumb cowboy like me can take a hint." He tipped his hat at her and sauntered away, cool and grinning, as if he were taking leave of her from her front parlor.

She stood staring after him, her fists clenched at her sides, shuddering. For the whole of her life, a loss of control had always been met with the most terrible of punishments. Anger certainly was not a genteel emotion. But it had felt so good to throw the plate at his head. She wished he would come back so that she could throw it again and this time maybe flatten his nose with it.

Gus materialized before her from out of the falling darkness. He picked up the plate and held it out to her. She couldn't see the expression on his face, but she could tell by the censorious quality of his silence that he'd witnessed at least the tail end of her temper tantrum.

"I wish you two'd make more of an effort to get along," he finally said.

She snatched the plate from his hands and tossed it into the wreck tub, even though it was coated with leaves and dirt. But the rage had left her now, leaving a burning in her chest. She pressed the back of her hand to her heated cheek.

"Can't I love you," she said, "without liking him?"

He stirred in the shadows and she thought she heard his breath catch. He took her hand, turning her palm to his mouth. His lips were warm, his mustache soft, tickling. "Do you love me, Clementine? You've never said the words before."

I don't know, she wanted to cry. *I think I do. I'm trying to love you, but I'm so afraid, so afraid.* She couldn't explain that her feelings for him had somehow gotten all mixed up with how she felt about Montana and, in some strange way she only dimly understood, with how she felt about his brother. And how could she explain this need she felt to hoard the deepest parts of herself, to keep her woman's secrets and fears and hopes to herself and apart from him?

Because the one thing seemed to lead to the other, although she wasn't sure in what way, she said, "I'd like for us to have a baby soon."

He laughed softly and tugged on her hand, pulling her into his arms. "I'm doing everything I can to make sure that happens."

Maybe it already had. She didn't know any of the signs and she was too embarrassed to ask Gus. She wished there was a woman she could talk to. But from the dim recesses of her memory she heard her mother's voice saying, "Never ask such naughty questions."

Her head fell back and she rose up on her toes, turning her face to his. It began as a chaste brush of his lips across hers; then his mouth pressed down harder, and her lips moved, opening beneath his. She arched against him, pressing her suddenly aching breasts into the hardness of his chest as he sucked on her mouth and mated with her tongue. She dug her fingers into the muscles of his shoulders and felt him shudder. He pushed his aroused body into her belly, but when she moaned and rubbed against him, he thrust her away.

"Not here, girl," he said. He was panting hard. "One of the others might come upon us."

She wrapped her hands up in her skirt and stared at the ground. She felt such a burning shame she was glad of the dark that he couldn't see her face. "Of course not, Gus. It isn't proper."

He expelled a loud, shaky breath. "No . . . It was my fault. It's just that the more I have you, the more I want you. I can't get enough of . . . of touching you," he amended at the last moment. But she knew what he'd been about to say. He couldn't get enough of what they did together in bed at night, and surely that was wicked. *"He that soweth to his flesh shall of the flesh reap corruption."* The marriage bed was for procreation, not pleasure. And yet, wicked though it might be, there'd been times when she hadn't been able to remain still and ladylike in her marriage bed, when she had actually whimpered and squirmed and moaned because of the things he did to her body and the way it felt. Pleasure . . . oh, yes, there was undeniable pleasure in what a man could do to a woman with his lips and his hands and those parts of his body that made him uniquely a man.

Clementine so embarrassed herself with the intimacy of these thoughts that she couldn't bear to look at her husband. She turned her hot face away from him while he picked up the wreck tub, tucking it under his arm. And she kept a careful distance from him as they walked together back to camp. Her muscles felt languid, heavy. She ached, wickedly, wantonly, for him to kiss her again. She wanted him to ease her down right there on the hard ground and make her whimper and squirm and moan.

Sometime while they'd been at the river the last of the day had bled from the sky. The cookfire had sunk to a mound of white coals. A feeble glow came from a moth-haunted lantern hanging from the mess-wagon tongue. With the coming of the night, the air had turned cool. It was filled with the smell of burning cottonwood and the riffle of shuffling cards.

Nash and Pogey were playing poker using dried beans for chips, and they barely glanced up when she and Gus returned. Rafferty lay stretched out flat, with his head on his saddle, his dog curled up nose to tail at his feet. She thought he was asleep until his hat brim tilted up and the lantern light caught the cold brassy shine of his eyes.

Unconsciously she brought her fingers to her mouth.

Her lips smarted as if scorched. It was the feel of his beard-roughened cheek that her lips remembered.

She stood at the pasture fence a week later, her head held high, her gaze on the wide sky, looking out over the valley as if it were a promised land. And yet to him she seemed frail and achingly lost, standing alone as she was in that great rolling ocean of grass.

Sometimes he wanted to stop the world and look at her forever.

He ambled his horse up behind her, letting his eyes dwell on the way the wind played with a loose strand of her hair and pressed the skirt of her riding habit to her thighs. The way Gus's old hat cast a shadow on the sweet fairness of her cheek.

"Mornin'," he said.

She whipped around so fast her feet almost shot out from under her on the dew-wet ground, and she had to make a wild grab for the fence rail to keep herself upright. She pushed the hat out of her eyes with the back of her wrist and sighed. "Do you lie awake at night and plan it, Mr. Rafferty?"

He twisted sideways in the saddle and hooked one leg over the horn. He got tobacco and papers out the pocket of his leather vest and started working on a cigarette. If she knew what he lay awake and thought of at night . . .

He struck a match with his thumbnail, but he had trouble holding it steady. "What're you jawin' at me about this time, Boston?"

"The way you're always sneaking up on me."

"I wasn't sneaking," he said around the cigarette in his mouth. "Hell, I was making enough noise to stampede a plow horse. The fault's with those tenderfoot ears of yours. You probably couldn't hear the blast from a can of black powder if it went off under your hat." He squinted at her through wafting smoke. "Rumor has it you're ready to pick yourself out a horse."

"I would rather Gus be the one to—"

"He's busy. Which one do you fancy?"

She swallowed and straightened her shoulders. She turned back toward the pasture. The horses were bunched at the east end of it. A hawk flew low overhead, casting a running shadow on the riffling grass. The herd, showing off for her, erupted into a collective canter, an earthy rainbow of bucks, tans, sorrels, and roans, manes and tails streaming, hooves flashing silver in the wet grass.

"What about that spotted one?" she said.

That spotted one. Jesus. He eyed the horse she was pointing at, a pinto that was mostly white with paintlike splotches of black on his rump and flanks. "You only like him 'cause he's flashy."

She gave him a stubborn look. "He is the one I want, Mr. Rafferty."

"Yes, ma'am." He ducked his head to hide a smile as he gathered up his lariat. The cayuse she'd chosen could be as ornery as hell, and he had a nasty habit of bogging his head and bucking the minute you straddled him.

She opened the gate and came with him into the pasture. He showed off a bit himself, sidearming his loop and laying it neatly onto the pinto's neck without disturbing a hair. He led the cayuse up to her and then sat back and watched while she tried to make friends.

The pinto, living up to his contrary nature, made a liar out of him by behaving sweet as a sugar-tit, nuzzling her with his muzzle while she stroked his neck. She was making a sort of purring noise deep in her throat that was as erotic as hell, and cooing on about what a pretty boy he was and how they were going to fly like the wind.

She looked up at Rafferty with a smile so honest and real that he had to turn away from it. "Oh, I like him! Does he have a name?"

He had several names—jughead, broomtail, and

buzzard bait being the polite ones. "Why don't you name him?" he said. "Since you picked him out and all."

Her face brightened even more, as if someone had just lit up all the candles in the world. "Very well. His name shall be Gayfeather, after the prairie flower."

Rafferty made a snorting noise. "If I was a horse and someone stuck me with a name like that, I'd go looking for a cliff to jump off of."

"Lucky you're not a horse, then, or I would name you Prickly Pear." And she laughed, her nose wrinkling, her teeth flashing white behind wet lips.

He stared at her mouth long enough for her to know it, and for her lips to part and her breath to hitch. His gaze locked with hers, and it happened again—that invisible skein of lightning wrapped around them, catching them fast. Stopping the world.

This time he was the one to break it. He slapped the loose end of his lariat against his thigh hard enough to sting. "Come on, Boston, let's saddle him up. I ain't got all day."

She'd brought her tack out with her and had kept it out of the wet by slinging it over the top rail of the pasture fence. Rafferty shook his head now at the sight of it. He wondered where in hell Gus had found her a lady's saddle.

"Jesus Christ and glory," he said. "I seen britches patches bigger than that scrap of leather."

Small as the sidesaddle was, she still struggled with it, dragging the cinch along the ground, and she dropped the bridle twice before she got it on the pinto's bobbing head. Rafferty didn't make any move to help her. It was a good thing, he thought, that the grass was nice and soft. He figured she was going to become real intimate with that grass quick as her dainty little butt came in contact with her dainty little saddle.

He grinned as he watched her try to mount. The pinto had rediscovered his true nature and was now performing little crow-hops while she jumped around on one foot after him, struggling to pull herself up into the moving saddle. Just as he'd predicted to himself, the moment her rump hit leather the horse bucked, and she shot straight up in the air. Her bootheel stuck in the stirrup for an instant, so that she landed flat-faced, her dainty nose plowing a furrow in the pasture. When she stood up, she stepped on her hat.

The pinto snorted, shying backward. The reins started to slide out of her hands and she lunged, slipping and sliding. "Drat it all," she said. It wasn't exactly a shout, but it was awful damn close. "Stand still, you dreadful beast."

"I gotta teach you how to cuss better."

She bared her teeth at him. "Mr. Rafferty, will you kindly take yourself off to hell where you belong."

He matched her nasty little smile with one of his own. "'Pears like that spotted horse of yours likes to have himself a spree when the humor strikes him. You shoulda picked yourself out a nice, gentle hackamore colt like my Moses here. He's a real sugar-eater."

"And come winter he's going to be mine."

He almost laughed aloud. He liked it that she chose to hone the sassy edge of her gilded tongue on him. He had noticed that he was the only one so privileged.

She wasn't giving up on the horse either. But no sooner did she hook her leg around the saddle bow then the pinto pitched, and she was sprawled on the grass again.

He looked down at her and shook his head in mock sadness. "I'm thinkin' Hannah is going to look mighty fine in that brooch of yours. You gonna sit him this time?"

She stood up slowly, wincing a little. She wiped her hands on her skirt and held her head high. "You just stand back and watch me, sir."

The horse started crow-hopping again as soon as she put her foot in the stirrup, but somehow she managed to pull herself into the saddle. She clung to the horn for dear life. Her hat went flying, but she didn't. The pinto gave half a dozen little bucks, then quieted, lowering his head to pull on a clump of nettleleaf. She cast Rafferty a look of triumph.

Her eyes, he thought, were greener than buffalo grass after the first spring rain. Her hair was the pale yellow of a winter sun. His fist clenched on the reins. Over the smell of sweating horses and tobacco and pine-spiced wind, he smelled her.

"Not bad for a greenhorn," he said, his voice grating roughly. He seemed to have ground glass in his throat. "Next time, though, see if you can stick without grabbing for the apple." He leaned over and scooped her hat off the ground. "You give up yet, Boston? Bought yourself a train ticket heading east?"

She took the hat from his hand and wedged it back on her head. "I intend to *stick,* Mr. Rafferty. Any way I have to." A smile flashed across her face, and he ached inside.

Somehow their horses had wound up so close their stirrups rubbed together. So close his mouth was within a breath of hers. Her lips were cracked by the summer sun and wind. He wanted to wet them with his tongue. She was breathing hard, her eyes wide. A silence stretched between them, underscored by the crackling of grasshoppers and the moan of the wind.

He opened his mouth, and the words that came out were rough with the desperation he felt. "Now that you got that flower horse of yours tamed, maybe you'd like to come riding with me."

She lowered her gaze to her hands. They clutched the reins as if the pinto were still in danger of bolting, and not standing still munching quietly on the nettleleaf. "No, Mr. Rafferty, I do not want to go riding with you. I'll never want to go riding with you."

11

ONE MORNING IN LATE June, Clementine took a hickory pole down to the river to catch supper.

She followed the path that wended its way through cottonwoods to the river and the place where the fish lived. Here the water circled gently around big rocks, forming small pools where the big fish lived under the foam. Bluebottles rose off the still surface in small clouds. Cottony tufts drifted like snow from the trees. It was a hot day, the air soggy and limp.

A lone willow grew on a small island in the middle of the river. Its branches wept low, as if bowing to the ground. Its leaves shivered, promising a breeze.

She sat on a beaver-chewed log to take off her boots and stockings. She hiked up her skirts and, grabbing her pole and tackle, waded into the water. She gasped at its iciness and ran, laughing and splashing, to the little island.

The grass was cool and satiny beneath her bare feet, like the silk counterpane on her bed in the house on Louisburg Square. She dropped down beneath the willow's shade. She baited her hook as Gus had shown her and cast it out into the deep water beyond the rocks. The line curved, sure and graceful, flashing like a thread of silver.

She shut her eyes against the glare of sun on water. In the distance, over the softly rushing river, she could hear the pounding of Gus's hammer echoing in the thick air. He was building her the house he had promised.

She sat in stillness, growing drowsy from the heat and the lullaby of the purling water. She could feel each sinew and muscle of her body. Feel the young and vital strength of her limbs and the life's blood pumping through her heart, the air gently filling her lungs. She felt *alive.* She wanted to sing with it, to laugh, and maybe to try to fly, the way the chicken hawks soared and floated across the big blue sky.

She ran her hand over her bodice, from the cameo at her neck to the pinched velvet band at her waist. She could feel her breasts swelling, brushing almost painfully against the thin batiste of her camisole. And a heaviness deep in her belly, a warmth between her legs. She imagined she could feel a baby growing inside her.

She pressed her hand there as memories flickered through her mind like the cards of a stereoscope. Pounding feet, her mother's screams, and servants whispering outside the nursery door. Black crepe draped across windows and mirrors, a cold wind blowing leaves over gravestones. Her father's hand lying heavy on her head as they prayed . . . prayed . . .

Oh, God, how her mother had screamed.

But only the baby had died. Mama had lived, and she had laughed with relief that day when the doctor said she must never try to have another. Laughed and then cried. There were so many questions Clementine had always wanted to ask of her mother, but she never had.

Only two women—respectable, decently married women—lived within a few hours' ride from the Rocking R. Pleading a loneliness that was very real, she had prevailed upon Gus to take her to visit them. With each click of the buckboard's wheels, she had carefully composed the questions she would ask.

Mrs. Weatherby lived in a soddy dug into the side of a thickly wooded hill above a coulee that gushed water from the mountain runoff. Mr. Weatherby was a sheepherder, and the shack smelled of the woolly monsters and of rotting paper. Inside, the walls were covered with old newspapers in a vain effort to keep out the seeping damp. "I read them," Mrs. Weatherby had said. "I read my walls aloud, and that way I can't hear the wind."

Mrs. Weatherby was as plump and pale as a stewed dumpling, and the wind had driven her quite mad. She heard the cries of her two dead children calling for her in the wind. And sometimes the voice of her mother, gone these twenty years. While Clementine tried to speak to her of home, Mrs. Weatherby began to read aloud the wall above her head. An advertisement for stomach bitters.

The sheepherder gave Clementine precious packets of vegetable seeds as they were leaving. Clementine spoke friendly words of good-bye. But she could barely hear them herself over the wailing wind.

The sheepherder's wife was like a white mole hiding alone in her dugout soddy. But Mrs. Graham, the cattleman's wife, was a woman rooted firmly in the Montana dirt, tenacious and strong like a tree. She wore a mountain man's beaverskin hat and chewed tobacco like Nickel Annie. Her skin was weathered as brown as hickory, and five children in stepladder sizes clung to her skirts. She would surely know, Clementine thought, the signs of impending motherhood.

Clementine's hopes grew when Mrs. Graham invited her inside and served sage tea in chipped blue-and-white cups. But no sooner had Clementine introduced the topic of the woman's many children than Mrs. Graham interrupted her in a voice that had a vinegar tang to it.

"Oh, I know your sort, I do. I seen right off the way you looked at my man."

"I beg your pardon?" Clementine said, startled, for she'd barely noticed Mr. Graham, who seemed as nondescript as his cattleman's Stetson and faded brown jeans.

Mrs. Graham set her cup down with a rattle and drew herself up proudly. "My Horace is the handsomest man in these parts, don't think I don't know it. So I'm servin' you notice right here and now: if I ever catch you nearer to him than you oughta be, I'll pluck out your eyes and feed them to the buzzards."

And so Clementine had left the Grahams that afternoon as ignorant as ever about the birthing of babies.

Now, as she watched the fishing cork bob in the current, she thought she must bring herself to speak of it to Gus. It was he who pushed himself inside her at night where someday a baby must come out. Yet, strangely, each time she formed the questions in her mind, it was to his brother she imagined herself speaking, that profane and cruel man. There was nothing of life that man didn't know. It was in his eyes, those hard, cold, brassy eyes. Gus had once claimed to have seen the world, but it was his brother who had seen the guts of it. And she thought that if somehow she could bring herself to ask Zach Rafferty for the truth, he would deliver it without flinching before her innocence. She was a woman grown. Grown enough to lie with a man and breed a baby. Grown enough, surely, to be given the truth.

And so, because she had been thinking of him so intently, she wasn't surprised to turn her head and see him standing on the bank. Watching her.

The sun was hot overhead. It had rained during the night, and now the ground steamed like an Indian sweat lodge. Rafferty rode along the river, his dog trotting at Moses's heels. When he saw his brother's wife sitting on the ait, fishing, he dismounted and picketed his horse to a chokecherry tree.

She turned her head, and their eyes met across the water. She sat unmoving, as if she had been waiting for him.

He saw where she'd taken off her boots and stockings to wade through the water. She'd bought herself a pair of boys' riding boots, made of cowhide, dyed red at the top, and trimmed with brass at the toes. These things intrigued him about her. The way she'd given up her city shoes for practical footwear. And that old hat of Gus's that she wore instead of her fancy bonnets. A hat banded now with the skin of the snake he'd killed, as if she wanted to boast to the world that she could face down a rattler and an ornery cayuse and anything else this country could throw at her.

Yet in most ways she hadn't changed, and he couldn't see her ever changing. She still wore her hair gathered up in a thick knot that looked too heavy for her slender neck to bear. And her lady's clothes, the skirts that brushed across the cabin floor, making intimate sounds, soft as lovers' whispers. Like the wisps of gauzy white stockings that lay beside her boots, she was so fine, so dainty and soft and feminine, she made his chest ache.

He took off his own boots and stockings and, after a moment's thought, his gun belt. He wanted to be with her for a while without fear and tension shimmering in the air between them. He wanted to make her smile and maybe laugh a little, to speak to her man to woman, brother to sister . . . No, it could never be like that between them. Hell, it was ludicrous to think they could even be friends. A man didn't become friends with a woman whose smile, whose laugh, whose very smell left him heavy with want.

"You stay," he said to Atta Boy, who looked up at him with what seemed to be a big happy grin on his face, though Rafferty knew he was only panting in the heat. "Stay," he said again. The hound whined and collapsed onto the bank, burying his nose in his paws.

Rafferty splashed through the water and sat down beside his brother's wife on the grassy ait. But when he went to speak, he could find the thoughts but not the words or the courage to shape them. He caught her gaze for a quick, heavy heartbeat before hers veered away.

"Good morning, Mr. Rafferty," she said.

As welcomes went, it wasn't much. But it was more than he'd ever gotten from her before. She sat with her hands laced around her bent knees. In spite of the heat, her dress was buttoned tightly from throat to waist. But she'd rolled up the sleeves. The skin on the inside of her arm was as pale and delicate as eggshells. For the hundredth time he wondered what Gus had been thinking of to bring her out here. It was like putting a hummingbird into a mud lark's nest.

She wouldn't look at him again. For all her surface stillness there was a restlessness underneath, as if she was undecided about whether to flee or stay.

He leaned over and tugged on her fishing line, feeling it drag through the current. "What're you using for bait?"

"Salt pork."

"You won't catch anything, then. They're feeding on the bluebottles."

Even as he spoke, a black-spotted trout leaped out the water to snatch a fly on the wing. Her gaze focused intently on the ripples left by the jumping fish. He could read her thoughts as if they were written across her forehead in printer's ink. She was thinking she was going to have to twist her hook through the fat, hairy body of a big ol' fly. But he didn't make the mistake of assuming she was too squeamish to see it through. She was game, he had to give her that. One by one she had been confronting her tenderfoot fears, shooting them down like whiskey bottles off a stump.

Except for him. He was one fear she wasn't facing, and he thought he knew better than she the reason why.

"Clementine . . ." It was the first time he'd used her given name. It tasted wild and sweet on his tongue.

Again he sought out her gaze, and this time he was able to hold it. Her lips parted as if she would speak. He lost himself in the deep shifting shadows of her eyes. For a while he must have stopped breathing. He blinked and drew in air, feeling dizzy, as if he had spun around too quickly in one place.

"What did you do before?" she said.

He almost choked on the air rushing back into his lungs. "Before what?"

She slid her clasped hands down her legs and gripped her bare toes, lowering her shoulders and smiling a little. She looked like a young girl. Her feet were very white and slender. "Before here," she said. "Before Montana."

He was absurdly pleased that she cared enough to want to know about him. He could feel his cheeks growing warm. "I mostly trailed beeves, which is to say, I straddled a horse all day in the broiling sun and choking dust, ate son-of-a-bitch stew and vinegar pie every night for supper, and slept alone on the cold ground."

"Hunh." She pushed her lower lip out in a little pout that twisted his guts into knots. "I think you loved every bit of it."

"Hell, no." He shook his head, smiling. He plucked a stem of clover, twirling it between his fingers. "Well, maybe I liked night-riding." He cast a glance up at her. She was looking at him with a wide, still gaze that called to something sweet and sharp in his heart.

"I do remember some nights," he said, "when you'd think that if you had a dollar for every star you saw you'd be a rich man, and the air would taste better than whiskey in your belly. Nights like that, the time would pass by sweet, just ambling along with nothing but the jingle of your spurs for company. Sometimes it would get so quiet you'd swear you could hear your own heartbeat."

And the lonesomeness of it would build up inside you until the tears would come if you didn't shut them off. Times like that a man would feel himself reaching for something, and there'd be an emptiness low in his belly that was partly hunger for a meal that wasn't sowbelly and beans, and partly his body saying he needed a woman, and partly the old ache for a home of his own, a place to belong to.

And for something more, something Zach Rafferty hadn't been able to put a name to. Until now.

He looked up. She was staring at him, her mouth partly open, her eyes deep and dark. He let the wild yearning rise up within him and overflow, and he thought he might be seeing a need in those eyes, but it could only have been that he couldn't bear not to see it.

A pitiful wail disturbed the taut silence.

Her gaze snapped away from his, and a faint blush colored her cheeks. She waved a delicate hand at the bank. "Your poor dog," she said, and Atta Boy threw back his head and howled again like a coyote at a full moon. Her lips trembled on the verge of a smile. "I think he's lonesome."

Rafferty slowly released his caught breath. "You don't want him over here. He's been rolling in cow . . . mess. He stinks to high heaven."

"Whiffler than a dead skunk?" she drawled, in a fair Pogey and Nash imitation. And this time she did smile. It blazed across her face and was gone, too fast.

"Whiffler than a sheepherder's boots," he drawled back, and to his delight she laughed and topped him.

"Whiffler than Nickel Annie's hat."

Atta Boy growled. The brush rustled downriver. Rafferty caught out of the corner of his eye a patch of gray fur moving in the leafy shadows and he went still. You didn't usually see a lone timber wolf away from the pack.

Beside him Clementine stirred a little, but she hadn't seen the wolf. Her gaze flickered to his face, then away again. Her breasts rose as she sighed. "Mr. Rafferty, I—"

He covered her mouth with his hand, his eyes intent on the wolf that was now coming toward them at a rigid loping trot. "Be quiet, Boston."

She twisted her head away. She sucked in a breath, and then she, too, caught sight of the wolf. She tensed, but she didn't scream. Rafferty thought of his gun, hanging on his saddle horn, too far away. The lobo was definitely alone, a renegade cast out of the pack. It moved stiffly as if its limbs were frozen, and its ribs showed skeletally beneath its matted gray hide. Its lips were curled back from its teeth in a growl, though it made no sound. Saliva drooled in foamy globs from its mouth.

"Atta Boy, stay!" Rafferty shouted. But the hound charged down the bank at the wolf. They met in a brief frenzy of gray and pale yellow fur and snapping teeth before Atta Boy yelped in pain and ran off with his tail deep between his legs.

With a strangled snarl the wolf leaped into the river and came at them.

Rafferty thrust her to the ground and threw himself on top of her just as the wolf hit the island with a spray of water. Rafferty flung up one hand as the wolf lunged, his fingers digging into the animal's neck, while he groped for his knife with the other. Bloodstained teeth snapped, barely missing his eyes, spraying foam and strings of saliva and bathing his face with fetid breath. The flesh and fur beneath Rafferty's fist vibrated with the growls that were trapped in the wolf's convulsing throat. At last his free hand closed around the hilt of his bowie. He stabbed the blade deep into the wolf's neck and ripped it open.

Blood gushed, spilling over his hands, splashing onto Clementine's face.

She uttered not a sound, although she thrashed with her arms and legs, heaving against his back and shoulder, which had her trapped. He flung the wolf's body off them and hauled her to her feet. He dragged her into the deep part of the river and pushed her head under the water. She came up sputtering, then began to scrub frantically at her face and hair. "Get it off of me," she said in an eerily controlled voice. "Get it off."

He pushed her under twice more before he was satisfied that the river had washed away the wolf's blood and saliva. Shudders racked her body. Her hair was plastered to her skull. Her mouth fell open, her lips white and trembling. His hands hovered over her face, needing desperately to touch her.

"Clementine . . . Oh, dear Christ, Clementine. Did he bite you?"

She started to shake her head. Her gaze became caught

in his and she grew still. Her eyes were turbulent green seas, deep and dark and forbidden, and he fell into them. His hands clasped the sides of her head and, with a low sound of despair, he brought his mouth down over hers.

His kiss was hard and desperate. He was being too rough and he tried to soften the pressure of his lips, but he wanted her, oh, God, but he wanted her.

One of her hands clenched in his hair, the other gripped his waist. Her lips moved beneath his, hungry and seeking. They opened, inviting his tongue. He drank of her, growing dizzy from her woman's taste and smell. He crushed her against him, pressed the length of his body to hers, felt her quiver, swallowed her moans, and somewhere, somehow found the will to stop.

He tore his mouth from hers and thrust her away from him. He gasped for air, his heart and lungs straining.

She brought a trembling fist up to her swollen lips and turned her face away, as if everything inside her would shatter if she had to look at him. She pushed her knuckles hard against her mouth. He wanted to lay her down and undress her slowly, and kiss and touch every inch of her. He wanted to spread her legs wide and bury his face between them and lick and suck her there until she came with soft cries and small tremblings and deep yearnings.

His hand came up to touch her, because he could no longer bear another moment of not touching her. "Clementine—"

Her palm swung up and around, striking his cheek with such force that his head snapped to the side. She pulled back her hand to hit him again, but he grabbed her arm.

The slap kept echoing until it faded into the sounds of the river. They stared at each other, breathing hard. The fire surged and crackled between them again, raw and violent.

"Don't touch me!" she cried. She tried to pull away, and that was when he saw the smear of fresh blood, the gaping cut on the white inside of her arm. Terror whip-sawed through him with such force that he swayed.

"I thought you said he didn't bite you!" he shouted, his voice guttural with fear and unleashed hunger. "Dammit, woman, did he bite you?"

"I don't know, I don't know! Why?" She shuddered and backed away, pulling against his grasp on her arm. "Oh, *God,* I hate you."

He let her go and then gripped her face hard between his two hands. "Clementine, look at me, listen to me. That lobo had rabies."

Her head moved, shaking a denial. Horror filled her eyes. "Oh, God," she whispered, "what am I going to do?" And he knew the question, and her terror, had nothing to do with a rabid wolf.

He swung her up into his arms. She stiffened and pushed against him, but he pressed her head into the curve of his neck and spoke to her softly. "Lie still, lie still. I'm only taking you back to the cabin."

She went quiet as he waded across the river and climbed the bank.

Gus had just begun to nail the siding onto the framework of the new house. When he saw them emerge from the cottonwoods, he threw down his hammer. He cut across the furrows of the freshly mown hay meadow in an awkward, staggering run.

"Clementine!" Gus stumbled to a halt before them, his chest heaving. He saw the blood on her arm, and his face went stark white. "Jesus, Jesus, Zach, what's—"

"A rabid wolf attacked us down at the river," Rafferty said. He pushed past Gus, unable to look into his brother's face, to meet his brother's eyes when he could still taste his brother's wife on his lips.

He carried Clementine into the cabin and laid her on the coffee-case couch. Gus halted in the doorway. "You sure it bit her?"

"No, dammit, I ain't sure." The way he'd been

plunging her in and out of the water . . . The cut was ragged and deep. It could easily have been made by a submerged stick or a rock. Or teeth.

He reached for his knife and realized it was still in the wolf's neck. He swung around to Gus. "You got a toad-sticker on you? Give it here."

But he had to cross the room to take the knife out of the sheath at Gus's waist. Already a glazed look had come over his brother's eyes. Gus was running away inside his head as he'd done so often when they were kids.

"That wolf couldn't have been rabid, Zach. You said he attacked y'all down by the river. Rabid animals are scared of water."

"This one wasn't. He ran right through it to get at us."

"I'm going to ride to Deer Lodge for the doctor. Just in case." But he stood unmoving in the doorway, his hands hanging helpless at his sides. "I mean, he probably wasn't rabid anyway, 'cause rabid animals are scared of water. And you said yourself you don't even know whether he got to her."

Rafferty set the back of his teeth. He didn't say what he wanted to, which was that there wasn't a damn thing any doctor could do, whether the wolf had gotten to her or not. He used a poke to open the door to the round iron stove and squatted on his haunches before it. He dumped wood into its belly, then thrust the blade of Gus's knife into the freshly fed flames.

One day to Deer Lodge, one day back . . . And that sawbones over there was next to useless anyway. He spent most of his hours dead drunk in a whore's bed. It would take a whole day just to sober him up enough to fork a horse.

"There's an Indian cure I heard of," Rafferty said into a room so quiet he could hear Gus's harsh breathing. "They burn out the infected wound with a red-hot iron."

He looked over his shoulder. Clementine sat in stillness on the couch. She might have just been resting there, out of the heat of the day, except for the faint line between her brows and a tautness in her jaw. Gus still hovered at the door. He rocked from one foot to the other.

"Gus," Rafferty said, "you're gonna have to—"

"No!" Gus backed up, shaking his head. "No. No, I couldn't . . ."

"She's your woman, brother."

A retching sound tore out of Gus's throat. He whirled and stumbled outside.

Clementine's wide-eyed gaze, deep and still, fastened onto Rafferty. "You must do it for him," she said.

He swiveled around and thrust the knife deeper into the fire. His hand shook. A moment passed. The sound of a hammer pounding hard smacked through the heavy air. Then all was quiet except for the hiss and crackle of the burning wood.

"Do not tell me, Mr. Rafferty, that it won't hurt unbearably, that it will only singe off the hair and a bit of hide."

He shook his head, unable to force any words past the tightness in his throat. He put a tin cup brimming with whiskey into her hand.

"I don't know as how I dare to allow the devil's brew to touch my genu-ine, starched-up lady's lips," she said, staring up at him with eyes that were too wide and too bright.

"Drink it, dammit!" He drew in a ragged breath. "God, I'm sorry."

He laid his hand on the side of her face and tilted her head back. "I'm going to take a knife, Boston, a knife that will be hot enough to burn through leather, and I'm going to push it deep into that cut in your arm and hold it there while I count to ten and then count to ten again, and it's going to hurt much worse than any branding. Much worse than anything you could possibly imagine."

Her lips trembled, and her throat jerked as she

swallowed. "There are times, like now, when I think I must truly hate you. But you've always been unfailingly honest with me. Don't ever stop."

He allowed his fingers to trail down her bare neck. He didn't know the smile he gave her was full of pain and tenderness. "Drink up. And then I'm going to make you hate me even more, because I'll be tying down your arm before I burn it."

She swallowed again, hard. "Oh. Yes, of course."

When he took the knife from the fire, it was white and glowing. She watched him with eyes that were dark and heavy-lidded with whiskey and fear. And then he did just what he'd told her he would do. He pressed the searing hot knife deep into the wound and held it there while her flesh hissed and burned and her arm jerked against the bindings, and he waited for her to scream, waited for it with a scream choking his own throat, and yet no sound came from her at all except for the breath sucking harshly in and out of her nostrils. It wasn't until he was untying her arm that she fainted, and by then he was shaking so hard himself he could barely manage to undo the knots.

It took him a long time to bandage the wound, because he was still shaking, and because he kept stopping to look at her pale, still face. When he was done, he lifted her into his arms and carried her into the bedroom. He laid her on his brother's bed.

He brushed away the drying wisps of hair that had caught in her pale lashes. Then he stepped back and back until he was up against the wall.

The air hurt his skin. He could feel each separate stroke of his heart. He looked at her. At her hair spilling across the pillow like tangled sunbeams. The gentle curve of her cheek. The soft, full lips parted slightly in sleep. The white slope of her brow. Each part of her brought him pleasure.

Somewhere between the time at the river when he had touched her face and kissed her mouth and now, standing with his back flattened against the wall unable, afraid, to breathe . . . somewhere deep inside him something had been shattered beyond repair.

And outside, the sound of his brother's hammer, pounding, pounding, pounding.

The blue of early evening had settled over the room by the time she awoke. Her eyes, luminous in the half-light, rested on him a moment, then moved to the window. Her lips formed a word, breathing it more than speaking it aloud. It sounded like "lightning."

She lay still for so long he thought she'd dozed off again. He could still hear his brother's hammer, though it had surely grown too dark to see a nail. He told himself that he could leave her now, but he stayed. A rising moon cast light through the window, glossing her face with silver. He felt something inside him tear, and it bled and hurt. Oh God, it hurt. After an eternity she turned her head and speared him with her gaze. "Come here, Mr. Rafferty."

His legs nearly buckled beneath him as he crossed the room. He leaned over her, and she reached up and grabbed his shirt, pulling him closer. For a wild moment he thought she was going to kiss him, and he was convinced his heart had stopped. When it started up again it beat in unsteady lurches.

But she only wanted to see into his eyes. "How long does it take to die of the rabies, once you've gotten it?"

He let his fingers hover over her cheek, desperate to touch her. Forbidden to touch her. He breathed in her name on a stab of anguish. "Clementine . . ."

Her grip on his shirt tightened. "How long?"

"I don't know. Days . . . a week, maybe." Too long.

"If I go mad like the wolf," she said, "you must shoot me."

He drew in a breath that clutched at his chest. "Christ Jesus."

She shook her head, hard. "I don't want to die raving

and foaming at the mouth. Rafferty, please . . . Shoot me cleanly. Like you did the snake."

He could do that, he thought. For someone he loved.

The old biscuit-colored hound never came home.

Every day for over three weeks Rafferty rode out to look for him, in between the constant chores at the ranch. He always took his Winchester with him.

And Clementine knew the day he found him. When she spotted Rafferty from her bedroom window, riding into the yard in the middle of the afternoon. It was the way he sat his horse, stiffly and drawn deep inside himself.

He dismounted and the little orphaned calf came trotting up to him, but he shooed it away. Gus talked all the time now about how that dogie was going to be shipped off for slaughter next fall. It was some kind of test that Gus had set up for his brother. A dare. Like finding Atta Boy had been a test Rafferty had set up for himself.

He disappeared inside the barn. She didn't want to go to him.

Unlike Gus, he never tried to spare her or coddle her. He'd told her straight out it could be weeks before she would know if she had the canine madness. In the beginning she'd thought about it all the time, and her terror was like a moth trapped in her throat, fluttering there. But the sun rose and set and the days went on, and there was the washing and the cooking and the cleaning to get done and one couldn't live on the knifepoint of fear every moment.

And that kiss . . . She couldn't bear to think of it, of what he had made her feel. She didn't want to feel such things for her husband's brother. She was as much afraid of that kiss, of him, as she was of dying.

She didn't want to go to him, yet she found herself watching her feet as they crossed the yard, heading for the barn. It was a rainstormy day, the clouds dense and dark and heavy. And the wind . . . it roared through the valley, making the cottonwoods groan and give. It whipped foamy spray off the river. And it whipped up such terrible frenzied achings within her that she was sure the wolf's madness coursed through her blood.

Weak light seeped through the open doors of the barn. A swallow fluttered past her cheek and disappeared into its nest up in the dark rafters. Inside, the air was damp and cool. Straw rustled, a horse nickered softly. She had never ventured as far back as the stall where Rafferty slept when he stayed at the ranch. When he wasn't with the woman of the violet dress and red-tasseled shoes.

At the moment, he was outside the entrance to the smithy. He had his gray gelding's forehoof up on his thigh and was scraping caked mud and dung out of it with a hoof-pick. She remembered the day she'd seen him for the first time. He'd been half naked and covered with the orphaned calf's birth blood, and he had hunkered down on his heels in the yard and scratched his dog behind the ears and laughed like a young boy. And she had hated him that day. More than she had hated the mud and the sod-roofed shack and the hot, restless wind, she had hated him. She felt sorry for him now, and she thought with some satisfaction that he wouldn't like it even a little bit—her feeling sorry for him.

She looked down at his bent back. At the play of muscle beneath the thin chambray shirt. At the way his hair folded over his collar in soft dark curls. At the way he . . . was.

"You found him," she said.

He was quiet for so long she didn't think he would answer. Then he straightened up and faced her. There wasn't any pain or sorrow in his eyes. There was nothing. They were flat and cold and hard. If he felt anything at all, it was buried so deep no one was ever going to find it.

"He'd gotten to be pretty much of a useless old dog anyway," he said, his voice flat and cold and hard as well. "Blind as a snubbin' post. I shoulda put him down a long time ago."

"Did you shoot him clean, like the snake?"

His shoulders lifted in a careless shrug, but she thought his mouth tightened just a little bit. "I owed him that much."

She drew in a deep breath of air that was sour-sweet with the smell of hay and dung and sweaty horse. She nodded once, then turned on her heel and left him.

If he'd done it for Atta Boy, he would do it for her.

Gus behaved as if that day at the river had never been.

He talked to her constantly about the house: "I'm giving it two bedrooms, Clem, for when the babies start to come. And we can always keep adding on rooms—if we have a baker's dozen."

And about the ranch: "I don't care what Zach says. We're never going to amount to more than a cocklebur outfit here if we don't mix some grade blood with our herd. I've sent back to Chicago for some breeding catalogs."

And only once, obliquely, about the terrible dangers that lurked in the wilderness that was Montana: "I can't be with you every minute of the day, girl. So I'm going to teach you how to use the Colt, and I want you to take it with you from now on every time you leave the cabin."

As if by speaking enough about the future he could ensure that there would be one.

But on the day his brother found Atta Boy, the dreamshine left Gus's face. He watched her go about her wifely duties that afternoon, the cooking of supper and the cleaning up afterward, as if he expected her to start convulsing and foaming at the mouth at any moment. That night, with rain thudding like galloping hooves on the sod roof, and the noise and flash of thunder and lightning, she awoke to find him leaning over her, intently searching her face. He wasn't ruthless with himself, like his brother. He allowed himself to feel, and when he did, he wasn't always able to keep it from showing.

She wrapped her arm around his neck, pulled his head down to hers, and kissed him hard on the mouth.

She could feel a fine trembling going on deep inside him. He touched his mouth where, a moment before, her lips had been.

"What'd you do that for?"

"Why were you awake and staring at me in the middle of the night?"

"Why'd you kiss me like that for?"

"I guess I must have gotten the rabies and gone crazy. Now you got it, so we can both go crazy together."

"Stop it, Clementine."

She pressed her hand against his cheek. "My husband. I love you." *I have to love you. I am going to make myself love you.*

He lowered his head, pressing his face into her neck. His words were muffled by her hair. "I've been waiting forever to hear you say that, and now you have, and all I can think of is that you might die."

"I'm not going to die." She said it with conviction because she thought it to be so. Death was a stranger to her, and so she could not really believe in it.

Her hands moved over his broad shoulders and down his strong back. She wrapped her arms around his waist and held him tightly against her. Held him fiercely. "Tell me how it's going to be, Gus. Tell me how we're going to make the ranch into the best spread in all of western Montana. Tell me about the house you're building and how happy we'll be in it, you and I and all the babies we are going to have. Tell it all to me again."

She held her breath, waiting for him to speak. But all she heard was the wind and the drumming of the rain on the roof. And the drips where the sod leaked. Then she felt his chest move as he breathed, and she heard him building dreams out of words. And as she listened, she held him close to her heart, as if she could fill up the loneliness by an act of will.

"Tell me that one story, Gus. Where you are riding

through a snowstorm and there's a warm fire waiting for you at home and stew bubbling on the stove and—"

"A wife with hair the color of a wheat field in August and eyes like a pine forest at dusk."

"Yes . . ." The trouble with dreams, she thought, was that sometimes they came true.

Lightning flashed and he raised his head. She looked up at him through a blur of memory, seeing him as she had four months ago, when she was someone else. His was a good face, with strong bones and a wide mouth framed by a mustache that was not so thick and long that it could hide his smile. And his eyes, those laughing eyes, were as blue and open as the Montana sky.

The cowboy of her dreams.

She could love him; she would make it so. And she would never allow herself to think again about that day at the river.

12

CLEMENTINE TILTED HER HEAD back and looked up at the shanty's sod roof. A bed of sweet pink phlox had taken root there and burst into bloom overnight. A roof of flowers. The thought was so beautiful it made her smile.

Last night's storm had blown away, and the sun shone its heart out in a sky too blue to be real. It would have been a perfect day, but for the wind.

Clementine had taken a bucket down to the south meadow to gather the wild strawberries that grew there, before they could all be eaten by the jays and the flickers.

Red juice stained her fingers, lips, and tongue. The berries had tasted as sweet as the sod-roof flowers smelled. But it was too much sweetness too early in the morning, for they had left her stomach feeling queasy.

She heard a murmur of voices now coming from inside the cabin, and she paused at the door. Gus and his brother were usually out chasing cows this time of day, trying to keep the cattle from straying off the range and Iron Nose from straying onto it.

"You sure he had it, Zach? You didn't just shoot him because—"

"He had it."

Gus let out a long, shaky breath. "Well, then, don't you reckon she'd be showing signs of it by now, too?"

"Hell, brother, how're you ever gonna know? She's always acted crazier than popping corn on a hot skillet."

She stepped across the threshold with a deliberately heavy tread. They sat at the table, nursing steaming cups of coffee. The smell of the strong brew battled with the sweet scent of the phlox coming through the open door. Gus's head snapped up as she entered. He studied her intently, as though looking for signs of impending madness.

When she walked past Rafferty she caught the glint of laughter in his eyes, and she knew he'd sensed her all along, hovering outside the door, listening . . . *She's always acted crazier than popping corn on a hot skillet.* Hunh. She became flustered when he teased her. Gus rarely teased her, and her father certainly hadn't ever done so. It was a strangely intimate thing, this teasing. She wasn't sure she liked it.

She could feel the men's eyes on her as she set the bucket of berries in the sink. She spun around, hands planted on her hips. "What are you looking at?"

"Nothing," Gus mumbled down into his coffee. He blew on it, took a sip.

"You got berry juice all over your mouth, Boston," Rafferty said. His eyes weren't laughing at her anymore.

A gust of wind blasted the cabin. Clementine turned back to the sink just as a big piece of sod, soaked by last night's rain and shaken loose by the wind, fell with a sodden splat into her bucket of fresh-picked berries.

"Oh, *drat* this wretched roof!" she exclaimed. Wild laughter tickled her throat and she bit her lip. The tame curse, spoken in her fine diction, had sounded silly even to her own ears.

She whirled and caught them staring at her again, although they both quickly averted their faces.

She seized the bucket and advanced on them, growling and baring her teeth like Aunt Etta's snappish little terrier. When she got close enough she lifted the bucket high in the air and dumped muddy sod and mashed strawberries on top of her husband's head.

There was a stunned silence, and then the mud and berries began to slide off Gus's head and shoulders and onto the table. He stared up at her, his eyes wide, and he couldn't have looked more shocked if she had truly turned into a rabid beast like the wolf.

A great whoop of laughter built and built in her chest. She pressed her lips together and clutched at her waist and collapsed bent over onto the coffee-case couch. But she couldn't stop it. It burst out of her, a great loud sound of joy and wonder.

She laughed and laughed. She rocked back and forth, her feet coming off the floor and kicking at the air. Her hair came loose and her face turned red and her laughter filled the cabin.

She lay back limp against the old soogan padding. Her eyes brimmed with tears as she stared at her husband, at the mud and fruit that decorated his hair. She clapped a hand over her mouth.

Gus picked a muddy strawberry off his forehead. "Well, hell. That wasn't funny, girl."

Laughter burst out of her nose in a most unladylike snort.

Rafferty cleared his throat; he looked around the cabin and then at her, his expression wary. Gus half straightened off the nail-keg stool. "Clementine, girl, are you . . ."

Snorting and gurgling, laughing out loud, she jumped up and ran out the door.

She ran as if she were being chased by heel flies. She had never run like this before, never picked up her skirts and run all out, stretching her legs, straining her lungs. Running, running, running, with the wind blowing in her hair, pressing against her ears, legs pumping high, until she thought that maybe she wasn't touching the ground at all but flying above it.

She ran until she reached her favorite spot on the ranch, the meadow where the buffalo grass grew as high as her knees now and the willows bent thick and heavy over the river. She threw herself down into the grass, letting the laughter come. It was as if she had waited her whole life for a reason to laugh and, once started, she couldn't stop.

She squinted against the dense sunlight. The grass seemed to tremble with the light and the wind. Strange feelings stirred deep within her belly. She pressed a hand to her stomach. Perhaps she would tell Gus that they might be going to have a baby. Now that she wasn't going to go mad.

She rolled over, burying her face in the grass, digging her fingers deep into the root-woven earth. She felt like the grass, rooted to the red Montana earth, but not so deep that she couldn't be ripped free if she wasn't careful. She pulled loose a great clump of the grass, as if to show herself how easily it could be done. She tossed it away and pressed her face into the exposed dirt. She smelled its ripeness, felt its coolness. This dirt that was Montana.

She hated this place. It was too big, this country, too raw and wild. There were times when she thought she would be crushed by it. And other times . . . Times when she looked out over the prairie and saw herself astride a wild cayuse, chasing her shadow over the empty miles of grass, riding and riding until she fell off the end of the world. Times when she looked at the big Montana sky and saw herself flying like an eagle, spreading her wings against the vast and empty blue and soaring on the tail of the wind. Flying high, high enough to touch the sun.

A hot-blooded woman just waitin' for an excuse to bust out.

She dug her fingers into the damp earth. She didn't want to bust out. She wanted to be safe, to belong. To have roots. She wanted to have babies, and she wanted Gus to love her, and to live a decent, moral life.

She wanted to find peace in her heart.

She smoothed her hands out, pressing them against the Montana dirt. She hated this place, and she feared it. And she loved it fiercely.

She laid her cheek on the cool earth and slept. When she awoke, the wind had died and the sun burned noon-bright and hot. She sat up, stretching, feeling languid and sore, and yet humming with an odd excitement. She had dumped a bucket of mud and berries on top of her husband's head, and laughed, and run, and slept away a morning—all wicked, irresponsible things. She knew she ought to feel guilty, but instead there was only a strange sense of wonder and repleteness that she sometimes felt after Gus made love to her.

She walked slowly back along the path she had pelted down hours before. She could almost hear the larch needles falling to earth. The sun melted and flowed over her like hot butter. As she climbed the snake fence, she saw a plum-colored shay parked in the yard and a woman speaking to Gus, a woman wearing a dress the same bright ruby red as the wild strawberries. A woman with hair like antique copper, as tarnished as her virtue.

Clementine watched them a moment through the shimmering heat ripples. She could tell by the stiff set of Gus's shoulders and the way his hands were jammed onto his hipbones that he was angry.

Gus cut off a furious spate of words as she came up to them. Hannah Yorke's gaze met hers. Two bright spots of color enhanced her rouged cheeks.

"Clementine," Gus said, "get on in the house—"

"Mrs. McQueen, wait." The woman took a step forward. She placed a hand on Clementine's arm, then dropped it immediately when Clementine stiffened. "One of the women who works for me . . . her little girl died of the measles yesterday. She won't let us bury her. I thought if you could take little Patsy's likeness for her to have as a keepsake it might ease things for her, help her to let the child go. I know it's a terrible imposition and a . . ." She looked at Gus, and bitterness pulled at her mouth. "Saphronie might be only a whore, as you say, but she loved her little girl same as any woman would."

"But of course I will come," Clementine said. She had never photographed a dead child, but she'd heard of it being done. It had been the fashion ten years ago to mount tintypes on gravestones. "It will take me only a moment to get my equipment."

But as she turned, Gus blocked her path. His face was set harder than she'd ever seen it before. "If you think I'm going to let you ride into Rainbow Springs and right up to that house of sin, sitting alongside the town harlot—"

"Gus, you can't mean to be so cruel. A woman has lost a child, her *baby*. If I can do something to help her through her grief—"

He gripped her arm, his fingers pressing through the heavy brown serge of her sleeve. "I forbid you to do this, girl."

She flung up her head and met his angry eyes. "You are hurting me."

He let her go, but that was all. "You are not going to—"

"But I am," she said. "I am going to ride into Rainbow Springs beside Mrs. Yorke. I shall go into her house and photograph that poor dead child, and you will not try to stop me."

They rode in silence all the way to Rainbow Springs, Clementine and the woman of the red-tasseled shoes. Clementine had seen those shoes when Hannah Yorke lifted her skirts high to climb into the shay. Had seen them as she braced her feet wide apart like a man, to drive the buggy over a road as rutted as a washboard. They were a harlot's shoes, yet she could not stop looking at them.

Mrs. Yorke pulled the shay up to the front gate of her house, which was by far the nicest in all the RainDance country, with its spool-railed gallery and fanciful gingerbread. She helped Clementine unload her equipment, all in silence except for a simple admonition to mind the steps.

Clementine paused on the gallery to savor the loveliness of the house. The wicker rocker with its blue-flowered cushion. The fanlight over the door, leaded with blue, red, yellow, and green glass that cast rainbows onto the painted white wood. The front windows lined with delicate lace curtains and decorated with pressed ferns on the panes. Clementine's gaze met Hannah Yorke's for a brief moment, and then she followed those red-tasseled shoes into the house of sin.

The air inside was cool and thick with the scent of lily of the valley perfume. She got a glimpse of the parlor through a green glass beaded curtain: thick wine-colored velvet drapes under tasseled valances, a medallion-backed sofa upholstered in gold brocade, a tree of life carpet. She followed Mrs. Yorke upstairs and down a hall papered in red flock and lit by a pair of fringe-shaded oil lamps. Murmurs of memories stirred within her, of other houses, of another life. Of the amenities and luxuries that she had fled from without understanding all that she would be giving up.

She passed by rooms with closed doors with shiny glass knobs. It was a large house, much too large for one person to live in alone. But then, Mrs. Yorke didn't always live in it alone. She tried to picture Gus's wild brother in this house. Rafferty, who had always seemed much too uncivilized even for the confines of a rough sod-roofed cabin.

An image flashed across her mind and was gone, like

movement caught out the corner of one's eye, of that man and this woman of the red-tasseled shoes lying naked on a bed. A heat pulsated through her, and she felt the strangest awareness of her own body. Of the flesh of her thighs rubbing together as she walked down the hall. Of her nipples, like smooth, hard pebbles beneath all her proper layers of clothes. Of a rippling deep in her belly, like a lake suddenly stirred by a gust of wind.

"She's in here," Mrs. Yorke said, and Clementine started. She blushed, sure that her sinful thoughts were as plain as the face on the moon to such a woman. A woman so worldly, so sinful herself.

They entered a small bedroom that smelled of camphor and hartshorn and, underneath, the sick-sweet stench of decay.

The dead child lay in a plain iron bed beneath a colorful flower-basket petit point quilt. Her small golden head barely made a dent in the lace-slipped pillow. The room was quiet except for the tick of a long case clock and the sibilant whisper of a horsehair rocking chair, its curved slats rolling back and forth, back and forth, on the bare pine floor.

Mrs. Yorke knelt before the woman in the rocker and patted her knee awkwardly. The woman had her face buried in her hands. "Saphronie. I've brought Mrs. McQueen, who has kindly agreed to make little Patsy's photograph."

The woman made a strangled, mewling sound into her hands. An immense clot of pity clogged Clementine's throat. She turned away, toward the dead child in the bed.

Sunlight poured through the sheer lace curtains at the window, reflecting off the cranberry glass lamp that sat on a petticoat table beside the bed. The light gave the child's cheeks a glow of life. She was such a pretty little girl, it didn't seem possible . . .

A dizziness assailed Clementine, and a nausea, similar to what she'd felt after eating the strawberries. She hadn't known, hadn't understood what it would be like. She had felt sad for the woman and her loss, but only in

the abstract, as one stranger thinks of another. Now she felt
the woman's pain keenly. How can she bear it? Clementine
wondered. How can any woman bear it?

She drew in a deep breath through her mouth as she
studied the room. With the curtains pulled aside, enough
light would come in the two large windows so that she
wouldn't need to burn a magnesium wire, which produced
a flat, harsh image. For this she wanted a gentle, soft effect.
She didn't want the child to look dead in the photograph,
but alive and sleeping.

A wavering voice began to sing a lullaby, scraping like
a rusty chain.

Clementine turned and nearly gasped aloud in shock.
The woman had dropped her hands and lifted her head, and
her face . . . her face was horribly disfigured by tattoos, like
dark blue teardrops, that ran from her mouth down over
her chin.

The woman rocked and sang and wept. Hannah Yorke
straightened and stepped forward. "Will you need help?"
She gestured toward the cases at Clementine's feet.

Clementine blinked and swallowed hard. "No, no,
thank you, I can manage." Oh, God, she thought. Her face.
Her poor face.

She had to force herself not to stare at the woman,
not to be so unpardonably rude. "I will do a tintype for
her to mount on the grave marker," Clementine said to
Mrs. Yorke, as she went about setting up her camera and
portable dark tent. The woman rocked and sang, rocked
and sang. "And a paper print for her to keep with her always . . . Oh, whyever has she done that to her face?"

"It was done to her. Indians."

Clementine's head snapped up in renewed shock.

"Comanches stole her off a wagon train when she was
just a kid. They sold her to the Mohave, who like to tattoo
their girls on the chin and arms by piercing the skin with
sharpened bones and rubbing dye into the wounds. They
think of them as marks of beauty, I guess." She cocked her

head, studying Clementine's upturned face as if undecided whether to say more. While the woman still sang and rocked, lost in a terrible grief, Hannah pitched her smoky voice low. "Before they sold her, the Comanches did what they call 'passing her over the prairie.' I reckon even a lady like you can guess what that means."

Clementine nodded. Oh, yes, she could imagine.

"One of the Mohave braves eventually took her as his squaw. When our soldiers rescued her, they killed him and they killed the baby she'd had by him. Trouble is, by then she loved her man, even if he was an Indian, and her baby, too, of course. And after all that, her family wouldn't have her back. Not when they got a look at her face and heard what had been done to her."

"But that was hardly her fault," Clementine protested, her throat tight. Unable to help herself, she stared at the woman, at her ravaged face. Ravaged by torture and grief. They had killed her baby and now she'd lost her little girl. It wasn't right that one woman should have to suffer such misery.

"Finding fault doesn't change what is," Mrs. Yorke said quietly. "Any girl who lies with a savage, willing or not, is going to come away from it branded a whore. There ain't no man going to marry her, and no one's going to hire her to sell hats or wait on restaurant tables. You look at her and tell me how you're going to change what is."

But Clementine no longer looked at the singing, rocking woman with her ruined face and ruined life. She looked at Hannah Yorke.

Color flooded Hannah's lightly painted cheeks, and she shook her head hard. She raised a finger to Clementine's nose as if to scold her. "Oh, no, you don't. Don't you go putting feelings to me that I don't have. I ain't nobody's savior. Saphronie does the swamp work no one else'll do, and I get one dollar out of three for every trip she makes to my back room. 'Cause whatever Saphronie was on the

day she left that Indian camp, she's a whore now, plain
and simple. So I reckon you know damn well what that
makes me."

"I know what you are, Mrs. Yorke," Clementine said.

She held Hannah's angry gaze a moment longer, then
lowered her head and began to peel off her soft ecru kid
gloves. A lady's gloves that hid the scars made by her
father's cane. He had beaten her for looking at souvenir
cards. He would certainly think her beyond all redemption
now if he found her in a house of sin, speaking to a fallen
woman about such things as back rooms, which she wasn't
even supposed to know existed.

Her mother had warned her about all the ways a girl
could tarnish her virtue: speak to a boy who was a stranger
to her family, return his smile, return his kiss . . . The loss
of a girl's virtue was like a tar pit. If she dipped one little
toe in the black gooey mess she would be stuck fast forever.
Ruined forever.

And so Clementine had always believed that women
fell into harlotry because of a wickedness in them that
made them enjoy the carnal attentions of men. *"Grant not,
O Lord, the desires of the wicked."* But Saphronie with her poor
tattooed face wasn't a sinner; she had been sinned against.
And what about Hannah Yorke of the red-tasseled shoes?
What tar pit had pulled her down to a place where she
rented out her back room for the easement of men's lust?

Clementine looked at the two women—Saphronie
with her ruined face buried in her hands, Hannah kneeling
by the rocker, stroking the other woman's back—and she
felt something within her break away and die. Some of her
youth and innocence.

Her hands curled into fists, her fingers pressing hard
against the scars. She felt outrage at the tragedy she had
found in this room. Rage at men like her father who made
it possible. Oh, she could just imagine the Reverend Theodore Kennicutt standing high in his pulpit, pointing his

righteous finger at Saphronie and calling her a harlot for lying with a savage, condemning her to a life of swamping out saloons and selling her body to strangers. And rage at men like Mr. Rafferty who took their pleasure from women in houses like this one, without sparing a thought for the souls and hearts within the soft feminine flesh they craved.

And she felt a rage at virtuous women like herself, who condemned their own kind for the things that were done to them by men.

"Are you sure you aren't gonna need some help?"

Clementine looked down into Hannah Yorke's face. She saw a wariness there, and the stamp of a sleepless, grieving night. And she saw another woman grown. A woman who had loved probably, and lost certainly. A woman who had broken the Lord's commandments and the laws of men and now must forever pay for her transgressions. A woman who was ashamed of what she was and proud of what she had become. A woman just like any other woman born of woman. A woman like her.

Saphronie had stopped singing. Once again the only sounds in the room were the tick of the clock and the creak of the rocker.

It wasn't until she was outside on the gallery, preparing to expose the print, that she and Mrs. Yorke spoke again.

She had already sensitized the albumen paper and was now fitting it onto the negative plate in the printing rack, which she had set up on the unshaded end of the porch. "It shouldn't take more than half an hour of this bright sunshine before we have a print," she said. She was kneeling before the rack and had to tilt her head way back to meet Hannah's eyes. She produced a shy smile. "I guess you must find it hard to believe, but I really do know what I'm doing."

Hannah's answering smile was hard and brittle. "Oh,

I don't doubt you know what you're doing, honey. You might be an innocent, but you ain't nobody's fool. What I'm wondering is why such a genteel lady as you, such a *smart* little lady, would defy her husband and risk ruining her reputation simply to ease the grieving of a worthless whore."

"You asked me to come."

"You could've spat in my face. You *should* have spat in my face. Your Gus did, in a manner of speaking."

Clementine glanced up at the window, where ragged snatches of lullaby spoke of a heartbreak too terrible to bear. "That poor woman up there—she isn't only a . . ." But she couldn't bring herself to speak the vulgar word aloud, even though Hannah Yorke had been tossing it about all afternoon like rice at a wedding. She looked down at the printing rack. She felt the heat of blood rushing to her face. "She is also a mother. No matter in what ways you both have sinned, you are *women*. Like me." No, that had not come out at all right. It made her sound self-righteous, to talk of sinning like that. She looked up to explain herself and saw to her dismay that Hannah Yorke's eyes were awash with tears.

Clementine stumbled to feet. "Mrs. Yorke, please, I didn't mean—"

Hannah backed away, shaking her head so hard the tears splashed onto her cheeks. "Oh, my," she said. She pressed her fist to her mouth and, whirling, crossed the porch so fast her heels rapped like castanets on the wooden boards. But at the door she stopped and her spine stiffened. Turning, she said, "Will you come back into the house when you're done out here? I could serve you some refreshment while that thing . . ." She gestured helplessly at the printing rack.

Clementine thought of tar pits and the scars on her palms, prices women paid for defying convention, for disobeying the laws of God and of men, who were allowed to make up all the rules. She lifted her chin. "I would love something cool to drink, Mrs. Yorke."

Hannah sliced up two pieces of dried-apple pie. Not that she'd be able to choke down a single bite, her stomach felt so jittery. And her hands shook as she stirred the lemonade she'd made with citric acid crystals.

She entered her front parlor on legs as shaky as a newborn colt's. The room suddenly seemed ugly to her eyes. Too stuffed with things: plaster busts, cushions, gimcracks, and vases. Back before she'd taken over the house, there'd been lewd paintings in here as well, and a slate board with the menu and price list. *Cost you three dollars if you want it straight, cowboy. Five if you want it done the French way.* Hannah thought she could still smell the stale whiskey, the unwashed cuspidors, and the sweat of men in rut. No matter how much dried sweet grass she burned, the parlor of this former parlor house still stank of old sins.

Clementine McQueen sat perched on the end of the gold brocade sofa, her gaze focused on the giant grizzly bear rug spread out before the nickel parlor stove. But as Hannah entered the room, the girl turned her head and greeted her with an uncertain smile. It was a hot day, and the stiff, tight black collar of her dress butted up under her chin, yet she looked as cool as an ice-cream soda. She was so very Bostony, with her perfect manners and quiet courtesy. She'd been born knowing to leave her hat and gloves on when taking tea and never to leave the spoon in the cup, knowing what hour to pay a social call and how to address an invitation in a fine copperplate script. Hannah Yorke hadn't even owned a pair of shoes until she was twelve, let alone a hat and gloves.

Hannah set the tray of lemonade and pie on an oval mahogany tea table. One of the glasses teetered, and the sharp smell of the citric acid tickled her nose. She pressed a finger against her nostrils to stop a sneeze, and snorted instead. "Pardon me," she mumbled, and handed the lemonade to Clementine, along with a napkin and a tight little smile. "It ain't—isn't the real thing, I'm afraid."

Hannah settled down in a chair opposite her, wishing herself in a deep, deep hole somewhere on the other side of the world.

Clementine opened the napkin and laid it across her lap, rubbing her fingers over its pink-flowered border done with tiny, delicate Irish stitches. "This is very pretty. Did you embroider it yourself?"

"Lord, honey." The words gusted out of her, too loud. "I wouldn't know the sharp end of a needle if I sat on it."

Clementine lifted the lemonade to her lips and took a dainty sip. "Mrs. Yorke . . ."

Hannah leaned over and waved a hand through the air, nearly knocking over her own glass. "You might as well call me Hannah. The Mrs. business is a lie. Oh, I came close to it once, but someone forgot to remind me to keep my drawers buttoned until the ring was on my finger." She forced a laugh because it was such a tired old story—every whore had a similar one. Hers just happened to be true.

Clementine was staring at her now in that intense way she had that made Hannah want to wriggle like a cutworm. "I have a question I would like to put to you," the girl said in her very proper diction, which had Hannah despising the Kentucky twang in her own voice. "I don't mean to offer you insult with the indelicacy of it, but I . . ." She faltered. She ran a finger beneath the stiffened velvet edging of her high collar. A telltale blush stained her cheeks.

In the world where Mrs. Gus McQueen dwelled, women of breeding said "limbs" instead of "legs," even when talking about a piano. In that world women bathed in their shifts and made love wearing nine yards of flannel to a husband in a union suit. And in such a world there were no rules of etiquette for how to make polite conversation with a saloonkeeper and retired whore.

Hannah decided to take pity on her. "I've never been

with Gus," she said. At the girl's look of utter shock, she let out another hard laugh. "I guess that wasn't your question."

Clementine slowly shook her head, her eyes wide. "I'm glad that you and Gus never . . ." A tide of color now flooded her cheeks. She dropped her gaze to her lap. "Mrs. Yorke—Hannah . . ."

"You want to know how a sweet little gal like me got into such a business?"

"Oh, no, that wasn't what I . . . But I must confess I have wondered . . ." Hannah watched with amusement as the girl's perfect manners warred with her all-too-human curiosity.

"Listen, it wasn't any grand tragedy like what happened to Saphronie. I just listened to too many sweet-talking men. So what is it you want to ask me, Mrs. McQueen? You'll find we drink our liquor straight out here in the RainDance country, and we do our talking straight as well."

The girl lifted her chin and met Hannah's gaze squarely. "How does a woman know if she is with child?"

Hannah felt a stab of envy so acute it was an actual pain just below her heart. It left her breathless, and she thought she could actually feel all the blood drain from her face. A baby. This girl who had everything, who'd been born having everything, was now going to have a baby.

Clementine set down her lemonade and started to stand up. "I know, of course, how improper it was of me to introduce such an indelicate topic into the conversation, but you did invite me to speak frankly. I only thought that perhaps you might have had some experience with the condition—"

"Lord, honey, we weren't exactly having a delicate conversation to begin with." Hannah hurried over to the sofa. She seized the girl's hands, pulling her back down. She looked at their entwined fingers. Hers soft and white because she was careful to keep them that way, Clementine's covered with expensive ecru kid. She raised her head and met Clementine's gaze and actually managed a smile. "I've had experience with a number of conditions—'experience,' of course, most times being just another word for 'mistake.' "

Clementine was looking at her with eyes that were guileless and so very, very young. "So you have had a baby?"

"I . . . oh, Lord a-mercy, no. I ain't never made that particular mistake," she lied. "But in my line of work I've come across plenty of whor—women who have. After all, when it comes to what goes on in a bed, and what comes out of it, men and women all got the same fixin's whether they be paupers or kings. So, when did you last have the curse, honey?" At the girl's bewildered look, she smiled gently. "When was the last time you bled?"

"Oh." A hint of fresh color rose on Clementine's cheeks. "Not since before the first time Gus and I . . . since I came here to Rainbow Springs."

There was no privacy in a one-room miner's shack. Hannah Yorke had grown up pure, but not ignorant. There had been nights when she'd awakened to the sound of her parents coupling behind the curtain that shielded their bed. She had helped her mother bring two stillborn babes into the world and a little brother who had died before his first year. And those times when the women all got together, for weddings and birthings and funerals, Hannah at her mother's side, helping with the endless cooking, the women's work, had listened as they talked about their men and their marriage beds, their pregnancies and the cycles of their woman's bodies.

"Well, if you ain't bled since the first time you and Gus . . . made love, then you'd be, let's see, about four months along." She studied the girl's slender waist. "You should be showing by now."

Clementine looked down at herself. "I have gotten *rounder*."

Hannah hooted a laugh. "Honey, you're gonna get a whole lot rounder before you're done. All of you's gonna get as swolled up as a dead frog."

That ravishing smile flashed across Clementine's face.

"Oh, I shouldn't mind that, for I do so want a baby. But, Mrs. Yorke . . . Hannah, how does one *know*?"

Hannah struggled with the thickness in her throat. "Have—have you been feeling sickish in the mornings, and dizzy at unexpected moments?" She smiled at Clementine's eager nod. "And your breasts should be getting tender and your nipples turning darker, like blueberry stain, maybe."

Clementine stared down at her bodice as if she could see through the thick serge and cotton to her woman's flesh beneath. Her hand came up, hovered a moment, then touched. She smiled. "Oh, they are! They have been. I had thought it was because of what Gus—" She stopped, blushing furiously.

Hannah pursed her lips to keep from laughing. "Well, I expect you'll be experiencing other not-so-pleasant sensations soon. Why I remember how I . . . how this girl I knew belched and farted so much her first six months, she went around sounding like a locomotive going up a steep grade."

"Oh, my!" Clementine exclaimed, her face glowing red and yet she was laughing. And in that moment Hannah knew that for the first time in her life she'd found another woman she could love as a friend.

But Clementine McQueen was a lady, and she was . . . who she was.

"Tell me more," Clementine said. "Tell me everything."

Hannah's voice took on even more of a Kentucky drawl as she spoke of labor pains and water breaking and a baby's suckling. But she didn't talk about the whore she knew who'd died after drinking bluing to induce an abortion, or the opium addict who had given birth to a spastic child. Or the cones of cocoa butter and boric acid sitting on top of her own dresser, which she used to keep a baby from ever getting started. Or of her mother's stillborn babies, and her own little boy who'd been born when she was so alone and so scared. Whose first view of the world had been a room in a brothel.

Afterward, when Hannah thought about that afternoon, it was to marvel at how strange it would have seemed to anyone listening—a Montana whore imparting the facts of childbirth to a Boston blue blood. And when she was done, Clementine McQueen had stood up and thanked her with those polished, impeccable manners as if Hannah had simply been giving her the recipe for dried-apple pie.

They went outside, onto the gallery. The photograph as it came off the printing frame was a solid purple square with no image to be seen. But Clementine draped herself in the dark tent again, and when she emerged, the likeness of Saphronie's daughter was there in the sepia tones that Hannah was used to. It smelled of strange chemicals and varnish.

Clementine mounted the photograph on a stiff card with a pretty floral border. She held it in her hands, and Hannah looked at it over her shoulder. The sunshine gilded it like the light of her own memory.

"She was a beautiful little girl," Clementine said.

"Yes. Yes, she was . . ." Her own child's face, his dear little face, was only a blurred image in her mind, but she could vividly remember his smell. That baby smell of milk and talcum and soft, moist flesh. "I reckon surely Saphronie will let us put the poor thing in the ground now."

They looked up together at the clatter of wheels on the road. Clementine's husband pulled up to the front gate in the buckboard. He wrapped the reins around the brake handle, jumped down, opened the gate, and came toward them with long, purposeful strides.

Hannah watched him come, thinking she'd been wrong about him. Gus McQueen might have a stiff neck, but at least his head was on straight. He'd given his wife enough time to make her photographs before coming after her.

He stood at the bottom of the steps, his hands on his hips, and looked up at them. There was anger on his face, but there was something else there as well, Hannah thought. An uncertainty, perhaps. A dawning comprehension that his young wife was not at all as malleable and submissive as he might want her to be.

"You ready to come on home now, girl?" he said.

She looked back at him. If she was afraid of him, she didn't show it. "Yes, Mr. McQueen. I am ready."

Gus didn't help his wife pack up her camera and things. He went back to the buckboard and waited for her there, as if to linger too close to the former parlor house was to risk being sucked down willy-nilly into the jaws of sin.

"I won't bother you again," Hannah said to the girl when she was ready to leave. "Your Gus is right. You hadn't ought to be seen around the likes of me."

The girl walked across the gallery, her back as straight as a plumb line, her head high. Skirts rustling, shoes tapping.

But at the top of the steps she turned and looked back. "Mrs. Yorke, if I wish to pay a call on you, I shall."

She eased her horse down to a walk, breathing deeply, filling her lungs with air that was said to be better than whiskey in the belly. She could feel the pinto's heart thumping beneath her legs, feel his muscles trembling with the excitement of the run. It had been like straddling thunder and riding it across the sky.

She followed an old buffalo trail that had been washed deep by the rains in all the years since the buffalo had last used it. She rode out from beneath the pines and descended into a coulee with the sun warm at her back. A bawling calf disturbed the silence, and a man's slow, melodious cursing.

The mouth of the gulch was deep in shade cast by the yellow pines and larches above. There were still patches of winter snow where the sun never reached. The miry ground gave beneath her horse's hooves.

Her husband's brother knelt at the edge of an old buffalo wallow, wiping off the face of a calf with his bandanna.

He was calling it all manner of profane names, but in the gentlest voice she'd ever heard from a man. The calf must have gotten bogged down in the wallow and Rafferty had hauled it out. It was hard to tell which of them was wearing the most mud.

She thought he didn't know she was there, but he didn't act surprised when she spoke. "I've seen pigs that were dirtier, Mr. Rafferty."

He stood up slowly and turned, cuffing the worst of the mud splatters off his face. "Well, now," he said, his deep drawl making music of the words, "that's mighty cruel of you to say, Boston. I'd've thought you'd have more of a care for the tender feelin's of this here poor dogie."

She laughed aloud. Today felt wonderful.

He came at her, his gaze hot and intense in that way he had. He came right up next to her, so close the toe of her boot brushed his chest. He looked up at her and she thought he was going to smile, but then his eyes focused on the gun she wore around her waist, an old Colt that Gus had given her.

"What in hell you aimin' to do with that?"

She lifted her chin. "Protect myself."

"Uh-huh. I guess you figure if you meet up with trouble you can wave that in its face and scare it to death."

"I'll have you know that while I might not yet be able to shoot the head off a rattlesnake—"

"Lord, I bet you couldn't hit the side of a barn if you were standing inside it and had all day to aim in."

He was mean to her sometimes. Most times. And she wasn't very nice to him. But other times, like now, he'd tease her or suddenly smile in that way of his that creased his cheek and warmed his eyes, and she'd forget to be careful.

She laughed and leaned down to give the brim of his hat a playful tug. "What will you put up this time, Mr. Rafferty—your own six-shooter? You keep making wagers you're sure to lose, and come winter you'll be finding yourself left with little of not much."

"My, my, but if you aren't frisky and sassy as a clover-fed colt this mornin', Boston." His smile deepened, turned lazy and knowing. "You have anything in particular you're aiming to do with all that friskiness and sassiness? Otherwise, there's a place near here I'd like to show you."

And there were other times . . . other times when he was the one who forgot to be careful.

They rode in silence except for the squeak of saddle leather, the steady rush and pull of their horses' breath. They rode through a forest of cottonwoods and pines and huge larches that filtered the sun. They emerged onto a high grassy plain where the yellow sage bloomed and a hot wind blew.

She felt his eyes on her and she turned her head, met his gaze, though she knew it would not be wise. The look he gave her was like summer thunderclouds—dark, shifting, uncertain.

She looked away. At times he seemed to her a terrible man, wild and ruthless, crude and full of sin. But then he would do something so fiercely brave, so earthily decent, that the very splendor of him would make her ache inside. She longed to know how his heart and mind worked. She wanted to crawl inside his skin and see the world through his eyes. He haunted her, like the elusive memory of a dream that leaves you empty and restless when you awaken. And yearning for sleep so that you can dream it again.

It took her a moment to realize that he had pulled up, was swinging down from the saddle. He reached up and clasped her waist as she dismounted. And the feel of his hands resting on her hips, the brush of his leg against her skirt, the nearness of his face, his mouth . . . Though the sun beat down bright and hot on the parched prairie grass, she shivered.

An enormous larch stood isolated in the middle of the sea of grass. It had been decorated like a Christmas tree with beads and bear claws, strips of red calico, queer-shaped stones, and pieces of bone.

"This used to be a hunting ground, this plain," he said. "And that's a sacred tree. The Indians would leave gifts here to the Great Spirit, so that he would make the game plentiful and their arrows fly true."

Clementine felt the pull of the tree's majesty as she walked up to it. She stood beneath the canopy and looked up, and it was like the vaulted ceiling of her father's church—open and limitless and silent. She felt something here, a power ancient and beckoning, holy.

But some of the holiness had been defiled. A man by the name of Emory had been here in 1869 with a knife and tar bucket.

She knelt and tried to cover up the ugly black scars on the trunk with her gloved hand. "I must bring my photographic equipment up here some time," she said. "But I'll shoot it from another angle, where this can't be seen."

"Why? This tree don't belong to the Indians anymore. It's the white man's now, like the land it grows on. If you didn't show that, you'd be making a lie."

She looked up at him, startled that he would understand such a thing. She wanted to think of him only as a man of rough ignorance and lawless sinning.

The intensity on his face frightened her. Her gaze shifted down to his hand, which gripped one of the larch's low-flung branches. To those long, urgent fingers that were capable of such explosive violence. That had touched so many women.

He took her arm, to help her to her feet, and then his hand moved down her side and wound up pressing into the small of her back. She drew in a deep breath, heady with the smell of sage and sun-ripe grass.

She saw that the plain they stood on was actually the shoulder of a high bluff. About two hundred feet below them was a narrow canyon filled with knee-high grass that rippled in the wind. The canyon wound past cliffs the color of driftwood and hogback ridges of red rocks and stunted pines.

Her eyes picked out a skull first.

Like a cow's skull, only not exactly. And then she saw more bones, thousands of them, heaped in jagged weathered piles among the sere grass.

"A buffalo is pretty much a stupid critter," came Rafferty's voice from beside her. "And he don't see too good, either. Once spooked, he'll stop for nothing. When the Indians hunted here they used to stampede whole herds of them over this cliff."

"What a terrible thing." The thought saddened her. The poor dumb blind animals being driven so callously to their death.

"No more terrible than standing at the end of a railcar and shooting them down with carbine rifles like wooden ducks at a fair."

She turned her head to look up at him. "Did you do that?"

He thumbed his hat back a little. "Yeah. And it shames me to think of it, when I see how they're mostly all gone now."

There was a vulnerability in his eyes that she had never seen before. As if the tough shell he lived inside had cracked a little to reveal the meat of the man he was, behind the chaps and the Stetson and the six-shooter.

A loud snorelike grunt echoed up from the bottom of the canyon. She whipped around, clutching one-handed at her hat to peer over the cliff edge. Directly below them an enormous buffalo stood alone.

"Oh, look, Rafferty!" she exclaimed, grabbing his arm, her excitement making her forget herself. All these months out west and this was her first close look at a buffalo.

She had never seen anything at once so ugly and so majestic, with his huge head and dainty legs, his humped back and coffee-colored fur like an old matted rug. His long beard trailed in the grass. His quarter-moon horns were as thick as tree limbs. "How magnificent he is!"

"He's what you genteel Boston types would call a gentleman buffalo. These old woods buffalo, they winter up in the mountains near here. They're bigger and darker than the ones you see farther east, out on the prairie."

"Oh, I do so wish I had brought my photographic equipment." She turned her head in time to catch his disapproving frown. Because he had brought her here, she thought he understood. But he didn't after all, and her disappointment in him was sharp and keen. "You're like Gus," she said. "You think I'd do better to spend my time at the washing and the scrubbing and the cooking."

"Hell, you could waste all day crocheting them little divan tidies for all I care. I was only thinking that buffalo should be allowed to keep his dignity, instead of bein' immortalized on some piece of pasteboard for folk to gawk at. Folk who don't understand how he used to be. He ain't so magnificent anymore, Boston. He's sick and he's old. You can practically see his ribs poking through his hide. Buffalo are social critters, yet here he is roaming the canyon alone. He's the last of his herd and chances are he won't live to see next summer."

A sadness filled her, a sadness that seeped deep into the soul. It was as if she were in mourning for a friend she never knew. "My photograph would help you to remember him," she said.

"Maybe I don't want to remember him as he is now. Maybe it would hurt too much."

The sadness swelled, filling her, pressing on her chest until she couldn't breathe. She looked beyond, beyond the canyon, where flat pancake clouds skimmed along the tops of the saw-toothed mountains that reared, black and frightening, against the sky. This place, it was so big and empty. Too big and empty for the heart to bear, and too wild to love.

Standing here with Zach Rafferty beneath the big

Montana sky, she felt alone and fragile. As achingly lonesome as the last buffalo.

She spoke without thought, from her heart, "All this land and sky . . . how like a man it is in the way that it demands a woman's surrender."

"You'll tame it, Boston. And us, too, I reckon." His lips quirked into a half smile that creased his cheek and seemed to catch her beneath the ribs. "If I don't manage to chouse you outta here first."

She shook her head. She didn't want to tame this land, but she didn't want to leave it, either. And she wouldn't surrender to it—that most of all. She turned away from him, couldn't look at him anymore, but her gaze found no relief in the wilderness that only stirred the restless, yawning achings.

"Do you believe in God, Mr. Rafferty?"

He was quiet for so long that she thought he wouldn't answer her. His gaze was focused on the immense ridges of timber and grass. But unlike her, she knew, he had no fear of them, but rather loved them fiercely.

"Looking at this," he finally said, "you can't help but feel there's something. You take it all in with your eyes and your breath and the pores of your skin, all the beauty and the wildness of it, and you can't help feeling at one with the mountains and the plains and the sky, a part of it somehow."

A flush touched his cheeks, and into his eyes there came a look of searching, of wanting. "Whoever created all this, whether you call him God or the Great Spirit, I do believe he must've had a reason."

"What?" She leaned into him, desperate to know. "What was his reason?"

She thought a smile might have touched his lips. "Love."

The word hung in the air between them.

She drew in a slow breath, trying to ease the pressure in her chest. But when he spoke again his words sent her heart slamming back up into her throat: "Do you know what it is to have a heartfire for someone?"

She wanted to clamp her hands over her ears and

shriek at him that he was wrong, wrong. That this wasn't happening and that she hated him, because he was wrong. It was wrong, sinful, wicked, and it wasn't happening. She would not allow it to happen.

"Clementine—"

"No. I don't want to know," she said, backing away from him. His eyes were fierce and wild, and they called to the terrible wildness within her. She wrapped her arms around herself. She was shuddering hard from the inside out. "I don't want to speak of this. I won't speak of this."

His lips made a funny little twist that was barely a smile. "You know, for all your tender feet, Boston, you sure do have a tough head. I guess you figure you can't be held to account for the things you don't say. So you make me say them instead . . ."

Her whole body seemed to be straining, but whether it was reaching away from him or toward him she no longer knew. She was terrified he would do something, touch her in some way, and she would be lost.

"A heartfire, Clementine my darlin', is when you want someone, when you need her so damn bad, not only in your bed but in your life, that you're willin' to burn—"

"I am having your brother's child!"

She shouted the words so loud that they seemed to split open the air, and the echo of them drummed on the cliffs and in the canyon and against the wide and empty sky. She watched the blood slowly drain from his face, and his eyes go dark and hollow. She had chosen the one thing she knew would stop him. The thing she knew would hurt him the most.

He stared at her across the shaken-up air between them. There was a pressure pain in her chest, from not breathing and from wanting and from fearing the things she wanted. When the gunshot split the air, she thought for a moment that her heart had cracked.

Several more shots followed, spitting like a string of firecrackers. Rafferty's head snapped up; then he whirled and took off running for his horse. Hampered by her long skirts, Clementine lurched and stumbled after him.

"Stay here!" he shouted. He was already mounted and pulling his horse's head around. He slapped the broad gray rump with his hat, and Moses launched into a gallop, disappearing into the timber within seconds.

Somehow Clementine got herself up on Gayfeather and rode after him. The echoes of the gunshots had long ago faded into the buttes and hills. She clung to her mount's neck as branches whipped past her face. The pinto, wild now and out of control, plunged after Rafferty's horse.

When he pulled up to a more cautious walk, the pinto nearly plowed his nose into Moses's rump. He stumbled and then shied, and Clementine wrestled with the reins trying to calm him. Rafferty didn't look at her. He'd gone utterly still, but the air suddenly seemed to vibrate around him.

Through the trees Clementine could see shafts of sunlight that marked a clearing. A man shouted. Another answered with a short, sharp bark of laughter.

Rafferty took his rifle out of the saddle scabbard beneath his leg and laid it across his lap at half cock, his finger on the trigger. He nudged his horse toward the edge of the clearing, and she followed.

They crossed into bright sunlight that dazzled her eyes, blinding her for a instant. "Oh, dear sweet forgiving Christ," Rafferty said on a sharp expulsion of breath.

A man dangled from the thick limb of a cottonwood tree. His eyes bulged in a blood-engorged face that was the mottled purple of crushed grapes. His tongue lolled out a mouth that gaped open as if in a silent scream. Hot vomit rose in Clementine's throat and she almost choked. A dozen or so mounted men were gathered beneath the hanging man, wearing almost comic looks of shock at this unexpected arrival of guests to their necktie sociable. Clementine's horrified eyes searched their faces: Snake-Eye, Horace Graham, Weatherby the sheepherder, Pogey and Nash, and others, strangers she didn't know.

And Gus.

Smoke drifted over the clearing from a fire that bristled with branding irons. The place reeked of blood and spilled entrails. Scattered everywhere were the hides and carcasses of slaughtered cattle.

Two human bodies lay sprawled and bloody on the ground, guns clutched in their lifeless hands. Two others had been captured alive. One now hung from the end of a rope, swinging and swaying, the braided rawhide creaking in the sudden silence. The other was the Indian boy, Joe Proud Bear. He sat rigid on his horse, his hands tied behind his back, and Gus McQueen sat mounted beside him, a heavily knotted noose in his hand.

"No!" Clementine cried. She wrestled awkwardly with the gun at her waist, jerking it from the holster. "Let him go!"

13

RAFFERTY'S HAND SHOT OUT, grabbing her wrist. "You gonna shoot your own husband?"

"Make them stop." His hand squeezed, just hard enough to force her to drop the gun. She held his gaze, challenging him, and there was nothing in his eyes, nothing. "*You* can make them stop. He has a wife and child. No one should have to die just for stealing a cow."

His eyes still held hers. He spoke, in a silky tone she'd never heard before, yet it carried to the posse beneath the cottonwood tree. "Let the boy go."

Although it seemed like an eternity since they'd burst

into the clearing, in truth only seconds had passed. Gus and the others were frozen in a silent tableau, except for Joe Proud Bear, who must have figured a bullet in the back was a better way to die than slowly choking to death at the end of the rope. He leaned forward, kicked his moccasined heels into his horse's flanks, and bolted for the cover of the timber.

"He's gettin' away!" Horace Graham yelled and wheeled his horse, his hand falling to the revolver at his waist.

The ground in front of the cattleman erupted into a spurt of dust. The smack of the rifle shot hadn't quit bouncing through the air before Rafferty was levering another cartridge into the Winchester's chamber. Smoke from the barrel wafted across Clementine's face.

"I won't shoot y'all to kill," he said in that same cold, soft voice. "But that ain't sayin' accidents can't happen."

Joe Proud Bear had disappeared into the woods. Even the sound of his horse flailing through the brush had fallen into the well of stillness in the clearing.

Gus spurred his mount into movement. Not after the Indian boy but at his brother and his wife.

"What are you crazy, Zach?" he shouted. "We caught the bastards red-handed."

"The buffalo are gone. There's nothing left for them to hunt."

Gus's face was red and bunched up tight as a fist. He pulled up his horse to stare at his brother, his eyes wide and incredulous. "What in the blazes are you talking about?"

Rafferty shook his head. "Take your wife home. She shouldn't have to see this. I'll help your friends bury these bodies."

Slowly Gus turned his head, his gaze spearing her. And now his eyes flattened with fury.

Clementine jerked the pinto around and heeled it into a canter and rode away, away from Gus and the hanging man and the smell of gun smoke and blood.

She heard hooves pounding after her. Her whole body began to tremble. She pulled on the reins and slid from the saddle before the pinto had come to a stop. The sun blazed down, yet her hands and feet were numb with cold, and her chest was so heavy, her throat so tight, she felt as if she were choking. As if she were the one hanging at the end of a rope.

Gus rode up to her. He lifted his leg over the pommel and dismounted. "You gonna be sick?"

She shook her head.

He took off his hat, ran his hand through his hair, then jammed the hat back on his head. "Then what's the matter?"

"I . . ." She wiped her mouth with the back of her hand. It tasted coppery, like blood. She had borne his weight, taken his body into hers, and he had hanged a man for stealing a cow, killed him in cold blood . . . hot blood. Laughing Gus McQueen of the sun-bright face and sky-blue eyes. The cowboy of her dreams. "I feel as if I don't even know you."

He blew out a sharp, angry breath. He started to turn away from her, then spun back around. He loomed over her the way her father used to, trying to make the very air shiver with his man's big size and his man's great strength.

"You just won't quit in your defiance of me, will you?" he shouted into her face, and his mustache quivered with the expulsion of each hot, angry word. "I tell you Iron Nose and his rustling are no woman's business, yet you come busting in where you don't belong and shame me in front of the entire territory." He emitted a bitter, ragged laugh. "'My husband,' you say. 'I love you.' Yet you look me right in the face and set about doing just what you want to do."

"You don't own me, Gus," she said through stiff lips.

"The hell I don't. You're my wife, girl, and—"

"And I am not a *girl*. I am a woman grown. I have a mind and thoughts and feelings that are mine"—she thumped her chest with her fist—"*mine*, and they're nothing to do with you. You cannot tell me how to live my life—"

He hit her. He did it with the palm of his hand across her cheek, but he was a big man and his frustration and anger put violence into his swing. She went sprawling against the pinto. The horse neighed and shied, and Clementine landed flat on her back, the air gusting from her lungs.

Gus stood over her. His face seemed to collapse in upon itself, to crumble. "Oh, Jesus, Clem. Lord Jesus. I'm sorry, g— I'm sorry." He reached down to help her up, but she jerked away from him, lurching to her feet. Her chest heaved as she tried to draw in a breath. The whole side of her face burned.

His hand came up as if he would touch the mark he'd left on her cheek, as if he could soothe it away. A muscle jumped at the corner of his mouth. "I never meant to hit you."

"You did hit me, though, Mr. McQueen."

She felt behind her, her fingers grasping the stirrup. She watched him, watched his hands and his eyes, watched him until she was safely back in the saddle.

"Clementine!" he shouted after her. And kept shouting, but by then she could no longer hear him over the thunder of Gayfeather's hooves and the rush of the wind.

She sat on one of the nail-keg stools, hunched over, hugging herself, pressing her elbows hard against her belly. She wasn't crying, though. She never cried.

Her face throbbed. The tears she couldn't shed burned the back of her eyes, the sobs built and subsided, built and subsided, deep in her chest. Outside, a hammer pounded rhythmically—Gus working on the house, brooding. He probably had himself convinced by now that she'd brought the punishment on herself, and perhaps she had. *"Thy desire shall be to thy husband, and he shall rule over thee."* But her anger with him was a hot cloud in her mind.

"Clementine?"

She straightened and turned.

Rafferty stood in the doorway. His gaze fastened onto her face, and fury leaped into his eyes, hot and bright as a grass fire.

He spun on his heel and started across the yard toward the hay meadow and the house that Gus was building for her.

"No, don't!" she shouted, running to catch up with him, clutching at his sleeve to stop him. "Stay away from him, please. Please."

He swung around. "You're carryin' his child and he puts bruises on your face, and you want me to stay away from him? I ought to kill him."

"He is my husband. I belong to him. Not to you, Zach Rafferty. Not to you!"

She saw the hurt in his eyes before he lowered his head so that his hat brim shielded his face. "A man don't ride into another man's business and take over," he said. "It goes against the grain, against what's right. Yet you asked me to take a stand against my own brother, to stop him from doin' what he felt was just and right, and I did. For you, because you asked, and that *changes* things, Clementine, whether you want them changed or not."

"Don't . . ." She spoke as if her throat hurt. "Don't make me choose between you. It isn't . . . What happened between us that day at the river, it was wrong, a sin. I am *married* to your brother. Not only is that a tie made by God that only he can sever, but Gus . . . is what I want."

One corner of his mouth tightened. "Hell, you haven't a fool's notion of what it is you want yet." He stared at her now, his face hard. She tried to control her breathing, to keep from trembling. It seemed she could feel the ebb and flow of her blood in every part of her. "I ain't going to make you choose between me and my brother, but that's for his sake and has nothin' to do with you. Still, someday you got to make a stand on it, Boston. Inside yourself, if nowhere else. That's what it's all about out here. Having the freedom to decide just what sort of person you're going to be, and having the guts to face up to it when you do."

He half turned, then snapped back around and pointed a stiff finger in her face. "And here's another thing. Don't you ever, *ever* again pull a gun on a man—"

"But I wasn't going to shoot anybody. I was only going to fire into the air, to stop them."

He sighed and shook his head. He brushed his thumb along her cheekbone, just above the bruise his brother had given her. "Once you pulled that gun from the holster you should've been ready to kill with it if that's what it came down to. If you pack a weapon, you got to be big enough to carry its weight. You understand what I'm sayin' to you?"

She pressed her fist to her lips and shut her eyes, nodding. He was telling her that she had been behaving like a child and that she must begin to be what she was now. A woman grown.

"You goin' to go make things up with Gus?" he said softly, still stroking her cheek.

She nodded again.

"Then go do it."

She went past him, her eyes on the ground, walking toward the new house. The hammering had stopped.

Her feet felt heavy, weighted down, as was her heart. Thunder rumbled in the air. She looked over her shoulder at the mountains. Like jealous mothers the mountains had gathered up the storm clouds, hugging them close.

She had said she belonged to Gus and she knew this had to be so. *"Wives submit yourselves . . . he shall rule . . . he shall rule . . ."* God demanded that it be so. But she refused to live in fear like her mother. Her poor cowed mother who unlike the mountains had never hugged her child close. Her poor furtive mother who had filled a sachet with coins, one by one, trying and failing to protect her daughter from the pain of being a woman grown.

A mother who had told her daughter to go with joy, but hadn't told her how.

She walked through what would someday be the back door of the house in which she would probably live with Gus McQueen for the rest of her life. It smelled of new wood and her man's sweat. He sat on a sawhorse, his hands pinched between his knees. At the tap of her boots on the rough floorboards, he lifted his head. His mouth twisted, and he looked away.

She knew this time would pass. She had borne his weight, taken his body into hers. He was her husband and she would come to care for him again. But at the moment there was this vast emptiness inside her. She felt nothing, nothing at all.

She crossed the space between them and laid her hand on his shoulder. Rubbed her palm over and over the soft red flannel of his shirt.

His back hunched, he wrapped his arms around her waist, crushing her. He buried his head in her breasts. His words were muffled by the stiff bone and sateen armor of her bodice. "I swear I'll never hurt you again, Clem. I love you, love you, love you . . ."

She looked through the kitchen wall, which was only wooden studs framing air. Rafferty stood in the yard where she had left him, and seeing him, she felt a tearing inside, as though pieces of herself were breaking off. Jagged, jigsawed pieces that settled wrong, not quite fitting together again.

Her hand hovered over her husband's head, then fell, her fingers twining in his sun-shot hair. "Sssh, it's all right," she said, comforting him. Comforting herself.

August came, and the chokecherries hung sour and black down by the river. The days were warm and still, smelling of dust and summer and dry grass. The wind had finally quit blowing.

But on this day, although the sun beat down stove-hot on the cabin's sod roof, Clementine was next door in the coolness of the stone springhouse. She was watching an owl change color, from purple to red to lilac to a golden brown.

A hum of delight fluttered her lips. Oh, she had done well, if she did say so herself. The print was sharply focused and clearly defined from edge to edge, with rich gradations of light and shadow. Using a pair of tongs she moved the print from the toning bath to a hypo fixing solution. Windowless and with troughs of spring-fed water, the springhouse made a perfect darkroom.

She heard a holler out in the yard, and she leaned over to open the door. "Gus! Come see what I've just done."

His shadow fell over her as he came to the door, ducking his head beneath the low lintel. "You shouldn't be kneeling on that wet stone floor," he said.

She cast a bright smile at him and stood up from the troughs. Her pregnant belly made her awkward, and her knees creaked like an old gate. She blew a damp strand of hair out of her eyes. "I managed to make a photograph of that big gray owl that roosts on the stump by the corral every afternoon. He just sat there, Gus, unmoving, staring at me the whole time, while I set up my equipment and made the exposure, and he didn't so much as blink."

Gus looked at the print but he said nothing. Red dust filmed his mustache and the front of his hair that fell out from beneath his hat. He smelled of the dust and of sweat and horses.

"I thought you and your . . . and Mr. Rafferty were going to be rounding up the mustangs this afternoon."

"And I thought you were going to finish putting up the chokecherry preserves."

Angry heat flushed her cheeks. She pressed her lips together to dam back the words she wanted to fling into his hard man's face. She kept her silence as she washed the print and hung it on a line to dry, and kept her silence as she left the springhouse. The shock of walking out of the damp, stony coolness and into the sun-drenched yard made her shiver.

Gus fell into step beside her. "I thought I'd drive on into town, and I came to see if you needed anything." She kept her silence. "Well, you got time to think on it," he said. "There's a split in the buckboard's wheel rim that needs fixing before I leave."

He turned toward the barn as she went on to the cabin. A wall of heat and the sickening, too-sweet stench of boiled chokecherries and sugar syrup struck her in the face as she stepped inside. Jars and pots and purple-stained cheesecloth littered the table, just as she'd left it when she spotted the gray owl at his roost on the stump and knew she couldn't let another day pass without trying to capture the scene with her camera's eye.

She stared at the mess, her hands clenched at her sides, and then she spun around on her heel and strode back outside. She crossed the yard, passing Gus, where he'd rolled the buckboard out of the barn to work on it. He called out to her, but she ignored him and began to run.

She waded all the way out into the middle of the rich buffalo grass, where it grew as dense as a fur pelt. The sun beat down on her head, thick and hot. She'd forgotten to bring her hat.

She sat in the grass and drew her knees up, curving her back. She imagined that the grass grew so tall she was lost from sight in it, that she could lose herself in the grass forever.

She sat that way for a long time, listening to the snapping of the grasshoppers. Then she stretched out her legs and leaned back on her elbows. Her head fell back and she stared up into the vast and empty blueness of the sky.

"Clementine?"

Blinking, she turned and looked up into her husband's red, sweating face. "I called after you," he said. "You didn't answer."

"Because I want to be alone." She knew the words would hurt him, but she couldn't seem to help it. Perhaps she didn't want to help it. It seemed sometimes that she deliberately tried to show him the ugliest parts of her.

She held herself stiff, waiting for him to go. Instead he sat down next to her, his hands clasped together between his legs, his spread knees pressed into the crooks of his elbows.

"I wasn't scolding you earlier, Clem. Leastways, I didn't mean to. Oh, I won't deny I minded it some at first—the time you spend gallivanting around the countryside making photographs when you oughta be at your chores. But I've tried to understand. I mean, I can see that things might get tiresome and lonely for you, by yourself in the cabin all day long and with nothing but kitchen work to occupy your thoughts."

Clementine shut her eyes. Sunspots danced behind her closed lids; an insect chirred loudly, calling for a mate. Gus stirred beside her, and she turned her head to look at him. He was staring hard at the river where the sunlight dappled the willows like lace. His hands tightened their grip on each other.

"Why is it, girl, that every time I try to get close to you, you push me away? It's not enough that we come together in bed at night. We got to come together during the day, with words and feelings."

She sat up. "I don't know what you want from me," she said.

"I want you to be a true wife to me. A soul mate and a heart mate as well as a lover."

I can't, I can't, she wanted to cry. *Because I don't know what that is.* How could she give him what he wanted when it wasn't there within her in the first place?

He pulled loose a sheaf of grass, running it through his fists. "We got to start learning how to talk to each other or this marriage won't ever be an easy one."

She felt a renewed wave of panic. What could she say

to him? *Your brother unsettles me; he stirs things within me that are better left buried. But even though I don't want it to be so, even though I am trying to stop it, still there is something going on between us that you'd probably hate us for if you knew of it. And if you came to hate me I would want to die, because I need you so much. Truly I do need you, Gus. More than you can ever imagine.*

He pushed himself to his feet, leaving her.

"Gus!" she cried. She looked up at him, squinting against the glare of the sun. He was so tall, as tall as the trees and the mountains. As tall as any cowboy she had ever dreamed of marrying. "In that house on Louisburg Square we never talked to one another. All we did was pray."

"I am not your father."

She pushed out a big breath, relieving some of the ache, but only a little of the fear. "No. I know." She held up her hand to him as if she would hold him, keep him from leaving. "I can't speak easily of what I feel. I try, but the words stop up in my throat as if there's a dam there."

He clasped her hand with his big one and sat back down beside her. "Clementine . . . all I ever wanted, all I want is for you to be happy." He'd kept hold of her hand, and he was stroking the pad of her palm with his thumb. "But I don't reckon you are . . . happy."

She turned her head and looked at him, at his eyes, which were as open and blue as the sky. There were moments, like this one, when she thought he was wonderful and she was a fool. "Oh, no, Gus, I am, I am. Especially now that we're going to have a baby. I want us to have lots of them—a dozen at least."

She squeezed his hand, then slipped her fingers from his. "I do admit it was hard for me at first, coming here and finding out I was going to have to live in a log cabin with a sod roof. And the mud that was everywhere." She tried for a smile, but her throat had closed up so tight it hurt. "The way it got into everything, that mud, including the cracks between your teeth, so that you could taste it when you swallowed. But still and all, Gus, I wasn't so much unhappy as scared and, well . . . unsettled. Things have changed—"

He gave a harsh laugh. "Sure they have. The mud's all dried up now. Now you got the dust to complain of."

"That's unfair. I wasn't complaining." She began to withdraw deep inside herself again, where he couldn't see her, couldn't hurt her. It was a mistake to have encouraged this conversation. He thought he had married someone who would be a virtuous, obedient wife. A genuine starched-up lady. He would never come to understand what lay beneath her silk and whalebone.

"I should never have brought you out here," he said.

She turned her head away. Maybe he would find a way to divorce her, to send her back to Boston and her father's house. No, he would never do that, for he prided himself on being a man of his word, and speaking a marriage vow was like giving your word to God. But it would never be the same for him, never be right. She would be another one of his hopeless, improbable dreams.

"You talk about being scared," he said, and his voice broke. "Well, I'm scared I can never make things good enough for you, as good as what you're used to. That I can never be what you want."

She had said that to his brother, that Gus was what she wanted, and he was. Oh, yes, truly he was.

But when she looked up into his face, to tell him this and make him believe it, something in the universe slipped and she saw wild yellow eyes that wanted her, and a hard mouth that had spoken of heartfire and once had kissed her.

She reached out and recaptured her husband's hand, seized it hard, as if she were drowning. "But you *are* what I want. I am the one who is lacking. Oh, I am young, and a tenderfoot to boot, but I've never been so foolish as to think there wouldn't be some rough times mixed in with the smooth. We vowed to stay together through better or worse. I'll take your worse along with your better, if you'll take mine."

He brought their linked hands to his mouth, turning them so that her palm was against his lips and he could kiss the scars. His mouth was warm, his mustache soft. It moved as he smiled, and she felt the brush of his breath on her skin as he spoke. "Did you mean what you said about wanting lots of babies?"

"Oh, yes, Gus. I do, I do."

His smile widened. "Well, at least so far I'm doing that right."

He brought her hand down and pressed it against the swell of his belly. The baby, as if sensing it had an audience, stirred. She laughed. "Oh! Did you feel that, Gus? He moved!"

She took his hand and placed it so that he, too, could feel their baby's life. He looked deep into her eyes, his own eyes smiling. "It's going to be good, girl," he said. "You'll see."

She smiled back at him. "Yes, Gus. It will be good."

14

HANNAH YORKE'S DARK MAROON skirts rustled over the oiled floor like dry leaves. She stopped before the mirror above the mahogany sideboard in her hallway. She peered at her face and frowned, then noticed the little chicken-track wrinkles around her eyes and made her mouth relax.

Without the touch of rouge she usually wore, her skin looked sallow. She blew out a long, shaky breath. Her ribs itched beneath her tightly laced corset. The high-banded neck of her polonaise jacket seemed to be strangling her.

She had splashed rosewater beneath her arms, but already she could feel nervous sweat beginning to gather in every crease of her skin and clothes.

Lord, she was more jittery than a schoolgirl stepping out with her first beau. Not that she hadn't stepped out with plenty of men in her time, and she'd charged most of them a pretty price for the privilege of her company, too. But she couldn't remember the last time she'd been invited into a respectable home.

News of the jamboree had spread over the RainDance country and beyond. The Rocking R was holding a frolic to celebrate the finishing of their new ranch house and the beginning of the fall cattle roundup that was to start next week. Folk within a hundred miles would be coming. All decent folk, though, and no saloonkeepers like her. In a weak moment she had promised to come, and now, oh, Jesus Lord, she was so damned scared.

They would snub her, she was sure of it. Those respectable sheepherders' and cattlemen's wives. Up would go their noses, down would pull their mouths, and the next thing she'd see would be their stiff backs walking away from her. And there would be men at the jamboree, too, who probably wouldn't be real excited to come upon her face to face outside of her saloon. Men she'd cut the pasteboards for and served her hell brew to, men she'd seen disappearing into her back room with one of her girls.

Her hands trembled as she lifted the black linen hat off the sideboard. She anchored it down on her head with a quartz-studded hatpin, covering her scarlet hair. She adjusted the black muslin veil over her face, so that she now looked at her mirror image through a shroud. "Hannah, you are a fool," she told the veil-draped stranger in the glass.

Before she lost her courage entirely, she left the house and went out onto the gallery. The trunks of the quaking aspens shone silvery in the late morning sunlight; their leaves shimmered gold. A triangle of wild geese harrowed the sky. It was only early September, and the days were still warm and long, but the geese were a promise of the winter to come.

She tapped her foot in time with the tinny sound of a piano coming out of the open doors of her saloon: "Oh, dem golden slippers. Oh, dem golden slippers . . ." She'd finally found someone who knew how to make those ivories dance, a man called Doc, of course. She knew nothing about him, not even his name, and she wasn't going to ask. He was a worn-down soul, with the haunted look of a man running from something. But then, everyone out here was either running away from something or lusting after something else.

With Shiloh playing his fiddle at the frolic, she was leaving the tonk in charge of Annie, the most reliable of all her girls. The chippy would probably skim off one dollar for every four she took in, but Hannah would just have to consider that the cost of her holiday. Oh, Lord, she really did need to get away for a time from the smell of spilled booze and tobacco slop and old sweat.

And then over a burst of laughter and the tinkle of the piano, she heard the singing of buggy wheels, the rattle of a harness.

Zach Rafferty pulled up in the pretty little plum-colored shay she often rented from Snake-Eye. He swung down with a jaunty air and tied the horse to her front fence. She watched him come up her path, walking with that tight-hipped gait of a man who spent more time in the saddle than out of it.

The sight of him this morning took her breath away. She'd never seen him looking so fine, dressed as he was in striped pants, burgundy brocade vest, and pristine white shirt with a stiff linen collar set off by a black bolo tie. But when he caught sight of her, the smile slid off his face.

He stopped at the bottom of the steps and propped his hands on his hips, which looked strangely naked without a gun belt. "What the hell've you got on?"

She lifted her chin high, though it quivered a little. "This happens to be a very proper dress."

"'Proper' ain't the word for it. Too somber for a funeral is more like it."

"You're the one forcing me to go to this shindig. You gonna tell me how to dress for it now, too?" He came up next to her on the gallery. So handsome and so much of a man, and a good one, too, for all of his wild ways. "We're going to be seeing all your family and friends, Rafferty. And there I'll be, standing beside you, my hand on your arm . . . I don't want to shame you."

"Hell, woman, you think people believe I'm keepin' company with you because of your virtue?"

That hurt. She looked at his handsome face through the mesh of her veil. His hard face. Tears blurred her eyes. The words came spilling up from a dark, sad corner of her heart. "That's all I am to you, isn't it? A good poke. A warm and ready quim to ease yourself with when the mood takes you."

"No, that ain't all you are to me and you damn well know it. And quit talkin' dirty like that. You sound like a—" He cut himself off, but she finished it for him.

"Whore."

He thrust his fingertips into his pockets and turned away from her, blowing an exasperated breath out between his lips. She wanted to kiss those lips. And she wanted to kiss his cheek, tan, and shaven smooth just that morning. She half expected him to up and leave her, which would serve her right and likely please the good folk of the Rain-Dance country, who would be spared her sinful presence at the frolic.

But he didn't leave. He cast a sideways look up and down the length of her. His face might have been carved out of the granite of RainDance Butte, for all she could read of it.

"Putting on sackcloth and ashes ain't gonna change you into other folks' idea of what's respectable," he said.

"You want to sell your saloon and marry me, Hannah? Move out to the ranch and into that sod-roofed shanty, make me chokecherry preserves, scrub the sweat stains out of my shirts, and watch your belly swell up every year with my babes?"

The ends of his tie danced in the breeze. The scent of bay rum wafted to her beneath the veil. "Are you proposing, cowboy? 'Cause if you are, I oughta serve you the bad scare you deserve by accepting."

Oh, there wasn't a whore breathing who hadn't dreamed of a day when some man would walk into her sordid life, sweep her off her feet, and marry her. Make her magically into a lady of respectability and virtue. To be a wife, to have babies . . .

But not even for a baby would she give up all she had now to go back in time and live her mother's kind of life. She certainly didn't need a man to complicate things, telling her what to do and how to be and trying to do her breathing for her. Oh, there were some things she still wished for at times. A man's face smiling up at her over a stack of flapjacks of a morning. His longhandles flapping on her line. The feel of a baby pulling on her breast, to smell that baby smell again and have those soft arms cling to her neck.

To love and be loved.

Oh, Hannah, you are such a fool. How many years and how many men is it gonna take before you learn that love lasts only as long as the bedsprings squeak?

She made another little upward nudge with her chin. "What makes you know so much about me anyways?"

"You talk in bed." His mouth curled into a naughty-boy grin. "Keep me up, you do, you and that frolicsome tongue of yours."

His wicked words startled a laugh out of her. But the hurt lingered underneath, like the smell of bay rum in the air. "Someday I'll marry you when you aren't lookin', Zach Rafferty," she said, her voice rough. "And then you really will be sorry."

His hand slipped behind her neck, tilting her head. He lifted the veil so that she could see his eyes and he could see hers.

"Whatever happens with us, Hannah, I won't ever be sorry." He lowered his head and kissed her. He spoke into her open mouth. "Now go put on your dancin' rags, darlin'."

She knew better, but she just couldn't seem to help herself. She loved him most when he called her darling.

"You got your dancing shoes on, Mrs. McQueen?"

Clementine lifted her skirts to show off her French kid shoes, shiny with fresh blacking. They pinched some, for her feet had swollen over the summer months, along with her belly. "And what about you, Mr. McQueen?" she teased, smiling just a little. "Does a bowlegged cowpoke like you even know how to dance?"

Laughing, Gus shuffled his feet like a minstrel showman, making music with the jinglebobs and heel chains on his silver spurs. If he swung his boots just right he could make the rowels spin and ring against the wooden floor.

Clementine laughed out loud when he tried to jump and click his heels together and had to make a wild grab for the end of the bed at the last minute to keep his balance. Their new bed was of white iron fancied up with acorn knots. She loved that bed and her other new things: the walnut dresser with its marble top and the matching washstand, the blue gingham curtains she had made for the window, the pink-flowered china chamber set they had sent away for from the Altman and Stern catalog. Above the bed she'd hung the dream hoop Joe Proud Bear's woman had made for her, for the good dreams to come through and sweeten their nights.

And there was her man, trying to dance and make music with his spurs.

He noticed the way she was looking at him, and he

struck a rakish pose. He had on a white buckskin vest and a red silk bandanna, and his face beamed like a harvest moon. "What do you think?" he said.

"Beautiful. The house is beautiful and you're beautiful." Today even Montana was beautiful, for the wind was pretty much behaving. The sun shone like a new five-dollar gold piece and cotton-ball clouds floated across a blue, blue sky.

He came up to her and took her hand, fitting his palm to hers, entwining their fingers. "I want to make you happy."

"You have, Gus. You do."

"I only wish I could give you more. Three, four years from now, I swear I'll build you the biggest house in the territory with two stories and a double parlor." He rubbed his free hand on his canvas pants, laughing. "And a water closet, so's we won't get our feet wet every morning, running through the wet grass on the way to the privy. Would you like that, Clem?"

She brought their entwined hands up to her mouth and kissed his knuckles. He made her the happiest when he was like this, laughing and chasing after the next big dream.

A crotchety old-man's voice came bellowing at them through the open window. "Crucified Jesus! Ain't there supposed to be a frolic goin' on somewheres around here? Where in holy hell *is* everybody?"

This was followed by the whacking sound of a hat hitting a substantial belly. "Quit your cussing, you blasted fool. We ain't even here yet and already you're bluing up the atmosphere."

Gus winked at Clementine and put his finger to his lips. "Did you invite those two scalawags to our classy to-do, Mrs. McQueen?" he said loud enough to be heard outside.

Clementine had to suck on her cheek to keep from laughing.

"Reckon they must've invited themselves then." He heaved a mock sigh. "I guess I should go make 'em welcome anyway."

They were smiling at each other, she and Gus, as Clementine followed him into the parlor. But she paused a moment there to savor the silence of her new home before it was overrun with company. It really wasn't all that fancy a house, just a white frame box with four rooms and a tin roof. Gus fretted that it wasn't up to the civilized standards she'd been raised to, yet already she felt more at home here than she ever had in the crimson-draped gloom of the house on Louisburg Square. Her father's house had smelled of beeswax and wood oil and too much godliness. This parlor smelled of its new pine plank floor, and of hope.

She stepped into the kitchen, which was already beginning to smell of the yeasty crock of sourdough that had been brought to rest in its new place above the brand-new nickel-plate range, a range that had—blessed day!—a hot water reservoir. And next to it—even more blessed day!—was a washing machine with a hand-cranked wooden wringer.

She heard Gus calling to her that their guests were starting to arrive. A wave of shyness washed over her, and she rubbed her damp palms over the swell of her belly. She had altered her brown serge dress as best she could to try to conceal her pregnancy, but she'd had to loosen her corset to a shameless degree.

She walked out onto the porch that wrapped around three sides of the house, her pretty white porch with its spooled railing. Skeins of smoke drifted from a pit in the ground where a whole steer lay roasting, and the smell of it mingled with the smell of curing hay that came from the stacks lined up like giant bread loaves at the edge of the meadow. Squinting, Clementine looked across the yard and gasped aloud in pleased surprise.

Buggies and buckboards and men on horseback were

coming down the road and over the prairie toward their little house. Most of the RainDance country would show up for any sort of jamboree, so Gus had told her, but she hadn't quite believed him. They would come riding for miles, he'd said, some getting up hours before dawn to arrive by noon, wearing their Sunday finery and bearing kettles of pea soup, legs of pork, venison chops, raspberry pie, and dried-apple duff.

There was Mrs. Graham, gripping her Horace's arm as if she feared every woman present would jump on him and ravish his body beneath her very nose. And Mrs. Weatherby, her pale face made paler by a coating of flour paste that had begun to crack in the heat like a dry gulch bed.

There was Mr. Carver, who ranched the high country above the buffalo canyon, a man who had come to Montana ten years ago and hadn't yet found the time to go back to Philadelphia and fetch his wife. And Sam Woo, who had gotten involved in a cutthroat game of poker at the Best in the West last month and lost all the money he'd been saving up to buy a Chinese girl to marry.

There was Snake-Eye, for once without his leather apron, and Shiloh with his fiddle tucked under one beefy arm. Cowboys painfully attired in tight new boots and celluloid collars. Sheepherders with woolly vests and bells on their hats. And prospectors sporting new red flannel shirts and trimmed beards.

Clementine spotted two more familiar faces and she went to them. Pogey was trying to lasso his partner's arm with a blue bandanna, and Nash was having none of it. Gus had told her of this western custom: at dances where women were scarce, the men partnered each other and those playing the ladies in the set had to wear bandannas tied around their arms.

Nash, however, had snatched the bandanna from Pogey's hand and thrown it in the dirt, then stomped on it for good measure. "I ain't the one being heifer-branded this time, and that is that! What makes you think I'm gonna want to dance with a gimped-up old saddle stiff like you anyways?"

"God and all the little god-almighties!" Pogey flung back his head in an appeal to the heavens. "You'd dance with any old gazabo fool enough to ask you."

Nash shook his finger beneath his partner's nose. "Now, there's where ye're mistaken, you see. 'Cause I got standards. And besides, playing the lady ain't a job fitting to my talents. I'm more the courting swain type, being known as I am for my dash and vinegar and savvy-fair."

"Savvy-what the hell? There're times when you make no more sense than tits on a bull. Yappity-yappity-yip goes your tongue, on and on, till a man starts to wishing for a shotgun just so's he could shoot off his head and put his ears out of their damned misery—"

Nash whipped off his hat and flattened it against Pogey's stomach. "Hobble your lips. There's a lady present."

"Eh?" Pogey spun around. He took off his hat and made a surprisingly courtly bow, so low his long yellow beard swept his knees. "Mrs. McQueen—my, but if you don't look prettier'n a little red heifer this mornin'."

The heifers Clementine had seen thus far weren't pretty at all, but the sentiment behind the compliment couldn't help but make her smile. "Howdy, Mr. Pogey. Mr. Nash."

Nash grinned and nodded. Pogey pulled a woeful face and tugged at his ear as he resettled his hat. "I wish I could say I was fine, ma'am, but I ain't." He rasped his hand across his whiskery neck. "Got me such a touch of the dry throat I can't even spit without primin' the pump."

"What he's trying to say," Nash supplied, at Clementine's quizzical look, "if'n he had the vocabulary for it and weren't so all-fired concerned all the time with being pithy . . . is that he's thirsty."

Clementine laughed. "Oh, of course. Gentlemen, this way, if you please."

She led the two prospectors over to a pair of barrels sitting on a trestle table tucked beneath the shade of a giant cottonwood. Gus had taken a week to make this cider from the dried apples that came from Washington Territory, strung like beads on strings and looking like pieces of old saddle leather.

She filled a tin cup from one of the barrels and passed it to Pogey. The smell of apples was sweet and biting, but he cast a dubious eye at it. "Is this teetotal stuff?"

Nash sighed loudly. "What for you even wasting your breath by askin'? And you normally such a pithy man. You think that Gus, with his abstemious ways, is gonna pack any kinda wallop into his cider?"

Clementine pressed a brimming cup into his hand. "Nevertheless you must try it, Mr. Nash. You might be pleasantly surprised."

Both men took tiny, tentative sips, screwing up their faces as if they were being asked to take a dose of cod-liver oil. Nash swallowed first, and his owl eyes grew even rounder. Pogey choked as his went down. He stifled a grin behind the cuff that wiped dry his beard. "Now, that's what I call prime cider."

Clementine sucked on her lower lip to hide her smile. She had seen Rafferty dump six bottles of spirits into one of the barrels when Gus's back was turned. Her temperate husband, Clementine knew, was not going to be pleased.

She leaned into the two prospectors and lowered her voice. "Now, Mr. Pogey, Mr. Nash . . . may I trust you both to ensure that only those gentlemen so inclined to drink cider with any kind of wallop in it will fill their cups out of this particular barrel?"

"Eh? Oh, sure, sure." Pogey nodded so vigorously his beard slapped his chest.

Nash placed his hand over his heart. "You may trust us, ma'am, to your dyin' breath. Wild cayuses couldn't drag out the truth if we didn't want it told. You could hang our guts on a fence post and braid 'em for lariats, you could drag us naked over a cactus patch, you could whittle whistles outta our shinbones—unh!".

Pogey smacked him hard in the gut with his empty cup. "Try exercisin' yer arm instead of yer tongue and pour me some more of that deeelicious dried-apple cider."

Just then Clementine spotted Gus heading their way, and she hurried off to intercept him. He walked around the edge of the dance floor, which was a canvas sheet pegged down on the flattest part of the yard. The brothers had chopped down little pine trees and hung lanterns on them in a circle around the canvas, for the dancing would go on all night long.

"You tried any of my cider yet, Clem?" Gus said as he came up to her.

"Oh, well, I . . ." She searched frantically for a reason to divert his attention from his precious brew. A group of cowboys, she noticed suddenly, stood in the middle of the canvas, their thumbs hanging off the back pockets of their pants, their jaws working on plug tobacco like cows chewing their cud. She pointed a finger at them. "Why, really, Gus! Go tell those men not to spit on the dance floor."

Gus grinned and tipped his hat. "Yes, ma'am."

Clementine heard the sound of more carriage wheels and she turned. For a moment she was dazzled by the sun striking off the tin roof of her new house, and she shaded her eyes with her hand.

Zach Rafferty held the reins of the shay and he looked . . . different. More like a banker than a bank robber. He looked almost tameable today. Hannah sat beside him wearing a candy-pink-striped dress with a shockingly low-cut bodice and enormous leg-of-mutton sleeves. Her hat was laden with pink plumes and purple silk lilies, and her hair fell over her white shoulders in two thick dark red ringlets. Hat and head were both shaded by a pink calico parasol trimmed with lace.

Rafferty stepped down and held up his hand for Hannah. He was smiling, and the look that passed between them was not meant for others to see. A bittersweet ache pulled at Clementine's chest, startling and confusing her so that her steps faltered.

She looked away and saw then that the other women, who had congregated on the porch, were casting scowling looks in the shay's direction. They turned their backs and marched inside the house.

Hannah Yorke had seen them, too, and her face turned the color of sour milk except for the two bright spots of rouge the size of dollars on her cheeks.

"Mrs. Yorke . . . Hannah." Clementine stretched out her hands as she came forward, the ache in her chest swelling, filling her throat and making it difficult to get the words out. She took extraordinary care not to let her gaze slide over to Rafferty even for an instant. "I'm so pleased you are here." She grasped the woman's trembling fingers and gave them a reassuring squeeze. "You couldn't talk Saphronie into coming?"

Hannah shook her head, heaving a shaky sigh. She flapped a hand in front of her face like a fan. "Lord, honey, I barely talked myself into coming here. I swear I'd almost rather have to skin a skunk."

Deep dimples appeared in Hannah's cheeks as she smiled, and then she was laughing. To Clementine's surprise she heard herself laughing as well. She remembered her first day in Rainbow Springs and how Hannah and Snake-Eye and Nickel Annie had laughed as they tried to winch the piano out of the wagon and how she'd envied them because they were friends, and a revelation came to her then that was stunning and rather wonderful. We're friends, she thought. Hannah Yorke and I.

Hannah snapped her parasol shut and whirled around. She leaned over to pull something off the seat of the shay, and when she straightened up, her arms were filled with a beautiful hand-pieced quilt. "Where I come from, when a man and his woman move into a new house, their friends give them a welcome gift."

"Why, I don't know what to say . . ." Clementine's hand came up to stroke the quilt. The quilt was exquisitely made, with tiny, almost invisible stitches, the colors so bright and cheerful it reminded her of wildflowers. "Except to thank you, of course," she finished, and she smiled. *"Their friends give them a welcome gift"* . . . a friend. She *did* have a friend.

Hannah's dimples started to deepen, and then they vanished entirely and her eyes turned wary, like those of a dog too used to the feel of its master's boot.

Gus came striding up to them, his face tight. "Damn you, Zach. I told you not to bring her here."

"Last time I looked, *brother*," Rafferty said in that cold, silky voice that had Clementine's gaze darting to his hips to see if he wore his gun, "my name was on the deed to this place, right next to yours."

Clementine took the quilt from Hannah and thrust it at her husband's chest. "Look at the fine gift Mrs. Yorke has given us. Perhaps you should take it on into the bedroom now, though, before it gets soiled."

He swung his angry gaze onto her. "Clementine, if you think—"

"Please, Gus. And then we'll all try a taste of your famous cider, shall we?"

Gus's mustache quivered as if he would spit out more angry words. But instead he spun on his heel and headed for the house, and Clementine eased out the breath she'd been holding. She knew Gus; he'd been all primed to say something mean about Mrs. Yorke's past. Mr. Rafferty would have had to hit him then, and both brothers would've been sporting scrapes and bruises for days to come.

When Clementine looked around again she saw that Hannah now held a watermelon in her arms. "And this is from Nickel Annie," Hannah was saying. Her voice was a little trembly, but the dimples were back in place. "She carried it all the way here from Fort Benton, wrapped in bunting and nestled in an egg crate. She said she was sorry she couldn't be here herself."

"Oh, my . . ." Clementine said as Hannah passed the watermelon to her as if it were a swaddled baby. It wasn't very big and it was rather yellow at one end, but it brought another lump to Clementine's throat. This time she dared a glance at Rafferty, but he was looking at Hannah and smiling.

"Hey, Shiloh!" he shouted suddenly and waved an arm through the air. "What are you waiting on? Agitate them catguts and let's dance!"

"You asking this child to cut a jig with you, cowboy?" Shiloh yelled back at him.

"Hell, no, I already got me a woman!" Laughing, Rafferty slipped his arm around Hannah's waist and pulled her toward the dance floor.

Shiloh sat on a barrel, crossed his knees, swung one foot, and tapped the other. He put the bow to his fiddle and lifted his head . . . and his eyes went wide. All the laughter and gay talk halted abruptly as a band of Indians emerged from around a bend in the north road.

There were about a dozen men mounted on piebald and pinto ponies. An equal number of women and children were on foot leading more ponies that pulled lodge poles packed with tipis. A pack of mangy, underfed dogs barked wildly as they darted in and out among the horses' hooves.

The man who rode at the head of the band wore a turkey-red calico shirt and white-man's pants with a breechclout over them. A single white feather decorated his braided hair. Although the day was warm, all of the women and children and most of the men wore ragged blanket coats laced up tight beneath their chins.

"Flatheads," she heard Rafferty say to Gus, who had suddenly reappeared at her side, the quilt still in his hands. "They don't usually stray this far off their reservation."

"They appear to be a pretty tatter-ass bunch of bucks," Gus said. "I reckon they aren't out for any trouble—at least not if they know what's good for them. We got them outnumbered three to one."

Rafferty cast his brother a mocking look. "Yeah. So do you also reckon I should go and make a little high palaver with their chief first? Before we start exchanging gunfire with the women and kids?"

The Indians had turned off the road into the hay meadow. The lodgepoles, trailing behind the packhorses, rattled over the uneven furrows. A child began crying and its mother scolded, the dogs barked. But a silence had settled over the ranch; not even the cottonwoods were stirring.

Clementine shifted the watermelon in her arms, feeling inside her an old familiar fear. She was often haunted by thoughts of the savages; she had only to close her eyes to see the tattoos on Saphronie's face and the gouges in the wall of the buffalo hunter's cabin. And Iron Nose . . . he had not been caught and hanged with the rest of his renegade gang. He was still free and filled with hate. He and Joe Proud Bear, who with his family had disappeared into the emptiness of the western mountains. Only a yellow ring in the grass was left to mark the place where their tipi had stood by the Rainbow River.

The Indian chief held both hands in front of his body, the back of his left hand turned down. "He's making the sign for peace," Gus said, and she heard the tension ease out of his voice. "I told Zach they were tame Indians."

Rafferty returned the gesture. The two men spoke some more with their hands and a few monosyllabic words Clementine couldn't hear. She was struck by the sight of Gus's brother standing toe to toe with the Indian. Even in his fancy clothes he looked almost more savage, more capable of sudden violence, than the man with the white feather in his hair.

Rafferty rolled cigarettes for himself and the chief. Then he turned and made a sawing motion in the air. Shiloh drew the bow across his fiddle, and the jaunty strains of "Little Brown Jug" broke the silence. One of the Indian children, a boy, whooped and began to dance.

Rafferty came strolling back. "They're on a buffalo hunt and horsestealing expedition to the Crow lands southeast of here," he said to Gus. "I invited them to stay for the party."

Clementine stiffened, and Gus patted her shoulder. "It's for the best, girl. We'd do better to have them here underfoot, where we can keep an eye on them. Otherwise come morning half our beeves will be missing."

She would never conquer her fear of them. Capture, rape, enslavement by savages—a dread instilled in every white woman long before she ever set one dainty foot westward. But the Indians of Clementine's imagination, who crept on moccasined feet up to her bedroom window at night, hatchets and scalping knives clutched in their bloodied hands, seemed like made-up figures on souvenir cards when compared to the thin, ragged wanderers who now huddled in the middle of her hayfield. And out here, when a man and his family rode across your ranch, they were invited to stop and eat and rest up a spell. This land was too empty, too lonely, to turn anyone away.

"Yes . . . I can see they must be asked to stay," she said.

She felt Rafferty's eyes on her. She knew it all the time now, knew it when he looked at her. Oh, yes, she could feel it—a swift, sharp plunge of her guts that left her breathless and full of confounded, frightening feelings that had no name.

She turned her head, lifting her gaze to meet his. And though she was prepared for the fierce intensity in his yellow eyes, still she rocked a little on her feet when she was struck by the full force of it. When her mouth would let her, she said, "What's the chief's name?"

"White Hawk."

Clementine walked alone into the middle of the hayfield. The chief was a tall, bull-shouldered man with a stately dignity that matched anything she could muster. He had a seamed and rugged face, with a long blade of a nose, sharp as a tomahawk, and a wide, turned-down mouth.

"Mr. White Hawk," she said. "You and your people are welcome here."

He stared at her, his face as enigmatic as the mountains at his back. He grunted and pointed to her swollen stomach, then to the watermelon she still carried, forgotten, in her arms. And then he did the most astonishing thing—he pantomimed swallowing the melon whole and pointed to her stomach again. Color rose hot and fast on Clementine's cheeks, but laughter rose as well so that she had to press her lips together to catch it, in case the chief took offense.

She held the watermelon up to him and pointed to the knife in the sheath at his waist. "Perhaps you would like to try a swallow of it yourself."

Clementine shared her watermelon with the Indian called White Hawk. She stood in the meadow, crushing the hay stubble beneath the soles of her French kid shoes, watermelon juice running sweet and sticky through her fingers, and the September sun warm and gentle on her head. You take it all in, Rafferty had said, with your eyes and your breath and the pores of your skin. She looked from the Indian to the raw and lonesome mountains, and something opened up inside her, flowed into her and out of her, and for one trembling, exquisite moment she was White Hawk and the redolent haystacks and the music from Shiloh's fiddle.

She was Montana.

Her candy-pink-striped skirts flared like the lip of a bell as she twirled, showing off a purple petticoat and red-tasseled shoes.

Gus frowned. That woman . . . that woman hadn't once been allowed to catch her breath since Shiloh took up his bow. She went from one man's arms to another's, and those who hadn't taken a turn with her yet waited on the sidelines stamping their feet until their spurs jangled. But if Zach didn't mind that nearly every man in the territory was handling his whore, Gus thought sourly, then he didn't know why he should stew about it.

It was a wonder to him anyway that his calico-chasing brother had stuck all summer with one woman. At least it could now be said that Zach Rafferty was being faithful in his sinning.

Gus hooked his hip on the hitching rail and folded his arms across his chest. He cast a wistful look behind him at the open kitchen door, where Clementine had disappeared to do some more of the endless chores with the food. He wanted to ask his wife to dance, but it probably wasn't proper for a woman in her condition to do all that bouncing in public. Hannah Yorke's breasts certainly did bounce as she danced. They nearly spilled out of that scandalous dress she was wearing, like a pair of pink and dewy peaches. Large peaches.

Gus cursed beneath his breath and pushed himself upright. He straightened the kerchief at his neck and smoothed his mustache. He had to elbow his way through a crowd of cowboys, sheepherders, and prospectors to plant himself before her.

He offered her a stiff smile. "Will you try a turn with me, Hannah?"

A look of wary surprise crossed her face. But then her dimples creased with a knowing smile, and a laugh gurgled deep in her throat. "Of course, Gus," she said, and offered him her arm as Shiloh switched from the schottische he'd been playing to a waltz.

This was the first time Gus had ever touched Hannah Yorke. She felt soft and warm in his arms, and she smelled as sweet as a hothouse rose. He tried to keep his gaze off her breasts and off her mouth. Her ripe, wet mouth. Man must truly have a predilection for sin, Gus thought, because this woman stirred him. She *shouldn't,* and he didn't want her to. But, oh, Lord, she did. And he waited in embarrassed agony for the dance to end so that he could be free of her.

By the time Gus steered Hannah off the dance floor and toward his brother he was feeling more like his old self. He had looked on a woman and lusted after her in his heart, but he had triumphed over the sin and vanquished it.

A smile broke across his face when he saw that Clementine stood beside Zach. His sweet Clementine, who, unlike Hannah Yorke, was all that a woman should be. Modest and pure in her ways, gentle and submissive . . . well, perhaps not always submissive. But she was young yet and she would learn. As her husband, he knew it was his duty to guide her.

Clementine stood beside Zach with the hitching rail at their backs, the logs of freshly peeled pine shining white in the sun. They looked posed there as if for one of her photographs, but for all the attention she paid him they might as well have been at opposite ends of the earth. For a while it had seemed his wife and his brother had only to get within spitting distance and they behaved like a pair of alley cats fighting over the same fishbone. Now they rarely spoke, and he'd noticed lately that they couldn't even abide looking at each other anymore. It sorrowed him to realize the two people he cared most about in this world would probably always hate each other.

At least maybe the sore feelings would ease some now between him and his brother, Gus thought. It hadn't taken that much skin off his pride after all, asking Hannah Yorke to dance. And he could understand Zach's weakness for the woman better, now that he'd felt the tug of her lure.

"That Shiloh, he sure can kick up a tune . . ." Gus began, but his voice trailed off. Zach's eyes were focused on the road coming from town, and they shone with a bright, laughing mischief that raised the fine hair on the back of Gus's neck.

Slowly he turned and he felt his own jaw come un-hinged.

"Well, glory be and hallelujah," he heard Zach say, and the words echoed back at him from wells of memory, "if it ain't One-Eyed Jack McQueen."

15

JACK MCQUEEN SAT ON the back of a mule the color of dirty dishwater and regarded his sons out of his one good eye. "Well, glory be and hallelujah, the Lord has seen fit to answer my prayers. My boys! I've found my long-lost boys!"

"What are you doing here?" Gus said, his voice crack-ing. The father of his memory was a bigger man, but the face was the same: the life-chiseled canniness of it and the slyness behind the charming smile. The sparkling blueness of his eyes . . . eye. Gus felt a sick twisting in his belly that he knew was shame. He was supposed to be a man now himself, but he was always going to be ashamed to be the issue of a no-account like Jack McQueen.

Apparently the man was back working the salvation bunco, for he was wearing a swallowtail coat shiny with age, rusty trousers, and Geneva bands yellowed with hard wear. Always dress shabbier than the flock you are fleecing, he'd told them many a time when they were boys. Women especially are more willing to trust their pocketbooks, and their hearts, to a poor but pious preacher man.

The poor but pious Reverend McQueen drew in a
breath that expanded his chest. He looked around, taking in the cowboys and miners high-stepping arm in arm
around the enormous fiddle-playing black man, and the
trestle tables loaded with enough food to feed the entire
Sioux nation. He fixed Gus with his one-eyed gaze, and a
shrewd amusement creased his face. Gus knew that look.
It was the one he always got when he was all set to make
trouble and prepared to enjoy it.

"I am pleased to discover you are well, Gustavus. Lo
and all these many a year," he said with the seminary-
polished manner he always put on with the Geneva bands.
When he peddled patent medicine, he spewed fifty-dollar
words faster than any college textbook. When he sat down
to a card game, he became a good ol' boy, full of bluff
and bluster and oozing snake oil charm. When he sold
bogus mine shares, he was a posh East Coast swell full of
acumen and sincerity. "Yes, indeed, pleased and humbled
and . . . oh, all manner of things to see you, dearest boy,"
he said now. "And how is my dear and faithful wife, your
mother?"

"She's dead."

"Jesus reigns!" The reverend snatched the battered
stovepipe hat off his head. Sunlight glinted off the oil in the
long, dark hair that hung straight to his shoulders like an
Indian's. Hair that hid the nub of his ear, which had been
cut off for horse stealing when Jack McQueen was a boy. At
least that was what the old man had told them once, but
then, he made up crazy lies just to get in the practice.

"O Lord . . ." He lifted his eye to heaven, his face
turning all gentle and weary, as if the sins of the world lay
heavy on his heart. "We do pray for the soul of our dear
departed, Stella McQueen. 'Bone of my bones, and flesh of
my flesh,' and a sinner, alas, in the eyes of God. Deserter of
her loving husband, repudiator of the innocent child of her
womb. Have mercy on her, we beg of thee, O Lord. And
should she, by the miracle of your holy grace, be repentant

of her sins, then welcome her as is thy wont into the bosom of thy glory, amen."

He settled the hat back on his head. A tear gleamed in his eye; a soft, sad smile lay gentle on his mouth. "Did the bitch suffer before she died?"

Anger rose in Gus's throat so hot and fast he nearly choked. "What are you doing here?"

"Well, now, Gustavus, that is a fine story in and of itself. An example of the ways in which the Lord doth provide. I was riding the circuit in Missouri—and a tightfisted lot of infidels they are in that part of the country—when I was visited with a calling to preach the Word in Deadwood. The Lord appeared to me in a dream. He spoke of a city of sin, a city of souls ripe for conversion, a city—"

"Full of saloons," a mocking voice drawled, "where they play poker with gold dust for ante."

Gus looked at his brother. Zach leaned back on the hitching rail, with his arms straight, his palms braced against the rough wood. He had a devil-damn-you light in his eyes and a crafty, hold-on-to-your-pocketbook grin, just like their old man.

The reverend didn't acknowledge his younger son by so much as a glance, but Gus saw a tic begin to pulse below the black eye patch. "As I was saying, I was in Deadwood when one day the calling guided me into a sin parlor—strictly on the Lord's business, you understand—where I fell into conversation with a Mexican boy who allowed as how he had worked spring roundup for a Montana rancher by the name of Gus McQueen. I logically presumed there couldn't be two of you, so I ambled on over for a little visit," he finished, as if it were nothing more than a jaunt to the next county and not a matter of hundreds of miles.

He shifted some on the mule's back and looked then at his other boy. His hedge of shaggy black brows drew together over his hawk nose. "I must say I didn't expect to find you here as well, Zacharias."

"Life is just plumb full of sweet surprises."

The reverend pursed his lips. "A man can raise up a son, but only the Lord can lift up a man to the glory of his righteous image. God gave you the hearing ear and the understanding heart. But when you turned away from me, you turned away from the path of righteousness."

"Amen, Revver. But then, we can't all be saved. Otherwise there wouldn't be any need for a hell."

Jack McQueen thrust a clenched fist into the air and shook it at the sky. "'God is not mocked!'" he thundered, and Gus felt Clementine jump beside him. "When you smite his tidings, you are smiting the holy hand that sends it."

He dropped his fist, and his gaze went to Hannah, who looked back up at him with both wonder and laughter on her face. His eye sparkled with manly appreciation, and she smiled. His gaze moved to Clementine.

"That greaser boy, he said you had married, Gustavus. Yea, a merciful Providence has carried me through many a danger so that I may greet your fair wife, my daughter in grace."

He slid off the mule, a tall man with long, lanky bones and an air about him that inspired fascination. Gus watched his wife carefully, to see if she was fascinated. His father's smile was full of flashing teeth and dazzling charm. He lifted her hand and brought it to his lips. "'Who can find a virtuous woman?'" he said in the deep raspy voice that had separated so many women from their virtue. "'For her price is far above rubies.'"

Clementine regarded him with that wide, intent gaze that could lay a man open to the bone. Slowly she pulled her hand from his grasp and turned to Gus, a look of utter disbelief on her face. "Is this man truly your father, Mr. McQueen?"

"Lord, we are all poor worms in the dust, struggling for life and happiness."

"We are, we are! Praise God, we are!"

"Help us poor sinners. Help us, O Lord, to take the religion of Jesus into our hearts."

"Blessed Jesus! Blessed Jesus!"

The jamboree had been uplifted—or had deteriorated, depending on your point of view—into a revival meeting. Shiloh's fiddle had been silenced, and voices were now being raised in praise of the Lord. The Reverend Jack McQueen stood atop a wagon box and preached in a bull-throated voice fit to rouse amens from the angels. Gus paced at the back of the crowd, not wanting to be where he was, not daring to be anywhere else.

His father's only competition came from the barrel of whiskey-fortified cider that Gus wasn't supposed to know about. It was doing a roadhouse business with those few who were irredeemable, like Pogey and Nash and Gus's hard-drinking, hell-bound little brother.

"The Lord shall deliver us from the paw of the lion and the paw of the bear."

"Praise Him! Praise the Lord!"

Oh, he was so good, Gus thought. He had always been so good. His description of hell could make a brave sinner feel faint. His rendering of the glory of the Word could redeem Satan himself.

Gus's gaze searched out his wife and found her. She had distanced herself from it all and was standing on the porch of their new house to watch the preaching. No doubt comparing the Reverend Jack to her own illustrious Boston Brahmin father, who delivered decorous sermons from a white-painted pulpit in a granite church.

A hand fell on his shoulder, turning him around. It startled him so that he stumbled and his brother had to steady him. "Kinda takes you back, don't it?" Zach said, the whiskey burning wild in his eyes. "The old man up there, playing the revver better than Jesus Christ himself could do it, whipping and softening them up for salvation. I keep thinking I should be fanning pockets, looking for something to steal."

The tension gusted out of Gus in a sigh. "What is he *doing* here?"

His brother cocked an ear toward the wagon box. "Sounds like he's giving us the latest authentic news from hell."

"*He* is the latest authentic news from hell. You know what will happen, don't you? He'll try to seduce the wife of every man in the valley. He'll get caught cheating at cards in the Best in the West, and Hannah will shoot at him with that boob gun of hers." He emitted a ragged laugh, then added a little maliciously, "Unless he's screwing her to the mattress by then, of course. And if there's a widow somewhere living on a pension, he'll find her and chisel the money out of her—"

"But he'll show her one hell of a good time while he's at it," Zach said, with a grin that was so much like their old man's that Gus almost shuddered.

"We got to get him back on that mule and pointed south or west or any direction so long as it's away from here." The stovepipe hat was being passed around now. Even from where they stood in the back, they could hear the clink and rattle of coins. "Those are our friends and neighbors," Gus said. "He's taking money from our friends."

Zach lifted his shoulders in a lazy shrug as he fired up a cigarette. "Short of bushwhacking him, I don't know what we can do about it. Besides, soon as he gets wind you want him gone, he'll stick around just to rile you." He squinted at Gus through a haze of smoke. "He's probably got some swampland to sell us, or a silver mine just ripe for investing. He'll tell us how, since we're his kin, he's going to offer us the deal of a lifetime. But once he realizes the old dog's pups are wise to his tricks, he'll move on to easier pickings."

"Please God," Gus said.

The preaching had reached a fiery conclusion. Shiloh's deep voice began to sing, the sweet notes lingering in the hot afternoon air: "Amazing Grace, how sweet it is . . ." Gus patted the pocket of his white buckskin vest, looking for his watch. "We should start the bronco-busting now," he said, "before he passes the damn hat again." He searched his hip pockets. He was sure he had—

Zach pulled a nickel hunting-case watch from his own vest and flipped open the cover. "Three o'clock," he said.

Gus looked at the watch dangling from his brother's quick and clever fingers. He knew he should laugh, or at least smile, but all he could feel was sick. "He's going to sour things for us here. I can see it happening already."

His brother's mouth curved into a smile meant to be easy. He tucked the watch back into Gus's pocket where it belonged. "I only wanted to see if I could still do it."

"What are you wanted for?"

Rafferty looked his father in the eye and lied. "Why, nothing, Revver. I'm as straight as a Puritan's backbone."

"Of course you are, dear boy. And I still have cherry balls." He squinted up at Rafferty, his mouth twisted with a foxy smile. "Is there a man with a grudge looking for you, perhaps? If not, whyever are you hiding out in this pathetic backwater under a handle I've never heard of?"

"Maybe I just don't want anybody confusing me with you."

"You should be so lucky, my dear, dear boy."

Amusement tugged at Rafferty's mouth as he leaned over the fence rail. A white-socked chestnut danced around the corral, dodging the rope of the cowboy who was trying to hobble it. Gus had finally gotten the bronc-busting going, once the praying had run out of steam. They had caught the wild mustangs out on the range last week—the ones they would use for the fall roundup. A few had been broken already, but they all needed the pitch taken out of them and some of the men were making a contest out of it.

His father settled next to Rafferty at the fence. If Jack

McQueen wanted to look his younger son in the eye now he had to tilt back his head to do it. When they had parted company, Rafferty was still a gangly boy, three inches shorter and thirty pounds lighter than the man who had raised him.

"Are there many tin badges in these parts?" the reverend said.

Rafferty considered the question from every angle while he watched the cowboy in the corral try to slap a saddle on a moving target. The horse neighed and kicked at anything it could see, including shadows. The warm breeze carried with it the smell of churned-up dust and sweating horsehide. Rafferty decided that his dear father, being such a doting parent, was probably trying to find out if there was any money to be made by turning him in to the law.

"I got caught passing boodle in New Orleans," he said. "It was a piddling-ass crime, so I don't reckon there's much of a price on my head, but you're welcome to try for it." The story in itself was true enough, and he enjoyed playing the game of lying to his father with the truth.

Jack McQueen rubbed a hand over his jaw. "No, I hardly think so. Even if I were to take you in—and I'm not saying I couldn't, mind you—I wouldn't want certain individuals getting too close a look at my own face, if you get my drift."

"Yeah? Maybe *I* ought to take *you* in."

The preacher's lips pulled back from his teeth. "You could try." He made a small huffing noise in the back of his throat, shaking his head. "Passing boodle—oh, really, Zacharias. Nobody gets caught passing boodle. Why, I imagine those bills were so amateur they wouldn't have passed for ass-wipe in a crap house."

Rafferty would never admit that he was only seventeen when it happened and that someone he thought of as a friend, someone he trusted, had used him to pass the counterfeit. He'd always been ashamed of that one lapse in judgment. Any boy with Jack McQueen for a father learned young not to let himself get used by anybody.

In the corral, the cowboy had finally gotten the saddle on the chestnut, and now the horse was buck-jumping around in a wheel in a vain effort to be rid of it. Rafferty noticed that Gus was standing on the other side of the corral with White Hawk and his braves, pretending to watch the horse, but watching their old man instead.

The reverend rested his elbows on the top rail of the fence and hooked a bootheel over the lower one. Rafferty cast a sideways glance at his father. The man was almost fifty now and looking it. Small broken veins webbed his nose, and the skin sagged off his prominent cheekbones. A fold of belly hung over his trousers. Rafferty had seen a man break a bone in his hand once, trying to hit that belly. Now you could bury your fist in there like in a pillow.

His father felt him looking. A faint flush colored his cheeks and he hitched his pants up over the bulge at his waist. "You boys have yourselves a nice little spread here," he said, the skin around his eye crinkling with his roguish smile. "And there appears to be plenty of sheep in this valley just ripe for salvation. Perhaps I'll hang out my shingle—metaphorically speaking, of course. Do some work in the Lord's name."

"Don't say that where Gus can hear you. You'll spoil his day."

The reverend's head fell back in a deep and genuine laugh. "I do like you, boy. I've always liked your style. It's a pity you didn't stick with me instead of leaving me high, dry, and lonesome as you did. It was I, after all, who taught you everything you know."

Yeah, Rafferty thought, like how to cheat and steal from others before they can cheat and steal from you.

"Why, by the time you were old enough to make a bone in your britches, you could pull a bunco, buzz a pocket, screw a woman till she was dizzy blind, and play the sharpest skin game I've ever had the pleasure to

witness—and all without breaking into a sweat. I raised
you up in my image, just as the Holy Book says. I *made*
you, my dear Zacharias."

And those, Rafferty thought, were the truest words
the man had probably spoken all year. Jack McQueen was
in him, a part of him. It wasn't just a case of there but for
the grace of God, but rather only a matter of time. One day
he was going to look in a mirror and see his father staring
back at him. The life he hoped to make for himself, the
man he wanted to make of himself . . . it would all collapse
like a rotten pumpkin.

His ma had known the truth. She had stood on the
deck of the steamboat and watched him grow smaller
as the muddy water rose up between them, and she had
looked into his soul and seen nothing there worth taking
with her and certainly nothing worth coming back for.

"What I don't understand," his father was saying in
an aggrieved tone, "is why you took off, and in the manner you did—like a thief in the night, if you'll pardon the
expression. Apparently I was laboring under the misappre-
hension that you and I were partners."

Partners . . . my God. "Hell, I couldn't get away from
you fast enough."

"You are being hurtful, Zacharias." And the devil of it
was, the old man looked and sounded hurt. But then, you
could never tell with Jack McQueen what was genuine and
what was merely guile. "My old man used to whale on me
until I couldn't walk," he said. "But I never raised a hand
to either of you boys. Indeed, I treated you as if you had
brains and were tough enough to use them—although I
admit I often had my doubts about Gustavus. I did the
one thing a father can do for his sons: I taught you how the
game is played."

"You taught us how to cheat at it."

"That *is* how the game is played. Don't say you've
grown soft on me, boy."

The cowboy was riding the chestnut now, combing its sides with his spurs to make it pitch livelier, kicking up a whirlwind of dust. "Eehaw!" Gus yelled from the other side of the corral. "Stay with her!"

A stillness came over Rafferty. A feeling of suspended breath, of quiet waiting. He turned his head, knowing she would be there.

Clementine and Hannah were walking down from the new house to see the bronco-busting. Hannah was laughing, and there was a lilt to Clementine's step. The breeze blew her skirt against the swell of her belly, and sunlight glistened off her hair. He couldn't help watching her any more than he could help breathing.

His father's voice rasped in his ear. "Fancy Gustavus taking himself such a wife. I'll wager you he has to court her every time he wants to bed her. That redheaded filly, now, is more to my taste—long and snappy as a six-horse whip. She would give a man quite a ride."

"Hannah is mine."

His father's laugh was deep and easy. "Not only yours, she isn't. The good Lord, bless him, made women like her to be shared. And I lied when I said you have yourselves a nice spread here. Any fool can see it's barely making it. Any fool but Gustavus. He expects the dollars to start crawling into his jeans any day now, doesn't he? But you know you're only a cold winter or a dry summer away from being busted. Only you'll stick it because you're stubborn and you always did have to try to spare that pretty-pious brother of yours the pain of his illusions."

"That's right, Revver," Rafferty said, letting anger edge his voice. The old man had rarely given Gus any credit, never allowed him any pride. Gus was the heart and guts of the ranch. A bad year might break them, but the ranch wouldn't even exist if it weren't for his brother. "I'm sticking it."

"Of course you are, dear boy. Right up until the day he walks in on you in bed with his wife."

Rafferty went very still. In the corral the chestnut crawfished backward and the cowboy rode air, then hit the dirt with a bone-rattling thud.

Rafferty had spent the summer he was eighteen breaking bangtails like that chestnut at five bucks a head. One hot afternoon he had been given a coal-black bronc with the biggest feet he'd ever seen on a horse. One of those old-timers who hang on corral fences all day had observed that a horse with feet that big couldn't be ridden, but Rafferty had only laughed.

He had thought his tailbone was going to get pounded out through the top of his rattled head, but he'd stuck to that damn cayuse until its nose was hanging down between its knees, and he'd laughed again at the old-timer. "I thought you said he couldn't be rode," he crowed, and no sooner was the last of it out of his mouth than the bronc arched its back and plunged sideways through the air. One minute Rafferty had been sitting relaxed and cocky in the saddle, and the next he was lying flat on his back in the dust and biting down on the unmanly urge to scream from the pain in his dislocated shoulder.

The old-timer had stood over him, grinning like he'd just won first prize at a kissing booth. "That'll larn you, kid, never t' underestimate a horse or a man."

He had forgotten how dangerous it was to underestimate his father. Even with only one good eye, Jack McQueen could still see in a glance what it took most men years' worth of studying.

He made his fists open. He wrapped his hands around the rail, gripping the wood so tight the veins and sinews of his wrists stood out. "You son of a bitch," he said.

"You are being hurtful again, and I am not the one at fault here. 'Lust not after her beauty in thine heart; neither let her take thee with her eyelids.' If it were only you lusting after her, I would say the poor boy might be spared the humiliation of being cuckolded by his own brother. But I've seen the way she looks at you. She hasn't worked it all out in her mind just yet, but when she does, she's going to be lifting her skirts for you quicker than—"

Rafferty whipped around and grabbed the lapels of his father's coat, hauling him up on his toes so that they were eye to eye. "If I didn't already know there was such a thing as pure trouble in this world, you would alter my mind." He flexed his muscles once, then relaxed his grip, letting the reverend slide out of his hands. He smoothed out the wrinkles in his father's coat and spoke in a flat, soft voice. "You keep your thoughts to yourself and your mouth shut, and if you come even close to causing her misery in any way, I'll kill you for it."

Jack McQueen's clever mouth turned disdainful. "Such a display, dear boy. And all for naught. You can't seriously expect me to believe you would slaughter your own flesh and blood. You're tough, but not that tough."

Rafferty waited a beat, long enough to see the uncertainty settle over his father's face. Long enough to see the tic take up its pulse below the black patch. Then he smiled his meanest smile.

"Tell that to the man who took your eye."

The mustang bawled and pitched, squealing as it crashed into the poles of the corral.

The Reverend Jack cupped his hand around his mouth and shouted across the minced dirt of the arena, "He's too much horse for you, Gustavus!"

The brothers stood next to each other, watching as four men tried to saddle the crazed horse. "He's spoiled," Rafferty said. "Someone's already tried to break him and mishandled it." The horse was a claybank, the same color as a mountain cat and just as wild.

A muscle bunched along Gus's jaw as he stared at the bronc. Gus was a fine rider, but the fact was he didn't much like horses, and deep down in the guts of him he had a fear of the really raw ones.

Rafferty saw the fear in his brother's face, in the taut skin over his cheekbones and in his bright, shifting eyes. "Sun's close to setting," he said. "Might as well just turn him loose and call it a day."

"A man," the reverend said loud enough for all the other fence riders to hear, "shouldn't fork a saddle if he's scared of being throwed. Or so they say."

Gus's gaze stayed riveted on the bronc—all bunched and quivering eight hundred pounds of him. Rafferty felt a flash of irritation with his brother. Some days tormenting him was as easy as squashing an ant with a sledgehammer.

"You're all the time bragging that you can ride anything with hair on it," Gus said. "I'm surprised you don't have calluses from patting yourself on the back." He pointed his chin at the bronc. "So why don't you try that one?"

"Because he ain't worth messin' with." And he hadn't done any bragging, either, but Rafferty let that pass.

"Some men," Jack McQueen said, "can't help feeling a certain shame to discover they've fathered a boy with a weak gizzard. 'Be strong, and quit yourselves like men,' so saith the Lord. I, on the other hand, am more tolerant of human foibles. You have nothing to prove to me, Gustavus."

Rafferty started toward the mustang, to turn it loose, not to ride it. Gus caught his arm.

"Leave the saddle on him."

"How many times've you watched the old man stir up trouble just for the hell of it? Why are you letting him chouse you into this?"

Gus jerked his head in a hard, sharp nod. "You know why. Okay, so maybe I'm scared, and maybe it's harder to do it when you're scared. You wouldn't appreciate that, because you've never been scared of a blasted thing in your entire life. For once I'm going to prove it to him. I'm going to prove it to myself."

"Prove what, dammit—that you're stupid?"

Gus pushed past him, mouth and jaw set rigid.

"Ah, hell," Rafferty said, and followed him.

The bronc was snubbed to a corral post by a lasso tight around its neck. Two men with braced feet had either side of the hackamore. Held down as he was, the horse still looked ready to explode, crouched back on its haunches, ears flat, nostrils flaring. Gus was going to get his fool neck broken, and Rafferty was mad enough at him now not to give a good goddamn.

Rafferty slipped the lasso and took hold of the hackamore's left cheek strap, forcing the bronc's head sharp around toward its neck. The other men melted back, putting the fence between themselves and any flying hooves.

Rafferty stroked the trembling withers. "Easy, boy," he said softly. "Easy, easy, now." The horse snorted hot breath on his neck.

Gus approached the mustang's side, quirt in his hand, silver spurs glinting in the sun. The bronc's right rear leg flashed, the hoof slicing air. Gus tugged his hat down tight and low over his eyes, as if he actually thought he might still be wearing it after all this was over.

Rafferty gave him a taunting smile. "Hadn't you ought to take off that pretty vest of yours, big brother? You wouldn't want to be getting it all dirty."

The smile Gus gave back to him was tight and full of fear, but Rafferty was being careful not to look directly at him. "Are you implying, little brother, that I'm going to wind up eating dust?"

"Soon as your butt hits the saddle."

Gus gathered up the reins and with his right hand turned the stirrup for his boot. "Use the bucking strap," Rafferty said, pitching his voice low so that only his brother could hear.

Gus's mouth flattened, but he wrapped his fingers around the strap. The bronc snorted, hindquarters dancing.

The brothers' gazes met, and deep in Gus's eyes was

the same bruised and bewildered look he would get as a boy when the old man would lay into him like this, not with a strap or a fist, but with words that could hurt down to the bone. Gus hadn't understood it then and he didn't now—how cruelty could exist in the world without a reason. He just kept on thinking there should be a way to make his father love him.

Rafferty took a deep breath, trying to shake off the ache. "Gus, you don't have to do this."

"It's always been so easy for you," Gus said, the words coming out mangled from the tightness in his throat. "You're not only tougher than the rest of us poor sons of bitches, you *know* you're tougher. You make me sick—"

"Shut up and get on the fucking horse."

Rafferty released the cheek strap and whipped the blindfold off the mustang's eyes as soon as Gus's right foot left the ground. The horse jackknifed and Gus slammed into the saddle with such force Rafferty heard his teeth crack. The mustang bogged its head and boiled, lock-legged, its back arched like a bow.

And Gus flew off him like crack-the-whip.

"What do I do with this?"

Clementine looked up from the purple slabs of huckleberry pie she was cutting to the huge brown crock full of baked beans in Hannah's arms. "Oh, dear . . . ." Mrs. Graham's beans had been a dismal failure, which was not to be wondered at with men who, seven days out of seven, ate beans for breakfast, lunch, and dinner. "Perhaps White Hawk . . . ?"

Hannah shook her head, dimples flashing. "I already tried him. He pointed to the beans, down to his belly, back to the beans again, then bent over and made a noise like he was going to puke."

Clementine smothered a laugh with her hand. She darted a look out the open kitchen door to be sure none of the other women, especially Mrs. Graham, had heard what Hannah said, although there was little fear of that. Whenever Hannah came into the kitchen, the other women left it. As soon as Hannah left, the women came back. Like the tide, Clementine thought, in and out, in and out. And like the tide, they were wearing Hannah down. Her dimples had appeared less and less often as the day went on, and the easy laughter had left her mouth.

"Clementine . . ." Hannah set the crock of beans on the new round oak table. "I want to thank you for making me feel t'home here. I can tell it hasn't been easy." She nodded her head at the open door. "Those women, they won't soon forget that you took my part against theirs."

Clementine looked down at the pie. She licked a drop of sweet purple juice off her finger. "I get so lonely out here some days, Hannah, I go out and talk to the cows just to hear something besides the wind."

Hannah reached out to touch her hand, pulled back, then did it after all. Their fingers curled together, resting a moment on the table's shiny white oilcloth. "I get lonely, too," Hannah said.

Clementine cut another wedge of pie. A burst of manly yelping came from the direction of the corral. Someone shouted, "Ride 'im hard, Gus!"

"Hannah, do you think you might ever . . . that you and Mr. Rafferty might be married?"

Hannah twisted a thick curl around her finger. Bright color flooded her cheeks. "Funny you should ask that, since we talked about it ourselves for the first time this morning . . . Well, sorta danced around it like a coupla bears dancing 'round a beehive. I 'spect the whole idea of domesticity spooks the both of us."

Clementine was suddenly feeling a sick churning in the pit of her stomach, as if she'd eaten too much green fruit. She didn't want to think of Hannah and that man . . .

"I mean, marriage changes things, doesn't it?" Hannah said. "Being a wife can make for a whole lot of drudge work, not to put too fine a point on it. And when you're dead tired at the end of the day it's kind of hard to make your man whoop an' holler, let alone do any whoopin' and hollerin' yourself."

I will not ask her, she thought. I cannot. "Do you mean to tell me you actually whoop and holler when he . . . when you and a man . . ."

Hannah laughed. "It's kind of hard not to, honey. When the lovin' is so hot and sweet you think you're going to come bursting right out of your skin if you don't let it all out of you somehow . . . Well, you know that feeling."

The kitchen grew quiet. Clementine glanced up from the pie she was massacring and caught Hannah studying her. "Oh, *that* feeling," she said.

She suddenly became aware that the tenor of shouts and yelps coming from the corral had changed from laughter and cheers to cries of alarm. She and Hannah looked at each other and then started together for the door, knocking aside the new spindle chairs.

Hannah got there first and held her back. "They're bringing him up to the house."

"Who?" Clementine asked, her heart pounding so hard in her ears it drowned out Hannah's answer.

Three men carried Gus through the kitchen door. He was covered with corral dust and bleeding from a cut on the head.

"Where do you want him?" Horace Graham said, as if it were a sack of meal they carried, and not a woman's husband whose dust-streaked face was as white and waxy as a Christmas candle. A man whose dust-streaked face looked dead.

"This way," Clementine said in her most collected voice. A western woman, she knew, was never supposed to make a scene when her man was tossed by a bronc. It was a measure of a man's manliness—how he handled a horse. A man expected his woman to understand why he risked his neck trying to break one. Clementine looked at her man's pale face and wanted to pull it tight to her breast. But she was also angry enough to knock his head off his shoulders. She would never, she thought, understand what drove men to do the things they did.

She had them lay Gus on their new squab sofa, part of an upholstered parlor suite that had come all the way from Chicago. A good saddle horse had been sold for the money to buy that sofa. Dust rained off Gus onto the bottle-green damask. His spur caught, ripping the delicate material. Clementine put a needlepoint pillow under his bleeding head.

The men pressed around her, offering advice: wrap his head in brown paper soaked in vinegar; heat up a gummy paste of chewing tobacco and flour; make a compress of raw chicken; pour a slug of whiskey down his throat.

"He'll be all right," said the one person she had been waiting for. "If y'all will just step back, please, and give him some air."

Rafferty squatted down on his haunches beside the sofa. His hand hovered over Gus's hair, then gently fell, touching him in the way a father would touch his son.

Gus wrenched his eyes open, biting back a groan. A look passed between them, charged with something Clementine didn't understand. It was part of the game they played constantly, a sparring match of feints and jabs and occasional head-rocking blows. A game played deep in some masculine dimension that Clementine couldn't fathom. She thought she hated men sometimes, and these two men most of all.

"You ridden him yet?" Gus said.

Rafferty shook his head.

"Well, what the hell you waitin' on, a telegram from President Rutherford B. Hayes himself? Go peel the son of a bitch."

"Gus—"

"You scared? Is that it? You scared, little brother?"

"Yeah, sure I'm scared. Who wants to get his ass pitched clear into next week?"

Gus struggled to sit up. "Liar. You're a goddamn lying son of a bitch. Go on out there and break him. Go on, dammit. Go!"

Rafferty pressed his hands on his knees, pushing himself to his feet. He left without looking back at his brother, and the other cowboys all stampeded out the door after him. "Wrap them long legs of yourn twice around his belly," one of them shouted, "and mebbe then you can stick 'im."

Gus swung his legs off the sofa. He groped for Clementine's shoulder. "Help me up, girl. I want to watch this. The son of a bitch—always so damned cock-robin sure of himself."

She staggered as he put his weight on her and lurched to his feet. He swayed, groaning and wincing as he touched his head. "Son of a bitch," he said.

"Mr. McQueen, why are you behaving this way?" She had never heard so much cussing coming out of Gus's mouth. He trembled from a shakiness that came from deep inside him and had, she thought, only partly to do with having been thrown from a horse.

Gus looked up and saw Hannah standing in the doorway, her arms crossed under her full breasts. "I never met a man yet who wasn't stupid stubborn as a rock at times," she said.

Gus gave her a hard smile. "That horse fights like a polecat with its tail on fire, and your man is going to turn him into a pussycat. Don't you want to watch him do it?"

"No," Hannah said and went back into the kitchen.

Gus leaned on Clementine as they walked out of the parlor onto the porch. Gus's father stood at the bottom of the steps.

"I always thought you were all gurgle and no guts, boy," he said. "I'm beginning to see as how I might have wronged you."

A dark flush stained Gus's cheeks. "Yeah, well . . ." He straightened his back and pushed off of Clementine and hobbled down the steps alone. "Come on, Pa. Come let that brother of mine show you how it's properly done."

The setting sun cast a yellow glamour over the land, filling the sky with lariats of gold. A dust cloud hung over the corral. A dirty yellow horse lay on its side in the middle of the corral, its legs trussed like a Christmas turkey's.

Clementine did not like this bronco-busting. The little she had seen of it earlier had disturbed her so much that she couldn't bear to watch. If she were a mustang, used to running wild and free out on the range, she wouldn't want the intolerable degradation of a man on her back, either. And yet they were *broken* to it; there was no other word for it. A cowboy whipped the horse's haunches with his quirt and raked its flanks with his spurs each time the animal bucked, driving home the lesson: obey, obey, obey. Or suffer for it.

Rafferty went into the corral, telling the men behind him to leave the gate open. "Let him up," he said to the man who held the end of the rope that was cross-hobbling the bronc.

The mustang erupted out of the dirt in an explosion of dust. He stood, legs splayed, froth dripping from his mouth. He snorted through his distended red nostrils.

Rafferty stroked the horse's quivering neck, speaking to him in dulcet tones that sounded strange coming from such a hard mouth, such a hard man. He was still crooning sweet words in that soft, gentle voice when he grabbed the mustang's ear and twisted it cruelly, at the same time thrusting his boot into the stirrup and swinging into the saddle.

The horse stood frozen, head up in surprise and pain . . . then erupted into a whirlwind of muscle, hair, and bone. The bronc bunched and jumped and twisted itself into a corkscrew, and it seemed that Rafferty's head must surely be snapped off his neck.

"No bucking strap for my little brother," she heard Gus cry, pride and envy both deep in his voice. "He rides 'em slick."

The man won, as she had known he would, although it pained her to know, too, that the wild horse could be mastered. The bronc gave a last, mighty buck and then stood still. Foam flecked his chest. Sweat stained the man's shirt and dripped from his hair. Man and horse sucked in deep breaths that shook their chests and made their straining muscles quiver.

Clementine imagined herself going to him. She imagined getting up on that half-broken horse with him and riding into the wild and lonely mountains where no one would ever find them. She imagined being with him there, among the rugged peaks, sitting by a campfire with the stars for a roof, and having the courage to say to him the things she could never say to anyone else . . .

But she didn't go to him. He touched the horse's flanks lightly with his spurs. Then there was just settling dust where they had been, the whip of the bronc's tail as it flew out through the gate, and the flash of hooves before they were swallowed by the wind-stirred grass.

16

GUS MCQUEEN'S MUSTACHE CURLED UP around his generous smile, catching wisps of snowflakes out of the air like a feather duster. "This storm won't stick long," he said. "Why, we could still have ourselves another warm spell before winter really sets in."

"But I like the snow." Clementine leaned back to let it fall on her face, into her open mouth. Lacelike flakes floated out of the sky as if the clouds were crumbling. She wanted

to hurl herself into it, to roll in a tumble of skirts and petticoats and laughter, like a child.

"Clementine . . ."

Something in his voice made her lower her head to
look at him. A heaviness had come over his eyes, a tautness
to his mouth. He glanced over his shoulder at Pogey and
Nash, who sat bundled up side by side in matching buffalo
coats on matching gray burros. He pulled her to him and
kissed her long and hard and deep on the mouth.

She drew in a little gasp of pleasure when he was
through and steadied herself by grasping the folds of his
mackinaw poncho. He brushed the melting snow off her
cheek with his knuckles. His gaze fell to her stomach,
which strained against the soft gray wool of her dress. She
had only tossed an old brown wool shawl over her shoulders, even though it was snowing hard.

He felt the shape of her stomach with his palm. The
baby, as if knowing its father's touch, squirmed. "I'm going
to fret about you, girl, while I'm gone."

"There's no need to. Hannah says I'm as healthy as a
bee in butter." She let a peep of a smile show. "Though
Pogey says I look all swoll up like a toad in a churn."

"Still and all, I'm bringing that doctor back with me
when we pass through Deer Lodge," he said instead, "even
if I got to do it at gunpoint."

"Yes, Mr. McQueen. Thank you." She rather wanted
a doctor on hand when the baby was born, which would
not be for another month, although she felt monstrous, as
if she'd swallowed a dozen watermelons whole. She hadn't
told anyone, not even Hannah, how frightened she was of
what was coming. She dreamed some nights of her mother.
In the dream her mother would not stop screaming. She
screamed while they sealed her in the coffin and screamed
while they buried her in the cold, windswept cemetery, but
only Clementine seemed able to hear her.

"And you know what to do if there's trouble?" Gus
said.

"Yes, Mr. McQueen."

She resisted the urge to shiver. Gus had mounted an old fire bell on the roof of the new house. It made a ferocious clang and clatter when rung. Rafferty, living now by himself in the buffalo hunter's cabin, could hear it easily. All she had to do was pull on the rope and he would come. It made her feel safe and at peril, both at the same time. She trusted Zach Rafferty to protect her from Indians and wolves and grizzlies, but who would protect her from him? Who would protect her from herself?

The other times Gus had ridden to Butte Camp on mining business she had gone with him, but this time she was too bulky with child. It had taken six months and four trips before Gus had at last put together a consortium of investors to operate the Four Jacks. The final paperwork was to be signed this week, and the mining works and stamp mill would be in operation by spring. The investors, calling themselves the Four Jacks Consortium, had leased the mine from Pogey and Nash, agreeing to pay them half the profits on all the ore the consortium dug up and refined that yielded at least twenty-five percent silver. And Gus in turn would get twenty percent of the two old prospectors' share.

They didn't look to be getting rich off it any time soon, though. Gus had told her there was a saying that you needed a gold mine to keep your silver mine going.

He pulled on her lower lip with his thumb, a lip that was red and slightly swollen from his kiss. "I've learned to trust you least, wife, when you're yes-Mr.-McQueening me." His mouth turned serious. "I know you two get along about as well as a pair of polecats in a sack, but you *will* call on Zach if you need him?"

"Yes, yes, I shall. I promise," she lied. Iron Nose would have to burst into her parlor bristling with scalping knives and wielding half a dozen hatchets before she pulled that bell. It was comforting that, with half a hay meadow between them, whole days could pass now when she and Rafferty didn't even have to exchange a howdy. And as long as he stayed away from her, she didn't have to think about the sweet seizing she felt now in her heart when she saw him, and the way he made her soul tremble.

"Jeeeesus God!" Pogey bellowed, white clouds billowing around his head like steam from a locomotive stack. "We leavin' any time this week, Gus? My ass is already so frozen stuck to this saddle I couldn't crack a fart without losin' skin."

Nash whacked him in the stomach, causing a minor avalanche to slide off the brim of his hat. "Quit cussin'."

"What else is a man to do in weather like this, 'sides cuss? Cold like this sure do make a soul hanker for hell."

"You call this cold?" Nash scoffed. "Why I recollect the winter of 'fifty-two. It was so cold that year your spit'd freeze solid before it hit the ground. It was so cold the hair on your chest broke off when you scratched it. It was so cold icicles a foot long—"

"Ha! When a hen cackles, she's either layin' or lyin'. Who ever asked you for a blamed lecture on the subject?"

"A man can learn a heap of things if he keeps his ears washed and his mouth shut."

"I guess I better get," Gus said, "before those two melt all the snow with the hot air they're blowing and we find ourselves drowning in a flash flood." He squinted up into the floating flakes. "I reckon one good thing'll come out of this storm. It means the Reverend Jack will be crawling into a hole somewhere to drink away the winter, and we'll be spared the embarrassment of his preaching to our friends and neighbors while he fleeces them of their hard-earned coin."

Clementine brushed the accumulating powder off his shoulders. "I think perhaps Mr. Rafferty is right about your father. The best way to fight him is to ignore him."

"Hunh. At least that's one thing you two've managed to agree on." Smiling, he drew her to him to kiss her one last time. "I'll bring you a surprise from Butte."

"What?" she said eagerly. "What will you bring me?"

His laugh bounced across the snow-blanketed valley. "Now, if I told you, girl, then it wouldn't be a surprise."

She watched them ride away until they were swallowed by the snow. It was falling harder now. Big clumpy flakes swirled around her head, wetting her face and hair. She gathered the shawl closer to her. The air was raw and piercing, and dozens of chores awaited her inside, yet she lingered still.

She felt an odd tightening in her womb, and again the baby squirmed. Until yesterday she had felt as if her belly was almost up beneath her chin, but this morning she had awakened to a strange lightening. The baby felt alien to her now, like a thing apart from her.

She drew in a deep breath, smelling the cold that pinched her nose and the smoke from the chimney that rose blue against the sky. She lifted her face to the snow, tasting it on her lips, letting its coldness sting her flushed face. She opened her eyes wide, watching the flakes fall, one after the other, from the blank infinity above. She laughed suddenly, out loud, and stretched her fingers toward the sky, as if they could grow and turn into wings and carry her up into the crumbling clouds.

She heard the *snick* of wood rolling over crusty ice and frozen grass, and she felt a suffocating, heart-juddering jolt of panic before she turned.

Rafferty's long legs cut toward her across the hay meadow. He was pulling a cord of wood on a red pung behind him. She watched him come, squinting against the winter glare. Silhouetted against the stark and whirling whiteness, he was fierce and beautiful and frightening. She stared at his face, at the strong lines and angles of bone under the dark, taut skin. His black Stetson shaded his eyes from her, not letting her see how he was looking at her.

He suddenly seemed too fierce and beautiful to bear. Her gaze dropped to the braided frogs on his sheepskin coat as he stopped before her.

He had a bridle draped over his shoulder—a bridle of smooth, well-oiled leather and etched silver cheek plates and buckles. He slung it off and held it out to her.

It dangled from his hand, a hand that looked dark and naked against the cold white light around them. She didn't take it. "What's this?" she asked, though she knew what it was: Moses's bridle.

"This is the first snowfall, and you're still here."

"I have plenty of bridles, I don't need another."

He tossed the tack onto the load of wood. "I'm not giving you the bridle. I mean, I am, but only as a symbol of the horse it belongs with."

"I don't want that horse. He's big and he's ugly and he bites."

"He don't bite." He shifted his feet, his boots squeaking in the fresh snow. "You're hard on a man, Boston. Hard on his pride. I've played some crooked games in my time, but this is one bet I don't aim to welsh on."

A heavy silence fell between them. She felt an overwhelming urge to touch him, simply touch him.

She couldn't see his eyes, but she felt their heat like a caress on her face. "Do you still want me gone?"

"Yes." The word had left his taut mouth in a huff of white breath.

"Why?"

For a moment he stood there, not moving, saying nothing. But she saw his chest give a hard hitch. His voice broke over the words. "You know why, Boston. And God damn you to the hottest hell for it."

Something cracked inside her. Those jagged, jigsawed pieces of herself shifted again, shifted and came together in a way that couldn't, should never, have been possible.

He didn't fill the empty spaces in her heart, this man; he deepened them. He didn't calm the furies of her soul; he stirred them. And yet, oh, how she needed him. She needed him in her life the way the eagle needed the wind to soar with, and the buffalo the tall grass to roam in. The way thunder needed lightning to make a storm. He was, and she needed him to be.

She needed him, and he could never, ever be hers.

She lifted her head and with the tips of her fingers pushed his hat up so that she could see his eyes. But they never showed anything, those eyes, not really. Always hard and flat, and as cold as a winter sun. If he had mowed her down on the streets of Boston with a big-wheeled ordinary she would never have had the courage to run off with him. Not with those eyes.

"I will not take your horse, Mr. Rafferty."

"You damn well will take him."

She took a step back and then another. She stopped and scooped up a handful of snow, packing it into a ball. "I damn well will not," she said in the Bostoniest voice she owned, and heaved the snowball at his head.

She hit his chest instead, and the startled look on his face would have made her laugh, if she hadn't wanted to scream and scream and scream from the terrible, aching pain of needing him.

She bent over to gather more snow and straightened up, only to catch a ball of it flush on her face.

"You will," he said, panting a little.

She spat snow out of her mouth, shook it off her eyelashes and her hair. "I won't," she said as she threw one that hit him on the chin. She huffed a pleased little grunt when she saw him shudder as the snow went down inside the open collar of his coat.

He took a step toward her, and she whirled to run.

But she was bulky and clumsy and he caught her easily. His hands fell on her shoulders and pivoted her around so they were face to face. Her swollen belly made a space between them, but it was not enough. Where he touched her she burned, and where she wanted him to touch her, she burned even hotter. She wet her lips, tasting ice and the heat of memory.

His gaze fastened on her mouth. He lowered his head

and his hand stole up to frame her cheek, his thumb stroking the line of her jaw. Their breath entwined like white
wedding ribbons in the air. Snow fell between them, gentle and cold. She watched the crease in his cheek deepen as
his lips moved. "You will," he said.

"I won't." Her eyelids drifted closed and her mouth
softened, and she waited, waited, waited . . .

She heard him pull in a deep breath. When at last she
opened her eyes, he was gone.

Clementine looped the last string of popcorn around the
branches and stepped back to admire her handiwork. It
was a fine Christmas tree, so tall it brushed the ceiling.
Its heavy limbs dripped with candles, strips of paper, and
pieces of ribbon and lace. Its spicy scent filled the room.

But the sight of the tree brought her no pleasure, and
she turned away from it to the ice-latticed window. It was
a lead-colored day, still and cold. The clouds, dense and
soggy, promised more snow. She pressed the heels of her
hands into the small of her back, wincing from the pain,
trying to stretch it out. She glanced over her shoulder at
the calendar clock that hung beside the fireplace—nearly
three o'clock. It would be dark soon.

Sighing, she let her forehead fall to rest against the
chilled pane. Gus was over a week late coming home. She
worried about him, and she was lonely. The loneliness
seeped into her like the cold from the glass. It was Christmas Eve and her birthday, and she was great with child.
Monstrous and swollen and irritable with child. No one
should have to be alone on such a day.

She moved restlessly from the window to the fire.
She held out her hands to the flickering flames, but their
warmth brought her no comfort. On the stone mantel she
had put a milk-glass bowl filled with pinecones and wild
rose berries. The smell of the cones reminded her of Christ-
mases past. Two years ago, on the Christmas Eve when she

turned sixteen, they had gone to Aunt Etta's for dinner.
In the afternoon they had made that fateful visit to Stanley Addison's Photographic Gallery, and she had still been humming and crackling like an electrical wire with the excitement of it.

That day was also the first time she had pinned up her hair into coils on the back of her head and gone without a cap. She'd kept catching glimpses of herself in the mirrors and pier glasses and windowpanes, in the crystal balls that decorated Aunt Etta's tree, and each time she'd been startled. Was that grown-up girl really Clementine? When the family gathered around the tree in the parlor, Aunt Etta and her family had toasted the holidays with mulled orange wine in tall, thin glasses. Clementine had wanted so badly to join them, but her father's sharp negative shake of his head had stopped her.

It occurred to her suddenly that if someone were to hand her a glass of mulled orange wine she could drink it now and there was no one to shake his head at her. The thought brought her such a marvelous feeling of freedom that she smiled. Freedom, she decided, tasted like mulled orange wine.

She stepped back from the fire suddenly as the muscles in the small of her back and lower belly clenched and spasmed with another fierce pain. Her gaze flew up to the clock. Seven minutes had passed since the last one.

She drew in a deep breath, trying to ease the ache and her fear. She bit her lip as she looked at the rope hanging beside the front door, the rope that was attached to the fire bell on the roof. But she did not cross the room to pull it. She would wait awhile longer. Perhaps these were only phantom pains. Perhaps Gus was even now riding into the yard with the doctor. She waddled back to the window. She could barely see the hitching rail beyond the porch; it had started to snow again.

Seven minutes later her monstrous belly clutched and spasmed again. She balled up her fists to keep from screaming, not from the pain but with frustration. She felt betrayed by her body, humiliated, that it would do this to her, decide to bring her baby into the world early, without waiting for its father or the doctor. Her gaze strayed back to the rope. There was only he, and he . . .

He called on her three or four times a day to be sure she was all right. Most times he stood outside on the porch, keeping a tight rein on his mouth and his hat carefully shadowing his eyes. He looked different and yet like a cowboy still in his sheepskin coat and the winter chaps Gus called woollies, which were made of goathide and worn with the hair on the outside. On days when the wind blew hard, he tied his bandanna over his hat so that it folded the brim down to cover his ears. On any other man it would have looked silly, but not on him.

Because of her he left the ranch buildings only for very short periods, just long enough to make sure the cattle weren't freezing or starving. He kept busy, though. She knew this because she watched him as she hovered in the concealing shadows cast by the curtains on her parlor windows. He chopped so much firewood that it was now stacked as high as the roofs of both houses. He fixed the loose corral poles. He spent hours in the barn, mending tack, she supposed, and shaping horseshoes and tools at the forge. When he wasn't working, when he was inside the buffalo hunter's cabin, she watched the smoke drift from his smokestack into the winter sky. At night a pool of lampshine spilled from the cabin's window. Sometimes she saw his silhouette cross in front of it. And once she saw him leaning on the hitching rail outside his front door, his hand curled around the neck of a whiskey bottle.

When he had to, he would cross her threshold only long enough to fill her woodbox and take out the stove ashes. She did not like having him in her house. He filled it with his smell, that mixture of horse and leather and Rafferty. A smell that lingered long after he was gone. When he was in her house, she couldn't stop herself from watching him, noticing things, like the way his hips moved when he walked across her kitchen. The way he held his head when he stoked the fire in the range and set the damper. The way his hair curled over the collar of his coat, and the way the bones of his strong wrist showed above his glove when he reached for a piece of wood. The way he never let her see beneath the concealing brim of his Stetson, never let her see his eyes.

This morning he had surprised her by bringing her the Christmas tree and setting it up in a corner of her parlor in a bucket of river sand. Politeness demanded that she at least invite him to stay for a cup of coffee, but she never quite got the words out and she breathed easier when he was gone.

Another violent contraction squeezed her back and stomach and she sucked in a sharp breath. She looked at the clock—seven minutes. She could deny it no longer: she was freshening and the only one to see her through it was a hell-bent cowboy who knew everything there was about the making of babies and nothing at all about the birthing of them. A hell-bent cowboy whose dark, fine-boned hands had touched many women, but none in the way he would have to touch her. A man she could hardly bear to look at because he frightened her with the wild and forbidden feelings he stirred in her heart. Yet she would have to undergo the most indelicate and frightening experience of her life before his terrible yellow eyes.

She tried to take a deep, slow breath. She would not let herself be afraid. Her gaze went back to the rope. If she rang the bell he would come to her, but it would be hours yet before she actually gave birth. Her hands curled, her fingers tracing the scars on her palms. She would do what had to be done, but she could not bear to have him in her house, to see her . . . as he would see her. Not in the house her husband had built for her.

She dressed carefully, as if she were paying a social call. She covered her hair with her black beaver bonnet. She put on black Limerick gloves and her traveling cloak, the one she'd worn the night of her elopement. Its voluminous folds barely met across the broad expanse of her belly.

She thought she could feel the weight of the clouds when she stepped outside. The snow was coming down heavily now. She had to stop a moment on the porch and let the bite of another contraction pass. Her gloved hands grabbed the rail, crushing the tiny glittering icicles that were suspended from it.

The blowing snow shrouded the whole world. She stepped off the porch and into the storm. The sharp-edged wind lashed the snow into a fury of whirling ice clouds. Within seconds she was caught up in a maelstrom of cold, swirling flakes and white air. She couldn't see the buffalo hunter's cabin. She looked back to the new house. She couldn't see it, either, and she felt the grip of panic. She should have rung the bell. She should never have allowed her pride to keep her from ringing the bell.

She drew in a deep breath. She looked down and saw a path cobbled with frozen bootprints.

Yet she stood for a moment longer in the whirlpool of the storm, and a strange exhilaration burst inside her like a bubble rising through water and exploding on the surface.

She put her feet into the marks he had left in the snow.

Rafferty threw open the door. He closed his whiskey-blurred eyes for a moment as the wind-driven snow lashed his face. But not before he'd gotten a good look at the woman who stood before him—his brother's wife.

Melting flakes silvered the dark fur of her hat. Her face was a pale oval in the fading light, but her lips were full and very red. He could have dipped his head and kissed them. He was just drunk enough to think of kissing them.

Instead he hooked his thumb on his pocket, cocked his hip, and slouched against the jamb. "Well, 'pon my soul, if it ain't my starchy sister-in-law come a-callin'."

"Good afternoon, Mr. Rafferty." Her back was so stiff he was surprised she didn't break in the wind.

"It ain't, in fact, a *good* afternoon. And you don't have the sense God gave a prairie chicken. When a flurry kicks up like this, a body can get lost going from the house to the . . . woodshed," he amended at the last moment. He kept getting overtaken by this rather hopeless notion to try to watch his manners around her. To treat her like the lady she was and maybe show her that he had it in him to be the gentleman that he wasn't.

The snowstorm raged beyond them, but a tense silence filled the space between them. It thrummed like Indian war drums in his blood.

"I did not get lost, sir," she finally said. "I am right where I want to be."

He didn't know quite what to make of that, and he sure as hell wasn't going to ask. He took a stumbling step backward. It occurred to him how scruffy and disreputable he looked with his shirttail hanging out of his jeans and three days' growth of beard grizzling his jaw. He suddenly wished he was sober. He'd sure picked one hell of an afternoon to tie one on.

He gave her one of his surliest smiles. "Well, hell, step right on in and make yourself t' home." He started to perform a mocking bow and noticed the whiskey bottle in his hand. He drank deeply, then shot her a look that defied her to say something about it.

And for a moment he thought he saw fear in her eyes.

"You're drunk," she said.

"Nope," he said. "I'm still standing, and I'm still seeing only one of you. And I ain't got to feelin' randy as a tomcat on a hot night just yet. Definitely not drunk."

He took another swig of the whiskey, as if the situation could be easily remedied. He thought about belching and decided that would probably be pushing things too far. Christ, she really was driving him crazy. One minute he was trying to impress her, and with his next breath he was trying to disgust her.

She had knocked the snow off her boots and come inside, shutting the door herself and bringing with her the smell of wet wool and wild roses. She unclasped her cloak and hung it on the peg. She peeled off her gloves, then raised her arms to take off her hat. Her breasts lifted above the proud mound of her pregnant belly, and Rafferty's chest tightened, making it difficult to breathe.

Her lips parted as she tried to catch her breath. He wanted to take her face in his hands and kiss that mouth. He ached for her with a hunger that was a heavy hollow feeling in his gut. It didn't matter that she was great with his brother's child. He loved her. And he hated her for making him love her so, when it was so hopeless and so wrong.

He studied her out of angry, narrowed eyes. She had turned away from him, and her back was bowed slightly so that her shoulders looked small and vulnerable.

"Clementine . . ." He started to reach for her, then let his hand fall. "If you needed something why didn't you just ring the bell?"

She turned to face him. She regarded him out of wide, solemn eyes. "Because I cannot bear having you in my house."

His face tightened. "Yeah? Well, pardon me all to hell," he said. He took another long, hard drink of the booze so that she couldn't guess how her words had hurt him. The whiskey burned going down, and he almost choked on it. Her image blurred as he glared at her.

Then he saw a trace of a strange smile soften the severe curve of her mouth. "Oh, Rafferty," she said, her voice so low and aching that he had to lean forward to hear her. "What woman would be so brave as to open the door and invite lightning into her heart?"

He shook his head, thinking she must have said

"house" and not "heart." Something seemed to explode inside his chest in a gush of pain and yearning, so that when he heard the wet splash he thought for one astonishing moment that it had come from him, that his own heart had burst.

Clementine took a startled step back and looked down. A puddle of pale straw-colored liquid was spreading over the pegged floor; the front of her gray wool skirt was dark with it. Her gaze flew back up to his, more surprised than embarrassed.

Rafferty, however, had hurtled past every other emotion on the spectrum and gone directly to holy terror. "Jesus Christ!" he exclaimed.

She started to say something, but just then her body jerked and spasmed and a low moan escaped past her clenched teeth. He could actually see her stomach contracting.

"Jesus Christ," he said again, more softly.

She took a couple of shallow, panting breaths. He could hear his own breath coming out fast and uneven, and the sound they made together was like the sough of the wind through the cottonwoods.

"As you can see," she said with utter calm, "I am having the baby."

"Jesus God." He took a step back and then another, until he bumped into the sawbuck table. He shook his head again, trying to clear it of the pumping blood that suddenly roared in his ears. "You got to stop this now, Boston," he said. "Wait until Gus gets back with the doctor."

She actually had the brass to laugh. He was in a gut-panic and she was *laughing*. "Oh, Rafferty . . . having a baby is hardly something that can be stopped once it's started."

He carefully set down the whiskey bottle. He raked the hair back out of his eyes with his fingers. "But I can't . . . but I don't know . . . shit! What the hell did you come to me for?"

That strange smile still hovered on her mouth, but

he saw the fear now plain in her eyes. "Believe me, sir, if the good Lord had offered me any midwife other than an uncouth, drunken, and debauched excuse for a cowboy, rest assured I would have taken her."

A taut silence had come over the cabin, underscored by the hissing of the oil in the lantern and the spitting of the snow against the window. Clementine closed her eyes on a stifled moan of pain, and a flutter of renewed panic stirred Rafferty's guts.

"Should you just be standing there? I mean, shouldn't you be lying down?"

"Not just yet, thank you," she said, so calmly that he wanted to shake her.

"How long before . . . it happens?"

"Oh, I shouldn't think for hours yet."

Hours . . . He collapsed onto one of the nail-keg stools. He pressed his fingers against his closed eyelids. There was a pounding in his temples worse than a brass band. "God." He lifted his head and stared at her out of eyes that felt as dry as last year's tumbleweeds. "I ain't ever going to forgive you for this."

"Why, I do believe you are scared, Mr. Rafferty."

"'Scared' isn't the word for it." His throat clenched as he swallowed, but he did manage to fire a cocky grin at her. "I feel like I'm standing bare-assed naked in a nest full of rattlers."

On her face there was a softness now that he had never seen before. A tenderness. Her eyes were oceans deep, and he wanted to drown in them. "You remember that day I first came to the RainDance country?" she said. "You had brought that baby calf into the world after its mother was killed by timber wolves."

"I don't reckon it's the same, Boston."

"I don't reckon it's that much different, though, either," she said mimicking his drawl.

Her chin had gone up and she looked down her nose at him in that way she had that could make her seem so starchy. The thought of that little nose leading the way so bravely into the world made him want to gather her in his arms and hold her safe against his chest. She was hardly older than a child herself, and she was about to have her first baby; it was kicking up a blizzard outside, and she was alone, with no one to help her but an uncouth, drunken, and debauched excuse for a cowboy.

He got up and stood before her. He rested his hand against her face, tilting her head back until she could see his eyes. Then he let her go. "I'm not as drunk as I was behavin' earlier," he said. Her skin had been as soft against his hand as the down of a newborn chick. "I was just acting like that to rile you."

"I know."

His mouth pulled into a crooked smile. "And even if I'd been dead drunk, the sight of you messin' all over my floor like that would've been enough to sober up a peach-orchard sow."

She started to laugh but caught it with her hand. "How drunk do peach-orchard sows get?"

He laughed with her, feeling his heart grow warm. "Drunker'n boiled owls."

The laughter spilled out around her fingers.

"Drunker than a goose at a rooster fight," he said. "Drunker than the devil on a hot night in hell."

"You're making those up," she accused, laughing openly now. And stopping suddenly as pain twisted her face and her whole body contorted.

He gripped her arms as she swayed into him. The contraction was sharp and violent, and he felt it against his own stomach. And the intimacy of it was almost more than he could bear.

He looked down at her bent head, at the whiteness of the part in her pale yellow hair. An overwhelming feeling of tenderness rose and caught in his throat. "It's true I've pulled a lot of calves and foals," he said, his voice rough. "Enough to know it can't be done blind. It's going to be messy and painful, and there won't be any place for modesty or . . . delicacy."

She raised her head and looked at him with wide, serious eyes. "I know, Rafferty, and on this night, at least, I'm not afraid of you. Or of myself."

"Easy now, sweetheart." He poured the sweet oil over her belly, rubbing it in with his palms. Beneath his hands her muscles quivered and contorted. "Take it easy, darlin'. You're gonna be fine, just fine . . ."

Clementine clung to the rails of the iron bedstead until her knuckles turned white. Panting, she raised her head and stared at him out of bloodshot eyes. "Mr. Rafferty, you are speaking to me as if I were a dumb bronco you were trying to break. I am not, I beg to remind you, a horse."

"Yeah? You coulda fooled me, big as you are." He waited until she was done grunting and gasping and panting through another pain. They came so hard and so close together now that she was barely able to catch her breath between them. "I thought some sweet talk might help things along here. You're taking your own sweet time about having this baby. Like you was tryin' to make it last as long as an all-day sucker."

She shot him a murderous glare and gritted her teeth. "You, sir, can go straight to hell in a handbasket."

"You're getting the words down real fine now, Boston, but not the tune. There's still too much starch in your voice."

She grunted and huffed and did some more glaring, and he flashed a damn-the-world smile back at her. But inside, he was sick with fear.

She had been laboring hard like this for over sixteen hours now. Her chest pumped so violently with the effort of it that he feared her heart would give out. She was drenched with sweat. She had long ago undressed to her shift, and now it was soaked through and rucked up around her waist. Her legs were bent and spread wide and trembling from exhaustion. She was gutsy and beautiful, and he loved her beyond lust or even liking and into a realm of emotion too vast for words, too deep to understand.

And if she didn't give birth soon she would die.

He wet her dry, cracked lips with snow and mopped her forehead with a cool, damp cloth. *Please, God,* he prayed over and over, like a litany. *Please, please, please . . .*

He'd never begged anything of God before, but he was begging now. He was, in his heart at least, on his knees with his hands clasped in an agony of pleading. But the God he knew, the spirit of the prairie and the wind and the mountains, was an indifferent deity who believed in letting the nature of his creation take its course. So he prayed to Clementine's God instead, the God locked up in her green Bible with the gold clasp. Such a God, who proscribed and punished, must also, he thought, show mercy on occasion. So he prayed for mercy, for her sake and his brother's, and he was careful to leave his own name out of the negotiations.

Her back arched and her belly contracted violently. She gripped the bed rails until the corded muscles of her throat stood out like white ropes. Her teeth clenched together and her lips curled back in a rictus of pain.

Please, God, please, please . . . She grunted and heaved again, and a great ripping sound tore out of her chest, like a blunt saw being pulled through wet wood. He tossed the wet cloth on the floor and moved between her thighs, and he saw the top of the baby's head. His throat tightened and tears stung his eyes. *Please, God, sweet God . . .* "It's coming, Boston. I can see the top of its head," he shouted, relief welling in his chest to choke the words. Her stomach contracted and her back arched, her heels digging deep into the mattress. "I can see more of it. Jesus Lord. Push, sweetheart. That's it, darlin', push some more now . . ."

In the middle of all the panting and grunting and heaving she was doing, she had somehow pushed herself up on her elbows and was trying to see for herself. "What does it look like?"

"Like a baby." He took her hand, guiding her fingers between her spread legs to the soft honey-colored crown of hair. "Here, feel."

She grinned at him, breathing hard. "Oh, my."

"Yeah . . ." He turned his head and pressed his lips to her knee, tasting the salt of her sweat and his tears. "Oh, my."

She fell back, grunting and pushing and convulsing. Slowly more of the head emerged and then part of one shoulder. The loop of the navel cord was wrapped around the baby's neck, but before he even thought to panic he had hooked a finger under the cord and gently worked it over the small head. Suddenly the baby slid, slick and wet, into his waiting hands.

Rafferty's heart squeezed up into an area just below his throat. And where his heart used to be there was an aching sense of awe.

He wiped the mucus off its tiny face with his fingers, laughing at its loud, squawking cry. He laid Clementine's son on her belly. The babe was wrinkled and scrawny and so tiny. He wailed and thrashed his legs, indignant, Rafferty thought, maybe frightened, too, to be wrenched out of his mother's warm, soft womb. "Look at him," he said, his throat thick, as love for his brother's child swelled in his chest, swift and fierce and heart-soaring. "Look at your son, Boston."

She tried to struggle up on her elbows again and he supported her back with his arm. She was laughing, too, and he heard joy and relief and awe in her voice. "Oh, Rafferty . . . have you ever seen anything more wonderful?"

He turned his head to look at her. Her hair was plastered to her cheek in wet, sticky strands. Her face was pale and drawn, her lips cracked and chewed bloody in places. He could see himself reflected in the wide, black pupils of her eyes. "No," he said. "I have never seen anything more wonderful."

He cut the navel cord, and when the afterbirth came, he put it in a zinc bucket to be buried later. Using the water he'd been keeping hot on the stove for hours, he bathed the baby and he bathed Clementine. He touched her naked body, her breasts and between her legs. Every time he looked up, it was to find her eyes on him, wide and dark and filled with some raw emotion he couldn't name.

He didn't have anything proper to wrap the baby in. He finally settled on one of his soft chambray shirts. It curtailed the kid's thrashing some, but not his squawking, which was loud enough to peel the bark off trees.

He put the squirming bundle into Clementine's waiting arms and sat beside her on the bed. They looked down together at the red face, with its tiny wailing mouth and eyes clenched into tight, angry slits. "I don't think he likes me," she said in a small voice.

"Maybe he's just hungry."

She wet her cracked and swollen lip with her tongue. "I'm not sure I know how to feed him."

He dragged in an aching breath. He had to make fists with his hands to keep from taking hold of her face and kissing her poor ravaged mouth. "I reckon if you aim him in the right direction, he'll figure the rest of it out for himself."

Clementine unbuttoned his shirt, which he had put on her in place of her sweat-drenched shift, and put the baby's face to her breast. The light pouring in through the window turned her skin creamy and golden, like freshly churned butter. Dawn had come and with it the sun. It had stopped snowing, and the world outside looked white and pure and born anew.

He watched her nipple tighten and harden, and the baby's mouth turned toward it, latching on. "Oh!" she exclaimed softly. "He sucks hard."

Rafferty stared in wonder at his brother's son. The

transparent eyelids, no bigger than the nails on his little fingers. The little fists thrown back on either side of his head. The pink mouth sucking greedily.

"I wish he was mine," he said. The words slipped out without thought, but there was no taking them back.

She looked up at him, and he allowed his face to be naked before her. She looked at him forever, and the days flowed into nights, snow melted into spring. Then forever ended and began anew when she took his hand.

She turned her face away, and he saw the raw anguish pull at her mouth and darken her eyes. "I love Gus," she said.

Please, God, sweet God . . . Her hand on his was like sunshine on shadow. He was afraid if he so much as breathed, she and the world and the touch of her hand would disappear.

"I love Gus," she said, cutting him deep, deep. "Not only is he my husband, but he is honorable and noble and good, and I vowed before God that I would love him." She made a harsh tearing sound in her throat. "When I saw him that day, when he knocked me over with his bicycle, he was like something out of a dream, my dream." She looked at him, and her eyes glittered like shards of glass. "Oh, God, God, how could I have known, how could I have known? Up until that moment, you see, he was the closest thing I'd found to you."

She swallowed hard, her throat straining as if it hurt. Her hand moved, gripping his. "From the beginning of time it was you, Rafferty. Always it was supposed to be you. You are the fire in my heart."

He looked at their hands, his dark and large, hers white and small. Her flesh pressed against his, and it seemed as if her blood flowed into him, as if he could feel her heart beating in his own breast, as if she had taken his soul. The moment was more carnal than in all his dreams, when he'd laid her down on his bed and driven into her.

She let go of his hand, and her touch became a memory

that swelled and seeped into a pain that went bone deep. Soul deep. The world had never been so empty.

"Clementine—"

"No." She pressed her fingers against his lips, a moment and no more. "We can't be held to account for the things we don't say, remember? So you musn't say it. One of us must always be careful not to say it. This time it has to be you."

And so he said nothing. A man couldn't speak anyway of a thing that didn't exist. The flesh-and-blood woman on the bed would never be his. All he had was a yearning, and words that were never really spoken and then were denied.

He adjusted the pillows beneath her back, smoothed the damp hair from her face, and for her sake tried to make his mouth smile. "You ought to try to get some sleep now."

"Will you be here when I wake up?"

"I'm not leavin' you, Clementine."

He sat beside her on the bed, his gaze never leaving her face. When he was sure she slept, he leaned over and pressed his lips to hers. He said her name, letting his breath wash over her mouth.

But she was still his brother's wife.

Clementine opened her eyes onto his face. For a long time they simply looked at each other; then she said, "Merry Christmas, Mr. Rafferty."

They shared a smile. And then together they watched the baby sleeping in the crook of her arm, and their smiles widened to include the world.

She stared at her son's face. It was round and red and wrinkled like a gnome's, and yet it was the most beautiful face she had ever seen. The love she felt for him was so intense it was an ache in her chest. He felt so fragile in her arm, as light and ephemeral as sunshine. He was so incredibly tiny, so vulnerable and helpless, and a terror gripped her heart.

"Oh, what am I going to do?" she said, the fear gushing out of her in words. "I don't know how to be a mother. I didn't even know how to feed him."

Rafferty's hand drifted toward her and she thought he might touch her, but he stroked the baby's cheek with his curled finger instead. Then he looked up and touched her with his eyes. "I reckon you can do whatever you set your mind to, Boston. You made it to the first snowfall. To the first snowfall and beyond."

Bellows and shouts bounced off the clear winter air. He went to the window. "It's Gus," he said. "With the doctor." He lifted the sash and halloed, his breath wafting white smoke, waving Gus on down.

Clementine turned her head. She watched out the window as her husband and the doctor rode across the hay meadow from the new ranch house to the buffalo hunter's cabin. The doctor resembled an enormous canary with ruffled feathers, dressed as he was in a yellow plaid coat. A watch chain hung with gold seals stretched across a belly that filled his saddle from cantle to horn. On his head perched one of those English hunting caps with a bill both in the front and behind.

"A hat like that," Rafferty said, "you can't tell whether a fella's coming or going."

Clementine looked at his dark, taut profile and she felt a raw ache take root in her soul that she knew would be with her forever. Between them everything had changed. And nothing had changed.

She willed him to look at her again. She wanted him to turn his head so that she could look in his eyes one last time and see the heartfire.

I am my beloved's and his desire is toward me."

But he didn't turn his head and look at her, for his brother had come home.

Gus bounded into the cabin in a whirlwind of cold air and excitement. He stared down at his son nestled on his wife's chest and his face lit up brighter than a thousand candles. "Well, hell," he said, his laugh rattling the window. "Well, hell."

Clementine smiled up into her husband's laughing face and thought she could almost hear her heart tearing in two. He was all that she had said he was, good and honorable and noble, and she had just given him a son. She could never leave him. For so many reasons she could never leave him.

She handed their baby up into his awkward arms. Gus looked from the baby to her and then to his brother. "Zach . . . Lord, Zach, I don't know what to say . . ."

Rafferty lifted his shoulders in a careless shrug. "Shit, brother. It wasn't no different than pulling a calf."

She waited for his tawny eyes, which were at once beautiful and terrible, to find hers, and they did—briefly, before he wrenched them away and veiled them with his eyelids, since his hat wasn't handy. But for the length of a heartbeat, the tough shell he lived behind had cracked open and she had seen it.

For one flashing, burning moment, she had seen the heartfire.

PART TWO
1883

17

THE STAGECOACH LURCHED OVER the rutted road. A gust of wind slammed against it, rattling the leather curtains and sending a cloud of dust billowing through the windows and onto the eight men and the Chinese girl crowded together on the hard horsehair seats.

The girl shut her eyes against the stinging dust. But she wrenched them open an instant later as the sharp tang of whiskey assaulted her nose. The foreign devil who sat across from her shook a brown glass bottle in her face and smiled, rudely showing his teeth. The whiskey sloshed into her lap and onto the bulging leather mailbags stashed beneath her feet.

"You thirsty, li'l China gal? Thirs-tee," he bellowed at her as if she were deaf.

Erlan, the favorite daughter of the House of Po, kept her face as blank as an opera mask, hiding her disgust. Like so many of the *fon-kwei,* this man was hairy and big-nosed like a baboon and smelled just as rank.

She dropped her gaze to her lap, saying nothing. But though she had been obedient, saying nothing, doing nothing, showing nothing, still the leash tightened around her throat in warning.

The leash was the worst thing that had been done to her.

It had begun with her mother, who had done a thing so terrible, so shameful and dishonorable, that she'd had to die for it. A thing so shameful and dishonorable that Erlan, her mother's daughter, had been made to suffer for it as well. And so her father, in his vengefulness and fury, had sold her to a Foochow slave trader for one hundred taels of silver.

The slave trader had raped Erlan, and when she fought him he had scored her breasts with long cerise fingernails that were curved and sharp like the talons of an eagle. But when he ripped the earrings of precious white jade out of her ears, the earrings her father had given her on the day she became a woman, only then did Erlan weep for the first time.

The slave trader had her put in the hold of a ship with other slaves and indentured laborers bound for Gum Sam, the land of the golden mountains. They had been packed onto tiers of wooden pallets like mah-jongg tiles in a box. Her pallet was on the bottom, and in foul weather vomit ran down the wall beside her head. The stinking whale-oil lanterns swayed and swayed with the rolling of the ship, and the rats were so bold they sat on her chest and looked at her with eyes that glimmered like spirit lights in the murky darkness. One of the sailors raped her, too, and when she fought him he broke her rice bowl so that she had to fight just for the few handfuls of mush left in the bottom of the community pot. That night she dreamed she was in her father's garden, sitting with her mother on the stone turtle bench in the shade of the banyan tree, sipping warm rice wine and nibbling on slices of candied ginger, and she wept for the second time.

When she finally left the ship and set her bound feet on the fon-kwei land, she tottered and swayed like a drunken fisherman, and she was nearly blinded by the pearly white light. The air tasted crisp and tangy, like a cold melon. And the mountains were indeed golden, though not made of gold as the stories had said. One of the sailors told her they were in a place called San Francisco, and there was a whole village of Chinese in this fon-kwei city.

She was taken to the house of the Hip Yee tong whose province was the slave girl trade. There she was bathed and the private parts of her woman's body examined so intimately that she burned hotter than a cook's brazier from the shame of it.

"That turtle dung of a Foochow slave trader has ruined you!" the tong man had raged at her, and he slapped her face as if the fault were hers. "I could have gotten four hundred fon-kwei dollars for your maidenhead." He peered at her closely, the wisps of his white beard quivering. "Aiya, I have been truly cheated! You are eighteen if you are a day, and your golden lilies are a disgrace. Big as boats, they are. Wei, bigger than imperial junks. You are not one in a thousand as he promised me, but one *of* a thousand. Better I sell you outright to a mining camp, ma? Those whore-cunts are so desperate for wives they will take anything, even a dishonored old woman with bullock feet."

He had shown her the cribs in the alley of the whores, where girls like her thrust thin white arms through the window bars and made sad mewling sounds like lost kittens. A hundred men a day would have her, the tong man had said, if she did not accept her fate and become wife to a mining camp.

Surely, she thought, she must not be hearing him right. Surely she would not be given as wife to a whole *camp* of men. But she didn't ask for clarification. What the blind man doesn't see, so it was said, the blind man cannot fear.

The tong man gave her into the care of a *bock tow doy,* one of the hachetmen who enforced the tong's laws. If the *bock tow doy* had a name she did not know it. He told her she must call him Master.

The master raped her, and when she fought him he beat her with a stick of firewood. He put the leash on her so that she would learn obedience, and that was when she wept for the third time.

Oh, the gods did surely know the leash was the worst thing that had been done to her. It cut into her pride more painfully than it cut into the tender flesh of her neck, for it proclaimed to the world that which she wished to deny to herself: she was a slave.

Now Erlan sat as still as possible in the rocking coach, enduring the leash's bite. She knew the master must stop his torment eventually. The merchant Sam Woo of Rainbow Springs, Montana, had paid eight hundred fon-kwei dollars for her. The merchant Woo would have no use for a strangled bride.

The white demon who had offered her the whiskey pulled aside the leather curtain and for the hundredth time in as many minutes squirted a stream of black juice out the side of his mouth, which was but a small slit in the tangled hair on his face. The wind that blew through the window was hot and dry and smelled strange, like freshly lacquered wood. Erlan thought the smell came from the olive-gray bushes that grew on the hills and in the meadows of tall sere grass.

In the bays and rainy basins of her homeland of Foochow, this was the season of the monsoon. The air would be as hot as it was here, but steaming like a water pipe. The mists would hug the hills of tea shrubs and bamboo groves. Along the banks of the Min River, rice paddies would glimmer emerald and jade green beneath the haze-haloed sun.

But in this foreign land everything was brown and gray. The trees with their dark, clawed branches and sharp needles made her think of dragons. And others shed cottony tufts and roared in the constant wind. An angry river bubbled and spat as it ran through tall grass that was not green, but the pale straw color of a farmer's hat. This was a tormented land, lacking harmony. There were mountains near her home, but nothing like these great jagged and furious rocks that seemed to be trying to poke holes in the sky.

Suddenly her yearning for the scarlet pillars and green tiled roofs of her *lao chia* was so strong she had to press her lips together to stifle a cry. The master's grip tightened on the leash, pulling her head around.

His face was as expressionless as the stone guardians of her ancestors' tombs, but she caught the warning in his eyes: *Yield, Erlan.* She was to do nothing, say nothing, show nothing.

Erlan lifted her chin and gave the master a look that said he was like turtle dung beneath her feet. Her father was a great man. Other merchants bowed respectfully before the wealth of the Pos and their august ancestors. And she was her father's favorite daughter. She was . . .

She was a slave now. The favorite daughter of the House of Po was no different from a peasant child sold by her parents for a few strings of *cash.*

In defiance of the leash that restrained her, Erlan turned her head and looked out the window. An enormous bird of rainbow plumage burst out of the brush and took to the air with a slapping flap of its great wings. The white demon with the hairy face pulled a revolver out of his belt and fired. The bird exploded, raining red, gold, and blue feathers.

The sound of the shot smacked against the wooden panels of the coach. The master jumped as if a scorpion had bitten him, and his face turned as pale as a carp's belly. He hated the foreign devils, but he also feared them. His spirit kowtowed to theirs, and Erlan took pleasure from knowing that the master who controlled the end of her leash had masters of his own.

The demon with the hairy face leaned toward her and smiled, again rudely exposing his teeth, which were stained brown and smelled foul and rotten. "Wild turkey," he said. "Makes good eatin'."

Who would eat the beautiful bird that he had left dead on the side of the road? Erlan wondered. She had seen no peasants living on this land. It lay empty and desolate, like a forgotten tomb.

The stagecoach rocked around a bend, and a strange sight met Erlan's eyes. A large hat-shaped hill barren of grass or trees thrust itself straight up out of the valley like a fat blister on the land. And on the hill a skeletal black edifice, like a burned-out pagoda, poked into the smoke-hazed sky.

"What you're lookin' at there is the gallus frame of the Four Jacks silver mine. Four years ago this place wasn't nothing but a burp in the road. Now look at her—silver's done turned Rainbow Springs into a regular li'l boom-town."

In spite of the leash that restrained her, Erlan leaned over for a better look. The hairy-faced man's speech was so different from the dulcet rhythms of the mission school English her mother had taught her that she had difficulty understanding him. But her ears had picked out the words "silver mine."

It was an ugly hill, scarred and gray. In its shadow, on the raw barren ground, were weathered wooden houses more wretched than beggars' huts.

A wagon heavily laden with rock passed them on the road, obscuring her view. The driver shouted and cracked his long whip across the backs of the mules. Over the rattle of the wheels on the hard and rutted ground, her ears picked out a dull, rhythmical thudding.

"That thumping noise you hear is the stamp mill crushing silver ore," the hairy-faced demon said, patting her knee.

The shock of him touching her jerked Erlan's attention back inside the coach. Beside her the master emitted a low hissing noise like an angry goose. The fon-kwei were odd ones in this way, Erlan thought, always rudely touching one another, even strangers, shaking hands, clapping one another on the back, taking women's arms and pressing their palms into the women's backs. It was a terrible invasion of one's private self, this touching.

The demon grinned at her, oblivious of his hideous breach of manners. "No speakee American, huh?" His gaze shifted over to the master. "How 'bout you, you speakee American, China boy? Tell me what bawdy house you're takin' her to and maybe I'll pay it a visit. I heard tell yer

Chinee gals're built different than ours. That their slit runs sideways and is as tight as a sparrow's gullet."

The master flattered the hairy-faced man with the nervous smile he reserved for the fon-kwei. "She be married," he said in his badly accented English.

"Damn." The hairy-faced man sucked on his rotting teeth. "What a waste."

A horrible smell wafted into the window with the wind, a stink so rank it nearly made Erlan gag. The stagecoach had slowed and was entering a town where dogs and pigs rooted in piles of empty tins, animal bones, and rotting garbage. The baked mud of a road was lumped with discarded objects: an old boot, a kettle with a hole in the bottom, a stool missing one leg. They rolled past a row of log buildings, all with swinging louvered doors. Tinny music and laughter burst from them in loud claps of sound.

How strange it all was, strange and frightening. When she was a child she had longed to see more of the world than the view from the high garden walls of her lao chia. She had yearned for the sort of adventures told by the soup sellers in the market square. And how often her mother had warned her then: "Be careful what you wish of the gods, else they might grant it to you."

The stage stopped with a squeal of its axle, a billow of dust, and a bawling shout from the driver, "Whoa, you sons of bitches. Whoa!"

The master handed her a red veil. When she didn't take it, he pulled her head around by the leash so that she was forced to look into his eyes and see again the warning there: *Yield, Erlan. Yield as the bamboo yields to the wind and thus is never broken.*

She took the veil and draped it over her head. Red was supposed to be a happy color, a wedding color. Once she had looked forward with a child's innocent joy to this day. In her dreams she had journeyed from her father's house in a red-lacquered litter, seated on a throne surrounded by red silk curtains. Her bridegroom, handsome and young, had

waited for her at the moon gate of his lao chia, in his hand
the key that would unlock her chair and perhaps . . .oh,
yes, perhaps her heart. Her only worry would be whether
she would quickly bless her husband's illustrious ancestors
with a son.

She rubbed her palms over the rough blue cotton of
the chang-fu the tong man had given her to wear. In her
dreams she had worn a bridal robe of red silk, heavy with
embroidery, and a headdress of gold, lapis, and jade. In her
dreams . . .

Yield, Erlan.

She sat in a deep inner stillness, shrouded by the red
veil. The master tugged on the leash. She heard the thump
of the leather mail sacks hitting the ground, felt the sway
of the coach as it emptied and lightened. It was time to
meet the man who had bought her for his wife.

After so many hours in the cramped coach, she tottered on her tiny bound feet. Dizziness assailed her and
a blackness dimmed the red veil before her eyes. She dug
her nails into her palms, hoping the pain would keep her
from fainting. She must be a credit to her ancestors; she
must display no weakness before the man who was to be
her husband.

"Honorable lord," the master said with a smirk in his
voice, for the merchant Sam Woo was certainly no lord. "I
bring this worthless girl to be your wife."

By peeking beneath her veil she could make out her
groom's lower half. She had expected to see the white shoes
with thick paper soles and the silk chang-fu of a Chinese.
Instead she saw striped barbarian trousers and shiny boots
with pointed toes. She dipped gracefully in obeisance before him, her head bowed, her back straight, her right knee
nearly grazing the road, both hands lightly touching her
left hip.

Merciful Kwan Yin, she prayed, ashamed of her pride,
yet unable to help it, *let him at least be young and pleasant to
look upon.*

He removed her veil. A bride's face ought never to be revealed to her groom until after they were wed, but Erlan was beyond all shock at this breach of tradition. She did not keep her head down as was proper. Slowly she raised her gaze to his face . . . Oh, the faithless, cruel gods. He was old, and as ugly as a bamboo rat.

The merchant Sam Woo peered at her through spectacles as thick as Shanghai noodles. The years had creped his eyes and dug deep wrinkles around his mouth. He had grown a thin beard in a vain attempt to disguise his insignificant chin. She couldn't tell if his forehead was also insignificant, as it was covered with a barbarian's bucket-shaped hat.

Yield, Erlan. She must yield. She must banish all feelings from her heart until it was as empty as a hollow gourd.

Two white demonesses flanked the merchant Woo. One was small and as slender as a wraith, with hair the pale yellow of a newly risen moon. The other also had hair of a most remarkable color, deep red like the juice of the betel nut. No, more vibrant than that. Like the hottest coals reflected in the polished sides of a bronze brazier.

A group of curious onlookers had gathered on the street to watch the stage's arrival. Erlan saw other Chinese, in coarse cotton knee-length jackets, baggy blue *schmo,* and the broad-brimmed peaked straw hats of peasants. The fonkwei were everywhere, too, in their mattress-ticking shirts and coarse canvas trousers. Several of them were pointing at her. Erlan wondered what she had done to be the recipient of such a contemptuous gesture.

And then her gaze was caught and held by one man. Even among the big foreign devils, he was a giant. Like all the other devils, he rudely stared straight at her. He was not handsome. Although he was young, the strong bones of his face—what she could see of it beneath the pelt of hair on his cheeks and chin—stood out as hard and blunt as an old ax. There was a fierceness about him that was rather frightening. But then he smiled, and although he showed his teeth, she rather liked his smile. It was gentle and sweet, like the music of a pi-pa, and it made her feel warm inside.

The leash tightened hard around her neck, cutting off her breath. Without thought, she lifted her hand and clawed at the leather, trying to tug it free.

The giant white demon started toward her, and his face was such a mask of snarling fury that she stumbled back in fright. "He's leashed her!" the giant bellowed. "The bleeding bastard's leashed her like a dog!"

The master stepped in front of her. The giant demon punched him in the belly. The master went sprawling onto his hands and knees in the dusty, dung-littered street.

He scrambled instantly back to his feet, his hand flashing into the sleeve of his chang-fu where he had hidden a small hatchet, the weapon of his trade. *"Ta ma!"* he cursed through gritted teeth. But he didn't dare strike back at the fon-kwei, so like the cowardly snake that he was, he lashed out at her instead.

His hard palm smacked against Erlan's cheek, making a sound like the crack of a whip. She would have fallen if the giant demon hadn't gripped her shoulders from behind, steadying her. Tears of pain blurred Erlan's eyes. She blinked and saw to her astonishment that the fire-haired woman had suddenly appeared in front of the master. She was pointing a small pistol at his face.

"You do anything else besides breathe, Chinaman," she said in a voice like hot smoke, "and you'll be doing it without a nose."

Her husband-to-be meantime was hopping from foot to foot and wringing his hands. "Holy God, Mrs. Yorke! Mr. Scully, please! What are you doing?"

A foreign devil who was as fat as a rice merchant swaggered up to them, his belly leading the way. "Now, Hannah girl," he said, "why don't you put that gun of yours back in your pocket and let these Chinks here look to their own affairs." He turned, and the seven-pointed star he wore on his chest flashed in the sun. The star was such an evil omen that Erlan quickly averted her face. The gods knew she certainly didn't need any more bad joss.

"You, too, there, Cousin Jack," the fat man said, his gaze settling on the giant behind her. "Didn't I just hear the shift whistle blow? You wouldn't want to be losing a day's pay."

Erlan suddenly became aware that the giant demon was still holding her. His hands were heavy and warm on her shoulders. She did not find his touch distasteful, although it was strange. She leaned her head back against his chest, and he surrounded her with his heat like a powerful but friendly dragon who had made a lair out of his body and was protecting her against the world.

"I don't give a bloody damn about the bloody whistle," he said in the bell-toned English she was used to, although his voice was still edged with dragonlike rage. "That yellow bastard's been dragging a woman about on a leash, and there ought to be a law in this bleeding town to say him nay."

The fat man rubbed his chin with a hand that was like the paw of a bear. "If there is a law agin it, I ain't never heard of it."

The fire woman wagged her little gun beneath the fat man's two chins. "Marshal Dobbs, you are about as useful as a three-legged mule. Why don't you go on back to swattin' flies and scratchin' your ass, and leave Mrs. McQueen and me to sort out this mess?" She looked back over her shoulder at the merchant Woo. "I'm sorry, Sam, but you're not marrying this girl till we're satisfied she's willing."

"Holy God."

The fat man gave his belt a hitch. "Now, Hannah girl—"

"Quit Hannah-girling me before I shoot a hole in that tin badge of yours." She turned to Erlan, and her face softened. "Come along, honey . . ."

The master chopped the edge of his hand through the air. "*Tsao ni,* Lo Mo," he spat. "The Chink girl, she stay."

The woman with moon-colored hair stepped forward

then, putting herself between Erlan and the master. "Move aside, please, sir," she said to the master in a voice that was like the wind blowing over snow. She stared at him for a long, still moment, and to Erlan's shock, the *bock tow doy* was the one who backed away.

The giant's hands still lay heavy and warm on Erlan's shoulders. She felt strange inside herself, as if there were a bird trapped in her chest, beating its wings against the cage of her ribs, beating to be free.

Gently he turned her around. His fingers were gentle as he slit through the tight leather leash with a small knife, and his voice was gentle as he spoke. "You go off with Mrs. Yorke. I trust her to take care of you. But you be remembering this, little one: there's no one here can be making you do a thing you don't want to do."

Erlan said nothing, yet she couldn't look away from his eyes. They were like no eyes she'd ever seen, their color the dark gray of a rain-drenched sky. And there was that strange mixture of fierceness and gentleness in them. She felt a ridiculous need to reach up and touch him, to see if he was real. She'd actually started to do so when she realized what she was doing and made herself stop.

She jerked her gaze away from his and allowed herself to be led away by the two demonesses. It took all of her will not to turn her head for one last look at him.

She swayed on her tiny golden lilies as she maneuvered around the foul messes that littered the way before her. Aiya, this place stank worse than a night-soil collector's cart. Everyone in the Flowery Kingdom had heard of Mei-Kwok, the beautiful land of America, where gold was supposed to lie in the streets as thick as buffalo dung in a rice paddy. But horse dung was all that lay in these streets, and some fool must have mistaken it for gold.

A steaming, fly-ridden pile of it lay directly in her path. She lifted her chang-fu and took little mincing steps on her highly arched, carved wooden shoes.

"Oh, Lord!" the fire woman exclaimed. "Will you look

at her poor feet? She's had that done to her—what those heathens do to their poor girls' feet."

Erlan felt hot color flood her cheeks as the demonesses stopped to look down in horror at her golden lilies.

It was true that her feet were not all they should have been. But the fire woman especially should not be pointing her finger, Erlan thought indignantly, not with feet of her own as big as sampans. Erlan couldn't help it that her mother had done her a disservice when it came to the creation of her golden lilies by not allowing the foot binder to make the final cut. Erlan's feet weren't two dainty arcs barely three inches long, but a whole five inches. When she grew old enough to understand these things, she had worried that her inadequate golden lilies would diminish her value as a bride. For no matter how rich or beautiful she was, no man would marry a girl with big feet.

She thought of Eldest Sister, whose feet were so perfectly tiny she could not even walk without a slave girl's shoulder to lean on. How she had teased Erlan, calling her a horse-footed girl. But how would she have moved over this raw land on dainty arcs only three inches long?

This raw land . . . Erlan looked down the road toward the hat-shaped hill. Beyond it the land stretched wide and lonely, riffled with windblown grass, to huge mountains standing ragged against an immense sky. The enormity and emptiness of this place frightened her. She felt weightless of a sudden. Only her tiny feet keeping her from soaring like a kite, up and up and up into that endless sky.

"You will hate him at first."

These words, coming from the moon woman, startled her. Erlan forgot all modesty and turned her head to stare, and she was struck anew at the woman's fairness. Her skin was as white as cherry blossoms, her hair so pale in places it seemed transparent, like sunlight. Her gaze was focused on the vast land, as Erlan's had been. And as she spoke it seemed her voice came from the vastness. As if she had taken the vastness deep inside her to nurse it like a wound.

"I always think of Montana as a *he,* for this is every bit
a man's place, and you will hate him in the way that only
a woman can hate a man. You will hate the wind and the
dirt and the miserable cold winters, hate his harsh strength
and his lawless, violent ways. And then one day you will
realize that you have come to love him fiercely in the midst
of all your hate. Love him in a way that only a woman can
love a man . . ."

She came to herself, shaking her head. "Oh, what am
I doing?" Her gaze, friendly now and concerned, touched
Erlan's face. "Here I've gone all maudlin and philosophical, and you aren't understanding a word I'm saying." She
motioned to the door of a large rambling building with a
broad veranda, indicating that Erlan was to follow the fire
woman inside. "We'll go on into the Yorke House for now
and see what is to be done."

As Erlan mounted the hotel steps, its signboard
creaked in the wind. The pine floor oozed resin in sticky
lumps, and the unpainted walls were pocked by knotholes.
The fire woman went behind a tall desk and retrieved a
key. Erlan followed the two demonesses down a hall and
into a small room crowded with a plain iron bed, a pine
chest of drawers, and a washstand.

A slice of sunlight from the single window fell across
the bare floor. Erlan unconsciously went to stand in it. She
threaded her hands through the sleeves of her chang-fu and
waited.

The two demonesses spoke together in rapid English.
It made her head ache to try to understand them, so she
ceased listening, merely letting the words flow over her
like the tide on sand. Erlan had never felt more alone than
she did in that one moment, standing in that barren room
with oaths and whipcracks and the smell of dung coming in the open window, and the image of a merciless and
empty sky haunting her mind.

They were discussing what was to be done with her,
as if they had a say in the matter. She would marry the

merchant Woo—that was her fate. It had been her fate
since the day her father had sold her for one hundred taels
of silver. Perhaps it had been her fate since the night her
mother had come as a concubine to the House of Po and
stirred her father's old bone to produce Erlan, his last child
and another disappointing, worthless daughter.

The fire woman reminded Erlan of her mother. Not
in her looks, of course, but in her being, which was overwhelmingly yin—dark and female and of the earth. Her
wispy voice floated like smoke through the air, and she
shaped her words with her hands, her movements languid
and fluid. With her burnished hair and the bright yellow
dress she wore, she looked like a sleek golden carp swimming in a garden pond.

By contrast, the moon woman's dress was a dark burgundy silk, the color of a New Year's banner. And her face
was closed and cool. But although she was as pretty and
delicate as the flowers painted on a silk fan, there was much
yang in her. Erlan thought she carried in her heart a warrior's finely tempered sword.

Just then the moon woman rubbed a palm over her
belly and Erlan saw that it was swelling slightly with expectant happiness. Yet she wore no gold bracelets to show
she had a husband.

They must be daughters of joy, then, Erlan thought.
This ramshackle place was a house of leisure, and the fire
woman was probably the Old Mother.

Erlan parted her lips to speak. But she had been silent
for so long that her voice broke, croaking like a frog's. "A
thousand pardons, Lo Mo—"

The fire woman spun around, a hand to her breast.
"Land, you startled me!" She laughed, making a sound as
melodious as ju jade bells. "How rude you must think us,
talking over your head like that. We just didn't expect you
would speak English, being fresh off the boat like you are."

Erlan's gaze fell in shame to the hem of her chang-
fu. She had not meant for her silence to cause the foreign

women such loss of face. "This stupid girl understands only some," she said. "Speaks even less."

The fire woman was smiling as she came up to her, two tiny crescent moons deepening her cheeks. "My name is Hannah, and this is Clementine."

Erlan bowed and touched her chest with her finger-tips. "Erlan . . . It means Day Lily in your language."

"Day Lily. My, what a pretty name that is." She took Erlan's hand and led her to the bed, easing her down so they were sitting side by side. The woman's touch was gentle yet strong. Erlan could see the blueness of her veins beneath the milky skin.

Clementine, too, crossed the room and settled on the bed. Even with her unbound feet she moved with the grace and elegance of a dragon boat. Her eyes were a dark froth-ing green, like the sea, and when they focused on her face Erlan saw deep currents stirring.

"Why did that man put a leash around your neck?"

Erlan blushed with shame and looked away. "To teach me obedience," she answered in a small, tight voice.

"Then it is not your will to marry Sam Woo?"

Her will? It had been her father's will to sell her. Her duty was to obey. Destiny, he had once told her, had four feet, eight hands, and sixteen eyes. How, then, could one worthless daughter with only two of each hope to escape?

"I don't understand," she said. She met the moon woman's gaze, and she saw deep emotions hiding behind a mask of serenity.

"You are not a slave, Erlan. No one can force you to marry Mr. Woo."

"But if I do not marry, what will become of me?"

"There are ships that sail east as well as west."

A vast longing swelled in Erlan's chest. She could see herself being carried in a litter along the tall walls of her lao chia until she came to the gate. There, her father would be waiting. His gold-embroidered dragon robe would shine in the sun, but no brighter than his smile. "My daughter," he would say, "how my heart has grieved. I should never have sent you away . . ." But it was only a dream, and like all dreams, it was destined to disappear like dew in the morning sun. She was a dishonored daughter, disowned by her clan. There would be no red banners hung on the moon gate to welcome her home.

"There is nothing for me there," she said, and the truth of this hurt so she nearly gasped aloud.

Hannah squeezed her hand. "You don't have to go back to China, honey. But you needn't marry Sam Woo, either. You could run a laundry, maybe. That doesn't take much money to start up. Or a vegetable garden. There's a Chinese man who works a plot of land across the river, and he claims he could sell twice what he's able to grow."

Erlan shook her head, pain sticking like a fish bone in her throat. "I must marry the merchant Woo."

Once she would have gone with joy and virtuous obedience to wed the man chosen by her elders. She mustn't weep now because the gods had laid down a different path. To defy her destiny would be to dishonor herself, and she could bear no more dishonor. Already it was going to take Erlan a thousand lifetimes to atone for her mother's shame.

"If you're sure . . . ?" Hannah said.

"Yes. I will marry the merchant Woo."

Her head jerked up at a knock on the door. Hannah went to answer it. The merchant Woo stood at the threshold, a red satin chang-fu embroidered with flying yellow cranes folded over his arm. He said something to Hannah, too low for Erlan to hear, but the answer brought a look of relief to his face. The *bock tow doy* hovered behind him, his scowl threatening dire consequences if Erlan did not yield.

"Look here," Hannah was saying as she came back into the room. "Sam's brought you a new gown for the wedding." Hannah laid the red robe on the bed and took up a pitcher off the washstand. Erlan watched her pour hot water from a covered tin container that sat on a trivet. The merchant Woo and the master stared at Erlan until Hannah shut the door in their faces.

"The circuit judge is only in town for the afternoon," she said. "He's holding court in the hotel bar. We've already told Sam he's got to marry you legally, in the American way. You won't be his slave, honey, no matter what that shifty-eyed bastard out in the hall says. You'll be Sam's wife, which ain't the same thing as his owning you. Do you understand?"

"Yes. I understand," she lied.

Her gaze was pulled back to the moon woman, who sat in stillness beside her. Whose sea green eyes were wide and deep and restless as she rubbed a hand over the gentle swell of her belly.

Erlan wondered about the father of the moon woman's baby. If she was not a daughter of joy after all, if she had a husband, then had the marriage broker chosen someone kind, a man who was young and handsome? But perhaps there were no marriage brokers in this fon-kwei land. Perhaps the choice had been all hers.

Their gazes met and Erlan thought she saw sadness now in those ocean eyes. Perhaps even here the fates ruled and choice was only an illusion.

"Would you like to wash up in privacy?" Clementine asked softly.

Erlan swallowed, nodded. "Please."

She waited until she was alone before she touched the wedding robe. The red satin was smooth and cool beneath her fingertips. The cranes had been embroidered with gold silk thread using tiny, intricate stitches. Red and gold, the colors of happiness and good fortune.

But there would be no fortune teller to determine the luckiest day for this wedding, no moon cakes to feast on, no firecrackers to frighten away evil spirits.

She went to the washstand. Steam wafted into the air from the water in the pitcher. She poured a little into the bowl and, glancing up, caught her reflection in the small rust-spotted mirror tacked to the wall.

She hadn't looked at her face in a mirror since she had left her lao chia. She was herself, yet she was not. She touched the glass, expecting her image to shatter and disappear like a reflection in a pool.

She had no rice powder to whiten her skin, but then, she was pale enough, except for the bruise the master had put on her cheek. Her hair was dressed in a maiden's coils. She should put it in a matron's knot for the wedding, but there was no maidservant to help her with it, and no jasmine oil to make it glisten.

She wore brass earrings worth no more than a small string of *cash* in place of the jade ones the slave trader had ripped from her earlobes. The loss of the earrings still pained her so much that she couldn't bear to think of it without tears welling up in her eyes. Yet he had also taken her gold phoenix combs, which were much more valuable. And her virginity, which was beyond price.

She pressed her hands hard to her face, her shoulders hunching. She wanted to shed tears of blood.

"Then it is not your will to marry Sam Woo . . . Your will . . ." The words echoed in her mind like stones dropped into a well. Until now her whole life had been dedicated to making herself a credit to her ancestors, obeying her father, preparing for the day when she would obey and please her husband and serve her mother-in-law. She had thought of nothing but how she might please, how she might serve.

Your will . . . your will . . . What would it be like to serve herself, please only herself? It was a novel thought and it frightened her, and so she buried it deep inside her heart.

She washed the dust of travel off as best she could and replaced the tong's rough blue cotton chang-fu with her satin wedding robe of red and gold. The high collar hid the marks left on her neck by the leash.

The master was waiting for her in the hall. He looked

her over, gave a sharp nod, and gestured for her to precede
him. Perhaps he, too, feared that without the leash to anchor her, her golden lilies would pull free of the earth and
she would float up and away from him, into the bottomless
Montana sky.

A commotion of voices spilled out of the foyer. Hannah's and Clementine's and another, deeper, one. She
stepped from the shadows of the hall into the light that
came through the open double doors, and the fon-kwei
giant was suddenly before her.

"I'll be hearing it out of her own mouth," he said.

Truly he was the largest man she had ever seen. Her
gaze began with the brass buttons on his blue-striped shirt
and went up and up. A dark flush stained his high, flat
cheekbones. The hair on his face and head was the rich
brown of freshly tilled earth. He had the most beautiful
eyes. Soft and gentle as rainwater.

He fixed them on her now and she felt a sudden surge
in her heartbeat. "'Tes your desire to marry Sam Woo?" he
asked.

Her mouth was as dry as a millet cake. She had to
swallow twice before she could speak, and the words nearly
choked her. "It is my desire," she finally managed in a voice
she did not recognize. And the word echoed back at her,
like more stones falling into the deep well of her heart:
desire . . . desire . . . desire . . .

"It is my desire," she said again, as if by saying it twice
the lie would somehow become a truth.

Another man stepped up to them. He was younger
and slighter than the giant, his face sharp like a hawk's.
His eyes were the same dense gray, but harder, like stones
seen through a pool of clear water.

He laid a hand on the giant's arm. "Come, then, Jere.
We're late for work as 'tes, and you've heard her. She be
doing it of her own free will."

The giant shook off the other man's hand. Anger darkened his face. For all his gentle ways, Erlan thought, he had

a temper that lashed like a dragon's tail. "I'll not be leaving till I'm sure of it."

"Please," she said. "You are shaming me."

She jerked away from him with such force she nearly slipped on her tiny bound feet. She saw the merchant Woo standing in a doorway, waiting for her. He had removed his barbarian hat, and his shaven crown was not insignificant but tall and smooth and strong. He had a black silk ribbon braided neatly through his queue, which was tucked into his vest pocket. His eyes glinted at her from behind his thick spectacles. She did not think she could ever come to love him.

The room they entered was crowded with men standing before a long wooden counter, tipping glasses of foamy ale up to their mouths. The pine floorboards shone wet beneath the men's feet and emitted a malty smell. Erlan saw everything through a blur of tears she blamed on the thick tobacco smoke.

The merchant Woo led her up to a man who was lounging in a chair on his tailbone, his feet propped up on a table. He put down his glass and wiped his mouth with his wrist. His head was as round and bald as a rice pot, but hair grew like a foxtail along his upper lip.

"Well, hell, Chinaman," he said, and shot a stream of spittle into a wooden box filled with sawdust. The floor around the box was slimy and stained brown. "I see you've decided on gettin' yer spurs tangled up in holy wedlock after all."

He lumbered to his feet and took up a book. Erlan didn't listen to the words he spoke. "Say yes," he said at one point.

"Yes," she repeated obediently, although her cheeks felt stiff and oddly cold.

He ended by proclaiming loudly: "You may kiss the bride."

It was not a thing a Chinese would ever do—touch his wife, even his new wife, in public. But the merchant Woo took her arms and pulled her against him and pressed his mouth to hers.

The foreign devils clapped their hands, making enough noise to chase away an army of evil spirits without the help of firecrackers. Erlan's gaze fell to the hem of her red silk wedding robe. A furious trembling was going on inside her, a frothing, like waves being whipped by the mighty winds of a *tai-fung*.

This pressing of mouth to mouth was truly a disgusting thing. And his lips were as dry as rice paper.

The wind was starting to tatter the pall of smoke that hung over the butte as the Scully brothers climbed the road toward the Four Jacks silver mine. They had been in Rainbow Springs less than a month, fresh off the boat from England and ready to mine the golden land of opportunity. Thus far, though, the only digging they'd done was for three dollars a day working a ten-hour shift at the Four Jacks.

The brothers didn't usually talk much between them, both being quiet men. Jere's was the silence of a man content and easy within himself, Drew's the silence of a man too proud to show himself.

But the arrival of the noon stage had shattered Jere Scully's contentment. "She didn't want to marry him, Drew," he said, the brogue of their native Cornwall thick on his tongue. "You could see she didn't."

His brother heaved a sigh thick with exasperation. "My blessed life, she as much as told you to go scratch yourself. She walked in there and said her 'I do's' before the justice, and nobody was putting a gun to her head that I could see. You think she would choose to go off with you rather than stick with them of her own kind? Were you going to be marrying her yourself, then?"

"Mebbe."

Drew swung the gunnysack that held his work clothes

at his brother's head. "You've gone daft, you have, to even think of marrying a Celestial. And tedn't like you know the chit. The two of you've barely passed the time of day."

"Did you hear her voice? It had a lilt to it. Like she was warming up to sing."

Drew shook his head, although he had to admit the girl was pretty. Her eyes were as dark and smooth as river stones, her mouth shaped like those perfect red bows they painted on candy boxes. But Drew preferred a flashier sort of woman himself. The sort of woman with crimson hair and rainbow petticoats, come-hither eyes and a throaty laugh. A woman who loved hard and lived dangerously.

A woman like Mrs. Hannah Yorke.

He thought of the way she had pulled that derringer out of her pocket and threatened to shoot off the Celestial's nose with it. God's life, she was beautiful and she was bad. And he wanted her.

Thus far, though, Mrs. Hannah Yorke was having none of him.

Usually he and Jere and most of the other miners frequented the Gandy Dancer, an Irishman's saloon tucked in the shadow of the butte. But one night last week they'd gone to the Best in the West for the hell of it, and that was when he'd first seen her. But he hadn't gotten beyond a simple "Pleased to be making your acquaintance, lady." Not that night or since.

It was said she'd worked in a hookshop not too long back, and owning the Best in the West Casino hardly put her in the ranks of the respectable. But she also owned the town's main hotel and a couple of boardinghouses, including the one they flopped in, which had to mean she was in the chips. So having her wasn't going to be as simple a matter as laying down three dollars for her time.

Drew Scully smiled at the challenge. He would have Hannah Yorke. He would see her in his bed, or he'd see her in hell. But there would come a day, and soon, when she would have to look him in the eye and reckon with him.

His smile faded, though, a moment later when he looked up and saw the gallus frame of the Four Jacks looming before him—the black skeletal headframe where the ore was hauled up from the shafts, and where the miners were sent down.

The slope of the butte was rutted with the streams of ore tailings and lumpy with black slag heaps and mounds of waste rock. But beyond the butte the sky was a limpid blue that made the mountains look close enough to touch. He wished he had a reason to go riding up in those mountains today. A reason to do anything but what he had to do.

They moved to the side of the road as a wagon pulling a load of crushed ore rolled by going down the hill while one bearing a stack of shoring timbers passed them going up. Jere raised his hand to the skinners in greeting. The curses they hurled back at him showed such inventiveness that he turned to his brother, beaming a smile, and caught the look on the younger man's face.

"Drew, are you—"

"I'm all right. So hold your clack." He wasn't all right, though.

The rhythmical thud of the stamp mill thrummed in Drew's head. He could feel the first quivers of tension deep in his belly. He could also feel Jere watching him, and he tried to put a spring into his step. But he couldn't fool his brother any more than he could fool himself. The rank fear lay always deep inside him like a mortal sickness.

By the time they had gone to the foreman's shack and gotten their work assignments, the muscles cording his throat had drawn as taut as bowstrings. In the changing house, as he put on a pair of filthy trousers and tied them at the waist with a piece of rope, his throat was so tight he could barely swallow. He shrugged into a shirt, which he would take off as soon as he was down in the shaft, and sweat immediately began to crawl all over his body. He put on a felt fedora made stiff with tree sap, and the blood began to roar in his head.

He walked with Jere to the collar of the Four Jacks shaft. As they stood under the headframe on the metal sheets, he could feel the vibration of the pumps and hoisting engine. Iron cages descended into the earth in clouds of steam as if they were descending into the bowels of hell. And fear burned a hot path up his chest, choking him.

He went behind a timber car and vomited up the stack of flapjacks he'd had for breakfast. He knelt in the dirt, his head pressed into the rough wood of the car, his chest heaving. Sometimes when he was sick like that, he would spew up all the fear along with the food sitting heavy in his belly. But not this time.

He came out from behind the car and returned Jere's look with a grimace that just about passed for a smile. But he knew he was as white as cornstarch. He stuffed his hands in his pockets to hide their trembling.

Runnels of sweat coursed down his sides as he watched the red arrow on the dial spin around as the cage came back up, watched the hoisting cable wind around the enormous grooved spool. And then he was stepping into the iron cage, he and Jere, and the hoistman was pulling the bell to signal their descent.

And blackness swallowed them.

The fear was now a scream in his mind. He gasped for breath, and the sound of it filled the rattling cage like the slithering hiss of a steam pump. Light flared as Jere scraped a match and put it to the candle on his hat. It helped some to see the upward-fleeing sides of the shaft instead of nothing but impenetrable blackness.

He tried to breathe through his nose, but it felt as if his lungs had shrunk. The air was as thick as black wool and smelled of the deep earth. Maybe the bloody cage will crash going down, he thought, and put me out of my misery.

He'd heard of that happening. Of bodies ricocheting against the rocky walls until they hit the sump, the pit full of hot water that lay at the bottom of every shaft. They kept small grappling hooks on hand to pick up pieces of whatever was left of a man when that happened. They rolled the pieces in canvas and put them in wooden candle boxes to be taken above, where they were put into caskets and laid back into the earth that had killed them.

The odd thing was, he didn't fear death, not even a hideous, horrible death like that one. It wasn't the ways a man could die in a mine that frightened him, it was the mine itself. The thick and heavy darkness and the earth closing in on him, pressing and squeezing, trapping him, smothering him . . .

The cage jolted to a stop, and Drew stepped out into the main drift at the sixth level, his jaw rigid and his knees loose. And his heart working like a bellows in his chest.

Jere greeted the shaft boss with the easy smile that was his way. "How's she going, gaffer?"

"You're late," the boss snapped back. Casey O'Brian had a face like a rat's, his nose and mouth and chin all coming to a point below his small, close-set eyes. He studied the Scully brothers out of those eyes now, and the whole lower half of his face twitched as if he had whiskers. "And since you're late, sure you lads'll be advancing the face of the west stope today."

Yesterday Drew had told the boss the cribbing was going rotten on the west stope—that web of massive timbers that shored up the tons of rock above their heads. It had been groaning and creaking for days now, and the rats had been skittering about. Rats could always sense when the cribbing was about to go.

Drew knew the shaft boss was daring him to say something about the weak cribbing so that he could crack wise and nasty about Drew's courage and his manhood. Hard-rock miners were supposed to take pride in the bone-wrenching way they made a living and worked on the edge of danger, as if it were worthy of a bloody knighthood.

"You got something stuck in your craw, boy?" O'Brian said. "Spit it out."

Drew pulled his mouth into a hard smile. "I was

going to suggest you go and get buggered, sir. But then I thought you'd not be finding anyone willing to put it to an arsehole like yourself."

O'Brian's jaw bunched along with his fists, but he said nothing. The Scully brothers were not only big men, they were the best double-jack team on the whole butte, and a shaft boss would put up with a lot to have them on his crew. They could drill more holes faster than any other team, one holding the drill and the other pounding it with a heavy sledgehammer, driving the drill point into the hard rock face to prepare the hole for the blasting powder.

Most times Drew was the blaster, the man who loaded and tamped the volatile sticks of dynamite into the holes, set the fuses, and fired off the blasts. The other miners all thought Drew was nerveless when it came to handling the giant powder. Nobody but his brother knew that he was already so scared spitless, just being down in the smothering earth and rock, that being blown to smithereens held little fear for him.

They walked in silence down the drift to the west face. Drew focused on the candle on his brother's hat, at the way it drew smoke patterns in the air. He pictured tamping down the fear within him the way he tamped down the charges of dynamite, and that helped some, but the slime of sweat was still cold on his face and the scream was still locked high in his throat.

The air was heavy with that morning's blasting and the smell of decaying timber. And it was hot. As hot as the belly of a cookstove and as humid as a Chinese laundry. The brothers shucked their shirts as they went along. Still, when they got off shift they would be pouring the sweat out of their boots as if they were buckets.

Rolfe Davies, their nipper, was waiting for them at the face, sitting on a box of drills. It was the nipper's job to take loving care of their tools, keeping the drills—or bull pricks, as the miners called them—sharp, and the grips of their hammers smooth and free of splinters, the heads on tight. He greeted Drew with a big grin all over his cinnamon-freckled face.

"It is true you told the gaffer to get fucked?"

Drew shook his head and laughed, wondering how the gossip could have gotten out to the far reaches of the mine so quickly.

Jere ruffled the boy's carrot-top head with his big hand. "Have a care if you're going to go patterning yourself after my little brother, then. Don't you know he's destined to hang before he's twenty? 'Tes true," he said, laughing at Rolfe's incredulous snort. "Cross me heart and spit to die."

"Go on with you!" Rolfe aimed a mock punch at Jere's hard belly, then turned a worshipful face up to Drew. "Would you teach me sometime, sir, how to tamp a charge? Sometime when O'Brian ain't about?"

"Aye, sure," Drew said, shrugging, embarrassed at what he saw in the boy's eyes. He felt especially foolish to be called "sir" by one not all that much younger than he was. Drew was only nineteen, but he knew the hard, sharp edges of his face made him look older. And deep down, he thought, deep in his craven, churning guts, he'd never been young.

He remembered being a little tacker back in Cornwall, half the age of Rolfe, and his da talking about the copper mine of an evening, and how much he hated it. Yet back down the shaft he would go the next day to hate the same thing all over again. Drew had sworn then that, for him, life would be different.

And he had tried to make it different. He had gotten it into his head that the way to make it different was to better himself. *Knowing* things was what kept a man out of the mines. When he'd announced to the family that he was going to take lessons at the vicarage, the da had called him a sniveling coward and a lazy do-nothing. But his fear of spending his life in the mines was greater than his fear of the da's strap. To the vicarage he had gone until the da was killed when the seventh level of Wheal Ruthe caved in.

He was twelve and Jere fifteen, and they were the only

boys of working age in the large and hungry Scully family. And so by dying the da had gotten Drew down the shafts after all, to blast rock and muck ore.

They had lived for a time after the cave-in—the da and the other tut-workers caught in the Wheal Ruthe fall. The rescuers could hear the *ping-pang* signal of a hammer striking rock during the first two days of trying to dig through the rubble. Then the hammering had stopped.

Drew had often wondered if the da had felt afraid at the end, afraid of the suffocating darkness and the earth pressing in, strangling him. But he thought not. His father had probably died cursing the mine, not choking on the screams that made a man less than a man.

In the smoking, flickering light of the oil lanterns, Jere's bulging muscles glistened as he struck the drill head with the sledge, finishing off the last hole. The din of metal slamming on metal shivered through the heavy air to be smothered by the earth. In the silence that followed, Drew's ringing ears picked up the drip and trickle of water, the creaking of timbers, and his own harsh breathing. But it was the breathing of hard work now, not fear.

He was almost jaunty as he finished packing wet mud around the rattail fuse of the last stick of dynamite. "Lighting up!" he yelled as a warning that everyone should start moving away from the stope and down the drift. Rolfe Davies scooted around, gathering up drill bits and hammers.

Drew snipped off and lit a spitter, a length of fuse that was cut shorter than the shortest rattail in the face. He would use the spitter to light the fuses and to serve as a warning: when it burned down to his hand it was time to run like hell.

The brothers lit off the fuses together, working with practiced skill, doing twenty-five in under twenty seconds. As Drew touched his spitter to the last rattail, Jere boomed out, "Fire in the hole!"

Jere grabbed the lanterns and set off at a brisk pace back down the drift. "What's your hurry, then, my handsome?" Drew called after him, laughing and walking more slowly, deliberately cutting it too fine. "We've swacks of time."

The drift made a couple of oxbow turns before ending at the shaft. They rounded the corner of the last one and saw the candles of the other miners ahead of them. Just as they stepped into the circle of light they covered their ears with their hands, and a split second later came the muffled booms of the exploding charges. The air shivered, pressing against their bodies. The too-sweet smell of dynamite wafted down the drift, and smoke clouded the candles and lanterns.

Only the shaft boss hadn't covered his ears, because he was counting. "How many?" he asked when the explosions had ended.

"Twenty-five," Jere said.

"Easy as scratch," Drew added with a cocky grin.

O'Brian nodded. They had all blown. But then, the Scully brothers were too good at what they did to leave any sleepers behind them—holes drilled and packed with powder that never went off . . . until some other miner came along with a pick and blew himself into hell.

O'Brian left without another word, moving down the tram tracks in his skittering ratlike walk. Drew made a rude gesture at his back. "That was a proper shot, lads," he said, mimicking the shaft boss's squeaky ratlike voice. He bowed, scraping the floor with his hand. "Why, thank ye kindly, yer lordship."

The other miners all laughed, and Jere grinned at him, shaking his head. "I'll get the tea hotted up."

Drew waited until all the men, including his brother, had disappeared into the darkness, heading for the end of the worked-out stope where they gathered every day for supper. When he was alone he fished out the twist of tobacco he carried in his boot.

He called her Pansy. She was one of the mules who

pulled a train of six hopper cars, each filled with a ton of ore, from where it was dug out of the stope to the cages where it was lifted to the surface. The miners joked that the mules were treated better than they were, with their underground stables and the finest fodder and fresh water twice a day. But Drew never laughed. The mules hadn't been asked if they wouldn't rather be up in the sunlight and clean air. At least a man had the illusion of a choice.

Pansy had been down in the shaft for so long her hide had turned green. She loved chewing tobacco, did Pansy. Drew brought her some every day, and he scratched her ears while she chewed it. He was tempted to talk to her sometimes, but he never did.

Jere handed him a cup of tea as he rejoined the others, using a roll of fuse cord for a seat. "Where you been?" Jere asked too casually.

"Taking a piss," he lied. He bit into his letter-from-home, a Cornish pie made of beef, onion, and potatoes. "I didn't think I needed you to be holding my hand whilst I did it."

The brothers sat apart from the others, eating by the flickering light of a single candle set into a niche hacked out of the rock. Drew thought of Pansy the mule, who would probably die down here without ever seeing the sun again or feeling the wind ruffle her tail. He thought of the way the mountains had looked earlier, where silence and loneliness were the creation not of the darkness and heavy earth but of the light and the sun and the wind. He wondered what it would be like to get on a horse and ride out into the hills and the plains and keep on riding until he reached the edge of the sky.

He wished he didn't have these hankerings and frets. He wished he were more like Jere, who worked hard, drank hard, fought hard, and laughed hard, and looked for nothing else out of life.

He felt his brother's eyes on him and he looked up.

"I've been thinking . . ." Jere said, the last word

breaking as he coughed up the rock dust he'd been breathing all afternoon.

"You've been thinking, have you?" he said, forcing a smile. "And should I be worrying now?"

"I've been thinking we should try our hand at homesteading. There's all that free land here just for the taking. We should get ourselves out of the mines and become farmers."

Drew wondered where his brother thought they would get the money to work a homestead. They made three dollars a day in the shafts. A dollar of it went for room and board at the flophouse, and they kept out a few bits for themselves for whiskey and whores. The rest went back to Cornwall for Mam and the girls. Every month they got a letter from her—written by the vicar, although the words were her own—calling the blessings of God down upon their heads for saving the Scully family from the poorhouse.

And besides, they knew damn all about farming.

"You really have gone daft," Drew said harshly. "First you get a notion in your noggin to court a Celestial and now you're makin' clack about being a sodbuster. Where's the blunt going to come for seed and a plow and a harrow and a team and a stoneboat and a seeder and a binder, huh?"

"Since when do you know so much about it? 'Less you've been thinking on it same as I have."

Drew slammed the lid down on their supper pail with a loud clatter. "When a man goes down into the mines, he stays there."

"You sound like the da."

Drew's lip curled into a mean smile. "I reckon the da knew what he was talking about, because where is he now, my handsome? Buried under a ton of rubble in the seventh level of Wheal Ruthe."

A silence settled over the stope as the others stretched out on a timber pile for a half hour's nap. Jere pulled a penknife and a block of wood out of his pocket and began to whittle—he was always making little toys that he gave away to the other miners' kids. Drew sat and watched blisters of grease follow each other down the side of the candle. Above his head the cribbing creaked. The eyes of the rats gleamed in the dusky penumbra of the candlelight.

When a man goes down into the mines, he stays there.

The Scully brothers put on dry shirts against the chill of a Montana summer night as they waited their turn to go up the shaft. The other men were all laughing and making loud talk about the beer they were going to put away at the Gandy Dancer. But all Drew Scully could think of was that he'd made it through another shift without any of the others glomming on to what a coward he really was.

Rolfe Davies sat on top of a load of rock in the hoisting cage, a box of dull drill bits in his lap. Drew caught the boy's worshipful gaze on him and they shared a smile just as the cage jerked into motion—

And the hoist cable broke with a crack like a rifle shot.

The loose cable whipped at the rock and timber as it went up the shaft, and the loose car smacked against the rock and timber as it went down. The nipper screamed and went on screaming until he hit the boiling hot sump with a splash. And then there were only the echoes of his screams, going on and on and on until they were swallowed at last by the thick black earth.

The white-faced hoistman jerked nine times on the bell rope. Above ground the disaster whistle would be piercing the night.

Tears burned in Drew's eyes. His chest jerked hard as he drew at the thin air. Ashamed, he turned his face toward the earth and rocks where only the darkness was there to see his weakness.

18

EARLIER THAT AFTERNOON A thick, warm wind had caressed Erlan's face as she stepped out of the hotel's double doors at the side of the merchant Sam Woo, who was now her husband.

She took mincing steps on the warped and spit-slimed boardwalk. One of her tiny carved wooden shoes caught on an uneven board, and she stumbled. The merchant Woo steadied her with a hand beneath her elbow, then withdrew it.

He had yet to speak a single word to her.

She thought he was probably taking her to his house. She had no expectations. The buildings of this Rainbow Springs were all of gray and weathered logs or freshly peeled ones. Certainly there would be no green tiled roofs and scarlet pillars to remind her of her lao chia and all that she had lost.

The road they walked along led straight and flat as a rice mat out into the wide land and big sky. She wondered if perhaps the evil spirits were less powerful here than in China, so that the roads didn't have to be laid crooked to fool them. She wanted to ask the merchant Woo about this and many other things. But until her husband opened his mouth to her, she wasn't allowed to speak to him.

The merchant Woo stopped before a squat log building with a tin roof, but Erlan barely glanced at it. A group of Chinese men had gathered in a tight, tense knot in the street. A few were barefoot and others wore only straw sandals on their dusty feet. Their baggy *schmo* were rolled up to their knees, and their legs were sun-browned and as skinny as chopsticks.

None was so rude as to stare directly, but they all cast furtive looks, *hungry* looks, at her from beneath their conical straw hats. They shifted on their feet and whispered behind their hands, making a sound like mice feeding in a rice bin. "A beauty! A beauty! A beauty with lily feet!"

"Better I sell you outright to a mining camp, ma?" the slave trader had said. "Those whore-cunts are so desperate for wives they will take anything, even a dishonored old woman with bullock feet."

She stood in utter stillness, her hands stuffed up her sleeves, gripping her arms. The *ping-pang* of a hammer on steel echoed from a large, cavernous building across the street. The pounding seemed to resound in the pit of her stomach. She trapped a moan of fear behind her teeth.

The door behind her creaked open, setting off a jangle of bells. The merchant Woo stepped back for her to cross the threshold first. She had to hop on her golden lilies to climb the two sagging steps. She entered a room filled with so many things that it made her dizzy just looking at the jumble.

Candlesticks and boxes of candles. A barrel filled with straw brooms and another one full of onions. Tobacco twists and twisted coils of rope. Tin buckets and tin spoons. Familiar things, like a set of mah-jongg tiles and a red silk lantern. And things she'd never seen before, such as a coat made out of a slick yellow material and a box of something called toothache gum.

Shelves sagged under precariously stacked tin cans. The warped floor was covered with wooden kegs and bales of animal furs. The small-paned window cast bars of dusty sunlight over the front of the shop. But the back corners were shrouded in darkness and looked as if they hadn't been explored in years.

A rank odor came from one of the barrels just inside the door. Erlan leaned over for a closer look. It appeared to be filled with great bloody chunks of meat packed in brine. A hand-lettered sign pasted on the outside of the barrel identified it: Bear Shot Fresh Last Week.

The merchant Woo cleared his throat. Startled, Erlan whirled so quickly she swayed on her golden lilies. He held aside a tattered brown blanket that hung over the doorway into another room. She passed by him into darkness.

A match whisked and flared. He put the flame to a lamp and adjusted the wick, then nearly dropped the chimney when he went to put it back on its base.

They were in a kitchen with a table, two chairs, and a round iron stove with a vent pipe that ran out through a circle of tin in the roof. The room, which had no window, was close and crowded and smelled of boiled cabbage. Flies stuck to a strip of paper that dangled from the ceiling.

The merchant Woo hung the lamp on a wall hook and came to stand before her, so close that if he had breathed deeply his chest would have brushed hers. She thought of the wedding and the way his lips had felt on her mouth, and it was all she could do not to shudder.

"Have you eaten today?" he said. It was the appropriate Chinese greeting, but spoken in the harsh, guttural Yueh dialect of Canton.

She gave the traditional response in high-class Mandarin. "I am well."

He frowned at her, and his next words were in English. "Mrs. Yorke said you savvy how to talk American. What a big wonderful surprise this is. Good for business. From now on you talk only American, even with me. That way you can practice."

And that way your peasant ears won't have to struggle to understand my Chinese, she thought. But she only nodded in obedience.

He took a step back, sweeping his hand through the air. "Sit down, please. Your golden lilies must ache."

Erlan slowly lowered herself into one of the chairs. If she had been alone, she would have groaned aloud. Her feet were indeed sore. And all those days and nights in that rocking, jouncing coach had left her as stiff as an old woman.

The merchant began to lay out an array of wonderful food before her on the table, and to her shame her mouth began to water. Thanks be to the merciful Kwan Yin that her husband's embracing of the barbarian ways did not extend to what he ate.

She thought of the swing stations where the stagecoach had stopped along her journey, those crude wooden shacks where the horses were changed and the passengers were given a piece of tough meat thrust between the two halves of a soggy, bitter biscuit, and tin cups of coffee thick enough to lacquer a chest. Once they had been treated to a platter of rancid pork and something called corn dodgers, which resembled fried millet cakes. Inedible food served under conditions of indescribable filth, as nourishing as a beggar's soup made of nothing but bones.

But this . . . aiya, this was truly a feast fit for the gods. Bowls of pickled cabbage, ginger, and lotus root. Steamed buns and duck coated with plum sauce. A cool custard of green beans and a saucer of melon seeds. Steaming meat dumplings, lo mein and snow-white rice. Erlan's belly made a loud gurgling noise.

She was saved from embarrassment by the clatter of a stove lid. The merchant Woo tossed more sticks on the fire. He had to move aside a wok and a bamboo steamer to set a kettle on to boil. The lantern light gleamed off a razor-sharp cleaver that lay atop a chopping block. He must have prepared this wedding banquet himself, for she doubted he had a servant to do it for him. If he had need of her in the kitchen as well as in his bed, the jest was on him. She could embroider cranes finer than the ones on the robe he had given her, and she could coax pretty music from a pi-pa, but she was an abysmal cook. She couldn't prepare so much as a bowl of soggy rice.

She stared from beneath carefully lowered eyelids at

this man who was her husband. He knelt before the open door to the stove, jabbing with a poker at the smoking wood. His hands were small like a boy's, but spotted with age, his chin whiskers thick and stiff like the teeth of an ebony comb. His shaven crown shone in the lamplight. His queue was very long and a credit to him.

He turned his head, his spectacles glittering. He offered her a tentative smile.

Emboldened, she asked, "What is your honorable name?"

"Sam is my name now. You will call me Sam. I will call you Lily.

"Lily is a good American name," he went on when she said nothing. "As American as the Fourth of July and Yankee Doodle Dandy, yes? There was a chippy—a joy girl—who worked for Mrs. Yorke for a while and called herself Lily."

Shame burned in Erlan's chest. Once she had thought to marry a man of breeding and scholarship. Instead she must be obedient and pleasing to an old peasant from Canton who wished to call her after a joy girl. But she must stop thinking of herself as what she was. Her father had sold her, *sold* her to a slave broker. She thought of those haunted faces peering through the bars of those whore-alley cribs. How easily one of those faces could have been hers.

She looked down. Her hands were clenched in her lap, and she flattened them, smoothing them over the blood-red satin. A tremor of fear coursed through her. "Who are those men gathered outside the door?"

He rose to his feet, dusting off his hands. "There're not a lot of Chinawomen in the Montana Territory, so they're curious, you savvy? They envy this unworthy one such a young and beautiful wife."

"Perhaps it is your wealth they envy, that you were able to buy this foolish self."

He grunted in agreement. "Those little shits couldn't

put together a string of copper *cash* between them, no sir-ree jingle. They work the tailings and played-out placer claims on the hill, what the white man no longer has use for. They're not allowed to work in the Four Jacks."

She hadn't grasped all he had said, for many of the English words were unfamiliar to her. She couldn't imag-ine why anyone would choose to work deep in a hole in the earth, but it made no sense that the men would be forbid-den to do so. "Why are they not allowed?"

"Because they're Chinks." He studied her from behind his spectacles, his eyes unblinking. She thought that he would say more, that he had a secret to impart to her, or perhaps a sorrow. Instead he shrugged. "You will under-stand after you're here awhile."

She didn't want to understand; she didn't want to be here long enough to understand. She was overwhelmed suddenly by the thought that it might be years before she could go home. So many thousands of *li* of land and sea now lay between her and her lao chia. And a barrier of honor betrayed and honor lost that was wider and longer than the Great Wall itself.

She wasn't aware he had come up beside her until he laid a small box wrapped in red silk on her lap. "This is for you," he said.

She unfolded the silk, a little excited in spite of herself to be getting a gift. She opened the box to reveal a small hinged case of gold with a new moon and a star engraved on its round face.

"It's a picture locket," he said. He showed her how to pry it open with the tips of her fingers. "Look . . . This is Sam Woo, my photograph. Clementine McQueen took it of me. She shot me," he said, laughing.

His face sobered. "You wear it here," he said, this time in his rough Cantonese. And he touched her throat where the bone curved beneath the high collar of her robe. Her pulse beat so wildly she was surprised he couldn't feel it. He took the locket from her trembling fingers. He snapped it shut and pinned it on her breast, just above her heart. "Or here."

"I am unworthy of such a fine gift," she said. She was struck by what a strange sight it was—the fon-kwei locket on her red satin wedding robe.

The kettle shrieked, startling them both. He let out a short laugh and hurried to take it off the fire. She watched while he placed tea leaves in two porcelain cups, poured boiling water over them, covered the cups, and placed them in copper bowls. He set one before her and one at his place across the table, then took his seat.

He removed the lid and took the cup from the copper bowl, cradling it in both hands. She did the same. The steam of the dragon well tea wafted around her face, smelling of flower petals, sweet and soft.

"Empty cup," he toasted and drank his down to the last drop.

She took a sip. He was staring at her over the porcelain rim of his cup. There was something in his eyes, something she had seen before . . . Fingers of memory gripped her heart, of rough hands groping, squeezing, teeth nipping, lips slobbering, a prodding, and then a pain like a knife rending her open, thrusting into her, a heavy weight heaving on her breasts and belly, crushing her . . .

A scream filled her throat, sticking there. The skin of her chest pulled taut.

Her husband stood up abruptly and came back with an empty rice bowl, which he set before her. Above the bowl, he laid a pair of chopsticks neatly on their stand. "Thank you for honoring my unworthy table with your presence," he said.

He brushed his knuckles along her jaw while she sat in utter stillness. She had been taught always to appear serene, but inside, she wanted to scream at the feel of his hand sliding along her cheek and down her neck. She tried to breathe and couldn't. The scream . . . the scream was there, in her throat, choking her, and she couldn't, she couldn't—

"Now," he said, his voice rough. "I will lie with you now."

And something within her shattered. She lurched to her feet, thrusting him away from her. The table scraped hard across the floor, bowls and platters sliding, falling, shattering. She backed up and up until she slammed into the stove. She felt its heat through the thick padded satin of her robe. The scream, trapped in her throat, beat hard like the wings of a frantic bird.

"Stay away from me," she said, or might have. The scream was so loud, so loud . . .

He came at her, anger hard on his face, his spectacles flashing in the dim light. She groped behind her, her fingers finding the handle of the cleaver. The scream was now roaring in her head, darkening her vision.

She swung the cleaver in a wide, desperate arc, missing his face by inches, and he reared back, shouting, "Holy God!"

The scream in her throat subsided some. She felt herself breathe, felt words form and push their way out her mouth. "Forgive this unworthy girl, but I cannot let you touch me," she said. Polite words, proper words. She would be a dutiful, obedient daughter, but she would not, she could not let any man force his way inside her again. She would rather die. To die, to die, to die . . . was the only honorable way.

The merchant Woo stared at his wife, his lips folded tightly to his teeth. It was unthinkable that a woman would attack her lord and husband. That she would deny him the use of her body. "There will be nothing to forgive," he said stiffly, "if you put that down this instant."

The cleaver flashed again. He let out a snort of derision that turned into a grunt of surprise as she twisted the blade around and pressed it to her own throat.

"Stay away."

He drew in a deep, noisy breath. The oil in the lantern gurgled. A piece of burning wood collapsed with a hiss in the stove.

He took a step toward her, and she slashed with the cleaver, cutting through skin and flesh and sending a spray of bright red blood splashing through the air.

Drew Scully turned away from the bar, balancing two tin pails of beer in one hand.

He waited while a man jetted a stream of tobacco juice into a spittoon before he crossed the line of fire. He fended off the groping hands of a hurdy-gurdy girl and sidestepped around the jabbing elbow of a man shooting billiards. Jere was waiting for him at a table against the back wall, wearing a face down to his chin.

Drew said nothing when he put the pail of beer into his brother's hands. And he said nothing when Jere downed nearly all of it in one breath. They both had a bad case of the sours.

He sat down and let a groan run silently through him. He felt so dead tired and full of misery, and he had a pain so deep it was like a bruise on the bone. He wasn't one for drowning his guts in drink of an evening, because he didn't like waking up the next morning with a head that felt as big as a bushel basket. But he wished now he had gotten some whiskey while he was up at the bar, a whole bottle of it. If he didn't get stewed tonight he was going to wake up screaming.

As the nipper had screamed.

Tears pressed against the backs of Drew's eyes and he squeezed them shut. God's life . . . He couldn't remember the last time he'd cried. The boy's death had unleashed years' worth of tears. They kept filling his eyes, clogging his throat, and he hated himself for the tears. And for his cowardice.

He had cried earlier that night when he had at last stepped off the cage into the fresh night air. Air that had the bite and tingle of fermented cider straight from a cold cellar. He breathed it deep, tasting it on his tongue and in his lungs, and that was when the tears had come.

Later, sitting in a bathtub at Luke's Barber Shop, they had come again, running down his cheeks like rain on a windowpane, mixing with the sweat and the steam, and his chest had shuddered with the effort it took not to sob aloud.

He shook his head now, trying to shake off thoughts of the mine and death. He looked around the Best in the West, impressed by this Wild West pleasure palace, by the flocked wallpaper and varnished wooden floors, the glittering diamond-dust mirrors and the tinsel tarts in their silk stockings and short skirts.

But the Gandy Dancer was more his kind of place. Tawdry as a ha'penny peep show, it was, with sawdust on the floor and walls so full of bullet holes it wasn't weatherproof anymore. The whiskey was so cut down there it tasted like river water with a tang to it. But excitement always quivered in the air, as if all hell was about to break loose at any moment. It was a miner's place, where a man dropped his bucket on the bar and slapped down two bits for a shot of whiskey and a free beer chaser to celebrate surviving another shift underground.

The Best in the West, now . . . its clientele appeared to be mostly cattle and sheep punchers. He wondered what they celebrated, what demons haunted their minds that only the booze could chase away.

He twisted the pail of beer in his hands, watching it slop over the side. He drank some of it down, feeling the night settle over him, chasing away the mulligrubs. The frantic noise at least gave the illusion of gaiety. The click of chips and the clatter of billiard balls, the slap of cards. The loose laughter of loose women and the ripple of tinny piano keys. An odd sight caught his eye, a woman as heavily veiled as a mourning widow dancing with a man who groped her buttocks with a hook in place of a hand. This country attracted strange people, he thought. The freaks and the dregs and the drifters as well as the hardy and the brave. He didn't want to think about which category he fell into.

"I shouldn't have let her go and marry him," Jere said out of nowhere.

Drew slowly turned his heavy-lidded gaze to his brother. "You still strumming on that harp? 'Tes past too late, brother. She's his now. He'll treat her proper, will Sam Woo. You know the man for a good sort."

"Aye. I shouldn't have let her marry him, Drew."

"Only because you want her for your own self."

The lovesickness was known to strike the Scully men suddenly, or so the da had been fond of saying. Just like that it had been with the da the first time he'd seen Mam, like being felled in the heart by a sledgehammer. Drew laughed to himself whenever he thought of that story, because if you got the da to drinking enough he'd also tell you that the first time he saw his future wife she was swimming bare-arsed naked in the cove. So to Drew's way of thinking, it wasn't the da's heart that was struck at all; it was his cock and bobbles.

"I'm going to have her for my own."

"Aye . . ." Drew agreed, caught up in his thoughts, then his head jerked around. He didn't like what he saw on his brother's face. "You stood there and watched her marry Sam Woo and now you sit there cool as a frog on a stone and tell me you're going to have her."

Jere's look stayed stubborn. He lifted the bucket and swallowed off the last of his beer.

"She's a Celestial," Drew persisted. "There's probably some law against it. Not to mention the law there is against doing it with another man's wife."

"Then we'll find a place where tedn't any law."

Drew spread his hands. "Christ all-bleedin'-mighty. You're talking like she'll even have you. How d—"

"She'll have me."

Drew's hands fell to the table and made a pair of fists. He might as well converse with the head of his sledgehammer as the thick head of his brother.

Jere's chin had sunk to his chest. He was giving the bottom of his beer bucket a deep study.

A movement behind the bar caught Drew's attention—the gin-slinger had pulled open a small door and was speaking to someone beyond it. Drew craned his head, but the man's massive shoulders blocked his view. He saw the corner of a rolltop desk and a triangle of bright green skirt the color of tart spring apples.

The bartender started to pull the door closed, and Drew felt disappointment sink into him. Then the door opened wide and Hannah Yorke stepped out into the area behind the bar, and Drew's heartbeat quickened. She was all smoke and heat and long legs that could wind around a man's waist and make him explode like a charge of giant powder.

He pulled in a deep breath and shifted in his chair.

Beside him Jere huffed a soft laugh. "And will you look at who's squirming now? You be eyeing her like she was a goose all ready for the Christmas pot."

Drew pressed his hands down flat on the table and pushed back his chair. Jere laid a hand on his arm. "And where be you off to, then, my handsome?"

"I'm thinking the lady could use a drink."

"The lady has a whole saloon full of drink should she be wanting some. And she already has herself a man to pour it for her."

The muscles tightened along Drew's jaw, but he eased his rump back down in the chair. "I know 'tes said she has a lover."

"Aye. 'Tes said."

"Well, where's he at, then? The man must be a bloody ghost for all we've seen of him."

Jere pointed with his chin. "Does he look like a ghost to you?"

Drew's gaze swept along the men standing hipshot at the bar, stopping at a cowboy in a dusty black Stetson and

faded black britches tucked into worn boots. He looked
roguish and rowdy and violent, though he was handsome
in a hard-mouthed way. "That one? He's been leaning there
on his elbows for ten minutes if it's been one. She hasn't
looked his way once."

"'Tes the *way* she hasn't been looking at him."

The man wore his gun low on his hips and tied snug to
his thigh, which fit with what else Drew had heard about
Hannah Yorke's lover. He was a sometime rancher who disappeared for months at a time, riding shotgun for Wells
Fargo, some said. Others said hunting bounty.

Whatever he did for a living, he didn't look like the
sort of man to give up his woman without a fight.

"The bloody hell of it," Drew said, and pushed to his
feet.

She was now in front of the bar, talking to the bartender, who was pouring them both double shots from a
bottle expensive enough to have a label. Drew slowed his
steps, taking her in a little at a time. The sharp curve of a
cheekbone, the small bump on the end of her nose, the wide
mouth that deepened at the corners. The way her dress
dipped over the slopes of breasts the ivory white of summer
clouds. The way it slipped off one shoulder, as if a man had
just pulled it down to bare her for his mouth and eyes.

She turned her head when he came up, and her lips
made a little movement that wasn't quite a smile, although
it tugged at the crescents in her cheeks.

"Well, how . . . Mr. Scully, is it?" she said in a voice
that was wispy and husky like woodsmoke. "And what
makes you come slumming over here to the Best in the
West?"

"You," he said.

She arched a taunting eyebrow. Her brows were a deep
dark red, like cuts over her eyes. "My, my. Aren't you the
one for calling a spade a shovel?"

"Down in the shafts we call it a muck stick."

Her face softened and grew wistful. "Yes, I know . . .

My father was a miner." She was silent a moment, then lifted her shoulders in a small, careless shrug. "He was killed in a fall when I was ten."

"I was twelve."

She raised startled eyes to his, and her lips parted slightly. There was a vulnerability around that mouth that didn't go with the tough way she acted. And he knew in that moment that he'd been lying to himself, trying to convince himself it was only lust. Just like the da, he'd been felled in the heart by a sledgehammer.

Oh, he knew the good folk in the town thought her wicked, and maybe by their standards she was. But if they said a good woman could make a man good, then it seemed as if it ought to work the other way about. Maybe all she needed was a man who loved her to hold her in his arms at night and touch her sweetly. She acted tough all right, but he knew she wasn't. Maybe it took a fraud like him to see the lie in her.

"Might I be buying you a drink, Mrs. Yorke?" he said.

But she had turned her head, and her gaze had drifted down the length of the bar to the cowboy in the dusty black Stetson. The man's expression didn't change. All he did was look back at her, but her face became vivid, as if a gas jet had been lit deep within her.

"The way I was taught it, Mrs. Yorke, when a gentleman asks, a lady gives him the courtesy of an answer."

She started and spun back around, the smile that hadn't been for him still lingering on her mouth. "Oh . . . Thank you but, no, Mr. Scully. I was just leaving for the night. Perhaps Nancy—"

He laid his hand on her arm. Her skin was soft and warm. Her scent wafted up to him, sweet and summery like the violet posies they sold for a farthing at a Michaelmas fair. "I don't want to spend time with one of your sporting girls. I want to spend it with you."

She looked pointedly at the hand that touched her. At a hand that was nicked and scarred from the times the hammer had missed the drill head. A hand with the black dirt of the mines under its nails.

He was just stubborn enough not to let her go.

She raised her gaze to his face and he looked into her eyes. Eyes that were a deep, loamy brown. Her breasts rose, and a small sound eased out of her like a sigh. But then she saw the doors of her saloon swing shut behind the disappearing back of her cowboy.

And the next thing Drew knew, he was watching her bustle bounce away from him and the doors swinging shut again. A moment later the busy doors were swinging shut behind Drew's back as well, and he was cursing himself for being driven to this.

The half-spent moon cast off little light. But the wind eased through the aspens, and it carried the cowboy's voice to Drew where he stood deep in the shadows of the saloon's log walls: "Seeing as how you're so busy tonight, I'll be riding on home."

She had caught up with her man at the end of the boardwalk. She leaned into him now, pressed the length of her long body against his. She said something to him with that woodsmoke voice—pleaded with him, maybe—and he allowed himself to be talked into giving in.

The cowboy slipped his arm around her waist, and they walked that way, hips bumping as they turned down the street that led to her house in back of the saloon. He dipped his head and nuzzled her white shoulder left bare by her dress, and she laughed. A laugh that was almost all breath, lazy and low.

And just a little sad.

Erlan watched her husband undress. He took off his swallowtail coat and hung it on a wall spike. A gray brocade vest with pearl buttons followed, and a shirt with a stiff collar. Even in the shadowy light of the coal oil lamp, his chest looked as scrawny as that of a rooster fit only for a beggar's pot. He raised his head and their gazes met, then his fell to her neck and he scowled.

She touched the thick bandage that was wrapped around her throat. The cut throbbed, although it went no deeper than the width of a straw. But, oh, had it bled, and she was still trembling inside over what she had almost done. A soul had many lives, but this life was the only one she had at the moment and now suddenly she wanted to keep it as fiercely as she had sought to end it.

Still, she had brought the cleaver into the bedroom with her and laid it within reach by her pillow.

She stood now on one side of the bed, her husband on the other, and he eyed her warily, as vinegar-faced as a hired mourner. It was a terrible disgrace to cause another's suicide. If he had forced himself on her and she had killed herself because of it, he would have suffered much shame. And shame was to be feared more than tigers or dragons or evil spirits.

"I will not touch you, wife," he said. He licked his lips, and his eyes shifted away from hers. "But there is only one bed for sleeping."

"This silly girl does not mind sharing." She lowered her eyes meekly. In truth she felt giddy with relief and a heady joy to be living still and at no cost to her honor. "And she thanks her husband for his restraint."

"You will not try to . . . ?" He gestured at the cleaver.

She buried her hands up the sleeves of her robe and crossed her fingers to trick the listening ears of the gods. "Not so long as you abide by your promise not to touch me."

He heaved such a hefty sigh of relief that his chin whiskers fluttered. Suddenly, the whole drama struck Erlan as funny and she had to bite the inside of her cheek and cover her mouth with her hand.

Aiya, the man was nearly as foolish as she was. She had fainted at the sight of her own blood and awakened to the merchant Woo wrapping cloths soaked with ginger water

around her neck and cursing the gods for saddling him
with a madwoman for a wife. And when she had opened
her eyes and sat up, with the cleaver still gripped in her
hand, he had shrieked and reared back on his heels as if
she were a dead woman come back to life. More laughter
welled up in her now at the memory. She bit her cheek
harder and turned her face away.

He had turned his back on her anyway and was putting on a nightshirt. He coiled his queue neatly around his
head and covered it with a sleeping cap. Erlan removed her
wedding robe, but not the under-jacket she wore to flatten
her breasts so that she wouldn't be called a wanton.

She eased down on the bed, and the mattress sighed,
the grass stuffing rustling and filling the room with the
smell of hot sunshine. She had been on her golden lilies
a lot today and her feet were raw. She longed to put on
fresh bindings, but it was too intimate a thing to do in
front of this man she didn't know. She massaged the aching
muscles in her legs, swallowing a groan.

"Would you like me to rub your calves for you?"

His offer startled her and she looked up at him out of
narrowed eyes, mistrusting his motive. Eldest Sister used to
rub her calves for her, especially when the bandages were first
used to bind her feet. Oh, how they had pained her, as the
four small toes were curled underneath the sole and the sole
forced toward the heel until her feet were almost bent in half.

The merchant Woo took a step. Erlan snatched up the
cleaver.

"*Amitabha!*" he exclaimed, flapping his arms. "I will
do nothing but rub your calves, I promise."

She huffed a soft snort. "Everyone knows that you
Cantonese lie like dogs."

He pointed his finger at her, a gesture so contemptuous she gasped aloud. "And you . . ." he sputtered. "You
are a dead ghost!"

It was the worst sort of insult, to call a person a dead
ghost. She was surprised the gods didn't strike him dead for

uttering it. "Turtle fart," she muttered under her breath, but not softly enough.

He glared at her, his brows drawn low, his cheeks sucked hollow. She glared back. He rolled his eyes, seeking consolation from the Immortals.

"Have you not heard the proverb, you stubborn, useless girl: When the cat overturns the rice bowl, the dogs will feast? I bought myself a wife so that I might have sons to sweep my tomb after I am gone. Do you not know how sons are made?"

"I know, honorable husband."

"A wife is no good to me if she cannot give me sons."

"I know, honorable husband."

"Think on it, then."

"Yes, honorable husband. I will think on it."

He crawled into bed and turned the brass screw of the lamp, plunging the room into darkness. The rough muslin sheets rustled as he settled in. She lay down as well, but a moment later she was sitting bolt upright.

"Strike a light, please, my husband," she asked, making her voice as sweet as a late summer peach.

A match scraped and the lamp flared again. He held it up. "What is it? Is your neck bleeding again? Aiya, if you die on me, I— What are you doing?"

She had scampered out of bed and gotten down on her hands and knees to look beneath it. She saw a lot of dust balls as big as chrysanthemums, but no gourd beneath where her head would lie.

"There is no gourd under the bed," she said.

He heaved a huge sigh. "This is America. There is no need for gourds."

"But what will chase away the ghosts and keep them from choking me?"

"Ha! And this from the girl who tried to take off her head with a cleaver." He patted the space beside him and actually smiled. "Come back to bed and go to sleep, child. There are no ghosts in America."

Darkness once again enshrouded the room. The log walls trembled and creaked under the wind. Her neck throbbed and her whole body ached; that demon-cursed stage driver had aimed for every stone and rut in the road. Even lying quietly she could still feel the ceaseless rocking motion of the coach, as if it had entered her blood. She drew in a deep breath and rubbed her palms over her breasts and down her sides until her fingertips came to rest low on her belly.

Two years ago, when Young Uncle married, she had helped put the bride to bed. She remembered the bridal bed with its red silk canopy and curtains, and the rose petals and baby shoes, of every color in a peacock's tail, strewn on the red satin coverlet. But she remembered most vividly of all the small square of white silk lying on the ebony tray, waiting to prove the bride's virginity.

She would leave no virgin blood on any white silk. Three men had had her, so what should one more matter? Yet it did, it did . . . She pressed her fist tight against her mouth. She could not bear to have another man do to her what those others had done.

It was the worst sort of fate for a man—to die without sons. Since she would not lie with him tonight, the merchant Woo would certainly complain to the master in the morning. She would be dragged back to the tong man, and he would put her in the cribs or sell her again, this time to a mining camp. And then many men would do to her what those others had done. The dogs would feast.

"'Tes your desire to marry Sam Woo?" the giant had said.

What would have happened if she had said no? Would the fon-kwei giant have carried her off with him? If he had, he would have expected her to lie with him, for such was the way of men. She tried to imagine lying with him and could not. A foreign devil who was fierce, even if he did have beautiful gray eyes, as soft and gentle as rainwater. He had an ugly, hairy face, and he was too big, built like a water buffalo, a peasant animal suitable only for pulling plows and turning waterwheels. He would have crushed her, smothered her, and rent her open with his man's great root.

Her mind twisted away and got caught up in memories again: a hardness piercing her, heavy weight bearing her down, down, blind darkness and a coldness deep within her, so cold, so cold. She hated this violation men forced upon women. Wives, concubines, crib girls—she wondered how a woman learned to bear it, how she endured without wanting to die. How a woman like her . . .

Her mother.

Hot tears seeped out of the corners of her eyes and dripped down into her ears. She pressed her bunched fist hard against her mouth.

In the Flowery Kingdom when a daughter was born, her father prepared several barrels of rice wine and put them in his root cellar. By the time the girl was of an age to marry, the wine was of an age to be drunk at the wedding feast.

The tea merchant Po Lung-Kwong already had three wives, five imperfect daughters, and a root cellar full of wine when he brought the beautiful young concubine Tao Huo to his bed in the hope of begetting a son.

That Tao Huo failed to produce the desperately needed heir was of course all her fault. When two years passed and no fruit took root in her womb, the patriarch's three wives expected the concubine—no matter how young and beautiful she was—to be sent away. Instead, the merchant Po visited her bed more often than ever. And she wore out his old bone, leaving it limp and useless to his other women.

In the third year, Tao Huo at last showed signs of expectant happiness. The wives gritted their teeth behind their smiles. And when Tao Huo was brought to bed of another imperfect daughter, they hid their smiles behind copious tears. Surely now the patriarch would send the worthless concubine away.

Instead, he visited her bed again as soon as she was able to receive him. There was no hope for it, the wives all agreed. The patriarch was infatuated with his young concubine. Although he was in the sunset of his life, with her he had all the strength and virility implied in his name of Lung-Kwong. Bright Dragon.

The wives, miserable in their jealousy, could not understand Tao Huo's allure. It was acknowledged, reluctantly, that her face was that of a first grade beauty. But she had such big horse feet. Worse, she had been corrupted by fon-kwei ways. She had spent the first fourteen years of her life at the Foochow mission school where she had learned the devil tongue and swallowed the foreign religion. She was nothing but a bullock-footed, clanless country girl, the wives all complained, yet she behaved as if she were a Manchurian princess. And most astonishing of all, she got away with it.

The members of the Po clan all lived together in ten courts beneath their ancestral roofs. The men lived in the outer courts, which the women were forbidden to enter. The daughters of the House of Po lived in the inner courtyards with their mothers, where they learned the arts of homemaking and prepared themselves to be perfect wives.

One of Erlan's earliest memories was of sitting on the sandalwood chest to watch while her mother made herself beautiful for the patriarch's visits. Tao Huo would powder her cheeks until they were whiter than Himalayan snow and paint her lips the shiny red of dew-kissed cherries. She would make her long ebony hair glisten like wet moss with wu-mu jelly, arranging it in the elaborate shape of a lotus blossom. Then in the midnight blackness of her hair, she would put one large and perfect peony. And the sweet smell of the red and pink flower would waft to Erlan on the breeze stirred by a slave girl's gently waving fan.

Sometimes Erlan would sit beside her mother on the great rosewood bed, Tao Huo's green robe spread out like a giant fan on the blue silk counterpane. Tao Huo would rub her nails pink with rose petals while she taught her daughter the English words they used to converse privately with in a household of three jealous wives and many spies.

Listening to her mother's pi-pa-sweet voice, staring at a face that was painted to evoke the timeless delicacy of Ming porcelain, Erlan learned more than English. She also learned the power of a woman's beauty. And the power Tao Huo wielded in the great rosewood bed.

Erlan saw her father only rarely, but each of those precious moments was engraved on her memory like the dragon on the family's jade seal.

She would wait for him in the garden, sitting by the lotus pond on a porcelain taboret, wait for him to come and air his birds, the small brown larks in their bamboo cages. Together they would sit and watch the golden carp swim in the pond, Erlan chattering like a crow and watching his beloved face in the hope of catching a smile, her father puffing on his silver water pipe and indulging her childish questions about the world beyond the garden walls.

Once she dared to ask, "Who is your favorite daughter, Father?"

He smiled and touched her cheek, tracing the curve of her chin. "You are, Erlan. See all the day lilies I have had planted in my garden. Every time I look at them I am reminded of you."

But whenever she complained about Eldest Sister making a joke of her big feet, or of First Wife ordering her to pick out her embroidery and do it over again, he would only say, "You must learn to yield, my daughter. Only by yielding can a woman achieve self-perfection."

Erlan spent many hours hiding high up in the watchtower set in the garden wall, where the guard beat out the passage of time with his wooden clapper. From there she could see the city roofs of yellow and green pottery tiles rolling and peaking like waves and, between them, the narrow hutungs crowded with peddlers and rickshaws and litters. Beyond the roofs graceful pagodas nestled against hills covered with bamboo and tea shrubs. The oolong, black, and green tea that was shipped to the fon-kwei lands had made the House of Po rich.

On days when the sun burned away the mist, she could see the river and the huge junks with their matting sails and the great round eyes painted on their bows to frighten away the river demons. She was too far away to see the fishermen with their nets and the bamboo mats of cuttlefish drying in the sun. Or the bales of tea bricks marked with the dragon seal of the House of Po piled on the wharves, awaiting shipment to foreign and exotic lands.

She was too far away to see, but she could still imagine. And as Erlan looked to the hills and the river, she dreamed of a day when she would journey beyond the garden walls and see these wonders for herself.

In the fourth moon of Erlan's seventeenth year, Tao Huo shared a secret with her daughter. Motioning her to silence with a finger to her lips, she led Erlan along a hidden passageway through the forbidden courts. They stopped before a small round window concealed by a wooden lattice screen. The window looked into a room that was set aside for the reception of visitors. Erlan sucked in her breath at the treasures it contained: silver- and gold-inlaid cabinets, porcelain in peach bloom, oxblood red, and mirror-black, screens and boxes of deeply carved lacquer, cloisonné vases, Tibetan tapestries. All of it glittered and gleamed in the light of dozens of bean-oil lamps.

The room was vacant, but a moment later a door opened and a servant ushered two fon-kwei men inside. "They are from America, the Flowery Flag land," Tao Huo whispered. "They wish to enter into an agreement with the patriarch. Six shiploads of tea a year in exchange for many taels of silver."

Startled, Erlan looked at her mother with new eyes. It occurred to her that this was not the first time Tao Huo had stood behind this screen, watching and listening to what went on in the reception room. And the patriarch must know of this, for even a favored concubine would never dare to trespass into the forbidden courts without permission. Erlan remembered a time she had come upon her father showing her mother a document written in the fon-kwei way, asking her what message it contained. Erlan understood now why her mother had taught her how to read the English tongue as well as speak it. Tao Huo's woman's power and her value to the patriarch lay not only in the great rosewood bed.

The Flowery Flag devils wandered around the room, peering at the scroll paintings, rudely picking up a Ming vase from this table, a ceramic Tang horse from that one, as if checking their authenticity.

"Christ, what I wouldn't do for some whiskey," one of the devils said. A man with a rotund belly and the vacuous-eyed face of a water buffalo. "But I reckon all we're gonna get is more of that damned tea."

"Tea is what we're here for, after all," the other answered. He was a young man with a cap of short curls brighter than hammered gold and a smile as blinding as sun-struck snow. "Just humor the old devil. Remember, to these people, face is everything."

Filled with excitement that she had understood nearly every word the barbarians uttered, Erlan turned to her mother. But her thoughts withered unspoken on her tongue. Tao Huo was staring avidly at the young golden-haired devil, and the look on her face . . . the look on her face was the one she wore when she picked over a box of crystallized fruit, trying to decide which sweet morsel she would bring next to her red lips.

It was two weeks later that the household guards locked Tao Huo in her rooms. The concubine screamed and pleaded for the patriarch, but he never came. The guards placed screens in front of her door and no one was allowed to pass.

Throughout a night and a day and another night Erlan sat in the garden on the porcelain taboret. She watched the golden carp swim in the pond and took slow careful breaths that were filled with the cloying odor of peonies. And she listened as her mother's screams grew weaker and weaker until they faded into the songs of the larks in the cypress trees, the tolling of pagoda bells, and the peddlers' cries outside the walls.

An hour after dawn on the second day, the patriarch's first wife came toward her down the pebbled path. The enormous kingfisher feathers in Po Tai Tai's hair stirred in the gentle breeze, and she looked sly and pleased with herself.

Erlan was beyond all pride and dignity. She kowtowed deeply to the older woman, and her voice broke with her pleading words. "What has she done? Oh, please, tell me. What has she done?"

"That shuey-kee!" Tai Tai spat, swelling like a toad in her satisfaction, and Erlan stumbled to her feet in shock and anger. A shuey-kee was a waterfowl, but it was also a word for the worst sort of prostitute, one who specialized in pleasing foreign barbarians. "That shuey-kee has betrayed the House of Po by lying with a white demon."

This crime was so terrible that Erlan could not imagine it, could not believe it. And yet she thought of her mother's face staring hungrily through the lattice screen at the Flowery Flag demon with the golden hair.

On the heels of this thought came another that made her gasp aloud. "What . . . what will he do to her?"

"It has been done. She was sent the scarlet noose."

The scarlet noose, with which she must hang herself and so avoid the disgrace of execution. It would have been done by now. Erlan's mother would have tied one end of the red silk cord to the canopy frame of the great rosewood bed, the other end she would have wrapped around her slender neck. Then she would have stood on the sandalwood chest and stepped into the air and beyond, into the shadow world.

There was a loud, strange humming in Erlan's head,

like the singing of a thousand cicadas. And she kept getting sharp pains in her chest, because she forgot to breathe.

The funeral. What was being done about the funeral? The wives, who had always been jealous of Tao Huo, would do nothing to see that she was given a proper burial. It was up to Erlan, then, and there were many things to think of. She must put on a white mourning gown and slippers of white hemp. Blue and white streamers must be hung about the courtyard, and biscuits burned to make Tao Huo's journey to the shadow world easier.

"And as for you, you worthless little turtle's egg," Tai Tai said, "you are being sent away."

Erlan barely heard her. There was so much . . . so much to think of, and it was so hard to think with this terrible humming in her head. "But who will see that she is given a white coffin?" she said aloud.

Tai Tai's painted mouth twisted into a cruel smile. "The shuey-kee has been given a coffin. She did not make use of the scarlet noose, and so she was nailed into her coffin alive."

Erlan stuffed a hand into her mouth as the humming in her head exploded into a silent scream. Great sobs tore at her throat, threatening to break out, but she would not weep in front of her mother's enemy.

She straightened her back and lifted her head, drawing herself up tall. "Leave me," she said.

Tai Tai huffed, but she said nothing more. She turned and went down the path, her golden lilies leaving tiny doe-like tracks in the pebbles.

Erlan waited until First Wife had disappeared into the women's pavilion, and then she went in search of her father.

She waited for him in the shadows of the marble screen in the hall of the ancestors. She wasn't sure what she would do, what she would say. Her only thought was to beg forgiveness. And to promise she would do whatever was necessary to redeem her mother's honor, if only he wouldn't send her away.

Candles flickered on the red gilt altar, their flames reflecting a thousand times in the thick gold embroidery on the altar cloth. Soft-colored lanterns swung in the warm summer air, whispering, *"Shuey-kee . . . shuey-kee . . ."* The smell of incense was so thick she nearly choked on it.

At last he came. He looked as forbidding as an emperor in his long dragon robe, but his face was that of her father and she loved him so. She waited a little longer, until he was done kowtowing before the ancestral tablets. Then she ran out into the middle of the hall and threw herself at his feet, pressing her forehead into the hard stone floor. When he did nothing, said nothing, she dared to raise her head . . . and she quailed at the rage that twisted his face.

"You dare!" he snarled and struck out at Erlan with his foot, sending her sprawling onto her back. "You dare to approach me, you whore-cunt's spawn." He raised a clenched fist to the heavens. "I will curse you from the land of the spirits for all eternity!" And then he was gone, leaving her alone in the hall with only the ancestors to witness her shame.

The next day she was taken in a litter to the home of the Foochow slave trader.

Far now beyond the garden walls of her lao chia, much farther than she had ever wanted to go, Erlan lay beside her sleeping husband. Beyond the creaking log walls, an animal howled in loneliness. And the smell of peonies filled the room.

"Mother," Erlan whispered to the spirit hovering between darkness and light. "Why did you do such a shameful thing?" And she didn't know which shameful thing she meant: that Tao Huo had been shuey-kee and lain with a barbarian or that she had lacked the courage to use the scarlet noose and thus redeem some of her lost honor.

"Mother," Erlan whispered again. But the spirit didn't answer, and the scent of peonies faded.

The tears had long ago dried on Erlan's cheeks. She had wept for the fourth and last time.

He came high and hard and long in her.

Hannah collapsed against him, skin wet and slippery, chests heaving and sucking and sighing. She murmured his name against his mouth when at last he allowed her to breathe.

One of his hands cupped her bottom, and he began to knead it gently. She was on top, straddling him. She tightened the inner muscles of her thighs, squeezing him, prolonging the moment. It always made her sad, the ending. Sad and lonely.

It never lasted beyond that one sweet moment, that was the trouble . . . her trouble. Men—all they ever wanted was to have their hunger satisfied. A woman, though, she hungered to be wanted, and so she was never satisfied. Because what a man wanted and what a woman hungered for were never the same thing.

She let him pull her mouth over to his for an unhurried, easy kiss, strongly flavored with whiskey. Yet when he released her lips, they felt naked. And she felt alone and needy still. She wanted to be wanted; she wanted him to want *her*. She wanted to hear him say the words that made this so, the tender words.

She sat up, still straddling his hips, still holding deep inside her the only piece of him she would ever have. A faint light came from the moon shining through the window. It limned the planes of his chest and the ridges of his stomach with silver, and made his eyes shine like a pair of gold coins dropped in a well. She rubbed her hands over him, reveling in the feel of him. Hot and hard. She stared at his face. He was so beautiful. So beautiful and so cruel.

"What?" he said.

She traced the shape of his lips. "I was thinking how good you look lying in my bed."

Rafferty showed his teeth in a strange smile. "Yeah. What I want to know is who else's been lyin' in it while I've been gone."

She tried to hit him, but he grabbed her wrist. He glared up into her face, then brought her fist to his lips. "I'm sorry," he said. "I shouldn't have said that."

She pulled free of him. "No, you shouldn't have."

The mattress gave and the sheets whispered as she got up, releasing the musky smells of man and sex into the air.

She pulled on her silk wrapper and lit a lamp. She went to the window, but she could see nothing beyond the reflection of her own face in the night-blackened glass. The curtains moved as if a hand had stirred them.

That boy who had come up to her in the Best in the West tonight, bold as brass and wanting to buy her a drink . . . there was something about him that kept tugging at her thoughts. Maybe it was because he was a miner like her daddy had been. Like his own daddy had been before he, too, had been killed in a fall. They both had come from the same place, she and that boy. Maybe that was why when he'd looked at her, she'd thought for just a moment that he was seeing not the Hannah Yorke she was now, but the young girl she used to be. That girl who had been so full of big dreams and sweet hope.

Drew Scully . . . She said his name to herself, feeling almost guilty for doing it. He had the hardest, coldest eyes she'd ever seen.

Behind her Rafferty lay quiet, too quiet. "I thought we agreed a long time ago not to go putting brands on each other," she said to her blurred white reflection in the glass panes.

"I been comin' to this house for four years, Hannah. To this bed. In all that time I ain't ever fucked another woman."

She forced a laugh, turning from the window. "Lord, we're near to being married, you and I."

He said nothing, just lay on her bed, long and lean

and naked. The brooding slant of his hard mouth, his wild, golden eyes—when he looked like that she wanted at the same time both to hurt and to heal him, but it was beyond her to do either.

She turned away from him and went to her dressing table.

He heaved a sigh, a man's sort of sigh that said I-will-never-understand-women. "Are we having a fight, Hannah?"

"No. Pour me some whiskey, will you?"

She started to reach for her hairbrush, but her gaze was caught by the bell jar. She ran her palm over the smooth glass. Even in the soft light of the oil lamp, the wax flowers from her wedding cake looked old and yellow, a bitter legacy of the first time she had loved this deeply, and this badly. There had been other loves between her first man and Rafferty, and she supposed there would be more. But she was thirty-three years old this time around, and the emptiness in her womb was becoming a hole in her soul. She wanted another baby, someone to love who would never leave her. Oh, Lord, why not just admit it to herself: she wanted a man who would last. A gold-ring kind of lasting.

She cast a glance at Rafferty over her shoulder, her heart tightening. *Oh, Hannah, you have always been the biggest fool. Since when did just loving him one night at a time stop being enough?*

But the nights with him were getting fewer and farther between. At first he'd only leave the valley for weeks at a time. Now it was months. He'd take a job riding shotgun for Wells Fargo or hunting bounty, claiming they needed the cash to keep the ranch going. Or there'd be a herd of cattle he had to drive somewhere, and horses to pick up somewhere else. Probably it was in his nature to roam, but he'd never once told her the truth about why he left. And she wasn't what brought him back.

Even though he'd been gone for over six months this

time, she had believed him when he said he hadn't been with another woman. Why, he'd had her twice before they even made it to the bed, he'd been that hungry for her. The trouble was, she knew him so well. In many ways they were closer as friends than as lovers, and she understood that somewhere along the way he had gotten it into his man's head that by being faithful to her, he was being faithful to the one woman he did love and could never have.

The one woman he did love . . .

She shook her head, angry with herself, angry with him. Sad for him. Lord, how could she be jealous of his love for Clementine, when she loved that girl so much herself?

She wasn't sure when she'd first suspected it, maybe all the way back to that first summer. It was nothing they did, nothing they said, but she could feel it in the air around them whenever they were together. A thickening, a freshening, a wild wind-and-lightning storm raging just past yonder ridge, too far away to see but powerful enough to feel. They *yearned for* each other, there was no other word for it. It was as if they weren't two separate hearts and souls, but one heart, one soul, that had somehow been ripped apart and forced to spend eternity searching for their missing halves, and now they had found themselves in each other.

And she and Gus . . . they were the other loves, the also loves, the would have, could have, should have loves.

Her fingers tightened on the handle of her brush. Well, hell and damn, wasn't she the one who had said it so long and so often? She wasn't the marrying kind. Oh, no, not Hannah Yorke. Good ol' Hannah, how she does like her fun and freedom. She can look after herself just fine, can good ol' Hannah, and no man is ever gonna tie her down, uh-uh. Except that good ol' Hannah hadn't turned out to be so good at holding herself close during the bad and lonely times. And good ol' Hannah wasn't ever going to make up a family and a happily-ever-after all by her lonesome.

Deliberately she lifted her head and looked at good ol' Hannah in the fluted gold mirror. The lampshine was being especially kind tonight, but the wrinkles would come someday; no amount of strawberry cream was going to keep them away forever. The mirror showed Rafferty as well, a glass of whiskey balanced on his belly, cigarette smoke obscuring his face. Still long and lean and beautiful, after four years, lying naked on her bed.

Four years . . . She should end it now, leave him before he left her, and yet she just couldn't bring herself to do it. It was like Christmas Eve when she was a child. She'd always had all those dreams in her head of what she wanted— dolls and picture books and a pretty pink dress with lace ruffles—knowing full well her mother had barely scraped together enough pennies to stuff her stocking with some rock candy and an apple to fill up the toe. But still she'd had her dreams. And so she had stayed up throughout the night, wishing morning would never come, trying to draw out the moment and hold on to the hope of it.

Rafferty's gaze met hers in the glass. "Come here," he said.

She put on a seductive smile, a smile learned and practiced in a crib in the badlands of Deadwood, and went to him, discarding her wrapper along the way.

He took her hand and pulled her down beside him on the bed. "Hannah—"

"No," she whispered, laying her fingers against his lips. "Don't say anything. Just love me. Make love to me."

19

THE BEAR GRASS WAS in bloom the morning he came home.

She saw him from her kitchen window. A man riding long-stirruped and easy on a big gray. Before him spread the plain, frosted lilac with the flowering grass; beyond him stretched the sky. She walked out the door and onto the porch. She touched the cameo at her throat, feeling the wild throb of her pulse beating in time with his horse's hooves as he rode toward her.

As he reined up at the sagging snake fence, her gaze fastened onto his face that was so much like the first time she'd seen him, all harsh planes and sharp angles, the black Stetson shadowing his eyes. Something shifted and tore loose inside her, a letting go of the pain of missing him.

And then he was on the ground and coming toward her and she was going toward him, not running, but walking fast and smiling, smiling wide and laughing, really laughing, and if she hadn't loved him so much she would have thrown herself into his arms.

If she hadn't loved him so much.

"Howdy, Boston," he said, stopping first.

She said nothing, only smiled.

And so they stood like that, arms hanging empty at their sides, staring at each other across the space that separated them. A space that was the width of Gus McQueen's shadow.

She turned away from him, seeking an anchor in the familiar. The cottonwoods and larches, the ax-marked chopping block, the windrows of freshly mown hay curving like giant yellow commas down to the buffalo hunter's cabin. The wind came up, thickly sweet with the smell of the hay. It caught at her hair and snagged her skirts, whipping them around her legs. She raised one hand to her head to hold the flying strands of hair in place. The other she cupped beneath the swell of her pregnant belly.

Her gaze came back to his face in time to catch the flash of raw pain in his eyes before he shuttered them.

Moses thrust his head between them and butted her breasts. "Hey, now," Rafferty said, trying to smile but his mouth stayed tight. "That's no way to treat a lady."

Unable to touch the man, Clementine stroked the velvet gray neck of the horse. "Why don't you rub him down and come on into the kitchen? I'll put some coffee on the stove . . ." The words trailed off, caught in her throat as she stared up at his face.

"Oh, it's so *good* to have you home," she said, and for once she allowed the yearning in her heart to show in her eyes. "Please don't leave us again." *Don't leave me again.*

"I'll stay." The wind snatched at a lock of her hair, plastering it to her mouth. He plucked it free, his fingers just brushing her lips. Her eyes drifted closed as she reveled in his touch, which was stolen and wrong and dangerous.

His fingers drifted down her jaw to the throbbing pulse in her throat. "I'll stay," he said again, "as long as I can bear to."

Clementine added a fresh stick of wood to the fire, punching with it at the coals. She heard the rasp of spurs on the porch, and her heart stopped, then started up again, drumming hard behind her breastbone.

She dropped the lid back on the stove with a loud clatter. She looked up, her face flushed by the heat of the fire, her eyes dazzled by the sunlight pouring through the open door. He leaned against the jamb, his weight slung on one hip, a thumb hanging off his gun belt, and his hat dangling from his fingers. It always surprised her, and frightened her some to see him again after a time apart. No matter how tame the country became around him, no matter how much of the wilderness was whittled away, he still seemed wild and lawless.

He straightened, tossed his hat on a wall spike, and headed for the washbasin, with no words, only the breath of the air he stirred as he passed her.

She pumped water into a blue-speckled coffee pot, casting quick glances over her shoulder. As he bent over the basin, his soft, faded blue shirt pulled taut across his back. The swell and play of muscle, the breadth of shoulder, the dark hair that grew thick and curling over his collar. The way he was . . .

A trembling started deep inside her. She tried to still it by crossing her arms and gripping her elbows.

He dried his face, slicked back his hair with his hands, and swung around. Their eyes met and parted in the same breath.

He plucked an apple—they came fresh now on the train from Washington—out of the milk-glass bowl that sat in the middle of her table. He bit into the red fruit with a snap. Juice dribbled out the corner of his mouth and he licked it off. Clementine watched and thought how it would be to press her lips there, where his tongue had just been.

She jerked around and picked up the coffee pot, almost dropping it, knocking it with a loud clang against the pump handle.

She scooped a handful of ground beans out of the box mill and put the coffee on the stove. He prowled her kitchen, crunching on the apple. The sound was too loud in the quiet room, the smell of it too pungently sweet. He looked at the photographs displayed on shelves along the far wall. Gus had built the shelves to store tinned food and

jars of preserves. She had put her latest photographs there
not to irritate her husband or to defy him, but to make a
statement: this is who I am.

Rafferty studied the photographs, a frown tugging at
his mouth. Like Gus, he resented this other love of hers,
but not for the same reason. He was possessively jealous of
what she photographed, jealous of the wild and raw land
that he thought of as his. He didn't want to share it with
others. Those others who came with saws to cut down the
larches and the pines, with repeater rifles to pick off the
last of the bighorn and the buffalo, with giant powder to
pockmark the rugged buttes with mine shafts and defile
them with black heaps of slag.

"You caught an eagle in flight," he said, and she
warmed to the awe she heard in his voice.

She came up next to him, closer than she should have.

"I took it from the cliff that overlooks the buffalo canyon." In the photograph the cliff cast deep shadows on the
light, wind-flattened grass. Yet the sunshine limned each
feather on the eagle's magnificent wingspan. A bird silhouetted in lonely splendor against the emptiness of the sky.
"They've built a nest near there," she said. She could feel
the man beside her as if he were giving off a heat.

"I know, Boston." He turned his head, spearing her
heart with his gaze.

They both fell silent as their memories joined hands.
In the four years she had known him, she could count on
her fingers the times she had been truly alone with him.
Yet the most piercing memory to her was that day at the
buffalo canyon when she had seen Montana through his
eyes and understood a little why he loved it so fiercely.

She babbled now, making noise, piling up words like
stones, building a levee against the tide of emotion that
surged between them. "There's a marvelous new photographic invention that makes it possible to capture images in motion. It's a gelatin emulsion so sensitive to light

that it takes only an instant to expose the plate. And one doesn't need to develop the plates right away; so it saves having to lug that blasted dark tent everywhere . . ."

Her voice trailed off. The tension thickened between them, hot and heavy as a chinook wind. "L-look," she said, pointing blindly at another photograph. "Here's one of, uh . . . a calf, just born." The calf stood on wobbling legs, his mouth open in a bawl. "And one of Gus busting a bronc for the spring roundup."

He laughed. "You gotta be quick to have caught my brother still in the saddle."

As he reached for the photograph, his arm brushed the side of her breast. He went utterly still, except for his breath, which she felt on her neck, warm and caressing. She could not remember how she had come to be standing so close to him. Her breast burned where he had touched her.

A cloud smothered the sun, and the kitchen darkened. The coffee began to burp on the stove. The wind gusted through the cottonwoods, making them moan.

His arm fell and he took a step back. He was breathing fast, his chest rising and falling. Unconsciously she pressed her fingers to the side of her breast where he had touched her. His gaze followed the movement of her hand, then came up to meet hers. She stared into eyes that were wild and dangerous. The percolating coffee and the gusting wind faded until all she could hear was the sough of their breath rushing through the kitchen like a summer storm.

A great whoop split the air like the clang of a fire bell.

"Gus," Clementine said. "He . . . he must have just seen your horse in the corral."

She jerked around and went to the window. Early that morning Gus had gone to the south hay meadow with the sorrel team and the mower. Now he was back, leading one limping horse and riding the other, with no mower. He rode bareback with their son, Charlie, perched before him on the horse's withers.

Clementine felt the rush of relief she got whenever

Gus took her son away from her and returned him unharmed. She knew Gus was careful with the boy, but she never quite trusted him to watch Charlie as closely as she would. So much danger lurked in the Montana wilderness: rabid wolves and rattlesnakes and black bears and coyotes. He could so easily become lost in the tall grass or fall into the river. The Grahams' youngest child had died last spring in just that way. The river was her greatest fear.

Gus set Charlie on the ground and he hopped around on his sturdy three-and-a-half-year-old legs, chattering loudly. Clementine's breath caught as the sorrel mare shifted her weight and barely missed planting her hoof on Charlie's foot. These dangers were a constant thing, yet he was her baby no longer, and as Gus was always telling her, she couldn't coddle and protect him forever. Already she was losing him. To Montana, the land he was growing up to love as naturally as he breathed the wind-tossed air and ran through the tall grass and laughed beneath the big sky.

And she was losing him to his father, into that male world where cayuses were broken and rustlers hanged and calves branded. That masculine dimension that was so much a part of this place and that was still such an enigma to her, even after four years of dwelling uneasily within it.

She would lose him someday to that world, was losing him already. Yet she thought of the eagles that roamed the sky above the buffalo canyon. Her son would not grow up yearning to fly, yet afraid to try.

"He's growing up fast on us, Boston."

Rafferty's words, an echo of her own thoughts, pulled her gaze away from the window. He leaned in the open doorway again, his hat shadowing his face. But it couldn't hide the taut set to his mouth or the pulse that throbbed in his neck above the knot of his bandanna.

And she had heard the pain in his voice. He didn't leave only her; he left the land he loved and a brother he loved, and a little boy who meant as much to him as any son of his own loins.

Unable to bear it, she turned back to the window. Gus was leading the sorrel team down to the barn. Charlie pointed toward the house and said something that made Gus's head fall back in laughter. He bent over and swung his son up into the air. The sunlight glinted off two heads of caramel-colored hair.

Something broke inside of Clementine in a terrible gush of guilt and pain. She wondered what kind of woman it was who loved her husband most when she was betraying him in her heart.

Gus always touched her so sweetly. His whispers to her in the night were of love and were lovely to hear; they soothed her heart. In his arms it was easy to let the strength of his feelings carry her along. To convince herself that it was enough. He needed her, and she wanted to be needed, needed to be needed. In return she gave him all she could. Her body, willingly and with joy, and her love. But there were degrees, so many degrees, of love. He would never make her burn.

She pushed words out of her throat, not even sure what she was saying. "That Charlie. He's gotten to where he can't sit still a minute. I've taken to tying a sheep bell around his waist when I'm at my chores, to keep him from wandering off when my back is turned. And he's talking lots more since you last saw him. Wears your ears out, he does, with all his questions. Do you know how a fish's gills work? And why the larches lose their needles in the fall and the pines don't . . . ?" Her voice trailed off. There was only silence behind her.

She turned quickly and slammed into his chest. He steadied her with both hands on her shoulders. A stillness came into the room, a sense of breathless waiting and yearning. His eyes focused on her face and she held his stare, not daring to breathe, as the pressure in her chest built and built and built until it became unbearable.

His hands clenched hard, once, and he thrust her away from him. He looked sered by a fever, the skin pulled too tight over the bones of his face. His shirt fluttered with his heavy breathing. A crushing pain now filled the silence.

"You see why I got to go," he said, his voice raw. "Why I should've stayed gone for good this time."

"No!" She lifted her hand and he recoiled violently.

She let her hand fall. She snatched a half breath, feeling as if her lungs would burst. "Don't do this, Rafferty, please. It hurts me so much when you do this."

"Yeah, well I'm glad it hurts you, Clementine."

He took a step, not away from her but toward her, and her breath stopped again. His hand stole up to grip her chin. He brought his face so close to hers the moist heat of his harsh breath was like steam on her mouth. Her lips felt thick and hot, as if he had already kissed them.

His fingers tightened, hurting her. He brought his mouth closer still, almost touching hers. That close, but no closer. "Because loving you is killing me," he said.

And then he was gone and she was left standing in the middle of her kitchen floor, feeling shattered.

She heard the low rumble of the brothers' voices, Gus's laugh, and Charlie's piercing shrieks. "Raff'ty! Raff'ty! I was gonna help Papa mow the hay. But that stupid Daisy stepped in a gopher hole and hurt her foot. Papa's been teaching me how to rope, but he says you do it better. Will you show me now, Raff'ty? Now, now, now! Show me now!"

Her gaze focused on the kitchen table where a half-eaten apple lay, turning brown in the summer heat. She pressed her lips together hard to stop their trembling.

The hens ran squawking across the yard, their wings cocked, heads bobbing. Rafferty placed his hand beneath Charlie's upraised arm, adding his man's strength to the boy's, teaching him the rhythm of the swinging rope. The miniature lasso twirled above the bright gold head.

A fat bantam hen broke away from the flock, and Rafferty guided the boy's aim. "Okay, now let her fly."

The rope floated through the air and landed in the dirt with a splat and a puff of dust. The hen flapped madly, and the air rained red feathers.

"Oh, shit," Rafferty muttered under his breath. The damn bird was molting in her fright. She'd probably never lay another egg as long as she lived.

"I missed." Charlie's lower lip pouched out in a pout. "I always miss."

"It only takes practice, is all. Come on, reel in the rope. Let me see you build a loop and then we'll try again."

The boy watched the man gather up the short reata. He kept his eyes on the man's every move, mimicking his saunter and the way he cocked his hip, the way he tugged at his hat brim and squinted into the sun, the way he simply *was,* for he was pure cowboy.

Rafferty heard the crunch of footsteps behind him and he turned. Clementine came toward them from the house, walking with such purpose her heels kicked up her skirt. The sun gilded her hair, and she was as slim and graceful as the willows that shaded the river. The sight of her hurt so much he flinched.

"Just what do you two think you are doing?" she called out, an odd tightness in her voice.

"Watch me, Mama!"

Charlie let fly with the reata on his own and by some incredible chance the lasso snagged the fat, and now partly bald, bantam hen as she raced across the yard. Her neck snapped with a loud crack.

The other hens stopped their squawking and flapping all at once, as if shock had frozen their wings and wattles. Rafferty and the boy stared at the bird lying suddenly dead in the dirt among corn feed and red feathers.

"Oh, shit!" Charlie said, his voice piping loud in the silence.

Clementine's gaze flew up to Rafferty. The tightness he'd heard in her voice was reflected in her eyes, which were wide and dark, like a mountain lake beneath a stormy sky.

He grinned at her and shrugged. "I forgot how little pitchers got big ears."

"You forgot . . ." She planted her hands on her hips and stuck her nose in the air. She breathed out a thick sigh, puffing her lips, and Rafferty's gaze settled hard on her mouth. "You're back home less than an hour and already you have turned my son into a cocky, strutting, foul-mouthed . . . *cowboy*."

"You ain't gonna raise him up to be no tight-assed Boston gentleman out here, Clementine."

"Nor will I raise him up to be a barbarian, Mr. Rafferty."

His eyes narrowed at her. He really didn't like her much when she put on Boston airs, but that hadn't yet stopped him from loving her, wanting her.

Charlie tugged at his pant leg. "Mama's angry."

Rafferty's hand rested on the boy's head. His hair was down-soft, a darker shade of yellow than hers. "Not angry with you, button. With me."

"Were you a naughty boy?"

"Yeah, I was naughty." His lips curled into a smile that held just a tinge of meanness. He spoke to the boy, but his eyes were on her face. "But I'll let you in on a little secret: she likes me that way."

They stared at each other, he and Clementine, and he was reminded of the way a prairie fire could start up in the heat of summer—one spark and the world turned into a raging conflagration. When the hunger was like this between them, at the flash point, they could strike sparks off each other with just a look.

"Hey, little brother!" Gus shouted. He came toward them from the direction of the barn, where he'd gone to put up the sorrel team. A bright smile creased his face.

Clementine flushed and made a sudden jerking movement like a hooked trout. She snatched up the dead hen. She spoke softly, to Rafferty alone, and her voice sounded clogged with suppressed tears. "He's going to seduce my son away from me, isn't he? Damn Montana. He won't let me have even the smallest part of you, and now he's going to take my son as well."

"Who? Gus? What the hell are you talking about?" Rafferty said, but her heels were kicking up her skirts again as she took long strides back to the house.

Gus watched her go, wagging his head as if at a joke. "You two going at it again already? You're like two cats in a sack. Aren't you ever going to see your way toward getting along?"

Rafferty turned his face away from his brother. He saw where Clementine had tried to plant a vegetable garden on this side of the snake fence—carrots and some beans and squash. But most of it had been beaten to pieces by the wind, and what was left was wilting in the burning sun. Grasshoppers rasped in the encroaching weeds. Only featherlike wisps of clouds drifted overhead, offering no relief in the thin blue air.

He thought sometimes that Gus was so stupid blind he couldn't track a fat sow through a snowdrift. He wanted to grab his brother by the scruff of his neck and shout into his face: *You big, dumb son of a bitch. I want to fuck your wife. I eat, breathe, sleep, and fuck thoughts of fucking your wife, and if you weren't such a big, dumb son of a bitch you'd see it.*

He squeezed his eyes shut. Christ, he hated himself for even thinking like that. It dirtied what he felt for her. He loved her with an emotion that was to him akin to worship. He wanted to make love to her, not fuck her. There was a difference even in his own saloon-and-spittoon-dirty mind.

A small, grimy hand took hold of his. "Raff'ty, are we gonna throw the rope some more?"

He looked down into a pale, delicate-boned face with wide-spaced, slightly protruding eyes the shadowy green of a pine in winter. Her face, her eyes. The boy was all Clementine's.

Rafferty continued to avoid looking at his brother as he collected the reata and pointed Clementine's son toward the house. "Practice swinging it at the hitching post," he said, his voice a hoarse rasp. "You don't want to go killing any more of your mama's chickens."

Rafferty walked off then with no particular destination in mind, but Gus followed after him so that they wound up standing side by side with their forearms planted on the top rail of the snake fence and looking out over their land. Red-and-white cattle dotted the buff hills, the prints of the branding iron still showing fresh on the young hides of the calves. His brother smelled of hard-work sweat and sickle oil. It blended with the other scents of June, of sweet clover and mown hay.

"You're home just in time to help mow, buck, stack, and fence that hay," Gus said into the taut silence.

Rafferty made a face, and his brother laughed, too loud. Home . . . He was seized by the sick restlessness he'd felt so often as a boy. He remembered how he had felt it most sharply when he walked down country lanes and the sun-baked streets of southern towns, peering in the windows of the farmhouses and shanties that weren't his. They'd been mostly poor houses, poor families, but not in his memories. In his memories velvet-draped windows framed a father sitting in a wing chair before a fire, a pipe clenched between his teeth, the evening newspaper rustling in his hands, and a boy sitting cross-legged at the father's feet, chewing on the end of a pen as he puzzled over his lessons. In his memories a woman came into the room and trailed a loving hand across the man's shoulders and bent over to ruffle the boy's hair, and Zach would think that he had never been touched like that. And then the yearning to possess everything in that room, from the lush fern on its stand to the feel of a mother's hand in his hair, would become so powerful he could taste it, and it was bittersweet, like a lemon dusted with sugar.

Rafferty pulled himself back to the moment with a wrench that was physical. He turned his back on the cattle-grazed hills and on memories that were not even real memories, only memories of dreams. He leaned against the fence and looked at another house that wasn't his. The sun struck the tin roof, blinding him, and he blinked.

Clementine's son swung the rope at the hitching post and missed. There would come a day though, Rafferty thought, when the boy would never miss, and he felt the restlessness deepen into pain because he knew he would likely never see it.

And as if to pile on the agony, she came back outside. She'd put on an apron and filled the pockets with cornmeal, and now she was tossing it to the flock of laying hens he and her boy had tried their damnedest to scare to death a moment ago. The wind unfurled strands of her loosely upswept hair and pressed her skirts to her legs. The love he felt for her burned so hot and fast that his eyes blurred. She was beautiful. Beautiful in that fragile way that made a man wonder if such a thing was meant to last. If such a thing was ever meant to be.

Home. Everything he wanted was right here, and all of it belonged to his brother.

Beside him Gus pushed off the fence rail, gripping it hard with his big hands. Rafferty could feel his brother's eyes on him. He didn't have to look to know they were filled with a pained bewilderment. Gus sensed that things were wrong between them, but he was unable to understand what they were. And Rafferty vowed for the thousandth time to do all in his power to ensure that Gus would never understand.

She went back inside the house, taking the boy with her. Rafferty tried to clear the gritty feeling out of his throat and sought words to bridge the distance between him and his brother. "The snowpack was gone already from the mountains when I passed through," he said.

"And the hay is thin," Gus said, seizing the topic eagerly. "Could be there's a drought in the making."

"It's already been hot enough this summer to put hell out of business," Rafferty said.

"And only to get worse, I reckon."

"Speakin' of worse, I heard a rumor in Rainbow Springs that the old man is back in town."

"Well, hell." Gus frowned so hard his mustache quivered, and Rafferty smiled to himself. Jack McQueen had finally worn out his welcome in the RainDance country about two years ago, and they hadn't seen hide nor hair nor patch of him since. Until now. Their father did have a way of rubbing and pinching at Gus like a too-small boot, and it gave Rafferty a mean satisfaction to know his brother was going to have that aggravation back in his life.

Charlie banged back out the kitchen door just then, carrying a bucket of slops to the pigsty, a new addition to the ranch since Rafferty had left. The boy had to stand on tiptoe to empty the bucket of swill down the chute into the feeding trough. The pigs squealed, and Charlie laughed.

"I bought us a couple weaners while you were gone," Gus said.

Rafferty cocked a smile in his brother's direction. "Yeah, so I can hear."

He waited for her to come back outside and ached when she didn't. The hunger was constant within him, to be with her and look at her and talk to her, whether half a hay meadow separated them or a thousand miles. Yet it was torture to be with her and not touch her, and so when he could bear it no longer, he took himself away.

And when he could no longer bear being alone, he brought himself back.

The fence rail was rough against Rafferty's back, the wind warm on his face. The grass beneath his boots was springy soft, and it was his. At least his name was on the deed.

He cast a sideways look at his brother's profile. Not for the first time he wondered at the capriciousness of a fate that had brought him and his brother back together seven years ago. "You ever ponder the strangeness of it, Gus," he said aloud, "that you and I would come to cross paths in a country this big and empty?"

Gus's face broke into his sun-bright smile. "Not so strange, little brother. When I decided to go looking for you, a cattle drive was the first place I thought of. You had the cow fever powerfully bad the summer that . . . the summer Ma and I left. You used to talk all the time about running away and joining up with some outfit."

Did he? Trust Gus to latch onto a bit of idle wishing and build it into the sort of pie-in-the-sky dreams Gus had always befuddled his own mind with. No, the only dream the boy Zach McQueen had ever had he'd kept hidden deep inside himself, safe where it wouldn't get broken. Home. God, he wondered what his brother would say if he knew that all he had ever really wanted, all he'd ever dreamed about, was having a home.

"What happened to that dream, Zach?"

Rafferty started and the blood rushed to his face. Then he realized Gus's thoughts were still back on the cattle drive, and he huffed a shaky laugh. "Nothin'. I lived it. And it didn't take me long to figure out that punchin' cows ain't exactly the easiest way to make a living."

"And what about the ranch?"

He pretended to misunderstand. "You appear to be getting along just fine here without me, so I thought I'd chase up some mustangs and run them on over to the Dakotas between now and the fall roundup. I hear the army over there is buying and paying prime."

"Aw, Zach. You've only just got back." Gus paused to chew on the end of his mustache, and Rafferty thought he was probably trying to figure out a way to nudge the conversation in the direction he wanted it to go. "The dollars you bring in are welcome, but I reckon it's more a thirst for excitement and the chance to pass a good time that keeps pulling you away from us." He took off his hat and thrust his fingers through his hair. "Lord, don't you think it's about time you quit gallivanting around and grew up and settled down?"

Rafferty nearly laughed out loud. Gus thought he actually *liked* riding shotgun up on the box of a bone-jarring stagecoach, putting up with runaway teams and half-drunk drivers, getting his nose and mouth clogged with dust in the summer and freezing his ass off in the winter, catching sleep on a dirt floor, and wolfing down indigestible food.

Gus telling him to grow up and settle down.

Gus all the time thinking that his little brother was so damn tough.

Gus's hand fell on his shoulder, but he removed it when Rafferty stiffened. "Clem and I, we need you. We . . . need you here, with us, is all."

Rafferty looked at his brother's face, at the sky-blue eyes that were their father's, and the tawny hair that was their mother's, and the smile that was uniquely his. *What did you have to go and marry her for, brother? We were getting along fine just the two of us.* Except they hadn't been getting along well at all. They were too different. It was as if they looked at life through opposite ends of a telescope. Like most of Gus's dreams, the idea of the ranch and the two of them making up a family was too grandiose and beautiful to be real.

The old disquiet filled him again, gripping his chest like an actual pain. The yearning was keen within him to get on his horse and ride out of here, ride away from this ranch that wasn't really his and never would be. It would hurt to give up the dream, but he was tough enough to stand it. He was supposed to be tough enough to stand anything.

But he wasn't so tough that he could leave her. At least not yet.

Gus pushed out a sigh to fill the silence. "Well, at least stick around until after the Fourth of July. The town's fixing to put on some big doings this year."

Charlie banged out through the kitchen door again,

the zinc bucket clasped to his chest. It was his sixth trip to the trough with the bucket. Whatever Clementine was fixing for supper, it was generating a lot of slops.

One of the pigs rammed hard against the logs of its box and squealed loudly. Charlie dropped the bucket and ran shrieking to Gus. "Papa, that pig got angry!"

The pigs were making a lot of noise, too much noise. Gus swung the boy up on his shoulders, and they ambled over for a look at the sty.

The pigs, a sow and a boar, were pink with black spots, bristly backbones, rotund bellies, and big lop ears. The boar stood in the middle of the pen with his feet splayed and his eyeballs rolling in his head like balls in a roulette wheel, and squealing so loud his snout flapped. The sow was trying to stand up. She would get on her two front feet and try to hoist herself up on the back two, whereupon the front two would slide wide apart like a kid learning how to ice skate, and she'd collapse snout-first into the straw.

Gus gripped his son's squirming body to anchor him on his shoulders as he leaned over the fence. "They look . . ."

"Drunk," Rafferty said, and laughter welled up and out of him in great whoops that felt good. Good and cleansing.

"They're hungry!" Charlie bellowed in his father's ear. "Feed 'em again!"

The noise had brought Clementine running out of the house, although she slowed some when she saw that Charlie was safe in her man's arms. She, too, leaned over the fence for a better look at the distressed pigs.

The sow had finally gotten all four legs underneath her, but she swayed from side to side like a weathercock in a storm. The smell of beer, heady and yeasty, seeped up from the trough.

Clementine's fists landed on her hips, her nose went into the air, and she swung an accusing gaze over to Rafferty.

Laughing still, he flung up his hands as if she were

all set to spit bullets. "Hey, don't look at me. You were the one kept putting all them buckets of home brew into Charlie's innocent little hands."

Her mouth pulled and puckered. She covered it with her palm, but sounds escaped, giggles and gentle snuffles. "He kept saying, 'More, more. They want more, more.' I thought you two were out here tying on a big one."

Charlie shrieked and pulled at his father's hair.

"I reckon they'll live," Gus said around his own laughter. "But they're going to have one hell of a head come morning."

The boar lifted his snout in the air and trumpeted like a moose, then fell on his face in the dirt, and they all laughed some more. "I need to dig up some carrots for tonight's supper," Clementine said a moment later. Her gaze met Rafferty's for an instant, then skittered away. "To go along with the chicken we're having so unexpectedly. You'll share it with us, won't you?"

He flashed a careless smile at her. "I reckon my stomach can just about handle your cooking after six months of practice on stagecoach fare."

"Oh, you!" She laughed like a young girl and punched him lightly on the arm. And even that touch, innocent, done only in fun and without thought, brought the hunger bludgeoning through him with such force he shuddered.

Clementine whipped the spoon so vigorously through the cream it thudded against the wooden bowl. The motion stirred her skirts until they swayed around her small hips. The setting sun lanced through the kitchen window, tinting her cheeks. The smell of the fresh-baked apple pie they were having for dessert was sweet in the air, but underneath it he could still detect her own special scent: wild rose and warm woman. The breathy gusts of a late afternoon wind and the thud of the spoon were the only sounds to disturb the silence.

Rafferty didn't want to be here. It was too easy to pretend this was his kitchen, his wife. A hard, hollow ball of longing built and got stuck in his throat. He tipped a whiskey bottle over his empty coffee cup and poured it full. He drained the cup, trying to wash the longing back down with the booze. He ignored his brother's disapproving frown. Sometimes there just wasn't anything else to do but drink against the great loneliness that filled a man.

Rafferty sat sprawled in his chair, one arm hooked over the back. Gus sat across the table from him, hunched forward, his hands pressed together over his coffee cup as if in prayer. Clementine stood between them, beating at the cream to pour over the pie. The kitchen was definitely too quiet now without the boy's constant chatter. Charlie, exhausted from his busy day and the excitement over his uncle's homecoming, had fallen asleep during supper and been put to bed. The collection of arrowheads he'd been playing with lay scattered over the white oilcloth, the chipped obsidian glittering in the fading light.

She paused a moment in the whipping of her cream and smoothed her apron over the soft swell of her belly. The thought of her pregnant again left Rafferty feeling as if he'd been gutted. Barely a year ago she had nearly died from a stillbirth and here she was expecting again. Three babies in four years. What the hell was Gus—a rutting beast? A ruefulness twisted Rafferty's mouth. As if he would be able to leave Clementine alone if she shared his bed.

If she shared his bed . . . God, just once. If he could have her just once. There was a lot of what was noble and pure in what he felt for her, but it just wasn't in him to love a woman chastely. He wanted to feel her underneath him, he wanted to taste her skin, her mouth . . .

"Did you stop off and see Hannah on your way?" Gus said into the silence.

The spoon stopped in mid-beat. "I saw her," Rafferty said.

He toyed with the handle of his coffee cup. He knew

that if he looked up he would see pain in Clementine's eyes. Hannah was her dearest friend, but he sensed she had a hard time bearing the thought of him touching any other woman, loving any other woman. Good, he thought sourly. I hope it hurts you to think of me in bed with her. Because it sure as hell hurts me to think of you in bed with my brother.

He drank more whiskey to wash away the thought. It made it seem as if he was only using Hannah to punish Clementine, and that wasn't true. Even he wasn't that much of a son of a bitch. He was fond of Hannah—loved her, maybe—and he'd always tried to be as good to her as it was in his nature to be.

A frown was pulling at Gus's mouth, putting a crease between his brows. "You ought to marry her, Zach. It isn't right, your . . . your visiting her regular like you do and for all these years. She won't ever be thought of as respectable as long as you won't marry her."

"Hannah's not the marryin' sort. And neither am I." *And it ain't none of your business, brother,* he told Gus with his eyes. Gus's mouth tightened, though he said nothing more.

Rafferty thought of last night. They were both so damned afraid of being alone, he and Hannah, and so they clung to each other. In the beginning the loving had been so good between them, and there'd been plenty of easy laughter. But somewhere along the way the good loving and the easy laughter had stopped being enough.

He thought of that boy, that rock-buster, and he wondered if the boy would be the one to take Hannah away from him.

And thoughts of the boy led him to thoughts of the mine, and he said, "There was an accident at the Four Jacks last night. Cable on the hoisting car broke and a young nipper was killed."

Clementine gasped, the spoon clattering against the bowl.

Gus frowned, shrugging. "We got no say in how the consortium runs the mine, Zach. You know that."

"Oh, Gus," Clementine said. "I told you we should sell those shares."

His hand slammed down hard on the table, rattling the dishes. "And I told you, girl, not to concern yourself with it!"

A dark band of color stained her cheeks and her fingers gripped the spoon so tight her knuckles whitened.

Rafferty had to squeeze his coffee cup with both hands to keep them from curling into fists. A primal rage coursed through him that someone would speak so to his woman. It didn't matter that he had no claim to her, that the man who'd spoken was her husband. On a level that went deeper than what was right or real, she was *his*.

Gus and his wife shared a long, hard, angry look. "I want us to sell those shares," she said. She turned to Rafferty. "Tell him to sell."

"Sell," Rafferty said.

Gus swung his riled eyes onto his brother. "You got no say in it."

Rafferty drew in a deep breath and let it out in a silent sigh. He knew his brother's anger was born of his frustration at having seen so little money from the mine. Pogey and Nash—and Gus with his twenty percent share—were supposed to get half the profits on all the ore that yielded at least twenty-five percent silver, but the consortium was always careful to mix enough worthless rock in with the ore so that the books rarely showed a yield of over twenty-five percent.

Gus still dreamed of getting rich, though, and living the high life off silver ore. It probably didn't set well with these dreams to learn that a fifteen-year-old boy had died in the shafts he technically owned.

"With the money we are making off that mine," Gus said, "we can buy us some more thoroughbred bulls come fall."

"You got big plans, do you, brother?" Rafferty said. "There was talk in town about you looking to get elected to the Territorial Assembly."

The color came up hard in Gus's face, but he shook his head. "Naw, that's just talk, is all. I don't know about you, Zach, but I want to make my fortune whilst I'm young so's I can calf around in my old age. What are you going to do when you're too gimpy to bust broncs and rope cattle?"

"Shoot myself, I reckon."

He looked over at Clementine. She had set down the spoon, and now her hand lay on the table. He wanted to press his own hand hard on hers until they became one flesh.

He scraped back his chair, plucking up the half-empty whiskey bottle. "I think I'll turn in early. We all've got a busy week ahead of us if we're ever going to get that hay put up."

"Don't you want any pie?" Gus said.

Rafferty tilted the bottle at his brother's face and smiled, doing it just to irritate the man. "Whiskey makes a better dessert."

"Zach . . ." Gus stretched to his feet. He stuffed his hands in his pockets and looked at the toes of his boots. "It's true, what I told you earlier. I didn't just stumble across you, I went looking. Serious looking . . . It took me over four years to find you."

Rafferty turned startled eyes on his brother. Clementine wiped her hands on her apron, not looking at either of them.

Gus raised his head and Rafferty saw real feeling there. Love, maybe. Probably. "It's good to have you home again," Gus said thickly. "Maybe now you'll think about staying this time."

"It's good to be home," he said, promising nothing, but even so, the words tasted like alkali dust in his mouth.

Rafferty left his brother's house and crossed the hay meadow to the old buffalo hunter's cabin. When he got within the shadows of the cottonwoods he looked back. They had come out onto the porch to watch him on his way. Gus stood behind Clementine, his chin on her head, his arms wrapped around her just below her breasts. This far away it was hard to tell whether she welcomed her husband's embrace. But of course she welcomed it. She loved Gus. She'd told him that the one and only time she'd ever spoken of loving him.

Rafferty went into the cabin, shut the door, and leaned against it. It was dark inside, with only the one window and the sun having fallen behind the hills. The place smelled musty, unlived-in.

He poured what was left of the whiskey down his throat.

20

CLEMENTINE MCQUEEN'S FAIR BROWS drew together in a frown as she studied the fizzling brown liquid in her glass. Erlan saw the face she was making and eyed her own glass with trepidation. Because they were guests in the fire woman's house, good manners compelled them to drink this . . . this whatever-it-was down to the last drop and then smack their lips with pleasure.

Erlan took a surreptitious sniff of the drink. It smelled of the lily plant, so perhaps it didn't taste too terrible. But it was hissing like a serpent.

"What on earth is this foul brew?" Clementine said.

Erlan bit her lip to hide a smile. She had just caught the glint of laughter in the other woman's eyes.

Hannah Yorke's eyes were dancing as well. She planted a fist on her hip. "You know darn well that's sarsaparilla, Clementine—a la-di-da lady's drink. So don't go wrinkling your Boston nose at it."

"Yeah, but what I wanna know is why you're trying to choke me with this teetotal stuff," Clementine said in a gravelly voice that sounded as if she were speaking with a mouthful of beans. Erlan had to cover her own mouth with her hand to keep from giggling. "Break out the Rosebud, woman, and let's get pie-eyed."

Laughing, Hannah went to a lacquered bureau and took out a brown bottle. She fetched three fresh glasses and into each she poured two fingers' width of the fon-kwei drink called whiskey.

Erlan took a cautious sip. It tasted bitter, but it left a tingling in her belly more potent than rice wine. She took two bigger sips. A most pleasant drink. She took a generous swallow. Her lips nearly pulled back from her teeth and her belly buzzed. A most relaxing drink.

She cast a covert glance at the two women who sat across from her on the gold brocade sofa. The merchant Woo had warned her that she would never be accepted in this demon land, that they would call her insulting names and laugh at her lily feet. He had seemed surprised, and perhaps secretly pleased, when Hannah Yorke had invited his new wife into her home. But then, as the merchant Woo had explained, Mrs. Yorke had once been a joy girl and thus was an outcast herself.

Erlan bowed her head to her hostess. "I am honored," she said, "that you would invite me for a visit."

Hannah's smile put deep dimples on each cheek. "Well, Clementine and I did get to thinking you must be feeling awful lonely for some female company 'round about now, what with being newly married and all."

Clementine smiled as well and took a swallow from her glass. Erlan was pleased that good manners dictate she follow suit. This whiskey was a most pleasant drink.

Hannah was looking at Clementine with exaggerated round-eyed wonder. "Lord, girl, I don't know what's come over you. Sitting on my sofa cool as you please and drinking hell brew like a fish . . . Imagine what Gus would say—"

"The man can't suffer over what he doesn't know." She shook a finger in Hannah's face. "And don't you dare go blathering to Rafferty, either."

"I won't. I promise." Hannah licked a finger and drew an X over her heart.

Erlan watched with interest. It must be the fon-kwei way of fooling the ears of their listening gods. She would have to remember this ritual.

Hannah poured more whiskey into their glasses. Erlan took another deep swallow. "The merchant Woo shall also remain ignorant," she said. "I promise." She licked her finger and crossed her heart.

A breeze blew in the open window, stirring the fringed scarf on the piecrust table and the fronds of the fern on its stand. Although it was not what she was used to, Erlan liked this house. In this Rainbow Springs where all was in disharmony, where even the roads were dangerously straight, this house was like a lotus growing in a pond of choked weeds. Perhaps it was because a woman dwelled alone here, and so the atmosphere was overwhelmingly yin. She wondered what it was like to be Hannah Yorke and have only oneself to please, only oneself to serve. The thought was unsettling, and she put it away.

Clementine set her glass on the tea table in front of her. "Oh, dear, Erlan. I almost forgot." She picked up a square parcel off the sofa beside her. "It's the photograph I made of you and Sam on your wedding day." The stiff brown paper crackled as she unwrapped it. "Hannah supplied the frame."

Erlan took the gift and bowed low. "A thousand times a thousand thank-yous. It is a thing truly worthy of an empress."

She stared with wonder at the photograph in its silver frame. There she was in her wedding robe with the flying cranes, her features as stiff as an opera mask, and there the merchant Woo in his barbarian coat with the swallowlike tail. He looked pleased with his bride, but then, that was before she had put the cleaver to her neck.

"You know, Clementine," Hannah was saying, "you ought to do that more often—take people's likenesses at weddings, and for other occasions, too, like birthdays and such. Then you could sell them. Imagine all the little extras you could treat yourself to with a bit of money of your own."

Clementine folded the brown paper into a perfect square and laid it with care on the table beside her empty glass. "Gus's pride would never stand such a thing—his wife working to give herself luxuries he thinks he should be providing."

Hannah sniffed. "Most times I don't even see him providing you with the bare necessities, and I don't notice his pride sparing you from all the drudge work you do out on that ranch."

Clementine gave her friend a hard look. "Don't start, Hannah. Gus is good to me. You know he is."

A silence came between them then. A silence Erlan could feel, for it was thick with words that had never been spoken, with secrets too dangerous to share.

Hannah shrugged, lifting her chin, as if, Erlan thought, she could draw her pride around her like a tattered straw cloak. She raised her glass in the air. "I want to propose a toast. To something I'll always admire and never be—a true lady."

"Oh, Hannah." Clementine flushed, shaking her head. "You are foolish sometimes."

Now the two women shared a smile, calming whatever deep currents had been stirred between them. "If you like the photograph, Erlan," Hannah said, "Clementine can make you another to send home to your folks in China."

Erlan could not bear to look at the women now. If she wished to become a friend to them—and, oh, she did so wish it—then they would have to know her shame and come to accept her in spite of it.

"I thank you for your kind offer, but there is no family left to me. My mother is dead, and my father has cast me off." Erlan laid her palms on her thighs. She made herself lift her head, made herself meet their eyes. "He sold me to the Foochow slave trader for one hundred taels of silver."

"Oh, whyever would he do such a thing?" Clementine was suddenly in the chair beside hers, gripping her hand. Erlan felt the woman's yang strength, her warrior's spirit, and took comfort from it.

"My mother wore the green skirt of the concubine, and still the patriarch honored her by not sending her away when she bore him only a worthless daughter. But instead of repaying this kindness with veneration and absolute obedience, she dishonored the House of Po and heaped shame upon the ancestors by lying with a . . . with another. And then when she was given the scarlet noose, she soiled the purity of her own spirit by cravenly not making use of it. The patriarch was forced to nail her into her coffin alive. Her shame has become my shame. Her dishonor, my dishonor."

Hannah sucked in a sharp breath, shuddering. "My God. That is the most barbaric thing I've ever heard of."

Aiya, this whiskey did something to the tongue. She had meant to reveal some but not all. Erlan looked down at her hand, still held tightly by Clementine's slender white fingers. Their two hands seemed like bare wisps of things, boneless. Yet she could feel the strength of the other woman's grip.

Hannah had come over to stand beside her chair. She laid a gentle hand on Erlan's shoulder. This custom of touching was not such a disagreeable thing after all. "Did you leave behind a beau in China?" Hannah asked softly.

"A beau?"

"A young man you fancied. Someone you hoped to marry someday."

"In China there is no such thing as a beau. Marriages are arranged by Tai-Tai—First Wife. A girl does not see her husband until the day they are wed, when he lifts her red veil."

Hannah huffed a laugh. "I bet that makes for some mighty interesting wedding nights."

Erlan caught a smile with her hand. "Of course we say we wish only for a husband of good heart, but in truth no girl wants to find beneath the silk covers of her marriage bed an aged and withered root that not even a *tai-fung* could stir to life. Rather, she looks forward eagerly to one that is long and thick and quivering with excitement like a divining rod."

Erlan's smile faded as she noticed the startled looks on the faces of the two women. Embarrassment burned in her chest. It was like being a tightrope dancer, trying to maneuver her way through this demon land's strange customs and ways.

"I have given offense," she said.

Hannah snorted and choked as if she was trying to hold back a laugh. And then the laughter did burst out of her in great loud whoops, and she was joined by Clementine. The two women looked at each other and laughed harder.

Hannah clutched at her belly. "Oh, oh, Clem, just imagine! Quivering like a divining rod!"

When she had caught her breath, Hannah asked, "But what if a girl isn't ready to be married?"

Erlan was pleased that she had not made a fool of herself after all. "Getting married and birthing children are a woman's happiness. Of course a husband is not found for every girl. If there are many daughters and the clan is poor, the younger ones often are sold as concubines or to houses of leisure to be daughters of joy."

"Lord knows, being a whore ain't an easy life," Hannah said. "And I 'spect it's no different in China. But I reckon I'd rather be a—what did you call them?—a daughter of joy than be married off to some man I've never set eyes on before. Why, what if he turned out to be a beast, or a tyrant?"

"Even the lowliest peasant acts like a warlord beneath his own roof. It is the way of men. To be a woman is to be like the brown larks my father keeps as pets. We only exchange one sort of cage for another."

The two women fell silent, and Erlan wondered again if she had given offense. She raised her head and met Clementine's eyes. Sea eyes, frothing, shifting, restless. And Erlan had a strange thought: she understands; she understands all there is of me. In another life we might have been sisters.

"Don't mind Hannah," Clementine said. "She's always going on about single blessedness, but someday she'll find a man who needs her to take care of him and she'll go willing into the cage, just like the rest of us."

Hannah laughed. "Me, take care of a man? Hunh. That'll be the day." She made a soft clucking noise in the back of her throat and ran a finger along the curve of Erlan's cheek. "Look how chapped your poor cheeks have gotten already. With this wind and the alkali dust, if you don't have a care your skin'll get as dry as a sand bed. I'll make you a batch of complexion salve. I'll make some up for you, too, Clementine. You can get it when you come back for the Fourth of July frolic."

Hannah continued to stroke Erlan's cheek. A strange mixture of excitement and sweet contentment settled within her. It made her tingle inside, like the fon-kwei whiskey. She looked up and smiled. "What is this Fourth of July everyone is talking about?"

The first thing a body did on a Fourth of July morning in the RainDance country was to step outside and sniff the weather.

The old-timers swore up and down that it had been known to snow on the Fourth. 'Most everyone else, though, being new to the place, hadn't seen this particular phenomenon and didn't care to. But Montana weather had other tricks up its sleeve that could spoil a day. Howling wind and slashing rain and battering hail as big as hens' eggs, to name but a few.

So on that Independence Day morning of 1883, the RainDance folk poked wary noses out their doors and found to their relief a light, sage-scented breeze and butter-yellow sunshine. It was going to be a fine afternoon for the festivities.

Rainbow Springs, Montana Territory, had changed from the bob-tailed town it had been four years ago. Why, just last winter it had been incorporated, and in the words of that old prospector, Pogey, "she was struttin' regular city airs like a two-bit whore in a French silk gown." There had even been talk lately about putting up streetlights. Nash, Pogey's partner in mischief, predicted that within the first five minutes of a Saturday night any streetlight worth going by the name "would get itself shot deader'n a beaver hat just for being there and handy."

It was silver that had changed Rainbow Springs. The Four Jacks had proved to be a solid, steady little mine. It had brought people to what was once nothing more than a burp in a road heading west. High-toned, high-handed people like the managers and engineers who ran the workings. Hard-fisted, hard-drinking people like the miners who blasted the rock and mucked the silver ore, and the mule skinners who hauled it to the smelter over in Butte. Church-going, root-putting people like butchers, bakers, and saddlemakers.

Many were foreigners, people with thick accents and odd customs and a hunger to take advantage of the opportunities the West claimed to offer. They were mostly Irish and Cornish and Welsh, who hired on at the mine and lived within its shadow in the shacks and boardinghouses nicknamed Dublin Patch. And the Chinese, who worked the old gold placers and the tailings of silver ore waste the Four Jacks Consortium didn't care to mess with. The Chinese put up their shacks on the outskirts of town, across the river, where a circle of bare earth still scarred the grass from a long-gone tipi.

There was an air of permanence about Rainbow Springs that the town had never had before. Most of the buildings were still made of rough-hewn logs, but a few, like the Miner's Union Bank, had been constructed of milled lumber. The haphazard grid of streets that had sprung up willy-nilly around RainDance Butte had been named and their names put up on wooden signs for those folk savvy enough to read them. In Luke's Barber Shop a man could keep his very own shaving mug on a shelf, an act of faith that he would be there tomorrow and the next week and the week after that to use it.

Most of the old-timers recognized the flow of change, called it progress, and went along with it. Snake-Eye acquired a last name to go with the new barn he put up in 1881. Painted above the barn's big sliding double doors in bright red letters was a sign: Smith's Livery, Horses Bedded and Shod, Several Conveyances for Rent and Sale. Sam Woo carried giant powder and caps and fuses in his mercantile now next to the bags of seed and sheep shears and cowhide reatas. Nickel Annie had given up the open road and now drove her string of mules for the Four Jacks. And Hannah Yorke had fancied up the inside of the Best in the West Casino, putting in gilt mirrors and a brass bar rail and a parquet floor until it looked like the sort of high-toned den of sin a man would expect to find in San Francisco, or maybe even in New York City.

And there was a schoolhouse in Rainbow Springs now, painted red, and with a pine flagpole in the yard and a copper bell on its roof.

The schoolhouse proved to be a bit too much progress for some. "The country," Pogey told his crony Nash, over a bottle of Rosebud whiskey in Sam Woo's mercantile on the day the new schoolhouse opened for business, "done got tame on us when we wasn't even lookin'."

"Tame as a neck-wrung rooster," Nash said.

"Tame as an old toad in the hot sun."

"Tame as a toothless coyote."

"Holy God," said Sam Woo.

On that Fourth of July afternoon in 1883 a miner stepped out of his boardinghouse in Dublin Patch. He hooked his hands on his hips, threw back his head, and breathed deeply of the warm sage-spicy air.

"'Tes a fine day," Jere Scully said aloud to himself. "A fine day for a frolic." Jere rather liked the idea of celebrating an Independence Day, the Cornish being of an independent bent themselves.

He spotted little Meg Davies coming down the dusty road, a straw basket of posies on her arm, and he waved her over.

"You want to buy some flowers for your girl, Mr. Scully? Only cost you a nickel," she said, trying for a smile and not quite making it. Her red hair was twisted into such tight braids they curled out from the sides of her head like jug handles, and freckles splashed like spilled cinnamon flakes across her cheeks and nose. But bleak shadows haunted her eyes. She was taking the death of her brother Rolfe hard; the whole of the Patch had taken the nipper's death hard.

Jere bent over for a better look at the bunches of flowers in her basket. "What have you got here?"

"Bluebells and shooting stars and wood lilies. I picked them fresh just this morning. Which do you like best?"

Jere didn't know one flower from another, except maybe for roses. "I'll be having the orange ones, then," he said.

Meg Davies plucked a posy of the orange flowers out of her basket, at the same time dropping Jere's nickel into her pinafore pocket with a deft flourish. "Do you got a girl, Mr. Scully?"

Jere looked up and down the road, then bent way over

until they were nose to freckled nose. He put his finger to his lips. "Don't you be telling anybody."

The little girl pressed her lips together, but her eyes glinted with laughter. "I won't . . . Oh, look, here comes your brother!" she shrieked, and hurried off down the street, giggling.

Jere whipped off his derby and stuffed the posy inside the crown, slammed the hat back on his head, and turned with an easy smile. "'Tes about bloody time . . ." His eyes opened wide at the sight of his brother resplendent in a brown windowpane-checked suit, a stiff white collar, and a yellow four-in-hand. "Cor! But if you don't look prettier than the primroses on a lady's Sunday bonnet."

Drew Scully took an exaggerated sniff at the air, wrinkling his nose. "Peeyew! And who smells worse than a sailor on a Saturday night, then?"

Drew scrubbed at his cheeks with his big rough hand. "'Tes the bay rum I splashed on me face after I shaved. Do you think 'tes too much, then? Mebbe I should go and wash it off—"

Laughing, Drew gripped his arm, hauling him down the dirt road in the direction of town. "Come off wi' you, my handsome. There's beer to drink and ladies to seduce, and they won't start the frolicking without us."

The festivities were being held on the north edge of town in a big meadow that bordered the river. The air was sweet with the smell of crushed grass, gunpowder, and chicken with all the fixin's. The Miner's Union Band tooted away at a mournful rendition of "The Girl I Left Behind Me," but the music had to compete with the patriotic flap of dozens of flags, the crackle of firecrackers, the clang of horseshoes, and the shrieks of children dunking for apples in a horse trough.

"Look over yon," Drew said, pointing to a fresh wooden platform with a six-foot-thick block of granite sitting in the middle of it. "They'll be having a double-jack drilling contest later. What do you say we enter it?"

"What—in our Sunday-go-to-meeting suits?"

"If we win, they'll not care how we're dressed."

Jere ran his finger beneath his stiff paper collar. He was already sweating up a swamp. The sun was beginning to bake the open field, but Mrs. Yorke, enterprising woman that she was, had set up a tent beneath a stand of aspens, where Shiloh hawked beer and sarsaparilla to cut down on the heat and dust.

And it seemed that no sooner had Jere thought of the woman than she appeared before his eyes. She, along with a good part of the rest of Rainbow Springs, had gathered to admire the town's new fire wagon on display in the middle of the meadow. A scarlet woman with scarlet hair was Mrs. Hannah Yorke. Today she was dressed in layers of cream lace, all frilly and frothy like a sugared marchpane confection.

Drew had seen her, too, and his face took on a familiar sharp look. It was the look he'd always gotten, even when they were little tackers, when he saw something he wanted and made up his mind to go after it. There was no one as determined as Drew when he set his teeth into something. He stopped at nothing to get what he wanted, did Drew. Nothing.

Jere breathed a silent sigh. His little brother was after a bagful of trouble here, though. That Hannah Yorke was the sort of woman who'd chew up a boy like Drew, spit out the bones and gristle, and not even dull the edge of her appetite.

Jere caught his brother's arm. "I could be using a beer."

Drew's head swung around, his eyes intent and a little wild. "Could you, then?"

Jere's mouth kinked into an easy smile, but his grip tightened on the boy's arm. "Aye. A beer would be good. A nice wet something."

The hard, sharp look clung to Drew's face a moment longer, then he shook his head on a short laugh. "I'll get you your beer, then. 'Twouldn't do to have her thinking I'm too eager, would it?"

While Drew went to fetch the beer, Jere strolled over for a closer look at the new fire wagon. The bright red paint on it still looked wet, and the firemen, volunteers all, were button-busting proud in their matching red shirts. The brass pump had been polished to an eye-dazzling shine down to the hose screws. Jere hovered at the edge of the crowd a moment, then he turned aside, squinting against the glitter of the river between the trees, and he saw her.

He got quite close to her this time before she saw him. Always before, when he'd stopped by the mercantile, she would disappear into a back room and leave Sam Woo to serve him, and so he had been unable to say one word to her since that first day. This time her head jerked up like a startled doe's and she looked around as if she would flee, but in the end she didn't. She stood in trembling stillness, her hands stuffed up the sleeves of her blue high-necked quilted robe, her gaze riveted on the ground.

"G'day to you, Mrs. Woo," he said, softly, so as not to frighten her.

"Good day, Mr. Scully," she said to the grass.

He stared down at her, suddenly unable to speak. His gaze traced the graceful curve of her back, the small knob of bone at the nape of her neck. The sharp white part in her hair, which was so dense a black it was the absence of all light. He remembered seeing an etching in a book once of a wild black swan swimming on a lake in front of some fairy-tale castle. She reminded him of that swan, a delicate creature not of his world. A strange feeling clutched at his chest, a need to cherish and protect.

He took another step to bring himself closer to her. She smelled like a spring apple, crisp and green. "Mrs. Woo . . ."

She lifted her head. Her eyes were as dark and impenetrable as lampblack. "Yes, Mr. Scully?"

He swept off his hat, almost crushing the brim. Her eyes widened at the sight of the wilted wood lilies lying like a clown's orange rag wig on top of his head. She started to smile, smothering it at the last moment with her hand.

He'd forgotten about the flowers. A tide of color flooded his face, but he couldn't help laughing at himself. He plucked the posy off his head and folded his body into a bow. "These are for you. Pretty flowers for a pretty lady." And then he wanted to curse himself. He'd sounded daft, like a moonstruck schoolboy.

She took the flowers, her fingers brushing his. A strange, quivery feeling rippled down his spine. He thought she might have felt it, too, for she trembled and her lips parted on a sharp expulsion of breath. "They are lovely flowers," she said in her sweet, lilting voice. Her gaze slid away from his, and her lips moved slightly, as if she were smiling to herself. "Thank you, my *anjing juren.*"

He tried to say the Chinese words after her, mangling them badly. He laughed again. "And what was that you be calling me? 'Twasn't a slur on my mother's good name, was it?"

Her gaze flew back up to his, and a tiny crease appeared between her brows. "Oh, no, you must not think . . . It is an address of great respect. Truly."

"Hunh. So you say." He took another step, bringing himself closer still. She tensed, but did not back away. He pitched his voice low, touching her with his words in the way he wanted to touch her with his hands, with his mouth. "And what is something I can be calling you, then? An address, for instance, of deep affection."

She appeared to consider the matter seriously, the crease between her brows deepening. He imagined pressing his lips to it, kissing it away. "I shall allow you to call me Mei Mei, if you wish. It means Little Sister."

A firecracker popped nearby, and the smell of burned powder wafted between them. He drew in a deep breath, trying to ease the pressure growing in his chest.

The band suddenly struck up a loud martial song, and they both jerked around, relieved to have something to look at besides each other. Sunlight bounced off the brass wind instruments. The musicians' faces had turned scarlet from all that puffing in the heat.

Yet against his will his gaze slid back to her. Her skin was the pale cream color of antique ivory. Her eyes met his; he wished he could tell what she was thinking. He knew that what he was feeling for her showed on his face, but he didn't care. He wanted her to know.

"Little Sister . . . 'Tes not the kind of affection I have for you," he said, thinking how the words belied the depth of what he felt. He was in gut-love.

"In China a man does not look thus upon another's wife," she said, and for the first time he heard a strain in her voice. "Or speak to her so. Indeed, he would not speak to her at all."

He pushed a harsh breath out his tight throat. "And what are we supposed to do, then? Be forgetting about this thing that's between us simply because we met at the wrong time and in the wrong place? You shouldn't have married him, m' love, but 'tesn't a thing that can't be undone."

A taut silence stretched between them. A boy ran by, carrying a sparkler in his hand like a torch. The lighted stick hissed and crackled, shooting off miniature stars.

Her chest lifted in a silent sigh. "Where I come from, in Foochow," she said, "there is a pagoda that is one thousand years old, and it is only just beginning its sojourn upon this earth. Perhaps there will be another time and another place for us, my *anjing juren*. But not in this lifetime."

"To hell with that—"

She pressed her fingers against his mouth, stopping his protest. He grasped her wrist, holding her hand in place to kiss it. When he let her go, her hand fell to her side and her fingers curled as if she would capture his kiss and keep it forever.

But something flashed in her eyes. Anger perhaps. Or fear. "You don't understand," she said. "You do not understand me. A Chinese does not seek to undo her fate. She does not sacrifice her honor for the sake of her heart." Her hand started to come up and he thought she would touch him again, but then she let it fall. "It was not by chance the gods put a great sea between our peoples, a sea too wide for any bridge to cross. We are too different, you and I. No bridge can ever link us."

She turned then and walked away from him. She moved on her tiny feet as if she were treading on cinders, her hips swaying, her back straight, her head still. He looked down and saw the posy of orange flowers lying in the grass. He knew she hadn't dropped it accidentally. By rejecting even so simple and innocent a gift, she was rejecting him.

Jere's hands tightened into fists. He wasn't going to give up, not on her, not on what he felt for her and what he hoped she could someday feel for him. He didn't care how bloody wide a sea there was between them, he would find a way to build a bridge. And then he'd cross it, even if he had to do it on his knees.

The miner slammed his sixteen-pound sledgehammer onto the head of the drill with such force the wooden platform trembled, granite dust puffed into the air, and the clang of steel against steel bounced off the distant hills.

"Oh, my," Hannah Yorke said, as she twirled her white lace parasol and stirred the dusty air before her face with a Stars-and-Stripes paper fan. "I must say, there is something about watching a half-naked man beat up on a rock, the way his muscles bulge and go all shiny wet with sweat and the veins pop out against his skin . . . it gives me a tingling feeling low in my belly."

A blush spread over Clementine McQueen's cheeks, but she laughed out loud. "Hannah, what a thing to say! You are incorrigible."

"Mama, why is that man hammering a big nail into that rock?"

Clementine shifted her wriggling son from one hip to the other. "That isn't a nail, sweetheart. It's a drill. Now, you must stay back here, well out of the way."

"But I can't see!" Charlie shouted. "I want to see!"

"I think he is like some wild, magnificent animal."

This remark came out of Miss Luly Maine, the town's new schoolteacher. Her eyes were riveted not on the shiftless miner pounding a steel drill into a granite block and racing against the clock, but on Drew Scully, who still had all his clothes on. Indeed, he was all slicked up in the most garish brown plaid suit Hannah had ever laid eyes on. He was waiting, with his brother, for a turn at the double-jack drill contest with its twenty-dollar prize.

Miss Luly Maine was seventeen. She had glossy chestnut hair, lake-blue eyes, and the top of her head came no higher than the middle of a man's chest. Hannah had often wondered how such a little thing handled a classroom full of rowdy boys not much smaller and younger than she. But then schoolmarming was one of the few respectable occupations a spinster could pursue out West. And most folk, Hannah being one of them, figured a gal took it up and came out here for the sole purpose of hooking herself a man.

For a while a betting book had been kept in the Best in the West on how long a sweet little morsel like Miss Luly Maine would remain in the single state in a place where men outnumbered women twenty to one. But when a month passed, then three, and then nine months passed, and twenty-seven proposals had been tendered and refused, folk began to suspect Miss Luly Maine was one of those unnatural females who married themselves to a career.

Right now, though, Hannah would have bet every penny in her account at the Miner's Union Bank that the little schoolmarm had begun to hear wedding bells after all. She was looking at Drew Scully as if she were imagining the shape of the flesh beneath his shirt, imagining how it would feel beneath her hands.

Hannah whipped her fan through the air with such force the brim of her white leghorn straw hat lifted a good two inches. "Ain't it just like a man," she said, "to spend his holiday away from hammering a drill into a rock hammering a drill into a rock. I reckon they always got to be measuring themselves one against the other, men do. To see which one is the toughest."

"Oh, but I think it is *so* exciting," Luly said on a sigh. Her eyes were still on Drew Scully and they'd turned all misty. "An exhibition of skill and courage."

An exhibition of muscle and chest hair, and of men's damned foolish ways, more like, thought Hannah. She closed her fan with a loud snap.

Behind them the air popped with the noisy explosion of a giant cracker, but most people in the crowd were too intent on the contest to notice. The miners worked in teams of two, trading places every three minutes. One would swing the hammer, and with every stroke his partner, who was holding the drill upright, would raise and turn it slightly to keep it from sticking in the hole and costing them precious seconds. A slow-running hose attached to a barrel poured water into the hole to flush it out. The team that drilled the deepest hole in the granite slab in fifteen minutes won the contest and received the prize, a double-eagle gold piece.

A man with a big nickel-plated watch cupped in his hand shouted, "Time!" and the miner with the hammer followed through with his last stroke. The ringing echo of steel on steel faded into the noise of popping firecrackers and the brassy din of the band. The timekeeper flushed out the hole with the hose and measured its depth. "Twenty-two inches," he announced. The crowd applauded politely. Twenty-two inches wouldn't be winning any prizes. Thus far the best measurement stood at just under twenty-seven inches.

As the Scully brothers prepared for their turn at the granite block, Hannah maneuvered herself so that she was between Clementine and Miss Luly Maine. In her white sateen dress garlanded with red and blue ribbons, the little schoolteacher looked as pretty and snappy as the flags flying from the pine poles that encircled the meadow. Pretty and dainty and so very, very young. Beside her Hannah felt as old and hard and used up as a sodbuster's hobnailed boots.

The girl went all stiff as a fence post as she cast a sideways glance at Hannah, and Hannah smiled to herself. Miss Luly Maine didn't know quite what to make of her. She was a saloonkeeper, a true daughter of Eve, the kind of fast and loose woman the reverend back home had probably warned Miss Luly Maine against. But she was also a friend of Clementine McQueen, who was eminently respectable, of course, a rancher's wife, president of the Ladies Social Club, and the daughter of a prominent Boston family. As a result the young schoolteacher couldn't make up her mind from one minute to the next whether to snub Hannah Yorke or invite her over for tea and gingersnaps.

"Do you know Mr. Drew Scully?" Hannah asked casually.

The girl's cheeks turned berry red, and a shy smile softened her mouth. "We haven't been formally introduced, naturally, but I've seen him some. Around town. He smiled at me and tipped his hat."

At the moment the man was taking off more than his hat; he was stripping off his suit jacket, vest, tie, and shirt as well. He stretched out the kinks in his arms, rolling his shoulders and flexing a bare chest strapped with muscle. Miss Luly Maine sighed, and Hannah almost sighed right along with her. It wasn't as if she wanted that boy for herself. Indeed, if anything this poor girl deserved her pity. The little schoolmarm had been bitten by the love bug bad, and now it probably seemed to her that she would go mad if she didn't scratch the itch.

Hannah knew all too well where such feelings could lead. To a wax posy off a wedding cake now fading beneath a bell jar. To soul-rotting memories of a crib in the badlands of Deadwood with the name Rosie burned above the door.

Jere Scully carefully selected the spot on the granite block where they would drill, although, since they'd drawn last place, all the best spots had already been taken. Drew Scully unrolled a canvas bundle and took up a newly sharpened bull prick. He glanced up and caught her looking at him. He cast a swift white grin her way, and she tossed a be-damned-to-you-mister glare right back at him. And he . . . why, he had the audacity to wink at her! As if she were some sweet young thing like Miss Luly Maine, who got all chest-fluttery and weak-kneed just because a handsome young man paid her a little attention, when all he was really after was a ride between her legs.

He held Hannah's gaze as he crouched on his heels, his britches pulling taut over his wide-spread thighs. He clasped the drill close around the head. His brother stood over him, hammer in the air. The timekeeper touched Jere on the shoulder, and he slammed the sledge down on the tiny head of the drill. The drill point bit deep into the block of granite with a reverberating clang, and Miss Luly Maine jumped and gasped as if she had taken the blow herself.

After three minutes the timer again touched Jere on the shoulder. He flung his hammer aside, crouched down, and grabbed the drill while Drew seized up his own hammer, sprang to his feet, and brought it down onto the drill head all without missing a beat.

"Put 'er down, boy!" someone bellowed.

Miss Luly Maine heaved another loud and fluttering sigh, and Hannah's jaw tightened. She was back to being irritated with the girl again, although she had to admit the sight of Drew Scully wielding a sixteen-pound sledge was a splendid one. He was not as big and brawny as his brother, his muscles tending more toward sleek leanness. But there was no denying their strength and power as they flexed and bulged beneath his sweat-slick skin. The platform trembled and the very air seemed to vibrate with the fierceness of his blows. The hammer rose and fell, rose and fell, pounding, pounding, pounding the drill head into the unforgiving, unyielding rock. The rhythm of the pounding hammer entered Hannah's blood, and a warm, heavy feeling spread over her. It was the rhythm of a brass bed's headboard banging against the wall, she thought, of a woman being taken again and again and again by a strong, lusty man until she wanted to scream from the agony and the pleasure of it.

The feeling became so intense that Hannah was relieved when the timekeeper touched Drew on the shoulder and once again the brothers changed places.

Jere tossed his head, flicking sweat out of his eyes, and grunted with exertion as he hefted the heavy sledge high in the air. Something or someone down by the river must have caught his attention, for his gaze flashed in that direction for just an instant, but that brief lapse in concentration was enough to affect his swing. The hammer came down without hesitation, but it didn't hit the drill head true. Instead, sixteen pounds of steel slid down the length of the bull prick with a loud scream and smashed into the hand that held it.

The hammer had immediately swung back on the upstroke and it hovered now in the air as Jere's eyes widened in horror. The crowd groaned and gasped, and Drew shuddered from the pain that must have burst suddenly upon his consciousness like an exploding giant cracker. But he flung up his head and shouted at his brother, "Bring it down, damn you! Bring it down!"

Jere brought the hammer down.

Thick red blood welled out of Drew's bruised and lacerated flesh, but he still gripped the drill, turning and lifting it as was necessary with each successive blow. Blood ran into the hole and was flushed out with the water. The puddles around the granite block turned a bright pink. A fierce pain squeezed Hannah's chest. She didn't realize she was holding her breath until the timekeeper, his face pale, touched Jere on the shoulder. It was Drew's turn to swing the hammer.

Jere hesitated, but Drew was already back on his feet, with his own hammer in his fists. He raised the sledge in the air, and blood ran down his arm. He brought the hammer down, and blood sprayed in a fanlike arc, splattering those in the crowd closest to the platform. Again and again he pounded at the drill, although each blow must have sent pain flashing like fire up his arm. Hannah stared, so tense her whole body quivered, as the sweat and blood ran in slow rivulets down his chest, over the ridges of muscle, following the arrow of hair that disappeared into his britches.

Once again the brothers changed places, and the last three minutes seemed to crawl by. Hard white lines bracketed Drew Scully's mouth, and a glazed look had come over his eyes. Hannah dug her nails deep into her palm as if she could take some of his pain onto herself.

"Fifteen minutes!" the timekeeper finally bellowed, and Hannah's pent-up breath left her in a thick rush. The crowd burst into a loud and spontaneous cheer at the sheer courage and strength of will that it had taken for the Scully brothers even to finish the contest.

The timekeeper flushed the bloody water out the hole and inserted the measuring rod. The crowd was silent now, holding its collective breath. "Twenty-eight and one-quarter inches!" he shouted, and the air exploded with loud whoops and even some gunfire.

"Luly's gone to fetch the doctor."

Hannah's gaze jerked around to Clementine, her cheeks flushing as if she'd been caught doing something wicked. Clementine's own face was as pale as the granite dust that coated the platform, but wet, red drops speckled her forehead and her smooth golden hair. Hannah realized that she, too, must be splattered with Drew Scully's blood.

"Mama, that man's bleeding," Charlie announced.

Clementine turned her head and pressed a trembling mouth to the boy's cheek. "Yes, he is. Let us go down to the river and see if we can spot some trout swimming in the shallows, shall we?"

The timekeeper had the Scully brothers on either side of him. He was all set to raise their hands in the air, proclaiming them the winners, when Drew sagged to his knees. His head lolled and his face turned white and waxy, as if the blood now pooling on the platform was the last he owned.

"Give way!" Hannah heard someone shout. "Here comes the doctor."

Dr. Kit Corbett was as tall and skinny as a snake on stilts and ugly to boot. But he was young and he wasn't a drunk, two attributes that were hard to find in doctors out in western Montana. He was new to Rainbow Springs, but he wasn't new to double-jack drilling contests. He didn't even blink at the sight of the blood-splattered wood and granite. "You might have had the sense not to finish it" was all he said as he leaped agilely onto the platform and knelt beside Drew, opening his black bag.

The schoolmarm, who had escorted the doctor this far, did not climb the platform after him. She stood back in indecision, her teeth sunk into her lower lip. Hannah reckoned a sweet young thing like Miss Luly Maine was too shy and innocent and well brought up to approach a man she had yet to be formally introduced to, even if he was on his last breath.

Hannah Yorke had also been well brought up, but sure as man needed woman, she was no innocent. And that crib in Deadwood had finished whatever shyness she had once possessed. She pushed through the men who were now wedged in front of her around the platform. Drew flung his head up, flicking his sweat-wet hair back out of his eyes, and their gazes met with the force of a sledge slamming into rock.

He looked so hurt and vulnerable on his knees like that, cradling his injured hand. She wanted to do something to him. Smack him, maybe, for being such a fool. Or cradle his head against her breast and comfort him with sweet words and gentle kisses, which showed that she was the bigger fool.

Instead she said in a voice as tart as vinegar, "I reckon if you were able to grip a hammer, your hand ain't busted."

He flashed a cocky grin at her. "You're some fine comfort, Mrs. Yorke."

"And you are some fool, Mr. Drew Scully."

"A fool who's twenty dollars richer, though."

His brother put a bucket of beer into his good hand, and Drew swigged it down. The doctor was flexing his bruised and bleeding fingers, trying to determine if any were broken. Drew swore and pulled his hand free of the man's rough treatment. "Go on with you, you bleeding sawbones. I've been hurt worse."

What a boy he was, Hannah thought, chock full of brag and fight. From the hindsight of thirty-three years of rough and tough living, she saw Drew Scully's youth hanging out all over him, as obvious as his ready-made three-dollar suit. Yet something about him intrigued her . . . It was the pure, unadulterated guts of him. Courage came easily to some men, because they so rarely knew fear. But Drew Scully, she suspected with the innate sense of a fellow sufferer, was intimate with fear. He knew fear as she knew men—he knew the stink of it and the taste of it and the way it ate at your pride and slowly, like water dripping on rock year after year, corroded your soul.

The doctor settled for wrapping a bandage around the injured hand and consigned his ungrateful patient to hell. Men pressed around Drew, slapping him on the back and offering to buy him a drink, but he broke away from them, his gaze intent on Hannah.

He came to where she stood and looked down at her. "Will you be nursing me back to health, Mrs. Yorke?" he said. "I could be using an angel's sweet ministrations."

"What you could use is a clout on the side of the head, and then maybe you'd acquire some sense. And besides, I ain't no—"

"Angel," he finished for her, and he smiled. Not one of those cocky grins this time, but a slow, soft smile that changed his face and left her feeling as if she'd been punched in the stomach.

He squatted and, putting his weight on his good hand, swung to the ground. He hooked his butt on the edge of the platform and wrapped his arm around her waist, somehow maneuvering her so that she was between his legs. She was amused by this blatant trick and shocked at herself for letting it happen. His spread thighs brushed hers. Her breasts pressed against his chest. Her belly arched into his groin as his hand splayed across the small of her back, pulling her closer. His thighs were as solid as the rock he had drilled so proficiently. She drew in a deep breath that was thick with his scent, of male sweat and granite dust and the violent, coppery odor of blood.

And though it seemed their faces were but a breath apart, she couldn't look at him. Her gaze drifted over to the refreshment tent just as Zach Rafferty turned away from the makeshift bar, a tin pail of foaming brew in either hand. Across a meadow of crushed grass and wafting gun smoke their gazes met, and Hannah stiffened within the boy's light embrace.

Callused fingers gripped her chin, pulling her head around, and she looked up into eyes the hard, dark gray of the flint the Indians had once used for their arrowheads. They were old eyes.

"When you're with me, m' lass," he said, his voice low, and as hard as his eyes, "you'll be keeping those lovely brown eyes of yours on me, then, and you'll not be looking at him."

She pushed off his chest with such force that his head snapped on his neck. "You are sorely mistaken, Mr. Scully. I am not *with* you. Indeed, you may go straight to hell, and you may go there by yourself!"

"Aye." His smile came again and it was irresistible. She thought she probably hated him. She definitely wanted him. "I've been told to go to the nether regions often enough and by enough women. I suppose if they have any say about it a-tall, that sure enough is where I'm bound."

He brushed her cheek with the backs of his bandaged fingers. "G'day to you, then, Mrs. Yorke," he said, and sauntered off without a further by-your-leave. She stared after him, her chest heaving with anger and bludgeoned pride.

Blue and red ribbons flashed in the corner of her eye and she turned her head. Miss Luly Maine had come up beside her. The girl's chin trembled, but she managed to get it up in the air. She swept aside her skirts as if the ground around them had suddenly become defiled, and she, too, walked away, the twitching of her bustle more eloquent than any words.

Hannah watched her go. She wanted to call the girl back, but she knew it would do no good. When you are seventeen there are only good girls and bad girls and no in-between girls.

Every man's girl and no man's girl . . .

Hannah's eyes blurred, and she blinked angrily. She focused her gaze across the meadow, where the Rainbow River wound its way, sparkling like tinsel, through the aspens and cottonwoods. Oh, what she wouldn't give to be seventeen again. She wanted to be innocent and pure, with a heart that hadn't been broken and patched together so many times it resembled the last whiskey glass in the last honky-tonk on earth. She wanted to have it all to do over again, with her life stretching ahead of her, empty and shiny, just like the river.

And with love at the end of it.

21

ERLAN KNELT ON THE bank and launched a paper boat into the river, a plea to the river god to answer her heart's desire. She thought of the many times she had sat high on the garden wall of her lao chia, her back pressed against the rough, sun-warmed stones, hugging her knees as she dreamed of doing just this—setting her secret wishes adrift on the distant, mysterious river.

This river surely was different from the Min, which was muddy and silty, yellow as an old man's skin. This river was so clear she could count the stones that lined the bottom. White down floated like snow flurries from the tall trees overhead. And those other trees, those slender silver ones—their leaves glittered where they caught the light and shivered even when the wind was still.

Erlan rose to her feet and drew in a deep breath of air, filling her head with the smell of the river and the sun-baked grass. A string of firecrackers went off with a rat-a-tat-tat, and the new fire wagon's bell clanged like a bronze gong. The sounds reminded her of the New Year's Day celebrations back home. There had been fireworks then, of course, rockets that burst into stars and flowers of colored lights, dragons that writhed across the sky trailing green fire. And, oh, had they feasted! On steaming meat dumplings and long rice noodles for long life, on moon cakes and good-luck oranges.

At one time, even just a short while ago, these thoughts of home would have made her soul ache, but now she smiled. She could bear to think of her lao chia, now that she believed in her heart that she would see it again someday.

Her smiled faded, though, as her thoughts turned to her *anjing juren,* her gentle giant. A while ago, as she had walked along the river, she'd seen him up on a wooden platform, wielding an enormous hammer. As if possessed of a spirit of their own, her feet had started toward him. But then she had made herself turn away. In this life it was their fate to be like the moon and the sun, only passing in the vastness of the sky with no hope of ever being together. And though she thought perhaps she could come to love him, still he frightened her. He was too big, too fierce.

Lost in her thoughts, Erlan rounded a bend in the river and, lifting her head, saw a woman kneeling on the stony bank. The woman had a child with her, and she'd just finished cleaning his face with a white cloth. As Erlan watched, the woman dipped the cloth in the water and began to scrub at her own face, rubbing vigorously. Erlan took a step, and her golden lilies sent a trickle of pebbles splashing into the river. The woman's head whipped around. Erlan smiled and bowed when she realized it was Clementine.

"Good day to you, my friend."

"Oh, Erlan, I didn't see you there . . ." Clementine pushed to her feet, struggling with heavy dark green skirts. Her fingers shook as she pushed stray wisps of hair off her brow, tucking them beneath the curled brim of a straw bonnet. Her face was whiter than the cottony tufts that floated through the air, and there was a fine trembling going on inside her.

Erlan held out a concerned hand to the other woman. "Are you ill?"

"No, no. A man was hurt, and his blood splattered . . ." Again she smoothed back her hair, and her hand still shook. "Oh, it was nothing, really. I am being silly, but . . ." She shuddered hard. "Oh, God, I hate this country sometimes. I just hate it."

Erlan felt a tug on her chang-fu, and she looked down into the child's face, which was as round and bright as a moon cake. "You got funny eyes," he said. "They're skinny at the corners."

Clementine laid a hand on her son's head, drawing him back against her knees. "Hush, Charlie. It's impolite to point out another's differences."

A pair of young girls ran past them, just beyond the trees, pulling a kite through the air. The kite's rag tail was laced with playing cards and whistles so that it sang and hummed like a dovecote. The boy Charlie twisted out from beneath his mother's hand and went running after the girls with the kite.

Clementine started to follow, then she saw that the other children had gladly welcomed him into their game, even passing the flying line into his dimpled hands. The kite dipped and soared through the breeze-ruffled sky. Charlie shrieked with laughter, and the sunlight turned his head into a cap of gold.

"He is a beautiful little boy," Erlan said.

Clementine turned back, smiling now. "He's a bit wild, though, I'm afraid."

They began to walk side by side along the riverbank, following the children as they were pulled along by the kite. Clementine had stopped trembling, had even smiled, but Erlan sensed that a battle still raged, deep in the well of her being. There were too many spirits in this woman, Erlan thought, pulling her this way and that and allowing her no peace.

"Why, whatever do you have on your feet?" Clementine said.

Erlan lifted her chang-fu the better to show off her new shoes. "Do you like? They are called croquet sandals." She had found them tucked away in a back corner in the mercantile. The box they'd come in had said they had a vulcanized rubber sole with a canvas upper. Some of these English words were unknown to her, but she did discover that the shoes were wonderfully comfortable. She stretched out her curled and deformed toes, pushing them against the soft sides. "I am allowing my feet to become as big as boats, like a regular American girl."

She'd been loosening the bindings gradually, bathing her golden lilies in herbed water every night to make the calluses and bones soft again. The process was horribly painful, and her feet swelled up like melon gourds every time she walked on them. Her crippled toes would never lie completely flat again, and she would probably always walk like a drunken sailor, but with each passing day, as her feet broadened, she felt all of herself grow stronger. Strong in body and strong in spirit.

She nodded in the direction of the open field, where the band played and couples moved in a circle of swirling skirts and clapping hands, their heels tapping a gentle cadence on the packed earth. "Perhaps someday I shall dance like those ladies. What is it called—the poker?"

"The polka." Clementine flashed another one of her sudden smiles. "You seem happy today, Erlan."

"Perhaps it is more accurate to say that I am at peace. I have stopped cursing my destiny and have decided instead what I shall do."

"You will go home?"

"No. I shall stay. And then I will go home."

So many hours she had spent thinking about her fate, taking long walks, walks that hurt her golden lilies and her head. At times it seemed she had to hold on hard to her jumbled thoughts. She yearned so for the Flowery Land, for her home and for her father, for her sisters and cousins and aunts. Merciful heavens, she even missed her father's three wives. She could not bear to accept a fate that meant she would never see them all again. But she wondered, too, if she were only dragging the lake in search of the moon, if she was not destined after all to spend her life in exile in this alien land, where the gods had surely sent her as a punishment for her mother's shame. And then one day she remembered a proverb her father had once told her: "Many paths of honor lead out of a forest of shame."

She sought now for words to explain. "We Chinese believe that to be born is not enough, to live is not enough. And if that is so, what matters then? Honor matters, and hope." She looked into Clementine's strange eyes, that were wide and intent and full of restless, shifting currents. "I will go home someday because I must. I cannot bear to think I might never see the green tiled roofs and scarlet pillars of my home again. But there is honor involved as well, for what my mother has done will shame all future generations that come of my womb. I must return to the place of my ancestors and find a way to atone for her disgrace. Until then I have no face. I am unable to lift up my head."

"But it seems so unfair to hold you to account for what she did."

Erlan shrugged, for that was the way of things. You were tied to your ancestors and they to you, and what each did affected the honor of all. She would return to her father and seek redemption so that Tao Huo would know peace in the spirit world. Just how she would accomplish this she didn't know, but she couldn't let ignorance or fear cause her to stumble on the path of duty.

She noticed Clementine was studying her intently. "So you must go home for your hope and honor," Clementine said. "But why do you stay now?"

"Because there is also the debt of honor I owe to the merchant Woo, who paid the bride-price for me in good faith, thinking he had acquired a wife to give him sons for his old age. Hope—that I could not live without. But neither could I live with the disgrace of not having paid all of my debts."

"Hope and honor." Clementine smoothed a hand over the gentle swell of her expectant happiness. "Hope and honor. Yes, I see . . . I think. At least I understand why the thought gives you peace."

"And have you not been home since you wed?" Erlan

asked, for she knew from that day of whiskey drinking a part of the story of how Clementine had run away with her rancher lover, to follow him out here to this raw place.

Clementine shook her head. "No, not once. I used to send letters, but they were never answered. I thought that after Charlie . . . that when Father learned he had a grandson, he would relent. But I know in my heart he never will."

"And my father, too, might never relent. The gods don't always let us have what we want."

Clementine's gaze sought out her son. Her husband had joined the boy and the girls with the kite. He was a bright, laughing man with eyes the color of blue porcelain, and Erlan liked him. With him was the brother, a man Erlan did not at all like, for he was too hard and raw and wild, too much a part of the lonely mountains and the endless, empty miles of grass and the even emptier sky. And he had terrible yellow eyes, hard and predatory and fierce, like an eagle's.

"No, we don't always get what we want," Clementine was saying, her eyes on her husband and son, her voice low and rough. "But sometimes what we want isn't right or fair. Or even possible."

Erlan watched as her gaze shifted to her brother-in-law and he looked back at her, and for an instant they loved with their eyes. It was like lightning streaking across a stormy sky, a wild yearning for something the gods would never allow them to have.

Erlan's chest lifted in a sad silent sigh. Oh, Clementine . . . And Hannah, and her *anjing juren*—they were all alike. They seemed like children sometimes, unable to accept that all their rages and protests against the gods were as meaningless as raindrops falling into the ocean. That a soul could not resist its fate any more than grass could stand up before the wind.

Clementine turned, holding out her hand. The pained restlessness was back, biting deep within her now, and the

source of it was the brother-in-law with the empty spirit
and the eagle's eyes. She gripped Erlan's arm, holding on
to it too tightly. "We will be unpacking our picnic basket
soon. Would you care to join us?"

Erlan bowed her head. "This worthless girl is honored
that you would ask, and she . . ." The brother-in-law came
up to them then, and she felt Clementine stiffen as his
shadow fell between them. "She thanks you for your kindness," she went on, "but she must seek out the merchant
Woo. She has something important to say to him."

Clementine squeezed her arm, gently this time, and
managed a smile. "About hope and honor?"

"Yes," Erlan said, her lips curving into an answering
smile. "His, as well as this worthless girl's."

Erlan thought it strange that the Chinese of Rainbow
Springs helped to celebrate this American festival with
things Chinese—with cymbals and gongs, with painted
silk lanterns and dragon flags and baskets of boiled eggs
dyed red for happiness. Strange and sad, too, to celebrate
Independence Day in a land where, because a man was Chinese, he could not till the soil or dig for silver in a mine or
take himself a wife unless he bought a slave girl from the
tong man.

The Chinese had appropriated a distant corner of the
field well away from the foreign devils. The air around
them was filled with the rattling and scraping of fan-tan
beans and mah-jongg tiles, with the smell of duck frying
in peanut oil, green tea brewing, and hot rice wine. If Erlan
shut her eyes, she could almost believe herself back in the
courtyard of her lao chia.

A group of children—demon children—suddenly
dashed around her, forming a circle with their linked hands
to lock her in. "Chinaman, Chinaman, rode 'im out on a
rail!" they shrieked as they skipped around her. "Along
came an Injun and scalped off his tail!"

Laughing and hooting, they danced around her once more and then ran off in search of a fresh victim.

Erlan stood where the children had left her, trembling with an engulfing fear. It was only a game, she told herself, only children's teasing. They had meant nothing wicked by it. Yet she could not stop shaking. She would never belong in this place. Even if she lived a thousand years, even if her bones rested for all eternity in this red soil until they became bleached and weathered like pieces of sea wood, she would never belong here. It was why the Chinese who came to America, even those who never left, always spoke of themselves as sojourners.

At last she spotted the merchant Woo. He was sitting apart from the others, on the protruding roots of an old tree, and smoking on a water pipe. The merchant Woo was not liked by the other Chinese because he tried too hard to be an American, with his smart and sassy talk and his black barbarian suit with the flowery flag pinned to his lapel. But he, too, was only dragging the lake in search of the moon. He could not even own the mercantile he was so proud of; the title was in Hannah Yorke's name.

He looked up as Erlan approached, and no expression crossed his wrinkled, teak-colored face. Since the night she had tried to slit her own throat, the wall between them had grown as high as the one around the Forbidden City.

"There you are," he said, not in his harsh Cantonese, but in the English he forced her to speak. "Where have you been?"

"Walking."

He grunted. "Walk, walk, walk. That is all you ever do, worse than a Buddhist pilgrim, yes? It's a wonder your golden lilies do not ache from it."

"They are growing stronger."

He grunted again and shrugged. He emptied the smoked tobacco out of his pipe, took a fresh pinch from his tobacco box, and poked it into the bowl. He sucked deeply on the tube. The gurgling, bubbling sounds and the ripe tobacco smell brought back bittersweet memories of her father.

"I want to make"—she struggled to find the American word—"a deal. I want to make a deal with you."

He lifted his head and looked up at her out of eyes that were narrowed against the swirl of smoke from his pipe. "Ha. You are going to cut my throat now instead of your own. Instead of being shamed, I will be dead."

She nearly smiled. He was old enough to be her father and not handsome, but she was vain and shallow to let such a thing matter. The truth was, she rather liked him.

She knelt before him on the grass and sat back on her heels. They faced each other, eye to eye, knees almost touching. "This is my deal: you will pay me one dollar a day to work in the mercantile, to cook the meals and keep our rooms clean."

She was pleased with this part of her deal. She could see herself bringing harmony to the merchant's life. Right now all was chaos, which frequently happened when the yang spirit assumed ascendancy. Sam Woo was the sort never to toss out an old broom, never to waste a single grain of rice. She would take inventory of the store and arrange things according to their purpose in life. She would sweep the dust balls out from beneath the bed and scrub the kitchen from top to bottom. She would try very hard not to make lumpy rice, and she would set dishes of that rice before the kitchen god every day, a duty that had been shamefully neglected, doubtless bringing much bad joss.

"I shall work and you will pay me," she said. "One dollar American a day."

The merchant Woo was pretending to weigh her words, stroking his bristly chin whiskers, but she suspected he was secretly laughing at her. "And what do I get for this deal, eh?" he said. "Besides a bellyache and empty pockets?"

She sucked on her lip to hide another smile and modestly lowered her gaze. "My shortcomings are indeed grave, my husband." She smoothed the lap of her chang-fu, plucked at a blade of grass, and tossed it away. She did not look at him. "It will bring me great joy to give you a son."

There, the words were out, and they had not tasted so bitter on her tongue. At least, she thought, she would have the dignity of being a mother to a man's son—that was, after all, the reason she had been born a woman. She would give the merchant Woo a son, and through their son she would be honored.

She had expected her husband to be pleased with this portion of her deal, for without descendants a man was doomed to roam like a vagabond in the shadow world. But beyond going utterly still, he did and said nothing.

In the distance she could hear the strange discordant noise made by the fon-kwei's brass horns. Firecrackers popped and, nearer to them, a Chinese cursed the gods and the fan-tan beans. "And what will you do with all this money I pay you?" he said at last.

"Put it in a box beneath our bed, where the gourd ought to be protecting us from ghosts. And when I have enough, I will give you back my bride-price and buy passage on a ship to the Flowery Land." The ship's passage would cost six hundred American dollars, Sam Woo had paid eight hundred more for her bride-price. It would take many days to earn so much money. And many nights.

He carefully wound the tube of his water pipe around the bowl. They both watched the movement of his fingers, which were brown and wrinkled with age. He looked up at her, his eyes unblinking behind the thick, round spectacles.

He jerked his gaze away, and his chest expanded on a deep breath. "I know what you think of me, a garlic-eater from Canton," and he spoke now in the rough accent of that place. "And you . . ." He waved a hand at her. "Aiya, you are so proud, so high and haughty with your Mandarin ways. You were born to red satin and silver chopsticks; I was born to hemp and wood in a hut with mud walls and a straw-thatched roof. My mother whelped me, the fourth son, on an old rice mat in the morning and was back digging in the field that afternoon. Ha, I say it was a field, though it wasn't even a square mou of land."

He laughed suddenly, a sharp, bitter sound she'd never heard from him before. "Just one of your golden hairpins would have fed my family for a year—we who had but a single bowl of watery rice gruel a day, or a millet cake, if fortune smiled. I cannot remember a time as a boy when my belly wasn't bloated like a dead fish from hunger." His gaze came back to hers, and the bitterness she'd heard in his voice now darkened his eyes. "You yearn for what you have lost. Me, I care not if I ever see the yellow earth of China again."

She swallowed around a strange lump that had suddenly formed in her throat. He was asking something of her, but she didn't know what it was. It didn't matter anyway; she had nothing to give. "I cannot alter what I hope for," she said. "But I can and I shall repay my debt of honor. I will give you a son."

He leaned forward until she could smell his breath—not garlic, but tobacco and American beer. She could see the pits in his skin where the stiff whiskers grew, but she could see as well the brackets around his mouth that came from his smile. "You would make the cloud and the rain with me?" he asked.

"I . . ." Erlan felt like an acrobat trying to walk a bamboo pole. For a moment she was overwhelmed by dark thoughts of wet mouths and probing fingers, of a thrusting hardness pushing up between her thighs, tearing into her . . . She shut her eyes, trying to stop the terror that lashed through her, trying to stop the scream from building in her throat.

All wives do it, she thought. I won't die from it, or even want to anymore. The merchant Woo was a man of good heart. If she asked him, he would try to be kind. It wouldn't be so bad, not like the others.

She forced her eyes to open, and the shuddering ceased. She plucked at the grass again with restless fingers. "There is something you must know. After my father sold me, I . . . I was forced to suffer indignities."

She had expected him to be dismayed or disappointed to hear that he had purchased damaged goods. Instead he merely patted her arm as if her confession had been of no import at all.

"This is no big surprise," he said, once more in English. "You have been like a beaten dog, cringing at the sight of a stick." He stroked her cheek lightly with the tips of his fingers, and he smiled. "I will not hurt you, Lily."

She searched his eyes, seeing the hunger that frightened her still. And an innate kindness that she took comfort from. She lowered her gaze and rose up on her knees, bowing and touching her head three times to the ground. Showing him with this gesture the obedience and loyalty she would give him, as his wife, as the mother of his son, from now until the day she left him to return to her lao chia.

He could have stopped her. She thought he would stop her, for it was not an American thing, a wife kowtowing to her husband. But he didn't.

The trestle table that had been put up on the wooden platform groaned with the weight of the cakes. Apple and cinnamon cakes, macaroon cakes, walnut cakes, fancy ribbon cakes, and sour cream cakes. It was the same platform where Drew Scully had gotten a mangled hand earlier that afternoon, although someone had had the sense to scatter sawdust over the bloodstains.

The cakes were about to be auctioned off by the Ladies Social Club of Rainbow Springs. A man who bought himself a cake got—besides a confection for his sweet tooth—the company of the lady who'd baked it for the duration of the fireworks display later that evening. The money raised went to the school, to buy textbooks and primers and desks, and to pay Miss Luly Maine's salary of twenty-five dollars a month. All the good ladies of Rainbow Springs had, of course, baked cakes for such a worthy cause.

And that, thought Hannah Yorke, was where she was being a fool. She wasn't either good or a lady, and she never would be.

She had arisen well before dawn to bake her own contribution, a molasses cake with stoned raisins. It was the only kind of cake she knew how to make, the kind a coal miner's wife whipped up when there was no money for sugar or candied fruit. Now, seeing all these fancy confections the other women had brought, Hannah figured a molasses and stoned raisin cake—lumpy and lopsided and fallen in upon itself in the middle—fit in about as well as a rattlesnake at a roping contest.

And the fallen woman who had baked it fit in even less.

Hannah's white-laced gloved hands gripped her egg-shell china cake plate so hard it was a wonder it didn't snap in two. She felt almost sick from the sweet smell of all those cakes. All the ladies of Rainbow Springs, those *good* ladies all buttoned up to their chins in stiff disapproval, stood between her and that platform.

But before Hannah had taken more than a step forward, Zach Rafferty blocked her path.

He had a half empty bucket of beer in one hand and a surly look on his face. "I heard tell your new beau just won himself twenty dollars," he said. "Do you reckon I'm gonna have to rob the bank now if I want to buy me a piece of your . . . cake?"

A guilty flush burned her cheeks. "Mr. Scully ain't my beau. He's only . . . he's nothing to me."

"Uh-huh."

His mouth was set mean, but she could see a hurting in his eyes. She thought his jealousy ought to ease the aching tumult in her own heart, but it didn't. And the words slipped out before she could stop them. "Oh, Rafferty . . .

do you ever wonder if maybe being in love shouldn't feel so sad?"

He looked away from her, toward the river and the cottonwoods. "Is that how you're feeling, Hannah? Sad?"

She bit her lip, shaking her head.

"There's never been anything stopping you from leaving," he said.

"No. And that's the trouble, isn't it? There's never been anything stopping either one of us from leaving."

They were leaving each other, she thought, and they both knew it. Only neither one of them was ready to face it just yet.

Lord, she couldn't even bear to think of losing him, of being alone again. Alone and unloved.

She leaned into him and put on her sultriest smile. A smile that had never failed to stir him before. "Aw, honey, what are we talkin' like this for? Maybe we're both a little edgy because of the heat and the crowd, huh? What do you say to you and me taking this cake and goin' on home and puttin' on a fireworks show of our own?"

He tipped his hat to her, and the smile he gave back to her was mostly just a wincing twist of his mouth. "No, thank you, darlin'. Suddenly I ain't in the mood for something sweet."

Hot tears blurred her eyes as she watched him walk away from her. All she'd really done was a little harmless flirting, but right off he'd jumped to the conclusion that she'd be having that boy in her bed before the night was through. Just like all the rest of the world, Zach Rafferty probably figured that if a woman had ever once been a whore, she had lost her scruples along with her virtue.

Just like all the rest of the world . . . She realized that the ladies gathered around the platform had at last noticed her. One by one their heads had swiveled her way and their bright chatter had died. Hannah made herself lift her head and walk toward them.

Suddenly she was possessed with the urge to do

something truly wicked. Such as bare her bosom so that all
their husbands, who'd only been speculating before, could
look their fill; or hold a contest to see who could come up
with the most obscene word for a man's tally-whacker; or
explain to all these *good* ladies just what it was a man really
wanted when he asked for it done the French way. Hunh,
maybe then they would learn a little something that would
put their tongues to a better use than all the gossiping and
the snide remarks they were now aiming her way. *Good* ladies, Hannah thought with a sniff and a thrust of her chin
into the air, always seemed to bring out the outlaw in her.

It wasn't that she had anything to be ashamed of anymore. She was one of the richest people in town; her hotel
and flophouses and the Best in the West were making
money like a mint. But you didn't see any of the men who
owned the other saloons getting snubbed for what they did
to earn a living.

They still called her the town harlot, even though
she'd never been a harlot in this town. But she had allowed
a man into her bed without a ring on her finger to make it
respectable, and in the eyes of Rainbow Springs, that made
Hannah Yorke a fallen woman. And once a girl fell off the
pedestal of virtuous womanhood, there she stayed, because
shinnying back up was like trying to climb a greased pole.

She had almost reached Clementine's side when a
woman with a round mottled face thrust herself between
them. The woman gave Hannah a quelling glare and then
turned to Clementine. "I do certainly hope, Mrs. McQueen,
that you did not invite this jezebel to partake in our cake
social."

Clementine said nothing, merely lifted a brow in
haughty surprise that someone would dare to question her
good judgment, and Hannah almost smiled.

Another woman joined their intimate little circle.
This one was as withered and pinch-mouthed as one of
last year's prunes. "When it was first suggested to us, Mrs.
McQueen, that we invite you to join our society, there

were some who voiced loud objection because of your acquaintanceship with the strumpet. We were persuaded to overlook this lapse of morality on your part, in view of Mr. McQueen's standing in the community and your own Boston connections. However—"

"If you persist in this folly," Mrs. Martin chimed back in, "we very much fear we will be forced not only to remove you as president but to expel you from the society entirely."

Clementine looked down the length of her fine Boston nose with some of the sweetest disdain Hannah had ever seen. "You must do what you think best, Mrs. Martin, Mrs. O'Flarraty, and I must do the same. Now, if you will excuse me, please." And she turned her back on the women, cutting them dead.

"I reckon I ain't gonna be invited to none of their tea parties or church bazaars," Hannah said to her with a weak smile. She had seen Miss Luly Maine, too, hovering within hearing distance. Luly had a saffron cake—a Cornish specialty—in her hands and a look of smug triumph on her face. "Maybe you won't be invited either now, thanks to me."

"Good." Clementine tugged on her glove, smoothing it up over her bunched knuckles. The color was now high in her cheeks. "Then we won't have to come up with any more polite excuses for not attending." She pulled at the velvet Byron collar of her dress, trying to let in a little air. "Oh, heavens. I am so nervous I am perspiring worse than a horse thief at a hanging bee."

A startled laugh burst out of Hannah's tight throat. "Oh, Clementine! Wherever did you pick up such an expression?"

"From Nickel Annie. Really, Hannah, I am about to die of fright. I never would have joined this silly organization in the first place, let alone become its president, if I'd known I was going to have to stand up there and make a spectacle of myself."

Hannah patted her arm. "You'll do fine," she said, although she understood the reason for Clementine's attack of nerves. Respectable, well-brought-up ladies simply did not give speeches and conduct auctions.

Clementine drew in a deep breath and squared her shoulders, as if she were indeed a horse thief about to mount the gallows. "Yes, well . . . Perhaps the thing to do is go and get it over with."

Hannah's fingers tightened on her sleeve. "Auction off my cake first."

Clementine's gaze darted around the milling crowd. "But Rafferty isn't—"

"He ain't here, I know. And I don't expect he's coming. Go on and do mine first. Please. If no other man is brave enough to make a bid, I reckon your Gus will jump in with an offer."

Gus had only now come up to join them. He had his boy by the hand, and the look that came over his face as his gaze settled on his wife was one of pride and yearning and a little awe, as if he still couldn't quite believe even after four years that this paragon of all the female virtues was really his. "Won't you, Gus?" Hannah said, beaming him a smile bright enough to melt lead.

He blinked and looked at her as if only just noticing her existence. "Uh, yeah, sure, Hannah. Sure," he said, though she knew he hadn't the foggiest notion of what he'd just agreed to.

She had no fear, anyway, that Gus would have to come to her rescue. She had seen Drew Scully standing at the back of the crowd, and she knew what he was after. If that boy had to buy a lopsided, lumpy molasses cake with stoned raisins to get it, he would.

Clementine took Hannah's cake from her hands and climbed onto the platform. She set the cake among the others on the trestle table, pulled at her collar, and cleared her throat.

Hannah studied her friend, feeling proud of her. She

looked so much the fine lady up there in her classy dress of olive-green foulard silk. And it was so much like Clementine that, while the cut of the waist concealed her delicate condition, in her nervousness she was rubbing her palm over and over her rounded belly so that no one watching could possibly miss it.

"Education," Clementine began in a trembling voice that grew steadily firmer with each word, "is a prerequisite of civilization. We cannot afford to allow our children to grow up to be barbarians for want of the proper tools for learning . . ."

She paused and looked down at Charlie and the almost desperate love she felt for her child suffused her face and plucked at Hannah's heart. She remembered something Clementine had said to her once, years ago, when poor Saphronie had lost her little girl: "She is also a mother. No matter in what ways you both have sinned, you are *women.* Like me."

"Is Mama gonna eat all those cakes by herself?" Charlie demanded loudly.

"Hush, now," Gus said. "She's going to be selling them, button."

Charlie pulled against his father's hand, pointing at the pathetic-looking specimen Hannah had baked with her own two hands that morning. "I want that one. Buy me that cake, Papa!"

Gus restrained his son by planting two rope- and rein-callused fingers on the boy's shoulders. He tossed a grin at Hannah. "If my boy has anything to say about it, you'll be watching the fireworks with him tonight."

Hannah bit her lip, not sure whether she should smile back at him or not, though she could feel her dimples deepening of their own accord. She and Gus had been easier with each other the last couple of years. He still didn't approve of her, and he never would. But he had quit kicking against her very existence.

Clementine had finished her speech and had now taken

up the auctioneer's gavel. She began to extol the virtues of Hannah's cake, making it sound as if it had come from the kitchen of a prize-winning Parisian chef.

Hannah elbowed Gus in the ribs. "Bid."

"Huh?"

She poked him again. "Go on now, cowboy. You promised."

He squinted at her in confusion, then a sudden smile creased his face. He put a finger into the air as if testing the direction of the wind. "One dollar."

"Twenty dollars!" Drew Scully shouted.

Chock-full of brag and fight, he was. Hannah almost laughed aloud right then. She wanted to throw her arms around his neck and kiss him. She had the satisfaction of hearing all the *good* ladies of Rainbow Springs gasp with shock, and of seeing Miss Luly Maine's face crumble with disappointment. *Her* cake sure wouldn't fetch anything near like twenty bucks, and she wouldn't be spending the fireworks-watching time making sheep's eyes at Drew Scully, either.

"Sold!" Clementine slammed the gavel down so hard and fast that Miss Luly Maine's saffron cake almost slid off the other end of the table.

Drew Scully pushed his way up to the platform, slapped his hard-won double-eagle gold piece on the table, picked up his cake, and came for Hannah Yorke. Hannah took a step forward to meet him, slipping a hand into the crook of his arm.

"You gonna tell me what's going on?" Gus demanded.

"Nope," she tossed back over her shoulder, and then she did laugh.

She didn't look at the boy until they were free of the crowd around the auction, although she could feel his intent gaze on her. "Won't your brother mind that you've spent all your prize money on a molasses cake?" she said. She looked up in time to catch his soft, slow smile.

"I'll explain to the lad how it went for a good cause."

Another laugh gurgled up her throat. "And what cause is that, Mr. Scully?"

He widened his eyes in a useless effort to look innocent. "Why, schoolbooks and slates and such, I thought 'twas."

"How noble of you, sir. And for your reward you are to have my molasses cake, and an hour or two of my company."

"For now."

She started to pull away from him, but he held her hand in place on his arm. "Don't go getting your dander up. I didn't mean that how it sounded. I only meant you can expect me to be behaving myself for now."

"And later?"

"You'll be havin' to take your chances later on, my beautay," he drawled, exaggerating his Cornish brogue.

She laughed again, suddenly no longer caring what all those *good* ladies thought of her. She was Hannah Yorke, keeper of a thirst parlor and a fallen woman, and that damn pedestal she'd fallen off of so long ago could go topple into hell for all she cared. She might have wanted it to be different once, but it was too late for wishing and wanting. Now she had to take what she could get.

And at the moment what she had was the arm of a handsome young man who'd just tossed away twenty dollars for an hour or two of her company. She cast another sideways glance at him. She wanted to trace his sullen lower lip with the tip of her tongue. To push her fingers through the thickness of his dark brown hair. To watch the reckless hunger flash in his granite-gray eyes.

He selected a spot in the shelter of the cottonwoods along the river. He took off his coat and spread it on the grass for her sit on. He stretched out beside her and put the twenty-dollar cake between them.

He rolled up his shirtsleeves and loosened his tie against the heat that had built up over the afternoon. The sun was just starting to slip behind the western mountains, leaving red streaks in the sky. The wind would pick up soon, but the heat would cling to the earth for a while yet.

Beside them the river moved silently, sluggishly. Hannah felt suddenly sleepy, drugged with sun and air. She breathed and smelled horse. About a dozen of them were tied up to a rope fence staked out across the river. They dozed in the heat, tails switching at flies. It was hard to believe these docile creatures were of the same species as the mustangs that roamed the open prairie beyond the Rain-Dance Butte. But these saddle ponies had been tamed. The mustangs were the wild ones.

He was one of the wild ones, was Drew Scully. Once you'd seen a wild one running free through the tall grass, chasing the wind, no other would do. Only a wild one seemed worth having. But you couldn't keep him unless you tamed him, and once you tamed him you no longer wanted him, because he wasn't a wild one anymore.

She kept her eyes off the boy and on the horses, but she thought of him and something swelled within her, a yearning that brought swift color to her cheeks.

"What are you thinking, Hannah Yorke?"

Her head swung around, a frown pulling at her mouth. "How old are you? And don't lie."

"I wasn't going to lie. I'm nearly twenty."

She flipped open her fan and flapped it vigorously through the heavy air. "Land, a baby."

His fingers closed over her wrist, stilling her hand. His smile was part boy and part devil. "Not such a baby where it matters, Hannah. Care to give me a try?"

She couldn't help but laugh at the way he betrayed his cocky youth. But then, all men from eight to eighty took such pride in what hung between their legs, and they never stopped marveling at what it could do.

She pulled her wrist from his grasp. Yet the feel of his fingers remained, warm, tingling. "You ought to be calling me Mrs. Yorke," she said. "I'm old enough to be your mother."

He grinned at her. "You don't look like any mother I've ever known. And besides, you're not—old enough to be my mother, that is."

"Near enough." There was thirteen years' difference between them, a lifetime in every way that mattered. She knew what he wanted from her, what he would take if she let him. He would dally with her until he was ready to settle down and have a family. And then he would look around for the right sort of girl to be his wife, someone young and sweet-tempered. Someone virginal.

And someone like Miss Luly Maine would wind up with the gold ring.

Well, what did she want with a gold ring anyway? She wasn't the marrying kind, not Hannah Yorke. Hadn't she thought this whole thing through a hundred thousand times before? It was too late for wishing and wanting. Maybe she was the one who should be taking what she could get.

For a while, for the moment, she could make this boy love her, for if she was good at anything, she was good at that. The thought brought her a rush of fear and shame. It was a frightening and shameful thing—to realize that you wanted to be loved more than you wanted anything.

He drew up one knee, bracing his elbow on it, his hand dangling. Blood had started to seep through the bandage. But his other hand, the uninjured one that lay still for the moment in the grass, had scars on it as well, from where chips of blasted rock had nicked his flesh and other errant hammers had left their mark. Her father had had hands like his.

The hand that had been lying so peacefully in the grass moved suddenly and came toward her face. She held herself still as he threaded his fingers through the heavy ringlets that fell over her shoulder. He leaned into her. Her head filled with the yeasty smell of the beer he'd been drinking all afternoon. And the smell of him.

"Will you let me kiss you?" he said.

Her mouth thickened and burned beneath his gaze, as if he had already done so. She wet her lips. "No."

"I think you want me to kiss you."

She jerked her head away and drew in a deep, wit-saving breath. "I think you want me to slap your face."

"Am I never going to be getting you out of your corset stays, Mrs. Yorke?"

"I think it very unlikely, Mr. Scully."

Somehow his hand was back in her hair again, and then his fingers were sliding across her collarbone, which pressed against the creamy Belgian lace of her bodice. She swallowed hard, and the bone jerked beneath his touch.

His smile was knowing. "A challenge always does get my blood up. My blood and other things."

She smacked him on the arm with her fan, hard enough to leave a welt. "You, sir, are wicked."

"You, lady, are a tease," he said. His head fell back and a laugh burst out of him. A man's laugh, deep, sensual. Sunlight glistened off the sweat on his strong throat. It glimmered in the brown hair on his bare arms, arms strong enough to wield a sixteen-pound hammer, strong enough to hold a woman tight.

She took a breath, and as if one wasn't enough, she took another. Oh, Lord, Lord, Lord, what a fool she was. She shouldn't be sitting here laughing and smiling and teasing with him, knowing it was only a matter of time before they would be lying upstairs on her big soft bed, making the mattress groan and the springs squeak, making memories that were only going to hurt down the years. She ought to be running away from this boy as fast and far as she could.

This boy she could love in an instant, and with all of her heart.

A lone dust devil danced down the street, spun around a corner, and disappeared into the pale light of the setting

sun. Gus followed it down the row of saloons and bawdy
houses that lined the south end of Dublin Patch. It seemed
strange to see this part of town so empty. But then, everyone was up at the big meadow awaiting the fireworks.

He stopped in front of the Gandy Dancer. The saloon
was a new building, as most were in Rainbow Springs, but
it looked old enough to have quenched the thirst of Lewis
and Clark. The logs were weathered as gray as old buffalo
bones, and the mud chinking was crumbling. The signboard swung loose on one hinge in the wind and had been
riddled so many times by bullets it could have been used
to net trout.

Being mostly a teetotaling man, Gus didn't patronize
many saloons, and if he'd wanted to wet down a parched
throat with a beer or sarsaparilla, he wouldn't have picked
the Gandy Dancer. It was sure enough his little brother's
kind of place, though. The boy and Hannah must've had
a lovers' tiff, because they'd been avoiding each other all
day, and then she'd gone off with that rock-buster who'd
bid a double-eagle on her cake. Now trust Zach to crawl
off to the worst hellhole in Rainbow Springs to soothe his
wounds.

Except that Zach never was one for seeking company
when he was brooding. Uneasiness trickled down Gus's
spine as he looked up and down the deserted street. His
brother wouldn't have gone to the trouble to pay an old
Indian two bits to track him down and direct him here unless it was important.

He pushed open the swinging doors and blinked
against the sting of thick cigar smoke. Inside, the saloon
was just about what he'd expected it to be: air fetid with
whiskey and tobacco, sawdust on the floor to soak up the
spilled booze, deer antlers and curling brewery calendars
tacked on the bullet-peppered walls, chairs worn bare of
varnish, and tables circle-stained by wet glasses.

He searched the packed room, his gaze pausing a moment on the oil painting above the bar. It was of two naked

women making love to each other. Gus's lips pinched inward with disgust.

He found his brother at one end of the bar, near a bunch of men who were standing like cows around a salt lick, spectating a poker game in progress. Zach acknowledged him by lifting his glass. The whiskey was already flowing wild in his eyes.

"Trouble," he said, "is once again among us."

Gus followed his brother's gaze. It was trouble all right—sitting all slicked up in fancy duds in the midst of the poker game with a mountainous pile of silver and bills at his elbow. One-Eyed Jack McQueen leaned back in his chair and fired up a long, thin cigar while the dealer fanned the cards.

Lamplight glinted off his long oiled hair, combed back sleek as jet against his skull. A pearl stickpin the size of a man's thumbnail nestled in the snowy folds of his silk tie. A seal-heavy gold watch chain stretched across his red satin vest. A fine linen handkerchief peeked out the pocket of his black frock coat. And an ebony-handled cane was hooked on the arm of his chair.

"What the devil did he do—rob a bank?"

Zach tossed off the last of his shot, grimacing as the raw booze bit deep. "Most likely he just hornswoggled someone good."

Gus fought off a violent urge to slam his fist into a wall. He really thought they'd finally gotten ridden of the old man, and now here he was back again. For two years they had been held up to shame before their friends and neighbors while the Reverend Jack McQueen traveled the sawdust trail of revivals and tent meetings throughout western Montana, using his God-given gift of gab to wheedle money out of the poor, the sick, and the hungry.

Unfortunately, a propitious flash of forked lightning during an early preaching had convinced the country's shepherdless flock to open up their pockets. But it didn't take long for the Reverend Jack to fall back into his old sins of drinking, fighting, whoring, and gambling. Eventually even the most gullible sheep got wise, and the dollars stopped ringing in the old stovepipe hat. One day in the fall of 1881, he'd up and disappeared, and Gus had thought that at last his prayers had been answered.

Now here he was back again, as perennial and tormenting as fleas in summer. From the look of things, he'd given up on the sin-busting game and found another way to separate the world's fools from their hard-earned money.

The last hand had played itself out in a hurry and the deck had passed to One-Eyed Jack for the deal. Gus watched the graceful, long-fingered hands cut and shuffle the cards. When he was a boy the cards had seemed to take on life in his father's hands. Like magic, he could make them appear and disappear, turn a deuce into an ace, or shift a king from the bottom to the top of the deck. He had passed the tricks on to both his sons, but only Zach had had any talent for it. Gus thought of the hours he had spent watching Zach practice palming a card, learning how to cheat.

For the first time Gus took note of the other players in the game: Doc Corbett, Snake-Eye, and Pogey and Nash. The whiskey glowed like lampshine in their faces.

"They're playing no-limit straight stud, no joker," Zach said. He signaled to the bartender, who poured him another shot and drew a small glass of beer for a chaser. Zach took the makings of a cigarette out the pocket of his unbuttoned vest. "Big stakes and let losers cry."

"Big stakes?" Snake-Eye's livery was a mint in disguise, and it was said the doc had East Coast money. But all the two old prospectors had was their income from the Four Jacks lease, which kept them fine in whiskey and five-dollar-ante poker games, but didn't allow for any big-stakes doings. "What are Pogey and Nash playing with?"

"The old man bankrolled them. Five thousand dollars against their eighty percent of the Four Jacks claim. They've lost most it of back to him already."

"Lost it!" Gus's hands jerked into fists. "Lost it? My God, you know him, you know how he is. How could you just stand here and let it happen?"

Zach lit the cigarette dangling from his lips. "Because I don't fancy myself my brother's keeper like you do."

Gus growled deep in his throat and started to push past his brother, who laid a heavy hand on his arm. "You can't horn in on another's man's game," Zach said.

"I can if he's dealing from the bottom of the deck."

"He ain't."

"How can he not be? You know the man—he's as crooked and wily as a snake and always has been."

Zach's hat brim rose slightly as he peered at him from underneath it. "I've been standing here letting it happen, remember? He's shooting square."

"Well, hell." Gus shot a glare in the direction of his father and rubbed the back of his neck. He supposed that it took a scoundrel to know a scoundrel, and if anyone could tell if the old man was cheating, it would be Zach.

He also trusted his brother's sense of right and justice about as far as he could spit a brick. He narrowed his eyes the better to study the action at the table.

The Reverend Jack was drawing deep on his cigar, making its tip glow fierce. He nodded at Pogey, whose turn it was to ante or fold. Each man had one hole card and three cards showing. "It's back to you again, old-timer. Are you staying?"

Pogey took a peep at his hole card. He combed his beard, gave the hanging flap of his earlobe a tug, rubbed the shiny dome of his head, aimed a shot of tobacco cud in the general direction of the spittoon, then took another peep at his hole card.

Nash stretched and scratched at a fleabite on his skinny chest. "You foldin' or staying, Pogey?"

"I'm thinkin'."

"Well, think a little faster. You're so slow you'd miss your own funeral."

Pogey rubbed his nose. "Anybody ever tell you, pard, that it's hard to put a foot in a shut mouth?" He tapped his hole card with a gnarled knuckle. "A faint heart never filled a flush—I'm stayin'."

Every man stayed and every man held a pair in sight, except Pogey, who had three clubs. Nash had tens to a queen. Snake-Eye had a pair of jacks to a four. The doc had treys to a six. And the Reverend Jack had a pair of deuces to an eight.

He began to deal around the fifth card. "Here comes the train, gentlemen, rolling down the track. A queen matches a queen and two pairs in sight. A five to the jacks and no visible help. A heart for the clubs and the flush goes bust. Another trey and the doc is sitting pretty with three of a kind. The dealer draws a deuce." He set down the deck and looked over at Nash. "Your bet, sir."

Pogey pitched in his ruined flush. "I'm busted."

"Amen to that," Snake-Eye said as he turned over his cards.

"Three lousy treys don't like the odds of bucking two pairs in sight," the doc said. "But I'll ride 'em for a while yet. I'm in for a hundred."

Nash added a wad of crumpled bills to the pile in the middle of the table. "Call and bump five hundred."

Nash might have been an owl sitting on a fence for all the expression he wore. But his bet revealed what his face didn't. He had a full house, either queens and tens or tens and queens.

The Reverend Jack contemplated the coal of his cigar. From what showed on the table he couldn't beat Nash's full house, unless he had a fourth deuce hiding in the hole.

"I will see you and raise it fifteen hundred," he said.

"He's bluffing," Gus said out the side of his mouth. "He always could run a bluff and make it stick."

A half smile flicked across Zach's mouth. "Brother, never bet your convictions against a bluff."

The doc pulled a disgusted face and tossed in his hand.

"I knew these treys would last about as long as shit in a goose. I'm out."

Nash peered at his cards with his large liquid eyes. "What's it to me, then?"

"Fifteen hundred," the Reverend Jack said.

The money left at Nash's elbow looked shy of the bet. A silence settled over the table, as thick as the smoke puffing from the end of One-Eyed Jack's cigar. Pogey flipped through what was left of his stake and passed most of it over to Nash, leaving only a few forlorn bills.

"I'll see ya, then," Nash said, and the last of the Four Jacks silver mine went into the pot.

Jack McQueen blew another plume of smoke over the table and then slowly, drawing out the drama of it, turned over his hole card. It was the fourth deuce.

Chairs scraped across the rough floor as the game broke up, and players and spectators alike crowded around the bar in a hurry to make up for lost drinking time. One minute it seemed to Gus that Zach was finishing off the last of his whiskey, and the next thing he knew, his brother was so close to disappearing out the door that Gus had to take long strides to catch up with him.

He grabbed him by the shoulder. "Just where do you think you're going?"

The face Zach turned to him was as blank as a fresh snowdrift. "I thought I'd go and watch the fireworks."

"You send for me to come down and witness this . . . this travesty, and now you're going to sashay on out of here as if nothing's happened?"

"What do you want me to do—play a funeral dirge for you on the piano? I told you he wasn't cheating. Those two old fools fell into his hands like a couple of ripe peaches on a hot summer day, and he ate 'em all up but for the pits."

"Then you can just go and win it all back."

"Now, how in sweet hell am I going to do that? I've got maybe all of ten dollars to stake. That and my share in the ranch."

"You could cheat." Gus's mouth pulled into a tight smile. "I heard you were taught by the best of them."

Zach's dark brows lifted in eloquent mockery. "I ain't believin' I'm hearing this out the mouth of my big brother, who wouldn't say boo to the devil—"

"Dammit, Zach."

"Like you said, I was taught by the best of them and so were you, though you never were much good at it. Maybe I've picked up a few tricks he doesn't know. But then, maybe he knows a few tricks he never showed me. You want to bet the ranch on which of us is the sharper blackleg?"

Zach held his gaze for a moment, then turned on his bootheel, slapped open the door, and disappeared into the twilight.

"It looks like you and I are partners in a silver mine, son. Would you care for a cigar?"

Gus looked down into the open silver case, at the expensive cigars banded with silk, then back up into his father's canny blue eye. "You give up preaching to take up gambling full-time now? What happened—did the power of the Spirit desert you in the middle of the night?"

The reverend shook his head, clicking his tongue against the roof of his mouth. "Gustavus, Gustavus. For all your dreaming, you simply never have had any vision. 'I am the voice of one crying in the wilderness, Make straight the way of the Lord.' Except there isn't any wilderness anymore. It's been ruined by all these committees of elders with their building funds and membership drives. Organized religion has come in and taken all the fun and money out of preaching. So I followed the good Lord's holy promptings and took the pasteboards back up again in a serious way." He clamped his teeth deep into the butt of the cigar and looked himself up and down, his eye twinkling with mischief. "From the appearance of things, I would say I've found my true calling in this latter half of my interesting life."

Gus shook his head. Although he hadn't had so much

as a beer all day, he felt a little drunk. His father could do that to him—confuse him until he didn't know which end was up. "The only calling I've ever known you to follow," he said, "was to stir up trouble just for the sick joy you seem to get out of watching it mess up other people's lives."

"I suppose you'd rather see me spend my days facing the ugly end of a mule, busting sod, or button-holed up in some tiny room bent over a ledger, getting ink stains on my cuffs and putting a strain on the only good eye I got left. Why, if you had your druthers—"

Gus sputtered a hollow laugh. "If I had my druthers I'd see you run out of Rainbow Springs on a rail."

Jack pressed a hand to his heart. "You wound me, son—grievously, most grievously. And what have I ever done to deserve it? What have I ever done to you boys except allow you to find your own merry way to hell?" His mouth pulled into his wily smile. "If you go around seeking the light, Gustavus, you must also be willing to face the darkness."

Gus breathed a weary sigh. "I don't suppose it's ever occurred to you to try and earn your living by honest means?"

"'He that walketh uprightly, walketh surely.'" He took the cigar from his mouth, examined it, and tossed it into a sawdust spit box. "Maybe I will, now that I own a silver mine. Are you looking to unload your twenty percent? If you are, I'm buying."

Gus anchored his hat down on his head and put the flat of his hand on the door. "Too bad for you, because I'm not selling—"

He was interrupted by gunfire.

It was just a bunch of miners, who'd had a little too much beer and sunshine and who'd taken a notion to anticipate the fireworks display by displaying a few fireworks of their own. They'd hitched up an empty lumber wagon, climbed into the box, sent it careening down the street, and tried to see how many windows and signs they could kill. Bullets rained into the Gandy Dancer, clattering like hail, splintering tables and chairs, slapping into the walls, and busting open three full kegs of not-yet-diluted whiskey.

After the gunfire stopped, Gus picked himself up off the floor, brushed the broken glass, wood chips, and whiskey out of his hair, knocked the sawdust off his knees, and looked around, his heart pounding, to see if the old man had gotten himself shot.

But wild and ricocheting bullets weren't known for their discrimination. It was Nash who was laid out beneath the shattered front window, a dark red stain spreading over the lighter, faded red of his shirt. Pogey knelt over him, a look of disbelief on his face.

Gus slopped through gushing streams of whiskey to get there just as Pogey gripped his partner by the arms and shook him. "Nash, Nash, damn you, say something. God almighty, but if this ain't the one time in yore life when yore jaw ain't a-flappin', and I'd give my left nut just to hear you grunt."

Nash stirred, grunting loudly. "Pogey?" He started to sit up and then looked down and saw the blood leaking out of a hole in his chest, and his eyes opened wide. "Pogey, them sons of bitches went and kilt me."

Pogey rocked back on his heels. He scrubbed at the wetness on his face, which was about half and half tears and whiskey. "Your timin' stinks, ya know that, compadre? You go an' get yerself kilt on the day it decides to rain bug juice."

By this time Doc Corbett had made his way through the rivers of whiskey and the men who were trying to drink it up fast before it evaporated or got soaked up by the sawdust or ran down into the cracks between the floorboards. He hunkered down next to the gunshot man and peeled back the striped suspenders and blood-soaked shirt. He tsked and shook his head, and Pogey choked down a sob.

"He's not going to die," the doc said. "You're not going to die."

Nash creaked his head up, the better to aim his glare at the doc. "What d'you know about it? I'm gushing blood like a Yellowstone geyser and I hurt worse'n a blue bitch. If anybody oughta know when a feller's dyin', it oughta be the feller what's dyin'."

Just then someone with a bit of sense must have figured out that alcohol, burning coal oil, and flying bullets were a dangerous combination, for suddenly the lamps went out.

Nash's head fell back and he moaned. "It's growing dark. Give me your hand, Pogey." His own hand groped along the whiskey-sodden floor. "I'm fadin', fadin' fast now. I can't hardly see a thing——" This last word ended on a cough and he moaned again. "The death rattle, Pogey . . . she's a-buildin' in my chest. It won't be long now."

Doc Corbett looked up at Gus and grinned as he pulled at one end of his waxed handlebar mustache. "The bullet's lodged against the collarbone. Soon as I fetch my instruments I'll have it out quicker and slicker than a greased pig."

A tenor broke into a song about smiling Irish eyes and was soon joined by a bass and a baritone.

"I hear angels singin'!" Nash exclaimed.

Pogey snatched off his hat and whacked him on the leg with it. "Will you quit it, you larruping ol' fool? The doc says you ain't dyin'."

Nash, who'd had his eyes squeezed shut in anticipation of the glories of heaven, popped one open and then the other. "I ain't? Well, hellfire, what for are you dripping all over me like a wet blanket, Pogey? Push me on over beneath that there barrel. Time and whiskey's a-wastin'!"

Rapt faces turned toward the heavens, and mouths fell open in breathy oohs and ahs as the rockets burst into noisy rainbow blossoms in the deep blue well of darkness that was a Montana night.

Gus picked his way through the shadowy figures sitting on the grass. He reeked of whiskey, and he wondered how he was going to explain it to Clementine. She had expected him back in time for the fireworks, but he'd figured the least he could do was see Pogey through the trauma of having a bullet dug out of his collarbone—not only because the man was his friend but because it was his father who had cleaned out the poor old prospector's pockets just minutes before he was shot.

He found her sitting on a blanket with his brother. Charlie lay between them, so worn out he was sleeping through the noise. Zach leaned against the trunk of a cottonwood, one leg bent, his wrist resting on his knee. Clementine was leaning back on her braced hands, her face turned toward his brother's. They weren't talking, though. All they appeared to be doing was looking at each other.

"There you are, Gus," she said as he came up to them, and a sweet smile softened her face. She looked beautiful, her hair shining and her eyes sparkling with the bursts of colored fire.

Gus sat down and slipped his arm around her waist. A ball of fire streaked across the sky with a shrieking whistle and an exploding hail of sparks. Light rippled across the blanket in intermittent flashes of red, white, and blue. His brother turned his head and their eyes met, and Zach's face lit up with a splendid smile that was brighter than any rocket.

And yet, and yet . . . A thought came to Gus, came more as a feeling, as a tight ache in his chest. A thought that there had been something in the air between them, between his brother and his wife. Something he had shattered when he stepped into the circle made by the blanket they shared. Like taking a mallet to a sheet of the thinnest ice.

But the thought slipped away and was forgotten as Clementine put her hand on his knee and leaned into him, and he breathed deeply of the wild rose smell of her, and he felt the warmth of her body.

"Look at our Charlie," she said. "Sleeping like a little angel while the sky rains fire." And she laughed her laugh that was as soft and pure as a fresh snowfall. Together they looked at their son, and together they smiled.

22

THEIR CHARLIE DIED ON a day in late August when the chokecherries hung fat and black on the trees. The sky was so deep a blue, the air so clear, the mountains had that sharp, transparent look, and the river caught the sunlight, reflecting it back to the heavens. And the grass was long and soft, and the color of his hair.

In the days that followed, Clementine held the moment of it in her mind and lived it over and over, and the memory of it was like the loop of a lasso, twirling, twirling, twirling through her head. It always began with her standing at the kitchen window and the men in the corral mating a stud horse to a mare.

The kitchen smelled of the oatmeal she had fixed for breakfast that morning. The day was warm and the cotton-woods were turning their leaves up to the sun. Thieving jays were raiding the chicken feed scattered over the yard, and Charlie was pretending to shoot at them from between the porch rails with his wooden gun. "Bang!" he would shriek. "You're dead! Bang! Bang!"

The men had brought the stud into the corral. The mare stood with her hind legs spread, her tail raised to one side, winking her female opening. The stud pranced and strutted and whistled, for he had done this before. He advanced on the mare, his organ large and proud. He mounted her and bit her neck, and she screamed.

Caught up in her memory loop, sometimes Clementine would watch this happen, but not always. Sometimes she would turn away from the kitchen window, because she always hated how, afterwards, after the stud was done covering the mare, he danced away and curled his lip as if with disdain.

But whether she was looking out the window or had turned away, it is always the sound of Charlie's shrill laughter she heard next. And she realized he was no longer shooting jays from the porch. He was running, running toward the corral, where the stud was rearing and screaming and tearing at the air with scythe-like hooves. He was running and shouting something, and laughing, laughing, laughing.

And she was running as well, although it always seemed her legs were pumping through air as thick as sorghum syrup, and the world exploded into shouts and a horse's wild neighs, and the dust swirled up to veil the sun.

Then the dust cleared and Gus was on his knees in the corral. Terrible sounds were coming out of his chest, and a scolding jay was flitting from fence post to fence post, and the wind was crying wild through the cottonwoods, and Charlie wasn't laughing anymore.

And she was running, running until she hit the solid wall of her love's chest. His hands wrapped hard around her arms, holding her, and his face was the gray of the dust that still floated through the air.

"Let me go to him. I must see him," she said, and there was this coldness inside of her.

Her love tried to press her head to his chest, tried to shield her eyes with his heart. "No, darlin', it'd do no good. He's gone."

A part of her had already lived a thousand years into a future where there was no Charlie, where there was nothing but this moment, and if the memory of it had to begin with her standing at the kitchen window, then it also had to have an ending, a slip-knot in the loop. She had to see her Charlie dead to know that it was so.

So she pulled away from her love and walked slowly toward the corral. Gus had Charlie in his arms and he was rocking and howling at the sky. There was no blood, except for a small drop at the corner of his mouth. His eyes were open, but there was no light in them. There was no light in all the world, because his chest was caved in, and he was dead.

Clementine sat in a bentwood rocker and stared out her bedroom window. The cane seat creaked as she rocked, and the curved slats rasped on the rough pine floor. The world outside was bathed in harsh sunlight, but she pulled the pretty hand-pieced quilt that Hannah had given her tightly around her. For her there was no light in all the world, and she was cold.

It had been a summer of hot sun and little rain, and now it was a dry and bitter fall. The days had grown shorter and the shadows of the mountains fell hard across the buffalo grass. The larch needles had turned color and were falling, slashing and cutting through the air like thin gold daggers. The wild geese honked as they flew low overhead, and a chicken hawk drew lassos of memory in the sky, and she thought how Charlie would never learn to fly now, how all the things she had wanted for him he would never grow up to have.

And so she rocked, and at night the moon came up big and white and hard. Her eyes followed it as it floated through the thick blackness of the night, and the coyotes mourned, wailing and howling for her, since she could not. Hour after hour she rocked and looked out the window at the brutal mountains and the sun-seared, wind-flattened grass. And at the empty, empty sky.

She rocked, and from her window she could see the buffalo hunter's cabin, the fat, flat silver ribbon of the river, and the haystacks in the shade of the giant cottonwoods. And Charlie's grave. It had been two months since they buried him. On the day they buried him she had sat in this rocker and listened to the sounds of death: the grating of saw and hammer making the coffin, the clang and ring of the shovels digging the grave . . . her husband's sobs. But not her own. She wouldn't cry. She never cried.

She had stood by the open grave and smelled the raw pine of his coffin and the freshly dug earth, and each breath she took was an abomination. The world was dark, the world was in a shroud, the world was being put into a hole in the ground. The world was dark, but she could hear. She could hear the creak of the rope as it lowered the coffin into the grave and a soft thud as Charlie's body shifted within it. She could hear the wind crying through the cottonwoods, and rock and dirt falling on wood, and her husband's sobs.

She rocked and looked out the window, and she hugged to her breast a photograph album with a white lace cover. She never opened it. She didn't want to look at these Charlies made from light, when the world was all darkness. When the world lay sealed in a pine coffin in a hole in the ground.

She rocked and watched the leaves drift from the cottonwoods into the river. She watched them being carried away to the sea. She was dead inside like the leaves, dry and brittle. She wanted to fall into the river and be taken far, far away from the mountains and the wind and the endless empty miles of grass.

Once, she had taken the heart-shaped sachet of coins out of its hidey-hole. She had clutched it in her hand, intrigued by its weight, by the solid feel of it. She spilled some of the coins into her lap. Many were gold, like the cottonwood leaves. And she wondered . . . if she threw them in the river, would they be carried out to sea? Could she go with them?

She rocked, and the baby thrust against her belly. Her breasts felt heavy and swollen. She tried to think of this child being born, the sweet ache of it suckling and pulling the life-giving milk from her nipples. But all she could think of was its dying, of its being put in the ground alongside Charlie and the other she had lost when she was in her eighth month.

She rocked and looked out the window. Gus was across the yard, chopping wood. The ax flashed through the air and landed with a *whunk,* and the wood blasted apart and pieces of it spun away like shrapnel through the air. She thought how dangerous chopping wood was, how she must be careful to keep Charlie away from his father while he did it. And then she remembered. Charlie was dead.

They lived on, she and Gus, they ate and slept and did the chores that filled a day, but there was nothing between them anymore. They made words sometimes, but the words couldn't bridge the chasm, and she could not bear to have Gus touch her.

She rocked, and she watched her husband chop wood, and she heard the rasp of her love's spurs on the floor behind her. She could always tell when he entered a room; even now she could tell. He was still her love. He would always be her love. But she never spoke to him or looked at him, because she wanted to stop loving him, even though that was impossible.

He came up to her, so close she could see his jean-clad leg and dusty black boot, though she would not look at him. "I was wondering if you wanted to go for an easy ride up to the buffalo canyon," he said.

She focused her gaze on the swing of the ax and said nothing.

"You need to get out. You need to feel the sun on your

face and the wind in your hair. If not for yourself, then for that babe you're carryin'."

"In that hole where you put my Charlie there is no sun, no wind to blow in his hair. There is nothing but cold and dark."

She heard his sharp intake of breath and then the long, sad sigh as he let it out. The words had surprised her as they came out her own mouth. She hadn't wanted to say them. Words were useless, meaningless things anyway. Like his name—Charlie. She said his name over and over, but it only hung there in the empty air.

"Clementine . . ." He laid his hand on her shoulder. His fingers were strong and urgent as they pressed into her flesh. "You got to let it out. Cry, maybe. Or swear, or scream. But you got to—"

Anger surged up her throat, burning and bitter, and it drove her out of the chair with such force the rockers skidded and screeched across the bare pine floor, and the photograph album fell with a heavy thud. "How *dare* you tell me how to mourn! I carried him in my womb for nine months and fed him from my own breast. He was my baby. My *baby.*"

He gripped her arms and gave her a small, hard shake. "Damn you, woman. You're killing Gus." She tried to twist free of him and he opened his hands wide, letting her go, taking a step back. "You are killing my brother."

She felt her lips peel back from her teeth in a dreadful rictus of a smile. "Do you think I don't wish him in that grave?" She pointed a stiff, shaking finger out the window. "That I don't wish you both in there in place of my son?"

He was silent for a moment, only stared at her with those uncomfortable brassy eyes. He shook his head. "You don't mean that."

She could see it in his eyes. A part of her could see the pain and devastation that was as bitter and terrible as her own. But she didn't care. He could go to hell. Yes, she wished him in hell, with her. She wanted everyone in the world to suffer as she was suffering. To feel this pain that was in her bones and her flesh, in her blood. And this vast, vast emptiness inside her.

She closed her eyes against the suffering she saw in his face and made a small helpless sound. "Leave me alone. I want to be left alone."

"Ah, Clementine." She felt something brush her cheek, and she recoiled violently away from him.

"Don't touch me. I can't bear it."

"What do you want from us?" He turned half away from her, his hands gripping the back of the rocker so hard his knuckles whitened and his shoulders hunched. "We loved him, too. We're hurtin', too. Just what the hell do you want?"

She laughed, a harsh, brittle sound, like shattering glass. "What do I want? I want my son back. I want him *back*. I want to hold him in my arms again and watch him grow to be a man, I want to hear him laugh, I want to watch him smear chokecherry jam all over his face and get it in his hair, I want to kiss him to sleep at night and bury my face in the smell of him—" Her throat caught as the terrible, choking grief welled up inside her. "I want my Charlie alive and back with me where he belongs."

"He's gone, and we can't change that. Nobody can."

She tried to laugh again, but it got caught up with the hard ball of pain in her throat and came out as a sick, mewling sound. "Oh, no, you can't change that, certainly not you men. You men who can do everything except keep a stud horse from kicking a little boy in the chest."

She turned her back on him and waited to hear him leave. For a long time he didn't go, and she held herself stiff and clenched her jaw so that she wouldn't weaken, and then after he did leave she wanted to call after him, but she couldn't get the words past that choking ball of grief that clogged her chest and throat.

She stared out the window, at the river and the cottonwoods and the haystacks, and Charlie's grave. And then suddenly she was out in the yard, her shoes crunching on the chicken feed, walking across the yard, and Gus shouted something at her, but she didn't see him because she was looking at Charlie's grave, walking toward Charlie's grave.

The hot wind battered her and she staggered once, but she kept walking. The wind howled and shrieked in grief, and the grief tore through her, ripping off pieces deep inside her that bled and bled, ran in rivers of blood to the earth, to Charlie's grave, and then she was at Charlie's grave, scattering the wildflowers Gus had put there that morning, throwing them away in rage and hate and bitter, bitter grief, and she was tearing at the earth with her hands, and the pain drove into her like a fist, and the tears came gushing out of her, rolling and surging and swelling, great ocean waves of tears. She made a noise like a rag tearing and then a high, keening sound that was ripped away by the wind. She hugged her pregnant belly and rocked back and forth on Charlie's grave as the sobs came one after the other in crescendoing, wrenching, soul-searing grief.

Clementine had fallen to one side and was clutching at her belly, trying to curl up into a tight ball. Her sobs were thin and reedy now, like a gopher's whistle, and Gus's whole body shuddered as if those sobs were being torn from his own heart. Rafferty couldn't bear to look at her; he wondered how he was going to stand it.

"She blames me for what happened," Gus said.

Rafferty took the ax from his brother's limp hand and wedged it into the chopping block. "She blames everyone and everything, including herself and God."

"At least she's having her cry." Gus turned a desperate face to his brother. His eyes were red-rimmed and bruised. "It's a good sign, isn't it? That she's crying."

Rafferty gripped his brother's shoulder and pushed him in the direction of his wife. She was rolling on the fresh-turned earth of Charlie's grave now, and her cries were no longer human. "Go hold her. Go on, even if she fights you, but, dammit, hold her." *Go on, brother, before I do, because if I do, you ain't ever gettin' her back.*

Gus went and knelt beside her on Charlie's grave. He tried to gather her up against his chest as she fought him, screaming and flailing at him with her fists. But somehow he managed to wrap his arms around her and he hugged her tight, as if they both might die there. Rafferty felt his stomach ball up like a fist and he looked away.

The yard looked empty. He reckoned it would always look empty without Charlie running through it, laughing. He thought of the day he had tried to teach the boy how to rope by lassoing the chickens. Tears blurred his eyes and he blinked hard, pushing them back down.

She was still crying, but now Gus was crying, too, so at least they were doing it together.

Rafferty started walking aimlessly out into the prairie. A jackrabbit darted across his path and into a barrow pit. The dry, coughing song of the grasshoppers suddenly stopped, and a magpie flew by with a flash of white-barred wings. The wind stilled a moment, then gusted hard, bringing with it the smell of burning wood. An uneasiness prickled along his spine and he stopped, squinting into the south, from where the wind was coming, and where smears of smoke rose thick and black over the hunchbacked buttes.

The smoke blanketed the sky within minutes as the prairie fire raged their way. It grew so dark the lamps had to be lit. Curled, feathery ashes brushed softly against the windows like snow. Clouds built up, but they were empty of rain, and the wind blew so hot and thick that the very air seemed to ache and burn.

The men loaded butts filled with water and piles of blankets and gunnysacks that had been soaked in the river into a hay wagon and drove it out to fight the fire. They were back for more water within an hour, their faces scorched, their hair singed, their eyes full of worry. The third time they came back to fill the barrels, Clementine pushed Gus aside and climbed onto the wagon and took up the reins herself. Gus was too tired and scared to stop her.

She drove the wagon into a boiling cauldron of heat and smoke. They met animals fleeing ahead of the encroaching flames. Thick flocks of birds flew with the blistering wind, the flap of their wings sounding like hundreds of whipping flags; jackrabbits, grouse, and quail darted in frenzied circles as if they'd lost their heads; herds of deer and antelope galloped through the crackling dry grass, white tails flashing their alarm. And their own cattle stampeded through the brush-choked coulees and draws, tongues lolling and eyes white-ringed with fright. The fire ran with the unceasing wind and everything it caught in its path, it burned.

The flames licked through the tall grass like a thousand greedy, hungry tongues. Great columns of black smoke rolled up to meet the clouds, reflecting the fire back on itself like the copper bottom of a frypan. The sky rained burning cinders, and ashes seeped down like sifted flour.

Many of the other men of the RainDance country were at the front line of the fire. The Rocking R was the first of the homesteads threatened, but they knew the voracious flames would not be satisfied with only one family's land. They spoke about how the grass had been like tinder for weeks, how when it got that dry and hot, a spark from a campfire or the discharge of a gun could set the whole world ablaze. One man joked about how they could use a few Indians to do a rain dance right about now, but no one laughed. A couple of the valley's new sodbusters brought plows, and they dug a wide furrow to create a firebreak. But the flames spread too fast, the wind blew too hard, and the grass was too dry.

Gus ordered Clementine back to the house, but she stayed. The choking black smoke burned her throat raw and seared her eyes, the stench of burning grass stung her nose, and the falling cinders blistered her skin, but she stayed. And she fought the fire, standing beyond the firebreak with the men, flailing at the flying sparks with a water-soaked saddle blanket. She hated this country too much to let it beat her, and she loved it too much to let it be destroyed.

The fierce wind sent glowing cinders flying, swirling, jumping over the firebreak to spark dozens of small, flickering fires. They ran from one to the other, trying to tamp them down with the wet blankets and gunnysacks. Rafferty lassoed one of the fleeing cows, slit it open, and dragged it by his lariat along the ground, spilling its wet blood. Clementine thought he had never looked more like the devil come up from hell than in that moment, with his soot-blackened face and fierce yellow eyes and his dark, wind-tossed hair.

Fight fire with fire, the men said. Rafferty and Gus tied ropes soaked with coal oil to their saddle horns, set the ropes alight, and dragged them through the grass of their hay meadow, sacrificing their own land for the greater good. But the wind blew hard and gusty, and the grass everywhere around them was too dry.

By late afternoon the fire had spread into the timber. With an immense roar, it jumped into the crowns of the great larches and pines. They exploded like gunpowder, and the sky erupted into a volcano of burning cones and falling branches streaming death.

"We ain't ever stopping her now!" Rafferty shouted against the roar and crackle of the flames. Through shimmering heat waves, his tall frame loomed black against the wall of red light. "We're going to have to run for it!"

The rest of the men had already fled back to their own ranches and farms, wanting to save of theirs what they could. Clementine slapped at her smoldering skirt with her scorched blanket. "No! We can't let it beat us!" A burning twig landed in her hair and she carelessly brushed it aside with her blistered hand. The heat from the fire had enveloped her for so long that she felt seared, as empty and dry as a seed husk. "I won't let it beat us!"

Rafferty grabbed her arm, shouting into her ear as he dragged her over to the buckboard. "Drive back to the house and gather up pronto what you can't bear to lose! You've got maybe ten minutes!"

She looked wildly around her. "Gus! Where's Gus? I'm not going without you. Without both of you!"

"We'll be right behind you, Boston. Now move!"

He heaved her up like a sack of hops onto the wagon seat and slapped the horse's rump. The horse, wall-eyed with fright, bolted forward with a piercing whinny, so that Clementine had to scramble to gather up the reins.

She loaded her photographic equipment into the wagon first. Her eyes stung, and she panted hard against the breath-stealing heat. She took the quilt Hannah had given her and used it like a satchel as she ran through the house, frantically snatching up things: her Bible and the silver hairbrush etched with her initials, the dream hoop made for her by an Indian girl, a pair of elk-horn candlesticks that had been a wedding gift from the man she loved to his brother, a photograph album filled with images she would never be able to look at again, a heart-shaped sachet heavy with coins that hadn't saved her from a woman's hopes and fears, a woman's yearnings and losses. She paused in Charlie's room. Everything she had left of him was here, and yet they were all only things and they meant nothing without him to give them life.

Outside, the wind roared hot and loud, as if from a blast furnace, and the horse that was hitched to the wagon reared in the traces, whistling in fear. She grabbed Charlie's old candy box full of Indian arrowheads from underneath his bed and fled the house, the lumpy quilt banging against her legs and the vast, hard emptiness back inside her heart.

She felt the first deep, clutching pain as she was climbing back into the wagon. Her breath rushed from her chest as if she'd been kicked, and she doubled over, clutching at her heavy belly. She twisted her head around and looked over her shoulder at the galloping flames that leaped and licked at the sky and at the two horsemen galloping before them.

"No!" she screamed in rage and fear. Screaming against the cramping pains, screaming against the roaring wall of fire that consumed her men, screaming against the belching black plumes of smoke that swirled like a gauzy enveloping shroud around her eyes.

Screaming against Montana.

23

THE HEAVY POUNDING REVERBERATED through the still house. Hannah stumbled down the stairs as she belted a wool wrapper around her waist. "I'm coming!" she shouted, but the door continued to shake beneath the force of the blows. "Heavens, I'm coming!"

She flung open the door. Gus McQueen stood on her porch, his big shoulders blocking out the first rays of a rising sun. "I want to see my wife."

Behind him Rafferty was coming up the path, boots crunching on the frost-stiffened grass. A cold wind ruffled the river and the lemon yellow leaves of the aspens. Two saddle horses were hitched to her fence, and three pack-horses.

Hannah pushed her breath out in a deep sigh. "Oh, Gus . . . she only just now fell asleep." And Clementine so rarely slept. All day long she lay in Hannah's big bed, fighting for the babe that still clung to life within her womb, and she mourned. But she didn't sleep, and she rarely spoke.

"I expect she'll be wanting to tell me good-bye, though," Gus said. The lines of strain around his eyes and mouth made him look tougher, older. A muffled choking sound rumbled up from deep in his throat, as if he'd just swallowed something bitter. "But then, maybe she won't, seeing as how she's spent the last two months wishing me in hell."

Hannah opened her mouth to deny his words. Then the full sense of what he'd said struck her. "Leaving? You can't leave her now, you fool man. Damn you, Gus McQueen, where in hell are you going?" she shouted to his back, for he had pushed his way in without waiting for her to step aside and was now striding two at a time up her stairs.

"Wolfing," Rafferty answered for him.

Hannah swung around to him, shock pulling at her face. He had brought the crisp smell and cold of the late October air in with him. She shivered, drawing her wrapper up close around her throat. *Wolfing.*

The gray wolves spent their summers in pairs up in the timbered mountains, where they whelped their young in caves or under large rocks. But when it turned cold they collected in big packs and migrated down to the plains to follow the buffalo, except that the great buffalo herds were mostly all gone now. Now the wolves preyed on sheep and cattle, and so there were men who preyed on them. Men who poisoned and skinned the wolves for the cash bounties the stockmen's associations paid for their pelts.

Next to whoring, it was the lowest, filthiest way to make a dollar that Hannah knew of.

Rafferty's gaze had followed his brother up the stairs, and for the flash of a heartbeat, a deep, hard-suppressed longing tightened his face.

Hannah turned away, shutting her eyes against the pressure of a thousand unshed tears.

"He's running away," she said. "Away from Charlie's death and the ranch burning and the trouble in their marriage. This wolfing is just an excuse. Gus is running, and you're running with him."

Rafferty sighed and tugged his hat lower on his head. In his long-tailed black sourdough coat, with the heavy weight of the gun hanging easily from his slim hips, with a three-day growth of beard roughening his cheeks, and with his long, dark hair brushing his shoulders, he already looked wild and mean enough to be a wolfer. Wolfers had to be mean to do what they did, and to survive a plains winter and the Indians. Indians especially hated wolfers because the strychnine poisoned their dogs. An Indian would sooner scalp a wolfer than steal a horse.

"He's just doing it to make some money, Hannah. A man's got to provide for his family, and right now he's so broke he's close to selling his saddle. If we don't come up with some ready cash by spring we're gonna lose the ranch, or what's left of it. A man's got to fight to keep what's his."

"A man should also have to spare a thought or two for his pregnant wife. You *men* are leavin' her to have that baby by herself."

She swung her gaze back to his face in time to see something flash deep in his eyes, something wild and desperate.

"You'll take care of her, Hannah," he said, and his voice cracked on her name. "You and the doc. And besides, Clementine is . . . she's game. Gamer than all the rest of us put together. When times get tough she prefers to look to herself to see her way through them, and she does it without a whimper."

Hannah said nothing.

Rafferty thrust his fists deep into the pockets of his coat. He nudged an umbrella stand with the toe of his boot. His restless gaze roamed her hallway, settling on a gilt-framed chromo landscape. He was being extra careful not to look up those stairs again. "I can't stop him from going, dammit. And I can't let him go alone."

"He's running," Hannah said. "That's something you *men* are all good at."

"There's a bounty paid of five dollars for each lobo pelt, Clem," Gus said. He smacked his hands together, trying to pump more enthusiasm into his voice. "We could make maybe two, three thousand dollars if the season's a good one."

He paced the room, his boots leaving grooves in the thick Turkey carpet. From time to time he threw a look at his wife, where she lay on the big four-poster bed, braced up against a stack of pillows. Her hair was nearly as pale as the bleached linen. Her skin looked transparent against the vibrant richness of the walnut headboard and the blood-red silk wallpaper. He couldn't help but think of the years' worth of nights his brother had spent in this room, with Hannah. The sight of his wife in a whore's bed turned his stomach. The very air in here reeked of their sinning.

He stopped at the side of the bed and looked down at her. She looked back up at him with eyes that were wide and still and as remote as the moon. "You know I wouldn't leave you, girl, if I didn't have to," he said.

The fine lace and tucks on her night rail fluttered against her chest as she drew in a breath. "Of course you wouldn't, Gus." Her gaze fell to the hands she had folded limply across the heavy swell of her stomach.

He stared down at her bent head, and his fists clenched. He wanted to grab her and shake the life back into her, the love back into her. He was so afraid . . . God help him, he was so afraid, so filled with a gut-panic that he had lost her.

"I'm only doing it for you," he said, and his voice trembled from the weight of the failure that he felt. "I wanted so much to give you all the things, the big house and the luxuries, that I took you away from. And I will,

Clem—you'll see. The fire was a setback, sure, but with a little bit of ready cash we can start up a new herd of cows next year, and I won't let Zach talk me outta getting anything but the best breeding stuff this time. And come next summer, you'll see, I'll be out there building you a new house, even bigger and fancier than the last one . . ." His words trailed off to be consumed by the silence.

A piece of wood collapsed in the grate with a spray of sparks. A gust of wind rattled the panes. He would never be able hear the hiss and crackle of flames or the howl of the wind without remembering the fire. It had destroyed the house he had built for her the first summer of their marriage. It had devoured nearly all of their hay meadows and open rangeland; and over a thousand head of Rocking R cattle and saddle stock had either burned to death or smothered in the thick black smoke. The fire had taken almost everything they had to give by the time it turned toward the cottonwoods and the river and the buffalo hunter's cabin, and Charlie's grave. But there the wind had shifted, and the flames had turned back and begun to consume themselves.

That night, too late, rain had fallen and the fire had died.

He sat down on the bed. He picked up one of her hands. She didn't stiffen, but he could feel her withdrawing from him, pulling away deep inside herself.

"I'll miss you, girl."

She looked across the room to the windows, where the rising sun bathed the sky with honeyed light and the mountains already showed snow. Winter was coming. But then, Montana winters always came before you were ready. "Be sure you take plenty of warm clothes," she said in that remote, polite voice that she had used ever since Charlie died and that Gus had come to hate. "And eat more than just sowbelly beans and biscuits at every meal. And try to keep your brother off the whiskey."

He swallowed hard around the lump of fear and

despair that had been swelling like a goiter in his throat
ever since Charlie's death, since the fire, and maybe long
before then. Maybe since a time over the last four years
when he had finally understood that he was never going to
have this woman, not the part of her that mattered.

"Clementine . . ." He wanted to hold her in his arms,
he wanted to kiss her mouth and touch her breasts, he
wanted to lie beside her, just lie beside her and hold her
close. And he wanted to tell her how badly he needed her,
needed her to believe in him. How without her belief in
him, without her love, he was nothing. "I love you," he
said, and then he waited.

And as he waited he thought that if he had lost her,
then he would find a way to lose himself. Because he
couldn't bear the thought of going on without her.

Her hand stirred in his. Her fingers gripped his,
squeezing, and she brought his hand up to her face and
laid the backs of his fingers against her cheek.

"I love you, too, Gus."

A draft stirred the green glass beaded curtains that hung in
the doorway of Hannah Yorke's front parlor, making them
click slowly. Hannah sat stiff and cold on her gold brocade
medallion-backed sofa.

She strained her ears, as if there was a chance she could
overhear the conversation going on upstairs. "No doubt
he's up there right now trying to talk her into moving into
my hotel," she said, "or maybe staying with one of the
more respectable families in town."

She turned her head toward Gus McQueen's brother,
who stood gazing out the window. The floorboards of the
upstairs room creaked and groaned beneath the tread of
heavy feet. "Not that he gave a thought to scandal when
he brought her to my house the day of the fire, all scorched
and smelling like a chimney sweep and in a panic because
he thought she was miscarrying."

"She won't leave," Rafferty said, though he didn't turn to look at her, "unless she wants to."

"Not that she has anyplace to go to, except back to that old buffalo hunter's sod-roofed shanty in the middle of a burned-out ranch."

The footsteps above stopped their pacing. Hannah stared at Rafferty's silent back. "Oh, I know poor Charlie's death has hit your brother hard. And now here y'all are on the verge of losing the ranch because of the fire. Lord, even the Four Jacks must be giving him headaches lately. What with your father taking over the claim and working out a deal with the consortium to operate the whole shebang by himself, thinking to make himself the biggest toad in the puddle that is Rainbow Springs, I reckon—"

"One-Eyed Jack is the least of Gus's worries," Rafferty said, cutting into her nervous ramble.

And what are *your* worries? she wanted to ask him. All these years she'd known him, had him in her bed, and she'd never known what was really going on behind those wild yellow eyes. Right now he leaned on the gold flock wallpaper, his head brushing the dark maroon velvet drapery, staring at Montana's great outdoors. Even through the woolly thickness of his sourdough coat, she could see the tension cording the muscles of his back and shoulders. And she could feel it. It hovered in the air around him, thick enough to spread on bread.

"Rafferty?" He raised his head and turned it slightly, though he didn't look at her. "*Can* you save the ranch?"

"Yeah, sure. Easy as driving a swarm of bees through a snowstorm with a switch." His back stiffened suddenly, and his hand clenched on the wall, and Hannah's belly fluttered with a cold, unnamed panic. "What's that digger doing hanging on your garden gate?" he said, and though his voice was soft, the words had a bite to them like an ice-tipped wind.

She shot up out of the chair as if she'd been propelled

by a charge of gunpowder and went to look out the other window.

Drew Scully. He had settled against her fence, his hands stuffed in his pockets, his gaze on the ground. He was dressed for a day of work in the mines, in his rough twill pants, canvas coat, and heavy boots. He'd been courting her proper, like a regular gentleman, ever since the Fourth of July picnic, and she'd been letting him do it. And all the while pretending to herself that none of it was happening, that she didn't want it to happen.

"I don't know what he's doing out there," she said, guilt sending the blood rushing hot to her cheeks. Rafferty spun toward her with a sudden explosive movement, and she backed up a step, pressing her hand to her chest in an unconscious gesture of self-protection. "Truly I don't know!"

He dismissed her protest with a little curl of his lip. "At least he's man enough to let me know ahead of time that he's gonna move into my side of the bed soon as I'm gone."

Her head swung wildly back and forth. "No, no. You're wrong."

"It's the guaranteed article, Hannah." He took a step toward her, and she backed up two more. The distrust in his voice was thick, and his gaze was cold and mean. In this mood he was as volatile as a stick of dynamite.

Her hip bumped against a piecrust table, almost knocking over a plaster bust and a bronze dragon candlestick. She tried to scoot around the table, but she tripped over a paw of the grizzly bear rug, and he was suddenly upon her. His hand shot out and gripped her neck. His thumb pressed up beneath her chin, forcing her head back so that he could look into her eyes. "Am I right, Hannah? Are you gonna leave me for that boy?"

"No!" she shouted, as if she could drown out the lie she heard in her own voice. She thrust against him, breaking free and pounding his chest with her fist at the same time. "God damn you, Zach Rafferty, don't you go turn it all around onto me! I ain't the one who's been in love with my brother's wife all these yea—"

She cut the words off, but not soon enough. His head rocked back a little as if she'd struck him. His gaze flashed toward the beaded curtain and the stairs, his face going white.

Hot, scalding tears pushed against her eyes and she dashed them out of the way with the back of her hand. "Oh, hell, Rafferty, what'd you go and make me say it out loud for?" Suddenly she needed to get close to him, to be held by him. Her hands went around his neck and she pressed the length of her body against his. She nestled her face into him, breathed against his taut skin, inhaling his musky smell. He was breathing fast, his chest rising and falling. "I'm sorry," she whispered, her lips brushing against the pulse in his throat.

He exhaled a long breath through his teeth. "Hannah . . ."

"Did you think you could go on fighting it and hiding it forever?"

She felt him swallow hard. She looked up at his face. A muscle bunched and hollowed in his cheek. Her hand stroked the length of his neck, up and down. His flesh was so cold and the muscles cording his throat were so tense it was like touching a marble statue.

"Oh, Rafferty . . . I usually ain't one for handing out advice to the lovelorn, not when my own heart's been broken so many times it leaks like a rotten bucket." Her hands fell to the lapels of his coat, and she gave him a little shake. "But for once I'm going to tell you what you better do. First, you go on and keep Gus from getting himself killed out there on the plains this winter. Then you bring him back to her, and you leave. You leave before the day comes when your feelings get the better of you and you do to her for real what so far you've only done to her in your dreams.

You leave before Gus finds out that the woman he loves is in love with you, before he tries to kill you for it so that you wind up killin' him, your own brother." She shook him again. "Leave the RainDance, Rafferty. Before you go and break all our hearts, including your own."

A trace of sad tenderness eased the hard lines around his mouth. "Wise, Hannah . . . " He drew her back into him, his hand pressing her head deep into the curve of his neck. He stroked her hair, his fingers tightening in it a moment, then letting go. "We had us a time, didn't we, darlin'?"

Her heartbeat seemed to fill her throat. She nodded, her chin scraping against the rough black wool of his collar. "Yeah . . . we did have us a time."

Gus came pounding down the stairs and slapped his fist against the beaded curtain. "Let's go, brother," he called out, and slammed out the door.

Hannah and Zach broke apart, both looking a little bright-eyed. "You want to go on up and tell her good-bye?" she said. "Gus won't think anything of it."

He stood still, his hands hanging loose at his sides. He was holding his head stiff, so he wouldn't even look toward the stairs, and she had never loved him more than she did in that one moment. "If I saw her now," he said, "I wouldn't be able to leave her. Not even for Gus."

Drew Scully came to claim her one morning a month later.

He came when she was in her front parlor, watering her ferns. When Clementine, feeling stronger, had gone for a walk along the river. Hannah saw him out her window, leaning against her fence as he'd been doing the day she and Rafferty had said their good-byes. Only this time he didn't walk off down the road to his job at the mine.

This time he opened her front gate and walked down her path, coming for her. The watering can fell from her fingers with a loud clatter. Water splashed the hem of her poppy-red silk skirt and left a wet stain on her tree of life carpet.

The winter sun was out in all its glory, for a change. It poured through the stained-glass fanlight over the door so that the long shadow he cast on her oiled pine floor was striated with tiny rainbows of red, yellow, blue, and green. He pulled aside the beaded curtain and took a step into the room, and her heart thumped unevenly and every nerve in her body hummed taut.

His face was like a hawk's, stark and sharp, predatory. There was something intensely, dangerously sexual in his eyes.

He looked on the verge of losing control, and she suspected that this wasn't something he often permitted himself to do. She wondered what would happen if he did. She felt a reckless urge to find out, to make him break his own rules.

She watched his mouth move as he spoke and wondered what it would be like to kiss it. "There's talk all around town," he said, "that your lover's left you for the winter, that maybe he's left you for good."

She tossed the hair out of her eyes and willed the breathlessness from her voice. "That's nothing to do with you, Mr. Scully, and I'll thank you to get yourself on out of here this very minute before I—"

"He's left, Mrs. Yorke, and I'm claiming you." His voice was guttural with the hunger she saw on his face. He took a step and she crossed her arms over her breast as if she could still the wild thrusting of her heart. "I'm not waiting until you've decided you no longer love him," he went on as he came toward her. She shuddered as he touched her face, and again as he spread his fingers over her cheek, while his mouth hovered against her lips. And then shuddered once more as the realization slammed into her, winding her, that this man, this *boy*, could own her as no one else ever had. "I want you now, Hannah Yorke, while you can still taste him on your lips. That way, when you come, I'll know it's me you're coming for and not some memory of him."

And then he was kissing her.

He kissed her as if he were starved, sucking on her mouth, drawing the life out of her. He slanted his head so that his lips could cover hers more fully, and he kissed her deeper, slower now, yet hot, demanding. His breath tasted of soda tooth powder. It seemed a strange and sweetly human thing in the midst of all the raw passion pouring out of his mouth.

His lips rubbed hard against hers, pushing them open. She moaned deep in her throat and gave herself up to him, and she moaned again as he stroked her mouth with his tongue, stroking, stroking, stroking, a graphic promise of what was to come. Her breath caught as he tugged her head back and slammed his body into hers.

"You're mine now," he grated. The words slurred as his tongue moved around hers while he spoke.

"Yes," she whispered, but that one word had the shattering force of a scream. To want and be wanted like this.

And she wanted him. Oh, how she wanted him. She gripped his coat, clinging to him, her mouth seeking his, taking, devouring. They rammed into the wall, then staggered blindly into the piecrust table. Her mouth still locked with his, she fumbled behind her, her fingers clutching the Arab scarf that covered the table, pulling it down with her as they fell to the floor. The bronze dragon candlestick went flying with a loud clatter into the nickel parlor stove. The plaster bust was saved from shattering by the thick grizzly bear rug. A mother-of-pearl trinket case clunked her on the head, but she barely felt it.

She pulled at his clothes. He tore his mouth from hers long enough to rip off his coat and shirt and send them flying across the room. She ran her hands over his chest and felt the savage drumbeat of his heart. His flesh was hot, slick with the sweat of desire.

She looked up into his hungry, steel-hard eyes. She

kissed the rigid muscles along his jaw, tracing her tongue over the hard line of his mouth. There was a wildness in her, a greed and violence that staggered her. She could hear her own blood roaring in her head, her breath coming fast and uneven.

"Take me," she said, the words coming out of her on sharp, hot gusts of breath. "Take me now . . ."

He ripped open the front of her poppy-red silk dress and pulled down her corset and camisole, baring her breasts. His head fell forward, his hair brushing her neck as he drew her nipple into his mouth, sucked at it hard, greedily, and she cried out, entangling her fingers in his hair, wrapping her legs around his hips, trying to draw him inside her now, now, now . . . He reared back and yanked at the buttons on his trousers, pushing them down over his hips. His face was hard, his whole body shaking. She laughed and scraped her nails over the taut plane of his belly, and the muscles spasmed and his penis jerked against her thigh . . . inside her now. And she cried out, a long, keening wail as he drove into her. She arched her back, rearing up to meet his thrusts, tossing her head back and forth, whipping his face with her hair, digging her fists into the thick grizzly fur of the rug, riding him, riding it, riding the hunger and the need and the longing and the soaring, shattering peaks of pleasure that ripped through her again and again and again, now, now, now.

And as he sank down into her, she heard him say the tender words. She didn't believe them; she was much too wise for that. But they rang sweet in her ears nonetheless.

"I love you, Hannah Yorke," he said.

24

SLEET SPIT AGAINST THE glass, and the wind gusted down the chimney, fanning smoke into the room. The norther was blowing in from the mountains in wild counterpoint to the soft murmur of the women's voices coming from the bed.

Jealousy twinged in Hannah's breast as she looked at the heads, one ash fair and the other prairie dog brown, that were bent over an Altman and Stern catalog. She hated herself for minding that Clementine and Saphronie had become such close friends lately. They had both lost a child, after all. Her own hurt she had never shared with Clementine, for to speak of her lost baby would be to admit to wickedness and weakness and shame, and that she had never dared to do. Yet there was a heaviness within her, a pain in her soul, and she ached sometimes from holding it all inside her.

Hannah took the glass chimney off a big potbellied lamp, struck a match to the wick, replaced the chimney, and adjusted the screw. A soft yellow light now flooded the storm-darkened corners of the room, shimmering off the crimson silk wallpaper, the gilt mirror, and the heavily lacquered peacock screen. A room right out of a brothel, Hannah thought, minding suddenly that this was so.

She moved restlessly to the window. She looked out, cupping her hand to the pane as a shield against the lamp glare. It was a foul evening and would only get fouler. She went to the fire, pushed a stick deeper into the flames and moved a cheval fire screen with a petit point rose panel closer in to block some of the heat and smoke.

She breathed a guilty sigh of relief when Saphronie took a brass warming pan out from beneath the bedcovers and left the room, and she was left alone at last with Clementine.

"A norther's brewing up outside," she said.

Clementine shifted the catalog to the other side of the bed and patted the mattress in silent invitation. "I always think I'm not going to mind winter, and then it gets here and I find I mind it very much."

The crisp shamrock-green sateen of Hannah's skirts rustled as she sat down next to Clementine. The girl's stomach was monstrous beneath the bedcovers; the baby was due at any time. "Montana winters do try a woman's soul," Hannah said. "But I reckon no matter how hard the winter, spring always comes."

"I'll never forget my first Montana winter, when Charlie was born . . ." The eyes Clementine turned to her were like deep, dark seas, spilling over with grief. She pressed her hands hard against the bones of her face. "Oh, Hannah, I do so hate myself for all these tears. I couldn't cry for so long, and now I can't stop."

A tight band of misery seemed as if it would crush Hannah's ribs. Her eyes felt sore and raw, as if the tears were hers. She hesitated a moment, then leaned over and wrapped her arms around the younger woman, hugging her close. She breathed in a deep sigh that was soft with the smell of rose toilet soap.

"I should have died in his place," Clementine said, her voice muffled by Hannah's shoulder. "It should have been me."

Hannah stroked her back. "No, no . . . Oh, Lord, honey, there is no pain like losing a child. It is an agony no woman should ever have to endure."

"Yet you have endured it."

Hannah stiffened and jerked away, forcing out a laugh that sounded empty even to her own ears. "Land,

Clementine, whatever made you think such a thing? I never . . . I . . ."

The words piled up in her throat, getting caught on a heavy, choking knot of fear and shame. She'd always known this day would come. Funny how she'd just been congratulating herself on having kept the secret for so long, and here it was out. But then a woman's sins always caught up with her. No matter how far or how fast she ran, they were always there waiting for her just around the next bend in the road.

She squared her shoulders and lifted her head, blinking hard against the betraying tears that filled her eyes. "How . . . how did you hear of it? The only one who knows is Shiloh, and I don't reckon he would tell you."

Clementine was looking at her with that wide-open gaze of hers that could see so much. "Shiloh didn't tell me. I guessed from some things you've said over the years. And from knowing you so well."

Hannah felt her whole body flush. She forced herself to meet those cool, fine eyes, those *lady's* eyes, but inside she was dying. She had lost men before and gotten over it. But she didn't think she could bear losing Clementine. "He didn't die," she said.

"Oh, but I thought . . ."

Those lady's eyes had narrowed just a little, and Hannah felt herself die some more. "I lost my boy, my baby, but not to death." Hannah drew in a deep breath and prepared to let it out along with everything else. "To begin with, I wasn't married when I had him."

Clementine stirred. She patted Hannah's arm. "I know. You told me once a long time ago that you'd never had a husband."

Hannah's gaze fell to the hands she had clutched in her lap. She picked at a loose thread in the skirt, a flaw in the weave of the sateen. "I guess if I thought you knew the truth about me, you wouldn't want to be my friend no more."

Clementine gripped Hannah's hands and brought them up to her breast. "Oh, Hannah, don't you see? You are *my* friend. You can't know what that means to me—to have a friend. I don't care how many men you've lain with for money or for love, you are and will forever be as dear to me as the sister I never had."

Hannah emitted a watery little gulp of a laugh. "I never had a sister either. I never had much of anything in that Kentucky coal-mining town I grew up in. Why, Daddy used to joke that we were so poor, if we didn't skip eating twice a week, we'd starve to death." She laughed again and was rewarded with a smile.

"I don't think my father ever made a joke in his life," Clementine said.

"Well, we might have been poor as Job's turkey, but we had us some magical times." She picked at the loose thread again, her drawl thickening with the memories. "He died in the coal mines when I was ten, Daddy did. Ma and me went to live with her sister, who was married to the baker. So we had plenty to eat after that, but it was never the same. And then the world turned magical again when I met . . . him. He was the son of the mine owner, just back from a grand tour—that's how he put it, 'my grand tour,' if you can imagine that. I don't think I ever met anyone more high-toned in my entire life, before or since." She sighed softly. "He was a sweet-talking man."

"And he was the father of your baby?"

Shame burned a hot path up Hannah's chest, and she averted her face. The truth was . . . if she lost her friend by telling the truth, she couldn't bear it. She patted Clementine lightly on the mound of her stomach, forcing a smile. "Hannah Yorke ain't nobody's fool, honey. I was a virgin way back in those days, and I made him ask me to marry him before I spread my legs."

Clementine smiled again, a warm, slow smile, and the warmth of it spread down deep into Hannah's chest. Oh, Lord, it was hard, but it felt good, too, to be talking. She'd never shared herself like this with another woman. Only with men, and then it wasn't a sharing, but more of a giving up of something to them in the hope that she'd get a little something back in return.

"Ma made me a dress—she hocked her wedding ring to buy the lace for it—and my aunt and uncle baked up the fanciest cake you ever did see. I reckon that must've been one of the worst days of my life, waiting at the church for him to show and knowing as the minutes ticked by that I was just another fool in the long line of fools that men have made out of women. The bounder had left town on the morning train, and he left me with a bun in the oven."

Clementine took Hannah's hand, their fingers intertwining like the strands of a rope.

"Well, I sure enough couldn't bring that sort of shame on my ma, so I ran off to the big city, to Franklin. I got me a job selling gloves in a dry goods emporium until I started to show. Then I lost the job and my room at the boardinghouse. And when I got good and cold and hungry and scared, another sweet-talking man came along and took me up to this big fancy white house, and he said all my worries were gonna be over."

Clementine gripped her fingers harder, and Hannah took a strange sort of solace from the strength of them.

"I suppose you can guess what kinda house it was and what he wanted from me in return for putting a roof over my head and food in my belly. My boy was born in a brothel without a daddy to give him a name. And that was when I committed the worst sin of my whole misbegotten life." She stopped, unable to go on, the horror of it almost choking her. "I sold him."

"Oh, Hannah . . ." Clementine pulled Hannah's hand onto her lap, holding it hard against her pregnant belly.

"The midwife who'd cared for me—she brought a man to see me. He owned a bank or something. He told me how there was a law in Kentucky against keeping children under the age of ten in a brothel, and how he could give my baby a good home, he and his wife. Schooling and warm clothes to wear and plenty to eat. He just kept talking and talking at me, and I was so weak and tired and scared, worried, you know, about how I was gonna provide for him. Oh, Lord, Clementine, I was just so scared . . ."

Clementine stroked the back of Hannah's hand over and over. "Of course you were. You could have left with him, but what kind of work would you have found? Look at Saphronie. And if you'd stayed in that house, they would have taken him from you anyway."

"But I *sold* him. That banker offered me a hundred dollars and I took it."

"You gave him up into a good life, Hannah."

"You mean because he grew up with shoes on his feet and a full belly, and not ever knowing that he's a bastard and his ma was a whore?" Scalding tears welled up in Hannah's eyes. "But I loved him so much and I would have made him a good mother. I know I would have. I should have found a way. Somehow I should have found a way . . ."

"You would have made him a wonderful mother," Clementine said fiercely. "The best in the world."

A heavy silence filled the room. Then Hannah shrugged and sniffled, rubbing at her eyes. She wanted to get the rest of it over with now, so she talked fast, punctuating the words with brittle, bright laughter to chase away the pain.

"Anyways, I really didn't mind working in that brothel after a while. I guess I've always liked a good time, and I had pretty clothes to wear and plenty to eat. Why, I could make sixty dollars on a good evening. And on Sundays we'd all go riding out in a black brougham, dressed in our finest, and I'd feel like a queen.

"But one day another sweet-talking man came along, and I ran off with him and joined up with this dime show that he was manager of. You ever seen a dime show? I didn't think so. It's like a cheap sort of circus, with freaks and acrobats and song-and-dance numbers. We went to places too rube for the big tents. On the rag sheets—those are the handbills that go out—I was listed as the featured attraction. Do you know what a hootchy-kootchy girl is? As long as the men kept laying their money down, I kept taking the veils off. I didn't have to whore, though, not with the boss happy for me to keep his bed warm."

"When I was a little girl I used to dream of running away to join the circus."

Hannah looked at Clementine in astonishment. She couldn't imagine anyone wanting to run away from satin sheets and six-course dinners, from lace tuckers and silver hair combs and all those little luxuries that went along with impeccable manners and a hoity-toity way of talking. Yet Clementine had done the next best thing to joining a circus—she'd run off to Montana with a cowboy.

Hannah waved an airy hand. "Oh, well, I soon tired of the dime-show business, and so I took up with a sweet-talking riverboat gambler. We traveled up and down the Missouri together. He was handsome enough to die for, that man, and the biggest scoundrel ever born to torment women." A sad smile pulled at her mouth. "Honey, never trust a man who tells you he loves you and can look you in the eye whilst he's sayin' it."

"They do sometimes lie," Clementine said. "Even when they don't mean to."

Hannah's eyes widened again and a startled laugh burst out of her. "How'd such a genuine lady from Boston get to be so smart about men?"

"She grew up," Clementine said simply.

Hannah's smile faded, and she looked away. "Yeah, well, it takes some of us a good long while to do that."

Oh, Lord, but hadn't the world seemed wonderful in those days, she thought, traveling up and down the river with love on her mind. So full of the good things—good lovin', good times, and good booze. She had gone so far beyond the line of respectability that she couldn't see it anymore and so she didn't care. She had felt so free, free when other women were fenced in by their corset stays and the strictures of their ladies' societies. She'd developed a taste for freedom in those days, a craving that still tugged at her woman's soul.

But in living free she had discovered the nature of the beast: it had no heart. If you broke freedom open and looked at it too closely, you discovered that it was hollow.

"It was during my riverboat days," Hannah said, "that I wound up with my rose." She flashed a dimpled smile, jumping to her feet. "Look, I'll show you."

She reached beneath her green sateen skirts and pulled off her sheer muslin drawers, then hoisted her skirts and petticoats until they were all bunched up around her waist. She planted her foot on the bed and turned her naked thigh toward Clementine's astonished gaze. The rose tattoo was a stark blue on the paleness of her skin, disappearing into her woman's hair.

Clementine touched her cheeks with her palms. "Oh, my, how . . ."

"Naughty?"

"How deliciously naughty."

They laughed together as Hannah dropped her skirts and sank back down on the bed. Their hands became linked again as naturally as a hook and button coming together.

"I reckon I thought I was a pretty smart chippy, Clementine—at least in the beginning. And I hornswoggled myself into thinking I was happy. But I had nothing with that gambling man—no gold ring, no babies, no home, and no pride. That's the second thing I'm most ashamed of. I loved that man so much that I forgave him everything he did—his other women, his drinking too much and cheating at cards, his jealous rages whenever he'd imagine me so much as looking at another man. He never hit me, but he beat me up bad on the inside. One day he up and decided he wanted to try his luck at the gaming tables in Deadwood, and that was where he left me. In Deadwood. I woke up one morning and he was gone, and I almost killed myself over that."

Hannah felt suddenly as if a winch had tightened around her throat, cutting off the words that had been flowing as freely as the river she and her gambler had traveled on. She couldn't look at Clementine anymore. She was sure the younger woman's eyes would say: *How could you let him do that to you?* Yet when she did look, those still, deep eyes said: *I know. I know what it's like to love that much.*

Hannah cleared her throat and dropped her gaze to their entwined fingers. Like a rope, Hannah thought, they were like a strong, tough rope that had been woven and cured by life. "It got real bad again after that. Are you sure you want me to tell you?"

"Only if you want to."

"I . . . I started smoking opium to escape from the pain of losing him and the pain of . . . oh, losing myself, I guess." For a moment the sweet-rotten smell of it, like burned peanuts, was thick in her nose and the bitter taste of the smoke filled her mouth. The old yearning was there, as strong as ever, the fierce, hot yearning to dream, to escape into the hollowness of freedom . . . She blew out a deep breath, but the yearning remained.

"To . . . to get the money for it—for the opium and for the whiskey I was drinking like it was water—I took up whoring again. Only by that time no house wanted anything to do with the likes of me, so I wound up in a crib in the badlands, and that is about as low down far into hell as a woman can go without bein' dead."

Clementine's fingers stirred, but did not pull away from hers. "You aren't there anymore, Hannah. You escaped. And that took courage."

Hannah wiped a stray tear off her cheek with her free hand. "Naw. It was mostly pure dumb luck that got me out of the badlands. A prospector died of the spotted fever and left me his gold-dust poke, and Shiloh had already befriended me and was helping me to cut loose of the opium. To this day I'll never know why he did that for me." She sniffled, wiped at another tear, and produced a watery smile. "Shiloh's the only man who's ever talked to me straight, not sweet."

She was quiet a moment; then she sighed deeply. "I reckon I'm just a sucker for love, and it costs a lot of your heart to love a thing you're bound to lose. Either through death or them leavin' you or you givin' them up. It costs—whether it be the babe you've suckled at your breast or a man you've taken between your legs. Or the one man out of all the world's sweet-talking rascals that you've allowed inside your head and soul. Him most of all."

Clementine was silent for a moment, and then a small soft sound huffed out of her chest. It wasn't really a sigh—more of a low, tired breath. "Rafferty will come back to you, Hannah. He only left this time because of Gus, and he always comes back."

"Sure he does, honey. But not for me."

Clementine went utterly still, her gaze searching Hannah's face. The currents in those shadowy green eyes shifting, restless. "How—how long have you known?"

"Always." She smoothed out the line of pain from between Clementine's brows. "Now, don't you go fretting about it for my sake. I loved him like crazy for a while, and in some ways I always will. But it wasn't you who came between us, and I never once begrudged him lovin' you."

The currents in Clementine's eyes quickened, deepened. "It wouldn't have mattered, Hannah. Dear as you are to me, I couldn't have stopped loving him. Not for you, not for Gus, not for my immortal soul." A strange light suffused her face, as if she were filling up inside with the sun. She looked filled to bursting with her love, as if she would explode with it. "I have loved him my entire life. Even before I knew him, I loved him."

To be loved like that, Hannah thought . . . God help her, but she was envious. Of Rafferty.

The house trembled and creaked under the wind, and Hannah heaved a gusty sigh. "What a pair we are."

Clementine pressed the back of a lacy wrist to her

throat, as if feeling for her own pulse. Then her hand fell and she clutched at the quilt, twisting it suddenly into so tight a knot Hannah feared she would rip it.

"And yet I love Gus," she said, anguish darkening her voice, "I do, and he is my husband before God." She pounded at the bedclothes with her clenched fists. "Oh, God, Hannah, God, God! I am committing the worst sin every day of my life with my every breath . . . loving my husband's brother. 'Her belly shall swell and her thigh shall rot: and the woman shall be a curse among her people.' And so God took Charlie from me. He had to punish me for my terrible sin."

"No!" Hannah grabbed her hands, stilling them. "You mustn't say that, you mustn't think it. Ever!" Pain spasmed across Clementine's face. The quilt, where it was stretched taut over the mound of her belly, quivered. "Clementine? Are you laboring?"

She nodded, panting heavily. "For a while now."

"Oh, Lord, why didn't you say something?" The wind whipped the sleet against the windowpanes, making a crackling sound like footsteps through dry leaves, and Hannah laughed shakily. "You and Gus really oughta time these things better. It just don't make sense to bring a baby into the world when the weather's apt to be throwing fits."

Clementine smiled wanly and let her eyes drift closed. *I should have died in his place. It should have been me.* All the blood seemed to rush from Hannah's heart, and her chest tightened with fear. It was the one thing none of them had ever considered, especially not Rafferty with all his man's stupid talk about her being tough and game enough to face anything—that Clementine might *want* to die.

The coal-oil lantern cast a murky light over the interior of Sam Woo's mercantile. Erlan stood on the highest rung of a ladder, stretching to reach the highest shelf. She hung a bowie knife on a hook next to a pile of brass knuckles, then used the sleeve of her chang-fu to wipe the dust off a case of rifle cartridges.

Moving gingerly on her tiny feet she climbed back down the ladder. She looked up and cursed to see a coffee grinder still stuck up there among some rolls of fuse cord. She used the hook to fetch it down, since she didn't think her golden lilies could bear another trip up the ladder today. Although her feet were no longer dainty arcs, she still had trouble managing the ladder.

Erlan let out a deep breath, stirring the wisps of hair on her forehead. Although it was a wintry night, the big potbellied stove kept the mercantile toasty, and she wiped a trickle of sweat off her neck with the back of her hand. As concubine to a gentry house, her mother had never so exerted herself as to perspire. Aiya, certainly Tao Huo would faint if she could see her daughter now, with her sun-browned cheeks, spreading feet, and callused hands.

Yet the truth was, Erlan rather enjoyed the work she did to earn her one dollar a day American. Peddlers had often come to the kitchen yard of her lao chia to sell their wares and haggle. She had listened with her hand hiding a smile as the servants bemoaned the prices and scoffed at the quality, and the peddlers wailed and moaned and cursed the gods for sending them such niggardly customers. Oh, how Erlan had longed to take part in the game. Well, she had plenty of things to haggle over now, but to her disappointment the fon-kwei had no knowledge of the fine art of bargaining. There was no sport in naming a price and having it accepted without an argument.

She heard a step on the boardwalk outside and she started for the door, with scolding words already dancing on the tip of her tongue. She thought it was the merchant Woo, coming home for his dinner at long last. But the footsteps passed on by and became a black shadow crossing the lampshine that spilled through the window glass.

Erlan cursed the four gods of marriage that had seen fit to give her such a husband. If they had lived in Foochow, he would have frequented the teahouses. Here in America, it was the saloons. Instead of gambling at go or chess, he lost his money at poker. Nearly every night he came home with the long face.

Yet all in all, Erlan was pleased with her marriage, with her deal. At least she was the head of his house, with no mother-in-law to rule her. And since the sweetest tea was made with only the purest water, she had tried to uphold her end of the bargain. She looked around the mercantile now with a sense of deep satisfaction. She had finally achieved a measure of balance and harmony here, though it had taken her months to accomplish it.

Stacks of oilskins now rested next to rubber boots, bales of overalls next to work shirts. If someone was searching for a red hair ribbon, it was there, where it ought to be, next to the lace collars. Hatpins were with hatpin tablets. Tin washtubs next to folding bench wringers. Lanterns next to boxes of candles and kerosene in five-gallon tins. Stick candy, dried apples, crackers—all were up front next to the pickles. She looked down at the coffee grinder in her hands. A grinder should be near the beans, of course. Now, where were the—

The cowbell over the door erupted into a jarring jangle. Erlan whipped around so fast she nearly fell over a barrel of straw brooms. She drew in a sharp breath of air that was thick with the smell of oilskins and sour pickles.

"You!" she exclaimed. "How dare you come sneaking in here like that!"

"'Tes a little hard to sneak when there's a bloody cacophony of bells to announce your arrival like a bishop to a cathedral. You shouldn't be leaving the door unlatched this time of night. There are hard cases spilling out the saloons. And you shouldn't be alone. Where's Sam, then?"

"The useless one of the family is playing poker," she said, then flushed at the startled look that had come over Jere Scully's face. In China, for a wife to call her husband a useless one in front of others was to show her affection, whereas to compliment him in public was to embarrass them both. But Erlan kept forgetting that this was not the barbarian way.

She had to tilt her head way back to look at him. The size of the man always startled her. She would never find his features harmonious, but his hairy barbarian face didn't seem so ugly anymore. Perhaps she was getting used to heavy bones and big noses.

As crowded as the mercantile was, he seemed to fill all the empty spaces. With his great size and with his smell, of wet wool and leather, and barbarian man.

He took a step toward her, and she jumped back. Inside she felt all tight and hot, as if she were swelling and pressing against her skin, as if she would pop open at any moment like a roasted chestnut. He came closer, and she took another hopping step back. Aiya, she was behaving like a fool hen, and she made herself stop. Her gaze fell to the hem of her chang-fu, and she thrust her hands deep into her sleeves.

"Don't be frightened of me, Lily," he said softly.

Her head snapped up. "I am not frightened. And do not call me that. I do not like that name."

"'Tes what your husband calls you."

"You should address me as Mrs. Woo, if you speak to me at all. And even that is not the Chinese way." No woman ever took her husband's family name unless she was an orphan or a concubine. "In China I am Erlan, daughter of the House of Po."

"Aye, but then ye bain't in China now, be ye, Mrs. Woo?" he challenged, his Cornish accent growing as thick as sea fog. His rainwater eyes glimmered in the lantern light, and there was a relaxed curve of laughter around his mouth. He had stopped stalking her and was now leaning against the counter, one booted foot laid across the other.

Erlan's nervous gaze darted around the mercantile. She was at a loss as to what to do. Good manners dictated that she offer tea to a guest as soon as he arrived. But this man was no guest; he was an interloper to her peace of mind.

She drew in a deep breath, trying to center herself and banish all the turmoil roiling within her. She must strive for virtuous patience.

"Lily," he said and just the deep, rich earth-sound of his voice sent her composure flickering like the wick of a lantern in a strong wind. "You shouldn't have married him, lass." It was what he said to her every time he managed to get her alone, and she hated hearing it. She was afraid that one day she would come to believe it. "You shouldn't have let them make you do it."

"In China a girl never has a choice; the decision is made for her by her family. And even if she marries against her wishes, it is for life."

"Who's life, then, hers or his? Don't widows marry again in your China?"

"For a woman to marry again is to dishonor her widowhood. The marriage bond lasts beyond the grave."

He had pushed himself off the counter and was now prowling around the mercantile. He picked up a stereoscope and held it up to the lantern light; he opened a jar of Epsom salts and took a whiff, wrinkling his big barbarian nose; he flipped through a stack of patent medicine trade cards. His shoulders, she thought, must be as wide as the Great Wall. Melting ice sparkled in his hair, which was as thick as fox fur.

"I've made a present for you," he said, spinning around to face her suddenly. He pulled a piece of wood out of the deep pocket of his coat, and she sucked in her breath on a gasp. It was a carving of a holy temple, so exquisite she could make out each tile and stone, the tiny dragons on the corners of the roofs, even a miniature banyan tree outside the double-handled doors.

"Miss Luly Maine, the schoolteacher, has a book with pictures of China in it," he was saying. "There was one of those things you spoke of the day of the frolic, a pagoda. I used it as a model."

He was holding it out to her, but she was afraid to touch it. Afraid that if she touched it she would start to weep, and once started, she would never stop. She would weep and weep until her tears of homesickness drowned the world.

"You spoke that day of the pagoda and how 'tes been standing for a thousand years. I'll be waiting for you, Lily, for as long as it takes. Even if it takes a thousand years."

"No!" She pushed the beautiful, terrible gift aside and backed away. "No, you musn't. I will be leaving here. I will return to my lao chia to end my days."

"Then I'll follow you there, and you can end your days with me."

"Oh, you are as stubborn as a rice bin!"

He cocked his head, an amused squint creasing the corners of his eyes. "A rice bin? How can a rice bin be stubborn? How can a rice bin be doing anything other than just sitting there?"

"It is an old Chinese expression."

"And a daft one, if you ask me." He set the pagoda carefully down on the counter and took a step toward her, his eyes intent on her face, his own face as hard as the granite he mined. "You've a lovely mouth, Lily," he said, and his voice was like incense, rich and heady. "Even when it goes all tight and stubborn like 'tes doin' now. I want to kiss your mouth . . ."

"No!" She nearly fell over the barrel of brooms again in her effort to get away from him. "What you suggest is shameful, dishonorable. If you persist in this behavior I shall take extra pains to ensure that our paths never cross."

"You already do."

"I shall be even more vigilant." She meant it. She thrust her chin into the air to show him that she meant it.

He studied her face for an intent moment, then gave a

sharp nod. "All right, then, I'll not speak again of kissing you," he said, and she almost snorted aloud in disbelief. What fool would wager a single *cash* on that?

She looked up at him, at his mouth. His lips were too full and soft-looking to belong to a man. She wondered what it would feel like to kiss them. And would the hair on his face be stiff or soft?

A pounding on the door startled them both. Relief flooded through Erlan as she hurried to answer it. Surely in another moment she would have allowed him to kiss her mouth.

"Huan yin!" she exclaimed with false cheer as she pulled open the door, and then a genuine smile brightened her face. "Hannah! Welcome. Be pleased to enter. I will put a pot of tea on to brew." She stopped as the lantern light fell full on Hannah's face. "What is it? What has happened?"

Hannah pushed back the sable-lined hood of her cloak. Her hands were shaking, her eyes shiny with fear. "Cle-Clementine's time has come, and that fool of a doctor's out on circuit till the end of the week."

Erlan gave a low half-worded cry as she whirled and hurried to the shelves behind the counter, where the mercantile's medicinal items were stored. "I have some herbs that might help," she said as she opened drawers. She filled small paper packets with the herbs and tucked them into her chang-fu.

She glanced up and caught the barbarian giant's eyes on her. It was strange, she thought, that she could feel his gaze when he looked at her. Feel it burning and tingling, like swallowing whiskey. "Mr. Scully . . . would you be so kind as to mind the mercantile until my husband returns?"

"'Twould be my pleasure, Lily," he said softly, and for a moment she became lost in his warm and gentle smile.

She heard Hannah's step behind her and she turned her head, breaking the spell. "I've tarragon salve, feverfew leaves, ginseng, and Siberian wort," she said.

"Do you know what to do with them?"

"Oh, yes. My father has many younger brothers, each of whom has several wives and concubines. I have been present at many births."

"Thank God," Hannah said with a sigh of relief. "I tried some of the other women—Mrs. Martin, the minister's wife, and Mrs. O'Flarraty, whose man used to superintend at the Four Jacks. They wouldn't come with me because Clementine's in my house." She uttered a harsh, broken laugh. "As if they think they could catch some sort of loathsome disease merely by crossing my threshold."

Sleet poured out of the night sky, glazing the streets and boardwalks. Wind drove icy needles into their faces like tacks as they plowed through the ragged trenches of rimed slush. It twisted their skirts around their legs and slapped their hair against their cheeks. It set the signboards to creaking and swinging wildly, and drowned out the piano and banjo music spilling from the saloons.

They entered the warmth and peace of the house on a gust of wind. Lifting her chang-fu, Erlan hurried up the stairs after Hannah and entered a bedroom that reeked of vinegar water.

The tattooed woman was bent over the bed, sponging off Clementine's naked breasts and belly. She straightened and turned to them. Tears streaked her face. "I've drawn some warm water from the reservoir and put some more on to boil," she said. "I'll fetch it up directly."

The woman on the bed was laboring hard, her breathing whipping through the room louder than the wind outside. Sweat ran off her in rivulets. The contractions were coming hard and fast, her belly shuddering, her legs trembling, yet it seemed she was barely aware of them. Clementine, the essence of her, lay in dreadful stillness, as if remote from the woman's body that was struggling to give birth. Her face was as pale as old wax.

"Merciful Kwan Yin," Erlan said. "She is dying."

To Erlan's shock, Hannah bent over and grasped the woman's shoulders, shaking her so hard her head lolled. "What's the matter with you, Clementine McQueen? Are you too much of a starched-up lady to fight? You always talked so big about Montana being like a man and how we couldn't let him get the better of us. So are you gonna let him win, Clementine? You gonna let him beat you?"

Clementine's eyes fluttered open. They were as dark as bruises, and empty. "Leave me alone, Hannah."

Hannah shook her again. "Fight, damn you. Fight!"

The butchered buffalo desecrated the pristine whiteness of the snow, the bloody meat glistening with the strychnined lard they'd rubbed in it the week before. The carcasses of half a dozen wolves lay scattered around it.

Gus toiled up the trail ahead of him like a slow-footed bear, wrapped up in a robe made from a winter-killed buffalo calf, his head swathed in otter fur. He pulled a lizard sled that was already piled with stiff gray skins. They plowed through a fine, hard powder snow, knee-deep and glittery white, what the old-timers called cold smoke.

The air was grainy with the wind-swirled ice powder, which was as sharp as crushed glass to breathe. The sting of cold made his eyes water and rasped at his lungs. A half-hearted sun had just come up. The wind thundered past them like buffalo in a stampede, and tasted of more snow. It was cold as brass.

"Not as many as yesterday," Gus said, his breath puffing white. "Maybe they're getting wise."

And maybe we killed them all, Rafferty thought. Maybe we've managed to skin every goddamn wolf there is in the world.

He picketed his horse to a tough little juniper. He loosened the cinch and put a stirrup over the horn to remind himself the saddle was loose. He brushed the frost off the animal's back with his fur-mittened hand. The horse snorted, blowing smoke. Icicles tinkled on his mane and tail.

They had laid the bait out beneath a bluff, to protect them from the worst of the wind while they skinned. The bluff was now crowned with a heavy crest of ice-snow. It thrust into the sky above their heads like the curl of a giant, frozen wave.

The white plain stretched before him, wide as forever. A hawk flew straight into the deep winter-blue sky. Always the thought of her was with him, like a steady, constant hum. *Clementine . . .* He let her name form in his mind and he shuddered. The shudder was more from the longing than from the cold. The cruel and sweet longing for her that was so familiar, as much a part of him as breathing.

He shuffled over to one of the wolves, the snow squeaking under his boots. He worked at breathing through his mouth; even in a cold this biting, the buffalo bait stank of corruption. He heard the wolves' howls now even in his dreams.

He skinned his three, slitting belly and legs. Knife snicking through frozen hide. The ripping sound of hair pulling off flesh. His hands stiff with the bone-ache of cold.

As he tossed the last of the hides onto the sled, the wind blew a whisper of snow off the crest overhead. He pulled a whiskey bottle out of his pocket and popped the cork. He took a powerful drink. The red-eye worked deep and hot within him.

He lowered his head to catch his brother staring at him, disapproval lines cut deep around his mouth.

He saw that mouth open and the breath come out of it like a puff from a pipe. "You know what Clementine said to me the day we left? She said to try and keep you off the whiskey, and yet I swear you've been pretty much pickled since we got here. What do you do it for?"

"I do it just for what-the-hell, brother." Rafferty presented him with the nastiest smile he owned. "You wanna see if you can make me stop?"

Gus stood deep under the overhang of snow-laden rock, looking like some great hairy beast in his buffalo coat. Vapor shot out of his nostrils as they flared with each angry breath. He and his brother had been circling each other for days now, like dogs spoiling for a fight, bristling and tight-muscled.

Gus knocked the ice off his mustache. Long curling plumes of snow whipped off the ledge above his head. "She's been through seven kinds of hell and all you can think about is adding to her worries."

Rafferty squinted against the glare of sun on ice, and he stared at his brother like a man sighting down a rifle. "Since I ain't married to her, why should I give a good goddamn?"

The sharp-edged wind lashed snow into a fury of whirling ice clouds. Rafferty blinked the powder from his eyes and thought he saw the ledge of snow above Gus's head tremble.

"Gus," he said, his voice quiet.

"And what about Hannah?" Gus shouted, whipping at his anger. "Do you think that woman deserves the way you've treated her—"

"You don't know shit from gold dust about what Hannah wants."

"I don't reckon she particularly wanted to be used as your whore for four years."

"Jesus's suffering ass! Can't a man have a lay without you moralizing about it six ways from Sunday?"

"You're just like him, aren't you? Pa's son clean on through. Whiskey and whores. You're just a new, improved version of Jack McQueen."

Rafferty snarled, his breath coming ragged and hard, as the tightly leashed rage burst free within him. "God *damn* you!" he bellowed, and took a lunging step at his brother.

Gus reared back. His boot slid on a frozen patch of blood. He flailed his arms at the air as he started to go down. The wind gusted, swirling ice powder around them like a blizzard under the blue sky. Then the wind-sculpted crest of snow broke free of the bluff with a crack like a rifle shot.

It slid in thick slabs through the air, knocking them to their knees. The snow hit the ground with a roar and billowed into the air in a giant cloud. For a moment Rafferty was buried beneath the weight of the snow, and he thrust upward, hard, with his legs and arms, until he broke free. He dug the wet, smothering powder out of his mouth and eyes as he struggled to his feet.

Where Gus had been, closer to the overhang, there was nothing but white powder and silence.

The thought entered his head: *Just leave him lying there. Get on your horse and ride on home to her, and you'll have it all then—everything you've ever wanted.*

He fell to his knees and began clawing frantically at the snow with frozen hands.

25

"Lie still, ye young bastard, don't bother me so. Your father's off bucking another bronco . . ."

Hannah Yorke jiggled the fussing bundle of baby girl in her arms as she sang in a smoky contralto. But her voice trailed off, and the jiggling stopped at the tinkle of laughter that came from the woman seated in her horsehair rocker.

"That," Clementine said, with another soft gurgle, "is the strangest lullaby I've ever heard."

The sound of Clementine's laughter, so rarely heard these days, plucked at Hannah's soul and brought a wide smile to her own mouth. "But fitting, don't you think, for a babe born of cow folk in the Montana Territory?"

She laid the baby down carefully in an empty champagne crate that had been padded with pieces of quilting. Saphronie and Erlan immediately gathered around the makeshift cradle, making faces and little cooing noises, which young Sarah McQueen ignored, choosing to fall asleep instead.

She had almost killed herself and her mother coming into the world, Hannah thought, but little Sarah sure enough seemed determined to stay now that she was here. She suckled lots and often and had filled out so much over the last four months that she was starting to look like a link of fresh sausage, pink and fat.

And she was turning into a spoiled little mite, too, what with three mothers—Clementine, Hannah, and Saphronie—to fuss over her all day long. And Erlan, too, who frequenly came by early in the morning to share a cup of coffee. This morning, the first morning of spring, she had arrived with her hands over her ears, claiming she could hear the baby's wails all the way over in the mercantile. Little Sarah had been awake all night with a colicky belly, and she'd wanted the rest of the world to keep her company.

Hannah hooked her bustled hip onto the edge of her black lacquer writing desk and picked up her cup, blowing on the coffee to cool it down. "We better hope that putting little Sarah to sleep in a champagne crate don't give her champagne tastes. What was it you used for your last blessed event, Clementine—a cracker box, wasn't it? Next time you really oughta—"

"Next time!" Clementine protested. She was sitting in the rocking chair she used to nurse Sarah, and she gave a little push with her foot now, making the slats slap the floor to emphasize her point. "I should hope I won't be having to face another *blessed event* for a good long while yet."

"If ever a man even once had to endure childbirth," Saphronie said in all seriousness, "I reckon there'd soon enough be an act of Congress passed against it."

Erlan smothered a laugh with her hand. "In China the day of a daughter's birth is forever after remembered as the anniversary of her mother's suffering."

"Hunh," Hannah snorted. She sucked in a scalding sip of the coffee, which was strong enough to float a kingbolt. "Don't Chinese women suffer having their boys as well?"

"Of course. But boys are wished for; girls are not."

A chorus of female voices rose up in protest against this, and Erlan laughed out loud.

A cottonwood log popped in the hearth, releasing a woodsy smell into the room. A pang of sweet contentment pierced Hannah's breast, so intense it left her almost dizzy. She looked from one dear friend to another. Saphronie, in her satin whore's dress, with her tears inked permanently on her face for all the world to see and shudder over. Erlan, in her blue quilted Oriental robe and English croquet sandals, with her homesick eyes. And Clementine . . . Clementine, looking so very Bostonian in a plain black muslin mourning dress with a high, stiff cleric collar, looking so very sad.

How different we all are, Hannah thought. And yet how much the same, in all our woman's sorrows and fears and vulnerabilities. In all our woman's strengths, to have endured what we have.

Saphronie, who'd gone to look out the window, spun away from it suddenly, her hand flattened tight across her chin to cover the tattoos. "The men," she said. "They're back."

Their horses' hooves made sucking, squelching noises as they plowed through the spring mud and pulled up at her fence. The men were all hair: matted brown buffalo coats and thick beards and scalps that hadn't seen a barber in five months, and evidently not an Indian either.

The yard gate opened with a whine. Hannah crossed her arms over her breasts and watched from the gallery as they came up her path.

Gus stopped at the bottom of the steps and looked up at her. Rafferty stood in the shadow cast by his brother's back so that she couldn't see his face.

"Howdy, Hannah," Gus said. His gaze shifted away from her. He stroked his mustache and swallowed. "Where's my wife?"

She was tempted to tell the man that his wife was dead. She figured he deserved the few moments' suffering that lie would bring him, since he'd been spared the agony of a sleet-sheeted November night, a doctor who was out riding circuit, a baby that was a hard time coming, and a game, tough little woman who'd gone from wanting to die to fighting so hard to live that it had nearly killed her.

"You got yourself a baby daughter," she said and turned her back, going inside the house and leaving them to follow.

They brought with them the pungent smell of Montana mud and buffalo coats. Their boots clumped and their spurs clinked on the stairs. Gus shouted his wife's name, his booming voice bouncing off the walls, filling Hannah's house with noise and life.

By the time she made it back up to the bedroom, Gus already had his baby girl in his big hands. He stood with his feet spread wide, a huge grin unbalancing his mouth. "Isn't she just about the prettiest thing you ever did see?" he said. And his laughter flooded the room like warm sunshine.

Clementine sat in the horsehair rocker, her hands folded in her lap, staring with wide, still eyes up at her husband. She wasn't smiling, but she looked pleased to have him home. There was a lightness about her, as if a burden had been lifted. "I named her Sarah," she said. "I hope you don't mind."

"He'd have the devil of a nerve minding," Hannah

snapped, "since he was so proud to be there at the begetting of it and so careful to be gone entirely for the birthing
of it." She would never forgive Clementine's men for not
having been here when she needed them.

Hannah cut an angry glance over to Rafferty, who
stood with one shoulder propped against the doorframe,
a cigarette drooping from the corner of his mouth. He
looked tough and ornery with his dark beard and shaggy
hair, sharp and edgy as a new penknife.

Their eyes met. She saw shadows in those hard, brassy
eyes that she had never seen before. A haunted quality, as
if something had happened to him out there on the plains
that had frightened him to the depths of his soul.

Slowly his gaze left her and went to Clementine. And
Clementine, feeling the touch of his eyes, turned her head
and looked at him, and the air between them suddenly
became as charged as a lightning field on a hot summer
night.

"I should go put the horses up," he said, peeling himself away from the doorframe and disappearing down the
hall.

He left a hard silence behind him. The fire popped, a
log shifted and then fell with a muted *thunk*. After that you
could have heard a leaf drop in a forest.

"Well!" Hannah exclaimed on a big push of breath.
"I reckon I'll go on over and open up the Best in the West
early today. 'Pears like if spring is really here there oughta
be quite a crowd coming in wanting to toast its arrival."

Her throat was tight, her eyes stinging, as she walked
slowly down the stairs, fumbling her way along the banister as if blind. She felt a deep, hollow sense of loss, as if
someone had died. There was nothing to keep Clementine
here now, with her men back and spring coming, a ranch
to work and a new little baby to raise.

Hannah picked up her French beaver bonnet from the
sideboard and placed it at a jaunty angle on her scarlet
head, anchoring it in place with a jet-studded pin. She

leaned closer to the mirror, and smoothed back the corners of her eyes, pinched her cheeks, and rubbed some color into her lips.

She lifted her sable-lined cloak off the bentwood coat tree, threw it over her shoulders, and stepped out into the first day of spring.

There was no sadder sight, Hannah thought, than a saloon in the harsh light of a morning.

The sun poured through the fancy sheet-glass window she'd had installed last year and picked out every stain, every scar, every sin. All the wet stains and cigar burns on the green felt gaming tables. The crack in the diamond-dust mirror, put there last December by a fist that had missed the head it was aiming for. The greasy finger marks on the decanters, cigar vases, and jars of brandied fruit that stood in a row behind the bar. The place smelled of last night's beer and whiskey and of a winter's worth of mud and sweat. It was empty now, but soon the same old faces would be back in here drinking, smoking, chewing, spitting, and cursing around the potbellied stove.

Through the sheet-glass window she could see Rafferty crossing the street from the livery, the mud squeezing out from under his boots. By the time he came through the door, she was behind the fortress of the bar. He left his coat on, which meant he wasn't staying long. And he left his hat on as a shield for his eyes.

Hannah swiped at the bar with a towel. "You look about as cheerful as a hell's-fire preacher," she said. She poured four fingers of whiskey into a glass and pushed it at him. "How 'bout something to cut the mud?"

He turned the glass in his fingers, studying the brown liquid, as if it were a crystal ball and he had a future that he cared about. He emptied the glass in two quick swallows.

"Come here, Hannah," he said, his voice roughened by the booze.

She came, though she didn't know why.

He turned, bracing his back against the bar, and pulled her into his arms. The buffalo hide beneath her cheek was soft and smelled faintly raw. She tilted her head and leaned back, the better to look at him. A flush of heat touched his cheeks and his mouth curved into a faint smile, and she felt an echo of an old desire. He lowered his mouth to hers.

She pushed him away. "You can't just blow in here, Zach Rafferty, and take things up as if nothin' happened."

"I always could before. So what're you gonna tell me, Hannah, that you're not feelin' well? That you've got the monthly curse or you imbibed a little too much hell brew last night? I reckon about the only thing left between us that we haven't done is lie."

"You oughta know me better than that, cowboy. And you know something else about me, too. Except for those years when I was whoring, I only sleep with one man at a time."

He gave her a long, deep look. "So that's the way of it, then."

"That's the way of it."

She flushed beneath his steady gaze and started to turn away. He caught her chin with two fingers and turned her head back to face him. "You happy, Hannah?"

She nodded, then shook her head. A short huff of hollow laughter pushed out of her chest along with a sigh. "I'm plumb scared spitless. I love him so much, Rafferty. Too much."

He let go of her chin and picked up his empty whiskey glass. He tilted it at her and lifted one corner of his mouth in a smile that was both sad and mocking, of her and of himself. "I reckon you and I are two of the same kinda fool. Falling hard for the wrong person. It's too bad we couldn't have fallen for each other." He set the glass back down on the bar with a clink that sounded too loud in the empty saloon.

She covered his hand with hers. "We did in a way."

"Yeah." He turned his head and gave her a warm, sweet smile. "We did."

She leaned into him, to kiss him on the cheek, and found his mouth instead. Desire echoed again within her. The kiss deepened, turning exquisitely soft and tender, and lingered on her lips as they parted.

"So long, darlin'," he said, giving her a quick, light brush on the cheek with the tips of his fingers.

It was, Hannah knew, the closest a cowboy ever got to saying good-bye.

One day in late April the men rode out to catch some mustangs.

Clementine went with them. She wasn't sure why she did so. She hated the ranch; she didn't care if they kept or lost it. With Charlie gone, she didn't care much about anything anymore, except Sarah. And even with Sarah she was careful. Her heart was still near to bursting with bitter pain. She felt as if grief had crushed her like a great weight of stones until there was nothing left of her.

The morning they went after the mustangs, she carried Sarah Indian-fashion on her back in a cradleboard. The way the men captured the wild horses was to walk them down, not allowing them time to graze or drink at their favorite watering holes, until they were tired and docile enough to be easily herded. Gus had ridden ahead, to chouse the mustangs toward a valley to the south of them, and he left Clementine to ride there with his brother.

It was the first time they'd been alone together, she and Rafferty, in so long. Yet she could find no words to say to him. There was love in her heart for him, but no longer any tenderness.

They rode through a wood of larch, fir, and yellow pine. Just as she could feel the warmth of the sun and the caress of the grass-sweetened wind, so she could feel his gaze touching her averted face. She thought perhaps he was disappointed in her. He had called her useless once, a liability, like a dogie not worth the slaughtering, and she had proved him right. She wasn't cut out for this country. She had tried to show them all that they were wrong, but Montana had beaten her—walked her down and worn her out, just as they were doing to the mustangs.

Although it was early morning, the birds were awake and noisy, flying in circles and cawing. A creek, flowing high from the winter runoff, rushed over tumbled boulders with a lion's roar. But their horses' hooves made no sound on the damp and matted pine needles, just as they, too, were silent.

They came out of the woods onto a high ridge that overlooked a narrow grassy valley. Sunshine shimmered and glimmered off the snow on the surrounding peaks, making the sharp, jagged rocks look as if they were dusted with gold.

Rafferty eased his horse up next to hers, so close that their stirrups knocked. Moses clicked his teeth on the bit and jerked his head, jingling the bridle's rings and chains. Clementine kept her gaze rigidly focused on the fiery mountains.

"The first white men to see Montana called it Land of the Shining Mountains."

Clementine said nothing. It was very beautiful and she hated it, hated it.

"The old-timers who named this land also had a saying about it: 'Sometimes a body's gotta lean into the wind in order to stand up straight.'" He nudged his horse closer, until their knees touched. "Clementine, darlin' . . . Montana didn't kill Charlie."

She swung around to face him, so fast and with such fury that he flinched a little. "I hate you. I hate everything about this place, and I hate you most of all."

She tried to urge her horse into a trot, but his hand lashed out, grabbing the reins. Her horse snorted, his hindquarters dancing sideways. "Why do you hate me, Boston? Because I can't give you a certified guarantee that there'll be no more pain, no more losses? Or do you hate me because you can't keep the whole damned world locked out of your heart no matter how much you might want to?"

She met his challenging look with a wordless, rigid pride. He let go of her reins, and she yanked her horse's head around, heeling him into a canter.

She didn't go far. She went to the shoulder of the ridge, pulled up, and slid out of the saddle. She threw the reins over her horse's head and let them trail. She slipped the cradleboard off her shoulders and wedged it up into the roots of an ancient giant larch. She stooped over and kissed Sarah's plump cheek, but the baby didn't awaken. She walked to the edge of the bluff, stirring up a nest of ground larks with the kick of her skirts.

Below her a mist lay in a gray scarf along the valley of sweet-grass meadows and gently rolling hills. In the shadow of the mountains the land was all tans and blues and purples.

Her horse lifted its head, his nose quivering, and then she saw them—the wild ones. A band of mustang ponies crossed the valley, wheeling in a half-moon arc, kicking up mud, shying and snorting and ripping up the tender spring grass with their hooves. They were small and sinewy and mottled-looking, for they were shedding their rough winter coats. But their manes and tails were long and flowing like spun flax. And they were all the colors of Montana in summer: dun and buckskin, chestnut and sorrel and bay.

The lead horse, a stallion, stopped and began to graze, and so the others followed. Gus had told her once there was always only one stallion to a band of wild ones. The stallion ruled with the help of a wise old mare. Sometimes geldings or mules who'd escaped from captivity were allowed to join the band, but never another stallion.

Just then this stallion jerked his head up, and though she was too far away to see, Clementine could imagine his nostrils flaring as he scented the wind. At the north end

of the valley she could just make out the small figure on
horseback that was Gus, approaching the band slowly so as
not to alarm them into an all-out stampede. The stallion
whinnied and broke into a gallop, and his mares followed,
and within seconds it seemed the valley was empty again.
But the mustangs' escape was only an illusion. In the end
the men would have their way—the wild ones would be
worn down, captured, and broken to the saddle and the
spur.

An immense sadness pierced Clementine's soul. Suddenly the great wilderness that was so beautiful seemed
too huge and lonely to be borne. She stared at the dazzling,
deserted land and sky, and the sight made her dizzy. She
tried to breathe, her chest pressing hard against her corset
ribs. Something within her wanted to shriek.

In the blue canopy of sky overhead, a big golden eagle
glided low, casting his shadow on the ground. The eagle
screamed, and Clementine thought for a moment that the
sound had been torn from her own throat.

She tilted back her head to the sky, letting the sun
drench her in light and warmth, letting it seduce her. The
wind gusted, stopping her mouth as if with a kiss, stealing
her breath. She felt ravished by the wind.

There was no going back to the Clementine she had
been before that summer day of dust and flying hooves,
and the end of Charlie's laughter. Charlie was gone, and
she was so afraid that in losing him she had lost the only
thing she would ever be any good at: loving Charlie and
being loved by him.

Yet somewhere deep inside her she could feel a stirring,
like a tender green shoot just pushing its way through the
thick, rich earth. She could feel herself coming back into
the rhythms of life. Montana, hated and beloved, claimed
her and it always would.

"Clementine . . ."

She turned, her skirts flapping in the wind. He came

toward her, her love. The sunlight was in his eyes, narrowing them, turning them into chips of fierce, clear amber, and everything inside her seemed to give way. A huge hard mass of sorrow rose up in her chest and broke loose, dissolving, shedding off of her like a chrysalis.

She didn't know the tears were coming until she felt them on her eyelids.

He touched her face with his fingers.

That was all he had meant to do.

He had seen her standing at the edge of the bluff. And it was like this sometimes with her: he would look at her and his heart would catch. She seemed so fierce, with her head held high on her slender neck and her shoulders drawn back, erect and proud. She was so brave, his darlin'. Too brave for her own good. He had known a fox to gnaw off its own leg to escape a trap—such a fierce, snarling courage was Clementine's.

She must have heard him, or sensed his coming, for she turned just then, and the sight of her crying was like a kick to his heart.

And so he had touched her face with his fingers. To catch her tears, maybe, or to wipe them away. That was all he had meant to do.

But somehow his arms were around her and he was pulling her body flush up against his. Her hair was thick and silky under his lips. Her wild rose scent clung to her skin, to the air, to his senses. He breathed her in.

He was going to pull away from her, to let her go, and then he made the mistake of looking down at her face and seeing the passion flood her eyes. Her mouth opened beneath his, her breath gusting out of her in a helpless moan. She tasted hot, of tears and hunger. His hand slid to her waist and slipped down to grip her bottom, molding her closer. He kissed her deep, tongue to tongue, their breath mingling, and she made little wordless sounds and rubbed against him as . . .

Sarah let out a loud, impatient wail.

She jerked away from him as if they'd just been doused with icy water. For a moment he couldn't breathe, and then it came out of him in a rush, along with a wrenching shudder. "Clementine," he whispered.

With a sharp cry, she whirled and hurried over to Sarah, who was now turning the air blue with her hollering.

The leather of his saddle squeaked as he put his weight into the stirrup. He swung up onto his horse and rode away from her without looking back.

Clementine looked down at the top of her husband's head. There was some silver mixed in with the tawny gold, and it made her sad to think of it, to think of time passing, of days that were being lived and could never be lived over.

Gus sat on a nail-keg stool outside the door of the buffalo hunter's cabin, his hands sandwiched between his knees, his brooding gaze dissecting the ground.

"Sarah's down for her nap," she said.

He raised his head to look at her. "You going to talk to him?" he asked. Clementine said nothing. "You won't talk him out of it," he said.

"I won't try to talk him out of it."

As she crossed the yard she looked back once, not at Gus but at the cabin. The phlox was blooming on the roof, a promise of summer days to come. Around her the burned-off meadows were spotted green in places with new grass, new life.

The wild plum thickets were in bloom along the river, filling the air with their thick, sweet fragrance. The willows were swollen and sticky with brilliant red buds. Larks sang, frogs croaked, and the river made its own music, deep and rich, like a man's laugh.

She spotted the sleeve of his hickory shirt among the

trees. He was fishing. At least he had a pole in his hands and a line in the water, but there was about him a sense of restless waiting, as if he knew she would be coming. She stopped farther than an arm's length away from him, for she didn't dare get close enough to touch. She wasn't afraid of him; she was afraid of herself.

He stared at her hard with those cold, uncomfortable eyes. "I reckon Gus told you I'm leaving in the mornin'."

She tried to say his name, but she couldn't.

"This time I ain't comin' back."

She had known this day would come. Ever since she had awakened, after the mad wolf had bitten her, to see the raw need in his eyes and the wondering look of a man in love . . . she had known he would have to leave her.

He set the pole down and rose to his feet. She stiffened, but he didn't take a step toward her. He only looked at her, and that was nearly more than she could bear.

"I'm going to say this once. I shouldn't say it at all, but I'm not tough enough to ride out of here and leave it unsaid. I love you, Clementine. But it's not the noble, chaste sort of love you seem to want from me. I want to take you, to make you my woman and only mine. I want to feel your hair slide across my naked belly. I want to know the taste of your tongue in my mouth. I want to have you beneath me, to spill myself long and deep inside you."

Oh, God, I am not worth all this . . . this passion, she thought. I was never worth it, and you make me so afraid. You have always made me so afraid.

"Clementine . . ." He looked up the river, squinting against the glare of sun on water. Then he pinned her with his yellow eyes. "Come with me."

She went absolutely still. Even her heart stopped beating. The silence stretched long and taut between them. She watched his face tighten, harden. She watched his eyes turn the brassy cold of winter suns.

"I love you, Zach Rafferty," she said. They were the first words she'd spoken to him since he had kissed her.

He pushed out a breath that caught and broke. "I know."

"I love you," she said again. And as on that day when they had captured the mustangs, she had the feeling of having burst free. She loved him so much. Sometimes you had to dare to grasp the lightning. And sometimes you had to dare to let it go. "Will you write?"

"No."

"To Gus. You could write to Gus."

He shook his head. And he broke then. She saw it in his eyes first, and then the anguish poured over his face. He turned his head, but she could see the cords in his throat working to keep back the tears.

"You will think of me." She said it as a command. He must think of her, for she was his. She would always be his.

"Clementine," he said, and her name came out of him broken and mangled. "My love for you won't stop with my leaving. Come an evenin' over the years, when you step outside your door and hear the wind blowing through the cottonwoods, that'll be me, thinking of you, whispering your name, and loving you."

She stared into his eyes, absorbing his pain, enduring it with him. Knowing it would be the last thing they would ever share.

Slowly, her gaze still on his ravaged face, she unclasped the cameo brooch at her throat. She didn't put it into his hands, for she couldn't bear to come that close to him. She laid it on the rock where he'd been sitting, and then she walked away from him without looking back.

Gus sat on the nail-keg stool and watched his wife come back to him. She went right into the house, without a word, without looking at him. But he had seen her eyes.

Gus sat with his stomach quaking and his leg muscles tense. He wanted to go down to the river and see Zach, see if the same look of longing and loss that he'd discovered in his wife's eyes was there in his brother's. Instead he sat on the old nail-keg stool and watched the sun set.

He sat there through the night. Just as the dark was beginning to soften into dawn, Zach came back from the river, or from wherever he'd disappeared to. He looked right at Gus and there was nothing in his eyes, and there was nothing said between them. And then he went into the barn.

A half hour later he came out again, leading his saddled gray. Tears filled Gus's eyes. He blinked hard, trying to will them away before his brother saw them. For he knew to his shame they were tears of relief.

Clementine pushed aside the curtain she had made long ago of bleached flour sacks and embroidered with little yellow finches. He was in the yard, her love, sitting on his horse, and Gus stood beside him, looking up at him and saying good-bye.

Gus would always be the cowboy of her dreams, but Rafferty was her life's passion. The man she was put on this earth to love with her every breath, every heartbeat.

She closed her eyes. She imagined herself going out the door and crossing the yard, holding out her hand to him so that he could pull her up behind him in the saddle. She imagined herself riding away with him, being with him, loving him forever.

She imagined herself going out the door and crossing the yard, but when she opened her eyes again he was no longer there, and all she could hear was the beat of his horse's hooves as he rode away.

PART THREE
1886

26

GUS MCQUEEN LOOKED UP into a hard morning sky that had already been bled white by a relentless sun. He cuffed the sweat off his face and whacked his hat against his thigh, raising a cloud of dust off his chaps.

"God damn," he said. The word tasted foul, but he said it again, trying to ease the weight off his chest, which was heavy with failure. "God damn it all to hell."

He squatted on his haunches beside the river and scooped up a handful of water, splashing it over his face. The water tasted foul, too, so alkaline it was almost thick enough to chew. It was no relief against the heat.

The sun seemed to melt and pour out of the sky, shriveling the grass and beating relentlessly at the air, and drying up the once muddy riverbank so that it curled and cracked like old paper. In all the years he'd ranched in this valley, he'd never seen the Rainbow running this low. Hell, it didn't even run now, it trickled. If it didn't rain soon he would go bust. But then, with cattle prices so low it didn't pay to ship the beeves to market, he'd probably go bust even if the sky suddenly started gushing water.

He stood up slowly, feeling old, his bones creaking. He unwrapped his horse's reins from around a chokecherry tree that had borne no fruit during this summer of drought, and headed toward home. His mare plodded along, her head hanging so low her nose nearly scraped the parched ground. It was too hot and dry to do anything but suffer.

As he emerged from the shadows of the cottonwoods, he disturbed a black-tailed doe that was grazing off the withered grass beside the salt block. The doe lifted her head and bounded away, her ribs showing through her hide plain enough to count. But her coat was long and shaggy. Yesterday Gus had caught sight of a white Arctic owl sitting on the snake fence. The wild geese and ducks and songbirds were already flying south, and lately the stars had been flashing and glimmering brighter at night. Even his own beard was growing faster. These were all signs that a bad winter was coming—although he didn't know how he knew this. Maybe Zach had once told him.

Zach. A sigh stretched across his chest, leaving behind an ache. He couldn't think of his brother without feeling this ache that was a convoluted mixture of love and hate, jealousy and longing.

Sometimes he would awaken in the stillness of the night and he would be haunted by images of his brother: Zach astride a bronc, his hand reaching for the sky; Zach cradling a bloody newborn calf in his arms; Zach dancing with Hannah on a summer's night, their laughter floating up into a star-filled sky . . . Zach left alone on the Natchez wharf, his head held high in rigid pride as the steamboat's paddles began to churn. And in the stillness of the night Gus would look at his wife's face and want to touch her, and he would be afraid to.

In the stillness of the night, when he had nothing to listen to but his own thoughts, a man couldn't hide from the truth of what he thought about himself. Down deep in the guts of him, in that secret, vulnerable place where a man lived, Gus thought he would never be the man his brother was.

He stopped now to look up at the big house through the shimmering heat ripples. They called it the big house not because it was big—though it was of a good size, with two stories and four bedrooms, even a water closet with a patent toilet—but to distinguish it from the buffalo hunter's sod-roofed cabin, which still stood in the shade of the cottonwoods along the river. The house had green-painted shutters, a double gallery wrapped all around it, and a shake roof with a pair of gables. He had at last given his wife some of the luxuries he'd promised her, even if he was already on the verge of losing it all again.

The new boards of the gallery steps squeaked beneath his boots. He entered by way of the front door, his nostrils pinching at the thick smell of burned niter papers and ginseng steam. He paused a moment, his heart clenched, as he listened for the wheezing sounds that meant the boy was having another attack. And let out a sigh of weary relief when the house gave back nothing but silence.

Their baby son, Daniel, born just last New Year's Day, suffered from what the doc called spasms of the lungs. Burning niter papers helped a little, and Lily Woo had shown them a Chinese remedy that involved inhaling the steam from boiling water heavily laced with ginseng. This soothed the spasms sometimes, but not always. Sometimes the baby's lips turned blue and his chest heaved with the frantic beating of his heart, and his arms waved wildly as if he were trying to pull the air into his wheezing lungs with his little hands. In those moments the helpless terror they felt was almost unendurable. Gus didn't think Clementine could survive having to bury another child. He didn't think he could survive it.

He took off his hat and ran a finger around the inside leather, wiping out the sweat. He hung the hat on a steer-horn rack just as a murmur of voices floated out from the kitchen—one shrill and petulant, the other soothing and patient: Saphronie trying to coax his two-year-old daughter, whose middle name was Stubborn, into finishing her stirabout.

A year ago if someone had told Gus that he would allow a harlot, even a reformed one, into his house to tend to his children, he probably would have called them a liar and spat in their eye. But Daniel's birth had been hard on Clementine, and with her stuck out here alone on the ranch, with the one baby barely weaned and the new one being so sickly, and then Hannah arriving that day with the tattooed whore in tow and acting mad enough to hiss fire, and . . .

And she had gone at it with him nose to nose. "You so impressed with what you got in your britches, Gus McQueen, that you can't keep 'em buttoned long enough for your woman to get over the last babe before you're planting another one in her belly? I 'spect you go easier on your broodmares than you do on your wife."

Angry words had built up in Gus's mouth to be stopped by a rigid-jawed shame. He lusted after his wife, he always had, and he couldn't keep himself from taking her. It was a weakness in him that he admitted to and didn't even bother to try to overcome. In his selfish desire to satisfy his carnal urgings he was his father's son. His brother's brother.

"You're just damn lucky, mister," Hannah had gone on, "that Saphronie here has agreed to do the heavy work and help care for your two babies and all for only board and a dollar a week. So damn lucky that you're gonna keep your mouth shut and let it happen."

And so he had done just that.

But he had never gotten used to the sight of her ravaged face—those dark blue teardrops running silently and forever down her chin. This mousy, morose woman bore the marks of cold, rough handling on her mind and body. Although he'd occasionally come upon her laughing and chatting with Clementine, and the children obviously adored her, she was always sullen around him, drawn deep inside herself. Perhaps it was because she sensed his thoughts, which Gus had to admit weren't charitable. But he just couldn't help feeling that somehow she should have found a way to stop the savages from taking her. A decent woman, it was said, always saved the last bullet for herself.

Gus came into the kitchen just as Sarah bellowed, "No more stir'bout!" and turned her bowl upside down on the table. The milk-thinned oatmeal mush splattered over the table and made a fine mess. Sarah looked at what she'd done and grinned. It probably wasn't good for his daughter's character, but Gus couldn't help grinning along with her.

Gus's gaze went to his son. The boy'd had another lung spasm attack last night, but now he seemed fine. He sat on Saphronie's lap, chanting nonsense sounds to himself and waving a spoon through the air.

Saphronie had cast a swift covert glance up at Gus when he entered the room, and now she lurched awkwardly to her feet while holding Daniel tightly to her chest. "I'll put him down for his sleep now," she said to Clementine, who stood at the ironing board, pressing the flounces on one of her petticoats.

"No sleep!" Sarah declared.

Clementine's eyes were on Gus, watching him intently, even as she sprinkled water on the wrinkled cloth and the smell of lavender filled the kitchen. "You may help Miss Saphronie gather eggs," she said to their daughter.

Sarah climbed off the chair herself and marched from the room, her back straight, her arms swinging like a little general's, making Gus smile. Already she had the world figured out, and she was in charge.

Saphronie, with Daniel in her arms, followed her. The woman definitely had some strange quirks, Gus thought. Today she wore yellow-striped knickerbockers that reached to her boot tops.

Gus wondered if Saphronie would leave if he told her he could no longer afford to pay her a dollar a week. Somehow he doubted it. And besides, it was Clementine's butter-and-egg money that paid Saphronie's salary. His wife churned butter, which she sold for twelve cents a pound, and raised hens, whose eggs she sold for five cents the dozen. It was Clementine's butter-and-egg money that had kept the ranch afloat this summer, and he hated having to admit that, even to himself. It was supposed to be the man's place to provide.

Clementine turned to the hob on the range and

clamped a handle around a hot iron. She lifted it, and he saw the fragile bones and sinews of her hand stand out against the chapped and reddened skin. A fine sheen of sweat coated her face, and yet there was that stillness about her that had always come from deep within her and had always shut him out. Sometimes he hated the strength he saw in her.

Sometimes he thought he was married to a woman he didn't know, and didn't like.

"Isn't it a mite hot to be doing that sort of work?" he said.

"It's got to get done, no matter what the weather," she answered, causing his jaw to tighten. She made him feel responsible for the heat and the drought, responsible for the whole miserable, sorry state of the world.

She set the iron on a trivet and lifted her head in time to catch the look on his face. "Gus? Is something the matter?"

"Why, heavens no, Mrs. McQueen," he said, mimicking her Boston reserve and high-blown manners that she could use like a shield to force people to keep their distance. "Everything's just as fine as frog hair. I got cattle out there dying on their feet, and it looks to be another wonderful day of a hundred degrees in the shade and hot winds that shrivel up the grass and dry up what's left of the water holes. Why, I don't reckon I remember when things've ever been this good."

He stopped to catch his breath and glare at her. "Why don't you just go ahead and say it. Go on, God damn you, say it!"

He shouldn't have cussed at her. He never cussed at her. But he saw no condemnation in her eyes, only concern.

"What do you want me to say, Gus?"

"That I should've seen the beef-market glut coming, should've known a drought was on the way when it didn't snow more than a few flurries last winter. That I shouldn't've run amok and overstocked the range just because we had one good boom year. That I shouldn't've borrowed to buy that timberland I wanted just because it'd come up for sale. Or mortgaged my soul to build an eastern house for my eastern wife out in the middle of a godforsaken Montana prairie where droughts and bad winters and hard winds and grass fires are as common as weeds in June . . ."

His eastern wife was looking at him, saying nothing. Whatever she was feeling she had under control, buttoned up tight like her stiff collar. The only times he'd ever known Clementine to let herself go were in bed, in his arms, and that one time at Charlie's grave when she'd screamed her guts out in rage and pain. He wished she would let go now, rant and rail at him, maybe even cry. Hell, what kind of woman was it who never cried? He wanted her to act scared so that he could play the man and comfort her.

She took a step toward him, and he backed away from her, horrified at the sudden tide of feelings that surged in his chest. He was the one who wanted to rant and rail and cry. He was the one who needed comforting.

"Gus, what is it? What's wrong?"

His hip knocked into a chair, and he sat down in it. He went to bury his head in his hands and planted one of his elbows in a glob of Sarah's mush. "Well, hell," he said and started to laugh, but the sound that came out his mouth was a sob. He pressed his fist hard against his lips.

A hot wetness burned the backs of his eyes and he squeezed them shut. When he opened them again she was standing beside him. He couldn't lift his head, couldn't let her see his face, not with the stinging heat filming his eyes again. Her hand came up and touched the fist he still had pressed tightly to his mouth, and it was like pulling a bung out of a barrel.

The words spewed out of him, harsh and grating. "Oh, God, Clem . . . we're stone-broke, the taxes are coming due, and the whole blamed ranch is mortgaged from root cellar to chimney. The cattle aren't just thirsty any-more, they're dying, and what's still living are pure scrubs. I borrowed against the land to build this house, and I'm so blasted . . ." *Scared.* But he couldn't tell her that. He couldn't tell her how scared he was. He was the man. He was the one who was supposed to take care of her. He was the one who'd always been so full of big talk about giving her back all the things she'd given up when he talked her into running off with him, full of such big plans about how he was going to make the Rocking R into the best spread north of Texas.

Somehow her hand had wound up on his head and she was smoothing his hair over and over the way a mother would touch a child. Sweetly. It felt so good, her touching him like this, and it made him ashamed. Ashamed that he needed it so.

"How much do you need?" she said.

For a moment he misunderstood, and he almost said it aloud: *I want all of you. All of you, Clementine, including—maybe most especially—the parts of you I've never had.* And then he realized in the instant before the words left his lips that she was talking about money, and he let out a harsh laugh. "About all what's in the Miners Union Bank if we took a notion in our heads to rob it."

"For the taxes, then. How much do you need for the taxes?"

He rubbed a hand over his face. He was shaking, but deep inside himself, low in his belly where, thank God, she couldn't see it. "Around a hundred."

She left his side, and he almost reached out to pull her back. He heard her cross the kitchen, her heels click-ing on the pine boards. There was the rattle of crockery and then the click of her heels again, and then she was setting something between his spread elbows, something that clanked when it hit the table and smelled of flour.

It had been in the flour bin, *hidden* in the flour bin. He felt the flour on his fingers when he picked it up, this sacklike thing that was shaped like a heart and made of some silky material, this sacklike thing that clanked and was heavy and was filled with . . .

He lifted his head and stared at her. She stared back at him with that wide, still gaze of hers.

His hand closed around the silk sack, so tight he bruised the flesh of his palm. "Where did this come from?" And he thought in the next instant that if she said it had come from his brother, he would kill her.

"From my mother. There was more, but I've spent some of it over time. On my photographic equipment, because you disapproved of it so, and it didn't seem right to use your money, and . . . and on other things—"

"Other things I disapproved of?"

She drew in her breath, her shoulders stiffening. Yet she clamped her mouth shut, as she always did rather than argue with him. He wanted to shake her, he wanted to hit her. He wanted to make her *feel* something, damn her.

He didn't realize he had lunged up out of the chair, his hand raised in the air, until she flinched away from him. Her eyes were wide and dark now, her fists gripping the heavy black material of her skirt.

She lifted her chin, but the fear was still wild in her eyes, and he felt a certain satisfaction in it, God help him. "Will you strike me, Gus?" she said in a small, tight voice. "Will you go back on your word and strike me again?"

His hand fell to his side, balling into a fist, and he turned away from her. "No. But I ought to. I ought to."

He tossed the sack of money onto the table and flinched himself at the loud clatter it made in the suddenly silent kitchen. All these years . . . she'd had it all these years, and she'd kept it hidden from him. She'd had it the year of the fire, and the winter he and Zach had gone wolfing. He flung his head back, clamping his teeth together hard to hold back a howl of pain and rage. Inside him something felt torn. "Just tell me one thing: all those times we could've used it . . . why didn't you give it to me before?"

When she didn't answer, he swung around. "Why, damn you?"

"Because it was mine. *Mine.*" He watched her chest heave as she struggled to draw in a breath, watched her trying to contain herself, this woman who never cried, never broke, never gave in. "And because Mama . . . she made me promise, and I owed it to her to keep my promise. She—she said no matter what sort of man I believed you to be, I should keep it as my own secret. Otherwise you would think it yours by right and take it, and then if I ever had to leave, I wouldn't . . . I couldn't . . ." She drew her lower lip between her teeth and pushed it back out again, and to his utter self-disgust he was suddenly filled with a fierce need to press his mouth to hers, to take her mouth. And he hated her for it. In that moment he truly hated her.

"And has that crossed your mind, Clementine? Are you going to leave me someday? 'Cause if you are, then you may as well get while the gettin's good, huh? You don't do me any big favor by staying, you know. I got along fine before I met you, and I reckon I'll go on living if you decide to leave."

The blood drained completely from her face, as if he'd torn open her heart. She jerked her head back and forth, once. "Oh, Gus . . . how can you say such a thing? You don't understand—"

"You're goddamned right I don't understand! I gave you all that I had. Everything that was mine I gave to you. Everything I had to give, from heart to guts, I let you take it all, and willingly. I'm not saying I wasn't willing. But I swear to God, girl, I feel sometimes as if I'm looking at you from the other side of a hurricane fence. Is there a heart inside you? Are there any *feelings* beneath all that starch and all those manners?"

She took his words like blows, almost cringing. "I don't mean to be that way. I don't mean it . . ."

She didn't cry; she never cried. Yet her shoulders bowed and she clutched at her belly as if he'd driven his fist in there. He'd hurt her, just as he'd meant to, and now he couldn't bear it.

"Clementine . . ." He reached for her, pulled her into his arms.

And she clung to him as if she were drowning. She sought his mouth, sucked frantically on his lips as if she could draw the life out of him and into herself. She arched against him, pressed her body hard to the length of his. She breathed into him, spoke into his mouth. "Love me, Gus. Please love me."

He gripped the sides of her head and looked down into her face, searching for the truth. Searching for her. "Please," she said.

"Let's go upstairs."

A faint flush colored her cheeks, but she nodded and pulled away from him, breathing hard. She led the way out of the kitchen and up to their bedroom.

The green shutters had been pulled closed against the glare and heat of the sun. The room was dim, quiet. From outside he could hear the faint sound of his daughter's laughter and the mad cluck of chickens and the wind that rose up late every morning, a false harbinger of afternoon storms that never came. In all the years of their marriage they had never made love in the daylight. It wasn't the sort of thing a decent man asked of his gently reared, God-fearing, preacher's daughter, virgin-when-you-married-her, and every-inch-a-lady wife. But now it struck him, looking at her in that moment, that whoever he had always thought her to be . . . she wasn't that woman at all.

She stood at the end of the bed, facing him, her hands at her sides. She started to lift them, to let down her hair, maybe, or to unbutton her dress, but then she let them fall again. She looked so vulnerable, so ash-fair, frail, and delicate, so like the girl he had married seven years ago. He slowly let go of the breath that fought to leave his chest. "I'm sorry," he said.

"I'm not sorry, Gus." She shook her head hard, fiercely.

And the fierceness was in her voice as well. "I've never been sorry."

They weren't talking about the same thing, but it didn't matter, because she had crossed the room and come into his arms, and the feel of her was so familiar and he wanted her. She was Clementine and she was in his arms.

And still, it wasn't enough.

Clementine sucked in her stomach, grunting with the effort it seemed to be taking to hook her corset. Her Dr. Jaeger's combination undergarment, made properly out of wool to absorb perspiration, was serving its purpose—already it clung to her sticky skin. Onto the corset she buttoned a crinolette petticoat, and over this she tied on a horsehair bustle. She had to sit in a chair to fasten her half boots, which still smelled faintly oily from the fresh blacking she'd rubbed on them last week. She put on a plain black alpaca skirt and a matching wasp-waist jacket bodice. She pulled her hair into a snood on the back of her neck and covered it with a black slat bonnet. In spite of the stifling heat she put on a linen duster, for she could not afford to expose her clothes to the ruinous alkali dust. And Limerick gloves to protect her hands. Hands that had been ruined long ago.

She had started to leave the room when her gaze fell on the bed. Dusty bars of light cast by the sun slanting through the shutters fell across the rumpled sheets. The smell of sex was thick in the still, heavy air.

He had been desperate in his loving, almost rough. Well, they'd both been that way, going at each other like animals. It might have been, she thought, his own feelings of failure that had pulled Gus behind her up those stairs, into bed. A need to get back his man's pride. But she knew she was the one who had failed him, was failing him.

She turned her back on the bed and all the feelings of longing and loneliness that it evoked. She went downstairs and out into the yard.

Saphronie already had the spring wagon hitched up for her, the eggs packed with straw in their baskets, the butter crocks covered with cheesecloth against the flies. A Winchester rifle angled muzzle-down next to the plank seat, although the country wasn't so dangerous anymore. The wolves and panthers and bears had been driven higher up into the mountains. Iron Nose and his band of renegades had ridden into legend.

Clementine's gaze went to the buffalo hunter's shack. She had a sudden memory of herself standing at that old sawbuck table, up to her elbows in bread dough, and Gus smiling at her, saying, "I ought to get you a milch cow so's you can have fresh milk for your coffee. And maybe a flock of laying hens, too." And her thinking then how she didn't know the first thing about milk cows or laying hens.

What a child she'd been that day, feeling disappointed because Montana and the ranch weren't what her dreams had been made of. Yet she had been happy. She was sure, remembering it now, that she had been happy.

She held her hat down against a sudden gust of wind that whipped up the dust in the yard. She tilted her head back, squinting. The sky was flat and dull as a tarnished pewter dish. High herringbone clouds wreathed the sun. There would be no rain again today.

The door banged behind her and Clementine whirled, surprised, for she thought Gus had ridden out already. He hadn't even finished dressing. His braces dangled at his hips and his shirt was unbuttoned. He wasn't wearing his hat, and his sun-shot hair was mussed where she had raked her fingers through it. His forehead, usually covered by his hat, was startlingly white next to the rest of his face, which was as brown as a hazelnut. There were white creases around his eyes, too, from when he used to laugh. It was the thing about him she'd always loved—his easy and joyous laughter.

They looked at each other for a long moment in silence. His thick mustache fell over the corners of a mouth that hadn't smiled since the rain had stopped coming, maybe not since Charlie . . . He no longer had that bright unbeatable look about him. She wanted to bring it back, but she didn't know how.

"It's too late to be going into town now," he said.

"I thought we needed money," she said back to him, hating herself for fighting him unfairly when she shouldn't have been fighting him at all.

His face flushed and his mouth tightened. "I reckon we won't starve between now and tomorrow, though."

Once every week or so she took her butter and eggs into town to sell. And though she had planned on going today, she could just as easily go tomorrow. But the wildness was building inside her—those frantic, frenzied soul-yearnings that threatened at times to drive her mad. She had to get away, away from Gus and the ranch, out where the sky was bottomless and without end in any direction, where the cloud shadows chased each other across mile after mile of grass. Out where she could surrender to the loneliness.

She drew in a slow, deep breath and fought to still the trembling that was going on inside her. "Gus . . ."

She wanted to tell him that all this disquiet, this restlessness, this constant yearning for things she couldn't even name had nothing to do with him. It was all her fault. What he'd said about the hurricane fence—he was right. It seemed she'd always looked at life from behind a high, broad barrier. She wanted to talk to him about all that he had given her, how he had saved her, shown her, been the cowboy of her dreams.

She climbed into the wagon, gathered up the reins.

He laid his hand on her arm. "Clementine, don't be like this. If you're angry with me for what . . ."

She looked down into his eyes, eyes that were blue as the noon sky but full of reproach and hurt and the residue of anger. And questions she couldn't answer for herself, let alone for him.

"My going into town has nothing to do with . . . with what just happened," she said. She wished she knew what had happened between them. It seemed they had brought each other release, but they hadn't soothed each other's heartache.

I love you, Gus, she thought, *but not enough for me. And not enough for you.* And ironically, because it wasn't enough for him, because he had that sort of pride, he made her think she could love him enough after all, if she tried hard, really tried. And if she would only stop listening to the sound the wind made as it blew through the cottonwoods, and stop thinking of what could have been.

She clicked to the team. The iron tires crunched over the hard ground. The wind drove grit into her face, and she shut her mouth against the bitter taste of it. When she turned onto the road into town, she looked back. The dust the wagon had churned up was settling down, and Gus was gone.

The wind was blowing Montana-strong now. She had to brace both feet on the dash and lean into it. The horses walked with their heads down, tails whipping. She could feel her face drawing tight, like a cowhide stretched in the sun to dry. The dust burned her nostrils and stuck to her sweat-slick skin. The sunlight was bright, hard, and metallic, fading the colors of the land.

This land, this place. The fierceness, the heartbreaking emptiness. The wild loneliness of it called to what blew wild and empty and lonely within her. Perhaps, she thought, there were some spaces within a soul that could never be filled.

She stopped for a moment when she arrived at the new acreage Gus had bought. It was mostly beautiful buttes heavily timbered with yellow pine, black ash, and box elder. Running between the two biggest hills was a coulee choked with red dust and rocks and entangled with stonecrop and wild plum thickets. The coulee had been cut through the earth during the wet springs of earlier years.

Built into the slope above the coulee was an old sod house that had collapsed in upon itself. It was known around the RainDance as the madwoman's soddy because poor Mrs. Weatherby, who'd once lived there, had been driven mad by the wind. There were many such abandoned places throughout the valley. They were called "hope's skeletons." Clementine wondered if that would be said someday of the new house Gus had built for her—just another hope's skeleton. And found she could not bear the thought.

Suddenly she felt watched and she spun around on the seat. She raised her hand, shielding her eyes from the glare of the sun.

She thought at first he wasn't real, a dream created out of her mind from the dust and shimmering heat ripples. A man in a dusty black Stetson, on a big gray standing still beside the fingerboard that pointed the way into Rainbow Springs.

The reins went slack in her hands. She thought she could actually feel her heart slamming in slow, painful strokes against her breast. The wind blew wild, crying her name. But it was his voice . . . his voice.

The man on the big gray rode at her. She wasn't sure when the hope began to die. It was the way he sat the horse or held his head or simply was. Was not.

Yet she clung to the hope still, because she couldn't bear to let it go, up until the moment when the stranger drew abreast of her and lifted his hat, saying, "Howdy, ma'am."

"Sir," she said with a small nod.

She sat trembling on the plank seat until he was well past her, until he had enough time to ride past the madwoman's soddy and then some. Then she bent over, wrapping her arms around her middle. She took a deep breath, and then another and another, until her chest began to shudder with the tears she would never let out.

Clementine pulled the team up abruptly to avoid running over a whiskified man who had come flying out of the

Gandy Dancer saloon. Wagon axles squealed behind her. The air rang with whoas and curses.

Rainbow Springs had never been a pretty town, but now it was truly ugly. There were bald spots in the hills where the trees had been cut down to shore up the mine workings. The buildings were all ramshackle and weather-pitted. And over it all loomed the RainDance Butte, barren and scarred and rutted with erosion. The streets all ended in mounds of tailings and dirty slag piles. A pall of brown smoke hung listlessly overhead.

I reckon I'm seeing the elephant, Clementine thought with a sudden inward laugh, as another fighting drunk flew backward out the Gandy Dancer's slatted swinging doors. But she was no longer that girl who had grown up in luxury and suffocating godliness in that house on Louisburg Square, that girl who had yearned for grand adventures. She didn't know who she was anymore. She felt like a stranger to herself.

The air shivered with the harsh clang of metal banging on metal. Clementine looked southeast, where a pair of thin parallel silver strands ran into town from out of the prairie. A crew of Chinese toiled at laying the last few feet of track for the new spur line of the Utah and Northern Railroad. They worked barefoot, with their baggy blue pants rolled up to their knees and their queues coiled around their heads. Another Chinese gang was busy building a water tank. One man stirred a great black steaming vat of tar with a big long-handled paddle. The vat sat on a bed of glowing coals and emitted a suffocating stench. It was hot work, Clementine thought, to be doing under today's angry sun.

Just then she spotted Sam Woo crossing the vacant lot where the depot would soon be built. He carried, balanced on his shoulders, a pine pole with large covered metal containers swaying at either end. It had been Brian's idea to go after a contract with the railroad to dispense hot tea to the Chinese workers, and it had turned out to be a real moneymaker.

At the moment, though, Sam was having trouble making his way through the north end of the lot, where a crowd had gathered around an old dray. A man stood on the empty bed, shaking his fist in the air and shouting himself red in the face. Clementine called out to Sam, but he didn't seem to hear.

"The Chinese must go!"

The words, which had come blasting as if out of a bullhorn, startled Clementine. She had assumed the man on the dray was a temperance shouter.

"The heathen Chinee is a parasite!" he bellowed. He was a muscle-knotted man in homespun britches patched with buckskin, and a head of tangled gray hair. He punctuated his speech by waving his big hands through the air. "The Chinaman spends his time eating opium and worshiping his foul gods. He takes slave wages and cheats the American man out of his honest day's labor. I say let's rid this country of the pig-tailed hoards. Let's chase 'em back to China where they belong!"

The crowd stirred, rustling and shifting from foot to foot like crows on a fence. One man spotted Sam Woo and cried out, pointing. The ragged edge of the crowd surged toward the storekeeper, jostling him roughly! The tin containers tipped, sloshing steaming tea into the dirt.

"The Chinaman is no more a citizen than a coyote is a citizen, and he never can be!" the man on the dray shouted. "The Chinese must go!"

The crowd took up the chant. "The Chinese must go!"

Clementine tried to turn her wagon into the lot, but she was blocked by the crowd. She wrapped the reins around the brake handle and stood up. "Mr. Woo," she called out, "may I offer you a ride back to your mercantile?"

Sam turned toward her, puckering his shortsighted eyes. He bobbed his head, since he couldn't bow with the pole across his back, and his thick spectacles flashed in the sun. "Very kind of you, Mrs. McQueen," he shouted back, "but this Chinaman has business he must do."

"Mr. Woo, I really think you should ride along with me. Mrs. Woo would wish it."

"No can do. No sirree jingle."

Clementine unwrapped the reins and urged the team forward, feeling uneasy. But when she looked over her shoulder, she saw that Sam was all right. He had reached the railroad section gang and was already pouring out cups of hot tea.

She caught sight of a shiny black Peerless buggy parked in the shadow of the half-built water tower. The man driving the buggy was dressed fine enough to be seen in the grandest hotel in New York City. The brocade on his vest shone like gold bullion, and the studs on his shirt sparkled in the sun like diamonds. They probably *were* diamonds, she thought a moment later when the man turned his head and she saw the black patch that covered his eye. One-Eyed Jack McQueen, gambler and swindle artist and now primary owner of the Four Jacks silver mine, as well as numerous other lucrative business interests.

He tipped his silk hat to her, his roguish smile flashing as bright as his shirt studs. She wouldn't put it past the man to have been behind that soapbox orator and his anti-Chinese rabble-rousing. As long as she had known him, Jack McQueen had been stirring up trouble just for the pure deviltry of it.

She was damp with sweat and coated with red dust by the time she pulled up to the hitch rack at the Woo mercantile. She had one foot on the ground and the other still on the foot bracket when her stomach seemed to rise up into her throat. She bent over, drawing deep breaths as she fought the nausea down.

She straightened her back slowly, feeling chilled and clammy. The world tilted slightly and then settled. She drew in another deep breath of the dry hot air.

She took off her linen duster and shook it, and the fine red dust floated down like mist. It disturbed the flies that buzzed over the dung in the street, and they swarmed in a black cloud around her face. The nausea rose up in her throat again.

The heat burned through the soles of her half boots as she walked down the boardwalk. She had to lift her skirts high above the tobacco muck that smeared the bleached planks. The Ladies Social Club had persuaded the town fathers to pass an ordinance against spitting on public pathways, but thus far it was neither obeyed nor enforced.

When she reached Hannah's white picket gate she had to stop again and fight off another wave of dizziness. She gripped the wooden slats so hard she rammed a splinter through the heel of her glove.

"Clementine!" Hannah came tripping down the path in a flash of poppy-red skirts. "I was beginning to think you weren't coming this week . . . Land, gal. You look like you're about to faint."

"It's just this dreadful heat."

"Ain't it awful, though." Hannah looked up at the sky, squinting. "Lord, there's not enough rain in them clouds to douse a candle. I can't promise it's much cooler inside, but at least we can get you off your feet."

Clementine looked back at her wagon and the mercantile through shimmering heat ripples. Those two old prospectors, Pogey and Nash, were roosting where they did every day now, on a spindle-backed wooden bench beneath the store's fancy new sheet-glass window. Sacks of potatoes and barrels of salted pork and mackerel were lined up with military precision on either side of the door. Since his marriage, the whole of Sam's mercantile was like that, as organized as a trail cook's wagon. Just then Erlan stepped outside, her pregnant belly leading the way. Her expectant happiness—that was what the Chinese girl called her unborn baby.

Clementine realized that Hannah was talking to her. "What? . . . Oh, no, I must unload my butter and eggs first, before they spoil. And today I really mustn't dawdle. I need to get home well before dark or Gus'll start to fret."

Yet she lingered a moment, for there was something she needed to tell Hannah, and she was afraid she wouldn't get the chance later. She could feel her cheeks burning, and she knew it wasn't only from the heat. Even with Hannah she'd never found it easy to discuss sexual matters and bodily functions. She kept hearing her mother's voice saying, "Never ask such naughty questions."

She drew in a deep breath and let it out slowly. "Hannah . . . that female preventive you gave me—it appears not to have worked. I am with child again."

"Oh, honey . . ." Hannah slipped an arm around her waist, and Clementine turned into her, like a child seeking comfort. "Damn that Gus McQueen," Hannah said. "When's he gonna learn that he doesn't have to go mountin' you every time he gets the urge?"

Clementine stiffened and jerked away from her. "You've no call to speak so, Hannah Yorke."

The color surged high on Hannah's cheekbones, but she didn't apologize. She and Gus had always brought out the worst in each other. "I only meant to say he's wearing you to a frazzle havin' his babies."

"They are my babies as well." She bit her lip and looked away, her chest hitching. "Only I don't want this one," she said, and the words tasted like the foulest blasphemy in her mouth. Yet they were true. She was so afraid. Afraid of dying, afraid of having this baby only to lose it, to have to bury it out there beneath the cottonwoods beside Charlie. "Neither will its father want it when he comes to learn of it. He's got so many worries weighing him down, with the ranch and the drought and little Daniel being so sickly and . . . and all."

Her mind went back to what they'd done on that bed and the empty way it had left her feeling. The big walnut sleigh bed with its matching bonnet highboy and marble-topped dresser—all costing a pretty piece of change and bought with borrowed money because Gus had wanted to please her. And she had let him do it to please himself.

"You'll both feel different once the baby actually gets here," Hannah said. "Once winter is over and the spring rains come."

"Will we?" Clementine looked up at her friend's concerned face. Hannah's cheeks were shiny and flushed with the heat and coated with a fine layer of dust. "Will we feel different come spring?"

Hannah's mouth tightened, making her look suddenly old. "Maybe not."

Clementine felt a strange tension in her stomach. A restless fluttering, although it was still too early for her to be feeling life. Expectant happiness . . . She had a sudden memory of her mother sitting in a white rattan chair, surrounded by the smell of Easter lilies, laughing with relief, weeping with pain because there could be no more babies. How old had her mother been on that day? No older than she was now, surely. All those questions she had once wanted to ask of her mother, and most of them were still unanswered. That heart-shaped sachet filled with coins—her mother's only legacy. In the end she had given it up to Gus so easily, without a thought.

"Maybe you'll have another girl," Hannah said.

Clementine pressed a hand to her stomach, which was already growing round beneath the steel busks of her corset. "If she is a girl, Hannah . . . I will raise her to be different than we are. She will grow up strong and certain of who she is and what she wants. And she will never be afraid."

Erlan wrestled the pork barrel over the threshold and onto the boardwalk. It was not an easy task, for her pregnant belly kept getting in the way. And though her golden lilies were no longer two tiny arcs, she could still only move about in short hopping steps.

She moaned as she straightened up and pressed her fist against a sharp burning pain beneath her breastbone. She cursed the unlucky demon that had tricked her into eating those beans for lunch. They gave out wrong *chi* and caused great imbalance among her inner organs.

Oh, but it was as hot and dry as a dragon's breath today. And the dust! She frowned at the sight of the new sheet window. Only this morning she had washed it, and now you could barely read the words painted in gilt on the glass: Sam Woo's Emporium.

She wondered if it had ever been this hot or this dusty in Foochow. It was odd that she couldn't remember, for lately all her dreams had been filled with vivid images of home. But on waking she often wondered if her dreams had lied. Surely the mists had never been so white, the rice paddies so green, the sunshine so soft and golden. She wondered how it could be that her memories had grown shabbier than her dreams.

Soon, though, she would have no need for either dreams or memories. Her debt was nearly redeemed, the bargain fulfilled. In a croquet-sandal box beneath her bed were one thousand one hundred and sixty American dollars in greenbacks and silver. And growing big in her belly was a baby.

Except . . . except that when she had made her bargain with the merchant Woo, when she had promised to give him a son, she hadn't understood how much a part of his his son would be. How they would share the same body and the same blood, draw life from the same air. Now she wondered how she would ever be able to leave a child, *her* child, here in this alien land when it came time for her to return to her lao chia.

She thrust the thought away, unable to bear it. An expectant mother shouldn't dwell on sad thoughts anyway lest the baby be born to an unhappy life. To be with child was a lucky thing, and the gods were often spiteful toward those who had too much good joss.

A stream of tobacco shot through the air, interrupting Erlan's thoughts, barely missing her protruding stomach, and splatting with dead-eye precision on a knot on the hitching rail.

Erlan planted her fists on her hips and cast an exasperated glare at Mr. Pogey, who sat on the deacon's bench beneath the window, working his jaws like the rods on a locomotive. She had set the bench out in front of the mercantile to encourage customers to linger awhile and perhaps spend more money. But Pogey and Nash had established squatter's rights; most of the prospecting they did these days was for gossip, not gold.

"Good day to you, gentlemen," she said, shuffling up to them in her awkward, mincing gait.

The old prospectors stumbled to their feet, doffing their hats. "How there, Mrs. Woo," Nash said. He waved at the spot on the bench he'd just vacated. "You oughta sit down here and rest a spell. You're lookin' kinda peaked." The smile he gave her was so broad his store-bought teeth slid off his gums. "Reckon it's that heavy load you're carrying that's wearin' you down."

Pogey, who was in the act of resettling himself, stopped halfway to stare up, round-eyed, at his partner. "Good God and all the little god-almighties! What you want to go insultin' Mrs. Woo for? No woman likes a man pointin' out to her how ugly she's lookin'. Even Chinee women've got their sensitivities."

"I didn't say she was looking ugly. Only kettle-bellied. Like someone tried to draw her through a knot-hole headfirst."

Erlan covered her mouth with her hand to stifle a giggle.

Pogey gave his partner a long, slow look. "Shee-it, Nash," he drawled. "Once you get your toe in your mouth, I guess you figure you might as well shove your whole foot in."

"Can I help it if I still ain't used to bein' surrounded by women and their sensibilities ever' whichaway I turn?" Nash restaked his claim on the bench. He hooked his thumbs around his striped suspenders, stretched them out, then let them snap back onto his red plaid chest with a loud pop. "What you see when you look at me is one of the original items—a trailblazer extraordinaire. Why, when I first set foot in this country, there were few white men, let alone women, to take offense every time a body opened his mouth. Now we got ourselves ladies' societies and school-teachers and temperance shouters who damn a man for being a man. And no one can say whoa to 'em."

Pogey fingered the chawed cud from his mouth and put in a fresh one, stuffing it deep in his cheek to let it soak. "Yeah, well, that was then and this is now, and all your jawing won't make it any different. Trailblazer ex-traordinaire . . . Christ all get out. You couldn't find shit in a cow barn with a compass and a pitch torch. The hot wind you blow would put a chinook to shame."

Mr. Nash was truly full of windy talk, Erlan thought, and she turned her head so that he wouldn't see the laugh-ter on her face and think her rude.

She caught sight of a giant of a man walking among a group of miners bound for the Four Jacks and the after-noon shift. But if Jere Scully saw her he didn't let on. It had been months since he had come around to the mercan-tile. She had been so cruel to him, so cold, that at last she had driven him away. And she was glad of this. Oh, yes, truly she was glad—for he frightened her with his talk of kisses and forever-after.

She noticed Clementine McQueen unloading her but-ter crocks and egg crates from the back of a spring wagon. And Hannah was on her way over to help. Perhaps there'll be a whiskey party this afternoon, Erlan thought with sud-den pleasure. She enjoyed it so when the three of them got together to talk of their men and babies and the homes they had left behind and the homes they were making out of the raw Montana wilderness.

"Why is it you always got to start argufying with me?" Nash was saying in a loud, peevish voice. "Seems like

I can't open my mouth no more without you jumpin' on me like June bugs on cow paddies."

"You're the one who's gone all wrathy lately," Pogey shouted back at him. "You been as cantankery as a plucked jaybird ever since you were shot that time at the Gandy Dancer, that Fourth of July when it rained bug juice."

"When a man has a close brush with dying, like I did, it rearranges his thinking. Settles his priorities into new alignments, so to speak." Nash stretched out his skinny legs, laid one dome-toed boot on top the other, and settled back to chew on the topic. "For instance, once upon a time I was an excitable individual. The least little thing could agitate my nerves and get my choler to boilin'. But nowadays when folks see me a-strollin' down the street, they say 'There goes a man who's as calm as a hog on ice.'"

"Christ bejesus, Nash!" Pogey snatched off his hat and slapped him on the thigh with it, then whacked his own leg for good measure. "You ever *seen* a hog on ice, ya goddumb fool? Dewlaps flapping like flags in the wind and trotters flyin' all over the place till you can't tell t'other from which. You can say a lot of things about a hog on ice, but calm ain't one of 'em!"

Nash arranged his owl-eyed face into a look of great sadness and infinite patience. "If you ain't a prime example, Pogey, of a man who's gone and let his priorities get all skewed. Here I was havin' a nice quiet philosophical conversation with you one minute, and in the next instant—bang! if your choler don't start to boilin', which goes and makes your face red and your eyes watery, and causes great turbulences inside your belly . . ." His words trailed off as he straightened and squinted down the street, shading his eyes from the glare. "What do ya reckon that ol' polecat's up to?"

The old polecat in question was Marshal Dobbs. The fat man was going fast, for him, even leaving a bit of stirred-up dust in his wake. He pulled his belt up over his belly and unsnapped his holster strap. Suddenly the hot air seemed to vibrate with a strange rustling and humming sound, like a disturbed beehive. Or like a nest of rats, Erlan thought, feeling a prickle of unease.

Pogey let loose a long splatter of tobacco juice as he got slowly to his feet. He pulled hard on his pendulous ear. "I hear trouble coming."

Erlan stepped off the boardwalk. Pogey and Nash joined her. "I *see* trouble coming," Nash said.

A surging crowd of men came around the corner from the east end of town where the new railway line was being laid. The men were making a frightening baying sound now and Erlan noticed several of them were armed with ax handles, shovels, and picks.

At the head of the crowd was a strange apparition—a shiny black demon covered with feathers. The feathered demon was being prodded forward by a long black paddle. Beside her, Nash started and uttered a shocked cry of alarm.

"God and all his angels . . ."

Erlan let out a wail of horror. It was Sam! Merciful Kwan Yin, what had those sons of turtles done to him? He was stripped down to his socks and long drawers, and the top half of him was covered with a gleaming black treacly substance and clumps of chicken feathers. His skin, where it showed through in patches, was blistered red. His shattered spectacles had been wedged onto the end of his tarred nose, their wire temples twisted and dangling. He stumbled in advance of the prodding paddle, his mouth open and distorted, though no sound came out of him.

And then Erlan saw a worse horror, and another wail escaped her clenched lips. No queue! Sam's hair had been shorn off at the neck. To cut a man's queue was to doom him to wander forever from the land of his ancestors. No Chinese could return to the Flowery Land *woo-pien,* without a tail, for a man's queue was a sign of his respect and obedience to his emperor. To be without it was a thing so shameful that death would be preferable.

The mob stopped in front of the mercantile. The baying subsided a moment, then rose up again, like the cries of street peddlers all vying for a single sale.

"String 'im up!" someone shouted. And others took up the call. "String the Chink up! Hang 'im high!"

"Let him go, you lily-livered bastards!" Nash shouted. He started forward and took a punch in the jaw that sent his false teeth spinning through the air and knocked him cold. Pogey let out a roar that ended in a strangled chirrup when the point of a pickax jabbed him in the throat.

"Don't reckon a coupla Chinks are worth dyin' for, do you, old-timer?" the man at the other end of the pickax said with a mean smile.

The man with the paddle poked Sam hard in the small of his back. He was a big man with a head of bushy gray hair and a mad glint in his eye. "Let's hear you crow, China boy." He jabbed Sam again with the end of the paddle. "Cockle-doodle-do! Cockle-doodle-do!"

Sam began to shake violently, although he still made no sound.

"You spawn of camel's dung!" Erlan screamed and lunged at her husband to pull him away from the men who were tormenting him. She cried out in horror as her hands sank into the hot black goo on his chest.

"Let's teach these Chinks a lesson, boys," the bushy-haired man shouted. "Let's show the yellow-skinned bastards we don't want none of their kind doing business in Rainbow Springs."

Hunks of horse dung and rocks flew through the air. A brick crashed through the plate-glass window and a boy, laughing maniacally, tossed a lighted firecracker inside.

Rough hands gripped Erlan by the shoulders and tore her away from Sam. Her golden lilies became entangled together, and she landed on the hard-packed dirt of the road, with such force it drove the air from her lungs.

"Lily!"

She thought the cry had come from Sam, but his mouth was still open in that soundless scream, and this wasn't his voice.

"Lily!"

She struggled to sit up, fighting breathlessness and the gravity that pulled on her big belly. Through tear-blurred eyes she saw Jere Scully charge into the mob, fists swinging, his lips pulled back in a snarl. He fought his way to her side, heedless of the blows he took from ax handles and shovels.

Jere gripped Erlan's arm and tried to haul her to her feet, but his back and head were being pummeled, and he staggered under the blows.

"Save yourself!" she cried out to him. "They mean to kill us!" But she doubted he heard. The screams and roars of the mob were louder than the howling winds of a *tai-fung*.

She looked up and saw the bushy-haired man looming above them. He threw back his head in a bark of laughter, his eyes glowing wild. He swung his paddle in a wide arc, and its wooden blade hit Jere square in the forehead, felling him like an axed tree. Erlan tried to shield him with her body, but someone grabbed her by the hair and hauled her backward so roughly that she screamed from the pain of it. A hobnailed boot caught her in the hip and she screamed again. She rolled over and curled into a ball to protect her stomach.

Jere swayed to his knees. Blood from a long cut on his forehead ran in streams over his face. The bushy-haired man laughed again and raised the paddle high in the air to finish him off.

And the blade of the paddle exploded into a hail of chips and splinters.

The rifle shot smacked through the air with a loud echoing clatter like a stack of lumber dropping. The silence that followed was so sudden and complete that Erlan could hear the spent shell casing hit the ground.

"Get back," Clementine McQueen said in a soft high-toned voice that was at odds with the smoking rifle in her hands.

Hannah Yorke stepped up beside her, her derringer pointed into the belly of the mob. "I reckon you fellas oughta do like the lady says. And while this li'l gun of my own may not look like much, it's been known to shoot the pip out of an ace at twenty paces."

No one but Sam Woo noticed the gray smoke sifting out of the jagged gaps in the sheet glass window. He saw it through the cracked and prismatic lenses of his spectacles, and the smoke looked like damned souls floating out of the bowels of hell. He tried to open his mouth and realized it was already open. He tried to shout, but only a little squeak came out. He took a shambling step forward. No one tried to stop him. He took another. He felt on fire. Smoke . . . fire . . . Another little squeak popped out of his open mouth.

Marshal Dobbs waddled over from where he'd been safely hovering on the edge of things. "Hannah Yorke, and you, too, ma'am," he said, frowning at Clementine, "you don't want to get yourselves involved in this. This is men's business."

The horse trough beside the hitching rack suddenly sprouted holes and another loud crack split the hot air.

The bushy-haired man leaped backward and dropped the splintery remains of his paddle. "Christ Jesus!"

"We just made it women's business, Marshal," Hannah said in her smoky drawl. "And, being women, we're liable to be a mite excitable. So I suggest y'all don't make any more sudden moves."

Sam Woo tried to point at the smoke that was wafting out through the broken window. But his arm was tarred to his side. He took another step, hit the edge of the boardwalk, and almost fell.

Clementine slid another cartridge into the Winchester's loading gate and levered it into the breech. She gave the marshal a wide, cool look. "I suggest you exert yourself for once, Mr. Dobbs, and arrest these men for inciting a riot."

The marshal scratched his grizzled jaw. "Pardon me, ma'am, but it's you and Miz Hannah here I oughta be arrestin', fer waving guns around and endangering the lives of innocent citizens. The way I figure it, it's them Chinks what started the trouble."

"How start trouble?" Erlan cried. "By living?" She pushed herself to her hands and knees. A groggy Jere Scully crouched beside her in the churned, blood-splattered dust. He reached for her, but she squirmed away from him. She flung her head back and shouted at the men, who stood now in shuffling and abashed silence, their ax handles and shovels hanging forgotten in their hands. "What trouble is it to come to a place so big and empty that even the clouds get lost in the sky—"

A strange whistling noise pierced the air, sounding like a hen with its throat cut. Sam Woo stumbled onto the boardwalk and took three short, staggering steps toward the door.

Holy God! he cried, or tried to. But the only sounds coming out of his mouth were these awful little squeaks.

He hit the threshold just as the fire took hold, the fire which had started when the lit firecracker had landed on top of a bale of cotton batting, setting it ablaze. The flames had spread along the freshly oiled floorboards to the shelves in back, which held rifles, handguns, cartridge cases, and other artillery, and beneath which were stacked in categorical and perfect order fifteen cans of kerosene and five of turpentine. The fire hit those cans and Sam Woo's mercantile exploded like a geyser into the Montana sky.

27

"You are to lie still, you stubborn barbarian. The doctor says you have a crease in your skull."

Jere Scully hunched his shoulders and gripped the sides of his head with his hands. "Only a crease? Dear life, my head feels like it's been split in two."

Erlan tipped her rocking chair forward so she could build the pillows into a downy pile behind him. She pushed gently on his shoulder, urging him to lie back in the bed. A tenderness stirred in her as she looked at him. His big knuckles were bruised and caked with dried blood. His face was paler than the linen bandage around his head. His hands were smeared with petroleum jelly, where the skin had been blistered when he'd tried to pull Sam Woo's lifeless body out of the burning mercantile. Oh, what a fierce dragon he had been, charging to her rescue with roars and swinging fists.

How had she ever tricked herself into believing she would never come to love him?

The lamp cast a soft glow over the quilt on the bed and the rose-sprigged wallpaper of Hannah Yorke's spare room. A breeze blew in the open window, cool now that the sun had set. It smelled of burned wood and dust, and hate.

"Ah, Lily . . ." He turned his head to look at her, and several long, slow heartbeats passed between them. He cupped her cheek with his callus-roughened hand. "Are you all right, then?"

She turned her face away from him. She felt bruised both inside and out. And cast adrift. Once again, in one explosive moment, all that was her life had been destroyed. "I am frightened," she said.

His thumb moved across her cheekbone as his hand slid around her neck, beneath her hair. "Don't be frightened, m'love. From this day out, I'll be taking care of you. He's dead, Lily. You're free of him."

She sucked in a sharp breath. "Do not speak such words."

"'Tes the truth."

The truth. She thought of all the truths that had once formed her life. A woman was a lowly creature, an imperfect being, whose happiness was to marry and give her husband sons. A woman's husband was her lord, and her sole purpose on earth was to obey him, to serve him, to please him. A woman must learn to yield, to suppress her wishes. A woman belonged first to her father and then to the father of her sons, until the hour of her death.

But men were not infallible; they were not lords. They were only men. And a woman . . .

If a woman thought too much, she began to question truths. And when she questioned truths she became *ni,* a traitor to her ancestors. A traitor to herself.

My destiny is a circle that is still only half drawn, Erlan thought. For the sake of Tao Huo's spirit, doomed by her crimes to wander forever between the shadow world and this one, she must return to China. Somehow she must find a way to extirpate her mother's shame and dishonor. She must kneel before her father and obtain his forgiveness on her mother's behalf. But her soul shivered faintly, as a realization crept into her heart like mist during the night. The realization that *she* could never forgive her father.

Jere stirred. His hand moved across the star-patterned quilt and onto her lap to part her clenched hands and take one of them in his own. Erlan's pulse thumped, filling her throat. Yet she held herself still.

He rubbed his thumb in a circle over the bone of her wrist. "We can be married by the circuit judge when next he comes through."

Her destiny was a circle half drawn. She knew what she must do. Yet her resolve kept wavering and dissipating. In another life, another place, surely they would never have to part.

"I will never marry you," she said.

His face showed all that was in his heart: love and despair and, still, a desperate glimmer of hope. "How can you be saying never? There's no one, no reason, to stop you coming to me now."

She filled her lungs and expended the ache with the air. "For Chinese and fon-kwei to wed is forbidden by law."

His fingers tightened their grip on her wrist. "No law's going to be stopping me from pledging myself to you before God."

She jerked free of his grasp. "Your stupid god is nothing to me, and my fate is not here with you. I must return to my lao chia. And if this child I carry is a boy, he must return as well, to find his destiny among his own people, close to the tombs of his ancestors. I am bound to Sam Woo as wife until *my* death, not his. It is my duty to return his bones to his native soil so that his spirit will find peace. For all those reasons and more, I can never marry you."

His mouth pulled into a wry smile. But his rainwater eyes glittered wetly. "You haven't said you don't love me. That's one reason you haven't mentioned."

On one of her walks along the river she had come upon a trout stranded on the bank, flopping and struggling against the air that was killing it. Her heart felt like that fish, stranded and struggling now against her fate.

He reclaimed her hand, stroking, touching, making her love him. "Will you kiss me, Lily?" he said. "At least don't make me wait a thousand years for that."

His lips were even softer than they looked, and warm. And they fit perfectly with hers.

Outside, on the gallery, Hannah Yorke sat on a slatted wooden swing and watched the moon skim wildly across a windy sky. After such a hot and dusty day, the night had the bite and tingle of champagne.

From here she could see the stark gallows-like head-frame of the Four Jacks silver mine and the torchlights burning at the shaft head. The piercing wail of the shift whistle rose above the wind. In a few minutes men in mud-splattered boots and slouch hats would walk past her gate, and one of them would be her man. Surely he would come tonight. When he heard his brother had been hurt and was resting at her house, he would come.

He didn't come every night, and he hadn't come at all lately. For three years she had loved him with a kind of greedy wonder, and now she was filled with such a terror that she was losing him.

She had dressed with special care tonight in a gown of striped lilac India silk trimmed at the sleeves with dark purple cashmere lace. The skirt had a deep ruffle with organ-pipe pleats and a bustle that fell in a bouncing cascade over her rump. The bodice was modestly filled in with a jabot of pleated white Swiss muslin. It was a lady's dress, and she felt like a lady when she wore it.

But beneath it, in case he stayed the night, she had put on wispy-thin lisle stockings and a lace-trimmed scarlet petticoat with a matching chemise and drawers fashioned of the sheerest silk.

Surely he would come tonight. And when he did come, she would make him understand that she was not the clingy, demanding woman he'd last seen. The real Hannah was a take 'im or leave 'im sporting gal. A girl who was easy on the eyes and easy on the heart, and easy to stay with because she was easy to leave.

Easy to leave . . . She felt a twisting, clenching pain in her chest every time she thought of the stupid mistake she'd made the last time he came calling. The mistake that had driven him away and had kept him away for two weeks.

It had happened after the loving.

After the loving, she never stayed with him for long. She always got up and poured herself a drink and lit a cigarette—naughty, unladylike habits she'd picked up from former lovers. She always kept her face carefully turned away from him until she was sure she could control what he would see. She didn't want him to see what he meant to her. And she didn't want to look at his face and see all that she didn't mean to him.

But that last time she'd turned around and looked at him too soon. She'd caught the restlessness on his face, the heavy-lidded, unquiet eyes. And the words had come blurting out of her before she could stop them: "What's wrong?"

"It's the bloody stinking mine," he'd answered, a brooding sulkiness to his mouth reminding her just how young he really was. "That's what's bloody stinking wrong."

"So why don't you quit?" she'd said without thought. Her relief that it was the Four Jacks and not her that had put the moodiness on his face had made her muddle-headed.

He'd sneered at her, exaggerating his Cornish brogue. "Right, Hannah m'girl. Quit me job an' do what?"

"You could work for me. You could run the hotel and the flophouses for me as a sort of overall manager of my properties. And I've been thinking of setting up another livery here in Rainbow Springs—Snake-Eye has way more business than he can handle. We could do it together, be partners." *We could get married,* she'd almost said, God help her.

He'd leaped out of bed and come at her, naked and

beautiful. She'd watched, sick at heart, as the chilling hardness came over his eyes. "I'll be a ponce to no woman, *Mrs.* Yorke," he'd said, practically snarling the words. "You want to buy yourself a kept cock, you'll have to look to someone else's." And he'd cupped his penis, which was still half erect and wet from having just been inside her. "This one isn't for sale."

And then he'd put his clothes on and walked out of the room and left her standing there. And only pride had kept her from crying until after she heard the front gate squeal shut behind him.

Oh, my, had she ever scared him off proper just by offering him a job. Imagine how far and fast he'd have run if she'd asked him to marry her.

During all her time as an upstairs girl in that Franklin parlor house, and those down-and-dirty years in a Deadwood crib, not once had she ever really succumbed to the whore's fantasy that some night some John was going to begin by buying fifteen minutes of her time and end by asking her to marry him for life. No, good ol' Hannah Yorke had never let herself in for that sort of soul-ache. If she had dreamed at all it was that someday she'd be her own woman, able to take care of herself without having to do it by lying on her back. A strong woman, with no make-believe and once-upon-a-time loves that could hurt her heart.

But then an arrogant boy, a hard-eyed wild one, had come strutting into her life, and she had fallen in love. Deeply and forever in love. Now suddenly here she was wanting to marry him and have a child by him, to make a family and live happily ever after.

Lord, she was truly a fool. She was already thirty-five—imagine having a baby at her age—and he was only twenty-two, a mere babe himself. When he turned thirty-five, she'd be nearly fifty. Imagine a man still in his prime wanting anything to do with such a worn-out old hay bag. And that wasn't even the worst of it. Once upon a time she had been a whore, and wife or not she would always be known as a whore. She wasn't fool enough to think all those men she'd spread her legs for in the past wouldn't come crowding into their marriage bed some night.

What she had to do was put all thoughts of marriage out of her head. Being a wife wasn't for her and never would be. And besides, he was a wild one. She didn't want him tamed. She only wanted him.

The squeal of the front gate startled her so much she nearly jumped out of her skin. He came at her out of the night. A man with a long, youthful stride, with the wind blowing his dark hair, and the lampshine from the windows highlighting the masculine planes of his face.

He took the porch steps two at a time, then stopped abruptly when she stepped out of the shadows. "Hannah! They told me Jere's been hurt in a brawl and that he's here with you. What's happened, then?"

She gripped her hands together behind her back to keep from touching him. To keep from slipping her arms around his waist and pressing her face into his neck and breathing deep of the smell of him. "Some man started rabble-rousin' against the Chinese, and sentiments got outta hand. It ended with Sam Woo getting killed and his mercantile catching on fire and blowing up. Your brother came charging to the rescue and he took a powerful whack on the head for his pains, but he's all right. He's resting up in the spare bedroom, and she's with him now—Sam's wife . . . widow."

He stared at her hard a moment, then shook his head. "Christ. Well, I'll just go on up and see him. If I may."

She almost choked on the egg-sized lump in her throat. He was being so damn polite. A man was always at his most polite right before he got around to telling a woman that he'd up and fallen in love with someone else.

"Of course you may," she said, summoning from somewhere deep within her a bright smile to plaster on her mouth. She waited until he was all the way upstairs before she followed him inside and went alone to her own room.

She lowered the wick on the lamp and lit a braided twist of dried sweet grass to sweeten the air. She paced the room, her purple kid slippers and the train of her skirts brushing the carpet in soft, intimate whispers. She touched things: the matching glove and handkerchief boxes on the bureau, the button hook and garter buckle she'd left out on the bed stand. The razor, shaving cup, and brush she'd bought for him to use when he spent the night.

But not the bell jar. She didn't go near the bell jar with its yellowed violets and roses. She had promised herself that when her heart got broken this time, she would keep no fading mementos.

It wasn't long before he came to her. She'd left the door open a crack and he pushed it wide with his knock. A slow smile spread across his sweat-dirty face, and her heart melted. She loved him so much she hurt with it.

But she didn't throw herself into his arms as she wanted to. She had to be careful to be good ol' fun-loving Hannah. Easy on the eyes and easy on the heart.

Easy to leave.

"I thought Mrs. Woo was going to put a matching lump on my head if I didn't leave the boy in peace," he said. He didn't come all the way into the room or shut the door behind him. "It's fine of you to be taking him in for the night, Hannah. We'll be getting out of your hair come morning."

"Why don't we wait and see what the doc says, huh?"

He started to leave and she nearly flung herself across the room to snatch the door out of his hands and slam it shut, to keep him with her. "Where're you going?" she asked, her voice sounding shrill even to herself.

He looked back at her over his shoulder, but she couldn't read his thoughts behind the brittle glitter of his flat gray eyes. There was always an aura of danger about him, of a savagery just barely kept under fierce control. He was such an arrogant boy. But she'd often wondered if beneath that arrogance, deep within the core of him that hé always kept carefully guarded from her, if there was a man who was vulnerable and bruised.

"I need a bath," he said. "I'm not exactly smelling as sweet as the last rose of summer right now."

"I thought you might want to stay the night—'cause of your brother, you know, in case he needs you." She waved a hand at the peacock screen, behind which was a galvanized tub already filled. "I've a bath all drawn, and one of the girls is going to be fetching us some supper over from the hotel restaurant later."

He hesitated, then shrugged. "Aye, sure. Why not, then?"

She let out a low, shaky breath. "Want a jolt first?"

He turned and shut the door behind him, leaning against it. "Aye. Why not that as well?"

She went to a table that held a decanter of aged Kentucky bourbon and two glasses. The table was already set with white linen and silver. She wished she hadn't done it now. It made her look too anxious.

She poured the drinks and then turned with one in her hand, nearly slamming into him. "My, you startled me!"

He slipped the glass from her hand, their fingers brushing. He stroked the glass along her jaw, back and forth, back and forth, and the feel of it was smooth and warm and sent a tremor low and deep into her belly. "Here's to wives and sweethearts," he said, the old Cornish sailor's toast that he made every time. But instead of lifting the whiskey to his lips, he lowered his mouth to hers.

He kissed her long and deep, wet and lazy. And it was such sweet, sweet pain.

He released her mouth, and she turned quickly away from him. She snatched up her glass and drank deeply. The bite of the whiskey was strong, but not as strong as his kiss had been.

"There's been talk that you've been stepping out with Miss Luly Maine," she said and immediately wanted to curse herself. Lord, despite all her good intentions, here she was sounding just like a nagging wife. Like all those smothering, carping wives whose men had come to her for a little fun and comfort during her whoring days.

She turned back to look at him. His eyes and face were empty.

"She asked me to go with her to the church dance," he said, and she heard the care he was taking to sound nonchalant. "It would've been rude of me to refuse."

She was losing him. She had let herself fall in love again, and she was losing him. So many times she had told herself that when this moment came she would accept it. But it was happening too soon.

She tried to talk around the knot in her throat. "You've a fine nerve, Drew Scully, showing your face anywhere near a church."

"Now, there's where you're wrong, Hannah m'girl," he said with a sudden unholy smile. "When I was a lad I had it in my mind to be a vicar."

She actually managed a credible laugh. "Land, how the angels must've wept when the devil changed your mind."

He took the two steps necessary to bring himself up next to her. For a moment he just looked at her. Then slowly he lifted his hand and brought it to her mouth. He rubbed his fingers over her lips. She tightened every muscle in her body to keep those lips from trembling.

"I'm not stepping out with Luly," he said.

Carve that one in marble, she thought. And it didn't matter anyway what he said. She was out there waiting for him—if not Luly Maine, then some other girl. This girl who would be young and pretty, and as sweet as a sugar-tit. This girl he would fall in love with and marry and have babies with, make a family and happily-ever-after with. And he would be happy with this girl. In the way that men could be happy with young and pretty and sweet.

He set his whiskey glass down and began to shed his clothes. He stretched, flexing a back strapped with muscle. The lamplight bronzed his skin with a soft, warm glow. He crossed the room to the tub, his stride long and rangy.

He was so young and strong and beautiful.

And she was a fool.

She followed him behind the peacock screen. She knelt before the tub and took the soap from his scarred hands. She rubbed her palms over the planes of his chest, across the ridges of muscle and the soft dark hair that narrowed down to a flat, taut belly. His skin was soft, yet the muscle beneath was so hard. If she balled up her fists and beat against the muscle that encased his heart, she would only end up breaking her hands.

She hadn't even realized she was crying until her tears began to pock the soapsuds. They kept coming one after the other, and she couldn't stop them from falling any more than she could have stopped breathing.

He touched her face, gathering up the tears with his fingers. "What're these for?"

She turned her face away. "They're nothing. Just dismals in the mind is all."

He slid his hand beneath the fall of her hair, pressing the heel of his palm into the side of her neck and forcing her head back around until she was looking into his eyes. His eyes that for once were not flat and hard but soft and deep. Deep as wells, and she felt herself drowning in them, losing her will and her pride, being washed away by the tears that wouldn't stop.

"Drew . . . don't leave me."

"Ah, Hannah love, I'll not be leaving you. I love you."

She squeezed her eyes shut. In the silence of the room, she could hear the soft tick of the ormolu mantel clock. The sound of time passing between them. He would leave her, tomorrow or the day after or the day after that. But he *would* leave her one day, she knew.

There was talk that year in the RainDance country, as summer ended and the days grew shorter and the nights got colder—talk of how the beavers were piling up huge quantities of willow saplings for their winter food. Of how the muskrats were building their lodges twice as thick as usual. And how the snowshoe rabbits had all turned white weeks before time. Talk about how it was fixing to be a long, cold winter.

The first big snowstorm arrived before October did, a regular blue norther.

It had already been snowing for ten hours when the Scully brothers took the elevator cage down into the Four Jacks for the afternoon shift. Drew stepped out into the drift and shuddered. But it was only his body's reaction to the blast-furnace intensity of the heat. He could tell within the first few moments that the smooth, thick, smothering blackness of the earth wouldn't swallow up his manhood this day. It would be a day when he wouldn't spew up his food or sweat through his shirt before he'd even stepped off the cage.

Oh, the fear was there, of course, as always, but it was only a dull ache beneath the surface of his thoughts, and he could control it. It was an odd thing, but ever since Hannah had given him the polished claw of a grizzly bear as a safekeeper, he'd mostly been able to keep the terror at bay.

He thought of her during most of every shift, although he didn't always go to her afterward. Sometimes what he felt for her was so intense he made himself stay away. Some nights, after they made love, the words would push up against his lips, words of marriage. But he always let them die unspoken. He had nothing to offer her. She was rich and a property owner, and he made three dollars a day digging holes in the ground like a bloody mole. It was true she had a tarnished past, but he knew her to be all that was fine in a woman. Generous and loving, honorable and true. And she was the bravest person he'd ever met. Whereas Drew himself . . . he wasn't even half of a man. A bloody coward, scared of the dark.

"Still snowing up there?" The voice came at them from the edge of the lantern light. It was one of the muckers just coming off shift. The man tossed his stick into a toolbox and stretched, reaching for air and cracking his knuckles.

"Coming down thick enough to smother a duck," Jere said, laughter in his voice, and Drew smiled. His brother had been a happy man ever since fate had removed poor Sam Woo from his beloved Lily's life. At least she smiled at him now and traded words with him from time to time. But he hadn't gotten any closer to her bed than the coyote was to the moon it bayed at every night. She had given Jere a good-luck talisman, though, a jade disk with Chinese chicken scratches carved into it.

"Shit, I'd almost rather stay down here," the mucker said as he stepped into the cage. "A man can get pneumonia coming up from the broiling hot shafts into a fucking blizzard."

The cage was snatched up into the blackness of the shaft with a clang of bells and a clatter of metal. The drift was filled with the roar of ore sliding down the chutes and the crank of the windlass, the air heavy with the too-sweet smoke from the morning shift's blasting.

They walked bow-backed like gnomes down a narrow winze that after fifty yards spilled into a big cavern. A half-dozen muckers were already at work there, shoveling freshly blasted rubble into a short train of hopper cars.

Drew lifted a hand in greeting to an Irishman and fellow blaster by the name of Collins, who sat high on a scaffold in the cavern, drilling into the rock face up near the ceiling. The rim of the man's head lamp shone above them like a new moon in a black night. Most of the bigger mines had brought in compressed-air drills, machines that made blasting holes at a prodigious rate, faster than any double-jack drilling team could ever manage. Such progress hadn't reached the Four Jacks yet, but when those drills did arrive, Drew thought he would hate the mine even more. At least there was some pride in being a faceman and master blaster. There was none in being a mucker or car pusher.

The man on the scaffold called something down to

them, but Drew couldn't hear it over the din made by the muckers.

They left the excavation by way of a newly cut drift. The walls were water-slimed here, the air faintly fetid, like a long-empty grave. Cold sweat broke out on Drew's scalp and a flutter of the old familiar panic stirred in his guts, but he beat it down. *Hannah,* he thought, conjuring up her image. He rubbed his finger once lightly over the grizzly's claw that hung from the cord around his neck.

When they reached a split in the drift, Jere bore to the left, saying, "The gaffer told me we're to blast that new crosscut off the west stope today."

Drew touched his brother on the shoulder. "You go on, then, I need to take a piss."

While Jere continued toward the left, Drew went off to the right, beyond the protection of the new shoring timbers. He felt his way to the portal of a freshly blasted shaft, stepping over the muck that had yet to be cleared. As he urinated into the hole, a rank smell came up out of the deep earth, of stagnant air and dead things, and the fear surged into his throat like hot vomit. He swallowed it down, but his head bobbed with the effort and the light from his carbide lamp struck off the quartz crystal in the newly exposed rock, making it glitter.

He noticed a large patch of soft, pale green among the quartz. He turned his head slowly. The rock glowed iridescently as it caught the beam of his lamp.

He went out into the drift and fetched an oil lantern, then came back. He held the lantern close to the face, moving it back and forth over the patch of iridescent green. He leaned closer, his boot knocking an avalanche of gravel into the shaft.

He hung the lantern on a protruding lip of stone and pulled his hammer and drill out of his belt. He set the bit of the drill into the rock face and tapped it with the sledge, using just enough force to knock a piece loose. The rock was hot, but not so hot that it burned his hand, although a stream of steamy water trickled out the fresh scar he'd left in the face.

He heard a step behind him and he whirled, dropping the rock into his gum boot. It was the Irishman Collins, down off his scaffold, and if the man had seen what Drew had done, he didn't let on. More than a few of the miners did a bit of high-grading—bringing up a pound or two of silver ore in their dinner pails and boots every day.

"Where's your brother?" Collins said.

"He's drilling the face of that new crosscut. Why?"

Even in the dim light, Drew saw the miner's eyes suddenly widen. "Didn't you hear what I said, man? There's a sleeper on that face. The last shift left a missed hole that's yet to be picked out."

"Jere!" Drew screamed and began to run.

He scrambled over the rough rock, his shouts of warning bouncing down the drift. His shadow lurched ahead of him as Collins followed behind, so close he could feel the man's hot breath on his neck. The earth began to close in on him, squeezing, crushing, smothering him. He wanted to fall to the ground and curl up into a tight ball to keep the thick and heavy darkness from strangling the life out of him. But he kept running.

At last he saw Jere, the sweating muscles of his brother's bare back glistening in the lantern light. Jere must have heard the noise he was making, for he turned his head just as he pulled back his arm to strike the drill head, and his smile glimmered in the dark oval of his face.

"Jere, *no!*" Drew screamed. He watched with horror as his brother swung his face back around to the rock and the hammer began its downward descent. It seemed to move with a strange slowness, as if it were being pushed through air as thick as treacle. It moved so slowly that Drew thought he could stop it if he could just get there in time, and he tried to lunge across the space that still separated him from his brother. He stumbled over a pile of muck, twisting his knee violently and falling onto his side with a bone-rattling jar.

He saw Collins run past him, and in the next instant he saw Jere's sledge strike home. A tongue of flame shot out of the rock face, followed by a flash of brilliant white light. Shards of rock came hurtling out of a black hole in the earth, and a blast smacked against his ears like a sharp clap of thunder.

He opened his eyes onto a darkness that was as thick and absolute as the darkness on the other side of hell, and he would have screamed if he'd had the breath. He felt a shifting in the piles of shattered rock around him, and then the darkness was pushed away by the spill of a half-dozen carbide lamps and oil lanterns. Smoke clouded the air, and an unearthly stillness smothered his ears. He turned his head and saw a ragged bone thrusting through the bloody flesh of his arm, but strangely he felt no pain. He could feel nothing at all except the wild thumping of his own heart. And a screaming. He could *feel* the screaming, as if it were a fine wire that someone was plucking.

He sucked at the foul air. The gauzy film began to melt away from his eyes. He saw red spongy wet pieces of something splattered all over the rock and earth around him, and in the next instant he realized he was looking at what was left of a man. Collins . . . Please God, let it be Collins.

Someone bent over him. He blinked and brought into focus the ratlike features of Casey O'Brian, their shaft boss.

"My brother?" Drew gasped, choking on the smoke.

The gaffer said something, but Drew couldn't hear. He made himself look over to the place where he'd last seen Jere, and he was still there. Not smeared in bloody bits and pieces all over the drift. He was hurt, though, for Drew could see his brother's legs thrashing. But he was still living, thank God. Still living . . .

A hand touched his forehead. He watched O'Brian's mouth move, although he still couldn't hear anything.

"Fucking mine," Drew croaked. He reached up with his good arm and grabbed the shirt of the man who should have warned them about the sleeper, jerking O'Brian's face down to his until he was sure the gaffer could see his eyes. "We'll be wanting a full day's pay for this, you bloody bastard."

28

SAM WOO'S WIDOW TEETERED as she lifted the heavy yoke onto her shoulders. The baskets of laundry swung wildly on their chains off the ends of the pine pole, causing it to bite deep into her shoulders.

She set off down the road in the teeth of the wind, her eyes narrowed against the snow flurries that stung her face The short quilted jacket and cotton pants she wore were the same birch-bark white as the snow and the sky. White, the color of mourning, the color she would wear for the next three years.

She carried her two-month-old son, Samuel, in a sling of woven straw that hung over her chest from a strap around her neck. She struggled over the ridges of mud and snow. Once, she slipped and the yoke became unbalanced, slipping off her shoulders and nearly driving her to her knees.

She made her slow, clumsy way among the shacks where all the Chinese lived, a town within the town of Rainbow Springs. She smelled roast pork as she passed the chop suey house and heard the clatter of gaming tiles from the mah-jongg room. She saw steam wafting from a crack in the window of the tea shop. Its signboard, painted in gilt and vermilion, banged loudly in the wind. She passed the herbalist's shop and nodded respectfully to Peter Ling, the golden needle man, who stood in the window. He was the latest to ask her to marry him.

Although she was a widow, and thus bad joss, Erlan had received many proposals in the four months since Sam Woo's death. And not all her suitors were bachelors. Many had wives back in China. But the immigration laws prevented wives and loved ones from joining the men, and so they looked for concubines to bring them comfort in their exile.

She stopped before the black lacquered doors of the joss house. She set down her yoke in the shelter of the eaves, although the laundry was already well protected from the elements by scraps of oilskin tarpaulin. She shook the snow off her pant legs, straightened her straw hat, then slipped inside the temple.

The rush of cold air made the wicks flicker in the round blue silk lanterns and fluttered the red scrolls that hung on the walls. With her head respectfully lowered, she approached the altar with its five deities carved of wood and dressed in vermilion silk robes and gilt headdresses. Sacrificial bowls of rice and burning incense lay at the feet of the gods.

Samuel whimpered, thrusting his tiny feet against her chest, and she patted his head to soothe him. She bowed to the gods and lit a stick of incense.

"Please," she prayed. "Please ease the torment of my *anjing juren*. Teach him the wisdom of virtuous patience and bring him peace."

The deities stared back at her with blank, unseeing eyes. But then, why would Chinese gods interfere in the life of a fon-kwei? She should go into the temple of his Jesus god and pray there. But the thought of entering that white-painted building with its pointed roof frightened her. Who knew what demons resided in such a place?

A soothsayer had set up his table inside the temple doors. As she passed him on her way out, he shook his box of sticks at her, trying to entice her to have her fortune told. But she already knew her destiny: she was going home.

Erlan struggled against the snow and the wind for another block and then stopped again. A set of wind-bells hung next to the door of this house and they jangled wildly, filling the air with a joyful sound. Which was appropriate, Erlan thought, since this was a joy girl's house.

Before Erlan could knock, the door was flung open. Ah Toy opened her mouth and struck her cheeks with her palms in mock surprise. "Aiya! What a pleasure this is to have visitors just when I was feeling so lonely!"

Ah Toy frequently watched Samuel for Erlan while she made her deliveries, especially when the weather was bad. But to ask anything of consequence from a friend who could not refuse was uncivilized, so the joy girl was saving her from embarrassment by pretending it was Erlan who was doing her a favor.

"It is our pleasure to come," Erlan responded, following the ritual of politeness. "But are you certain you aren't busy this afternoon, Elder Sister?"

"Not at all, not at all," Ah Toy said, bowing Erlan inside. "That Ah Foock—he wanted to come today, but I told him to stay away. He makes me work too hard for my three dollars. He has testicles the size of a gnat's and a withered old root that no amount of flogging can stiffen."

Ah Toy helped to lift the yoke off Erlan's shoulders. Erlan removed Samuel from his sling, and both women fussed over him for a moment before she put him down in a white wicker bassinet that stood near the parlor stove. The bassinet looked strange among the Oriental lacquer and brocade furnishings.

Ah Toy pulled a red-lacquered chair away from a red-lacquered table and gestured for Erlan to sit. "I was so anxious for you to visit this worthless self that I already poured the tea. Stupid me, I hope it isn't cold."

Erlan took a sip of the tea and assured her it was just perfect.

She enjoyed coming to Ah Toy's house, for it was as richly furnished as a tomb. Bronzes and porcelains and carvings of jade, ivory vases, cloisonne boxes, and scroll paintings. And the smells: sandalwood and incense, and occasionally a sickly sweet hint of opium smoke.

Ah Toy had much status in the Chinese community because one of the gentlemen she entertained was One-Eyed Jack, who many said was the richest man in Rainbow Springs. In China such a wealthy, powerful man was often the local warlord and a man to be feared. A man who was feared was a man who was respected, and all who served him were respected as well.

Ah Toy was not a first-rate beauty, but she had a delicate face that was always wreathed with smiles. Today she was dressed like a Mandarin princess in a robe of midnight blue embroidered with peonies, and she wore abalone shell combs in her hair.

She was laughing now as she leaned over the bassinet to dangle a string of jade worry beads before Samuel's face. "So you have brought this worthless little flea to spend the afternoon with me, have you?" she exclaimed loudly, in the exaggerated tone of voice used for compliments. Samuel gurgled as he tried to grasp the beads. "What an ugly little worm you are!"

Erlan smiled. The Chinese always called a boy baby disparaging names, for the same reason that they put thin gold hoops in his ears and tied ribbons of the female color blue in his hair—to fool the jealous gods into thinking he was a girl so they wouldn't steal him for their spirit world.

Erlan spent a few more minutes drinking tea and chatting with Ah Toy, and then she pushed back her chair and stood up, wincing as pain shot through her feet. They were already raw, although the day was not yet half over.

"Ching! Ching!" Ah Toy exclaimed. "Please eat before you go." She gestured at the stove where a pot of congee sat

steaming. The smell of the sweetened rice was tempting, but Erlan politely declined.

Outside, the snow was coming down harder now and the temperature had fallen. An icy glaze covered everything, making the footing even more treacherous. She groaned as she lifted the yoke. It was so heavy it often left weals and bruises on her shoulders after a long day. All of her body hurt after hours bent over the washtub and ironing board. But it was her heart that ached the most. She had never thought she would miss the merchant Woo so much. She missed his gentle ways and his many kindnesses and even his odd eccentricities—like his desire to make himself over into a one hundred percent American. A Yankee Doodle dandy.

Oh, she had wailed loudly at his coffin for three days and three nights, as was proper. And though she'd had no money to spend on his funeral, she had done what she could to show him honor, burning red paper money to provide for his journey in the afterlife, and sweet incense sticks to propitiate the gods. And then, two months later, fortune had given them a son. A son who would live to feed his father's spirit in the shadow world.

But the one thousand one hundred and sixty dollars American that she had kept in the shoebox beneath her bed was gone. Blown out into the prairie, or stolen by those sons of turtles, may their ancestors be cursed ten thousand times. Now she must begin all over again to earn the money for her passage home, and she must do it in this place where the Chinese people were despised and tormented. This empty land with room enough for everyone but them.

Opening a laundry was one of the few businesses allowed to Chinese, and it required little capital. One needed only soap, tubs, a washboard, an iron, and an ironing board. But last year the town council had passed an ordinance that all laundries had to pay a licensing fee of fifteen dollars a quarter. They called it the Chinese tax, because few whites were in the laundry business. At two dollars the dozen, Erlan had to boil and iron ninety shirts just to pay the tax. She understood now whence came that American expression: a Chinaman's chance.

She lay awake at night doing sums in her head to determine how long it would take her to make enough profit to buy passage home for herself and her son. At least she no longer had to repay Sam Woo her bride-price. She would repay her debt to him in another way, by taking his bones with her to be buried in the soil of China where they belonged.

A gust of bitter wind buffeted Erlan and sent her slipping along the troughs of snow. There had already been so many storms this winter that she had lost count. No sooner would the snow start to melt than it would freeze again, so that all was covered with a thick, crusty ice.

A snowball caught her flush on the neck, sending ice crystals shivering down inside the collar of her quilted jacket. She spun around so fast she nearly slipped again. A shadow flitted around the corner of one of the miners' shacks, and then she heard a child's mocking chant: "Chinaman, Chinaman, rode 'im out on a rail . . ."

She had left the Chinese part of town and was now in Dublin Patch. The smells were different here—sowbelly beans and coffee. But the shacks were the same, made from old shoring timbers and planks that had been thrown onto the trash piles near the mine.

She stopped now before one such shack and this time, too, the door opened wide before she could knock.

Drew Scully stood on the threshold, facing her. He stared at her a moment, then nodded and motioned for her to enter. His left arm was in a sling. But he had the strength in his right hand to lift the heavy yoke off her shoulders and set it carefully on the floor.

"How is he?" she whispered.

"Drunk."

"Already?"

"Already isn't the way of it, Mrs. Woo. He hasn't been sober since it happened. But then, you can't blame the man for not wanting to shout hallelujahs because he's been left stone blind." Drew rubbed a hand over his mouth as if he could wipe away the bitter taste of the words. "He wants the world dead, and himself first."

"Drew!" bellowed a voice from the back room, dark and bitter with rage. "You tell her to get herself lost, d'ye hear me, brother? I don't want to see her . . . *See* her." He laughed, a sound that was like a rag tearing. "Bloody, bloody hell."

"I told him you were coming," Drew said, keeping his voice low. "I thought it best. He's apt to get . . . violent when he's surprised. The physician finally took the bandages off for good and all a few weeks ago—" Something caught in his throat and he had to stop and swallow it down. "'Tesn't a pretty sight." He turned his face away, blinking hard. "Are you sure you'll be all right doing this alone, then?"

"It was your suggestion, Mr. Scully."

He sighed deeply. "Right. I'll be leaving, then. If he tries to murder you . . ."

"He won't," Erlan said. She was sure of that, though she was sure of nothing else. He was her *anjing juren,* her gentle giant, and he would never try to hurt her.

The one time she had seen Jere since the accident, he had been unconscious, the whole upper half of his head swathed in bandages. Afterward he had begged his brother to keep her away. Now she and Drew Scully had concocted this plan together. She only hoped it wasn't a mistake, for she couldn't bear to bring him any more pain after all he had already endured.

She waited until the door shut behind Drew. Then she called out a polite greeting to the man in the back room. But she didn't go to him right away. She had brought some herbal tea with her, made of jasmine, wild cherry bark, and wahoo root, and she set about brewing it on the shack's small cookstove. While she waited for the water to boil, she talked to him. She talked of Samuel, of how he could roll over now and how just last week he'd laughed out loud. She told him about the gift of a red jade necklace that One-Eyed Jack had given Ah Toy. She related a funny story about Pogey and Nash, who had gotten drunk at the Gandy Dancer last week and tried to rope a skunk.

He said nothing. But every time she paused for breath he made a rude noise, like the sucking sounds a horse made while trotting in mud.

She strained the tea and poured it into a big handleless cup, and then she could postpone the moment no longer.

With the shade pulled down over the window and no lamp lit, it was dark in the room. Jere sat in a willow rocking chair with his back to the door. His ragged hair hung down to his shoulders. A rank smell soured the air, and his blue chambray shirt was grease-marked, and stained with old sweat. As she approached him, she wished she had an opera mask to hide her face. Then she remembered: he couldn't see her.

Once he'd had a smile as broad as a moon bridge, but no longer. Once he'd had the strength of ten tigers. Now he sat in a chair all day and allowed his muscles to grow wasted and flabby. Once he had been brave, now he drowned his spirit in whiskey.

One of the bare pine floorboards squeaked beneath her feet, and he whipped his head around. And she saw his eyes.

Once his eyes had been beautiful, like rain-drenched skies. Now they were ugly weals of raw flesh.

She tried to make her lips and tongue work, to say something to him, but she couldn't. She imagined that she could see his heart working in his chest and his breath sucking in and out, and she knew the bitterness was like vinegar in his belly. She stared at his compressed lips because she couldn't bear to look at his ruined eyes.

She took a step toward him and then another. She held

the teacup out to him, waiting for him to take it, and when she remembered that he couldn't see what she had done, she almost sobbed aloud.

She lifted the clenched hand off his lap, the one that wasn't wrapped around the whiskey bottle. She pressed the cup against his knuckles.

"Get out!" he snarled, and knocked the cup out of her hand. It shattered against the wall, splashing the tea in a dark stain over the white-washed boards. "Get out of here, you Chink bitch, and leave me the bloody hell alone!"

Drew Scully cradled his left arm against his chest as he slogged down the snow-choked road. In weather like this the bone ached like a rotten tooth. The break hadn't healed straight the first time so his arm had been re-broken and set again. He didn't want to think about what would happen if it still didn't come out right. At least it was his left arm.

Yellow light spilled from the windows of the Gandy Dancer saloon, along with the giddy strains of banjo music. He was no more than a flea's leap away from going in there and buying himself a drink, and then another and another. Joining his brother in the sweet, dulling comfort of the bottle.

When he passed by the butcher shop, he had to turn his head away from the sight of the bloody slabs of meat hanging off iron hooks in the window. One of the other miners had told him the drift where the sleeper had blown had had to be dusted with quicklime before work could be resumed down there.

No power on earth would get Drew back down the shafts. The fear was so strong in him that he could taste it all the time now. It was the taste of dynamite and blood, and a black hole in the ground.

Drew Scully took a deep breath and tried to get ahold of himself. His self-respect, his pride, was breaking to bitter pieces inside him.

He trudged up the butte through the falling snow. As he turned down the path to the office of the superintendent of mines, he passed the men on the rustling line applying for work. The line was long. The Four Jacks had been doing more laying off than hiring lately. Rumor had it the silver was playing out.

The mine office occupied a small shack next to the changing house. Drew asked the secretary, who was sitting behind a desk made out of empty dynamite boxes, if he could see the superintendent. He was told to take a load off and wait.

He sat down and looked around a room cluttered with rock samples, canvas bags, map cases, a broken time clock, and a gold nugget press. The walls were covered with drawings of the works below, geological charts, and risque *Police Gazette* calendars. The room was cold but he could feel a runnel of sweat run down his side.

After about a half an hour the secretary got up and left through the front door. Drew got up and went through the back door, which he assumed led to the super's office. He didn't bother to knock.

The superintendent sat in a hooded leather chair behind a mahogany desk. A six-point rack of antlers hung on the wall at his back. A long case clock, its painted face orbited by moons and stars and comets, filled the room with a steady, sonorous ticking.

It was said the super owned the bulk share of the mine he was now running for the consortium. It was said he'd won it in a poker game. It was also said the man had once been a traveling parson. The black eye patch gave him the air of a pirate, but he'd always put Drew in mind of those slick drummers who wandered the countryside selling consumption-killer.

He was a sleek-looking man with a sharp face and long, oily bootblack hair that hung straight to his shoulders. His belly swelled against an expensive sealskin waistcoat, worn hairy side out.

The long case clock struck two o'clock. The super drew a dollar-sized stem-winder from his vest pocket and checked the time. He looked up and saw Drew. "Who the devil are you?"

"Drew Scully." He thought about adding "sir," then didn't.

"Scully?" The super puckered his mouth, as if thinking required some effort. But Drew saw a gambler's wits behind that single pale, flat eye: assessing, analyzing, calculating. It was as if life to him was one big poker game involving strategy, bluffing, risk, and reward.

He flashed a sudden charming smile. "You're the tough Cousin Jack who had the balls to demand a full day's pay after breaking an arm and putting in less than an hour on shift." On the desk sat a miniature gallus frame made of silver. He stroked it almost lovingly with his finger while he stared at Drew. "If you're worried about having a job once that sling comes off, you can tap her light. So long as you can still swing a sledge, you can do it at the Four Jacks."

Drew helped himself to a chair and produced a be-damned-to-you smile of his own. "We'll talk about what you'll be giving me later. After you take a look at this." And he tossed the ore sample at the super so fast the man had either to snatch it out of the air or allow it to smash his face.

He caught the rock one-handed without even blinking. He frowned at it. "What am I supposed to do with a piece of gangue—use it to weight papers?"

"That's no piece of worthless quartz. 'Tes the red metal."

The super's face took on a look that was half bored, half patronizing. "Copper? And you expect me to dance a jig and ooze delight from every pore over this? I'm afraid the fact that you found the green blight in my workings is hardly news and it isn't welcome." Copper was considered the bane of any silver-mining operation because it was a mineral that had to be extracted and dumped from the profit-producing ore.

Drew stretched out his legs, crossed his feet, and hooked a thumb in his vest pocket. "Aye, there's copper down there, all right. Big ruddy green veins of it."

Jack McQueen's mouth pulled into a wry smile. "Whoopee."

"Let me tell you about copper, Super." The older man lifted a haughty brow at this effrontery, and Drew smiled again. "Right now it sells for twelve cents a pound. Maybe 'tedn't a big market for it out here yet. But back in your eastern states, they're putting in electric cables and telephone wires all over the place. They're calling this the age of electricity. All those telephones and Edison's electric lights require miles' worth of the red metal. One, two years from now I figure copper'll be going for twenty cents a pound, maybe more."

Jack McQueen lifted the cover off a sandalwood humidor and took out a cigar. He examined it, bit off the end, and spat in the direction of a brass cuspidor. He lit up and sucked greedily on its smoke. Only then did he take a jeweler's loupe out of one of the desk's numerous drawers. He stood up and went to a cracked, dirty window, taking the ore sample with him.

He fitted the glass to his one good eye. "Where did this come from?"

"The west stope of the four-hundred-foot level. I already had it assayed over in Butte, but you can let your own man have a look. It'll prove so pure you could ship it to China and back for smelting and still make a profit. And this hill is full of copper. I'd stake my rep as champion double-jacker on it."

"Would you? But then, you won't be winning any more double-jacking championships, will you? Not with your brother as blind as a mole in a blizzard."

"You bloody bastard—" Drew leaped out of the chair and lunged for the man, only to be brought up short by the pocket derringer aimed at his middle.

"Sit down," the super said.

Drew put a finger under the gun's short barrel and lifted it until it was pointing between his own eyes. He smiled. "You going to shoot me, then? After half the morning shift has just seen me come calling?"

One-Eyed Jack tried to stare him down, and when he couldn't, he laughed. "You do have some sand in your craw, don't you, Drew Scully? Sit down, please. And notice I'm even saying it with a smile."

He slipped the gun back in his coat pocket and studied the ore sample again, turning it over and over in his hand. "Normally I abhor violence, especially when it's aimed at me. But it's unsettling to jump at a man's back like that, Drew Scully. It makes him jumpy, and then accidents are liable to happen."

He resumed his seat behind the mahogany desk and rested his chin on his steepled fingers. He studied Drew with the hot, intense stare of a conjurer. "A few months from now, when copper is discovered here at the Four Jacks, you will act as surprised as a nun with a bellyful of baby. That will be your play."

"And what's yours, then?"

"'Thou shalt not curse the deaf, nor put a stumbling block before the blind, but shalt fear thy God: I *am* thy Lord.' Five dollars a week to your brother—we'll call it a pension, shall we? This way he will never have to beg for pennies on a street corner. He'll have enough to keep him in whiskey and leave him with just enough pride not to put a gun in his mouth."

Drew pretended he hadn't just been given what he'd wanted most to come of this visit. "That's all well and good for poor Jere," he said. "Now what about me?" He had no intention of being greedy or a fool. If he demanded a percentage of the claim, he'd only wind up getting dry-gulched, shot in the back, and dumped in some brush-tangled coulee. But he was getting himself out of the mines. One way or the other he was getting out of the bloody mines.

One-Eyed Jack got slowly to his feet. "The Lord raises up the virtuous and casts down the wicked," he intoned in a preacher's voice, but his eye was smiling with mischief. "It so happens one of my gaffers—a fellow by the name of O'Brian—was jumped on and beat up by persons unknown a couple of weeks back. He was worked over so badly there isn't much of the man left in him, I'm afraid. Indeed, talk is, he can't even crawl out to the shithouse now without whimpering with fear."

Drew stood up as well. "Aye, Rainbow Springs is truly a wicked town," he said with mocking solemnity. "I don't want the gaffer's job."

"I had no intention of offering it to you, Drew Scully." A smile pulled at the super's mouth, and his eye narrowed with a mixture of amusement and guile. "What would you say to being town marshal of Rainbow Springs?"

Drew leaned over the desk. He lifted the top off the humidor and helped himself to a cigar. "Mr. Dobbs's thinking of retiring, is he?"

The super laughed. "I do so like a man who can see where I'm going and who tries to get there ahead of me. It keeps me on my toes. Yes, indeed, Drew Scully. The good marshal wants to buy himself a nice piece of property somewhere and raise chickens. I and some of the other businessmen in this town have been thinking things have gotten a bit too lax around here lately. Too many men have been had for breakfast, and that's apt to make those with money to invest in . . . in certain projects a bit leery, if you get my drift. We need a town marshal who's not afraid to lay down the law a bit, someone young and tough. A real scrapper."

Someone you can own, Drew thought, but he still said nothing. If he had to sell himself to get out of the mines and secure a pension for Jere, then he would sell himself.

He smiled at the super as he held a match to the end of the cigar. He sucked in his cheeks, drawing deeply. He thought the expensive smoke would burn the bitter taste out of his mouth, and it did. Somewhat.

She had cleaned up the mess he'd made of the tea, and then she'd left the room. But not the house. He heard the clatter of china and her singsong voice muttering to herself in Chinese, probably cursing him to hell and back, he thought.

"To hell with you, too!" he shouted.

She answered him by dropping a lid back on the stove with a loud clatter.

If she came in here again, he'd knock over the slop jar. Aye, he thought, that would make her good and sorry. Except that she might not do the cleaning up this time, and he'd have to live with the stink until Drew came home, since he was bloody useless at doing anything for himself. Could barely find his poker to pee with without fumbling. Bloody useless . . .

He heard the shuffle of her feet moving across the floor, coming toward him, and he stiffened. She stopped in front of him. At least he thought she was in front of him. Maybe if he reached out and grabbed her, she'd scream and run off and leave him alone.

He kept his hands clenched in his lap and stared into the thick, soughing ocean of blackness that was all he could see and all he would ever see again.

He heard the rustle of her clothing and felt a subtle shift in the air, and he thought she might have knelt on the floor next to his chair. Her lilting voice came up at him out of the black ocean, although the words were not sweet.

"You grow fat and petulant like an imperial eunuch, and you are disturbing the virtuous harmony of this house. Instead of tea, I ought to give you a snake potion to cleanse your bowels of their ill humors."

She pressed the hot cup against the backs of his fingers as she had the last time, to let him know it was there. "If you spill it again, there is a whole pot of it on the stove, and I will empty it all onto your head. You need a bath anyway. You stink."

"Get . . . out."

She took his hands and wrapped them around the steam-wet porcelain. "Empty the cup."

Silence gripped the room like a fist. He could taste the foulness of his bitter rage on the back of his throat. His hands trembled. He wanted to hurl the cup into the bloody black void before his eyes . . . before where his eyes used to be.

He waited for her to leave. He strained his ears listening for the rustle of her clothes, her shuffling footsteps. For the sigh of her breath, the beat of her heart. He almost jumped when she spoke.

"I know what you are thinking."

"Do you, then?"

"You are wailing at the moon over the unfairness of a fate that would take your eyes. But what foolish god promised you life would be fair? Ask the legless beggar in the market square if life is fair. Ask the barren wife who burns seven *ris* of incense day after day beseeching the gods for a child, only to be cast aside by her husband instead . . . ask her if life is fair. Ask the starving peasant's daughter who is sold into slavery for fifty coppers if life is fair."

He curled his mouth into a sneer. "And that's supposed to make me feel better?"

"No. But such is the way of life's treacheries. You must come to accept what has happened, because it cannot be undone."

He gripped the cup so hard that the scalding tea sloshed onto his hands. "And if I won't bloody well accept it?"

"It still cannot be undone."

For a moment the horror of it almost choked him. He

was a blind man, maimed and useless. *Blind.* He would never be able to put things back the way they were before, the way they were supposed to be. *Blind, blind, blind . . .* Oh, God, he was drowning in the horror of it and he wanted to reach out and cling to her. He could never have her now, now that he was so bloody useless as a man. Now that he was *blind.* Still he wanted to cling to her, to the dreams he'd once had for them.

Suddenly he wanted desperately to talk with her, simply talk with her and keep her with him for a while. "Were you sold, Lily?" he said, and the words came out rusty, raw. "'Tes that how you came to be here?"

"Yes."

He lifted his chin, stretching out his neck, trying to ease the tightness in his throat. "'Tes sorry I am."

"Why are you sorry? If my father had not sold me, we never would have come to know each other in this life."

He took a swallow of the tea, grimacing at its bitter taste. He felt with his elbow for the table beside his chair, then set the cup down. "And if your da hadn't sold you, if you'd stayed in China to be marrying some rich man, would you have felt still 'twere something missing? Would you've awoken in the silence of the night and wondered why your soul was always empty, your heart always sore?"

He didn't breathe while he waited in the darkness for her answer.

"Yes," she finally said. So softly he barely heard her.

"And would you've consoled yourself with the thought that 'twas just another one of life's treacheries?"

She punched him hard on the thigh. "How dare you mock me through the back door, you blithering baboon?"

She startled a laugh out of him. And he startled himself with the sound of it. He felt a rushing sensation against his ears and a fierce pressure in his chest, as if he were hurtling headfirst down a shaft.

She struck him again and he grabbed her wrist, hauling her into his lap with a force that punched the air from her lungs. He gripped the sides of her head and slammed his mouth down onto hers, not even getting that right, so that his teeth grated roughly across her lips. She gasped and pulled free of him. But she didn't leave him. He could feel her hovering just beyond the edge of the darkness.

Tension thickened the air until he couldn't breathe. Then her hands were sliding up his thighs, and her breasts were thrusting against his chest, and her lips were pressing against his, but gently. He opened his mouth, thinking he would die from the sweet taste of her, wanting to die so that his life would end now with this moment, this ecstasy. Her lips slipped apart and he traced their shape with his tongue. He swallowed her sigh.

He realized he wasn't touching her, except with his lips. The blood pulsed in his fingertips, and his hand shook as he pressed it against her chest. He could feel the swell of her breast beneath the thick quilted material of her jacket. She breathed and his hand lifted with the filling of her lungs.

He tore his mouth from hers. "Lily, I want . . ."

"Yes!" she said fiercely. And then gently, "Yes, my *an-jing juren*. Please."

But now he couldn't move. He didn't think he should even be breathing, because he wanted to pant and moan like some great hungry beast, and yet he didn't want to frighten her away. If she left him now he would not be able to bear it.

So he sat stiff in the chair, one hand gripping the armrest, the other still pressed flat against her breast. His breath whistled in and out of his clenched teeth.

She took his hand and, linking her fingers with his, slowly rose, bringing him up with her. She tugged gently on his hand, and he followed her. He felt like a shuffling old man, clumsy, too big for his skin. His thighs bumped against the bed and he tumbled onto it awkwardly. But she fell with him, and they were in each other's arms, lying on a bed, and this was Lily, Lily, Lily, and he'd wanted her for so long, wanted her so desperately.

Her breath bathed his cheek and he turned his head, seeking her mouth. The coarse muslin pillowcase scraped across the back of his neck. Silk . . . She should be lying on a bed covered with silk, on a down mattress, not one stuffed with horsehair and straw. He wanted to tell her he was sorry he couldn't give her silk and feathers, and a man who could at least see her face to know if he was pleasuring her, but he didn't want to let go of her mouth.

They kissed for a long time and when he eased his lips from hers, it was only to slide his tongue along her jaw and down to the pulse in her throat. It leaped and throbbed against his open mouth, pumping to the hard rush of his own blood.

She leaned over him, unbuttoning his shirt, and her hair fell into his face. It was as soft as he had known it would be. As it had been so many nights in his dreams. Ah, God, if pity had brought her to this, he didn't care.

The mattress rustled as she pulled away from him. "Lily!" he cried, panicking when he reached for her and got nothing but air.

She pressed her fingers against his mouth, then they drifted over his face, stroking his beard. "Your beard is so soft. I thought it would be prickly, but it is soft, like a kitten's fur. I am only going to undress so that you may touch me. I want you to touch me everywhere."

A sob of anguish and glory rose in his throat and he almost choked on it.

He listened to the sounds she made as she undressed, whispering sounds, seductive sounds. He tried to imagine what she would look like naked. She would be small-breasted, with copper-colored nipples. Her hips would be slim, her belly concave, of a perfect shape to cradle his head once he was done loving her. The down between her legs would be the same dense black as her hair.

She lay back down beside him and he turned his head, burying his mouth in the softness of her throat. The crisp green-apple smell of her came in sweet bits and snatches.

He touched her everywhere, and the feel of her beneath his hands and lips spread through his body until he ached.

He opened his trousers, desperate to fill her hands with the heavy swell of his erection, and she held him, stroked him, brought him to a quivering, shuddering ecstasy. Then she straddled him, sliding his penis into the opening between her legs. She was wet and hot and hungry like a mouth. She sucked him deep inside her.

He bucked and she rode him. Her hands caressed the taut muscles of his belly, her silky hair slapped his chest. God, he wanted to see her, to see her . . . She was kissing him, her mouth urgent and frantic and hot. He could feel the helpless tremors coursing through her body. He heard the blood roaring in his head. Every muscle tightened violently and he felt his seed explode within her.

She collapsed on top of him. Her breath struck his face in hot gusts. He kissed the damp tangle of her hair.

He waited for her to leave him. She sighed long and soft, her breath fluttering over his throat. It seemed he could still feel her hands in his hair.

If he'd had eyes and still been a man, he would have thrown her words in her face again. All that blather about acceptance, the way of life's treacheries. If she believed all that, then she would quit thinking she had to go back to her damn Flowery Land. She would understand that her fate had brought her here because he was here, and from the beginning of time they were meant to be together. But he had wanted so much to give her more, show her more, promise her more. And now he never would.

He touched the scarred flesh that covered the empty sockets of bone.

If he had eyes . . .

29

IN LATER YEARS FOLK would come to speak of what happened that winter as the Great Die-Up. It was a time when the cattle dropped out on the snow-choked range like leaves after a frost.

Range horses could survive a bad winter by eating the bark off trees. But cattle would rub their noses blood-raw in a vain attempt to break through the crusty snow-ice to get at the stubby dead grass underneath. And when a norther blew in, they turned their tails to the snow and wind and drifted until they hit something that stopped them—hillsides, coulees, fences. And there they stacked up to freeze and starve to death.

That winter did seem to be one long, hard snowstorm. But on this particular day, six more inches of fresh snow had fallen in the night and blown into drifts. Gus had ridden out as soon as it was light to chop through the ice crust at the water holes and to herd what cattle he could find to those places where the wind had scoured down the snow to the brittle gray grass.

As Clementine stood on the porch that morning and watched him ride out of the yard, she thought of how like life itself a marriage was—with droughts and raging storms coming in between long sunny days filled with love and laughter.

Like on that hot, dry day last summer, when she had given him the sachet of money, and she thought he might have hated her. She would not have been surprised to return from Rainbow Springs that day to find him gone. But it was not Gus's way to quit on his dreams, to quit on her.

He had been in the corral, trying to train a yearling to the hackamore, when she drove back into the yard. She got off the wagon and went right up to the corral fence. He kept his back to her.

She had intended only to tell him about what had happened in town, about the mob blowing up the mercantile and Sam Woo's death. Instead other words came out of her mouth, words that broke with the desperation she was feeling. With the fear that she had irrevocably lost him.

"I do love you, Gus," she said.

He swung around. His mouth was tight, his eyes wary. "So you keep saying."

Tears built in her eyes. She had to blink hard to keep them from falling. "I'm sorry for . . . for everything."

He stared at her a long time, and then he came to her. But only as far as the corral fence that still separated them.

His gaze broke from hers. He took off his hat and wiped his forehead with his bandanna. "It isn't that, Clementine. It isn't a matter of who's sorry or which of us was wrong. Maybe . . . maybe it's just a matter of you deciding what you want."

She knew what he was trying to say: that no matter what he did for her, no matter how much he loved her, he could no longer believe she was ever going to give him all of herself in return.

She looked at him, at the way the corners of his mustache didn't quite hide the bitter curve of his mouth, at the way his eyes were more hard and brittle than the sun-baked sky. She wanted to reach through the fence and touch him. She wanted to tell him that even though he didn't have all of her, already he had more than she could almost bear to give. She loved him. She loved him enough that, for him, she had given up the only man on this earth she would ever love more.

He wrapped one of his hands around the fence rail, gripping the wood so tightly the veins and sinews of his wrist stood out. "Maybe you'd like your money back," he said, "so's you can be quit of this place. And quit of me."

Her breath shuddered in her throat. "Oh, Gus . . . you know I'll never leave you."

Again he stared at her hard, trying to read her thoughts, trying to see down into her soul. "I don't know whether I do know it," he finally said, "but I guess I have to believe it. If I'm going to go on."

She reached up and laid her hand on top of his. The fence was still between them, but they were touching. A drought, she thought, doesn't end with a single drop of rain. But when that one drop is joined by another and another and another, they can become enough water to turn the land green again.

"We are going to have another baby," she said.

She watched the emotions cross his face: surprise, and then that wariness again. And finally a warm and gentle joy.

For him, for his joy, she smiled. And then she realized that she was smiling for herself as well. It would be good to have another child, she thought, and she would not let herself be afraid. She would try not to let her heart dwell so often on that grave beneath the cottonwoods.

Gus slid his hand out from beneath hers to cup her face. Slowly, he lowered his head and kissed her. And although the fence was still between them, neither of them noticed it.

The rain never did come that summer to feed the land, but the drought in their marriage had ended that day. Each touch, each word spoken since, had been like so many raindrops nurturing the life they shared.

She thought of that now as she watched her husband ride off to rescue their dying cattle. She thought that in spite of the bad winter and the failing ranch, she and Gus had at last found happiness and an ease with each other.

And they had found love.

Later, Clementine was alone in the kitchen baking bread when she heard the jangle of sleigh bells. She narrowed her eyes against the snow glare. A cutter was turning off from the road into town. The driver was dressed richly, in a beaver bowler and a dark plaid woolen greatcoat. He lifted his head and turned his face toward the house.

"What is that old polecat up to now?" she said aloud to herself.

Gus was in the yard, having just come in from the range. She watched the two men meet and disappear into the barn together, then she banged out the door and set off after them without even bothering to put on a coat.

The frigid wind drove itself right to her bones and she shivered, hugging herself. Her shoes crunched over a path already cobbled with frozen footprints. The cottonwoods were popping with the cold.

The barn smelled of wet horse, old hay, and manure. A coal-oil lantern that hung on a hook just inside the door cast a murky light, glinting off scythes, oiled harnesses, and old spiderwebs. Clementine walked into a silence that was as thick as winter molasses. Gus was leading his horse into its stall and he looked up at her, but she could tell nothing from the expression on his face.

One-Eyed Jack McQueen flashed her his beguiling smile. "It is always a pleasure to find you looking so pretty, daughter-in-law." His gaze dropped to her belly, now five months swollen with child. "And you're increasing again, I see. 'Be fruitful and multiply.'" A knowing look glinted in his eye. "Yes, indeed. Pretty and fruitful, and yet faithful and virtuous as well. 'A virtuous woman is a crown to her husband.' Is she a crown to you, Gustavus?"

Gus slung his bridle over a peg and swung his saddle up onto an empty stall door. "What do you want?"

Clementine produced for her father-in-law a most virtuous smile. "'He that hideth hatred with lying lips,'" she said, "'and he that uttereth a slander, is a fool.'"

Genuine delight flashed across Jack McQueen's face. He nodded, as if granting her a victory in their little skirmish, then turned his attention back to his son. He slapped his gloved hands together, shivering dramatically. "Turning out to be a bad winter, isn't it? When the sun bothers to show up at all lately, it seems as if it's only long enough to say good-bye."

Gus pitchforked a mangerful of hay to his horse. "You going to tell me what you want?"

"My, what a surly young'un you are, and after all I've done for you. Raising you up tenderly, putting food in your belly and a shirt on your back . . ."

Gus's lips pulled back from his teeth. "When you scalp a man more than once, you begin to run out of hair."

His father tsked and shook his head. "Such bitterness doesn't become you, my boy. But then, it's been a bitter year for you, hasn't it? And it's only going to get worse. You're looking to be about as poor as a blanket Indian come spring. I hope you weren't counting on your twenty percent of the lease money from the Four Jacks to bail you out."

Gus's hands clenched around the handle of the pitchfork. He drove it into a hay bale with such force it twanged. "I've heard the rumors."

"Well, it was hardly likely to stay a secret for long, and it won't be the first time a promising vein of silver petered out over time. The ore we've been mucking out lately has mostly been low-grade stuff, full of zinc. The cost of transportation and smelting is taking too big a chunk out of the profits, and the market's drying up. No, the sad fact is, Gustavus, the Four Jacks Consortium has decided to allow its lease to lapse."

The income from their twenty percent share in the Four Jacks had waxed and waned over the years, but Clementine knew the closing of the mine would be a sore blow to Gus. Another dream turned to dross.

"Once we shut her down and allow her to fill with water," Gus's father was saying, "your share will be about as useful to you as a pot of cow pee. So what do you think about selling it to me?"

Gus laughed. "When pigs fly."

Jack McQueen heaved an exaggerated sigh. "Now, why did I just know you would prove to be stubborn?" He pulled a small square leather satchel out the deep pocket of his coat. From the satchel he removed a stiff sheaf of papers. "When the latest ore samples gave such a poor showing, I hired an engineer to crawl all over every drift, crosscut, and winze. The silver is exhausted, Gustavus."

He held out the engineer's report. When Gus didn't take it, he set it down on the hay bale beside the pitchfork. The report had been prepared on a typewriter and was even embossed with a seal.

"I am wondering, Mr. McQueen," Clementine said into the silence that stretched between father and son, "why a smart businessman like you would want to acquire another twenty percent of something that is worthless."

He threw Gus an amused glance. "Do you always let your woman do your wondering for you?"

"Why don't you answer her?"

He waved a resigned hand through the air. "Oh, very well. I'll lay my cards on the table. I was thinking I could unload the Four Jacks onto some unsuspecting eastern syndicate. Those suckers back in New York hear the words 'silver mine' and they almost piss in their longhandles with excitement. It would be easier to swing a deal if I had a hundred percent of the whole caboodle to peddle."

Gus stopped his puttering to stare hard at his father. "That's it, huh? Cards on the table. You tell me you're going to try to swindle someone and you want me to think that someone isn't me." He grinned, showing his teeth again. "Now let me see the card you got up your sleeve."

Jack McQueen looked wounded. "What makes you think I have one up my sleeve?"

"Because you always do."

A wry smile pulled at Jack McQueen's mouth. "I always figured a pretty-pious boy like you couldn't peddle ice in hell. Now here you go and prove me wrong. Maybe you got more of me in you than I ever gave you credit for." He paused a moment as if pondering hard, stroking his chin, then shrugged as if coming to a decision. "Well, hell. This time I really will put all my cards on the table." He winked at Clementine. "Even that ace I had up my sleeve . . . There's copper in the Four Jacks."

Clementine could see Gus trying to figure out what sort of bunco his father was working this time. "I thought copper was supposed to be bad," Gus said.

"It is if you're mining gold or silver. But not if copper is what you want in the first place." With two of his slender, clever fingers Jack McQueen tapped the report that lay on the hay bale. "The silver might be played out, Gustavus, but she's plumb loaded with copper. Now, you don't need to tell me copper is only selling for twelve cents a pound, which makes it hardly worth the cost of digging it out. But that's today. I'm looking to the future."

Gus poked his tongue in his cheek. "Seems like I remember hearing this patter once or twice before in my life. You got a way to make me rich, and all's I gotta do is put up a little seed money to get things rolling."

"If you don't choose to believe me, that is your prerogative, and ultimately it will be your loss. But to get this venture off the ground I'm going to need investors, big investors. If you want to keep your twenty percent share of what I'm calling the Four Jacks Copper Mine, you'll have to put up, say, two thousand dollars. And in case you think I'm cheating you, let me tell you right now that my share will be fifty thousand. So you can see I'm offering you a fine deal." He flashed his roguish smile. "You are my boy, after all."

Gus's head fell back in rafter-shaking laughter. "You think I'm going to give you two thousand dollars to invest in a copper mine that even you don't quite have the balls to claim is a sure thing. Man, it would almost be tempting just to finally be quit of you . . . if I wouldn't also be quit of my hard-earned money."

Jack McQueen's mouth hardened. "If the play is too deep for you, my dear boy, then deal yourself out. I'll give you that two thousand dollars right now, cash on the barrelhead, for your share to the claim."

Still laughing, Gus hooked his hip on the hay bale and picked up the report. Clementine brought the lantern closer. To her surprise he gave the papers over to her to read when he was done with them.

"You think I should sell out?" he said, looking over her shoulder as she studied the report.

"You must do what you think best, Gus."

He made a snorting noise, and then his mouth broke into a sun-bright Gus McQueen smile. "You're only saying that now so's you can point the finger of blame at me when it turns out to be a dumb-ass mistake."

Clementine looked up into his laughing eyes and that was when she knew it didn't matter what sort of deep and devious game One-Eyed Jack McQueen was playing at. They didn't have two thousand dollars to invest in the venture anyway, and they could sure use the two thousand the man was willing to pay them for a sale. Gus needed that money to keep the ranch alive, and she wanted that for him. No, she wanted that for herself. This was her home, her dream as well as his, and she would fight at his side to see it through.

Jack McQueen had slipped more papers out of the satchel. "I took the liberty of having my lawyer draw up the deal, giving me your twenty percent share in exchange for two thousand dollars. I even brought along the tool to sign it with." He shook a small cork-stoppered ink bottle. "I hope this didn't freeze on the way out here." He pulled out the cork with his teeth, dipped the pen, then carefully drained the ink from the nib before handing it, along with the bill of sale, to his son.

Gus's eyes narrowed on the paper. "You were so sure I'd want to sell out that you had this all written up ahead of time?"

Jack McQueen shook his head, huffing a melodramatic sigh. "That suspicious mind of yours must truly be a burden to you at times. I had two different documents drawn up, Gustavus. One if you decided to sell, another for full partnership in the newly formed Four Jacks Copper Mine. It's not too late to change your mind."

"Sure, change my mind and give you that two thousand dollars I don't have and that I'm just pure anxious to throw away into your pocket." Gus took the bill of sale from his father and read it over three times before he rested it on the hay bale and scratched his signature across the bottom.

"I have this niggling little feeling you will regret this someday," said Jack McQueen with a sad smile. "And then inevitably you will blame me for it. You'll twist it all around inside that righteous head of yours until I come out the villain, just so you won't come out the fool. Here's the money, all in treasury notes, no greenbacks. I expect you'll want to count it."

"Damn right."

Gus carefully examined every note. He even held one up to the lantern light as if he suspected it of being counterfeit. His father made a show of leaving slowly, as if he didn't want them to think he was in a hurry to get away.

"I'm durned if I can see it, Clem," Gus said as they stood together in the barn and watched One-Eyed Jack's sleigh cut through the yard. "But I know somehow he's hornswoggled us good."

"At least we have some ready money now, when we need it most. And you're free of him."

He slipped an arm around her waist, and she turned her head to look up at him. His face was hard, almost bitter. And his eyes were dark with an emotion she couldn't read. Not fear, exactly, or anger. He looked almost haunted.

"Gus?"

His arm tightened around her, pulling her close. "I don't know if I can ever be free of him, girl. He's in my blood."

The next morning Gus showed her a newspaper that had come out of Deer Lodge only last week. A sodbuster was selling hay—at a dear price, but as he told her, they had money now and matters were desperate. As in other years, they'd only put up enough of their own hay to see their saddle horses through the snow months. This winter they needed more.

"I can get there and back in two days if I push it," he said. "The beeves just aren't making it on what little range grass they can find. If I can hand-feed 'em during the worst of these storms, enough of them just might make it."

Clementine slipped the newspaper out of his hands to take a closer look at it. "How scandalous!" she said with a little sniff.

"What's so scandalous about hay?"

"Not hay. This." She tapped the paper with a mock-indignant finger. Her lips worked hard to keep from smiling. "An advertisement for red flannel drawers for ladies. And they come all the way from Paris. Imagine that."

Gus widened his eyes and twisted his mouth into a lustful leer. "I'm imagining it."

Laughter bubbled up out of her. She tried to stop it with her hands and he stopped it with his mouth. They clung to each other a moment before separating.

She made sure he dressed warmly, fussing over him as if he were one of the children. Everything wool and fur from the skin out. Wool longhandles and three pairs of wool socks. A red-checked woolen shirt and California pants and a sheepskin jacket, and over all that a buffalo coat. Knee-high buffalo boots worn with the hair on the inside and fastened with leather snaps and brass buttons. A sealskin cap and sealskin mittens lined with wool.

He went into the kitchen, where Saphronie was boiling the week's laundry and the children were playing within the circle of warmth cast by the stove. "Daddy!" Sarah shrieked as he bent to kiss her good-bye. "You look like a bear!"

"If he isn't careful," Clementine teased as she put on her own sheepskin coat, "he's liable to stampede the cattle."

Sarah gave her mother a disgusted look. "You are silly, Mama."

Clementine and Gus were laughing together as they left the kitchen and went out into the yard. Last month, when the snow got deep, Gus had put the ash-hub runners on the hay wagon, turning it into a sled. Now she helped him add the hayrack. The air shimmied with the cold, and a fresh snowstorm brewed darkly against the mountains. The clouds were heavy and murky, the color of wet slate.

"At least it isn't snowing yet," she said. He'd finished hitching up the team and was rolling the wagon-turned-sled out into the frozen yard.

"Don't hex the weather." He shook his finger at her, laughing, and she thought suddenly that they had been doing that a lot lately—laughing. Laughing and being in love—so in love they were almost giddy with it.

He climbed into the sled and wrapped the leather reins around his mittened hands. He looked down at her and she saw the flash of his teeth beneath the tawny brush of his mustache. "If I get a chance while I'm in Deer Lodge," he said, "I'll buy you a pair of them scandalous red flannel drawers . . . Gee-up!"

The horses jerked into motion, harness chains jangling, the runners crunching over the snow. She watched, shivering in her baggy sheepskin coat, until he disappeared over the crest of the rise. A lone magpie flapped across the sallow sky. Her breath smoked, wreathing her face.

She told herself she was being foolish, but suddenly she felt very much alone. And scared.

He'd been gone only an hour when it started to snow.

It snowed fitfully, lacy flakes sifting out of the cloud-swollen sky. By noon, it had grown so dusky the lamps had to be lit.

And it was cold. Cold enough, Saphronie said in Montana lingo, to make a polar bear unpack his longhandles.

Clementine hung asafetida sacks around the necks of the children and slathered goose grease on them to ward off the grippe. She bundled them up into so much wool and fur they could barely move. Sarah didn't like this restriction on her freedom one bit. She stomped around the house like a martinet, trailing scarves, her little body lumpy with fur wraps, determined to show that no winter storm was going to cramp her style.

At such times Clementine would look at her daughter and wonder how she had ever managed to produce such a child. Opinionated and outspoken, demanding and bossy, insatiably curious and brave enough to face down a grizzly. So at ease in her own skin, so sure of herself that she insisted on trying to impose that certainty onto others. "I don't want to" or "I don't care" was her answer to any demand that went contrary to her own will. She never said it defiantly, only matter-of-factly. She truly didn't care. Sarah McQueen pleased only herself.

She is all that I once had it in me to be, Clementine often thought, before my father and life beat it out of me. And she worried for her little girl's future. She wished she could wrap Sarah up against the pain that was coming as easily as she had bundled her up against the cold. For as sure as night ended even the sunniest of days, life would try to break her daughter's spirit. The world was cruel to little girls who didn't want to please, and to grown-up women who bravely spoke out and went their own way.

And she worried about Daniel as well. His was such a gentle, dreamy spirit, not at all like Charlie, who had been pure cowboy from the minute he drew his first breath. This was a country that demanded hardness from a man, a tough body and a tough heart. Men broke horses with spurs and whips, and pressed hot irons into the hides of little calves. Men hanged other men from cottonwood trees. Looking at her son now, she couldn't imagine him growing up to do these things, these tough-man things. His health alone would brand him a weakling in the western code.

At least he didn't seem to suffer as much from the lung spasms during these cold months. Right now he lay before the stove content to be wrapped up like a silkworm in a cocoon. He babbled nonsense sounds to himself, although every now and then Clementine caught the word "bear." It was the only one he knew, besides Mama and Dada, and she couldn't imagine how he'd come to learn it when they'd had no trouble with bears around the ranch since he'd been born.

Clementine wished she could wrap herself up into a cocoon. She could use another pair of drawers, no matter what their color, although she already had three pairs on, so that she waddled when she walked. But cold air billowed up from the floor as if the earth were breathing ice. She finally put all female modesty aside and followed Saphronie's example, putting on a pair of Gus's trousers under her skirts. With the trousers, the three pairs of shimmies, two wool petticoats, a wool skirt, Gus's socks, which were as thick as saddle blankets, and a belly swelling with baby, she no longer waddled when she walked; she rolled like a log in water.

Sarah and Saphronie came back just then from a trip

upstairs to the water closet. Their breath wreathed white around their faces even here in the kitchen, which was always the warmest room in the house. Clementine began to worry about what they would do if it got much colder. The fire crackled in the wood cookstove, but it didn't seem to put out enough heat to beat back the frigid air that poured right through the walls. She and Saphronie had to keep stoking the stove, and they all stood before the open door, turning themselves like chickens on a spit. Earlier Saphronie had gotten too close, and her skirt had caught fire. They'd all had a fine laugh over that . . . once the flames were safely put out.

Because it had grown dark so early that afternoon, Clementine set about making a supper of bachelor fare: a stew made of canned beef and camas root and seasoned with sage. And Saratoga chips, dried apricots, and sourdough bread to go with the stew. She rattled the pots and pans and shouted "Grub pile!" just like a roundup cook, and they pretended they were out on a cattle drive.

When the children had been put to bed, huddled beneath fur robes on the hooked rug in front of the kitchen stove, Clementine took out the bottle of whiskey she kept in her remedy chest for medicinal purposes and spiked the coffee with it. She and Saphronie pushed the sofa from the parlor into the kitchen and huddled on it side by side beneath a mackinaw blanket, drinking the whiskey-spiked coffee and talking in hushed tones of past winters, both good and sad.

"Of all the winter holidays, I think everyone loved New Year's best when I was a girl," Clementine said. "It was one time when a gentleman could safely go calling on a lady without arousing talk, you know, of whether he was seriously courting her. He would pay his call between two and four. And he always took off his hat and overcoat, but left his gloves on. He partook of a refreshment of tea and cakes. No intoxicating drinks, of course. And he stayed only fifteen minutes, not a second longer."

Saphronie looked up from the sock she was trying to darn in the dim firelight while at the same time keeping her hands warm beneath the blanket. Her forehead pleated in puzzlement. "What's the point of going visiting when you don't stay above fifteen minutes? And what kind of feed is that to offer a guest—tea and cakes? A man can't properly fill up his belly on tea and cakes."

Clementine thought about trying to explain the rules of Beacon Hill society to someone who lived in a country where your nearest neighbor could be a two-hour ride away and your larder was always open wide, along with your front door. She wasn't sure she understood all those strict and strained rules of etiquette herself anymore. "That's just the way it's done," she finally said.

Saphronie sniffed and thrust her needle into an apple-shaped pincushion. "Well, it seems a waste of time and effort to me. To get all dressed up to go a-calling and not even get fed a decent supper for your pains."

"Silly," Sarah declared from beneath the mound of furs. The two women exchanged smiles; they had thought she was asleep, although they should have known better.

"I don't remember much of when I was a little girl, before I was captured," Saphronie said. "But I do have this, like . . . picture in my mind of my mama lying down in the snow and making an angel, waving her arms and legs like little kids do, and my daddy looking at her and laughing—"

A rattling thump on the kitchen window cut her off in mid-sentence.

"Maybe it's someone lost in the storm," Clementine said after a frozen moment of breathless quiet.

"They'd knock on the door."

"Maybe they can't find the door. But they would see the light leaking out of the window."

She got up slowly and went to the window, with Saphronie hovering over her shoulder. Earlier she had tacked a blanket over the glass to cut down on the draft, and now, trying to be as silent as possible, she pulled it free.

For a moment she saw nothing but the reflection of her own face and the root crystals of ice that webbed the glass. Then her eyes focused on a movement beyond the window, and an image took shape—tawny fur, whiskers, pointed ears. A mouth opened wide, showing off big pointed yellow canine teeth. It let out a loud wail, its breath fogging the glass.

Saphronie shrieked so loud she woke up Daniel and started him crying. She went dashing into the parlor for the rifle that hung on the wall above the hearth. Clementine would've screamed herself if she hadn't been ruthlessly trained from the earliest age to suppress all emotion, even fear.

Sarah hadn't had such training, but hers was a different sort of backbone. She flung off the furs, got up, and marched over to the window. She crossed her arms over her chest and thrust out her chin. "Mama, I want you to shoot that painter."

Saphronie thrust the gun at Clementine, who was by far the better shot, then snatched up Daniel, hugging him so tight that he cried even louder.

"It was only attracted by the light, sweetheart," Clementine said, having to raise her voice above Daniel's wails. "It's probably cold and hungry because of the storm, but it can't get inside. Don't be frightened."

Sarah's chin went up another notch. "I'm not." She glared at the window where the cougar had been. "I want my daddy."

Clementine exchanged a look with Saphronie. She wanted Sarah's daddy, too. But even more, she wanted him safe. The window had shown her more than a cold and hungry cougar. It was snowing harder than ever now. The Lord willing Gus would be in Deer Lodge, snuggled inside a hotel bed. Tomorrow morning he'd buy the hay and load it up and start for home. But only if the weather didn't look bad. She hoped he would use his common sense and stay put if it was kicking up a blizzard come morning.

"The mercury's at minus thirty and falling," the sodbuster said as he helped Gus tie a tarpaulin down over his load of hay bales.

"I reckon maybe the snow will let up, then," Gus argued, though more to convince himself. "It usually does when the temperature drops so low." Cold like this was going to make for a ball-busting trip back home, but then, a man took what he had to take. "I reckon that about does it," he added as he threw the last diamond hitch and hauled tight the slack, damp rope.

The sodbuster stuck out a hand to seal their deal, the snow icing the beard around his grin. "You're welcome to stay until the weather turns."

Gus looked at the man through a shimmer of tears brought on by the bite of the cold. He clasped the proffered hand, nodding his thanks. "That's generous of you, Mr. Laurence, but I got a pregnant wife waiting for me and two little ones. And, besides, if I hung around till the weather turned, you might still have me on your hands come spring."

The farmer laughed and stepped back as Gus hauled himself up into the sled. "That's Montana for you," the man said.

Gus's laughter joined the sodbuster's, and clouds of white smoke billowed around their heads. He took up the reins and geed the reluctant team into motion, toward Rainbow Springs and home.

Within seconds he was cold enough to spit icicles. His face felt pinched, the skin drawn tight and numb over his cheekbones and nose. He kept sucking at the biting, ice-spangled air, but he couldn't seem to draw a deep enough breath. His lungs felt clogged with ice, and his mustache kept freezing his lips shut. His hands and feet were like dead stumps, and his joints grew as stiff as a new saddle.

It was a silent cold, like having your ears stuffed with cotton. The falling snow and the still, heavy air muffled all sound, except occasionally the jangle of the harness chains, the cutting rasp of the runners, and the crunch of the horses' hooves breaking through a crust of old snow. And, once, a raven calling out as it flew overhead, although he couldn't see it.

But in a way, he thought, the cold itself was a sound. A shriek that a man heard only in his mind. Or deep in the guts of him where the fear dwelled.

He looked out over the winter-ravaged land. The river was smothered under a blanket of fresh snow; the willows, cottonwoods, and pines were all fringed with it. The prairie was like a sheet of beaten silver. The whole world was frozen dead.

He knew this country as he knew the curves and lumps of the face he shaved every day. But landmarks could become invisible during a blue norther, buried or shrouded by the wind-driven snow. The snow was drifting down lightly now and there wasn't any wind. But the practical, cautious side of him, which he hadn't wanted to listen to before, knew that could change at any minute. There was an ominous weightiness to the air now. And a stillness.

That's Montana for you.

No sooner did the thought seep into his head than it began to snow harder. Great wet clots of flakes as big as fists. He looked back over his shoulder, blinking hard to get the ice crystals off his lashes. He could still see the holes left in the snow by his horses' hooves and the parallel grooves of the hub runners, but they were filling in fast. Sometimes in a bad blow a man could lose sight of the horizon, lose his sense of direction and wind up going in circles.

He snapped his head around and peered through the curtain of falling snow ahead of him. He saw plainly the

blinders and collars and straps of the harness, the backs
of his cinnamon-colored horses. And beyond them—just
barely, but he could still see it—the tree-lined river that
would lead him home.

An hour later there came the first shrieking, biting
gust of wind. It sent the falling flakes spinning and whirling crazily and whipped at the loose snow on the ground.
The knife-slash of the wind ripped through his clothes and
shredded his lungs.

He resisted the urge as long as he could before he
finally looked back over his shoulder again and saw . . .
nothing. Nothing but icy flakes whipping past his face. He
scrubbed his eyes with his sleeve, knocking off the icicles
that had formed on his brows. No tracks, no horizon, no
ground, and no sky. Only snow. It must be snowing, he
thought, even on the moon.

A strange feeling of utter and horrible aloneness
gripped him. Slowly he turned back around . . . and saw
nothing ahead of him except his reins, disappearing into a
coiling swirl of whiteness.

The wind smacked against the house, startling Clementine
awake. She was disoriented for a moment, aware only of the
cold that lay thick and deep around her. Then a fresh gust
slammed against the north wall, making it moan. She sat
up on the sofa, the blankets crackling as she disturbed a
layer of frost.

Saphronie slipped a fresh cup of whiskey-spiked coffee
into her hands. She and Saphronie had taken turns staying
awake during the night, making sure the children's noses
and ears stayed covered so they wouldn't freeze.

The blizzard that had threatened throughout yesterday and last night had finally struck. The walls trembled
and creaked beneath the battering force of the wind. The
noise roused the children. Daniel whimpered, and Sarah
demanded that the fire be made hotter and no amount of

talking convinced her the fire was as hot as it was going to get. Clementine fed them some hominy, which quieted them some, and then Saphronie got them interested in playing bears-in-a-cave beneath the furs.

Although the house was tightly built, still the driving snow sifted in around windows and beneath the door. Saphronie remembered some old canvas tenting down in the cellar, and they nailed it up where they could to keep out the invading blizzard. But they couldn't keep out the cold. Even with the stove stoked like a blast furnace, the inside pump froze. They weren't likely to die of thirst, though. There was so much snow out there, Clementine thought, that, melted, it would have drowned the world.

"You don't think he'll try to make it back today?" she said, voicing aloud a fear that had nagged at her all through the long night and morning.

Saphronie pursed her lips in thought, wrinkling the teardrop tattoos on her chin. "Say, give him time to find the sodbuster, buy the hay, and load it. By then it would already've started to get real bad. He's lived here long enough not to try to set out for anywhere in the middle of a blue norther."

Clementine nodded, but she wasn't so sure. Her husband had always been likely to lose sight of an unpleasant present when he got his eye fixed on a promising future. In his head he'd have himself home and toasting his toes before the fire and with his cattle all fed, before he'd gone even a mile down the road.

She was pulled to the window, as if Gus might already be turning into the yard, even though she knew it was impossible. She pried loose the piece of blanket, but she saw only darkness and the reflection of lamp-shine. A half an inch of ice coated the glass.

Suddenly she felt imprisoned and panicked, as if she'd been buried alive inside a cave. When she couldn't stand it anymore she heated a flatiron and held it against the glass to thaw the ice and let in some light. But all she saw beyond the oval-shaped melted spot on the window was the driving snow.

By midafternoon they had run low on wood for the stove. She and Saphronie tied lariats together and then argued about who would make the first trip out to the barn and the woodpile. Finally they flipped a coin and Clementine won. She added more clothes to her bulky figure, knotted the rope around her waist, and set out into the blizzard.

Even after seven Montana winters, she hadn't known it could snow this hard or be this cold. It seemed the wind blew the stinging, biting flakes right through her, as if she were invisible. This country had always had that ability, she thought—to make a body feel insignificant before the awesome forces of nature.

She fed the animals while she was in the barn. There were only the saddle horses—the chickens had all died long ago, during the first big freeze, and the hogs had been butchered even before then. The horses stood in their stalls, hunched and sad against the wind that slashed through the cracks in the barn walls. She worried about the broncs out on the range, and the cattle that were probably stacking up like cords of wood against the drift fences.

Her hands were as clumsy as clubs, her arms and legs stiff, as she pitched hay to the horses and broke the ice in their water troughs. She stacked as much wood as she could onto the red pung. With all the moisture freeze-dried out of them the logs were so light she could have juggled them like balls. But every time she drew a breath of the icy air into her shrunken lungs, it felt as if a knife were sliding into her chest.

She made countless trips back and forth to the woodpile. Then Saphronie made countless trips. After that they looked at their stockpile and figured they had enough to see them through until the following morning.

It had been dark a good hour when they heard the knocking noise. With the wind blowing hard enough to peel the bark off trees, Clementine thought it had peeled something loose off the house. Then the wind stilled a moment, as it did sometimes, as if sucking in its breath to blow even harder, and they heard it again.

It was a definite knock, and on the door. A thump-thump that could have been made by nothing but a human fist.

Clementine started for the children, ready to comfort them if they awoke frightened, but they both remained asleep. She met Saphronie's startled eyes. "It could be Gus," she said, except that she knew it wasn't Gus. Gus would've been banging the door off its hinges and bellowing to be let in.

"Maybe whoever it is will go away," Saphronie whispered, as if whoever had knocked could hear them through the door with a blizzard howling outside.

"We can't turn a body away on a night like this, no matter who it is."

Clementine picked up the rifle and made sure it was loaded. Saphronie lifted the lantern off its hook. They had to use their combined strength, pulling on the door, to break the ice seal.

The storm snatched the door out of their hands and banged it against the wall. A drift of fresh snow fell over the threshold. The wind's roars turned shrill.

"Who's there?" Clementine called out, the words getting snatched away by the shrieking wind.

Saphronie lifted the lantern. It threw a pale glow on the ice-glazed gallery. Something was hunched deep inside a blanket coat and furs, hovering at the bottom of the steps on the edge of the light. A small dark figure in whose face no mouth was to be seen, only the gleam of two narrowed eyes.

"Indians," Saphronie whispered.

Gus McQueen pounded his arms with his fists, which accomplished nothing except to dislodge the snow caked on his buffalo coat. He ached with cold deep inside the bones and heart of him.

His hand was a frozen claw wrapped around the hames on the harness collar of the near horse. Some time ago he had gotten off the sled to walk beside the team. He told himself it was to ensure they followed the meandering line of the river. But maybe it was also to be close to something else living in the howling white void.

And besides . . . he hadn't seen the river in some time now.

He trusted the bale-laden sled to be connected still to the traces that disappeared into the swirling veil of wind-driven snow behind them. It had been a while since he'd been able to see the sled as well.

The team slogged through the shifting dunes of snow, floundering and staggering as if drunk. The horses' sides heaved, matching his own labored breathing. Icicles hung from their snoots, and white clouds rose like steam around their heads. He thought he must look like the horses, though he could no longer feel his face.

Although it seemed he'd been walking for years in a perpetual dusk, he sensed the hour was truly getting late. When night fell it would be as dark as a plugged barrel. And he'd be done for then.

He slogged on. The wind struck in volleys, driving the corn-hard pellets of snow into his face. He stumbled, went sprawling, and got mired up to his knees in a fresh drift. The horses jerked free of his frozen hand and went on without him, disappearing.

Scythes of snow slashed at his eyes. He saw nothing, heard nothing but the constant scream of the wind. And underneath, the whoosh and suck of his breath and the heavy thumping of his heart.

He thought he would stop a moment, here in this drift. Maybe lie down and rest a little while. He was so tired . . .

He had to get home, couldn't leave her, couldn't leave

Clementine alone with a dying ranch and three children to raise. Had to get home to that roaring fire and that pot of some good-smelling thing bubbling on the stove. To that girl with hair the color of a wheat field in August and eyes like a pine forest at dusk. Clementine . . . She needed him. He couldn't die on her, couldn't die on himself, couldn't die.

He told his legs to move and they wouldn't, and then they did, somehow on their own, fighting free of the sucking, clinging snow. He slogged forward, fell, got up, and slogged forward, hit something . . . the sled. Oh, Christ, the sled. The horses had stopped, then, and he felt his way up to their heads and clung to the harness collar, sobbing with fear and relief and then fear again.

He couldn't see the river. The river was nowhere, and he was nowhere, lost in a world of white light, white cold, and white ache.

Indians!

Clementine almost ran back into the house and slammed the door. But then the flickering lantern light flashed off the frightened faces of two children lying on a skin hammock hung between skid poles . . . An instant later they were swallowed by the driving curtain of snow.

The figure with the narrowed, gleaming eyes took a step forward, and two other bigger, bulkier shapes materialized behind it. A voice, high and tremulous, floated on the wail of the wind.

"Mrs. McQueen . . . do you remember me? Joe Proud Bear's woman."

Saphronie hissed something behind her that Clementine couldn't hear over the thundering beat of her heart. She had to swallow twice before she could speak. "And the others? Who else is with you?"

"My children and my man . . . And his father, Iron Nose. Please. We need warmth and shelter or we will die."

Clementine took the lantern from Saphronie's stiff hand and gave her the rifle. "Take this and go inside by the children." Saphronie turned a frightened face to her, and Clementine gave her a little shove. "For mercy's sake, we can't turn them away."

She stepped farther out onto the snow-smothered gallery, holding up the lantern to give them light while the half-breed woman unbundled her children from the travois. One was small enough to rest on her hip. The taller one had to be the little girl Clementine had last seen sitting outside a tipi beside the Rainbow River over seven years ago.

Joe Proud Bear took the youngest child from its mother's arms and started for the door. Iron Nose melted back into the biting wind and ripping snow, a hulking figure draped in a buffalo robe.

"What about . . . him?" Clementine said. She felt a macabre curiosity, an urge to see the man's face, to see if he truly had an iron nose. And to discover, perhaps, if he was as horrible as the monster who had once haunted her nightmares.

Joe Proud Bear's woman looked to the place where the old Indian had disappeared into the wild night. She shrugged. "He has chosen to live off his pride."

Clementine swallowed around the fear lodged in her throat. "There is an old cabin down by the river . . ." Her voice quavered into silence. If the stories were true, Iron Nose knew already of the cabin and of the buffalo hunter who had died there . . . tomahawked into so many pieces, it was said, they'd had to gather him up in a bucket to bury him.

They plowed into the kitchen, bringing with them drifts of snow that turned into puddles as it struck the warmer air. Clementine had to wrestle with the door to close it against the force of the wind.

Saphronie sat on the sofa with the rifle gripped tightly in her hands. Daniel, wrapped up in his cocoon of blankets, lay on one side of her. Sarah sat on the other, self-contained and fearless, her wide eyes taking it all in, her stern little mouth for once offering no opinion.

Joe Proud Bear turned in a slow circle as he looked around him, his gaze stopping a moment on Saphronie and the rifle. His lips pulled into something that wasn't quite a smile. "Where is your man?"

Clementine's gaze flashed around the room as if she could suddenly will Gus's presence into existence, along with a troop of U.S. Cavalry.

The half-breed's dark eyes narrowed on her frightened face, and he laughed.

His wife stepped between them. "I would cut out his heart before I let him harm you," she said, and shot her husband such a harsh glare that color flooded his face and his gaze dropped to the floor. Clementine suspected it had been a while since Joe Proud Bear had dared to rope his woman.

For a moment they all stared at one another, and then Clementine jerked into movement. She served them bowls of stew from the pot she'd kept going on the stove. The Indian children, swaddled in faded scarlet trade blankets and pieces of buffalo hide, ate as if half starved. Joe Proud Bear helped himself to a chair and braced his booted feet on the fender of the range. He kept his eyes fastened on Clementine as he shoveled the stew into his mouth.

"Lot of dead whoa-haws out there," he said. "Maybe your man's dead, too."

His wife pried the empty bowl from his hands and handed it to Clementine along with her own. "Don't listen to him. Like the naughty dog who steals the meat and then growls to hide his crime, he is ashamed. Already he owes you his life, and now he comes begging for it again." She said something to him in harsh guttural syllables; then she turned back to Clementine and smiled. "I tell him that some white people are good. Maybe as good as Indians."

Clementine tried to find a smile of her own, but she

was still too ill at ease. No, "scared" was the word. She was plain scared.

She busied herself pouring them some of the hot black coffee. Too late she remembered the whiskey in it, and she backed away from them until her hip struck the kitchen table. She'd heard gruesome stories of what Indians did when they were drunk.

She wondered if they carried weapons. Surely they did—hatchets and knives if nothing else. She thought about asking them to toss their weapons out the door, but it seemed such an inhospitable thing to do. She nearly laughed out loud at what a fool she was being, worrying about good manners at a time like this.

They all jumped when the youngest Indian child suddenly began screaming and pulling at his fox fur cap.

To Clementine's surprise Joe Proud Bear was the one who went to the child. He removed the cap with gentle fingers, then turned to Clementine with eyes that shone with worry. "My son . . . the cold has bitten his ears."

"I—I have some glycerin in my remedy chest," she said.

She warmed the glycerin in a pot on the stove, then applied drops of it to the boy's ears with a turkey feather. She filled a shallow washpan from the hot reservoir and prepared a mustard bath. Together she and Joe Proud Bear's woman knelt and unwrapped the strips of woolen blanket from around the little boy's moccasined feet and then the girl's. The Indian children smelled of goose grease, just as Clementine's children did, and of smoke from long dead campfires. Their dark eyes watched her, shining like shoe buttons in the lantern light. The only sounds in the room were the drip and splash of water in the pan and the wail of the blue norther beyond the walls.

"To be out in a storm like this," Clementine said when she could bear the silence no longer. "It's God's miracle you're still alive."

Joe Proud Bear's woman turned her head and the light

shone off her wide cheekbones. "We had been sleeping with the dogs, but then the dogs died."

Where had they been sleeping with dogs? Clementine wondered. Where had they been hiding all these years? Up in the foothills, no doubt, and they'd probably been helping themselves to Rocking R cattle all this time. Heavens, Gus would be furious if he knew. For some reason—hysteria, probably—the thought made her want to laugh.

It was, Clementine decided later, the strangest night she ever spent. She and her family on one side of the kitchen, Joe Proud Bear and his family on the other, with the heat and crackle of the fire and the howling, snow-laden wind outside the only things they shared. Only the children slept.

Near dawn it stopped blowing. She went to the window and pulled aside the blanket to look out. The sky had cleared and the moon cast a cold blue light over the frozen land. Now that the wind had ceased, she could hear the cottonwoods snapping and crackling. And the yapping of the coyotes, a lonely and beautiful sound. She couldn't see Iron Nose. She wondered if he was still out there somewhere; if he was alive, or if he had escaped being hanged from the limb of a cottonwood tree, only to die in a blizzard because his pride wouldn't allow him to accept an enemy's charity. She remembered her first year here, how frightened she had been by tales of that renegade Indian, by the very idea of red painted savages and their gruesome atrocities. But now those fears were dim and ragged, scarcely more than echoes of fears. Other horrors had come to take their place in her mind.

She heard a rustle of movement behind her and she turned. Joe Proud Bear's eyes glittered at her, bitter and black as chokecherries. The hard will of him showed in his chiseled cheeks and chin, his hawk's nose that caught a reflection of the stove's light. She didn't fear him now, but she wondered if in another time and place he would be capable of killing her, even though she had twice saved his life. If his hatred ran that deep.

"I've been wondering," he said, as if he'd read her thoughts, yet he spoke softly so as not to wake his children, "why it is that your yellow hair isn't decorating some brave's war club long by now."

She lifted her chin. "And I have been wondering, Mr. Joe Proud Bear, why it is you weren't hanged years ago for a cattle thief."

His smile flashed white in his dark face. And his next words surprised her, and pleased her as well. "The years have changed you, white woman. Once, I think, you had the heart of a straw squaw put among the corn to frighten away bears. Now you are the bear."

The sun came up in a sky that was hazy with frost. The air shimmered so with the cold that it was like looking at the world through a sheet of oiled glass.

"We go now," Joe Proud Bear said, and they did. They disappeared back into the white wilderness whence they had come. Clementine did not see Iron Nose rejoin them, and she wondered if he had ever existed. If she hadn't dreamed it all.

But when she went back inside she found, lying on her kitchen table, a pair of white gloves decorated in the Blackfeet fashion with beads and bits of colored glass and dyed porcupine quills. Each glove was beautiful and distinct from the other, yet somehow they belonged together.

"Well, land!" Saphronie said as she rubbed a finger over the intricately embroidered design on one of the gloves. "There's something to be said for Boston ways. I was never so glad to see company go in my life."

Clementine pressed her lips together to keep from laughing and snorted instead. Saphronie giggled, which made Clementine snort again, and soon they were laughing so hard they woke the children.

"You two are being silly," Sarah said.

"Bear!" Daniel shrieked. "Bear!"

Which set them to laughing again, laughing until their sides ached and the kitchen rang with it.

They almost didn't hear the rasp and crunch of the sled runners, maybe wouldn't have heard it at all if Clementine hadn't left the door open a crack to let some fresh air into the kitchen despite the cold.

She saw the horses first, their coats caked with snow and foot-long icicles hanging from their bits, and behind them a sled that appeared to be filled with a mountainous pile of snow and ice. Beside it stumbled a creature that looked like the sculpture of a bear carved of ice and come to life.

"Gus!" she screamed, flying out the door. The brightness of sunlight on snow stabbed at her eyes. Bulky and clumsy with all the clothes she was wearing, she nearly foundered in the drifts, her feet getting tangled with each other. "You fool of a man—what possessed you to set off for home in the middle of a blizzard? You could've been lost or frozen or . . . You could have died, Gus. You could have died . . ."

He looked at her with eyes narrowed against the snow glare and glittering with fever. "Couldn't die on you, Clem," he said. "Wasn't gonna die on you."

He tried to smile, and the icicles that dripped from his mustache quivered. "Die," he said, and sagged to his knees at her feet, then fell face-first into the snow.

Gus was wrenched back into consciousness by the fiery sting of a hot mustard-and-linseed poultice being slapped onto his bare chest.

He opened his eyes. Two female faces hovered above him. One belonged to his wife. She was frowning. The other belonged to his daughter, and a tiny crimp of concentration marked her forehead between her straight little brows.

He saw his daughter's mouth open and heard her voice as if it came up at him from the bottom of a well. "Daddy, your nose looks funny."

"Sarah, go play bears-in-a-cave with your brother, please—see if you can get him to hibernate. Help keep him quiet and let me tend to your father."

His daughter's face disappeared, and in its place was his wife's hand, wielding a dripping feather. His eyes crossed trying to see what she was doing to him. He opened his mouth to talk, surprised the words didn't come out right away, and that when they did they were so raspy. "What's wrong with my nose?"

"It's frozen solid as a brass knob, you idiot man," his wife said, and he almost smiled, knowing that Clementine only scolded him when she cared. "A well-aimed punch would probably break that nose right off your face. Of course, Snake-Eye can always fashion you a new one out of iron."

He drew a breath to speak, and a harsh cough shook his chest. "Sounds like you want to be the first one to take a swing at me . . . Reckon you must be mighty glad to see me home."

"Oh, Gus . . ."

Another racking cough exploded out of him, this time with such force it wrenched his chest and bent his belly double. He tried to draw in a breath and coughed again, his lungs gurgling.

He sagged back and realized he was lying, not upstairs in his bed as he'd thought, but in the kitchen. On the parlor sofa. He wondered what the parlor sofa was doing in the kitchen. And the kitchen itself looked strange, with pieces of old canvas nailed all over the walls and blankets over the windows. A fresh spasm of coughing bent and wrenched him, and when he could finally breathe again he was gasping.

Clementine leaned over him. She brushed back his sweat-damp hair and laid a wet cloth reeking of vinegar on his forehead. To his surprise her eyes brimmed with unshed tears. "God damn you, Gus McQueen, you could have died out there."

He lifted his hand, surprised at how heavy it felt. He

brushed her cheek, catching the lone tear that had managed to escape in spite of all her best efforts. "But I didn't . . . And since when did you take up cussing?"

"Since you started running such a fever I could fry an egg on your forehead. I've sent Saphronie for the doctor."

"Aw, Clem, what'd you want to do that for? It's only the grippe. Weather like this she's liable to come back sicker than I am."

She disappeared for a moment and was back with a cup of something steaming. "Drink this. It's onion syrup."

He struggled to push himself up onto his elbows, hacking and coughing. "The horses . . ."

"Saphronie saw to them before she left. Gus, *please.* Drink this or I shall pour it down your throat."

He made a face, but he drank it, and then the cough took him again, rumbling and gurgling through his chest. "Well, hell," he said. He pulled in deep drafts of air to keep from coughing again and tried to sit up . . . and fell back down.

His eyes burned. His whole face felt strange, sunken and collapsed in upon itself, his joints all loose and floppy as if his bones were tied together with baling twine. Out there, fighting the blizzard, he had thought even the fires of hell would never make him warm again. Now he felt so hot he wanted to run outside and jump in the snow buck naked.

Out there . . . It must, he thought, have been the good Lord that had led him through it. Because he'd lost the damn river, lost sight of everything but his own two feet, slogging through a black night of wind-whipped snow, slogging, slogging, slogging . . . And then the wind had died and the snow had stopped and when the sun came up, there he'd been, still following the river and less than a mile from home, and only the good Lord could've managed that. A miracle. He wanted to laugh. A son of the Reverend One-Eyed Jack McQueen had been the beneficiary of a genuine miracle.

But the miracle could turn out to be as bogus as one of his father's if he didn't see it through. He wrapped an arm around his wife's waist and tried to use her to boost himself to his feet.

She staggered beneath his weight, and her hip bumped into the kitchen table. Something splashed, and a chair went skidding across the floor. "Gus, whatever are you doing? Lie still. Look, you almost knocked over the vinegar water."

"Help me up, Clem . . . Got to feed the cattle . . . Be blamed if I walked through a blizzard . . . only to see 'em die 'cause I couldn't get the hay from my yard out to where they're at."

She gripped his shoulders, pressing him back. "All right, all right, then," she said, speaking to him in the soothing voice she used on Daniel when he was suffering through one of his lung spasms. "I'll get the hay out to the cows, Gus. You just rest easy."

He tried to laugh and coughed instead. "Now look who's being the fool. You're five months gone—"

"Not so gone that I couldn't drag you in here after you'd fainted out in the yard and looked all set to drown in the snow." Her hands tightened, and she shook him a little, surprising him with her strength. "Not so gone that I couldn't make umpteen trips back and forth between here and the woodshed to keep us all from freezing during the most miserable weather Montana could dredge up. Not so gone that I . . ." She stopped, and the color came up high in her face. "Not so gone that I can't pitch a few forkfuls of hay to a few hungry cows."

It would be more than a few forkfuls, but he said nothing. He wasn't getting up; he could tell that now as he tried and failed to fight down another bout of bone-wrenching coughing. He let his head fall back, shutting his eyes. His chest hurt. He heard Clementine telling Sarah to mind Daniel and sing to him if he woke up fussing, and have a care not to get too close to the stove. And he struggled to keep from coughing again so that she wouldn't know how sick he really was, because then she wouldn't want to leave him alone.

His eyes drifted closed. When he opened them again she was leaning over him. "Gus, are you well enough to watch the children? I can't leave them if—"

"Yeah, sure, I'm well enough. Only resting easy is all, like you said . . . Clementine . . ." He groped for her hand, found it, and held on tight. "Out there last night—I did a lot of thinking. Not much else to do when you're slogging through snow and trying to keep your mind off how cold you are . . . A lot of the thinking I did was about you, about us." He swallowed hard, fighting down another urge to cough, and his chest burned. "I did you wrong, girl, taking you away from your home and family when you were so young. Bringing you out here to this hard, rough country, when you were raised to so much better . . . So many things I wished I could've given you and I never did. I did wrong by you, Clem, but from the first moment I saw you, I wanted you. I just didn't see a way I was going to get through life without you."

She knelt and brought their clasped hands up to her mouth to kiss his knuckles. "You didn't do wrong by me; you did right. And what makes you think I would have wanted to go through life without you, Gus McQueen? If I had it to live over again, I would do all of it, *all* of it, in the exact same way." A gentle smile softened her face, and she touched his lips with her free hand, following the drooping curve of his mustache with her finger, stroking it. "You are the cowboy of my dreams."

"I am, huh? What's that supposed to mean?"

She lowered her head and kissed his mouth. "It means I love you."

Their entwined hands fell apart. She stood up and backed away from him. A small woman, delicate as heired china, elegant and graceful even in a long, ragged buffalo coat. But then, she'd always been prime, a real lady.

She opened the door and winter billowed inside. The cold air felt good on his hot face and he breathed it in. She paused a moment to look back at him. Then the door shut behind her and she was gone.

His thoughts drifted, making him smile. He had those red drawers in his saddle pack . . . meant to give 'em to her. Would get them out when she got back and make her put them on for him tonight. Only the drawers and nothing else. She had a fine pair of legs, long and slender, like a colt's.

He thought of how she'd looked, standing in the doorway with the snow-bright winter light behind her, and she'd been smiling. She didn't smile all that often, but when she did it was like turning on a gas jet. It lit up her whole face. So pretty. Just like the first time he'd seen her.

Clementine stood tall on the sleigh seat and looked back at the big house. Smoke puffed from the chimney. The icicles on the eaves glittered wet in the sun—a lemon-colored sun, shining without heat in a hard blue sky.

Ice crystals swirled and sparkled and flashed in the air. She could hear a faint tinkling sound, like glasses clinking in a toast. She wondered what caused it. Perhaps it was just the earth being cold.

Since the storm had come from the north, she drove the sled south toward the coulees and draws where the cattle would have drifted. The snow cried as it was cut by the sleigh's ash runners. The horses' hooves sent the loose flakes rippling like sea sand. The RainDance country was sheathed in ice, shimmering like a crystal pendant. The mountains stood out in stark relief like a long line of white tipis thrusting into the sky, clean and cold and beautiful.

And it *was* beautiful, she thought. Hard and cruel and frightening, yet so beautiful.

She found a bunch of cows piled up against the line

fence. Most were dead, but a few lived, standing huddled together, shivering and hungry. Their coats glinted with hoarfrost, vapor shot from their snouts, and icicles dripped like fringe from their dewlaps and flanks. They tinkled like wind-stirred chandeliers as they unlocked their frozen legs and came toward her, drawn by the smell of the hay.

A wolf pack was feeding off the pile of stacked carcasses. Made brave by hunger, they hadn't even run off when she drove up. So she killed one cleanly with the Winchester, and the others scattered into the surrounding pines. She looked at the dead wolf and knew a sense of pride. Pride that she had made herself learn how to shoot long ago and then practiced until she could do it well.

She wrestled a bale off the load, cut through the baling twine, and began spreading the hay with a pitchfork. It smelled of summer. Last summer during the drought, when money was too tight to hire extra hands, she'd helped Gus put up their hay. She thought of how it felt to swing the scythe through the tall grass, the way the sharp blade sliced the hay and laid it down in perfect rows. It had been like making poetry with her body. And though she'd been clumsy at first, she'd learned to do it well. She could do many things well now. Montana things.

I am the bear, she thought and she laughed. She threw back her head and shouted it aloud. "I am the bear!"

She breathed deeply, scouring her lungs with the cold air. She kept her face turned to the sky. A big, wide Montana sky with no wind, no clouds, just still air and cold sunshine.

She sensed a charged feeling in the air. And then it came, a warm gush of wind from out of the mountains. A wind that smelled of the earth, and of a sea that was hundreds of miles away. She turned her face to the southwest, where it came from, the warm dry wind. The chinook.

The balmy wind roared out of mountains, blowing the loose hay over the snowy field. The ice crust glistened, reflecting back the sun in prisms of glorious color. Chinook. A warm breath from the dark mother, so the Indians used to say. It was as if the earth wept. But if the earth was weeping, it was with joy.

You take it all in, with your eyes and your breath and the pores of your skin, all the beauty and the wildness of it . . . Once, a man she loved had told her that. She hadn't really understood it then, but she did now. The missing things had been there within her all along. They were there in the land, and in hard work and good living, and the birthing and raising of children, and the love of two fine men.

She wanted to ride all over the range and feed all the cattle in the world while the warm wind blew in her face. But it was winter still, and darkness would come early, and Gus would be needing another dose of onion syrup soon. So she finished feeding the cattle she had found and turned for home.

She ran into the house, laughing, calling out to Gus, saying, "Gus, Gus, do you feel it? It's as warm as summer. There's a chinook blowing outside, a real snow-eater, and . . . Oh, God."

Gus lay on the floor, his chest heaving as the breath rasped and rattled out of his throat. Sarah sat next to him, with Daniel beside her. Daniel was quiet, sucking his thumb. Sarah had been singing, but she stopped when Clementine burst through the door. "Daddy's fussing," she said, "and I can't make him be quiet."

"Gus! Oh, my God, Gus . . ." Clementine fell to her knees beside him. With trembling hands she lifted his head and laid it in her lap. She brushed the hair out of his face and pressed her mouth to his, as if she would give him the breath he fought for. Rubbed his swollen, fever-cracked lips with hers. His lips that knew how to smile and how to hurt, and how to love.

"Gus, please don't leave me." She clasped him to her chest and rocked. "Please don't, please don't, please don't, please don't . . ."

She had left the door open to the chinook. She held him in her arms as the lush, warm wind lapped at the snow. She thought she could almost see the frozen land take heart and begin to live again. She held him in her arms, and it was the strangest thing. One moment he was there with her, in her arms, and in the next he was not.

PART FOUR
1891

30

SHE WAS STRAINING A bucket of fresh milk when she saw him across the prairie, a man on a dun-colored horse.

He didn't appear to be in a hurry, ambling along, sitting tall and easy and graceful in the saddle.

She set the foaming milk down to cool and poured a can of soured cream into a barrel churn. She fired up the stove and put on some coffee before she took the churn and a chair out onto the gallery and sat down.

The man had turned toward the ranch and was cutting through the hay meadow. She liked the way he rode, as if he'd been born to it. She hoped he was a saddle bum in need of work, a cowboy down on his luck. They could use some help with the spring roundup.

She had milked her cows in the muddy corral that morning and had broken a colt to the lead there that afternoon. She looked a fright now, with muck on her boots and on the divided skirt of her riding habit, and with her hair falling loose from its chignon. Once she would have rushed upstairs and tidied herself up for company; now it didn't seem as important as making the butter.

She pulled the churn up between her legs and began to crank the handle, turning the barrel end over end.

She narrowed her eyes, the better to make out the approaching rider. He was a cowboy surely by the look of his buckskin coat and dark Stetson hat. The late afternoon sky rose high and wide and gray in back of him, brooding up for another rain. A flight of drakes, bright in their courting feathers, pierced the low clouds above his head, bearing north.

She felt a strange uneasiness that she couldn't attribute to anything in particular, a restlessness. She paused a moment in her cranking to watch him come, then shrugged. If she liked the looks of him and he was willing to work for his thirty dollars a month plus beans and bacon, if he could handle a rope and bust a bronc, then she would definitely take him on for the roundup.

She and Saphronie, with the help of Pogey and Nash, had managed by themselves during the last four springs, mostly because there hadn't been many cows to round up. That first spring after Gus had died, that winter of the Great Die-Up, most of the RainDance country's cattle had wound up as carcasses stacked and stinking in the coulees, food for the buzzards and wolves. The few left living had been ragged and starved and hardly worth the slaughtering. But if a rancher couldn't find a meat market for his beeves, he made what money he could from selling their hides. It was called a skinning season. They'd had mostly skinning seasons since Gus died.

This spring would be different, though, especially if she could hire herself a man to help out. That man on the dun for instance, who was riding alongside the snake fence now and would soon be turning into the yard.

If he wasn't averse to working for a woman, which most men were.

If the Four Jacks Copper Mine and its offer of four dollars a day didn't hire him away.

She stopped cranking and peeked through the small glass window in the churn, and saw that the butter had come. But she didn't open the end of the churn, fling some cold water in it, and go on cranking as she should have. Instead she wiped her hands on her skirt and went out into the yard to meet the stranger.

He disappeared for a moment into the long shadows cast by the cottonwoods, then emerged into the wan, cloud-shrouded light. He must have seen her just then, because he checked his horse hard, as if he'd been surprised or startled. The dun reared and Clementine's steps faltered. There was something about the way he handled the horse, the way he held his head and shoulders, the way he was . . . She pressed her fist to her chest, because it felt as though her heart had suddenly stopped beating.

The dun was shedding its rough winter coat, and the man looked winter-worn as well. His dark brown hair hung long over the collar of his buckskin jacket; his boots were badly run-down and scuffed. The hat pulled low over his eyes had dents in the crown and a frayed brim. As he swung down from the saddle and looped the reins over his arm, she saw he wore a Colt slung low on his hip. And there was a Winchester rifle nestled in the boot holster. He came at her, walking like a cowboy, narrow hips swiveling, long muscular legs eating up the ground.

She sucked in a deep breath, feeling almost dizzy. She didn't want to believe it. To believe and then have it not be true would be more than a soul could bear.

He stopped while there was a good six feet still separating them. He thumbed up his hat a little, and she looked into a pair of fierce yellow eyes.

"Clementine," he said and his voice broke over the syllables.

She could say nothing at all. Only look at him. It hurt and it was wonderful to look at him.

The wind came up, tugging at the loosely knotted handkerchief that sagged from his throat and stirring the shaggy strands of his hair. His gaze broke from hers and moved back out into the open prairie.

"Where's that big brother of mine? Out chasin' cows?"

"It happened four years ago, during the winter of the Great Die-Up. He caught the grippe, and it settled on his lungs and he . . . died."

She had buried her husband beneath the cottonwoods, next to her son. The wolves had been so bad that winter they'd had to cover the grave with rocks, and the rocks were still there, mottled now with moss and lichen.

Gus's brother stood with his head bowed, his hat off and hanging from two fingers of the hand he had hooked on his gun belt. She studied his face—the fierce, strong lines and angles of bone under the dark, taut skin. A face that was imprinted on her soul, and yet a face she knew not at all. He'd always been good at keeping his feelings to himself, and whatever kind of life he'd been living during the last seven years had made him better at it.

Suddenly he whipped his head up and around to pin her with his intense gaze. "You out here all by yourself?"

She swallowed around the thickness in her throat. For so long, so long she had waited for this moment, for the day he would come home. Now he was here, standing so close to her she could have reached out and pulled his head down and pressed her mouth to his. And yet she could not, for he was a stranger.

"Saphronie's been living with us for a long while now," she finally managed. "And there's the children, of course."

One corner of his mouth lifted in what was almost a smile, but those yellow eyes burned hot, like a fire that had been fanned. A shock of recognition crimped her chest, and a shiver of the unknown.

"Children?" he said. "Y'all had more, then, after Sarah?"

"Two more. Two boys." She made a hard, jerky movement, as if a rope stretched taut between them, holding them together, and she had to break it with force. "I imagine you'll want to be alone with him for a while, to say good-bye. When you're done . . . there's coffee on the stove."

His gaze went back to the grave. He stood in silence, his eyes shielded now by his hat. "I already told him good-bye," he said, his voice flat and hard. "On that day I left here seven years ago."

He walked beside her across the yard, pausing to look up at the big house.

"Gus built it for me," she said, "not long before he died."

"He always worried that you'd get to missing that fancy house and all those fine things you left back in Boston."

"He was wrong about that."

"I know."

His gaze went to the Studebaker sheep wagon parked in the middle of the yard. A sign, bolted to the struts, stretched across the full length of the canvas top: Temple of Photography in large black block letters. And beneath that, in smaller script: Views of all Kinds, Family Groups and Individual Portraits, Parlor Gatherings Taken by Flashlight, Taken Either Stereoscopic or Plain.

He looked from the wagon to her, then back to the wagon again, shaking his head. "Boston . . . Lord, Boston . . ." The severe line of his mouth softened and curved, indenting the faint crease in his cheek. His eyes focused on her with breath-stopping intensity. Slowly his hand came up and he brushed the backs of his knuckles along her jaw. "You've always been a wonder to me," he said, his voice rough, "and I reckon you haven't changed."

He leaned against the doorjamb, one long leg crossed over the other, his fingers stuffed into his pockets, that damn hat still shadowing his face. His gaze roamed the room, taking in the maple breakfront cabinet filled with its white-and-blue patterned china set. The pie safe and the modern nickel-plated range. She wondered what he would say if he knew how much of it had been bought since Gus's death, with money she'd earned herself with her photography.

He wasn't likely to miss seeing her photographs, for they literally papered the walls.

Every summer she took the sheep wagon, which she'd converted into a portable photographic gallery, out on the

road. Like a tin peddler, she and Saphronie and the children
traveled all over western Montana, selling prints for fifty
cents apiece. If he wanted to know, she had funny stories
she could tell him, about keeping sticking wax on hand for
pasting down those wing-shaped ears that stuck out like
jug handles from so many men's heads. Or about the wads
of cotton called plumpers that she stuffed inside the sunken
cheeks of sodbusters' wives—those women so worn down
by work and weather and hunger, and not wanting their
folk back home to see them that way. About how an old
woman of ninety, with a face like a withered apple, had
insisted that every wrinkle be smoothed away by chemical
magic before she would buy a final print.

If he asked, she would tell him that those were only
portraits she made to sell, and so if the customers wanted
pretty they got pretty, even if it was a lie. But there were
times when she knew she had captured the truth of the
person on the other side of her lens, and she was proud.

Those portraits she made to sell, and they were what
kept the ranch going. But these others, the ones on her
walls, she had made for herself.

If he asked, she would tell him about these others.
About how she had discovered, through light and shadow,
the rhythms and patterns and truth of life. The soft gray
light of a foggy day, the bright, harsh light of a noonday
sun, the cold and cheerless light of a winter afternoon. In
every detail of these images—in the crumbs of ice around a
cow's eyes, in a cattail bowing before the wind, in the rawhide texture of an old squaw's face—she had found a truth.
If he asked, she would tell him that she had discovered
where to look for the truth, because she had at last found
the truth within herself.

If he asked, she would tell him . . . but he didn't ask.

He didn't even come all the way into the room. As if
he thought he needed to keep the open door at his back,
so that he could turn around and be through it fast, before
she could stop him.

The silence stretched taut between them. The coffee pot burped its strong smell into the air. She stood with the stove at her back, facing him. He propped up the doorjamb, saying nothing. For so long, for forever, a yearning for him had filled her days like a haze. Now he was here in her kitchen, and the years had made a stranger of him.

She saw his chest move as he drew in a breath. "Clementine," he said, and she felt Gus's shadow fall between them, even before he said the rest. "I'm sorry about him. That you lost him."

"You lost him, too."

He shrugged, his mouth tightening. "Yeah. But like I told you out there, it was a long time ago."

He was trying to sound rawhide-tough, the way a man was supposed to be. But her photographer's eye could see beyond his man's hard face to the raw places in his heart. To the truth.

He had, after all, loved Gus so much that he had ridden away from her and stayed gone for seven years.

She took the coffee pot off the fire and set it on the chrome fender of the stove. She went into the parlor and came back with another of her photographs, this one in an ornate silver frame. She held it out to him and he took it, but with a reluctance so deep she thought she saw him shudder.

"This was made the summer before he died," she said. That had been a bad summer for Gus, for them both, but you couldn't tell it by the picture. A laughing smile brightened his face, curling his mustache and crinkling his eyes. A shock of sun-tipped hair fell over his forehead, making him look young and boyish. Caught forever joyous in this picture, he was gilded with sunshine, as he was by the light of her memory.

"It's a good likeness," said his brother. But he set the photograph on the nearby windowsill, facedown.

"It was Gus you came back for." She said it flat out, knowing it to be so, yet wanting him to deny it.

He shrugged again, but his mouth stayed hard. "I thought maybe I could get something for my share of the ranch."

"Oh." She shook her head, trying to pull some air in through her tight throat. "The thing is, we're doing all right here . . . but we haven't so much extra put aside that—"

"I can see how you're doin', Clementine." He looked out the window. At the pine poles of the corral that had started to rot last winter. At the buckboard sitting in the shadow of the barn with its busted wheel. He would have seen the scarcity of Rocking R cattle as he'd ridden across the range.

"I suppose you thought . . . I suppose that after all this time you got to hankering for a spread of your own," she said.

His gaze caught and held hers, but only for a moment, before shifting away again. "I've been roamin' some while. A man can get tired of it."

A silence fell between them then. A silence heavy with the weight of years passed apart. She could have told him this place had always been his home and his leaving hadn't changed that. But *life* changed things. Time passed and it was like what winter did to the land. Cold snaps killed and blizzards ravaged the earth. The chill, bleak days wore and withered and wasted the fields. And come spring the land was never quite the same as it had been the spring before.

"Ma! Ma!"

The child's cries shattered the tense quiet.

"Ma, lookit!" Her younger boy burst into the kitchen, carrying a string of trout and tracking mud onto her oiled linoleum floor. "Saphro and me caught a whole mess for you to fry up."

She saw the shock register on Rafferty's face as he took in the boy's dark hair, tawny eyes, and single-dimpled smile. This last child of hers and Gus's had come out of the womb looking so much like the man standing before her that she had hardly been able to bear looking at him at first. Now she loved him so fiercely she had to take extra pains not to favor him over the other two.

She rested a hand on his head, trying to still him for a moment. "Zach, this is your daddy's brother, your uncle . . . Rafferty."

"His brother? Honest to gosh?" The boy looked up, wonder brightening his face. "Did you know my daddy when he was little?"

Rafferty squatted on his haunches, so that they were eye to eye. "Howdy, button," he said. "And, yeah, I knew your daddy when he was little." He flashed a look up at her, one she couldn't read. Then his gaze fell back to the boy, searching. "Looks like the fish were really biting this evenin'."

"Naw, I'm just good at catching them."

Rafferty laughed and stood up, but he kept his face averted from her.

"Gus died before this one was born," she said, "but he'd always said the next we had he wanted to name after you. I don't know what would've happened if he'd turned out a girl." Somehow she had made her voice sound sweet and easy, and she got her mouth into a smile. She was tough now herself. Montana tough. "I guess there'll be fresh trout for supper . . . If you're aiming to stay, that is."

He smiled back at her, a smile that reached all the way to his eyes. "Well now, Boston, maybe I'd better think on that a moment," he said, his voice rough, the way it always got when he was teasing. "You gotten any better at cookin'?"

She could feel the heat of a blush on her cheeks. That teasing of his—she didn't think she'd ever gotten used to it. Yet it brought a rush of hope welling in her chest. This was the Zach Rafferty she had once known and loved.

But then his smile faded and his eyes emptied, and he was a stranger to her once again. "You got a place for me to pass the night?" he said.

She wiped her hands on her skirt, feeling suddenly

more awkward and nervous than she'd ever been with Gus at seventeen. "We had us a hired hand for a while after you left. Gus turned part of the barn into a bunk room for him. You can bed down there."

"I'll show 'im where it is, Ma!" The boy ran for the door, swinging his fish and splattering slime on her kitchen wall.

Clementine herded her son in the direction of the yard pump. "You go on and get those fish cleaned up. And clean yourself up while you're at it."

The boy stuck out his lower lip. "Well, hell."

"And quit your cussing, Zach McQueen, or I'll be scrubbing your mouth out with soap."

Beside her, Rafferty made a soft huffing sound that might have been laughter or a sigh of sympathy. But when she looked over at him his face was empty. Even his eyes seemed empty now.

"He's a fine-lookin' boy," he said after a moment.

"He looks like you."

He said nothing to that, and she went on, merely talking to fill the silence as they crossed the yard to the barn. "My other two will be home from school soon. There's Daniel—he's five. And Sarah, of course. Wait until you meet her. Gus used to say there wasn't a man born she wouldn't scare to death. She's going to be tall, like her father . . . and you. You won't believe how near to being a woman grown she is. Why, she was still just a babe in arms the spring you . . . left."

She remembered suddenly that very first summer of her marriage. Rafferty had bedded down in the barn that summer, too, in an empty stall, leaving the old buffalo hunter's cabin to her and Gus. He'd gone out of his way to avoid her in those early days, and she'd been glad of it. For he'd frightened her, and she was sure she hated him. She'd been too young and foolish to understand what she was really feeling for him, her husband's brother.

Now here she was, sending him back out to sleep in

the barn. It seemed they had come full circle, to start over at the beginning. But of course that wasn't so. Time had passed, years of it. He had left, and she had grown up and borne children and suffered and laughed and lived and dreamed. And Gus had died.

She led the way into the barn. The room was in the back, where tack used to be stored. It didn't actually have a door, only an old moth-eaten buffalo robe hanging from the lintel. She held the robe aside for him. He passed by her so close his sleeve brushed her chest.

"No one's been back here in a while," she said. "I'm afraid it's a bit dusty." It was more than dusty. It was like a dead place, desolate and lonely.

His eyes flicked once at her and then around the room. "It'll do."

A small stove stood at one end, a plain iron bedstead at the other. There wasn't much else to the place beyond a wolfskin on the bare plank floor next to the bunk. The bedding had long ago been stripped, but for tonight he could spread his soogan out on top the straw mattress. Maybe tomorrow she would give him sheets and a blanket . . . if he stayed beyond tomorrow.

He tossed his bedroll and saddlebags onto the bunk, then thrust his hands into his rear pockets. His dark face looked drawn and fiercely beautiful in the room's muted light. It was so quiet she could hear her own wild heartbeat and the wind rushing thickly through the cottonwoods. Moaning, sighing, whispering.

Such a gut panic gripped her chest that for a moment she couldn't breathe. Seven years was too long. Long enough for a man to forget a woman, long enough for feelings to wither and die. So many days, so many nights, she had heard his voice in the wind blowing through the cottonwoods. But he could have stopped whispering her name a long time ago.

"Well!" she said and the word came out of her like a gasp. "I mean, I expect you're just thirsting for that coffee."

She fled that small and lonely room, almost running for the sanctuary of her kitchen. Running from him and all that he made her feel.

"It never used to be like this," Hannah Yorke said as she tipped a bottle of Rosebud whiskey over three barroom tumblers. "Why, that year I first came to the RainDance country the air was so clear and crisp you could practically drink it like water."

Clementine looked out Hannah's gingham-curtained kitchen window at a sky that was the faded sepia of an old photograph. Her boy Zach and Samuel Woo were playing among the aspens, trying to shoot at squirrels with slingshots. The day was so thick and heavy that even the silver-backed leaves weren't stirring. The world outside looked blurry, as if she were seeing it through a piece of gauze.

"It's that damn heap roasting pit," Clementine said, shocking even herself, for she rarely used profanity. The heaviness of the day was making her edgy, she supposed. And Zach Rafferty had come home.

She opened the door so they could keep an eye on the boys, before joining Erlan at the kitchen table. Hannah had prettied it up with a lace cloth and put a cranberry-glass bowl in the center. Hannah had always had nice things.

"Aiya," Erlan said, wrinkling her nose. "It stinks out there worse than three-day-old fish."

Hannah set a plate of sponge cake and bread spread with oleo on the table. "It's that damn pit," she said, echoing Clementine. She slid into an empty chair, plucked a match from the safe, and lit up a machine-rolled cigarette. Clementine thought it made her look delightfully wicked. "I swear it's gotten worse since the Four Jacks fired up that new heap last week."

Next to the big mines over in Butte, the Four Jacks produced more copper than any other place in the country. And the cheapest, most common method of refining the red metal was heap roasting, where alternate layers of logs and copper ore were burned off day and night in a giant open-hearth smelter. The trouble was, heap roasting like that poured funnels of sludgy brown arsenic-laced smoke into the air.

Clementine sipped at her whiskey. It went down smooth and burned when it hit bottom. She wondered what Rafferty would say about their whiskey parties. But then, he would never come to know of them if he didn't stay.

She looked at Hannah and Erlan . . . dear familiar faces. It was this fear that he would leave her again, she supposed, that was keeping her from telling them that the man she'd loved all her life had come back into it again. It made her feel strange, as if she were keeping a secret from herself.

Though it was midday, it was dark enough indoors that Hannah had to light a lamp. Its flame glinted off the pressed-tin ceiling and the green enamel tiles on the stove. Lampshine highlighted the valentines that Hannah had framed and hung on her wall. Fringed, embossed, pearled, laced, and beribboned valentines. One for every year that Marshal Scully had been her lover.

"The smoke is so bad some days my laundry comes off the line gray and sooty as an old stovepipe," Erlan was saying. "And Samuel had the croup all of last winter because of it."

"We ought to do something about that pit," Clementine said.

Hannah widened her eyes and looked behind her, as if checking to be sure there wasn't someone else in the room. "Who, us?"

"There's no reason why the Four Jacks can't build a proper smelter."

"Money's one reason I can think of without even breakin' into a sweat."

"But the smoke is poison," Erlan said. "It makes us all sick."

Hannah finished off her whiskey in one swallow. "Copper's made Rainbow Springs into a boomtown. Folk don't mind putting up with any amount of dirty smoke long as they're getting rich. Especially the men who run things around here . . ." She gave Clementine a penetrating look. "Like Jack McQueen. Why don't you have a little chat with him about it and see how far you get? He's your kin, after all—even if the two of you ain't exchanged more'n a howdy since Gus died."

"It's the miners themselves we should be talking to," Clementine said. "If they refuse to dig up any more copper until the heap pit is buried and a new smelter is built, then the men who run things won't have any other choice. And if the miners won't do anything about it, we can go to their wives."

Hannah snorted. "As if the good ladies of Rainbow Springs would listen to the likes of us . . . Well, me, anyway."

"Their wash hangs on the line and gets gray from the smoke, as Erlan said. Their babies get the croup from it. Why shouldn't they listen?"

Hannah sighed. "Lordy, why am I always letting you chouse me into trouble like this?" She scraped back her chair and stood up. "But I reckon if we're gonna come up with a plan to take on the Four Jacks, we'll need a second round of whiskey to see us through it."

As she straightened up, a surprised look crossed her face and her legs wobbled and collapsed beneath her. She grabbed wildly for the table, snatching at the cloth and sending glasses and plates crashing down on top of her.

"Hannah!"

Clementine and Erlan scrambled onto the floor, kneeling on either side of her. Erlan lifted her hand and patted it. "She only fainted, I think."

"I'll get some vinegar water," Clementine said, but Hannah was already stirring.

Her eyelids fluttered and opened. She still wore that

surprised look. "I reckon it was all that smoke in the air made me dizzy all of a sudden," she said, her voice thick. She sat up gingerly, pressing a shaking hand to her stomach. "Land, my belly's all a-queasy."

"We must do something about that pit," Erlan said.

Clementine sat cross-legged in the muddy yard beside the softly bleating calf, so newborn it was still steaming.

The mother was licking her baby, which she would do sometimes for hours, until it stumbled to its feet for its first taste of milk. Clementine was content just to sit and savor the sweet joy she'd felt as she watched the life come into that calf.

The mud she sat in was cool, and goopy enough to stir with a stick. The yard smelled of blood and manure. Smiling, Clementine leaned over and patted the heifer's white face. "You did fine, lady. Just fine." The mother cow licked and huffed and blinked her long white eyelashes.

A prairie chicken came whirring across the yard, clucking madly. The heifer didn't stop her licking, but Clementine looked up to see Rafferty riding across the hay meadow. Her chest tightened with the bittersweet ache that it did every time she saw him.

In the three days he'd been back, he'd kept mostly to himself, settling into old patterns. She knew he'd been riding all over the ranch, as if he had to see for himself how she'd been managing on her own, and it angered her to be judged by him.

And it worried her some to think he might be totaling up the worth of his half with the intention of selling out, to an East Coast syndicate, maybe, or to some English baronet in search of a Wild West adventure.

He reined up beside her and swung down from the saddle. She pushed herself to her feet, shaking the mud off her skirt. For a moment they simply stared at each other, saying nothing. They were finding it hard to stir up words between them, she thought. It seemed too soon to talk about anything that really mattered. Maybe they would never be able to talk about what mattered.

The calf, as if he'd only been waiting for the man's arrival, lurched up onto its tiny hooves, bleating and nudging at its mother's red belly. The cow, pleased with herself, tossed her head and let out a low bawl.

"I wonder what possessed that heifer to come in off the range and into the yard to calve," Rafferty said.

Clementine looked down at the spindly-legged creature, busily suckling his mother's milk. "I suppose to her it seemed like a safe place to have a baby."

"That one looks a mite ganted. But then, most of the younglings I seen out on the range today looked poorly."

"Cows that pasture in timberland that has been logged, they eat the pine needles from off the downed tree-tops, and it makes for sickly calves."

"So, since when have you been logging?"

She brushed the loose hair out of her eyes with the back of a hand that she suddenly noticed was stained with blood. She walked away from him, heading for the yard pump.

He fell into step beside her, leading his horse. "Clementine—"

"You can't come waltzing back here after all this time, Mr. Zach Rafferty, and expect things not to have changed."

"Hell, I know that."

"And expect me not to have changed."

She felt his gaze move over her like a touch, though she wouldn't look at him.

"I don't see as how you're any different," he said. "Still starchy and prickly as a boiled shirt."

Which showed, she thought, how little he knew her. But then, neither of the men she'd loved had ever really known her.

He worked the pump handle for her while she washed the birth blood off her hands. A moment ago she had caught the head of a calf as it emerged from its mother's womb and laughed aloud as it took its first breath. A year from now she'd be sending it off to slaughter without a pang or a thought. "There once was a time when I couldn't even bear to watch a baby like that one get branded," she said, speaking the tail end of her thought out loud.

A muscle pulled at the corner of his mouth, deepening the slash in his cheek. But it wasn't a smile. "I never once said you weren't game."

She looked at him. She wanted to touch the hard edges of that mouth with her fingertips, feel them soften and part, feel the heat of his breath—

She swung her head around sharply at the sound of pounding hooves. A pinto gelding galloped wildly down the road from town with Sarah and Daniel mounted double on its back.

Her children rode old Gayfeather back and forth to school every day, and Clementine hadn't known the animal still had it in him to go that fast. She saw that her incorrigible daughter was once again not wearing her bonnet, for her hair flew loose behind her like a Gypsy's child. Then she saw the blood on Daniel's face.

She ran back out into the yard, her heart thundering with fear. Sarah already had helped her brother to the ground, her hands on his shoulders to steady him. The blood ran down the side of his head and neck and dripped onto his shirt, staining it scarlet.

"It's only a little graze," Sarah said, her voice unnaturally loud, and Clementine caught the sharp warning in her daughter's eyes. Daniel still suffered from lung spasms, and one of the things that could trigger a bad breathing spell was hysteria and fear. Sarah squeezed the boy's shoulders. "He isn't scared, are you, Daniel?"

"Uh-uh," Daniel said. His lower lip trembled a little, but his breath came slow and steady.

"No, of course he isn't scared—a little scratch like this," Clementine said, forcing her voice to sound calm. She tilted her son's head up the better to examine the wound, feeling dizzy at the sight of so much blood. It was more than a little cut; it was long and ragged, but not dangerously deep. She put her arm around his bony shoulders and led him up onto the gallery and into the chair where she sometimes did her churning.

Little Zach came banging out the kitchen door, followed by Saphronie. The boy was wearing a ring of chokecherry jam around his mouth, and he held a milk cracker dripping with the stuff in one sticky fist. For a moment the syrupy sweet smell of the jam rose up and almost choked Clementine. "Saphronie," she said, "will you fetch my remedy chest, please."

"Oh, heaven preserve us." Saphronie's hands gripped her apron. "Oh, heavens . . ." She cast an imploring look at Rafferty, then lifted her skirts and ran back into the house.

"Wow, Danny, you're bleedin' like a stuck pig!" his little brother exclaimed.

"Zach, you hush up," Clementine said. She noticed that Rafferty had pulled her youngest up against his legs as if to protect him, and the boy had allowed it. Her children had taken to the man as if they'd known him all their lives. Even Saphronie didn't bother to cover up her tattoos around him.

Clementine made herself look more closely at the gash in her son's head. The blood seemed to be thickening on its own, although the wound still looked ugly. "Sarah, you will tell me now how this happened."

Sarah's wide, serious gaze shifted up to Rafferty, as if he was the only one she deigned to answer to, and Clementine wanted to shake her. "They're logging again on our land—those Four Jacks men. We only rode up for a closer look at what they were doing, and they shot at us. We didn't mean to sneak up on them . . . well, not exactly . . . but I think we kind of surprised them when we rode out from behind the madwoman's soddy."

Four Jacks men . . . A cold, engulfing wrath swelled in Clementine's chest. The Four Jacks. First they poisoned the air and stripped her land of trees, and now they were shooting at her children.

Saphronie appeared at her side with the remedy chest. "Thank the Lord Mr. Rafferty's come home," Saphronie said in a low voice. "You can let him take care of them Four Jacks men."

Clementine said nothing as she bathed the cut in her son's head with witch hazel. Her hands shook as she thought of how much worse it could have been. She cast a sharp look up at her daughter. "Sarah McQueen, you disobeyed me by not riding directly home from the schoolhouse, as you know you're supposed to."

The look Sarah gave back to her was typical of the child—wide and still and edged with contempt. Her daughter, who was so fearless and independent, and unmerciful to those weaker than she.

"Those are our trees they're cutting down," Sarah said. *"Somebody* should make them quit it."

Clementine finished dressing the gunshot graze with aloe vera gel and comfrey. "Saphronie, you take the children on into town this afternoon just like we planned," she said. "Stop by Doc's and see if Danny needs this cut stitched up. We'll all be staying the night at Hannah's."

Saphronie lowered her voice to a bare whisper. "You really are gonna do it, then? What you all decided the other day at the whiskey party?"

"I said I was, and I am. Only now I'm going to make a little detour on the way."

"Oh, mercy. Take Mr. Rafferty with you," Saphronie said, but Clementine was already on her feet and striding into the house to fetch the jacket to the riding habit she was wearing, and the Winchester rifle. The man she'd loved all her life could come with her or not.

When his dun pulled up alongside her, Clementine urged her own mount into a flat-out gallop. They tore down the road toward town, their horses' hooves making sucking, squelching sounds in the spring mud. She felt frantic inside, as if demons were chasing her and she dared not stop.

She eased up after a few minutes, though, when she realized he intended to keep up with her. She wouldn't look at him.

"Are we riding out to kill someone?" he said.

She breathed to ease the ache in her chest. "I would like to, truly I would."

"You gonna tell me what this is all about?"

"Sarah just did. The Four Jacks Copper Mine is logging our land, and somebody has to stop them."

The loggers had set up their day camp on the west slope of the coulee, near the ruins of the madwoman's soddy. Once, the surrounding hills had been thick with yellow pine, alder, cottonwood, and larch. Now whole acres of trees had been shorn down to bare shale earth or reduced to slash piles. In the coulee that had been so dry the summer of the drought a creek now flowed three feet deep from the recent rains and the runoffs in the mountains.

One of the picket horses whinnied, announcing their arrival, although they had already made noise enough as their horses' hooves popped and sucked through the soft slough where the melted snow had run down from the buttes and foothills into the coulee. The loggers were all busy farther up on the hillsides. Only two men remained in the camp, standing around a small cookfire.

Clementine's gaze went first to Percivale Kyle, superintendent of the Four Jacks Copper Mine. As usual, he was dressed like an escapee from a Wild West show: white Stetson, fringed jacket, and a white leather vest with a braided horsehair chain looped from a buffalo-horn button to his watch pocket. He was a fair, elegant man with a spade-trimmed blond beard and winter-gray eyes.

Clementine had seen him a few times packing a silver-plated revolver with a pearl handle. But today, like most days, he was unarmed. The Four Jacks liked to present itself as a peaceful, law-abiding company.

But one look at the Mick, she thought, changed that impression. He always wore a tam-o'-shanter over his big bullet-shaped head, and he kept his mustache clipped short and stiff, like a boot brush. The skin on his face hung loose and his eyes were beady, making him look mean. Clementine didn't know his real name; she'd only heard him called the Mick.

For a moment all was silent but for the click of the horses' teeth on their bits. Then Percivale Kyle took a step toward her, his own teeth showing in a smile.

"Mrs. McQueen. Somehow I knew that little accident we had here would bring you hotfoot after us." He had a strange way of talking through his nose while barely moving his small pink lips. "Please believe me when I tell you that no one regrets more—"

"Which one of you polecats shot at my son?"

Neither man volunteered, but no one had to. Not only was the Mick the only man wearing a gun, but Kyle's gaze flashed over to the Irishman, all but pointing a finger at him.

In one quick smooth motion, Clementine brought the Winchester up to her shoulder, sighted, and pulled the trigger. The sound of the shot punched through the air, its echo muffled by the rain-heavy clouds.

Her horse had danced sideways at the sudden explosion of noise, its ears back and its eyes showing white, but she easily kept control of it with her thighs and knees. She swung the barrel onto Percivale Kyle and levered another cartridge into the breech.

From behind her, she heard a click as Rafferty cocked his revolver. "Don't," he said softly, and the Mick, who had started to reach for his gun, changed his mind.

A bright red stain had appeared on the sleeve of the Mick's buff wool coat. He touched his arm and then stared in astonishment at the hand that came away bloody. "Christ, she shot me! Did you see that, Kyle? She shot me."

"And I will do so again if you ever harm another child of mine. Only you won't hear the next one." She raised the rifle barrel until it was aimed between the dandy's eyes. "They say you never hear the shot that kills you. Isn't that true, Mr. Kyle?"

Percivale Kyle lifted one elegant blond brow and spread his hands out at his sides to show that he was unarmed. "You've made your point quite adequately, Mrs. McQueen. But as I attempted to explain to you, the wounding of your little boy was an accident. One that will not be repeated, I assure you. The Four Jacks doesn't make war on innocent women and children."

"No, only on innocent trees." Another shot smacked through the air, and Kyle's pristine white Stetson went sailing backward off his head with a gaping hole in its big crown. Even Clementine was a little surprised by how close she'd cut it—she'd missed putting a crease in the top of the man's head by the width of a fiddle string. "Get off my land," she said.

Kyle kept his hands spread wide at his sides, but his pale eyes narrowed and a muscle bunched along his jaw. His voice, however, remained calm. "Now, now, ma'am, be reasonable. The court has determined the ownership of this parcel to be in dispute between the Four Jacks and the Rocking R, and until a final ruling can be made we have sanction to continue cutting."

"From *your* court, *your* judge."

"The law is the law. However, we both know that if you were to accept the generous offer the Four Jacks has made and give up all claim to the parcel in question, then any legal suit would become a moot issue." Kyle had been slanting glances at Rafferty ever since they'd first ridden into view, and finally he could stand the suspense no longer. "Who the devil is he?"

Rafferty's saddle creaked as he leaned forward. He rested his left wrist on the cantle, but his right hand still held his Colt trained on the Mick. "He's the devil who owns the Rocking R."

Percivale Kyle's surprised face swung back to Clementine. "I thought you owned it."

"I do," she said. And she pulled her horse around and heeled him into a trot, leaving Rafferty to follow. Or not.

She waited until they were well clear of the coulee, and then she reined in and gave him a long, penetrating look.

She could read nothing of his thoughts in his face. Nothing. "My name's still on the deed, Boston," he finally said.

All those hard and lonely years of relying only on herself, answering only to herself, coming to believe only in herself—after living through those years, she wasn't sure she could bear to turn her life and her heart over to any man. And to a man like Rafferty, so wild, so irresponsible, so dangerous . . .

She had a hard time getting her throat to work. "I don't see as how you have a right to it. Not after seven years."

She looked at him and waited. Waited for him to tell her she was the all and the only of what he had come back for. But what had their love ever really been, beyond a scorching heat and a wild yearning? Many a wild mustang was untamable, and if you tried to put a saddle on one, you only risked getting hurt. Or you broke the spirit you were seeking to own.

She waited, and she supposed she was waiting for him to say he loved her, but what he said was "Since when did you become such a dead shot?"

"There are a lot of things you no longer know about me."

"I know there's no quit in you, Boston. I've known that about you ever since that first year, when I tried to chouse you away from here and you stuck like a cocklebur on a blanket. All the way through the first snowfall and beyond . . . remember?"

For a moment their eyes met with all the hurt and pride and pretense stripped away. And then she hardened her mouth, along with her heart. "But we both know there's quit in you."

She didn't expect an answer, and she didn't get one.

Farther down the coulee, concealed within a stand of pines, Marshal Drew Scully had watched the altercation between Mrs. McQueen and the Four Jacks men. He'd kept his hand on his gun, ready to intervene, although he was relieved when it hadn't been necessary.

He didn't want anyone to know he was out here. And he particularly didn't want anyone to witness what he was about to do.

When he was sure he wasn't being watched, he went down to the new creek that flowed through the coulee. He had a saddlebag draped over his shoulder and he walked stooped over, peering at the rocks that were scattered in the creek bed and along the banks. These were rocks that had been carried along with the melted snow and excess rainwater down from the surrounding hills and buttes. From time to time he bent over to pick one up, before tossing it away. Finally one caught his attention enough that he fixed a loupe into his eye to study it more carefully.

He rubbed a spot on the rock clear of mud and grit and looked at it again, and a smile tugged at one corner of his mouth. His thumb continued to stroke the stone over and over, even after he'd allowed the loupe to dangle and swing idly from the cord into his neck, and the smile had long since vanished.

His gaze went up the ravine, following the direction of the runoff. He began to climb.

About halfway up the steep, slippery slope, a scattering

of boulders thrust up out of the soggy earth. He carried a sledge and bull prick in his belt, and he used them to chip a fist-sized piece off one of the rocks.

He slipped it into his saddlebag and then he went quickly back down into the gulch, heading for the stand of pines and his hidden horse. For a moment only, no more than a second or two, sunshine burst through a break in the clouds and flashed off the seven-pointed tin star that was pinned to his chest.

31

THE KNIFE FLEW THROUGH the air, striking the wall handle-first and clattering to the floor.

"Bloody hell!"

Erlan Woo thrust another comb into the smooth ebony coil of her hair, ignoring the flying knife and the savage fury in the man's bellow. But she winced a moment later when she heard the crunch of wood being smashed and shattered by a heavy boot.

Holy God. First he flings his knife at the wall, and now he is destroying the beautiful carousel he spent all of last month carving. She took a deep breath and closed her eyes for a moment, reminding herself that a woman should always strive for virtuous patience.

She turned away from the mirror and looked across the small bedroom at the man she lived with. Most days he was himself, her *anjing juren,* sweet and gentle. But there were other days when his ill moods lashed out like a dragon's tail.

She felt her love for him swelling warm and tender in

her heart. He had tried, was trying, and she knew he did it for her. His fingers bore many scars where the knife had slipped, and the wall showed many nicks from when his temper had slipped, but he tried.

His head swiveled around just then to face her, although she hadn't moved or made a sound except to breathe. It was something he often did. She thought it was because he could see her with his heart. They were no longer two, but one.

"I'm forgetting, Lily," he said. "I'm forgetting what things look like. Even you. Your voice, the feel of your hair, the clean, sweet smell of you—they're all engraved in my heart. But not your face. I try to put your face into the black ocean and all I see is a blur, like looking into a clouded mirror."

She crossed the room to him, shuffling on her crippled feet. She gave him the smile she smiled for him alone, although he never saw it.   .

She knelt beside his chair and picked up one of the wooden horses that had been part of the carousel he had destroyed. Her loving gaze went from the ridges of scar tissue where his eyes used to be, over the broad flat bones of his cheeks, to the thick, strong throat that rose above the open collar of his chambray shirt. She watched him swallow.

She curled his scarred and bleeding fingers around the wooden horse. "Feel how the wind flies through its tail, how its hooves prance high. Can you not tell that you are getting good?"

"I'll never be as good as I was."

"You will be better."

His face knotted into a frown, but he said nothing.

"In China, today is the Festival of Pure Brightness. It is the day we *sao mu*—we sweep the graves of our ancestors and make offerings. Samuel and I . . . we would like you to come with us while we pay respect to his father's grave."

He sat very still, and beyond the silence of the room she could hear the suck and splash of wagon wheels plowing through the muddy road, and the distant rumble of thunder. The bedroom, which was nothing more than a lean-to added on to the shack where she ran her laundry, always smelled like this—of soap and starch and steam.

He felt for her lips with his fingers and softly brushed over them. "'Tes not that I don't want to be with you and Samuel, you understand. 'Tes that . . ."

She licked his fingers, tasting him. "I know."

His eyes were badly scarred and people stared, and although he couldn't see them staring, she knew he felt them. But she knew that, even more, he hated the shame of having to be led around. "Like a bloody little pug dog on a leash," he always said.

She stayed with him a moment longer and then she rose and went to fetch her son. She washed and dressed him in fine American clothes to please his father, and she put on the gold bracelet of a married Chinese woman because she was still married to Sam Woo and always would be.

Then she went back, with Samuel's hand in hers, to the door of the lean-to. "We are leaving now," she said to her lover who sat in the shadows beyond.

He turned his head and nodded. She saw the need on his face to ask her how long she'd be gone, to get some sort of assurance that she would be back. And she saw, too, the pride that kept him from asking.

Erlan dropped her son's hand and crossed her arms over her chest as if to protect her heart. He was getting good again with his carving. And when he did get good, truly as good as he had been before, then he would have something to live for besides her, and she would have no more reason to stay. She would have to leave him, and this time he would let her go without trying to stop her. Because he no longer believed himself worthy of her.

My destiny is a circle that is still only half drawn.

She would have to leave him.

Outside, the sludgy smoke from the copper smelting pit hung overhead, as smothering and smelly as a wet wool blanket. She and her son struggled through the sloppy mud as they trudged out of town, toward the Chinese cemetery.

"Aiya, these roads are as muddy as rice paddies," she said to Samuel, who had never seen a rice paddy. Her memories, too, were dim of the paddies she had only observed from the high garden wall of her lao chia.

The citizens of Rainbow Springs wouldn't allow the Chinese to bury their dead in the town cemetery, so they had established a burial ground of their own, on land no one else wanted at the base of RainDance Butte, among the tailings and slag heaps and waste rock. It was as if a dragon had breathed upon this place. Not even a weed grew in the scorched earth.

Erlan gave Samuel a willow branch, showing him how to sweep his father's grave and so drive off any harmful spirits that might be lurking about. Then together they laid out the bean-curd cakes and rice dumplings and a single precious orange. As she arranged the burning incense sticks and small wax candles around the wooden grave marker, she told Samuel of the strong and honorable man the merchant Woo had been. And how it was now his duty to nurture his father's spirit in the shadow world.

This year Samuel was old enough to handle the kite by himself. Fashioned of red silk and kindling sticks, it was flown on the Festival of Pure Brightness to honor one's departed ancestors. Erlan watched the kite swoop and soar like a lazy bird across the smoke-hazed sky. She wondered what it felt like to be as free as that kite, free of always having to yield to the clinging hands of a fate she was no longer sure she wanted.

Free to serve only herself, please only herself.

The kite rode the wind, but still it was bound to the earth and to the hand of her son by its flying string. Its freedom was only an illusion. And if someone were to cut the string, the kite would float up, up, up into the vast and empty Montana sky to disappear forever.

A movement on the road leading into town from the lower valley caught Erlan's eye, a man and a woman on horseback. The man she couldn't know from this distance, but the woman she recognized by the fairness of her hair, and because she had been expecting her.

Her gaze went from the woman on horseback up the butte to the stark skeletal gallus frame of the Four Jacks. And then back down and out into the flat prairie, where the new copper heap roasting pit spewed its foul brown smoke.

She took the kite from her son's hands and began to reel in the flying line. "Hurry up, Samuel. We must hurry and find Auntie Hannah."

Zach Rafferty allowed his gaze to roam slowly over the woman who rode beside him. He let the feeling of looking at her settle deep within him.

Gus was dead.

The truth of it, the reality of that stone-piled grave, gripped at his chest like a fist and twisted. But he couldn't get his mind to settle on that yet—on Gus being dead.

Four years, she'd said. That rock-piled grave had been lying beneath the cottonwoods for four years, and all that time she'd been alone. Alone and . . . He couldn't bear to think of those four years wasted, couldn't bear to think he'd come back too late for her. Too late, maybe, for himself.

The temptation to do it, to come back, had been part of his every breath and heartbeat. He'd driven himself near crazy at times, trying to imagine what she was doing at any moment of the day. In his mind were a thousand memories, and he'd lived them again and again. Clementine with a fishing pole tucked between her knees. Clementine beating a bowl of cream, skirts swaying. Clementine smiling down at the head of the babe that suckled at her breast. Clementine doing things he'd never seen her do, only

imagined. Like taking down her hair and pulling a silver
hairbrush through its thick length again and again, her
breasts rising and falling with each stroke. Or unrolling
a black stocking up her calf and knee to the middle of a
slender, creamy thigh. Clementine . . . Clementine living
and doing none of it with him.

Each moment, each hour and day, had been one more
spent without her, until all the miles and years that separated them had become unendurable. There were days
when he'd been so lonesome for her he had shuddered with
it, like a drunk too long without a bottle.

And now here he was and here she was . . . and here
Gus wasn't. He looked at her face, so heartbreakingly familiar. And as cold and distant as the stars. He'd never
been gut-sure of her love for him. Never really believed
it would endure. The one and only time he'd asked her
to come away with him she had chosen to stay with his
brother.

He still wanted her, though. Lord, he still wanted her.
But having a woman in your bed wasn't the same as having her in your life, as *making* her your life. Her and her
children and a struggling ranch, another man's dream. His
brother's dream.

He looked at her closed face and thought how the hells
on earth were usually of your own creation.

Hell was what he thought he was seeing a moment
later when they topped the last rise before town and his
eyes beheld a pit of flames. His second thought was that
it was a prairie fire, except that it couldn't have been, not
with the ground wet enough to bog a butterfly. As they
drew closer he realized he was looking at an enormous bowl
in the earth filled with glowing coals and burning wood.

"Jesus God," he said.

The burning pit released a fumy smoke that smelled
like souring hides and made a brown sludge that smothered the sky. The surrounding countryside was as bare and

pocked as the face of the moon. The once pine-studded buttes had been logged almost bald, and the few trees left standing were stunted and dying. The grass was leached-looking. The Rainbow River ran swift from the heavy spring rains and snow runoff, but it was foul and foamy, like dirty soapsuds.

"It's called heap roasting." She turned in the saddle and cast him a look so sharp he felt it. "It's how the mine—the mine your father owns—smelts its copper, by burning layers of logs and the ore in a big pit. This one's a new and improved heap they fired up only last week, and it's twice as big as the last one. There's sulfur in that smoke, and arsenic. On hot summer days when the wind doesn't blow, the smoke can spread all the way out to the ranch. It's killing the land."

His gaze followed the streams of slime and tailings that ran from the mine. The butte was ugly with heaps of gravel, erosion ditches, and gray stumps. Huge piles of cut timber were stacked around the headframe and among the mine buildings.

"It burns up voracious amounts of wood—that pit," she said. "As does the mine itself, what with all the timber needed to shore up the miles of underground workings. If the Four Jacks has its way, there soon won't be a tree left standing in all of the RainDance country."

In town the raw, suffocating smoke was so thick he could barely see from one false-fronted building to the other. The lamps were lit against the dusk, although it was still midafternoon. Shadows cavorted behind the windows of the saloons and dance halls, and tinny music floated on the thick, heavy air.

"Rafferty."

He turned to look at her. Her face was a pale oval floating in the murk. "You were here in the beginning when the town was new," she said. "Tell me it doesn't hurt to see it like this."

He wished he could see her face, but even if he could have, he knew it wouldn't have changed things. It would never tell him what he wanted to know.

"It hurts," he said.

Hannah Yorke had spent most of that morning kneeling on the carpet in her bedroom being violently sick into a chamber pot.

As the bouts of nausea came and went, she'd thought of how tired she'd been lately, of how she'd fainted at their last whiskey party. Of how she couldn't remember the last time she'd suffered with her monthly curse, she who'd always been as regular as an eight-day clock.

She'd wiped her face with a wet cloth, and her lips puckered as if pulled by a drawstring. She pressed her knuckles to her mouth, not sure if she wanted to laugh or cry.

She pushed herself to her knees, swaying dizzily. She caught a movement in the large mirror with its fluted gold frame. Her own startled image stared back at her, as if they both saw a stranger.

A baby. She was going to have a baby. There's buck in this ol' hoss yet, she thought, and had to stifle another hysterical laugh.

The woman in the mirror raised her hand and pushed her sweat-dampened hair out of her face. My, what a hag! Although on any other day Hannah knew she looked good for forty, young still, not like those sheepherders' and sodbusters' wives. She had stayed out of the sun and off the booze for the most part, and she'd kept her figure. She wouldn't have her figure much longer, though, and there were those fine-drawn lines around her mouth and eyes that no amount of strawberry cream had been able to keep away.

She was forty years old and she was going to have a baby by a man practically young enough to be her son. It was ridiculous, scandalous. Why, the whole town would reel in horror at the thought. Most respectable women still averted their eyes and drew their skirts away when Hannah Yorke walked past. Imagine how they would behave when her belly got big enough to shade an elephant.

There were ways . . . But she wouldn't think of them. She pressed her hands protectively over her womb, as if even stray thoughts could do it harm. She still hadn't forgiven herself for giving up her first baby; she would have this one if it killed her. She *wanted* this child. It seemed she wanted it more than anything had been wanted since time began.

She tried to imagine what the proud daddy would say when she told him. She wouldn't tell him. Lord, what was she thinking? He would be able to see it for himself soon enough.

And he would insist on doing right by her, she was sure of that. When you shared a bed with a man for seven years you came to know at least some things about him. Drew Scully wasn't the type to father a baby and then walk away from the responsibility of it.

Another bout of nausea struck her and she fell to her knees, groping for the pan. She couldn't remember being so sick the last time. They said it was a good thing, a sign the baby was taking. If that was true, she thought with a shaky laugh, then Hannah Yorke was damn good and pregnant.

Drew . . . Oh, God, what was she ever going to do about Drew?

Never mind that she was much too old for him, she wasn't near good enough. As marshal he was well liked and respected by the town. He was a man on his way up in the world. Hannah knew how other men looked down on a man who was fool enough to marry a whore, even a reformed one. It was a matter of pride, of being content with other men's leavings. If he walked down the aisle with her, he would walk himself right out of the life he had made for himself here.

And if he had wanted to marry her for herself—really wanted to, and the town and everything else be damned—he'd have gotten around to asking her long before now.

So she would have to be looking after herself, again, and looking after herself meant leaving Rainbow Springs. She couldn't raise her baby as a bastard in a town where everyone knew its mother for a whore.

By late afternoon Hannah was feeling well enough to go out.

She dressed with care in a dusky rose linen gown and an enormous net-swathed hat trimmed with burgundy silk lilies. She went to the window and looked out, trying to peer at the sky through the heap-smoke haze, to see if it was likely to rain soon. In the end she decided to take along a black lace parasol lined with oilcloth. Over her shoulders she threw a purple-and-rose-striped silk shawl with black fringe that matched the fringe on the parasol.

She had just started down the stairs when her stomach began churning again. She gripped the banister tightly, drawing in great gulps of air. Her stomach turned over and settled. She released her breath in a long sigh.

She had reached her front gate when she saw Erlan coming toward her down the road, as near to running as she could come in her shuffling gait. She had her little boy in her arms, and the kid was using the wind they made by their rush to trail a red kite along after them. It was a strange sight, making them look like a big, awkward red-winged bird trying to take flight.

"She is here!" Erlan cried. She was breathless from having to struggle through the thick mud on her crippled feet. "She is going to do it."

Hannah felt a smile break across her face, and her blood stirred. A good down-and-dirty scuffle was just what she needed to take her mind off her own troubles. "Then I expect she'd like her friends standing at her side when she does do it," Hannah said. "Are you willing?"

Erlan looked toward the scarred, ugly butte, then up into the grimy yellow sky. The pall of smoke that hung over the town had grown much thicker since morning. The new heap roasting pit was half again as large as the last one, but it seemed to be releasing four times as many noxious fumes into the air. Just then the shift whistle blew, and Erlan started. But she straightened her shoulders and shifted her son's weight higher on her hip. She met Hannah's gaze, her eyes serious and a little worried, but resolute. "I am willing," she said. "We had better hurry, though."

Clementine McQueen was already standing beneath the gallus frame when they arrived at the Four Jacks. The morning shift was coming up in the cages and the afternoon shift was waiting to go down. She must have asked a nipper to stop each man coming and going, for a towheaded boy went from miner to mucker to skinner, and every time he spoke a head would swivel around to stare at her. The collar sheet and the area around it were already crowded— with cable spools and reels, boxes of muck sticks, picks and drills, and hopper cars full of giant powder and timber.

As more and more damp and sweating miners congregated around the shaft head, the gallus frame began to smell like a roomful of wet dogs. The carbide lamps on the miners' hats shot beacons of light into the murky haze. Hannah wondered how Clementine was going to make herself heard over the ringing bells, the clattering cages, the ore being dumped into the holding bins, the rhythmic throb of the pump rod, and the steam hissing from the boilers.

Clementine had climbed atop an empty cable spool. She stood tall, her head held high, like a queen about to address her subjects. Hannah, who knew her well, understood that Clementine gathered her ladyhood around her like a mantle only when she was most afraid. But folk had a tendency to find it off-putting, mistaking her shyness for conceit and maybe being a tad insecure about their own lack of polish. At least Clementine didn't look so Bostony today; in truth, she looked disheveled and muddy, as if she'd just ridden in off the range.

As Hannah and Erlan approached her makeshift platform, Clementine noticed them. Her face lightened with a quick and dazzling smile, and some of the stiffness eased out of her shoulders. The miners had also spotted the other two women, and their murmurs rose from a hum to a beehive buzz. Not even hurdy-gurdy and red line girls hung around the gallus frame during a shift change.

"They're as fired up as a January stove," Hannah said to Erlan. "They're not going to want to listen to what she has to say."

Erlan set Samuel on the ground, keeping a tight hold on his hand. The worry in her eyes had intensified. "Perhaps we should have tried to talk her out of it."

"Have you ever known anyone, man or woman, more gut-stubborn than Clementine McQueen when she gets her sights set on a thing? I'm only worried our being here'll wind up harming more than helping. We ain't either one of us exactly upstanding citizens of the community."

"Merciful heavens." Erlan fingered the high, stiff collar at her throat. "I feel as if I am wearing a brand on my forehead like a Taoist monk. But Clementine said the battle cry must come from us women. So far we three are the only women willing to make any noise."

"I suppose you're ri— Oh, my lord. Speaking of needing mercy, will you look who's here?"

Erlan followed Hannah's gaze toward the man who leaned against one of the headframe's iron struts, a battered Stetson deeply shadowing his face. "Is that not the brother of her husband?" Erlan's forehead wrinkled. "Is this a good thing?"

At the sight of that dark, reckless face, Hannah's eyes had blurred a moment and her heart had clenched with the sort of bittersweet ache a gal got when she ran into a man she'd been crazy in love with a long, long time ago. It was hard to tell from this distance, but he looked pared down. More hardened, if such a thing was possible. "It could be good," she said, her voice cracking. "But then, it could also be real bad. With a sweet-talkin', heart-breakin' scoundrel like Rafferty, you can never guess."

If Clementine even knew he was there, she didn't let on. She nodded at the nipper, and he gave a short toot of the shift whistle, silencing the miners. "Gentlemen," she began in her fine diction, "I wish to speak to you about how the Four Jacks is poisoning your lives . . ."

"Come on, honey," Hannah muttered under her breath, "let 'er rip."

Hannah's gaze swept over the miners. She spotted Marshal Drew Scully lingering in the back of the crowd, his stance calm but watchful. Her heart surged up into her throat, and a warmth spread all over her, as if she'd just slipped into a hot bath. She wondered if there would ever come a time when she wouldn't react this way to the day's first sight of him.

At that moment he noticed Rafferty, and the two men eyed each other warily like two bull elks deciding whether to butt or back off. Then Drew's gaze found hers. She gave him an uncertain smile that he didn't return.

An angry bellow interrupted Hannah's thoughts, and she realized with a start that she had missed most of what Clementine had said.

"We all know the Four Jacks has offered to buy your timberland and fer a fair price, only you ain't sellin'," one of the miners was shouting back at her. "If you ask me, all this talk about poison is just a lot of sour hay."

The man's cronies laughed and hooted, banging on their lunch pails. From the back of the crowd someone let fly with the soggy remains of a letter-from-home. The gravy and meat-filled pastry landed with a splat on Clementine's chest.

She swayed, a look of utter distaste and horror twisting

her face. But before Hannah had even thought to react, Erlan launched herself forward. "Did you forget you ever had a mother, you pile of turtle dung?" she shouted. "How dare you treat a woman with such disrespect? You are all mannerless pieces of dog vomit!"

A hoot of nervous laughter erupted out of Hannah's throat. "I reckon you boys've just been properly cussed out, Chinese style," she drawled.

The men, at least those standing in the front, looked sheepish. A few looked back over their shoulders to scowl at the culprit. But one turned around to address the others. He was a red-haired mucker with a long, sharp jaw and a big mouth that had started more than one fight at the Best in the West.

"What the hell are we listenin' to these women for?" he demanded. "Hannah Yorke here, who's no better than she ought to be, this slanty-eyed laundry girl, and a widow who probably just needs a good beddin' to get the hysterics out of her system."

Hannah lifted her parasol in the air and advanced on the man. "You're sucking wind, mister——"

"That's all right, Hannah," Clementine said. Her voice trembled a little, but she squared her shoulders, tugging at the peplum of her grease- and gravy-spotted riding habit. "You can throw your garbage at me and say all manner of vile things, but you can't change the truth."

"You cause trouble like this, lady," one of other miners put in, his tone more concerned than angry, "and you could be responsible for throwing two hundred men out of work. We can't afford to see the mine shut down, no matter what it's doing to the land."

"Who cares about a few acres of grass and trees any-ways?" the red-haired mucker said. "It ain't like we're run-nin' low on the stuff." And the men all laughed.

"I don't want to shut down the mine," Clementine said. "Only stop the heap roasting. There are alternative methods of refining copper ore, such as smelters with flues and smokestacks. But nothing will change until your union leaders raise the issue with the Four Jacks.

"Look," she went on, conviction coloring her voice and cheeks. "I've brought along with me some scenic views I made of this valley when I first came here twelve years ago, before silver and copper were discovered . . ."

She leaned over and handed the photographs to a miner standing in front. He gave the top one a dismissive look and passed them on. "Lady, them alternative methods you talk about take money to build, and if you don't know how their cost'll come in the way of jobs and wages, then you don't know diddly about how things work. I got me a wife and six young'uns to feed, and if I got to put up with a bit of stinking smoke and a few bald hills to do it, you ain't gonna catch me kickin' and squawkin'."

"Damn right!" the man next to him shouted and the others joined in.

They had a point, Hannah thought, feeling a pang of disloyalty as she did so. In the coal-mining town where she'd grown up, the soot covered everything, so that the whole world looked like the bottom of a scuttle. A mine dirtied up a place; that was a fact of life, like a man needing a job to feed his family was a fact of life.

But there was going to be no stopping Clementine, certainly not the men's indifference and resistance, which they'd talked about and expected anyway. She nodded to the towheaded nipper, who scurried in back of the spool and dragged out a burlap sack. He reached inside and pulled out the stiff, gray-furred carcass.

"This dead jackrabbit," Clementine said, "was picked up only a few moments ago out on the prairie."

One of the muckers let out a yelp when the boy put the animal into his hands. He flushed red with embarrassment at his overreaction, and the other men laughed. The boy held a dead blue jay up by its feet before another man's face. The miner smiled weakly, his eyes shifting away.

"And this," Clementine said as the nipper produced a

dead steelhead from the gunnysack, "I found floating in an eddy right where the Rainbow passes through town. No natural causes killed that trout. It was the heap.

"And this"—she tossed something into the crowd, which one of the miners caught reflexively—"is a set of teeth that came from the skull of one of my cows. Those teeth are copper-plated from eating poisoned grass and drinking out of a poisoned river. Do you honestly believe this can be happening to the livestock and wildlife of the valley while nothing is happening to us? You and your families drink the same water and breathe the same air. With this new and bigger heap that has been fired up, how long do you think it will be before your wives and children fall ill from the fumes?"

She paused and seemed to capture each man's eyes in turn with her wide, still gaze. "You men pride yourselves on taking care of your families. But what if you're participating in a thing that is killing them? . . . That is all I have to say to you."

With an innate grace she descended from the empty cable spool and walked off the collar sheet, not looking back. The miners watched her go, silenced and not meeting each other's eyes.

Drew Scully had almost made his way to Hannah's side when a hand fell on his shoulder, turning him around.

"I don't know as how it was a good idea to allow the lady to go orating on like that, do you, Marshal? Orating and passing out party favors like at a church social."

Drew looked into the sleek, one-eyed face of Jack McQueen. He gave the man an easy smile. "There's no law against telling the truth, Jack."

The man's mouth broke into an answering smile that was all foxy charm and didn't come close to warming his single pale eye. People in town called him Mr. McQueen, and some who'd been around long enough to remember his salvation-show days called him Reverend. Behind his back a very few still called him One-Eyed Jack. But no one dared call him just plain Jack to his face, which was why Drew did it. But Drew knew it was only a way of making himself feel as if he was still his own man, even if he wasn't.

"'I have no greater joy,'" Jack McQueen quoted in his preacher's voice, "'than to hear that my children walketh in truth.' But the question that plagues us, Drew Scully, the question that has always plagued us is: What is truth?"

"Come on, boys!" the mine super, Percivale Kyle, was calling out to the dispersing men. "Come on down into town with me and there'll be a bucket of beer for every man jack of you. Line up at the brass rail, boys, at any saloon but the Best in the West, and the drinks'll be on the Four Jacks."

Drew saw a flash of dusky rose and heard Hannah's husky voice saying, "You were magnificent," and Clementine McQueen laughing softly and saying, "Look at my hands. I believe I'm shaking. But that's on the outside. Inside, I feel rather magnificent."

Drew wanted to talk to Hannah and started for her, but Jack McQueen smoothly put himself back into Drew's path. "I would like you to see our dear friend the judge about getting an injunction to shut her up," he said with another of his foxy smiles.

"Get one of your errand boys to do it."

Jack McQueen still smiled, but the rest of his face smoothed and hardened. He leaned into Drew, so close the younger man could smell him—expensive cigars and hair oil.

"Allow me to jog your memory, Drew Scully. First think on how you turned a blind eye when I neglected to mention to the consortium—when they were all panting and eager to let their lease lapse—that there was a great ruddy lode of copper lying just quiet and waiting down in the Four Jacks. And then think on how all I have to do is say the word and that pride-saving stipend your brother collects every week goes as dry as a bull's tit.

"When you're the only game in town, Drew Scully, you get to set the rules. Rainbow Springs was a one-towel she-bang before I came along, and you were just another digger." He tapped the tin badge on Drew's chest with a stiff finger. "I own the both of you now—heart, soul, skin, and guts."

Drew's eyes took on a sudden sharpness. "Why not just be shutting down the heap, Jack? Like the lady said, there are cleaner ways of smelting, and I expect there's plenty of room in your profits to allow for the building of a stack-and-flue refinery."

"When I want the benefit of your business acumen, Drew Scully, I'll ask for it. In the meantime you're paid to uphold the law around here, and one of the ways you can do that is to see the judge about that injunction."

Having delivered his order, Jack McQueen turned on the heel of his expensive patent leather shoe and walked away. A soft hand touched Drew's arm and a familiar wood-smoke voice spoke into his ear. But her words had a bite to them, and he felt their sting: "How is it you could never stomach the idea of working for me but you don't mind crawling on your belly for that toad-sucking swine?"

As he turned to her, Drew could feel his face growing closed and cold and empty. "Rainbow Springs pays my salary, not the Four Jacks. And as for me coming to work for you, Hannah m'love, haven't we danced that jig before?"

Her face, always pale, went even paler. "Forget I brought it up."

"You're always bringing it up."

"Yeah, and I'm always sorry afterward."

She planted her parasol on her shoulder, lifted her head, and started down the haphazard path of planks that led through the gumbo toward town. She stopped and swung back around so fast her bustle bounced. "You know, Marshal, even a blind pig manages to find an acorn once in a while."

"Aye?" He stuffed his hands in his jacket pockets and thrust out his chin. "And what's that supposed to mean?"

"You think on it a spell. Maybe it'll come to you."

This time she kept on going. Drew watched after her, wondering what it was he'd done. The woman sure did have a mood on today, and only last night they had made some of the sweetest love he could remember out of years' worth of sweet loving. To him it seemed they had never been closer, and now apparently they were having a fight, though he was damned if he knew the cause of it.

His hand had closed over the rock in his pocket. He rubbed his fingers along its rough edges that were gritty still with dried mud. He stared into the distance a moment, thinking, and then his gaze focused on the super's office, where an old assayer's scale was barely noticeable in the grimy window.

He had turned and started back down the hill when he noticed Pogey and Nash, coming toward him. It was unusual to see them up and about this time of the afternoon; most days found them sitting on their favorite bench on the veranda of the Yorke House until sunset. Somehow the words "drinks are on us" must have carried to them on the wind.

He pulled his hand out his pocket and waved the two old prospectors over. "Pogey, Nash—might I speak with you a moment?"

They came reluctantly, Pogey cuffing his beard. "Can't it wait, Marshal? I've got me got a terrible dry."

"This'll only take a moment. I've been thinking I could use your help."

Nash's owlish eyes blinked slowly, and a pleased look settled over his seamed and haggard face. "You want to deputize us? I reckon you must've heard about that time I worked alongside of Wild Bill Hickok and the two of us cleaned up Abilene slicker'n spit."

Pogey glowered at his partner. "Kee-rist. The closest you ever been to Wild Bill Hickok was when that patent medicine drummer came through town and charged you a nickel to look at the bullet what killed him."

Drew sucked on the inside of his cheek to keep from smiling. "I won't be needing to deputize you, but I would like you to keep what I'm about to tell you under your hats."

Nash laid his finger next to his nose. "We'll be quiet as a stone cow, Marshal."

"As quiet as a hoss thief after a hangin'," Pogey added.

"As quiet as a dropped feather," Nash said. "As quiet as a tree full of owls—"

Pogey snatched off his hat and whacked his partner on the back of the head with it. "Who ever heard of a tree full of owls being quiet? Why there'd be so much hootin' and hooin' going on a feller wouldn't be able to hear hisself think." He wedged his hat back on and turned to Drew. "Don't mind him, Marshal. The man was born stupid and he's been re-gressin' ever since."

"Aye, well . . ." Drew took the rock out of his pocket and held it out to them on his palm. "Would you boys be knowing what this is?"

Pogey tugged on his flapjack ear. "It 'pears like just another chunk of copper ore." He pointed with his chin toward the shaft head. "There's whole hoppers down there full of the selfsame thing."

Drew's hand closed into a fist around the rock. "No, this one is different. This is a piece of the truth."

That evening the Best in the West was as deserted and lonely as a cemetery in the middle of winter. Hannah Yorke looked into the mirror in back of the bar and saw a reflection of unoccupied tables and chairs, still billiard balls, and a pair of hurdy-gurdy girls lounging against the wall, their painted faces stiff with boredom.

"Y'all may as well take off, Shiloh," she said. "I don't expect we'll be doing much business tonight."

For a moment the gin-slinger looked as if he had something important he wanted to tell her. Instead he shrugged, then took off his leather apron and slung it over the end of the bar. His teeth flashed white in his face. "There's a new li'l gal at Rosalie's with skin like melted chocolate and a mouth that oughta be declared illegal. Reckon I'll go pay her a call."

Hannah winked at him. "You go have yourself a time, Shiloh."

"Oh, I intend to, boss-lady. I intend to."

Shiloh's booming laughter followed him out the door. Smiling, Hannah made a shooing motion at the hurdy-gurdy girls, and they eagerly disappeared in his wake. Hannah stood alone in the empty saloon, awash in a thousand memories so vivid she could almost hear the slap of cards and the gaudy trill of women's laughter, almost smell the tang of tobacco smoke and the bite of spilled booze. Regrets? Oh, she knew she had them, but in that moment for the life of her she couldn't remember what they were.

She was on her way to her tiny office in back of the bar when she noticed a shadow move in the lamplight spilling out of the card room.

He sat at one of the felt-covered tables, where her customers—when she had them—retreated to play serious poker or buck-the-tiger. Tonight, though, he was alone. His elbows rested on his widespread knees, and he was turning his battered hat around and around in his hands while he studied the floor. It wasn't the same hat he'd worn before. But then, a lot of years had passed since she'd last seen either him or his hat. Seven of them.

She leaned against the doorjamb and crossed her arms over her chest. She took the time to study him, noting the lines of strain around his eyes and mouth that made him look tougher, more dangerous. He had helped himself to a bottle of her better whiskey and had already emptied half of it.

"My, my," she cooed, "look what an ill wind blew in."

His head came up. Their gazes locked hard for a moment. Then he gave her a lazy smile and leaned back, hooking the heels of his boots over the chair rung. He tossed his hat on the table and laced his hands behind his head. "You're like an old trail buddy, Hannah. I wouldn't pass through without stopping to say hey."

She pushed herself off the jamb and went to a gramophone that sat on a small table against the wall. She wound it up and put on a tube. "I don't reckon we've shared too many trails lately, though," she said. *Passing* through. He'd said he was passing through.

The gramophone crackled out a tinny rendition of "The Man on the Flying Trapeze." She let it roll through a verse before she tossed him a sidelong glance laced with a hint of a smile. "I don't know if there's a lonelier sound than music playing in an empty dance hall."

"The night's still a pup. They'll remember your charms when the revver's free booze runs out."

"Ain't that the truth." Another smile tugged at Hannah's mouth. She had forgotten how easy he was to talk to, how much alike they were.

She picked up a pack of cards and sat across the table from him. She slid the cards from the case, riffling them through her fingers. He was slouching and drinking slowly and trying to look for all the world as if he hadn't a care. But there was a tension pulling at his mouth, and taut, shadowed lines around his eyes.

She began to lay out a game of solitaire. "And speaking of your daddy—that man sure is shiftier than a dance hall fiddler. You know he euchred your brother out of his share in the Four Jacks? Paid him two thousand bucks for it and, lo, six months later, if copper wasn't discovered running thick as blood through the whole butte and East Coast investors all lined up to start the new venture. 'Course by then your brother was dead and his widow had enough on her plate just trying to keep body and soul together. Now he's poaching on her timberland and trying to pressure her into selling that."

She moved a red queen onto a black king and let a small silence develop between them. The gramophone had long since wound down. She watched him carefully from beneath lowered eyelids. "You'd think having you come riding back into her life would be about as welcome as a spring thaw," she said. "So how come she don't seem happy about it?"

"You've known her real good for a long time now, Hannah. Why don't you tell me?"

She flashed him an easy smile and turned over another card. "It don't take a genius to figure it was either some fool thing you said or some smart thing you neglected to say." She held a three of hearts poised in the air as a thought came to her, and her smile slowly faded. "Lord, Rafferty, don't tell me you've up and married someone else?"

Color spread like a stain over his cheekbones. "There'll always be only Clementine for me."

It was sweetly said, and typical of him in a way. Unlike a lot of men, Rafferty never had any trouble admitting it when he cared for a woman. Hannah started to smile again, but there was something in his eyes that stopped her. He'd always been a little edgy and wild, but tonight there was a tautness about him that almost had a smell to it, sharp and metallic, like blood.

"Well, land, I know that, honey," she said, making her voice light and easy. She laid the red three onto a black four, uncovering a ten she didn't need. "But it's lonely out there and . . . Oh, what am I saying? There's some women who don't mind being second choice, and some men who'll settle, but you ain't one of them." Her hands paused over the cards as another thought struck her, this one stealing her breath.

She stared hard at him, at the tight mouth and the hooded, wary eyes. "You went and got yourself in trouble with the law, didn't you?"

He averted his face, reaching for the whiskey bottle. He slopped some into his glass, but then he huffed a laugh that was genuine, even if did still have that sharp edge to it.

"I'm not on some wanted poster if that's what you're saying, though it's not for want of trying. I only know how

to do but a few things and most of 'em not very commend-
able. Like punching cows and hunting bounty"—he cast
a rueful grin at her—"and dealing from the bottom of the
deck. Well, hell, you can guess which it was I did the most
of. And all the while that good and decent brother of mine
was here running the ranch and raising up a family and taking care of the woman I . . . taking proper care of his wife."

The knuckles of the hand he had wrapped around the
glass had bled white. He knocked the whiskey back in one
swallow. "So I don't know as how I can just ride on in and
take over Gus's life. Take her over like she was part of the
stock and the outbuildings."

Hannah slapped the ten of clubs down with such force
the table rocked. "You expect her to act like those years
never happened, like Gus never happened? She was married to him, she bore him five children . . . buried two
of them. Lord, isn't it just like a man to go on insisting
she choose between the two of you long after there's no
point to it anymore? Instead of just being grateful God's
arranged it so's both of you could have her."

She reached across the table and touched the hand that
clenched the empty whiskey glass. "Gus might be dead . . .
but you aren't."

He shoved the glass across the table and buried his
head in his hands, lacing his long fingers through his dark
hair. "Aw, shit."

Men! thought Hannah with a wrenching smile that
came mostly from sadness. You had to love them. But she
knew what he was feeling, because she had those same
feelings herself whenever she thought of Drew and the
baby. Wonderings if whether you can ever really change,
whether you even want to anymore. Worryings that you'll
settle back into bad old habits, that you'll wind up failing
the one you love, wind up failing yourself. Again. Wonderings if maybe that other person just isn't better off without
you in his life.

A lot of years of living apart had passed between

Rafferty and the woman he loved, a whole lot of denied feelings and tamped-down urges. And if there was one thing the tumbleweed life taught you, it was that for all the roads there were on this earth, very few of them ever really brought you home.

The game was hopelessly lost. She shuffled the cards into a haphazard pile and pushed herself to her feet. She looked down at his bent head and thought that she did love him still, and more than just a little bit.

She touched his head once, lightly. "Lord, Rafferty, you always were a hard case." She walked away from him, feeling shaky inside.

Two years ago she had bought a melodeon for the front room and moved the old piano back here. A long time ago one of the many Docs she'd had working for her had taught her how to pluck out a single tune. She went to the piano now and began to play it with one finger. The notes jangled in the silence, sounding obscene.

"Hannah." She looked up. He stood close beside her, his hat back on, and his face all shut up tight again. "It must have been rough on her after Gus died," he said, "and I expect you did some watching out for her. So if I can't . . . if we can't work things out between us . . ."

She couldn't bear to look at him. She ached so for him, for Clementine. And maybe for herself. Maybe a lot for herself. "You know her," she said, her voice breaking. "She's always been able to take care of herself just fine."

She plucked out more notes, putting words to the tune. "My love is a rider, wild broncos he breaks . . ." Her fingers stilled on the keys and her voice trailed off. She looked up at him, her vision blurring. "You quit being stupid about things, Zach Rafferty, and beg that girl to marry you, even if you got to do it on your knees. Maybe you don't think you're good enough for her, but a good woman can make a man good."

Smiling sweetly, she laid her hands on his shoulders. "Besides, you forget how well I know you, cowboy. There's a part of you that's always wanted taming." And she rose up on tiptoe and pressed her lips to his.

A movement flashed in the corner of her eye and she jerked back. "Drew!"

Rafferty swung around, his hand going for his gun, as if he was used to reaching for it first and looking later to see who had come up behind him. Hannah grabbed his arm, but he had already relaxed when he recognized the marshal.

Drew Scully's attention, though, was focused only on his woman. Hannah held her breath as the two men exchanged bristling looks. Then Rafferty stepped away from her, pulling free of the hand she still had on his arm.

He tipped his hat at her. "See you around, Hannah."

Rafferty walked straight through the doorway without acknowledging the marshal, and Drew Scully remained planted in the middle of it. Neither man gave ground, and so they wound up knocking shoulders as Rafferty passed.

Hannah listened to the receding footsteps and the front door slamming shut. She said his name again on a sharp expulsion of breath, and the sound of it in the aching, stretched-out silence made her jump.

He advanced on her, his stride long and rangy, his breath ragged and hard.

She cleared her throat, licking her lips. "We were only talking . . ."

"Uh-huh. And what were you telling him with that kiss, Hannah?"

"Nothing. It was for old times' sake, is all. Howdy and good-bye."

She watched the anger and the wildness leap into his eyes and she fed off it. Excitement and fear pulsed through her blood, so whip-quick it made her dizzy. Tremors were shimmying through him. She could see in his face, in his eyes, the eruptive violence that she'd always known was in him. And she knew that at last she had done it; she had pushed him too far.

She pulled her little boob gun out of her pocket and pointed it at him. But for once her hand trembled wildly and her voice trembled even more. "If you lift so much as a little finger with the idea of hurting me, Drew Scully, so help me God, I'll kill you first."

He kept coming until only scant inches of charged air separated them. He dipped his head and rubbed his open mouth, his hard and beautiful mouth, against the muzzle of the gun. "Do it, then, Hannah. Kill me. You might as well, if you've decided to be leaving me and taking back up with him."

The gun fell from her stiff fingers, clattering as it struck the pine floor. "I won't leave you, Drew. I love you—"

His mouth closed over hers, kissing her hard, and her hip crashed into the piano in a jangle of discordant notes. "I love you," she said again, or tried to say. He wouldn't let go of her mouth.

He took her there on a green felt-covered table, among a deck of playing cards and with the smell of spilled whiskey in the air. Or she took him.

Afterward she decided it was she who had taken him.

The bore of the Colt pressed hard against the scar of One-Eyed Jack McQueen's missing ear. His arm jerked, knocking over an inkwell. And his knee jerked, banging hard into the big African mahogany desk that sat in the study of the gaudy fifteen-room mansion he had built with copper money at the edge of Rainbow Springs.

He watched the ink puddle soaking into the green blotter. Even with the gun pressed against his mauled ear he heard the hammer cock.

"Jesus fucking Christ," he said.

"Amen, Revver."

He turned his head and looked into a pair of cold yellow eyes. Even when he was still in petticoats, the boy had

had eyes like that. Inhuman. Jack McQueen held little faith in the God he'd so often used to his advantage. But looking into his son's eyes, he had no trouble believing in the devil.

"For heaven's sake, Zacharias," he said. "Why can't you come calling through the front door like everybody else?" The boy said nothing. The smell of the spilled ink was sharp in the room. The drape on the fireplace mantel stirred, and Jack dared to move his head another inch. His gaze fell on the open window and the smears of red mud on the blue floral wall carpet. "And see if you didn't go and track gumbo in here. Have you no respect for another man's property?"

"Nope."

Father and son exchanged knowing smiles. Jack waited for the gun to be moved away from his face, but it stayed right where it was, pointing at his nose. His son gave him a slow once-over. His smile turned mean, and his eyes glinted like a cat's in the gaslight. With his other finger, the one that wasn't wrapped around the trigger, he poked Jack in the belly. "You've gotten a bit fleshy, old man."

An embarrassing noise popped out of Jack's throat, a high-pitched grunt, like a startled hog. "And you look hard-used, dear boy. These last years haven't been so good to you, have they?"

"Been good to you, though." His son looked around the octagonal room, pretending to be impressed with the chandeliers and their milk-glass globes, with the ornately framed paintings and the Venetian mirror, with the walnut bookcases filled with leather-bound books and with the copper casework on the walls, with the stained glass between the windows fashioned in the pattern of a jack of diamonds.

"About the only place I ever seen fancier than this was a whorehouse in St. Louie. And look at you," he drawled the words, loading them with mockery. "All slicked up like a tenderfoot dandy. Almost as dazzling and miraculous as a traveling salvation show."

The remark stung, but Jack McQueen was much too experienced to let it show. He produced his flashiest smile. "I'm not complaining . . . So what has you in such a pucker that you come sneaking in here to shove a gun in what's left of my ear?"

His son's smile didn't lose its mean edge, and his voice didn't lose its mocking drawl. "I told you if you ever caused her any misery I would kill you for it."

Jack pushed out a slow breath, trying to push out the uneasy fear he was feeling along with it. He'd always hated these nasty confrontations. Except for one bloody and violent night, he'd always been able to talk his way out of trouble.

"The Four Jacks has offered her better than a fair price for that timberland, and this is in spite of the fact that there's some dispute as to who actually possesses title to it. And as for that unfortunate incident this afternoon, the man who provoked it has been disciplined. Good Lord, Zacharias"—he tried to turn his head and bumped his nose into the gun barrel—"do you think I like it that my own dear grandson, my own flesh and blood, had a crease put in his head?"

He paused to swallow and draw breath. The damned gun pointing in his face was making him cross-eyed, if such a thing was possible with only one eye. "I've offered her a fair price for that land, dammit. Ask anybody. Hell, ask her."

"Like the fair price you paid for Gus's share of the Four Jacks?"

Jack heaved a louder, more exaggerated sigh. "I just knew the blame for Gustavus's stubborn foolishness would wind up falling on my head. Why, I even said as much to him at the time." He sucked his lower lip into his mouth. There was a gun in the desk drawer, but he didn't even think of going for it. He had no doubt Zacharias was capable of shooting him in the heat of a moment, or after cold calculation, for that matter. After all, he was the one who'd raised the boy up not to be weakened by any sort of sentiment.

"I gave Gustavus every chance to invest in this venture," he said, and he even let a hint of petulance creep into his voice, playing on it. "But he wouldn't hear of anything but selling out. All right, so maybe I didn't try real hard to convince him to do otherwise, but the fact was, I didn't want him and his twenty percent in there messing up my game. Hell, even you got to admit, my dear boy, that when it came to the game, that pretty-pious brother of yours was always so useless he couldn't fish floaters out of a swill barrel, for all that I tried my damnedest to teach him better."

"He wasn't useless. He was just born without a mean streak, and nothin' you ever taught him was able to take the good out and put the mean in." His son's voice had gone very soft and very dangerous. "Now, me, I'm a whole different story. I reckon I'm your boy clean through. And any true son of yours can stomach doing just about anything." He rubbed the Colt's barrel along the hanging fat of his father's cheek. "Let her alone, my dear Pa, or when I'm through with you there won't be enough left to bait a trap."

Jack could feel his face go slack. The tic beneath his eye patch picked up its beat. "'Be sure your sin will find you out.' You kill me and you'll swing for it."

The gun barrel moved along the bridge of Jack McQueen's nose, across his cheekbone, and up until it was centered on his one good eye, so close he couldn't have blinked without catching his lashes in the target sight.

"There are some things worth dying for," his son said in that same silky voice. "I reckon sticking you like a hog on a slab might be one of 'em."

Blood-soaked images came at Jack McQueen from the dank recesses of memory. A knife slashing at his face, moonlight leaping along the blade like a stream of fire. A boy's screams and then a man's, and a rank smell, like butchered meat. And, years later, Zacharias's voice saying,

"Tell that to the man who took your eye." He could feel the tic beneath his patch thrumming now.

His lips pulled away from his teeth. "You don't booger me, boy."

The hammer fell on an empty chamber with a loud click. Jack jumped, the breath coming out his clenched teeth in a whistle.

His son smiled. "Leave her alone," he said. "Or hell is gonna hear you holler."

Jack McQueen had never seen the sense in shouting fire after the blaze was out. He waited until his son had left the way he came, through the window, and then he went in search of Percivale Kyle. But the man wasn't where he expected to find him, in the butler's quarters in the back of the house.

The night was pretty much shot anyway, so Jack walked over to the Gandy Dancer, where he had two whiskeys and listened to the mining gossip, which was flowing especially thick tonight because of the free booze, and which was always a revelation, but even more so tonight.

Once again he felt the urgent need to talk to Percivale Kyle. This time he took the trouble to track the super down at Rosalie's parlor house, and he had no compunction about rousing the man out of bed.

"Write these names down," he said to Kyle, who was struggling to button his trousers over his unfinished business and blinking like a fish in the sudden harsh light. "Zach Rafferty and Zacharias McQueen. Tomorrow morning I want you to start sending out telegrams. Find out if he's wanted for anything, even if it's only for farting in church. Then when you're done with that, I want you to find out just what it is those two old-timers, Pogey and Nash, intend to have assayed over in Helena and where it came from."

He fixed the super with his crafty one-eyed stare. "And in the meantime, thanks to my daughter-in-law and her crusade on behalf of nature and all of God's little creatures,

we need to take the town's mind off that heap roasting pit.
Do you have any suggestions?"

Kyle stroked the point of his beard, and smiled, and
Jack smiled back at him. "The Chinese are always good for
rubbing up a sore."

32

THE BOY GASPED, CLAWING at the air. His chest heaved
and jerked, and his neck arched, the tendons drawing taut.
A tight, shrieking silence filled the room as they waited,
waited, waited for him to breathe, waited while his face
turned red and then purple and his whole body strained,
reaching, reaching for the air he couldn't take in.

He choked—a strangled, desperate sound. And then
he wheezed and his lungs filled, and Hannah let out the
breath she'd been holding, unable to breathe herself until
Daniel did.

"Oh, God, Clem . . . maybe we ought to send for the
doc," she said.

Clementine set a fresh cone of saltpeter-soaked blot-
ting paper alight, waving it in front of her son's red and
sweating face. "There's nothing he can do. We just have to
see Daniel through the attack and hope . . ."

Her voice trailed off, but Hannah finished the thought
for her: *hope for the best.* Hannah marveled at her calmness.
If Daniel were her boy she'd be hysterical by now, in need
of the saltpeter paper herself. But then, little Daniel had
suffered from these lung spasms all his young life. She supposed Clementine had taught herself to remain strong like

this, to keep from transmitting her fear to the boy, and to keep from going mad with it herself.

"It's that new heap roasting pit," Hannah said. She felt hot, her chest tight with anger at the Four Jacks and at the stubbornness of men who saw only profits and progress. "That pit has made the air so foul it's a wonder we all don't have spasms."

Even with the room closed up tight they could smell the raw fumes, could feel a scratchiness at the backs of their throats, a burning in their noses. Hannah knew that if she went to the window and pulled the drapes aside, she'd be able to see the fires of the heap glowing like a giant bed of coals against the night sky.

Clementine lit another saltpeter cone and waved it slowly like a fan beneath her son's nose. The lung spasms seemed to have passed as quickly as they had struck and he had fallen off into an exhausted slumber.

Hannah watched the paper curl and burn in Clementine's fingers. "I heard somewheres," she said, "that others who suffer with their breathing as Daniel does have taken to wearing muskrat skin over their lungs."

"I tried that muskrat cure. It didn't seem to work worth beans. Besides, it itched him so, he couldn't bear it. And the other children teased him unmercifully about his furry chest when they saw it. Children can be so cruel."

People can be cruel, Hannah thought. She felt a sharp and sudden fear for the life she carried. Would he be born healthy, not only with all his fingers and toes, but sound in his mind as well? She remembered back home in Kentucky there was a boy who'd been what they'd called a little tetched in the head. One day some of the bigger boys had doused him with coal oil and set him alight. They'd been sorry afterward, claimed it was just teasing that had gotten out of hand, but that poor boy had died . . . And folk had always said that tetched boy was a late-life baby, born of a woman who was already a grandmother.

Her first baby was a man grown now, could even be

married and with a child of his own. Lord, she could be a grandmother and not even know it. In her mind's eye she could see a young man sitting in a velvet-draped parlor, bouncing a little curly-haired girl on his knee and singing "Ride a Cock Horse" just like her daddy had done with her. She wondered if he ever thought of her, her boy. But no, he surely didn't even know she existed. He'd grown up thinking that banker's wife was his mother. Any kids he had now would be calling that woman Gram.

Which was just as well for him. What a terrible mother good ol' Hannah Yorke, the calico queen, would have made. And just what sort of mother did she think she was going to make this time around? She imagined the other boys teasing her son for having a saloonkeeper for a ma, claiming maybe their own fathers had *known* her back in Deadwood. And if the baby turned out to be a girl . . . when she grew old enough to have gentleman callers, wouldn't they think: Like the mare so goes the filly?

And where did Drew fit into all these imaginings?

She pressed her tightly laced fingers against her belly. It was flat now, but it wouldn't be for much longer. Nowhere, she told herself. Drew fit in nowhere at all.

"Hannah, are you all right?"

Hannah started, grateful for the darkness that hid her face. "Sure, I'm fine," she said. And then her face crumbled in upon itself as a sob burst up out of some empty, aching place in her chest. "No, I ain't. I'm going to have a baby."

"Oh, Hannah, are you really? Oh, I'm so happy for you!" Clementine laid aside the remnants of the saltpeter cone and hugged Hannah tightly, squeezing her arms. "You're happy for yourself, aren't you?"

Hannah's throat spasmed. She nodded, pressing her cheek into Clementine's. For a moment they just clung to each other in the dark. She had known Clementine would understand, that she'd see the baby as a good thing, even if it would have to come into the world a bastard.

Hannah made a funny little gurgling sound in her

throat, as if she'd swallowed wrong. "It's like I've been given a second chance, you know. To make up for what I did the last time, selling my other poor boy like he was a crop of cotton or something." She pulled away, wiping at the wetness in the corners of her eyes with her fingers. "Only I'm scared as spit about it, too. Imagine having another baby at this late date in my life. And then there's the problem of what I'm going to do about telling Drew—who had a whole lot to do with the cause, even if he might not want nothin' to do with the result."

"You haven't told him? Oh, Hannah, you must. Truly I believe he'll want to marry you and be a father to that baby, to make a family with you. And if you love him, as I know you do, then you must give him a chance to prove he loves you."

Hannah shook her head hard. "He could've asked me to marry him anytime in these last seven years. I reckon the fact that he hasn't done so says something."

"Perhaps he hasn't asked the question because he's been unsure of the answer. Why, how often have I heard you say we'd never see Hannah Yorke hitched to the post alongside of any man?" She'd drawled the last words, and Hannah could feel her smile coming soft out of the night. "You can't blame Marshal Scully for behaving like a man and believing that tired old lie of yours. We women might always look for the lie in what they say to us, but a man would rather believe a woman's lies than risk hearing the truth, and if you can make sense out of what I just said, you're doing better than I am."

Hannah choked down a laugh, rubbing hard at the tears that had dampened her cheeks. She tried to make out Clementine's face in the murky dark. She'd heard that edge to Clementine's voice, talking of the lies men and women told one another. She wondered if now would be the time to bring up the touchy subject of Zach Rafferty's homecoming. But then she knew Clementine. That girl never talked about a thing until she was damned good and ready to, and even then she put up fences you didn't dare cross.

"Lord, I don't know what to think anymore," Hannah said instead. "Maybe it's this wretched weather along with that wretched heap pit that's making me edgy as well as giving Daniel spasms. Those clouds've just been hanging there for days over our heads doing nothing. If only it would rain."

"Or the wind would come up."

Hannah laughed. "Heavens, did you ever think to see the day? Imagine a Montana woman *asking* for the wind to blow."

The next day dawned dark. The clouds were a liverish purple, dense and heavy, holding the heap smoke in the valley like a blanket over a campfire.

"It's black enough to blind a bat out there," Hannah said to Clementine over morning coffee. It was only a slight exaggeration.

Even indoors with the windows shut up tight, the air was close and raw. The smoke floated listlessly over the town in slow brown drifts, thicker than fog. It was like trying to breathe through dirty flannel.

"An old woman died of it during the night. Choked so hard on the heap smoke, so her folks're claiming, that her heart gave out."

The coffee cups lay scattered on her kitchen table. Saphronie had brought the children downstairs for breakfast and was now sitting between Daniel and Zach, who were having a running fight over something. Sarah was ladling hominy into Hannah's best Spode bowls.

"Mrs. Wilkins, the baker's wife—it was her mother," Hannah went on. "But there must be about a dozen others confined to their beds with chest pains and raw throats, so the doc said. I know our plan was to wait awhile, give the men a chance to digest what you fed 'em yesterday, but I reckon none of us figured on the new heap being this bad. I say we do it now."

Sarah's spoon knocked against her bowl as she laid it down. "I'm coming with you."

Clementine looked into the face of her daughter, nut brown from never wearing her bonnet. As stubborn, her father would have said, as a rat-tailed cayuse. "I need you to stay here with Daniel and Zach."

"They're coming, too." Sarah gave her mother a penetrating look. "Daniel *needs* to come."

Hannah reached out to pat Clementine's hand and wound up gripping it tightly. They sat like that a moment, then their fingers fell apart and Hannah pushed back her chair and stood up. "We'll split up; that way we can cover more territory faster. I'll start by telling Erlan, and she can rouse the other Chinese women."

It began with the four of them—Clementine, Hannah, Saphronie, and Erlan—going from door to door. But before long they were joined by other women, until it was like a snowball rolling downhill, picking up mass and power. They spoke of Mrs. Wilkins's mother and of the others who had fallen ill during the night, but they really didn't need to say much. The rank smoke draping over the town, the jays and meadowlarks falling dead out of the sky, and their own tearing eyes and raw throats were persuasion enough.

Some of the women, expecting trouble, strapped on their husbands' revolvers or carried rifles. They all brought shovels and other dirt-breaking tools, and many brought their children with them as well.

Pogey and Nash watched all this to-ing and fro-ing from their bench on the veranda of the Yorke House. "Lot of women scurrying about this morning," Nash observed. "All looking busy as one-armed monkeys at a flea farm."

"Busier'n tumbleweeds in a stampede," Pogey agreed. He gave his ear a good tug. "What do you figure they're gonna do with all them shovels and muck sticks?"

Nash studied the situation carefully, sucking on his store-bought teeth. "Bury somebody, I reckon," he finally surmised.

Pogey considered the suggestion for a while, then nodded. "Let's hope he's dead first."

"Maybe it ain't a body they're gonna bury; maybe it's a thing."

"Have to be a *big* thing, to need all them shovels."

"Bigger'n a red barn, I reckon."

"Bigger'n a twenty-mule freight wagon."

"Bigger'n a politician's lie."

"Bigger than . . ." But the rest of Pogey's simile was drowned out by the ascending wail of the Four Jacks' big whistle that normally shrieked out a shift change or a disaster in the shafts.

"Whatever's going on around here," Pogey said when the whistle finally petered out, "with all them women riled like that, I reckon it spells trouble for whatever man is fool enough to put his head in the way of them shovels."

Nash watched his partner pull a twist of tobacco out of his boot and tear off a chaw. "I say the smart man is the one who sits pat and hears all about the excitement afterward."

"And I say that for once in a lifetime of flappin' your lips, compadre, you finally done said something that makes a particle of sense."

The women marched out into the prairie where the heap roasting pit spewed its foul smoke in brown funnels that rose up to be snagged by the low flat-bottomed clouds. "March" was the word for what they were doing, Clementine thought. Like soldiers off to a war, but armed with more shovels and muck sticks than guns. Her gaze went from face to face. Some were young and as fresh and pretty as a bouquet of wildflowers, others were as worn and seamed as the buttes. Three of those faces, Erlan's and Hannah's and Saphronie's, were as dear to her, as familiar, as the faces of the sisters she'd never had. The strength she saw in all of them, stranger and friend alike, left her awed.

She looked down at her daughter, at the determination in Sarah's small pointed chin and the fierceness in her eyes, and her awe deepened into a pride.

As they walked by Snake-Eye's livery she saw a man at the hitch rack, saddling up a shaggy dun . . . Rafferty. She turned her face quickly away. When next she looked around again, he was coming at her with that sauntering cowboy walk, his hat shading a face that probably wouldn't have shown her anything anyway. She thought that if he tried to stop her, she would never forgive him or love him again.

He fell into step alongside of her. She wouldn't look at his face, but she could see his legs flashing in and out of her view of the muddy road. Long-shanked and lean, the muscles bunching and flowing beneath the worn cloth.

Her throat felt too raw to talk, but when he said nothing she could finally bear the silence no longer.

"I thought you'd left town," she said. She looked up at him. "Yesterday evening when I didn't see you after . . . I thought you'd left."

His mouth curved faintly. "What, and miss all the fun?"

His eyes were full of tears from the fumes, but she heard an edge to his voice. A ragged wildness that had always both drawn and frightened her.

The sight of some fifty women converging and marching out of town armed with a few guns and a lot of shovels had not escaped notice. Those of their men who weren't already down in the shafts began straggling after them in twos and threes, but with a wary, nervous air about them. Clementine would have smiled if one of them hadn't been Marshal Drew Scully, and if she hadn't seen the stark anguish come over Hannah's face as she looked at her man.

We might wish we could do without them, Clementine thought. *We might even try to do without them. But we can't. Yet so often they end up leaving us. We lose them to death or to indifference or to another woman or . . .* She looked up for one swift moment at Rafferty's hard profile, but what she saw was the dun waiting saddled back at the livery. *Or to the wildness in his soul.*

A murmur arose among the women when the shriek of the Four Jacks' whistle cut through the air. A few faltered, but then Mrs. Pratt, one of the miner's wives, fired a pistol into the murky clouds. "Come on down and face the medicine, Jack McQueen, you one-eyed scalawag!" she shouted, and the laughter that followed eased the women's nerves.

Mrs. Pratt soon got her wish. The mine owner arrived driving his Peerless buggy, Percivale Kyle and the Mick riding horseback on either side of him.

"I reckon there's about to be more excitement around here than in a corral at brandin' time," Hannah said into Clementine's ear. She was now carefully ignoring the marshal and wearing a tight-lipped smile.

Without even having to talk about it among themselves, the women formed a living corral in front of the heap pit. It was as if, Clementine thought, they were of one mind and one heart. As if all the cumulative moments of their women's lives, all their women's tragedies and triumphs, had come down to this single, suspended moment in the middle of a Montana prairie.

And it seemed as if all the earth had gone quiet, holding its breath. The women of the RainDance country stood shoulder to shoulder, their children interspersed among them. The fumes stung their eyes and scratched their throats, but they held their heads high.

The men had stopped when there was still a good bit of red Montana mud between them and their women. They stared in wonderment at the shovels and weapons in the women's hands. But to Clementine's surprise not one demanded to know what they were doing, not one ordered his wife home. It was as if they sensed that, perhaps for the first times in their lives, they wouldn't be obeyed.

Jack McQueen pulled his buggy up within twenty yards of the women and the heap roasting pit at their backs. He looked the situation over, his lips pursed in smirking amusement. "Aren't you ladies out roaming a little far from your kitchens this morning?" he drawled. The Mick and Percivale Kyle both laughed. "Who's minding the stove and doing your chores?"

"Don't listen to the one-eyed son of a turtle's whore," Erlan said, loud enough for him to hear her.

Jack McQueen dismissed her insult with a laugh. He pointed the butt of his whip at Clementine, his mouth still smiling. "I don't need to guess that you're the cause of this latest trouble, daughter-in-law. I'll be durned if you aren't taking on the nature of being a sore trial to me. Just what do you aim to do with this congregation you've assembled?"

Clementine took a step toward him, her chin leading the way. "We aim to bury this pit."

Jack McQueen poked his tongue in his cheek and looked around him in exaggerated wonder. "Do you, now? And do you figure to shut down the mine whilst you're about it?"

The miners all stirred at this, making a low rumbling noise. The Mick's hand settled on the butt of his gun. Percivale Kyle was still trying to look smugly bored, and not succeeding all that well, what with the tears streaming down his pale cheeks from the fumy smoke.

Jack McQueen waved his whip at the empty space on the seat beside him. "Why don't you climb on up here, Mrs. McQueen, and I'll take you on back into town and we'll talk this over all reasonable-like."

She didn't trust him. He was all wily smiles and pleasant, *reasonable* words that would melt like mist once he got her away from here. She could feel the women standing solid behind her, feel their steadiness and their courage.

She raised her shovel into the air like a standard. "We're burying this pit now."

Jack McQueen leaned forward, gathering up the reins. "I don't think so—"

"Haw!"

A twenty-mule freight wagon rolled out of the

smoke-filled prairie. Nickel Annie stood on the lazy board, snapping her rawhide whip through the air. "Haw, you whoring bitches and whoreson bastards. Haw!"

She pulled up at the edge of the smoldering heap and cackled a laugh. "Mornin', One-Eyed Jack," she said into the sudden, quivering silence. "Wish I could say 'twere a pleasant mornin', but it ain't—not with this heap smoke chokin' the life out of folk."

Jack McQueen's mouth pulled back into his conjure-man's smile. "Annie honey, I thought you'd be wanting to line up on my side. How many years is it you've been hauling freight for the Four Jacks?"

"Too damn many. Now, I got me a hundred pounds of giant powder connected to a mighty short fuse in this here wagon of mine." Her cheeks were stuffed with chewing tobacco, and she paused a moment to unload some juice. "I figure to set her alight and drive her right at you and your boys, Jack *honey*. So the way I see it, y'all've got two choices: either stand yer ground and meet yer Maker, or run like the snake-belly cowards I figure you to be, and leave us women to do what we've set out to do, and that's bury this gol-damned pit."

Nickel Annie brayed another laugh as she broke a kitchen match off a block and scratched it alight on the knee of her leather britches.

Hannah gripped Clementine's arm. "Oh, Lord have mercy. This wasn't in the plan. Tell me it wasn't in the plan."

Clementine shook her head. "She can't blow up her wagon and Mr. McQueen without hurting her mules, and Annie would never do that. They're her babies."

"But the revver don't know that, does he?" Rafferty said from beside her, startling her so that she jumped. She thought he had joined the men, but he was here, he was with her, and the laughter was wild and dangerous and seductive in his voice.

Jack McQueen's eye had taken on a sleepy cast as he

contemplated the mule skinner. He smiled. "Better men than you have failed to run a bluff past me, skinner. Let's see what you got in those britches of yours."

Nickel Annie's face split into a wide grin. "I was hopin' you'd say that." She put the burning match to the fuse. The wick sputtered and flared and began to burn.

The Mick's hand tightened around his gun, pulling it half out of its holster. "Uh, boss . . ."

"Gee-up, you devil-damned offspring of whores and pimps!" Annie bellowed. The deep-bed wagon lurched forward. "Haw!" She swung the team into a wide left-handed circle, picking up speed. The left rear wheel hit a deep hole; the wagon dipped wildly and almost toppled.

Hannah flapped her hand in front of her face. "Oooh, my . . . I feel faint."

Annie's whip cracked. Her curses snapped through the smoke-choked air. The cask of dynamite rattled around in the big empty bed like a marble in a bucket. The wagon swayed and groaned, mud squeezing out from under its large red iron-rimmed wheels. It bore down on One-Eyed Jack and his men, with Nickel Annie's hands firm on the reins and her lips pulled back from her brown teeth in a maniacal smile.

The smile was melting off Jack McQueen's face faster than snow in a chinook. "Well, hell, Annie . . . Well, all right then . . . God damn it, *stop!*"

The bull-throated roar carried through the thick, bitter smoke. Annie hauled hard on the reins, and the wagon's back wheels slithered and slewed in the mud.

The mule skinner stared, grinning at the man, for an interminable second while the fuse continued to burn. Then she shot two thick, gloppy, and well-aimed streams of tobacco juice at the sputtering cord. It fizzled and went out.

Jack McQueen's face was wine-red, and his chest pumped as he sucked at the rotten air. He was half standing in the buggy, as if he'd been about to leap out of it in a panic. The Mick, either too stupid or too scared to move, sat stiff-legged in the saddle, wide-eyed, his mouth hanging open. Percivale Kyle was already halfway back to Rainbow Springs, going at a dead gallop.

Nickel Annie threw back her head and let out a great bray of laughter. "I reckon I had you pegged proper, One-Eyed Jack. You still had a whole five seconds to spare when you started yellin' chicken. A real man—and not one with a yellow stripe down his back—would've stuck with calling my bluff and took his chances on meetin' me in hell."

Jack McQueen eased back into his seat. He puffed an obsequious laugh. "All right, you've had your fun, Annie. Now why don't you go on home? Why don't all you good ladies go on back to your homes now and leave us men to settle things here?"

Hannah startled Clementine by hooting a laugh of her own. "Like every fool man I've ever known, Jack McQueen," she shouted, "there comes a day when durned if you don't wear out your welcome." She thrust her shovel into the ground, leaned on it with her foot, and scooped up a blade-ful of Montana gumbo. "Ladies . . . we got work to do." And she swung around, flinging the mud into the smoking heap pit.

Clementine had half turned when from beside her Rafferty erupted into a blur of movement. A whacking crack split the dense air. She spun around in time to see the tam-o'-shanter go sailing as the Mick's whole body jerked hard and he flopped rag-doll loose off the back end of his horse, a red stain blossoming in his chest. His hand still gripped the vulcanite butt of his drawn gun.

For a moment no one moved, except Rafferty, who trained the smoking muzzle of his Colt on his father's chest.

"Don't make me kill you," he said, but so low Clementine wondered if the man even heard him. It didn't matter, for suddenly a dozen or more guns were being cocked, making a noise like crickets in July, as those women with weapons all pointed them at One-Eyed Jack McQueen.

The breath left him in a whine through his teeth. Slowly he eased his hand out of his pocket, bringing with it a white square of embroidered linen. "'He that diggeth a pit shall fall into it,'" he said with a bold attempt at his old beguiling smile. "I was only going for my handkerchief, ladies."

For a moment longer the women of Rainbow Springs stood with their weapons trained on the mine owner. Then, as one, they understood the danger had passed and they put their guns up. Those with shovels and muck sticks started pushing mud into the burning pit. They worked in silence, sure and united in their purpose.

Hannah laid her palm on Rafferty's back. "I don't know which one of us the Mick was aiming to shoot," she said with a shaky smile, "but if it was me, I reckon I ought to thank you."

Rafferty said nothing. His intense gaze had locked with Clementine's. He had moved so fast. So fast and so lethally. And now he just stood there looking at her with that gun still hanging from his hand as if it were a part of him, and his eyes on fire and his mouth so . . . She wanted to kiss that hard mouth until it softened and moaned and surrendered to hers.

Clementine felt a hand on her arm. She looked down into her daughter's serious face. Without a word, Sarah pried her mother's fingers loose from their tight grip on the handle of her own shovel. The tool was nearly as tall as the girl, and she struggled with it a bit. The blade made a loud scraping sound as she pushed it through the rocky mud.

Clementine's gaze was pulled back up to Rafferty's. "You got one of those for me?" he said.

He wasn't smiling at her, and that dun-colored horse was waiting saddled back at Snake-Eye's livery. "Are you asking me for a shovel, Mr. Rafferty?"

"Yeah, a shovel will do . . . for now," he said. He still wasn't smiling, but the air between them suddenly seemed to be humming with a wondrous and frightening feeling of promise.

Drew Scully and Doc Corbett walked up to the body lying on the ground and looked down at the Mick. "Why, the poor fellow appears to be staring at the sky and seeing nothing," Drew said, shaking his head as if at the wonderment of it all.

The doc sighed deeply. "Another man who's been had for breakfast."

The doc did check, though, to make sure the Mick was dead before he went to join his young bride, who used to be Miss Luly Maine, the schoolmarm, and was now Mrs. Kit Corbett, the doctor's wife. Without a word he took the muck stick from her small lace-gloved hands and began to throw mud into the pit. For a moment longer the rest of the men of Rainbow Springs stood and watched their women shovel. And then they came, one by one crossing that bit of red Montana mud that had separated them, and the murmurs and whispers rose to excited chatter and intermittent bursts of laughter, and it began to sound like a Fourth of July picnic.

"Why aren't you arresting those men, Marshal?"

Drew looked up at the man who sat alone on his fine Peerless buggy. One-Eyed Jack McQueen's one good eye was weeping from the heap fumes, and his face was mottled and sweaty, his voice hoarse and scratchy.

Drew laughed out loud. "Arrest them for doing what, Jack? If there was a law against filling up a hole, I suppose come Saturday night I'd be having to arrest every randy young buck in the RainDance country."

They paused, she and Rafferty, on the rise overlooking the dip in the valley that sheltered the cabin and barn and pastureland of the Rocking R. The timothy grass was coming up green and sweet, thick from such a wet spring. It would make a good hay crop this year.

On the wide horizon the mountains surged black and ominous like swelling waves. Montana. This place, so wild and raw and beautiful, had always seemed able to take her or reject her, never allowing her a say in the choice.

Like him.

She shifted her gaze from the mountains to the buckboard loaded with Saphronie and the children as it rolled down the road and turned into the yard. With every mile she had been waiting for him to say something, anything, until the anticipation was like a scream, a shrill relentless shrieking in her mind.

It had taken them most of three days to bury the copper roasting heap. Now the wind, which had come up at last that morning, blew fresh. The rain clung to the sooty clouds still, so close they could smell it coming.

"It's done now," she said. Not sure if she meant the heap being buried or the terrible certainty she felt that everything was wrong, forever wrong, between them.

She felt him stir beside her, heard him draw in a breath. She thought she could sense his heart beating in syncopation with hers.

He pushed the heels of his hands against his saddle cantle, stretching out the kinks in his arms and shoulders. "You seem mighty pleased with yourself," he said. "Like a hen at roostin' time."

Casual words, empty words. When he could have said that he loved her. That he would stay with her and love her forever. The sound of the wind through the cottonwoods was like the ebb and rush of her yearning.

"The heap's buried." She fought to hold on to her pride. If he wouldn't say it, then neither would she. "The fire's out, and that's all I wanted. I don't feel pleased with myself, only tired."

"Yeah, well, you better be perking up pretty damn quick, then. Because the revver's still got himself a hired gun left, and odds are he'll be sending him out here quicker'n scat to put out the fire in you."

She swung her head hard around to stare at him. His words might have been empty, but his gaze was focused on her with that darkly intense expression she had learned to love. And fear.

"And what do you think I ought to do about that, Rafferty? You took care of the Mick for me. Perhaps I should hire you and your gun to take care of Mr. Kyle as well."

"I guess you probably figure you've gotten good at taking care of yourself." He looked pointedly from the rifle in the boot behind her saddle to the Colt strapped around her waist, and his voice was hard with a tight anger. "But if you miss, you're dead, and there's no use talking about your lightning-quick draw. The fact is, there's only one sure way to send a man to hell, and that's to dry-gulch him in the back."

She looked into eyes that were now as cold and flat and yellow as brass. Those eyes reminded her of what she'd always known about him: he was a hard and dangerous man, cruel and mean when he had to be.

She swallowed around the sudden dryness in her throat. "So you're suggesting that I lie in ambush and murder your father? A man who, however crafty and full of guile and probably no good at bottom, is still grandfather to my children? 'The land cannot be cleansed of the blood that is shed therein, but by the blood of him that shedeth it.'"

"You sure are in a bloodthirsty frame of mind, Boston. All I'm suggesting is that you take precautions. One-Eyed Jack has never played by any rules but his own. And I might not be here—"

He cut himself off abruptly. His gaze shifted off her face and out to the prairie, windswept and empty.

"To protect me," she finished for him. The tight band of misery, which had been wrapped around her chest ever since he'd come home, was twisting now as if it would crack her ribs. "Because you're not staying."

She pulled her horse's head around to ride away from

him, but he stopped her, leaning over to grab hold of the shank of the bit. It brought his face so close to hers she could see his nostrils flare with each hard breath, and the faint lines that bracketed his sharply sculpted mouth. She could feel, as if holding her hand to a flame, the heat and intensity in his terrible yellow eyes.

Her gaze was riveted to his mouth, and she saw his lips move before she heard the words. "I haven't said I wasn't staying."

"You haven't said you were."

"Dammit, maybe I'm waiting for you to—" He cut himself off again. He drew in a swift, hard breath. "You always got to be fighting something, Boston. Before, it was my brother and Montana. Now it's the revver and the Four Jacks. And me. Mostly you've always done a lot of fighting against me."

She drew in a deep breath of air that was thick with the smell of the coming rain, and of him. She wanted to drive her fist into that mouth. She wanted to cup his lean, beard-shadowed cheeks in her hands and draw that mouth to hers and kiss it. She wanted to make him suffer, and she wanted to show him that with her to care for him, to love him, he would never know suffering again.

And she wondered: if Gus hadn't found her first, if from the beginning there had been only this man, would there still be all this turmoil and tension between them? All this heady and frightening ecstasy?

"It's either fight or surrender," she said, her voice breaking. "With all of you men, it always comes down to that. Either fight or surrender."

She watched his lips tighten and curve a little, but not in a smile. She had always been able to remember what they felt like. She wanted to know what they felt like now.

"You really do think you're pretty tough, don't you?" he said, that familiar thread of meanness in his voice.

A harsh laugh tore out her throat. "Oh, you bet I'm

tough. You men have always got to be holding contests to see who's tougher. Bronco-busting and roping contests and drilling contests and drinking contests. Well, we women *know* who's tougher. It's the mother who buries a beloved child and still finds the will to get up in the morning and see to the cooking of the flapjacks and the milking of the cow and the washing of her man's shirts. It's the sodbuster's wife who somehow keeps her family going through all the die-ups and the droughts and the blizzards and the prairie fires when what she most wants to know is what in God's name they're doing out here in the first place. It's the miner's wife who follows her man from camp to camp while he's searching for that one big strike she knows is never coming. *She,* Zach Rafferty, is tough."

The words had spewed out of her, leaving her feeling seared and empty. For a moment she thought his eyes had flashed with a bright yellow light, but then he tipped his head down so all she could see of his face was his mouth. He said nothing, and she could see by the set of that mouth that he wasn't going to.

She thrust her chin into the air. She felt it quiver, but she didn't care. "So maybe you should just ride on out of here right now, because I don't need you. I don't need any man."

She wheeled her horse around and sent him into a canter down the hill. She didn't look back.

It started to rain. Big drops that made dollar-sized pocks in the mud. She rode straight into the barn.

She unsaddled her horse, ignoring the man who had followed her.

"I'm tired of sleeping out in this barn," he said.

She hung her bridle on a peg and turned to look at him. He leaned against a stall door, his arms folded across his chest, his long legs crossed at the ankles. Rafter shadows lay in bars across his face. His eyes were dark and heavy-lidded. A tautness had come over his mouth. She could feel her heart pounding against her chest.

"Clementine," he said, his voice breaking a little on her name. "I've been wanting you my entire life."

It was raining harder now. It drummed on the roof, and the wind sent it splashing through the half-open doors. It smelled of mud and wet grass.

She knew he was waiting for her to say something, but the words seemed trapped in her chest along with an enormous ache. She wrapped her arms around herself and squeezed, as if she could push it all up out of her, along with her breath.

He snatched off his hat and thrust his fingers through his hair. "Well, damn it all to hell and back!"

It was a gesture so reminiscent of Gus that she almost smiled. She almost stopped aching.

"You're just like your brother," she said. "You even argue like him."

"And damned if he still isn't standing between us, huh, Boston?" He pushed himself off the stall. Something raw blazed in his face. He came at her and she held her ground, although inside she was scared right down to the bone. He'd always held such a power to shatter her heart. To shatter her life.

She watched his mouth move, felt his words come at her. "He'll always have a claim on you."

She wanted to tell him he was wrong about Gus and her and about the claim the past had on her, wrong about so much. But she'd never been good at putting into words what she thought, what she felt.

"Oh, why?" she said softly. "Why is there all this . . . this anger between us? Is it because, when I didn't ride away with you that day, you decided I didn't love you enough? Because I wouldn't choose you over Gus and my own honor?"

He stopped when he was but a hand's width away from her, and she stared up into yellow eyes that were wild and dangerous. "If I had tried, Boston . . . really tried, I could have taken you away from my brother, and him and your honor be damned."

The rain suddenly slashed hard against the side of the barn; the old wooden walls shivered. "Then why did you come back?"

She thought surely he would say "For you." But he said nothing. And when the silence dragged out to be filled by the beat of the wind and the drone of the rain, and still he said nothing, she whirled and ran from him again. By the time she made it to the house, she was soaking wet.

In the days that followed, it rained every minute of every hour. Sometimes a slow, seeping rain and other times a gully washer. It was as if the heavens had gotten on a crying jag and couldn't stop.

The women of Rainbow Springs, with the help of their men, had buried the heap beneath two feet of Montana mud, and it stayed buried. The managers of the Four Jacks met with the town council and agreed to do no more open-hearth smelting. But certain other plans that had been set in motion marched forward.

Clementine, Hannah, and Erlan had another whiskey party. They talked about babies and the latest fashions pictured in *The Ladies' Home Journal*. They didn't talk about their men. And of the three of them, two were holding to themselves the bittersweet belief that these moments together might well be their last.

The afternoon of the heap pit altercation Pogey and Nash had disappeared off the Yorke House veranda, which had some speculating they'd discovered a rich strike somewhere. A supposition that was pretty much scoffed at until a valley drifter passing through mentioned having seen the two old prospectors at an assayer's office way over in Helena.

The Four Jacks still maintained a logging camp on the disputed land near the madwoman's soddy. A few folk thought it odd that while there was usually somebody around the camp, no one was seen to be cutting any more trees. But then it was so damn wet, the consensus was they were waiting for a break in the weather.

The real interest in town anyway—now that the heap pit was good and buried and folk had quit choking to death—was the series of meetings the town council was holding to determine what to do about the Yellow Peril. Even so, the town councillors weren't known for leaping to conclusions and making up their minds quickly, even on a good day. Things pretty much chugged along slowly like a locomotive going up a steep grade, mainly because it wasn't precisely clear what sort of peril the Chinese were causing . . . that is, until the murder happened.

A miner by the name of Paddy O'Rourke had announced to his buddies at the Gandy Dancer one night that he was going to pay a call on the Chinese prostitute Ah Toy. The next morning he was found in the gutter not far from her shack with a hatchet buried in his back. An old vegetable vendor by the name of Ah Foock was arrested for the crime. The town council, full of steam now that the peril had gotten serious, held an emergency session.

The Chinese were always good for rubbing up a sore.

At least, Erlan Woo thought, she had been prepared deep in her heart for the knock on her door when it finally came. In many ways she had been hoping for this moment. It was as if the path of her destiny, which had been running so twisted and crooked of late, now lay straight before her again and with the end in sight.

Still she jumped when the warped boards rattled beneath the heavy fist. *"Hoy man!"* a voice shouted. "Open up!"

She opened the door to Peter Ling, the golden needle man. His face was wet with the rain, his long, wispy white mustache floated up and down with each laborious breath. Already many Chinese clogged the road behind him. Some pulled small donkey carts or pushed wheelbarrows, but most had all their worldly goods rolled up in straw mats, which they carried on their heads or beneath their arms.

"What are all those idiot dogs running from?" Erlan demanded of the golden needle man. She crossed her arms over her chest as the anger and shame burned through her. If her people were going to be chased away, at least they should contrive to leave with some manner of dignity.

Peter Ling said nothing, merely handed her a flyer printed in a form of Chinese shorthand called grass writing. She wondered what traitorous turtle dung of a calligrapher had written this out for the Rainbow Springs Town Council.

"I cannot read it," Erlan said and almost laughed. It suddenly seemed absurd to her that she could read the demon tongue and not her own. In China a girl was never taught to read, for what would be the purpose when her use was only to marry and give birth to sons? In China a girl could be sold as a slave by her father, and no one ever thought to say to her: "'Tes your desire?"

Peter Ling cleared his throat, his mustache quivering. "Oh. So sorry," he said. As he took the flyer back from her, both their hands were trembling. He cleared his throat again and read in Cantonese: "'Notice is hereby given to all those of Oriental blood residing under sufferance in the RainDance country and its environs to leave by midnight on this, the twenty-fifth day of April. Any who fail to comply shall be moved by the force of arms.'" He lifted his thin shoulders in a pathetic little shrug. "That is all it say."

"Isn't that enough?" One did not need to be a Hanlin scholar to know who was in back of this, Erlan thought. One-Eyed Jack McQueen and the Four Jacks Copper Mine. They all should have remembered that wise old Chinese adage: There is no one more treacherous than a cornered foe.

"You can probably stay," the golden needle man was saying. "Your boy, he was born here. That make him American citizen. Yankee-Doodle dandy, *ma*?"

Yankee-Doodle dandy . . . Erlan looked around her, at the shack's single tiny window with its white lace curtains trimmed with crocheted lace. At the bright hooked rug spread over the rough plank floor before the cookstove. At the round oak table covered with shiny white oilcloth. The room smelled, as usual, of starch and soap, and the fried trout coated in cornmeal that she had cooked for dinner. There was little to tell anyone that a Chinese lived here. When, she wondered, had she lost the essence of what she was?

"What's happening, Lily? What's all the commotion about?"

Jere Scully's big body suddenly filled the doorway to the back bedroom. At times he moved about in their tiny shack as quietly as if he had eyes, especially if she and Samuel were careful to leave things where he was used to them being.

Erlan made shushing, shooing motions at the golden needle man and then rudely shut the door in his face. "Oh, it is only another Chinese celebration, like New Year's," she said, trying to make her voice as bright and joyous as a firecracker. "With lots of happy shouting and noise. The . . . Festival of the Joyous Rice Planting. Yes, that is it. It is to celebrate the day rice is first planted in the spring."

She thought her voice sounded hollow, but he didn't challenge her lies. Even though this was the first such festival ever held in Rainbow Springs, and even though no rice would ever be planted in Montana.

He stared at her—she always thought of him as staring when he did this, turning his face toward her and concentrating hard with all his other senses, so that his forehead furrowed and a muscle ticked along his jaw. He smiled, a brilliant smile that flared and was gone.

"I-I thought I would take Samuel and watch the festivities for a little while," she said. "Do you mind this?"

"Nay, of course not, m'sweet. And if there's any of those little moon cake things being passed about, why don't you bring me back some?"

"Yes, yes, I will. I will bring you many moon cakes."
A smile trembled on her mouth. *Oh, my love, I would bring
you the moon itself if I could. I would make all your wishes come
true, for I know your first wish would be for me to stay. And then
we would both have our hearts' desires.*

"Samuel!" she said loudly, startling the boy, who had
quietly been putting a picture puzzle together on the table.
"If you wish to fly your kite at the Festival of the Joyous
Rice Planting, then we must hurry. For I've a dozen more
shirts to boil and press before the day is done." She bustled
about, chattering to Samuel like a berserk magpie as she
tied his straw hat on his head and shoved wooden pattens
on his feet, while Jere stared at her in that way of his, a
tense, silent presence in the doorway.

With him there, she couldn't go into the back room
and collect their clothes and personal things. It didn't matter anyway, for all she really needed was the oilskin bag of
American dollars hidden beneath the starch vat. She was
glad now she hadn't put her hard-earned money in the
Miners Union Bank, as Hannah had so often urged her to
do. Those water-buffalo farts probably would be finding a
reason not to give it back to her now, she thought, and then
where would she be—penniless again and without even a
demon-cursed laundry to earn passage back to China.

She lifted her chang-fu and tied the bag of money to
her waist with a rope. She was grateful for once for her
love's blindness, since he couldn't see what she was doing.
He wouldn't try to stop her leaving, though, for he no longer thought himself worthy of her. And, oh, he was wrong,
wrong, for he was worthy of an emperor's daughter.

She made herself go to him with a light step. She
pulled his head down to her mouth and kissed him, not as
she wanted to, but in the way of a cheerful wife who was
off to do a bit of haggling with the shopkeepers and would
be coming back to her lord in an hour or two.

His big hands spanned her hips, and he drew her
tighter to him. "Lily . . . ?" She waited for his question

with her heart choking her throat. "Have I told you yet today that I love you?"

She laughed too loud in her relief. "Indeed you have, twice already. And have I told you?"

He touched her lips with his fingertips so that he could feel her smile. "Only once."

"Then I will say it again, so that we might be even. I love you, Jere Scully."

She kissed him hard this time, as if she could brand the taste of him, the feel of him, onto her heart forever. Samuel, sensing something wrong, clung to Jere's legs and began to whimper. The man swung the boy up into his arms, laughing and teasing him back into giggles and smiles. A wrenching pain clutched at Erlan's heart as she realized she was tearing her son away from the only father he had ever known.

No, no . . . His destiny, like her own, was not in this place. He wasn't Yankee Doodle Dandy. He was Samuel, son of the merchant Sam Woo, grandson of Lung-Kwong, patriarch to the great House of Po. Her son's duty was to return to the land of his ancestors and do honor to them there.

She took the boy out of her lover's arms. "Come along now, Samuel. We must hurry. The sooner gone, the sooner back, yes?" She touched Jere lightly on his bearded cheek. "Perhaps you can peel some potatoes for supper?" He smiled and nodded, turning his head so that his lips brushed her hand. She often gave him chores to do, for it pleased him to be of use to her.

She paused at the door, one hand on the latch, the other holding Samuel. "Good-bye, my love," she said, putting a smile into her voice. "I will see you soon."

Only not in this life. Never again in this life, my anjing juren.

For a while after the door had closed behind her, Jere stood where he was and listened. The rain pattered hard on the tin roof, but he could hear other sounds coming at him from the road outside, rising and falling in volume like the rush and suck of the tide. Frightened cries and shouts, the rumble and splash of wagon wheels. A horse's panicked whinny.

Fear rose up like a black cloud in his mind. He lunged across the room, not concentrating, so that he knocked into a chair and banged his hip into the corner of the table. He groped for the latch, found it, and flung the door open so hard it banged against the wall. The cries and shouts, mostly in Chinese, beat at him like waves now. Running feet, hoofbeats, the screech of wheels and ungreased axles . . . horses and wagons going somewhere in a hurry.

He stepped out onto the stoop. Wind-driven rain splashed into his face. His boot crunched on a piece of stiff paper. He bent over, feeling along the wet, splintery boards until he found it. But of course he couldn't read it, damn it all to bloody, bloody hell . . .

"Hey!" He stepped out into the road, waving the paper in the air. Something slammed into him. He grabbed wildly, clutching at the sleeve of a wool cloth coat. A coat that covered the scrawny arm of a wriggling boy.

"Who are you?" he shouted, knowing his big size and the scars on his face were probably terrifying the child. But the panic he felt was now shrieking like a runaway train through the black tunnel that was his world.

A boy's trembling voice came up at him from out of the darkness. "R-Ross Trenowith . . . sir."

"Can you read, lad? Tell me what this says." He kept one hand heavy on the boy's shoulder and thrust the paper down where he thought a face ought to be, his fist accidentally clipping the boy's head.

The boy took the paper from his shaking hand. "It's in Chink writing—nothin' but squiggles and lines and dots. But I reckon I can guess what it says. The town council had a meeting yesterday, after Paddy O'Rourke got hisself hatcheted to death by that Chink. They decided all the Chinese gotta get theirselves outta town. So that's what they're doing. They're all gettin'."

A terrible liquid feeling clutched at Jere's guts. "How? How are they leaving?"

The boy's shoulder rose and fell beneath his hand in a shrug. "They're just walking. Since there ain't no stage due till Friday and the train's done come and gone already, I reckon they ain't got no choice but to walk. Less'n they got a horse."

The bony shoulder slipped out from underneath his hand. "Wait!" Jere cried, but the boy was long gone.

Jere stood alone, trembling in the terrible darkness. He flung back his head and shouted up into the rain that fell out of the forever damning blackness. "Lily!"

Find her . . . He would find her . . .

Rough hands shoved him, sending him reeling into the iron-banded side of a wagon. Pain stabbed at his ribs, cutting off his breath. He spun around, his bootheel slipping in a mushy pile of . . . a stink rose up at him—horse dung.

He lurched and staggered like a Saturday-night drunk, his hands groping wildly at the air. His thighs slammed into a hitching rack, and he fell over it, his head landing hard on the edge of the boardwalk.

He lay there, his raucous breathing drowning out all the screams and neighs and the squealing wagon wheels. He could feel his heart thundering like fury in his chest.

"Lily. Oh, God, Lily . . ."

He pressed his cheek into the weather-roughened board of the walk. If he had eyes . . . If he had eyes he would be weeping now. She couldn't leave him. If she left, then there would be only the darkness.

He made himself get up. He pushed against the air with his palms until he hit the log wall of a building. He felt along it, using it as a guide, going from one building to another. The great soughing darkness lay before him, familiar now even in its terror.

And out of the dark came the whistle of the 12:07 pulling out of the Rainbow Springs railway station.

The boy was wrong—the train hadn't already left. It was leaving now.

God, God, what if she was on that train? He'd never catch up with her, never find her out there in that vast and empty ocean of blackness.

"Lily!"

She pulled the fringed shade down over the window, shutting off her last sight of Rainbow Springs as the train blew steam and huffed its way out of the station.

A big ball of tears was wadded up like a wet rag in the back of her throat, but she was determined not to let herself cry. It had been her choice, after all, her last gift to him. In spite of what she had promised that night they'd made wild, abandoned love on a poker table in her back room . . .

In spite of her promise, and in spite of that night, she was leaving him.

She sat stiffly on the train's uncomfortable slat-board seat, dressed in widow's weeds. A black grosgrain silk dress that made her skin look positively sallow. Not that anyone could see her complexion, with a mesh veil draped in front her face. The widow's weeds were appropriate, she supposed, if one had a macabre sense of humor. But then, if she was mourning the death of one life, she was also celebrating the birth of another.

She'd bought a ticket all the way through to the end of the line, but she wasn't going there. Even she didn't know for sure where she would be getting off. And where she did get off, she wouldn't stay longer than it took to get on a stagecoach heading any direction, as long as it wasn't east. She wasn't sure what sort of place she was looking for. Only that she would know it when she found it.

She had always thought that when this moment came she would be sad, and sad she was. The bone-ache kind of sadness that made a person realize just how lonely and empty a place this old world could be. But underneath all the misery of leaving him, an excitement hummed. The one thing she'd wanted all her life, even when she hadn't been able to put a name to it, was now within her reach. A family. They'd make a family, she and the baby. Well, a small one, but a family nonetheless.

She figured she could easily lose herself in a place like San Francisco, but she was too used to the wide-open spaces to settle happily in a big city. So it would be a small town, this place she would pick to settle. Oh, the townsfolk would probably guess she was only a grass widow—anyone could buy herself a black dress and a gold ring, after all. In the beginning they might have their suspicions, but they'd be too polite to voice them aloud and to her face. And once her lawyer sold off all her businesses in Rainbow Springs she'd have enough money to buy herself all the respectability she would ever need. Why, she might even invent a whole history for herself and the baby, like something out of a storybook. There was no reason for the kid ever to know his ma had once lived the sporting life, or that his family tree was no more than a shrub.

She shut her eyes, swaying with the rocking-chair motion of the train, listening to the click of the wheels, and she let herself imagine how it would be.

Like in one of those parlor photographs Clementine took when she traveled the circuit in her portable photographic studio . . . Herself, Mrs. Hannah Yorke, sitting in a plush green velvet chair in a room all done up genteelly like one of those you see drawn up in a mail-order wish book. Her little boy—for some reason her child was always a boy in her imaginings—would be sitting astride a wooden horse that had a red saddle and real horsehair for the mane and tail. And he would be laughing. Always in her imaginings he was laughing. And he had dark hair and gray eyes, and she would raise him up to be a wild one, just like . . .

Suddenly a man's face appeared, surprising her, cropping up in her parlor and hovering there like some ghost.

She ripped him out of it, as if tearing the photograph in two. She had to make herself forget him.

She would make herself forget him.

She clutched at the leather Gladstone traveling bag in her lap. She would think of the baby. Good ol' Hannah Yorke, sportin' gal and fancy gal, every man's gal and no man's gal . . . Hannah Yorke was going to have someone who would care about what happened to her, who would care when she was hurt or if she was happy or scared or feeling blue.

Hannah Yorke was going to have someone all her very own to love.

She leaned forward and flipped up the shade. Montana rushed by, all grass and mountains and sky. The grass was flattened, made soggy by the rain, and the mountains were murky with the low-lying clouds. It was a wet, dreary day, and the skies were dark. But Hannah smiled.

Every once in a great big beautiful while someone really did get ahold of the gold ring.

Samuel was too big and heavy to carry in her arms, but the press of fleeing people, horses, wagons, and carts was too dangerous for one no higher than a wheel hub. He was crying, great whooping cries, as if he knew she was taking him away from the only home he'd ever known.

It rained harder now, the water splashing against her face, running in streams off the round brim of her straw hat. Erlan slogged through the thick mud, her feet already aching as if they, too, knew what bitterness she had in store for them. The road stretched straight and wide and forever before her, out into the prairie and beyond, to the raw and black jagged mountains.

In China scholars spoke of a place where the sacred mountains held up the heavens. Surely these must be such mountains, she thought, for no others could be so awesome and majestic. So wild and frightening and beautiful.

And if, as the scholars said, the order and rhythm of heaven flowed through everything, then no place ought to be foreign to a soul at peace. And no single place ought to be called home.

Her feet slowed.

The worst lies, Hannah Yorke had once said during one of their whiskey parties, were the ones you told yourself.

No red banners were hanging from the moon gate of her lao chia awaiting her return. There was nothing there for her anymore. There had been nothing there for a long time now.

What her father had done to her was worse than what her mother had done to him. So of what value was his forgiveness? What was done was done and couldn't be undone, not in this life. And if such was the way of life's treacheries, then such could be the way of life's bounties. Sometimes the hardest lesson was learning to let go.

And sometimes . . . sometimes it was knowing when to reach out and take your heart's desire.

She stopped in the middle of the street. She looked west, toward the mountains and China. Then slowly she turned and looked east, where the sun rose. Where life began anew each day.

"Lily!"

A giant of a man stumbled off the boardwalk, almost into the path of an ice wagon.

"Watch where you're goin', you blamed fool!" the driver shouted. "What's the matter—are you blind?"

She began to run, her deformed feet twisting and tripping over the ruts in the red mud. She tried to draw breath to call his name, but her lungs thrust up against the walls of her chest, threatening to burst. For a moment it seemed she ran and went nowhere, and then it was as if her feet had pulled free of the earth and she was floating toward him, floating with him, together, up, up, up into the bottomless Montana sky.

And even when she stopped in front of him and set a suddenly quiet Samuel onto his feet, even then she couldn't find the breath to speak, although his name was on her lips and the sight of him filled her world.

He saw her, though, with his heart, for he turned his face toward her and he smiled. "Lily."

My destiny is a circle that is still only half drawn.

His strong arms came around her, and the circle was closed.

33

CLEMENTINE STEPPED OUT ONTO the gallery. The boards were cold beneath her bare feet. The wind snatched madly at her night rail and tore at her hair. She wondered when she had gone from hating the wind to loving it.

The roiling night sky bellowed and crackled, spitting fire, and the rain poured. She gripped her elbows, hugging herself, as lightning cut jagged streaks before her eyes. Booms of thunder thrummed from mountain to mountain, resonating in her blood. The wind blew wild through the cottonwoods. Love's whisperings.

Lightning flared again, bright as an exploding camera flash. She saw him through a curtain of rain, standing beneath the cottonwoods, looking down at his brother's grave.

Her heart was thundering in her chest now, beating as wildly as the storm. She longed to go to him, to get back what she'd once had and given up for love of his brother, for love of him . . . for fear of him.

She wondered if he thought Gus's grave neglected, if he read something into the moss-covered rocks and lack of a headstone, something that wasn't true. And something else that was. She had loved Gus, but not perfectly, for there had always been something safe about the love she'd felt for him. And something empty. And she could rarely bring herself to go near his grave, because he rested so close to Charlie.

The old pain, the eternal pain, of Charlie's dying clouded her grieving for Gus, as it had clouded all of her life since it had happened. The pain of his loss was still nearly unbearable, and would always be so. He would have been eleven years old this last Christmas, edging up on becoming a man. She had missed all those days of his growing up, and she would never know now what sort of man he would have made. She had lost a part of herself when Charlie died; once she had thought Rafferty could give that part back to her, if he dared. If she dared . . . He'd always had the ability to mend the broken pieces in her while shattering others.

She went down the gallery steps and into the yard.

She didn't know how he could have heard her footfalls amid the howling madness of the storm. But he spun around as soon as she neared, his coat whipping open to expose a flash of white shirt. The wind blew the rain in drifts, the water sluicing off his hat. In the long shadows between lightning flashes, he looked more dangerous than ever.

He came right at her without warning, like a wildcat pouncing.

He gripped her shoulders and hauled her up against him, his mouth coming down hard onto hers. There had never been anything tender or gentle in the way he kissed her. Those other two kisses had been violent and cruel, full of fire. And this one was no different.

She pressed her fists against his chest and tore her mouth free. "Don't . . ."

"Don't say that, Clementine. Don't tell me 'don't' no more."

He lowered his head again, but she turned her face aside. "Not here."

Lightning flashed. His eyes glowed hot and piercing and slightly wild. "Here, dammit."

Her protest dissolved against his lips. His tongue plundered her mouth, scouring it of all pride, of all resistance. She surrendered to the power of his hunger, and her own. Gus was dead; he could no longer be hurt.

Bracing his legs apart, he pulled her hard into the cradle of his hips, their mouths locked together. The night was black and wild around them. The wind seemed to be coming from every direction at once, roaring through the cottonwoods, dashing the rain into misty swirls like a waterfall.

"Jesus," he moaned into her open mouth. "Jesus, Jesus . . ." He rubbed his lips over her cheekbone, licking at her eyes. "Don't cry."

"I'm not. No, no, I'm not." But her face felt odd, as if it were melting like tallow beneath a flame.

She laid her open mouth against the shadowed hollow beneath his jaw. She felt the wild throbbing of his pulse. She tasted a wetness too salty to be rain. "You're crying, too."

His throat moved beneath her lips as he swallowed hard. "I grieved for you, Clementine. I've grieved and grieved for twelve long years, ever since that first day I saw you sitting up there on Snake-Eye's buckboard and lookin' so proud and so fine. For so long I've wanted you that I've thought I was going to die from it. And prayed sometimes that I would . . ."

"There's no need, no need. Not anymore—"

He gripped the sides of her head and stopped her words with his mouth. His breath filled her, followed by the words she'd been longing for, waiting for, forever. "I love you, Clementine."

He bent and, catching her behind the knees and back, swung her off her feet. He crossed the yard, heading for the barn with her in his arms. He was taking her to his bed. It was where she wanted to go.

The coal oil lantern cast a soft yellow pool of light onto his bed. The straw mattress rustled as his body covered hers. He kissed her deeply, a kiss that thrummed through her blood like the thunder beyond the walls. His lips slanted roughly back and forth across hers, forcing her mouth open so that he could fill it with his tongue. He tasted now of the cool wetness of the rain, and of the fire in his heart.

He raised his head. She looked up into those strange brassy eyes that had always frightened her and did so still. Frightened her and drew her.

"Clementine . . . I've wanted you for so long. So long . . ."

She wrapped her arms around his neck and pulled his mouth back down within reach of hers. His hot breath bathed her lips. "Love me," she said. "Just love me."

She kissed him, a light, sweet kiss, and turned her face into his neck. His hair smelled of the night. His buckskin coat was slick beneath her hands. A shudder racked her.

"You're cold," he said. "Christ, I gotta get you warm—"

"No," she cried as he started to pull away from her. "Don't leave me. Not even for a moment, don't leave me."

He stared down at her and she saw that the hunger raging within him burned closer to the edge now, bordering on fury. He had never been a gentle man, and she didn't want him that way. She wanted him as he was now, full of wildness and sin.

He flung off his jacket, but his shirt had gotten wet and it clung to his chest. She rubbed her hands over it, tearing at the buttons so that she could touch the warm, hard flesh underneath. Their harsh breathing soughed together, wild as the wind, nearly drowning out the drumming rain. Lightning flashed in intermittent brilliants of fire that were caught fast in his eyes, intense and beautiful. The way he was . . .

He reared up above her, straddling her, his knees pressing deep into the mattress on either side of her hips. The wet cloth strained across his thighs. It reminded her of how he looked riding a horse, so strong, so powerful. So much a cowboy.

She watched as his strong, fine-boned fingers unfastened one by one the pearl buttons of her night rail. He spread it open, the fine batiste snagging on his callused fingers. He looked down at her, a rough groan tearing out of his throat. He cupped her breasts in his palms, his thumbs sweeping back and forth over their tips. Her breasts seemed to swell and throb in his hands, and she arched her back, wanting to give him more. Wanting to give him all of her.

"Aw, Jesus, you're so soft," he said, the words broken and raspy. "I used to look at you and wonder what it would feel like to touch you."

"Sometimes I couldn't bear to look at you, it hurt so much."

He stared at her as if everything about him was arrested, even his heartbeat. His need showed like anguish on his face, and he began to shake with it. As she was shaking, with joy and fear that at last, at last, he was going to take her with him over the edge, into the wildness. Where she had always longed to go, and never dared to.

"Clementine, I want . . ."

"Yes," she said fiercely. "Oh, yes."

He stretched out his legs and settled over her, giving her his weight. He lowered his head and closed his mouth over a nipple. She almost screamed as he sucked, bathing it with the heat of his breath, nipping it gently. She clung to him, feeling the solid muscles of his shoulders and back beneath the damp cloth of his shirt. His hair fell forward, lapping and caressing her neck, gentle and whispery as a sigh.

He made love to her breasts, lavishing attention on them with his lips and tongue. Scraping the sensitive skin with his day-old beard so that there was a sweetly keen edge to the pleasure as well. He slid his hand beneath her night rail and up her thigh. His hand drifted over her, tracing the hollow beneath the bone of her hip, cupping her belly. Her body felt thick, melting, her skin fiery and tight. And when his fingers lightly, lightly, became entangled in the triangle of her woman's hair, she gasped aloud.

He breathed a ragged laugh, and she felt the warmth of it sweet on her neck. "So you like that, do you, Boston?"

"Yessss," she said on the soft gust of a sigh.

"That's good, darlin'. That's good, 'cause sure as hell is hot, you are gonna be gettin' a whole lot more of it."

He gathered her night rail up around her waist. The air was cool on her naked skin, and yet she was hot, so hot.

She opened her eyes to find him staring down at her, his face hard, almost cruel with his man's need. He kept his eyes riveted on hers as he knelt between her legs, and sliding his hands beneath her hips, he lifted her. Slowly he lowered his head and kissed her belly. And slowly he moved his lips lower, and lower still. Lower and lower, and she twisted her fingers in his hair to stop him, but she didn't want him to stop. And her chest got tighter and tighter until she couldn't breathe again, couldn't breathe as she waited, waited, waited for him to put his mouth there, knowing that when he did, she would burst all apart. Burst apart and die like an exploding sun.

She shuddered hard when he pressed his hot open mouth between her thighs. And a great scream burst open inside of her, a scream that was somehow caught up and swallowed by the storm outside.

"Touch me," he grated harshly. "I want you to touch me."

He took her hand and put it where he wanted it. Her

fingers closed around the hard ridge bulging against the fly of his jeans. His erection was a swelling, throbbing, pulsing heat.

He gasped, a sharp, sucked-in breath. He arched his back so that he could unbutton his jeans and push them down over his hips. His penis sprang free, thrusting up thick and raw red from the dark nest of hair below his belly. He lowered himself and eased into her, stretching her wide, filling her all the way up to her heart.

He moved inside her, a slow thrust and drag that began to build and build and build in tempo with the driving rain. Lightning burst in white-hot flashes and the thunder rolled. She wrapped her thighs around his hips, gripping him tight. His hands interlaced with hers, their arms stretching above their heads. Together they gripped the iron rungs of the headboard. It moved against his grinding thrusts, pounding, pounding, pounding into the wall.

He let go and tangled his fingers in her hair, pulling her head back. He brought his face close to hers, still moving hard within her.

"I want you lookin' at me, Clementine." He ground into her, pushing deeper. "I want you knowin' it's me who's inside you."

"I know, I know . . ." Yet she looked at him. His face shone with sweat. His mouth was hard and twisted as if in pain.

Her legs fell open and her hips lifted to meet his plunging strokes. She tried to keep still, but she couldn't. She didn't want to keep still.

He flattened his palm against her stomach, his fingers inching down, finding her in the tight tangle of blond curls, rubbing her in rhythm with his pounding thrusts. She felt another scream pushing up the back of her throat.

He lowered his head, his mouth brushing hers. "You're mine now."

"Yes."

He drove into her. "Mine."

Her head thrashed and her hips bucked, her heels pressing deep in the mattress.

"Say it. I want to hear you say it."

"Yours."

But she didn't say it. It was more like a wild shout.

He stayed inside her a long time, for she was warm and wet and welcoming, and he wanted to stay in her forever. He held her to him tightly, unable to let go of her as tears burned his eyes. Tears born of a joy and of an ache, and both so fierce he couldn't bear them, and he had to hide the tears in her sweet, rose-scented hair.

But nothing good like this ever lasted, he thought. It always ended, and it always seemed to end with a hurtin'. He eased out of her, hitching his pants up over his hips, leaving them unbuttoned. He lit a cigarette and then washed away the harsh taste of the smoke with the open bottle of whiskey that he'd left sitting beside the bed.

He made himself look at her. She lay staring at him with that wide, still gaze of hers that could swallow up a man. He had made her say she was his, but there was, he knew, more to possessing a woman than bedding her.

"I shouldn't stay," she said when the silence between them had gone on almost beyond bearing.

"It's just that Daniel has bad dreams sometimes," she went on when he said nothing. "And when he wakes up scared he needs me."

And what if I wake up scared? What if I need you? "You'd better get on back to the house, then," he said.

She averted her face and stood up slowly, smoothing her wet night rail down over her thighs. She raked the tangled mass of sunshine-colored hair off her face with her hands. She looked down at him and he could see in her eyes the need to ask him for the words to go with what they had just done. And the pride that kept her from it.

He listened to her footsteps as she walked away, and

the creak of the barn door sliding open and then closed. Listened to the sounds of her leaving him alone.

He lay staring up at the knot-pocked ceiling until the cigarette was gone and the bottle emptied. He rolled over and pushed his face into the soogan. It was damp from her hair, and smelled of sex and wild roses.

Every morning since he'd been sleeping in her barn, he had come into her kitchen for breakfast, and she had fed him at her table like he was her man. And every morning she had thought that this couldn't go on. That something would have to give between them, to break, so that it could either be mended or cast aside forever.

And then last night they both had given and taken, had broken and had been broken, and come together at last, and it had been so wild and so sweet and so perfect, except for the ending. And now this morning they would face each other across her table and she would say to him whatever words were needed to make the ending right.

All the things she had never said to Gus and should have. All the things she'd always wanted to say to him and hadn't dared to.

But this morning he didn't come.

She had to put on a slicker to go out to the barn, it was still raining that hard. She pushed aside the buffalo robe and crossed the threshold. For a moment she simply stood still, accepting the absence of him. It was as if a great hole had opened in the world and swallowed all the light.

Her footsteps echoed on the bare floor. She sagged down on the bed. An antique ivory cameo brooch lay on the black-and-white-striped ticking as if it had been carelessly dropped there and forgotten. Once she had given this to him so that he would never forget her. Never forget her love.

Her fingers closed tightly around the brooch. *I won't cry,* she told herself. *I never cry.* She clutched the cameo to her belly and curved her body over it, as if protecting a wound.

Drew Scully looked up at the man taking his ease on the white wicker rocker on Hannah's front porch. Rainwater cascaded off the eaves, splashing into the muddy yard. Shiloh squinted through it and tipped his bottle of sarsaparilla at the marshal. A grin flashed white in his face.

"If you're looking for Miss Hannah, she done left town."

"Left?" For a moment the word meant nothing to Drew, and then he felt the blood leave his heart. *Left town.* He had been expecting this moment for years, but he still felt as if he'd just been coldcocked with a roundhouse punch. Maybe he'd heard the man wrong, misunderstood. He'd been pretending for so long, maybe if he just went on pretending . . . He made himself smile. "How long did she say she was going to be gone?"

"She didn't say. But it'll be pretty close to forever, I reckon."

Drew climbed the steps onto the porch with boots that felt weighted down with more than mud. Beneath the roof's overhang the air was dry but cool. He sat down on the damp floor next to the rocker, with his bent knees supporting his elbows. He leaned back against the white clapboard siding.

She was gone.

After a time he raised his head and stared at the gin-slinger. "I suppose she made you promise not to tell me where."

"She went looking for a place where she can raise her baby and folk won't know it's a bastard or think of its ma as a whore."

Her baby.

Shiloh pushed on the floor with his foot, and the rocker creaked. "Aren't you gonna ask if it's yours?"

"I know bloody well it's mine." Drew pounded on his knee with his fist, though he would rather have been smashing it into the wall. Or maybe into his own face. "Why didn't she tell me?"

"She probably thought you'd try and talk her out of leaving. And she didn't want to take the chance that you might just succeed."

"Bloody damn right I would have talked her out of it!" He scrubbed his face with the heels of his hands, shoving his hat to the back of his head. "Shiloh . . . tell me where she's gone."

Shiloh met his gaze with wide-open dark brown eyes that told him nothing. "She didn't let me know where she was headed, Marshal Scully. And that's the God's honest truth. I think she was busy pretending awful hard to herself that she didn't want anyone coming after her."

"I would've married her, even without the baby. I was going to ask her . . ."

The rocker creaked. "Uh-huh. Well, it's a pity *going to* didn't happen yet."

Drew stared at the floor between his spread knees. *Aye, sure you were going to ask her, Drew Scully. On the grand day when you woke up richer than she was. On the day when you could look yourself in the eye and not want to spit in it.* "It was her damn money that kept stopping me. One of the things . . . She has so bloody much of it."

Shiloh laughed softly. "Man, she sure enough does. She wound up owning a good part of this here town."

Drew pulled in a deep breath. His ribs hurt, as if he'd been kicked in the chest. "I just could never stomach the thought of living off her. Of living off any woman."

"Now, you and me differ on that point, Marshal. Me, I've been looking for a rich woman to support me my entire life. Once I find her, I figure on retiring and spending my days fishing and snoozing." He laughed and upended the neck of the sarsaparilla bottle into his mouth, draining it in two big swallows. He smacked his lips. "And maybe doing a little boozin', too."

He paused, turning the empty bottle over and over in his hands. The rain pounded on the roof above their heads. Shiloh's dark forehead wrinkled and pulled as if his thoughts were heavy. "There's so many ways of being a fool, I reckon a man can't expect to avoid them all. It's in the repeating of his mistakes that a fella can start to get tiresome."

"I told that woman I loved her so many times I wore out the words. Next time I see her I won't be bothering with that. I'll tell her to shut her clack and marry me."

"Now you're talking."

"Provided I do see her again. Provided I go after her."

Drew had never been one to go begging for a woman's affections. He was too proud for that, and too cock-robin sure of himself when it came to everything. He was even sure about his being a sniveling coward, for he'd sure had enough proof of that every time he went down the shafts. Maybe that was why she'd left him—because she'd seen through him to the man that he wasn't.

He remembered that night at the Best in the West, her pointing that silly boob gun at him, and him taunting her to go ahead and shoot if she was going to leave him. And that hoarse smoky voice of hers saying back at him, "I won't leave you, Drew . . . I love you."

So much for her promises. He should just let her go, then—aye, it would serve her bloody right. Or he could go after her and maybe have a few things said to him in that woodsmoke voice that he didn't really want to hear.

It could take months, maybe even years, to track her down, and he was no Indian scout. It would mean quitting his job and cutting Jere loose to fend for himself . . . Ah, hell, he was only using his brother as an excuse. Jere had his Lily now.

It was a big place out there, out beyond the Rain-Dance Valley. A lot of empty country where a man had no choice but to come face to face with himself and find out just what sort of man he was and wasn't. He would have to face the cowardly Drew who was afraid of the dark. And the Drew who had turned himself into a bootlicker for the Four Jacks while lying to himself that he was still his own man. And at the end of the trail he just might find a woman who really hadn't wanted him after all.

Drew pushed himself to his feet, resettling his hat on his head. It was still raining. All of a sudden he couldn't remember the last time it hadn't been raining.

"Thanks, Shiloh," he said. His throat felt thick. It was a good thing he was a high-and-mighty marshal with a gun strapped around his waist and a tin badge on his chest. Otherwise he just might be crying 'long about now.

He started down the steps, then turned back. "Did she give you this house?"

The gin-slinger grinned. "Yes, sir. She said a long time ago that if she ever left, be it feetfirst or headfirst, this place'd be mine."

Drew nodded. "She's a damn fine woman."

"Yes, sir. She's the best."

Drew stood there a moment longer, looking up at the house, at the window of the bedroom where they'd shared so many nights, and then he stepped out into the rain.

Before him the road rolled long and empty out into the prairie grass. And beyond the grass, the mountains shot up into a sky that was bigger and emptier still. But none of it was so big and empty anymore that a woman with a woodsmoke voice and a head of wine-colored hair could disappear for good and all.

Especially if she wanted to be found.

Clementine looked at the rock that lay in the scarred palm of her hand. "Explain it to me again."

Pogey gave his partner a great tharrumping whump in the ribs with his elbow. "Lemme do it this time, you blathering slack-jawed jackass. You done got her head filled up now with so many buzzing syllabic words it ain't no wonder she can't hear herself think." He turned to Clementine. "I'll give it to you straight and in two pithy words, ma'am: it's the apex law."

"Them's four words," Nash said. "Five, if'n you count the apostrophe."

"Shuddup!" Pogey bellowed, thumping him again.

While the two old prospectors stood there looking pleased with themselves and dripping rainwater on her kitchen floor, Clementine rubbed her thumb over the rough-textured rock. A rock that an assayer over in Helena had just certified as being almost pure copper ore.

She'd heard of the apex law and she had a general notion of what it was. The ownership of a vein of ore was determined by the ownership of the land on which the vein surfaced, or apexed, no matter how deep or far it spread underground. Sometimes, as in the case of the Four Jacks Copper Mine, the spot where the vein apexed was never discovered. And sometimes it was discovered on land not owned by those doing the mining, and when that happened . . .

"You say you found this near the madwoman's soddy?"

"We didn't find it—ugh!"

"Shut your leaky mouth, Nash. Why is it every jack-ass thinks he's got horse sense? . . . Yup, Mrs. McQueen, that there chunk of rock you're lookin' at is a piece of the Four Jacks Copper Mine that's come bustin' up out of the ground on that timberland of yourn. Which explains why One-Eyed Jack's been camped out there, making like he's logging trees when what he's really been doin' is ensuring nobody else stumbles across that apex."

And why the Four Jacks had been pushing at her so hard to sell that land, even going so far as to shoot at her children to frighten her off. Because if the copper lode was apexing on her land, then she had a legal claim to it.

"Someone else *has* stumbled across it," she said. "Who was it that gave this to you and told you to get it assayed?"

A sly grin deepened the leathery wrinkles on Pogey's face. He tugged at his ear and studied the big round toe of his boot. Outside, the wind gusted and the rain splashed against the windowpanes. "That would be confidential, ma'am. Privileged information, so to speak."

"It doesn't matter anyway." Clementine whirled and headed for the door, grabbing her slicker and hat off the wall hook on the way. "What I need to do is have a look at it for myself."

"Now hold on there," Pogey cried. "Don't go off all haywire."

"Snooping around the Four Jacks' hired guns can get you leaded," Nash added. But they were talking to an empty room.

Zach Rafferty sat in his saddle in an uncomfortable state of sogginess. His yellow slicker was so old it had developed cracks that let in water worse than an old sod roof. And the wind set the brim of his hat to flapping, sluicing cold water down the back of his neck.

He looked through the dripping, scraggly pines to the wide gray sky and the line of broken, rain-black bluffs. He shook himself hard and got rid of some of the water. But he couldn't shake off his thoughts.

He rode to the top of the highest bluff. From here he could see the madwoman's soddy and all of Clementine's timberland, mostly bald now, thanks to the strip logging. He'd ridden over every inch of that timberland this morning and all he'd discovered was a bunch of slash piles and stumps. No logging was being done here now, and hadn't been since before the heap pit altercation. Still, the Four Jacks always seemed to have at least one man around, watching over the place. Sure enough the revver had to be pulling some sort of bunco out here, Rafferty thought. But whatever it was, he was damned if he could see it.

He pushed his legs out straight in the stirrups and

drew in a breath big enough to stretch his chest. The Rain-Dance country had changed a lot since he'd first laid eyes on it. It had been grazed and mined and logged, its lonely emptiness filled up with towns and people. He supposed some would say it had been tamed.

But the jagged snow-dusted peaks still threatened to poke holes in the sky, and there were places in those mountains he knew of where the trees still grew thick enough to block the sun. And come summer, he knew, the buffalo grass would still grow as high as a man's waist, and the chokecherries would still hang fat and black on the trees down by the river.

This country . . . God, he loved it. Though it sure could make a man ache inside, make him feel good and sad, and a little wild sometimes. Country like this could make a man believe that anything was possible. And it could make him hurt deep inside to know how he was wasting all his possibilities.

He could feel his love for her swelling inside him, like there was another being in there trying to burst through the bone and muscle and skin, trying to get out and be the man she needed, the man she deserved.

He had just started to pull his horse's head around when he heard the gunshot.

The water roared as it rushed through the coulee. It was swollen now, as deep as a man on horseback, and it cut through the steep-sided ravine, carrying along with it rocks, chunks of earth, the slash piles, and even good-sized pine and cottonwood saplings. The rain continued to pour down in wind-tossed sheets that flattened the grass and bowed what was left of the trees.

Nash had said the ore sample was found on the hillside about fifty yards downstream from the madwoman's soddy. Clementine tied up her horse and made the climb on foot. She carried her Winchester with a round in the chamber, even though it was dangerous, what with the going so rough, the rocks greasy with rain, the mud slick and crumbling. She wasn't sure what she would do once she found the apex. Just look at it, she supposed, and savor, for Gus's sake, the sweet irony that they had been the true owners of the Four Jacks Copper Mine all along.

She had scrambled maybe halfway up the slope when the two men rose up out of the black rocks like specters out of a grave—Percivale Kyle and One-Eyed Jack McQueen. She saw the pearl-handled revolver in Kyle's hand, saw him raise and point it at her.

And she shot him.

The smack of the rifle explosion echoed up and down the coulee. Kyle spun around on his toes like an opera dancer, flinging his arms wide as he fell down into the ravine, taking mud and rocks and branches with him.

Clementine looked wide-eyed at the man lying sprawled on his back over the rocks, his long yellow hair trailing in the rushing muddy water. Then she turned her gaze, and the Winchester, onto her father-in-law. Between them the rain slashed down like a silver beaded curtain.

Jack McQueen clicked his tongue against his teeth, shaking his head. He hadn't even bothered to glance at Kyle. "Damn me, woman, but if you aren't turning out to be a revelation. 'I have appeared unto thee for this purpose, to make thee a minister and a witness.' Yes, indeedy. Smart as the crack of a whip, you are, and with the guts to go with it. A pure revelation." His lips pulled back from his teeth in a cagey smile. "Why, I'd almost consider taking you on as a partner . . . if I thought I could trust you."

His one eye watched her with the intensity of two. He took a step.

Clementine tightened her grip on the Winchester. Her stomach clenched and spasmed, and her legs kept wanting to shake. And she was cold, so cold. She kept thinking of that yellow hair floating in the stream, and she felt a terrible need to look at him again, to see if he was really dead. Yet she didn't dare to, couldn't bear to.

Jack McQueen took another careful step. "You've discovered the existence of the apex, haven't you, my dear daughter-in-law. I was afraid you might."

The rifle trembled in Clementine's hands, then stilled. "Don't," she said.

"So now what are we going to do about it?" he said. He took another step.

The crack was so loud Clementine thought it had come from a cannon rather than a gun, and she hadn't even pulled the trigger. The ground gave out beneath her feet, and there was a great thundering rumble as if the earth were splitting in two.

The hillside came sliding down on top of them.

34

THE WET RED MONTANA mud smothered her, burying her alive, even as it carried her down the ravine like so much debris.

She felt as if she were tumbling end over end inside a great churn that was thick with mud. She was trapped in a suffocating blackness, the weight of the gumbo pressing on her chest, pressing, pressing, pressing her ribs into her lungs, crushing her like a pile of stones.

She clawed at the mud, thrusting, digging, pushing through it, and at last, at last, her head popped free. Still, the mud clogged her mouth and nose and eyes, blinding her, choking her. She pulled one arm loose of its sucking hold and rubbed at her face, trying to clear a way to breathe.

She drew in great drafts of rain and air. And still she was being carried along by the heaving, churning mud. She could hear the wild rushing of the water through the coulee below her and knew that if she hit that rock-filled chasm she would die. A pine tree, too small to be of interest to the Four Jacks loggers, whipped at her face, and she grabbed for it. Needles and branches scraped through her hands as the sliding mud tugged her along with it, but somehow the tree held.

Wasn't holding . . . for she could feel its roots begin to give way. She stretched out a desperate hand, trying to grasp another, bigger tree that remained just out of reach. And then she saw it, coming out of the rain-drenched sky—a rawhide rope looped into a lasso. She lunged, just as the tree gave way, trusting to the rope and the cowboy who wielded it.

And the lasso swung true, settling over her head and shoulders. She gave a little cry as it jerked hard, tightening and cutting into her flesh, and she was pulled out of the sucking, clinging mud.

She crawled onto blessedly firm ground. A strong arm supported her as she struggled to push herself half upright, bracing her weight on her straight, outstretched arms. She retched and spat the mud out her mouth as her heaving lungs fought for air.

"Lord God, Boston, what the hell were you doing?" He hauled her up against his chest and held her so tight she couldn't breathe again.

Her fists gripped the wet leather of his jacket and she burrowed into him, rubbing her face against his chest. "You left me again," she said. "You left me."

"I thought I'd lost you. Dammit, Jesus Christ, and God almighty, I thought I'd lost you . . ."

She pushed him away from her, so hard he rocked back on his heels. "You left me without even a 'So long, darlin'.'"

The rain poured over them, mixing with the red mud. He'd lost his hat somewhere, and his hair clung sleekly wet to his head, dripping water. The whole front of his chest and face looked like a mud pie.

"Well, shit," he said, "I didn't get far."

She spat the grit out of her mouth. "What if I don't want you back?"

"You want me." She lifted her hand to push the mud-logged hair out of her face, but he did it for her and his touch was so tender, so gentle. "Quit it. Jesus, we've got to quit this. It's like tempting God or something."

Suddenly she was shaking so hard she had to hug herself. She looked around her. The slope of the ravine where she'd been standing only moments before was now a scooped-out cavity in the earth, and the ravine was now in the bottom of the coulee, damming up the mountain runoff and creating a lake that was drowning the logged-off stumps and slash piles, the logging camp and the mad-woman's soddy, and the apex of the Four Jacks Copper Mine.

There was no sign of One-Eyed Jack McQueen.

"Rafferty . . . your father was standing right in front of me when that hillside went."

He was trying to wipe the mud and water off her face with his bandanna. "I know. I saw him . . . I only had the one rope."

She touched one corner of his hard mouth with her fingers. He rarely showed what he was feeling; a man like him never did. But she'd lived out here long enough to understand the code he lived by. His father had been killed by the land that he had so callously raped and plundered. A man, if he was man enough, didn't kick about it when it came time to pay the price for what he had done.

He dropped the bandanna and wrapped his fingers

around her wrist. He held her hand in place so that he could turn his head and brush his lips across her knuckles.

"I'm scared," she said, and her voice broke with the force of what she was feeling. "You scare me, Rafferty. I love you too much, and you're hurting me."

He smiled, and it was a smile that wasn't like him at all. It was sweet and wistful. "I ain't gonna tell you not to be scared, or that I'll never hurt you again." His hand still held hers, and he was rubbing her palm with his thumb in slow, gentle circles. "Hell, I don't know why I rode out on you this morning, except that maybe I had to try to leave, just so I could understand why I had to stay."

Tears welled in her eyes, blurring his image until he seemed less real than a dream. *You love him,* she thought, *and then you lose him to the wildness in his soul.* Her throat was so tight it hurt to talk. "It shouldn't be so hard—"

He let go of her hand and pressed his fingers against her lips, stopping her words. "It's hard, Clementine. Hard for a man to look into a woman's eyes and see love lookin' back at him. And to know that when she's lookin' at him, she's seeing not what he is, but what he ought to be."

"You are the world to me."

He laughed raggedly. "And you say you're scared." He gripped the sides of her head and stared at her a long, still moment. "I ain't like my brother. I ain't responsible like he was, or godly, or any of those other things that makes a woman a good husband. But I got to hope there's a man like that buried somewhere inside of me if I have the guts to go lookin' for him. I want to become that man, Clementine, if only for myself."

He was looking at her with his heart and his pride naked in his eyes, and she thought of how she had searched so long for those missing places in her own heart, and of how she had found them. "I am the bear," she said.

His thumbs were stroking the sensitive skin behind her ears. His eyes had turned hot and intense in the way they did just before he kissed her. "You're the what?" he said, his voice husky with desire.

She shook her head within the embrace of his hands, smiling through her tears and happiness and hope. "Nothing . . . I love you."

He lowered his mouth over hers in a kiss that was rough and hungry and desperate. He kissed her forever, and she wrapped her arms around his waist and held on.

His hands fell to her shoulders and he set her back, and she thought it was so that she could see his face and know the truth of his words. "I love you, darlin'," he said. "So much, so much . . ."

By the time the first shot was fired over the stage driver's head, Hannah Yorke would have committed highway robbery herself if it would have gotten her out of the belly of the lurching, swaying coach.

She'd been sick all the day before on the train and sick all day today on the stagecoach. An hour ago the rain had finally stopped and the sun had come out hot and started baking the damp, mildewy horsehair seats and leather curtains. And Hannah Yorke had bent over and spewed up the oily coffee she'd drunk at the last swing station into the zinc bucket between her legs.

She was still bent over the bucket when the shooting started.

"Heaven preserve us, we'll all be killed!" the woman sitting next to her screamed, and Hannah fervently wished this would be so. The woman smelled of old talcum powder and canned sardines.

Although there was a man riding shotgun up on the box next to the driver, the stagecoach slogged to a stop after that first spurt of gunfire. Through a haze of fresh nausea, Hannah heard men's voices raised in consternation and then gruff acknowledgment. The coach dipped as the driver descended, and a moment later the door jerked open.

Hannah pushed the widow's veil out of her sweating face and raised her head and looked with blurry eyes at a whisker-grizzled face. "There's a marshal out here from Rainbow Springs, ma'am," the driver said, giving her a look full of sly curiosity. "Says he's got a warrant fer yer arrest."

"I knew she was no better than she ought to be," the woman huffed to her husband, who was slat-rail thin and smelled of pickled beets. "The hussy!"

Hannah was willing to surrender to Wyatt Earp himself if only she could first set foot on solid ground and breathe some fresh air. She held out her hand for the driver to help her down, then swayed dizzily a moment as she straightened her back. A man sat on a roan horse at the side of the road. The horse was blowing and sweat-foamed as if it had been ridden long and hard.

Hannah raised her head high enough to meet the man's eyes. They had always been the coldest, hardest eyes she'd ever seen.

Marshal Drew Scully kept a tight rein on his horse and his mouth while the driver climbed back on the box and sent the stagecoach along on its journey west without her. The great iron wheels squelched and sucked through the red gumbo, leaving deep ruts in the road, and still he said nothing.

Finally he stretched his legs out in the stirrups and half rose in the saddle as if taking a look at the countryside. "Turned out it wasn't as hard to find you as I thought it would be," he finally said.

Hannah thrust her chin into the air so fast and so high her neck cracked. "Yeah, well, now that you've found me and said howdy, you can just turn right around and ride on back to Rainbow Springs."

He pushed out a slow breath like a sigh and rubbed at his unshaven jaw. "The thing is, Mrs. Yorke, I was prepared to spend years looking."

"You were?" She swallowed hard and tried to quell the shaking that was going on inside her. She didn't want to hope, and knew already that the hope was in her so bad she hurt with it. "The thing is, Marshal Scully, there's something you ought to know before you start laying down conditions or . . . or making offers: I'm pregnant."

His eyes crinkled faintly at the corners, as if he was thinking about smiling. "That's good, because I've always wanted to be a da. A little girl might be nice, if you could arrange it, Hannah. A little redhead with dimpled cheeks."

A gust of prairie wind buffeted her, whipping at her widow's weeds and clutching at the black net veil of her hat. "I'm forty years old. When you're forty, I'll be fifty-three."

"Aye, and our daughter will be thirteen. Close to being a woman." He drew his eyebrows together in a frown as if at a sudden thought. "Bloody hell. I suppose I'll have to be practicing my quick draw between now and then. I'll put up with no riffraff sniffing around the skirts of my little girl."

The hope was in her now, roaring and gusting like the Montana wind. She wanted to shout to the skies with it. "I've been with dozens of men. Hundreds, maybe."

"So I've heard. And how many men is it, then, that you've been with in the last seven years?"

"Damn you, Drew Scully. You know there's never been anyone but you since that day you took me on my bearskin rug and without even a by-your-leave."

He grinned down at her. "My point exactly."

"I wasn't only a whore. There was a time—I'm not proud of it, mind you. Truth is, I'm bitterly shamed. But there was a time in my life when I was a drunk and a . . ." She squared her shoulders and lifted her head as high as it would go. "And an opium eater."

"Aye? Well, you've nothing on me, Hannah Yorke. Since we're confessing our sins, I'll be telling you plain— I'm probably the sorriest coward you'll ever live to meet.

Near most every day I spewed up my guts and sweated buckets when I went down the shafts, I was that scared."

She stared at him in utter wonderment. "All those years . . . you worked down in that mine for all those years feeling like *that*?"

His mouth tightened and his gaze shifted away from hers. "I knew hearing it would give you the disgust of me."

There was this lump of sadness and joy all knotted up in her throat as big as a turkey's egg. "Oh, Lord, you men . . . always thinking you have to be so tough all the time. It would be a fine thing for y'all if we women didn't love you in spite of your foolishness."

He turned his head back around and looked at her, and something swelled within her, something sweet and scary and precious. "Do you love me, Hannah?"

She couldn't say it just yet. She was doing it again, dragging out the moment, holding on to the hope of it. She did smile at him, though.

"You told that stagecoach driver you had a warrant for my arrest, Marshal Scully. Just what is it I'm supposed to have done?"

"You broke my heart, Hannah. Leaving me like you did."

The lump in her throat was definitely going to choke her. "I only left you 'cause I loved you. And it's gonna be too bad for you, now that you've come after me, because I reckon you're stuck with me." She gripped his stirrup iron, giving it a rough shake. "Get on down from there, you. If I'm going to accept a man's proposal of marriage, I'll be doing it eye to eye."

He swung off the horse with as much grace as she'd ever seen in any cowboy. He removed his hat with one hand, took her own hand with the other, and got down on one knee in the middle of the Montana prairie. "Hannah Yorke," he said. His mouth was set serious, but those gray eyes of his were as warm as a summer sun. "Would you be doing me the honor of becoming my lawful wedded wife?"

She thought she was going to start crying if she wasn't careful. Land, she was crying. "Oh, Lordy . . . oh, yes," she said.

He kept hold of her hand while he stood up, dusted off the knees of his britches, resettled his hat, and fished something out of his vest pocket. "This is to keep things looking respectable and permanent until we can round up a preacher," he said. "I'll not be having you forget that I've asked you to marry me and that you've said yes."

Hannah looked down at her hand, where it lay trembling and looking so small in his. And she had to blink hard, so dazzled were her eyes by the sunlight flashing off the gold ring he'd put on her finger.

The oil lamp cast a warm glow over the kitchen where they sat together at the round oak table, a little uncomfortable in the rush-seat chairs but reluctant to move just yet. The night had settled deep and still around them.

She had poured coffee into her blue-and-white-patterned china. He held his cup cradled in his palms, blowing on it, his gaze caressing her face. "I love you," he said.

"Say it again."

"I love you, Clementine."

She felt shy of a sudden and she looked away. A bowl of her chokecherry jam, which they'd spread on her supper's biscuits, still sat on the table. She toyed with the spoon, making patterns in the thick pureed fruit.

"That first summer I was married," she said, making talk, delaying what was coming because the anticipation was so sweet, "I swear it was a pure mystery to me how berries could end up in jars to be spread on bread. Now I could put up a whole pantryful of preserves in my sleep."

"You remember the day you upturned a bucket of strawberries over Gus's head?" he said. "Lord, I don't know when I ever saw that brother of mine more surprised."

She pressed her fingers against her lips. "I don't know when I ever laughed so hard."

She looked up. His gaze was fastened hard on her mouth in that fierce, intense way of his. It made her lips soften and part and grow warm, as if he were already kissing her. But she saw a darkness in the shifting depths of his eyes, and a hurting. She didn't want this—there was no place for Gus between them anymore.

"He never knew," she said. "I'm certain he never knew. Oh, he always suspected there was a part of me he could never have. But he never knew it was the part of me that belonged to you."

His cup made a small clink in the quiet room as he set it down. He ran his finger along the rim of the saucer, his gaze still on her face. "There were times when I thought of him dying. I stopped short of wishing it, but I thought of it."

His words shocked her some. But the lawlessness in his nature that had always so fascinated her meant that not all of God's commandments were always going to be kept. And there was nothing he could ever say or do that would make her stop loving him.

His hand lay on the white oilcloth, dark, with long strong fingers that could swing a rope and break a horse. And love a woman. She closed the space between them and covered his hand with her own. "Come, my love," she said. "Come to bed."

He looked down at their entwined hands and then back up to her face, and he smiled.

They left the kitchen hand in hand like an old married couple. His boots made no sound on the striped stair carpeting. But when he took them off and dropped them by the bed, they made a soft creak and clunk, like settling wood in a beloved old house.

Discover how Western hearts were tamed...

Bestselling Historical Romance from Pocket Books

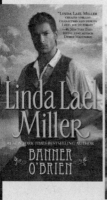

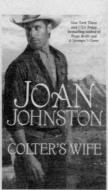

Available wherever books and eBooks are sold.